Dreams

Susan Lewis is the bestselling author of twenty-two novels. She is also the author of *Just One More Day*, a moving memoir of her childhood in Bristol. She lives in France. Her website address is www.susanlewis.com

Acclaim for Susan Lewis

'One of the best around' *Independent on Sunday*

'Spellbinding! ... you just keep turning the pages, with the atmosphere growing more and more intense as the story leads to its dramatic climax' *Daily Mail*

'Mystery and romance *par excellence*' *Sun*

'The tale of conspiracy and steamy passion will keep you intrigued until the final page' *Bella*

'A multi-faceted tearjerker' *heat*

'Erotic and exciting' *Sunday Times*

'We use the phrase honest truth too lightly: it should be reserved for books – deeply moving books – like this' Alan Coren

'Susan Lewis strikes gold again ... gripping' *Options*

4012354

SUSAN LEWIS

Chasing Dreams

arrow books

Published by Arrow Books 2007

10 9

Copyright © Susan Lewis 1998

First published in Great Britain in 1998 by William Heinemann
First published by Arrow Books in 2001
Arrow Books
Random House, 20 Vauxhall Bridge Road,
London SW1V 2SA

www.rbooks.co.uk

Addresses for companies within The Random House Group Limited can be found at: www.randomhouse.co.uk/offices.htm

The Random House Group Limited Reg. No. 954009

A CIP catalogue record for this book
is available from the British Library

ISBN 9780099517825

Penguin Random House is committed to a sustainable future for our business, our readers and our planet. This book is made from

Pri   plc

For Jill and Gary

Chapter 1

'I don't believe it,' she cried, pressing a hand to her mouth. 'Oh my God, I just don't believe it.'

Tears were welling in her eyes as she clutched the letter to her chest and tried to make herself accept what she'd just read. It could be that she was dreaming; this could be a cruel and faithless trick of her mind, or it could be that after all this time of waiting, and hoping, and trying to get up the courage to make it happen, her entire life was about to change.

She pressed the heels of her hands to her temples and tried to make herself think. Then, sinking down on the bottom stair, she considered reading the letter again, but didn't, for fear that she might have misread it. She took a breath. Thank God she was alone. She didn't want anyone else to see the letter, she'd rather die than let any of them know what she was planning to do.

Minutes ticked by. Outside she could hear next door's cat mewling to be let in. Old Hodgkins, across the road, was having trouble starting his clapped out Fiesta again. Someone shouted from down the street, telling him to chuck the bloody thing in the knackers' yard. Sandy didn't have to look out to know that a dank grey sky was lying heavily over the forlorn terraced houses that she called home and the Post Office called Fairweather Street.

She looked up at the hall clock. Five past ten in the

1

morning. Maureen, her recently divorced sister, would be back from cleaning the factory at eleven. Her other sisters, Sharon and Glenda – one was a bus driver, the other worked breakfasts and dinners in the canteen at the depot – would come in for an hour at half past twelve. As it was Friday they would bring bags of curry sauce and chips from Mo and Joe's on the corner, then spread themselves out across the yellow plastic table cloth and eat with their fingers as they gossiped about their workmates at the Beddesley Heath bus garage. Neither Sharon nor Glenda lived at home any more, both were married, no kids yet and lived over on the Wexford Estate. Coming here Fridays was a habit they'd fallen into, even though their mother, Gladys, was hardly ever there to see them. Since the Legion had introduced bingo at lunch-times Gladys rarely made it back to the house before it was time to return to the number five check-out at Safeways.

Sandy's brothers, Gordon and Keith, invariably made their way to the King's Head over at Cadworth on Fridays, where they exchanged a good portion of their plasterers' wages for cloudy pints of bitter with a dash. Gordon, who was just eighteen, still lived at the house, but Keith had recently moved in with Laura, a hairdresser who had her own flat on the same estate as Sharon and Glenda. The boys might make it back some time today, most of Gladys's children did at some point on a Friday, if only to pop a quid or two in the old-fashioned teapot Gladys used for the Christmas Club fund. As for Bob, their father, well, it was anyone's guess when he might be home, as no one had seen him for close on five years. The saddest part of that was that he'd been gone for almost a week before anyone had seemed to notice and the day was yet to dawn when anyone gave a sign of caring.

Sitting there at the foot of the dimly lit staircase, Sandy thought about her family and tried to muster some feeling. It was hard, for they seemed like strangers, people she'd never known, even though she'd lived with them all her life. Each of them, including Sandy, bore a clone-like resemblance to the other, with Gladys's pale oval face and upturned nose, and their father's lank fair hair. Not one of them was over five feet six, Sandy was the tallest of the girls at five feet four. She came fourth in the line-up, meaning she had three sisters older and two brothers younger. Perhaps she should have been a boy to even out the numbers; she might have been noticed then. As it stood, she was simply a lesser nobody in a family of nobodies.

She started as someone rapped on the front door. From the clink of milk bottles on the step outside she guessed it was Ron, the milkman, looking to be paid. She drew herself quickly in against the wall in case he peered through the letter-box. She wasn't supposed to be here, no one knew she'd got the sack from her job at the building society and there was no way in the world she was going to use any of her savings to pay Randy Ron. She'd been with him once, in the old shed over by Miller's Farm, where everyone went to have it away when they had nowhere else to go. She'd been there plenty of times, because there was never anywhere private in this house and there was a time when she'd been really popular with the boys – probably still would be if she hadn't decided to give sex up for a while.

She waited as Randy Ron's footsteps retreated down the path, then, taking heart, she looked down at the letter again. If it really did say what she thought it said she was going to have to move fast to be out of here before Maureen came home.

As her eyes moved rapidly over the five neatly typed lines, her heart started to swell and her hands to shake. 'Oh God, thank you, God,' she whispered as she read

3

the final words. 'Thank you, thank you, thank you.' Her lips were trembling as tears of joyous disbelief swamped her eyes. Then suddenly she was on her feet, racing up the stairs to the cluttered back bedroom she shared with Maureen. Quick as a flash she was up on the dresser, opening the trapdoor to the attic and hauling out her suitcase. It was heavy, heavier even than she expected. It hit the ground with a thud and burst open.

She leapt down from the dresser. The stylish, expensive-looking clothes were neatly folded in tissue, all bought from second-hand shops and lovingly reshaped, rebuttoned and retrimmed by Sandy's own hand to fit her petite figure and newly refined taste. She worked in the privacy of her bedroom, while listening to self-improvement and voice tapes on Glenda's old cassette machine.

Carefully folding back the top layer of clothes, she eased out a Prince of Wales check dress and held it up for inspection. Her turquoise-blue eyes glistened like jewels in her pretty though pallid face, while currents of dread and anticipation shot through her nerves. *This* was her going away dress.

She had already showered, so throwing off her old candlewick dressing-gown she rummaged in her drawer for underwear and tights, slipped on white knickers and bra, then emptied the rest into her case. Her hairbrush was where Maureen had dropped it, on the stool at the foot of their bunk beds. Sandy snatched it up. She hated the way her sister used her things without asking; even more, she hated the fact that Maureen and Maureen's bloody fags had returned to their cramped little room after Maureen's eight-month marriage had failed. Those eight months had been as close to bliss as Sandy had ever reached in her life.

Hurriedly she brushed the tangles from her hair, knowing that by Monday it would be short and chic

4

and gloriously blonde. Her heart was floating between thuds as, from the lining of her case, she took out a small flowery bag full of brand-new make-up. She sorely wished she had more time to do this, but it wasn't to be, and standing the mirror up against the window she began to apply an enlivening Rimmel foundation. When it was done she smiled. Darkening her complexion made her teeth look whiter, but she had good clean teeth anyway, which was more than she could say for the rest of her family. Thank God she'd never smoked, at least not actively, passively she'd probably done several thousand by now.

It took her no more than five minutes to apply the shadow, liner and mascara to her eyes, blusher to her cheeks and crimson gloss to her lips. As she worked she was thinking about Clive Baxter, her old boss at the building society, whose George Clooney eyes and Tom Cruise smile had driven the female customers wild. Of course, he still had his job even though *he* had been caught screwing *her* in the ladies lav. It had been a single lapse from the self-imposed celibacy she had started a couple of months ago and she'd had to go and get sacked over it. She'd been really upset at the time, as she'd been doing so well at the society that there was talk of her being promoted to assistant manager. But then Clive Baxter, the manager, had to go and get fresh after a few too many at someone's birthday and Cilla Radford had to come walking in right at the crucial moment. It was just typical of Cilla the Righteous to go and blab what she'd seen to head office, though she was bloody lucky Sandy hadn't spilled the beans on her, for Sandy knew a few choice things about Saint Cilla that Cilla certainly wouldn't want getting back to her church-going chums. Funny how many people told Sandy their secrets when she never did anything to encourage them.

Still, she had this new job to go to now, but if it

5

hadn't come up she might well have sued the building society for sex discrimination, or wrongful dismissal, or whatever charge suited the circumstances, like she had when Marmons, the big electrical company, had kicked her out for stealing from the petty cash. They'd settled out of court on that one and given her three hundred quid, which she was probably mad to have accepted when everyone knew who had really taken the money, but as Julia Starky was the boss's daughter no one was going to fire her. So Sandy Paull had been the scapegoat and Julia had paid her an extra fifty quid for taking the rap. Now she came to think about it she could probably have got a lot more out of Julia than that, but she'd learned for the next time.

Putting away her make-up she checked herself in the mirror and tried fluffing out her hair. It was a real pity she couldn't have it done before she left, but a London salon would be ten times better than any of the local ones and now she was on her way she didn't want to hang about.

Again from the lining of her case she took out a black leather purse. Her heart was thumping as she unzipped it and looked inside. She almost choked with relief as she saw the money was still there. Seven hundred and fifty-three quid; she just had to pray now that it was going to be enough to get her started. She knew already it wouldn't be, because there wasn't only her bus fare to the station, her rail ticket to London and a taxi fare to a hotel to pay for, there was the hotel itself, a deposit on a bedsit, food for a month and all her fares to and from her new job as well. But she'd find the money somehow, because nothing, just nothing, was going to stop her now.

It was ten to eleven by the time she hauled her suitcase down over the stairs. Settling it next to the front door, she rummaged in her bag for her front door key, put it on the hall table, then steeled herself to go and say the only goodbye she intended saying and the only one that was going to cause her any sadness.

Daisy, the long-suffering, devoted old mutt, who'd already turned fourteen, was lying in her basket in the corner of the kitchen. As Sandy came in, Daisy's stubby little tail started to wag and her huge brown eyes gazed expectantly up at the only member of the family who ever remembered to walk her. Seeing that beloved whiskery old face was almost Sandy's undoing. Tears seared the backs of her eyes and the love she felt for the poor, dying old dog almost overwhelmed her. But she couldn't allow herself to cry, her make-up would run and Maureen would be home any minute.

'Hey there,' she said, trying to sound cheery as she stooped down in front of the dog. 'You remember that job I told you about? The one that agency sent me for when I went down to London a couple of weeks ago? You know, when everyone thought I was going on a beano with a gang of girls from the office? Well, guess what? I got it. I start a week on Monday. Isn't that great?'

Daisy licked her wrist, then nestled her face into the palm of her hand.

'Oh God,' Sandy choked, dabbing the corners of her eyes as she stroked Daisy's face. 'Try to understand, OK? I can't stay. I've got to go and get myself a life. I mean, I'm twenty-four on Sunday and I can't go on living here like this for ever, can I?'

Daisy's big eyes gazed forlornly up at her mistress.

'Oh, don't look at me like that,' Sandy said shakily. 'I don't want to think about you being all lonely here. I've got to forget you and you've got to forget me, OK?'

Leaning forward, she kissed the top of Daisy's head, then, forcing herself not to look at the dog again, she turned and walked down the hall.

All the way down the garden path she struggled with her tears, seeing Daisy in her mind's eye, nose

7

pressed up against the door, waiting for Sandy to come back. Sandy guessed she'd never stop waiting until the day, which thanks to Sandy's departure wouldn't be long in coming now, that Gladys took her to the vet and had her put down.

She took the long way round to the number forty-four bus stop, past Dewhurst, the butcher, and across Fiveway Roundabout where British Gas had the road up again. If she went the shorter way she'd probably bump into Maureen, puffing on a cigarette as she hurried along Fullers Lane towards home. Fortunately, her other sister, Sharon, didn't work the forty-four bus route, but there was a good chance that the driver who did would recognize Sandy and tell Sharon he'd seen her get off at the station, all dolled up and carrying a suitcase. But she'd be long gone by then and though they'd probably guess she was headed for London, because she'd been talking about it for long enough, no one would ever know exactly where in London even if they cared to find out, which they probably wouldn't.

As she stood in the shelter waiting for the bus to arrive she bunched her hands in her pockets and stamped her feet to keep out the cold. She was a lot more apprehensive than she wanted to think about, so she tried buoying her confidence with reminders of all the positive and encouraging things people said about her. Most often it was her ability to pick things up so quickly that got her noticed, which was how come she'd had three managerial positions in three different fashion boutiques, a supervisor's job in a typing pool and a couple of other jobs that had started off lowly until she'd begun working her way up the ladder. In general she got along well with other people, though she was a bit of a loner, probably because she'd jumped a couple of years at school, so had never really mixed with people her own age. She'd taken her GCSEs at fourteen and two A levels at sixteen, then she'd left, bored with exams and wanting to earn her own money, so she could go out to pubs and discos with her sisters. But she'd soon got fed up with that, couldn't see any point to it, unless she wanted to end up pregnant and down the aisle with one of her brothers' mates and stay stuck in this place for ever. So she'd suffered her sisters' teasing and started a three-year night-school course in business studies, which she didn't actually complete, but had got a lot out of anyway. Except, what was she supposed to do with it, stuck here at the back end of beyond? So that was how come she had decided to go to London, just like she'd always said she would. But talking about it and doing it were two different things, and until now she just hadn't been able to find the courage to go, for as blasé and confident as she often appeared, underneath she was really quite shy, and horribly aware of how embarrassingly unworldly she actually was.

At last the bus came and after stowing her suitcase, she went to sit at the back, where she could hopefully ignore anyone she knew if they got on. The bus didn't travel fast so she had plenty of time to take a last look out at the small North-Midlands town she had lived in all her life – the drab, tired-looking houses; the garage that had sacked her brother Keith after catching him selling off spare parts cheap; the old church where her sister Glenda had got stood up at the altar and all the Paull children were christened. Granny Marge was buried in the cemetery there, but no one ever went to visit her grave, except Sandy and Daisy, every once in a while.

Allowing her eyes to lose focus, she pushed out the depressing images she was passing and let the excitement of where she was going come flooding in. It took only seconds for her heart to start beating with hope and, as the blood of the person she was about to become began to flow through her veins, it was as though she was rising up like a phoenix from the fag ash of this turgid existence to become her real self, a smart and educated young woman who, as she'd told them at her interview, had helped her father run a lively little bookshop and coffee bar in their country village home, until he had died a few months ago. She had sold the business now and after many years of caring for her sick father she was ready at last to start living. And having just landed a job with McCann Walsh, one of the most important theatrical agents in London, she didn't see how she could fail to do just that.

She shivered as a frisson of excitement eddied through her heart – the future was suddenly so filled with possibilities and promise that her imagination was whirling out of control. But stranger things had happened than a little Miss Ordinary being plucked from anonymity to become the latest stage and screen sensation. OK, she'd never acted, but it couldn't be that hard and, like everyone said, she was nothing if not a quick study. Or maybe she was going to be a businesswoman and head up her own agency, provided she didn't meet a stinking-rich playboy first, of course, who wanted to fly her off all over the world and pamper her with all his manly attention and millions of dollars. Actually, that was a nice idea, but what interested her more was Michael McCann, one of her new bosses. She hadn't met him yet because he'd been out of the office when she was there for her interview, but she'd seen plenty of photographs dotted around the walls of him with dozens of famous faces and the minute she'd laid eyes on him she'd known that it was for a man like him and the kind of life he was leading that she had to go to London. It was meant to be, her getting this job, she could feel it in her bones, just like she could feel the trip in her heart every time she thought of Michael McCann. It was like that thing across a crowded room, except he hadn't actually been there, of course, but there was just no way she could have reacted to a photograph like that without there being something to it – and she was just dying to find out if it was going to happen to him too, the minute he saw her. It would be so incredible if it did, because he was absolutely drop-dead gorgeous, in a Ralph Fiennes kind of way, and from the very little she'd managed to find out from Zelda, the woman who'd interviewed her, he was still single.

A bolt of nerves suddenly shot through her as the grim reality of what she was going to do when she actually got to London crudely blocked out her dream. It wasn't going to be easy and she knew it, for she had to find herself somewhere to live in a city she'd only ever been to once and where she knew absolutely no one at all – except Zelda Frey, the woman who'd interviewed her. And Zelda Frey wasn't going to be interested in seeing her until Monday week, when her job was due to start, by which time she should have moved in with the cousin she had assured Zelda she could live with until she found herself a place.

Her throat started to ache as the apprehension in her heart expanded. God, how she wished that were true, that she had a cousin in London, or a friend, or even the friend of a friend.

She was only two stops from the station now. She didn't want to stay here, but she was suddenly terrified to go on. Her hands were tight on the strap of her bag, her knees were pressed hard together. She wished there were someone she could do this with, for she suddenly felt so horribly alone she wasn't sure she could go on with it now.

The bus went through a tunnel and catching her reflection in the window she felt her courage make a hesitant return. She looked good, she had an air about her that didn't belong to dead-and-alive holes like this.

11

And besides, she had it all worked out. She was going to get off the train at Euston, go straight to a newsstand and buy a copy of the *Evening Standard*, where all the flats for rent were listed. Then she was going to find a tourist information office and ask them to recommend a cheap hotel. She might have to stay there a couple of nights, but at least she'd have a roof over her head and somewhere to leave her suitcase while she went out looking for a place to live.

Filled with the dread of how much even a cheap hotel might be, she got up from her seat and rang the bell. Two minutes later she was carrying her case through the drizzle, across the road to the station. It all seemed to be happening so fast now and she had never felt so scared in her life. The part of her that was electrified and excited and unbelievably courageous had beaten a cowardly retreat. But it would come back, she told herself firmly, it was only hiding to give her the chance to realize that, OK, it would probably be tough at first, and there were doubtless going to be times when she might want to chuck it all in and come running back home. But she wouldn't, she'd handle it, because destiny had her marked down for something big, she was sure of that, it was only getting started that was a problem. But she had a good job now and once she got going there would be no stopping her, for she really didn't care what she had to do to make things work, she'd do it, because she was never coming back here again – not ever.

Chapter 2

Ellen Shelby was sitting in her favourite spot on the porch, swaying idly back and forth in the old iron swing as she watched the setting sun drag those final fiery rays into the far horizon. She sat with one foot tucked carelessly under her, the other skimmed the dusty porch boards as she rocked. Her arms were spread out across the back of the seat, her thick, shiny brown curls were twisted into a band at the top of her head. Between her and that far-away edge of the world was nothing but space, and carpeting that wide, wonderful space was acre upon luscious acre of ripe, almost ready for market, soybeans.

The leaves of the plants fluttered like tiny wings in the breeze. Thin furrows lined the sandy loam, as though a giant comb had descended from the heavens and run itself through the disorderly plants to tidy them up and stand them to attention for harvest. It had been like this for as long as Ellen could remember, planting in spring after the frosts had gone, harvesting in October once the leaves had fallen. It was as regular and monotonous as the endless loop of the sun and she had come to rely on it in much the same way. It never changed, only the weather cast different shades or different patterns upon the ceaseless tangle of lush vegetation.

The house didn't change either, always dust on the

13

porch, a couple of brooms propped up behind the fly screen, a pail lying on its side, a supply of logs stacked against the wall. Suspended over the handrails were her mother's cherished clay planters, filled with impatients and cyclamen, and snaking up the posts were the pretty bell flowers of pink and purple fuchsias. One of the steps descending into the yard was missing. It had been like that for years, if anyone replaced it now it was likely someone would take a fall.

Ellen yawned and resting her head on the seat-back gazed out at the darkening sky. A tiny sliver of moon was peeking through a drifting cluster of cloud. A jet plane, way too high to be heard, passed on to an unknown destination. The scent of damp earth rose into the night air and mingled with the pleasing smell of home baking. If she were to close her eyes it would be easy to imagine she was still only five years old, or twelve, or sixteen.

In three months she would be thirty. She wasn't sure whether to be concerned about that or not. Sitting here right now she couldn't have cared less, but this wasn't LA where things like age, laugh lines, gravity responses and hair loss mattered more than God. This was Nebraska where the only thing that mattered more than God was the harvest.

She was here, spending a short vacation with her folks, before flying on to New York to finalize a movie deal for Ricky Leigh, the stand-up comic who, just last year, had turned his successful club act into a smash-hit sitcom for NBC. The guy wasn't only a great performer and a great star, he was a great big pain in the butt, but Ellen was well used to pains in the butt now, they came with the territory of being an agent, much like paranoia and ego.

Closing her eyes she inhaled deeply, as though to absorb the rich, soothing calmness of home. The thought brought an ironic smile to her lips. She'd been here two days now and her father had yet to speak to her directly. Everything he had to say was relayed through her mother, even though Ellen was standing right there. It had been like that for years, ever since she'd returned from college and announced she was leaving again to go join her cousin Matty in LA. Matty was an actress, which, in their house, was the same as saying Matty was a harlot; and now Ellen was an actors' agent, which, according to her father, was just a fancy way of saying she was a begetter of flesh for the devil.

The first time he had said that Ellen had made the grand mistake of laughing. Not noted for his humour, Frank Shelby, the giant bear of a soybean farmer who drove fifteen miles to church every Sunday and read to his wife from the Good Book every evening, had reached for his belt. There was no place for the devil in his house and if his daughter, his own flesh and blood, thought she could bring him here, then he, as God's servant, was going to drive him out.

He hadn't whipped her, he never did; he just thwacked his belt on the table a couple of times, making both her and her mother jump, then took himself off in a rage to go pray for God's guidance on the matter of his fallen daughter.

Ellen's heart ached for him, as deep down inside she knew he loved her, though never in all her twenty-nine years had he been able to to tell her that. She knew too how deeply hurt he had been when she had chosen to study literature and dramatic art at NYU, when the University of Nebraska had some of the finest agriculture and economics teachers in the world and Lincoln was just a couple hundred miles down the road.

The college battle had been fought and won a long time ago now, but it still saddened her to think of how badly let down he felt that she hadn't chosen to stay on the farm and marry Richie Hughes, the boy next door, the way everyone had expected her to. She'd known Richie all her life. He lived with his folks further along the road to North Platte, the small town where everyone hereabouts shopped for their groceries, picked up the local gossip and placed a weekly bet on the lottery. Richie and his family were their nearest neighbours and closest friends. Richie was a good and dutiful son who had gone to college in Lincoln, got all his diplomas and degrees in subjects that mattered and was back home now, preparing for the day he would take over the farm from his father. He'd have married Ellen if she were willing, they'd been sweethearts since high school, their families expected it, and no one would be happier than Frank Shelby for Richie Hughes to become the son he'd never had and combine the Hughes' precious four hundred acres of the world's most important bean with the Shelby four hundred when the Good Lord saw fit to call Frank to the great farm in the sky.

Ellen had adored Richie and still did. He was kind and funny, steady and dependable, deeply moral and far too handsome to be buried away in Nebraska. For years she had thought she would marry him, they'd talked about it often enough, especially as teenagers, when he would borrow his dad's truck after church and take her over to the bluff near Laramie for picnics. At first, as they ate their mothers' home- made pies and drank Pepsi from bottles, he used to entertain her with stories about the pioneers who had ground their wagons along this route towards the Oregon trail. She had loved those stories and doubted she would ever forget them. Nor would she forget the first time he kissed her, a real, grown-up kiss, using his tongue and pressing his body against hers. It had turned her breathless and weak with feelings she had never experienced before, but though she'd wanted him to carry on as far it could go, she'd been too shy to say

16

and he too respectful to try. It had taken almost a year for them to pluck up the courage to go all the way, but it had happened right there on the bluff, with the bubbly, rocky river rushing along below and the huge, billowing clouds sailing by overhead.

She'd broken his heart when she'd told him she was leaving. It hadn't been easy for her either; never in her life had she left Nebraska and the only time she had ever spent away from home was when she had been taken into the hospital to have her appendix removed. But she had promised her cousin Matty, a promise sealed in blood when they were eight years old, that one day they would go to college together in New York. As Matty and her brothers lived in White Plains with Aunt Julie and Uncle Melvin, Matty's side of the bargain hadn't been hard to keep. For Ellen it had been the most difficult step she had ever taken in her life.

But that was a long way behind her now; Richie had married a girl from Omaha three years back and just yesterday Ellen had stopped by to say hello to the newest member of the family. Richie's wife, Mitzi, who was as addicted to showbiz as anyone Ellen knew, had wanted to hear all about Ellen's wildly glamorous life in LA, how many big stars she knew, which famous places she went to and whether or not it was true what they were saying about Bruce and Demi. Even before she had a chance to answer Mitzi was telling her what was happening in Melrose Place, then declaring how she just didn't understand why everyone raved about The Nanny, when the woman's voice was like a cat in a garbage can and what she knew about kids had been tossed out with towelling diapers. Richie, who obviously loved his wife a great deal, teased her for getting so involved and tried not to seem embarrassed when he asked Ellen if she'd met anyone special yet. Ellen had merely winked and tapped the side of her nose,

17

before changing the subject to much more important matters, like what they were going to call the new baby.

Now, as she sat there on the porch, her tall, slender body curled up on the seat, her lovely face turned to the moon, she wondered what they would say if she told them the truth. A smile curved her lips as a current of excitement stole through her heart and closing her eyes she felt herself sink into the tingling warmth of her secret.

Hearing the TV go on inside, she was tempted to escape the noise and go wander round to the barns, maybe check on the horses or sit a while with the dogs. Her mother was addicted to TV. If she could, she'd watch it around the clock, but Frank wouldn't allow that. It was a miracle he had allowed a TV in the house at all, considering his views on it, but as softly spoken, pliable and easily dominated as Ellen's mother appeared to be, when it came to wanting something badly she knew how to get her way. And over this she'd really done herself proud for there were now TVs in the living-room, kitchen and two of the four bedrooms; and if Ellen had to lay bets on who knew more about *Seinfeld*, *ER*, *Savannah* or any of the other soaps and sitcoms currently bombarding America, she'd probably have to put her money on Frank. How he reconciled this with the Good Lord she had no idea, but she imagined he'd found a way.

Of course, with her parents watching TV as much as they did they'd know exactly who Clay Ingall was, were she to mention his name. Anyone would, for not only had Clay played lead guitar for the Stones, Pink Floyd, Led Zeppelin and the Doors in his time, he'd also starred in three major hit movies in the past three years and was currently, thanks to a messy divorce, making most of the gossip shows and all of the tabloids on a pretty regular basis. It was amazing, in fact quite unbelievable really, that no one had gotten hold of his

18

romance with Ellen yet, particularly as Ellen was something of a name in her own right and the affair, such as it was, had been going on for the best part of six months.

Of course, they had gone to great pains not to be discovered, for if Clay's wife, Nola, were to get wind of Ellen then God only knew how many more millions she would add to her alimony suit, nor how much more bitter her attacks in the press would become. Already she had labelled Clay a lousy lover, a recovering alcoholic and a wife-beater, none of which was true, though Clay had not uttered a single word in his own defence, for fear of making it any worse than it already was for his children.

He and Ellen had met at a party hosted by American Talent International, one of the top-ranking agencies in LA where Ellen now worked. She'd started out, five years ago, as a booking clerk at a much smaller agency over on Olympic where the owners, Phil and Flynn, two wicked old gays, taught her the basics of agenting, introduced her around town, hyped her up to the press and promoted her to full-blown agent within a year. They'd also brought her to the attention of Ted Forgon, the owner of ATI, who had approached her soon after with an offer Phil and Flynn wouldn't hear of her refusing. It was time for them to pack up and retire to Palm Springs anyhow, so Ellen didn't only get herself a new job, she also got to take the cream of Phil's and Flynn's client list with her. Now, thanks to some ruthless manoeuvres and a remarkable gift for discovering new talent, as well as recognizing great scripts, she had a list to rival many in LA and a reputation for pulling down a deal and promoting her clients that had made her the talk of the industry. Being as beautiful as she was, it seemed the press were forever on her case, taking shots of her coming and going from restaurants or night-clubs and taking great delight in pairing her name with anyone from Ted Forgon, her boss, to Felix Moselle the disgraced California senator whose wife was currently doing any talk show that would have her, telling the story of how she had caught her husband writhing around the bed in a Hollywood hotel with three budding bimbos and a couple of chihuahuas.

Hearing the theme tune for *Lucy* start up inside, Ellen picked up her cellphone and, wandering down from the porch, walked across the yard and round to the back of the machine shed. It was dark now, but she knew this place like the back of her hand and since her parents would be engrossed for the next half-hour it was a perfect opportunity to make a call without being overheard. Her stomach was already churning, her muscles were tensing and her heartbeat was starting to race at the prospect of hearing his voice. The disappointment that he hadn't yet called when he'd said he would was lessened by the understanding that he was busy with a new band this weekend and had probably got so engrossed he'd forgotten what day it was, never mind what time.

'Hi, this is Ellen,' she said, as he answered his cellphone. 'Oh, hi, honey,' he responded, sounding genuinely pleased to hear her. 'How're you doing? You still with your folks?'

'Yeah, still here.' She smiled, so easily able to picture his humorous dark eyes, dishevelled silver hair and unbelievably sensuous mouth that she melted back against the tractor shed, hugging an arm to her waist. 'How about you? How are you doing with the band?'

'With the band, OK,' he answered. 'But I've got to tell you, I'm having a real tough time otherwise. I mean *real* tough.'

Ellen's smile faded. 'Nola?' she said, wishing the woman's name didn't have to come into every conversation they had.

20

He chuckled softly. 'The woman's name is Ellen,' he told her, 'and I'm missing her like crazy.'

Immediately the light returned to Ellen's eyes, and the insecurity fled. 'But she's only been gone a couple of days,' she reminded him. 'And you're supposed to be catching up with her in New York tomorrow. Is that too long to wait?'

'Damn right it is,' he said gruffly. Then, after a pause, 'Listen babe, I'm sorry, but I'm not going to be able to make New York. Something's come up here. Vic Lovell, you know the guy who's supposed to be taking over the rewrites on *Prizewinners*? He's backed out and all hell's breaking loose around here so I feel like I ought to stay. Do you mind?'

'Of course,' she answered. 'I miss you too and I was looking forward to seeing you. Why did Lovell back out?'

'Oh, it's kind of complicated to go into right now, but he's not getting along with the director and a couple of the other guys wanted to fire him anyway. It's crazy-ville, but we'll work it out. How's it going down there? How're your folks? Did you tell them about me?'

'My mother swooned and my father's coming after you with a shotgun,' she told him.

He laughed. 'When do you get back to LA?'

'Next Tuesday,' she answered. 'Ted Forgon's asked to see me as soon as I get in.'

'Does that mean something?' he said.

'I'm not sure,' Ellen responded, loving him for caring. 'I had a bit of a run in with Faith Berry, one of the seniors, before I left on Thursday, it could have something to do with that.'

'What was it about?'

'Oh, you know Faith, you never get to the root of what's bugging her, but it was something to do with the way I'd spoken to her at a meeting we had last week. She thought I'd made her look foolish in front of the guys from Universal.'

'Because you closed the deal for a higher figure than she was prepared to ask,' Clay said. 'I can't see Forgon having a problem with that.'

'No, but Faith's been stacking up the complaints since I arrived and you know what this business is like, one day you're in lights the next you're in history.'

Clay laughed. 'Tell me about it,' he said. 'But take it from me, honey, Forgon's not letting you go anywhere, 'cos if anyone knows when he's onto a good thing in this town, Forgon's the man. And you're one hell of a good thing. So good I can hardly believe my luck or what's happening to me right now, just thinking about how god-damned beautiful you are.' As his voice dropped, taking on a sleepy, much more intimate quality, Ellen felt an instant response flare through her loins. She knew what was coming next and already her heart was starting to pound, as her nipples stiffened and the desire turned almost to a pain.

'You some place private?' he asked.

'Kind of,' she responded. 'I'm outside, by the barn.'

'What are you wearing?'

'A shirt, cotton pants.'

'Undo the shirt,' he said huskily.

Ellen's fingers moved to the buttons and began to twist. 'It's undone,' she told him a minute later.

'You wearing a bra?' he asked.

'Yes,' she answered, gazing blindly out at the night. 'It's a front fastener.'

'Then undo it, honey,' he said. 'Show those big, beautiful breasts to the moon. Did all those cowboys go home yet?'

'There might be a couple still around,' she answered, knowing it was what he wanted to hear, even though the farmhands had taken off much earlier in the day.

22

'Touch yourself, honey,' he whispered. 'Squeeze those nipples and tell me what you're thinking.'

Ellen's pulses were racing as she leaned back against the barn, stroking her breasts and imagining it was his fingers pulling at her nipples. 'I'm thinking about how hard you must be by now,' she told him, 'and how much I want you inside me.'

'It's where I want to be,' he groaned. 'Christ, I miss you.'

'Are you touching yourself?' she asked.

There was a smile in his voice as he said, 'Hard and fast.'

'I think there's someone watching me,' she whispered, looking round at the dark, empty night.

'One of the cowboys?'

'Yes,' she said.

'Do you want him to fuck you?'

Ellen's breath caught in her throat.

'Do you want his cock?' he said.

'Yes,' she murmured.

'Then pull down your pants.'

Obediently Ellen pushed her pants down over her hips. She could feel the cool night air like a caress on her skin and the need for him slaked through her in piercing waves. 'They're down,' she told him, barely able to speak.

'Is he still watching you?'

'I think so. Oh God, I wish you were here,' she gasped, pushing her fingers between her legs.

'So do I, honey,' he said softly. 'If you let the cowboy touch you, I'll kill him.'

Ellen smiled. 'My fingers are where you should be,' she told him.

'You got me there,' he said. Then his voice sounded strangled as he said, 'Jesus Christ, I'm going to come just thinking about being there.'

'I can feel you filling me.'

23

'Oh God, Ellen,' he moaned. 'I'm there. I'm right there.'

'Do it harder,' she begged. 'Really fuck me.'

'I'm coming, honey,' he panted.

Ellen's fingers were moving rapidly back and forth, bringing on her own shuddering climax.

'Are you with me?' he said.

'Yes,' she gasped. 'Oh, Clay.'

There were several moments of silence, then his voice came over the line, saying, 'I want to kiss you real bad.'

Ellen's eyes were closed, her lips were parted as the breath shook from her lungs and the climax shot from her fingertips right into her body. Only with Clay had she ever had sex like this and until now she'd never have believed it could turn her on so much.

'Are you OK, honey?' he asked.

'Yes,' she answered weakly.

He chuckled. 'I guess you really were doing it,' he said.

She smiled. 'It was you who did it,' she told him.

'Me and the cowboy.'

She laughed. 'Can I get dressed now?' she asked.

'Hell, I really want to say no,' he answered, 'but this is the third time the bleep's gone, telling me someone's trying to get through. It could be the kids. I'll call you later, OK? Love you,' and he was gone.

'Love you too,' Ellen echoed as the line went dead and, taking the phone from her ear, she began to hike up her trousers. Now that his voice was no longer there, egging her on and arousing her so much, she felt faintly embarrassed at what she had done and suddenly afraid that someone might actually have seen her. But it wasn't very likely and, refastening her bra and shirt, she gazed out at the moonlit fields. It was strange how sometimes when she spoke to him she ended up feeling so miserable after, especially when there didn't seem any reason to, but as a wave of dismay coasted through her heart she forgot all about the intimacy they had just shared and gave in to the bitter disappointment that he wasn't going to make New York, even though she'd already guessed he wouldn't.

Sighing, she thought of how they never went anywhere together. They only ever saw each other at his house where the security was tight and totally ignored each other if they were ever at the same parties. Even worse was that sometimes as much as three, or even four, weeks would go by without them seeing each other at all, which was of course how come they had got so good at telephone sex.

Pushing herself away from the wall, she started slowly back to the house. The wind was picking up now and in only a pair of check, seersucker pants, a thin shell top and one of her mother's hand-knit cardigans she was starting to feel cold. Not that she noticed particularly, for her mind was still full of Clay, wondering exactly what he was doing now, where he had been when she'd called, and if he'd really meant it when he said he was missing her. She hated giving in to her insecurities like this, but she'd had such a rough time with boyfriends in the past – with the exception of Richie, of course – that despite her success as an agent, she sometimes wondered if there wasn't something seriously wrong with her character. Maybe there was something in her that made men treat her badly, for she'd yet to meet one who didn't, even though they started out as besotted with her as she was with them. And none of her friends seemed to have the kind of problems she had, so she could only conclude that she was doing something they weren't. Or maybe not doing. She wished to God she knew which, or what, because it was playing hell with her self-esteem and Clay, with his interminable divorce case and obsession with secrecy, wasn't really doing much to help.

But now wasn't the time to be dwelling on her problems; her mother would only detect something and though Ellen rarely held anything back from her, she knew that her mother wasn't yet ready to accept the hell-raiser Clay Ingall as a part of her daughter's life. Of course he'd changed a lot since those early days when his reputation had been as wild and crazy as any other rocker from the sixties, but compared with the allegations his wife was throwing out about him these days, his past was starting to appear pretty tame. Indeed, if she didn't know him so well, Ellen guessed she'd probably have him labelled too, because neither his looks nor his image did much to portray the kindness and sensitivity she had come to know.

The moment she walked in the door of the farmhouse her mouth started watering, as the delicious aroma of her mother's special pot-roast was filling up the house. Her mother was right there in the kitchen, absently stirring gravy as her eyes stayed riveted to the TV.

'Anything I can do?' Ellen offered, stealing a taste of the gravy.

'Set the table, honey,' her mother answered, still watching *Lucy*. 'And take your father a beer.'

Ellen glanced up at the clock over the washer. At six fifteen every evening her father had a beer. And sure enough, even without looking Nina Shelby had known it was time.

Amazing, Ellen thought, pulling open the refrigerator and taking out a Budweiser. Most other evenings the workers would still be here and they would drink a beer too, out on the porch, while Nina served some of her bite-size home-made pies and hot potatoes. As it was Saturday they were alone as a family.

Helping herself to a carrot, Ellen carried an open bottle through to her father and set it down on the cherry wood table beside him. His eyes didn't move from the TV as his hand went out to take the bottle. Ellen crunched loudly on the carrot. The bottle paused at Frank Shelby's lips, then he continued to drink as though nothing had happened and no one was there.

As soon as the programme was over they sat down to eat at the old pine kitchen table that was engraved with names of workers and children from along the years. Ellen searched for and easily found her cousin Matty's name, carved much bigger than the others with a diamond around it and a flower beneath. Matty had come to stay every year since she was five and Ellen four. She had always come alone as her brothers had other places to go and Aunt Julie wasn't allowed in the house – nor was Uncle Melvin since the day he'd married Aunt Julie. Aunt Julie, in her younger years, had been a dancer in a Paris night-club where, Nina Shelby had once confided to Ellen, she had danced topless in front of crowds of men. It was only when she went to college that Ellen had actually gotten to know her aunt and uncle, until then she'd never even met them, for Matty had always been put on the plane in New York to fly alone over to Nebraska. Ellen had so envied her that freedom, and as much as she loved her parents, she couldn't help wishing, once she got to know her aunt and uncle, that there had been as much fun in their house as there was in Matty's.

'How's Matty, dear?' her mother said, as though picking up on her thoughts. 'Is she still running the coffee bar?'

Ellen nodded as she took a mouthful of food. 'Mmm,' she said, then, waiting until she had swallowed she went on. 'She had an audition last week for a regular singing spot at a club on Sunset.'

Nina Shelby's eyes slid over to her husband whose face remained stony. 'That's nice,' Nina said. Then turning back to Ellen, 'I thought she wanted to act.'

'She does,' Ellen confirmed. 'But she's not getting a

lot of work and she has to pay the rent somehow. Oh, that reminds me, I brought some photographs of our apartment in Valley Village. I'll get them after dinner.'

Nina nodded and took a mouthful of food.

'Actually, I've been looking around for a place of my own,' Ellen went on. 'If Matty gets the singing job then I'll probably move out, but I don't want to do that until I know she can manage the rent.'

'Could she find someone else to share?' Nina asked.

Ellen was about to mention that Gene, Matty's boyfriend, was dying to move in, but realizing that would be too much for her father, she simply said, 'Sure, I expect so. She just has to find the right person.'

They ate on in silence for a while, the crackle and pop of the logs on the fire and the faint hum of the wind outside making the kitchen seem cosy and safe and very far from the rest of the world. After a while Ellen and her mother fell into conversation again, years of habit steering them safely around subjects that would either offend or upset Frank. Once in a while he spoke, addressing himself only to his wife as he asked about one of the workers, or talked about the upcoming harvest and the weeds that needed to be cleared before they could begin. Though Ellen could see how deeply it pained her mother to keep switching her attention between the two people she loved, she knew that to try to force her father to acknowledge she was there was pointless. He was too stubborn to shift, had come too far with this now to back down.

'Do you think you'll make it home for Thanksgiving?' Nina asked, as she and Ellen cleared the table after a blueberry pie dessert.

Ellen thought about it, then nodded. 'Mmm, there's a chance,' she answered. She was thinking of Clay and wondering if he was planning on spending it with his kids. She knew he would if he could, but he'd have to get Nola's agreement on that and it was doubtful she'd give it. Whether he would come here instead, though, was another matter altogether.

Taking a clean tea cloth from an overhead rack, to wipe as her mother washed, she couldn't help smiling as she tried to picture the forty-six-year-old rock star with his movie-star good looks, shabby denims and crocodile boots, sitting at a table with Frank and Nina Shelby of Willoughby Farm, Nebraska. The image almost made her laugh, though Clay would love it here, she felt sure of that, for being the kind of man he was it wouldn't suprise her at all to see him motoring off to church with her father on Sunday, or helping chop wood, or walking the bean with the workers. He'd get a real kick out of getting involved in something so different from his normal life and meeting the kind of folks he never came across in LA.

What her parents would make of him, though, was almost beyond imagining, and just thinking about it got her feeling sorry for her father to think of how awkward and out of his depth he would be in the company of a man like Clay – and how horribly distressed it would make him to discover how deeply involved she was with a man so at odds with his own hopes for her future. After a time, though, he might come to accept the guitar and the Oscars and the denims; what he would never be able to handle was the fact that Clay was married. OK, Clay and his wife were split up, but that wouldn't make it any better for Frank; if anything, it would probably make it worse, as divorce ranked right up there along with all the other deadly sins.

Not until late the following morning did Ellen see her father again when he and Nina, all spruced up in their Sunday best, set out for church. By the time they returned, Ellen and her rented car would be gone, so the goodbyes had to be said now before Frank and Nina climbed into the truck.

29

The parting was never easy, as Ellen hated leaving without having resolved things with her father, even though, in the last couple of years, she'd more or less given up trying. Nina always said that he would come round in time, but more than seven years had gone by now and Ellen couldn't see it getting any better.

As she and her mother walked outside to the truck a chill wind was blowing across the land, dancing dead leaves around the yard and whistling merrily through the cracks in the old tractor shed. It was a crystal clear, bright sunny day making the sky seem bluer than ever and the beans about ready to explode.

Frank had already brought the truck round and was standing in front of it, looking awkward and impatient and slightly pale in the face. Ellen was surprised to see him there as normally he made himself scarce when the time came for goodbyes.

Nina's eyebrows were raised, showing her surprise too as she turned to take Ellen in her arms. 'You'll call us when you get to New York,' she said, hugging her. 'Let us know you've arrived safely.'

'Of course,' Ellen answered. 'And you take care of yourself, do you hear? Don't go overdoing it at harvest, the way you usually do. And I'll try to get back for Thanksgiving.'

Frank cleared his throat loudly. Ellen and her mother turned to look at him. He was staring past them towards the house, as though neither of them was there. 'Tell her she should stay with Matty,' he barked. 'It's not safe in that city. She shouldn't live alone.'

Nina turned to Ellen. Ellen was looking at her father. 'The apartments I've been looking at all have private security,' she told him.

'That city's not safe,' he growled, glaring at Nina.

Ellen glanced at her mother, then, turning back to her father she said, 'Why don't you come to LA and help

30

me find a place? That way you'll know where I am and then you won't have to worry.'

Frank was already walking round the truck to the driver's door.

Ellen looked at her mother in dismay. But inviting her father to his idea of Babylon wasn't clever and not necessary either, for there was every chance that when she moved out on Matty she would actually move right in with Clay, provided the divorce was settled, so it was unfair of her to worry her father about living alone. She supposed she had just hoped to get some reassurance from him that he still cared and here, at the eleventh hour, he had given it.

'I love you, Dad,' she called out as he got in the car.

The door slammed, but she knew he had heard her.

'Don't tease him,' her mother chided, giving her another kiss on the cheek.

'Who's teasing?' Ellen responded.

'You. Asking him to Los Angeles and telling him you love him, you know that's not your father's sort of thing. Ah, ah, don't argue,' she said, holding up a hand. 'Just look after yourself and promise to call when you get to New York.'

'I promise,' Ellen said.

'And tell Matty that her Uncle Frank and Aunt Nina would love to see her at Thanksgiving if she's not going home to her folks.'

'I'll tell her,' Ellen said, linking her mother's arm as they walked the few steps to the truck.

She stood, waving and blowing kisses, until the truck was on its way to the horizon, then hurried back inside out of the cold. She'd be leaving herself in less than an hour and had several calls she needed to make before she got on the road to the airport. She looked at her watch to check the time in New York, then took out her cellphone and a heap of annotated contracts and started to dial. She shuddered to think what her father

31

would say if he could see her working on a Sunday like this, but fortunately he would never know and what he didn't know wasn't going to hurt him.

Several lengthy and interesting phone calls later, she packed up her briefcase and carried it out to the car. It was clear that the next thirty-six hours were going to need every iota of negotiating skill she possessed. Not that she was sorry for that; she enjoyed a good fight and she could certainly do with something to take her mind off Clay for a while. She had lain awake until the early hours going over and over all the reasons she had to believe they would work out and trying desperately not to mind that he hadn't called back as he'd said he would.

The fact that Ted Forgon wanted to see her the moment she returned to LA was playing on her mind too. It was rare for Forgon to summon one of the agents individually, though it was true he had singled her out for special attention in the past. But he hadn't done that for some time, and feeling as vulnerable and uncertain about things as she did right now, she was scaring herself into thinking that he was intending to involve her in his ongoing battle with the British agent Michael McCann. That was a vendetta she definitely didn't want to be a part of, especially not when three of her colleagues had already lost their jobs as a result of it and certainly not when she was so concerned about where her relationship with Clay was headed.

Chapter 3

Sandy's heart was thudding. Her small, anxious face, flushed from her walk in the wind, looked around the semicircle of offices that occupied the penthouse floor of Harbour Yard, one of the several towering office and apartment blocks of the exclusive Chelsea Harbour complex. The McCann Walsh suite was a bit like half an amphitheatre, with glassed-in offices around the upper level that looked out on one side to the river and the other to the cluttered arena of desks, filing cabinets, partitions and state-of-the-art technology.

The lift doors closed behind her and she walked uncertainly across the neutral carpet to the edge of the three steps that descended to the well. There was no one in sight, but she could hear a voice coming from somewhere behind one of the partitions. Her eyes scanned the walls and she felt a quiet excitement steal through her. So she hadn't imagined all the famous faces on the giant posters and photographs, in fact there were even more than she remembered. She wondered if she was actually going to get to meet any of them and wished she had someone to boast about it to if she did.

She stayed where she was a while longer, hoping someone would notice her or even, remembering she was starting today, come to find her. She continued to look around, her hands hanging awkwardly at her sides, her Sunday market bag over one shoulder and her long black coat buttoned up to the neck. Her eyes were heavily made up in an effort to disguise their puffiness; the result of all the crying she had done these past seven days. She wasn't going to think about that now, though, or she'd only start again. Instead she thought about her great new hair-style and how pleased she was with the way it looked now it had been cut short and highlighted. It was helping to make her feel a bit less nervous than she might have, though the fact that it had cost almost a hundred pounds was a shock she was still trying to get over. She'd never dreamed a haircut could cost so much. Her sisters had always thought Wendy the mobile overcharged, but at twelve quid for a cut and blow dry, and twenty to touch up the roots, Wendy was bargain basement.

The person the other side of the partition laughed loudly. Whoever it was was obviously speaking on the phone. Sandy put a foot out as though to go down the steps, then thought better of it. She couldn't interrupt a phone call, so she'd better just carry on waiting.

She looked at her watch. It was only a quarter to nine, so she was fifteen minutes early. It had taken her over an hour and a half to get here, starting out with the District Line from Barking to Sloane Square, then the number eleven bus down the King's Road to the humpback bridge by Chutney Mary's, the Indian restaurant that the bus conductor had said was famous. From there she'd had to walk in her four-inch-heel ankle boots through the cold, wind-trap streets of World's End where auction-house stock-rooms and very posh-looking art galleries were starting to open up business for the day. She'd known what the journey would be like, though; she'd done a practice run last Friday, after plotting it all out with her maps and timetables, to make sure she wouldn't be late on her first day. The tube fare was really expensive, but she didn't have enough to get a season ticket so she would have to continue with daily peak-hour returns for now. A bolt of dread suddenly twisted her heart and tears stung her eyes. All she had left was enough to get her back to her bedsit tonight. She had nothing for food and no means of getting in to work tomorrow.

She turned as the lift doors opened behind her and a crowd of people, all talking at once, spilled out into the office. Sandy watched as they passed, hoping one of them would be Zelda, the only face she would recognize, but there was no sign of her.

'Hi, is someone taking care of you?'

A tall, thin-faced girl in fluffy blue earphones and a lime-green parka had come up behind her.

'Oh, um, no,' Sandy stammered, feeling suddenly very dowdy in her plain black coat and Victorian boots.

The girl's friendly eyes widened in invitation for Sandy to continue.

'I'm supposed to be starting work here today,' Sandy explained.

The girl's smile grew bigger as she held out a hand to shake. 'Then you must be Sandy Paull,' she said, pumping Sandy's hand up and down. 'I'm Jodi Webb, Michael's secretary. You'll be sharing an office with me. Come on, I'll show you where it is,' and linking Sandy's arm she led her down into the well where the others, still gossiping, were taking off their coats and opening up the steaming styrofoam cups of coffee they'd brought in with them.

'Hey everyone,' Jodi shouted, 'this is Sandy, the new clerk.' Everyone turned to look at Sandy and Sandy felt her cheeks burn. 'Sandy,' Jodi continued, 'this is Frances, Janine, Bertie, Thea and Harry. The only one you should remember is Harry. He's an agent and has the office over there, at the far end of the crescent.'

'Hi, Sandy,' Harry said, holding out his hand. 'Welcome to McCann Walsh.'

'Thank you,' Sandy said shyly, taking his hand. He

had a cheerful-looking face, slightly scarred from teenage acne and liberally freckled. His auburn hair was thinning on the top, but curled thickly around his collar and he had a sparkle in his pale-blue eyes that warmed Sandy to him right away.

The others came forward to shake her hand too, the first being Janine and Frances, the booking assistants who were around Sandy's age and dressed as way-out as Jodi. The way they gave Sandy the once-over put her on edge, but she was careful not to let it show. Then came Bertie, another agent's assistant, who was over six foot tall, as thin as a pole and camper than a row of tents, as Sandy's brothers would say. Last was Thea, Harry's assistant, who, with her stark white face, burgundy lips and straight black hair was a dead ringer for Mortitia in the *Addams Family*.

'Don't worry,' Jodi laughed, as she led Sandy up the steps to the glassed-in offices, 'they're not as scary as they look. Now, I think the best thing is for us to take off our coats, get some coffee going, then I'll show you round, OK?'

'OK,' Sandy answered, liking the cheery cockneyness of Jodi's voice and wondering if she shouldn't have studied that rather than the accentless one she'd got off to a tee within three months of starting the tapes. But then, she always had been good at mimicking.

'Here we are,' Jodi said, using a foot to push open a door that was mostly obliterated by a poster of Ruskin, the TV cop everyone was currently raving over.

'Do you know him?' Sandy asked, pausing to look at the familiar, craggy features that came on the telly every Friday night at nine.

Jodi turned. 'Who, Peter?' she said. 'Oh yeah. He's always in and out of here. He's a great friend of Michael's, actually, though he's one of Zelda's clients. You're sure to get to meet him. So, this is our office,' she continued, as Sandy followed her into an oblong room with two desks in the centre, a row of filing cabinets against one wall and an overflowing bookcase under the window. 'Your desk is there,' she said, pointing to the furthest one that contained a computer screen, keyboard and a pile of books called *Spotlight*. 'And the ladies, when you need it, is just along next to the lifts.'

Sandy wished she could think of something to say, but couldn't. In fact, her feelings of inadequacy were suddenly weighing so heavily on her that the only thing stopping her from running out the door was the fact that she'd have to pass all those people on the way out. Glumly she unbuttoned her coat and copying Jodi, hung it on the back of the door.

'Oh, nice suit,' Jodi commented and Sandy flushed to the roots of her hair. Jodi seemed like a really nice person, but there was a chance she was being sarcastic as, next to her own citrus-yellow leggings, red boots and pink top with zips all over, Sandy's navy C&A pinstripe looked exactly what it was, a cheap, second-hand attempt to look like a career girl.

'So you're from Shropshire?' Jodi said, going over to the coffee machine.

'Uh, yes,' Sandy answered, only just remembering that was what she had said at her interview.

'Is that near the Lake District?' Jodi frowned.

Sandy had no idea. 'Not far,' she answered. 'Where are you from?'

Jodi laughed. 'London. Can't you tell? I was born and bred in Catford.'

'Is that where you live now?' Sandy asked, not having the faintest idea where Catford was.

'God no,' Jodi chuckled. 'My mum does, but I live with my fella in Balham. Have you got a boyfriend?'

Sandy shook her head.

'Oh well, I'm sure you'll find one soon, London's full of men on the look-out for mother replacements. Now, this'll be the first thing you have to do every morning,' she continued, holding up the empty coffee pot. 'You wash it and fill it up in the ladies, the coffee and sugar is in the cupboard just there, under the fax, and the milk you have to buy on your way in every day. Shirley will reimburse you from petty cash. I got some this morning,' she said, digging into her bag and pulling out a pint carton. 'We keep it here in the little fridge next to the cupboard.

'Oh, get those faxes will you? That'll be part of your job too, giving out the faxes. Most of them go straight into people's computers, but those that don't, have to be delivered. I'll come round with you the first couple of times so's you get to know who everyone is. I expect you got the lay-out of the place, did you? All those desks down there in the well, the ones facing out towards the agents' offices, they belong to the agents' assistants and the others belong to the bookers and secretaries and administrative types like contracts and rights. I've got an office up here because I work for Michael. His office is next door that way, to the right. And Dan Walsh, the other partner, has the office to the left, which he shares with his assistant Shirley, because he's hardly ever here.

'Dan's finance, Michael's talent, so Michael's here most days, when he's not travelling, and Dan splits his time between here and the other companies he's finance director of. Shirley, the one I mentioned, takes care of wages and staff records and all that kind of stuff, so she'll probably want to see you later. Oh, that reminds me,' she said, going to the phone as a light started flashing, 'Michael's got three lines that come straight into this office and one other that goes direct into his. You never give out his personal number, obviously. Only he gives that one out. We can pick up calls for everyone else from here too and they can pick up for us. Michael McCann's office,' she said into the receiver, while rummaging hastily in a drawer for pad and pen.

'Oh hi, Ricky,' she said. 'I'm fine, thanks. No, he's not here yet. Not until eleven, maybe even twelve. He's got a meeting at the BBC first thing, then he's going on to a viewing somewhere in the West End. I can get a message to him if it's urgent. OK, I'll tell him you called.' She rang off, made a quick note on her pad, then picked up another call.

It continued like that for the next few minutes, so Sandy took the coffee pot and went in search of the ladies. By the time she came back, Jodi was off the phone and yelling out for someone to let Marlene know that Michael wanted her to call him at the Beeb the minute she got in. Whether anyone registered was impossible to say, as there was a lot of noise coming from that area now, as the usual two-way blizzard of phone calls got underway.

'Great, you got the water,' Jodi said, taking the pot from Sandy as Sandy came back into the room. 'I'll show you how to work the machine, then we'd better get started. I've put a pad and a couple of pens in your top drawer so you can take notes as we go along. The phones are pretty straightforward. The panel there, on your desk, operates like a kind of switchboard. Everyone's got one and we all answer the phones for each other and take one another's messages. There's a board over by the lift where you can pin messages for anyone who's not in. The stationery cupboard's over the other side, next to the gents. Help yourself to anything you need, but don't forget to note it down. In fact, it'll be one of your jobs, keeping the stationery records and to order in new stuff when it's needed. Your main job, though, is to fill in for me when I'm out of the office, which is rare, but sometimes Michael likes me to go to meetings with him and take notes, especially when there are lawyers involved. Do you do shorthand?'

Sandy's heart gave a thump of unease. Was she supposed to? No one had mentioned it at the interview. 'I'm not very good,' she said hesitantly.

Jodi shrugged. 'Doesn't matter. The only time you'll need it is to take minutes when the agents are in conference, but you can always use a tape.' As she was talking she was looking past Sandy and starting to grin. 'Look who's just walked in,' she drawled, putting her hands on her hips as an extremely striking young man, with an unruly shock of blond hair and exquisite blue eyes, strolled into their office. 'Sandy, let me introduce you to Craig Lovell, the greatest loss to womankind since they banned the douche. Craig, this is Sandy, our new clerk. Craig is our literary agent,' she told Sandy, 'meaning he represents all our screenwriters, script editors, script associates and creative consultants. Bertie, who you've already met, is Craig's assistant.'

'Hi, Sandy,' Craig smiled, shaking Sandy's hand. 'Nice to meet you. It's a bit of a madhouse around here, but most of us don't bite.'

Sandy laughed and felt as instant a liking for Craig as she had for Harry.

'Is Michael around?' he asked, glancing over to where the coffee was starting to sputter.

'Not until eleven or later,' Jodi answered. 'Anything I can do?'

'Not unless you want to get heavy with Tom Whitehead over at Limehouse,' he answered. 'Has Michael got his mobile with him?'

'Yes, but he's in a meeting at the Beeb right now,' Jodi said, looking at her watch. 'Give it half an hour and he should be in a cab on his way to the West End.'

'OK.' Craig turned back to Sandy and smiled. 'My office is three doors along, after Zelda's,' he told her. 'If you've got any faxes for me bring them over, bring some coffee too and we'll have a chat. I'll fill you in on the real truth about Jodi and the crush she's got on Harry.'

Jodi's face turned beetroot. 'Sssh,' she hissed, only half laughing. 'He'll hear you.'

'Well I won't be telling him anything he doesn't already know,' Craig grinned.

'Don't take any notice of him,' Jodi told Sandy, starting to push Craig out the door. 'He's got a vivid imagination. If Michael calls I'll tell him you want to speak to him,' she said to Craig, 'now get lost.'

As Craig passed the window he looked in and blew Jodi a kiss.

'If I didn't love him I'd kill him,' Jodi muttered.

Sandy was laughing. 'He's really easy-going, isn't he?' she said. 'And he looks really young to be an agent.'

Jodi sighed. 'Doesn't he just,' she said. 'How old would you put him at?'

'Twenty-four, twenty-five,' Sandy guessed.

'Thirty-two,' Jodi corrected. 'Doesn't it make you sick? It's the blond hair and baby-blue eyes that do it, and those rosy red cheeks. But if you think *he's* good looking you wait 'til you see Michael.' She thought about that for a moment, then said, 'Well, I suppose it depends on your taste. Craig's blond, Michael's dark. Craig's gay, Michael's straight. In fact the only thing they've got in common is their age and being an agent.'

'Craig's gay!' Sandy said.

'Strictly,' Jodi replied. 'Sorry to disillusion you, but I've seen too many fall into that trap to want to see it happen to you. He's really friendly, gets on great with women, but when it comes to true love and the dastardly deed he only leans one way.'

Sandy looked across to Craig's office again, and seeing his assistant carrying a pile of paperwork up the steps she said, 'Are he and Bertie . . . ?'

Jodi laughed. 'God, no. Craig's much more subtle

41

than that. In fact I don't even know if Craig's got a boyfriend. No one seems to know anything about his private life. He never talks about it, but it's hard to imagine someone who looks like him going without, don't you think?'

Sandy nodded. 'What about Dan?' she asked. 'Michael's partner. What's he like?'

'Dan,' Jodi answered, sitting back down at her desk, 'is an absolute sweetheart. He's married to Michael's sister, Colleen. They've got two kids, another about to arrive, and Michael's mother Clodagh more or less lives with them.'

Sandy smiled. 'They sound like a close family,' she remarked, sitting down too.

'Oh, they're definitely that,' Jodi confirmed. 'Clodagh calls at least once a day, which is generally an excuse to have a gossip with whoever answers the phone, because she usually ends up forgetting to ask for Michael. She's a doll, though. Everyone loves her. Bit mad, but she's Irish so what do you expect? There's another son, Cavan. He's in his early twenties and the real darling of the family. He's got a different father to Michael and Colleen, but you'd never know it. They all dote on that boy. Every one of them. And if you met him you'd know why. It's not something you can put into words, it's just like something you feel, you know. Like you just love him, because he's the most lovable person you ever met. He looks a lot like Michael, but younger, and the last I heard he was rescuing otters somewhere in Norway.' She frowned. 'I might have that wrong. You never know with Cavan, he's always into something weird. Not that otters are weird, but you get my drift. Hello, Michael McCann's office,' she said into the phone.

By the end of the morning Sandy was feeling much more confident and at home than she'd ever have dared hope when she first arrived. Everyone was so open and friendly and eager to show her how things were done that her initial shyness had almost completely vanished and she hoped it wouldn't be long now before she managed to laugh without blushing. In fact, she was feeling so good and enjoying answering the phones and learning the computer so much that she had all but forgotten that she had no more money in her purse than it took to get home. Indeed, she might not have remembered until it was time to leave, had Dan's assistant, Shirley, not called her into her office to go over her records.

Sandy's misery was total as she sat in the spacious, shiny office with the same view of the river as hers and Jodi's, watching Shirley enter all her lies into a computer. The ridiculous part about it was now she was getting to know them she didn't think these people would mind that she was a no one. In fact, she couldn't imagine them thinking that way about anyone, no matter who they were. Well, perhaps Bertie might, and Janine and Frances were pretty thick with him, but on the whole these were the easiest-going people she'd ever met. Even Adrian Fisher, the bloke who hosted the morning breakfast show, had been really nice to her on the phone when he'd rung in earlier. In fact, he'd said he was looking forward to meeting her, but whether he meant it or whether he was just being polite, she wasn't too sure.

'So, you're a Shropshire lass,' Shirley beamed, her lined, powdered face reminding Sandy of her mother. Not that her mother ever smiled like that, but she wasn't much good at putting powder on either. 'Such a lovely part of the country,' Shirley said. 'My sister lived there for a while, we used to go to visit every summer.'

Sandy continued to smile, while silently begging God not to let Shirley ask if she knew anywhere in Shropshire. She wondered now why she had chosen it, when she didn't know the first thing about it. In fact, for all she knew, it could be even worse than Beddesley Heath. It seemed not, though, from the look on Shirley's face.

'And you and your father ran a bookshop,' Shirley said, consulting the screen in front of her. 'What a wonderful thing to do. I've always fancied it myself, retiring to the country and surrounding myself with books.'

'It had its moments,' Sandy responded, astonishing herself with such a slick reply.

Shirley's eyes twinkled. Then, returning to the screen she said, 'OK, we have most of your background details, so what we need now is to confirm where you're living in London and get a home telephone number for you and one we can call in case of emergency.'

Sandy's smile remained, but the warmth was draining. 'Oh, yes,' she said, thinking fast. The address she could give, as she'd found herself a poky little bedsit in Barking with shared shower and toilet and there was a phone box on the landing that took incoming calls. But the number for emergencies was a problem as she didn't know anyone yet, never mind their telephone number, and she'd said at the interview that she had a cousin in London. Quickly she gave the details she could, then added the first eleven-digit number that came into her head, for emergencies.

Shirley was nodding happily. 'Lovely,' she said, hitting the enter key. 'I'm glad you managed to find yourself a place so quickly. I'm not familiar with Barking. Is it nice?'

'Oh, very,' Sandy lied. 'I mean, my flat isn't anything special, but it'll do until I find somewhere else.'

Inside she was crying, for the crummy little bedsit had cost her four hundred pounds in advance rent, with another thousand payable in four weeks to cover the following month's rent and a security deposit. She

44

was lucky that the landlord had agreed to wait for the deposit, though where on earth she was going to find a spare six hundred pounds when finally she got paid she had no idea. But that was four weeks away yet, and right now she had more to worry about than rent, when she was ravenously hungry and all that was in her purse was enough to cover her fare home at the end of the day. If she could she'd walk, but even if she knew the way, which she didn't, it would take her half the night and by the time she got there she'd have to turn around and come back.

She looked at Shirley and was right on the point of asking for an advance when her nerve failed. What reason could she give for needing an advance, when she had just sold a bookshop and presumably inherited whatever other assets her father had owned? Come to that, with all that money, why would she be living in a place like Barking? She wished desperately that she'd never told those lies now, but she couldn't think of a way to take them back.

'Oh, just one last thing,' Shirley said. 'Sandy? Is that Sandra or Alexandra?'

'Alexandra,' Sandy replied, lying again.

Shirley typed it in, then clicked a few times on the mouse. 'OK, well that's us done,' she said, getting up. 'I hope you're going to be very happy here at McCanns. We aren't without our faults, but on the whole I think you'll find us a pleasant bunch. Dan should be in tomorrow, I'll introduce you then. Michael, I believe, is due in any minute.'

Sandy nodded and felt her heart turn over at the prospect of meeting her new boss.

As she returned to her office Jodi was on her way out. 'Ah, there you are,' she cried, tugging on her coat. 'Michael's just arrived. He's in his office with Zelda. I've got to go and get some sandwiches, can you take them in a coffee and answer the phones while I'm gone?'

'Yes, of course,' Sandy said, hiding her panic well. 'Uh, what kind of coffee do they take? Black? White? Sugar?'

'They both take black, no sugar. Zelda likes to have her own mug. It's the dark-green one next to the coffee machine. Can I get you a sandwich while I'm there? They do everything. Tuna, prawn, chicken, you name it.'

Sandy's mouth watered. 'Uh, no thanks, I'm not hungry,' she said. It was now almost twenty-four hours since she'd last eaten and she didn't even want to think about how much longer it was going to be to the next time.

'Jodi, are you still there?'

Jodi turned and running back to her desk pushed a button on the intercom. 'Still here,' she confirmed, winking at Sandy. 'Michael,' she mouthed.

'Bring me in the file on Don Portman before you go,' he said, 'and make sure his number in the Cotswolds is there.'

'Will do,' Jodi responded and let the button go. 'The file is in the second drawer over there,' she said to Sandy, spinning her Rolodex. 'If you get it . . . Ah, here we are, Don Portman, Tetbury.' She passed the card to Sandy. 'Write that number on the inside cover of the file and take it in with the coffee. I'll be back in ten minutes, fifteen if there's a queue.'

Sandy did as she was told, her hands shaking slightly as she wrote down the number, then went to pour the coffee. Her face felt strained and there was a slight dizziness in her head and strangeness in her stomach that had as much to do with nerves as it did with hunger. She so desperately wanted to make a good impression on her new boss, yet she felt almost sick with apprehension at the prospect of meeting him.

The file was tucked securely under one arm as she carried two mugs of coffee the short distance to his office. The inner circle was emptying for lunch now and none of those left appeared to notice her, and even if they did they'd never guess how she was feeling. Perhaps if she weren't so hungry she'd have a better grip on herself, but feeling so empty and weird inside she was finding it difficult to keep her mind on one track.

Fortunately the door was slightly ajar, so giving it a gentle nudge with her foot she peeped round to see if it was all right to go in. There was no sign of anyone, then a voice behind the door, the same voice she'd heard on the intercom, said, 'I hear what you're saying, Bob, but I've got the schedule in front of me and it's not looking good. He's shooting in Sunderland all that week. Hang on, let me see ... It's dated a couple of weeks ago, so yeah, things might have changed. I'll check it out and get back to you. OK? Yeah, later today.'

Sandy stayed where she was, half in, half out of the door, not knowing which way to go. She couldn't knock, because her hands were full, but she didn't feel right about going in unannounced.

'Beep, beep,' someone said behind her.

Sandy started, slopped the coffee and turned to find Zelda smiling down at her. Her heart filled with relief.

'Och, it's Sandy!' Zelda exclaimed, her round, sparkly eyes reflecting the warmth in her throaty Scots voice. 'How are you, dear? Glad you managed to get here all right. Settling in OK, are you?'

'Oh, uh yes, thank you,' Sandy stumbled. 'Um, I was just bringing you some coffee.'

'Terrific,' Zelda intoned, already gesturing for Sandy to go on in. 'Have you met Michael yet? Where is he?'

'Right here,' Michael answered, pulling the door open wide.

'Michael,' Zelda said, 'this is Sandy, our new recruit. Sandy, this is Michael McCann.'

Sandy turned to look at him. For the moment she could only see his profile as he was standing over a table behind the door, his chin resting on a mobile phone while he studied a chart in front of him. He lifted a hand and pushed it into his untidy dark hair, then pulled a face as he muttered something under his breath and scratched his chin. Sandy wondered if she should say something, but he seemed so deep in thought that she didn't like to interrupt.

At last he seemed to sense she was there and turned to look at her. The confusion in his arresting blue eyes was only fleeting as he belatedly registered what Zelda had said. Immediately he broke into a smile. 'Hello, Sandy,' he said, putting a hand on her shoulder and steering her towards the desk. 'How are you settling in? Have you met everyone? Here, why don't you put those down there?'

Sandy put the coffee down, then took the file from under her arm. She waited as he walked around the desk, saying something to Zelda who was talking on the phone. Sandy's heart was pumping faster than ever, her face felt unbearably hot and all her senses seemed to be reeling.

Michael was looking at Zelda, listening to what she was saying. Then he turned back to Sandy and smiled again. His teeth were slightly uneven, but seemed only to make his smile more striking. His nose was in perfect proportion to the rest of his face, his eyebrows were thick and almost joined at the centre, and his eyes were so intensely blue that she almost missed the way they were simmering with humour. He needed to shave and his tie was skewed to one side, but there was no question in Sandy's mind that he was the most gorgeous man she had ever laid eyes on.

'Is that Don Portman's file?' he asked.

Sandy looked down at the hand he was holding out. His fingers were long and slender, there was hair on the back of his hand. 'Um, yes,' she said, passing the file over.

His smile grew wider and Sandy blushed so hard it hurt. There didn't seem much doubt that he knew exactly what kind of effect he was having on her, which was probably, Sandy guessed, the same effect he had on every woman he met. The idea of how glamorous and sophisticated those other women must be in comparison with her made her feel faintly sick inside. Yet being different might be just what would attract him to her.

'Why don't you go and get yourself a coffee, then come and let us get to know you?' he said, sitting down and opening the file.

To Sandy's dismay, no sound came out as she made to answer. She tried again. 'I have to answer the phones while Jodi's out,' she said quietly.

He was looking down at the file. 'It's lunch-time,' he said, 'there won't be many calls. Tell him the deal didn't go through,' he said.

Sandy frowned, then belatedly realized he was talking to Zelda. She continued to stand awkwardly where she was, not sure what to do now. He was leafing through the file again and Zelda, perched on the edge of his desk in a huge, flowery dress and beaded headband, was engrossed on the phone. In the end she decided to go back to her office.

As she sat down at her desk she could hear him talking in the next room and wondered if she should do as he'd said and get herself a coffee to take back. A part of her wanted to desperately, but another part was telling her that he had already forgotten he'd mentioned it. She poured herself a coffee anyway to help ease the hunger pangs which, for the moment, didn't seem quite so acute as they had.

A fax came in for Bertie so she took it to his desk. The lower circle was deserted now: everyone, it seemed, had gone for lunch. She went back to her office and carried on entering addresses into the computer.

'Sandy, are you there?' Michael's voice suddenly came over the intercom.

Sandy leapt to her feet and leaned quickly across to Jodi's desk. As her finger hit the button her arm hit the coffee. 'Yes, I'm here,' she said, whisking a set of photographs out of the way before the coffee could reach them.

'See if you can get hold of Pat Roseman at Freeman Banks, will you?' he said. 'The number should be on the Rolodex, probably under F or R. If it's not, come back to me and we'll try again.'

Sandy found the number, dialled it and asked for Pat Roseman. The voice at the other end told her that Mr Roseman was at lunch. Sandy asked her to hold and buzzed through to Michael. 'Pat Roseman is at lunch,' she said, 'shall I leave a message for him to ring back?'

'Yes, why not?' Michael said. 'Tell him it's about the Mantree project.'

Sandy went back on the line, gave the message, then rang off. She felt so ridiculously proud that she had suggested the message that she couldn't stop herself grinning. And what luck to have had the opportunity to show off her initiative so early.

'Are you joining us?' Michael said. 'Or are you too busy cleaning the furniture?'

Sandy stopped mopping up the coffee and stared at the intercom. How on earth did he know what she was doing? Then realizing he was standing behind her she turned and started to laugh. 'Sorry, I thought . . .' she said, waving towards the intercom.

He grinned. 'No, it's the real thing. Any sign of Jodi with those sandwiches? I'm starving.'

'Not yet,' Sandy answered. 'Shall I go and see if I can find her?'

'No need, she's here,' he said as the lift doors opened and Jodi came rushing out. 'I forgot to tell you,' he said to Jodi as she bounded up the steps towards him, 'I saw Butch Wilkins this morning, he said to send his love.'

'Very droll,' Jodi remarked.

Michael was laughing.

'I hope you're not intimidating Sandy,' she said, dropping the sandwiches into Michael's hand and starting to take off her coat. 'You've got mine there as well, before you go,' she told him. 'Did you remember to call Kate?'

Michael pulled a face.

Jodi sighed. 'She specifically said you were to call her before one o'clock,' she said.

'OK, I'm sorry,' he grimaced. 'I forgot. So who do I make it up to? You or her?'

'Both,' Jodi answered, taking her sandwich. 'Where's Zelda?'

'Meditating.'

'Then I'd better take her some ice and lemon.'

Laughing, Michael watched as Jodi took ice and lemon from the fridge, then went past him to pop it along to Zelda. 'Meditating,' he told Sandy as he walked over to Jodi's chair and sat down, 'is a useful euphemism where Zelda is concerned.'

Not knowing what a euphemism was, Sandy just smiled.

'Not eating?' he asked, unwrapping his sandwiches and propping his feet up on the desk.

Sandy shook her head. 'I'm not hungry,' she said.

He bit into his sandwich, chewed slowly as he looked her over, then, swallowing, he said, 'So, tell me about you. Where were you working before? Zelda mentioned something about a bookshop.'

51

'That's right,' Sandy answered. 'I ran it for my father.'

He took another bite of sandwich.

Sandy watched him, almost drooling at the thought of how good it must taste, then, suddenly realizing he was waiting for her to continue she said, 'Uh, he died a few months ago, so I decided to sell up and come to London.' She smiled self-consciously. 'I wanted something a bit more exciting out of life and this job seemed a good place to start.'

Michael nodded. 'Are you ambitious?' he asked.

She wasn't too sure how to answer that, as she'd never really thought about it before. 'Uh, yes, I think so,' she said.

'Are you planning on becoming an agent? Is that why you chose us?'

Sandy flushed and glanced away. 'I'm not, uh . . . Well, yes, I do want to become an agent,' she answered, suddenly realizing how much greater an impression she would make on him if she were, 'but I know I've got a long way to go yet.'

He shrugged. 'Depends how hard you're prepared to work,' he said. 'So where do you live?'

'Barking,' she answered. 'Where do you live?'

His eyebrows flickered. 'Me?' he said. 'Just along the river, on the other side, near Albert Bridge. Do you know it?'

Sandy shook her head. 'I don't really know anywhere yet,' she confessed. 'Do you live in a flat or a house?'

His blue eyes were starting to dance and she wasn't entirely sure why. 'A flat,' he said. 'What about you?'

'A flat. Not a very big one, but it'll do for now. Have you always been an agent?'

His head went to one side as he thought about that. 'Yes,' he said in the end, 'I suppose you could say I have. At least, it's the only real job I've had. Dan, my partner, and I came down from Oxford at the same time, moved to London and started working for a friend's father who was having trouble keeping his agency afloat. Considering Dan and I had graduated in economics and business studies, but had had no experience of the real world, we were the right and the wrong choice to help bail this guy out. But what we lacked in hands-on we made up for in zest and Franklyn, the friend's father, needed all the help he could get. His problem was gambling, not agenting, so we didn't have a huge problem getting the show back on the road, and while I concentrated on pulling together the right agents and clients, Dan took over the financial side. We bought Franklyn out a couple of years after we joined him, called ourselves McCann Walsh and in the same year pulled off a major coup by getting the great Zelda Frey to come and join us. She was with Sylvesters at the time, probably the biggest agency in London and had, still has in fact, a list that reads like a roll-call at BAFTA. So, I guess you could say that we owe most of our success to Zelda, who resolutely refuses to accept a partnership because, so she claims, she prefers gin and tonic.'

Sandy laughed.

Winking, Michael put down his sandwich and went to pour himself another coffee. A painful zing dug into Sandy's taste buds as she gazed longingly at the rich, succulent chicken and creamy mayonnaise between two thick slices of granary bread.

'Would you like one?' he offered.

Sandy spun round, appalled that he had seen her hunger, then relaxed as she saw he was holding up the coffee jug. She shook her head. 'No, no thanks,' she said.

As he walked back to Jodi's desk he started talking again. 'You've probably gathered by now,' he said, 'that we don't only look after actors here. We've got a pretty extensive list of writers, which Craig heads up, and directors and producers which Harry mainly takes care of.'

'What about you?' Sandy asked. 'Who do you take care of?'

He shrugged. 'A dozen or so directors,' he answered, 'and the rest of the business. On the whole I tend not to take people on myself, I just bring them into the agency and Zelda or Craig or Harry or one of the other agents looks after them. Obviously, all the clients have access to me, whoever they are, but I try not to get involved unless I have to.'

'Oh, I see,' Sandy said.

Michael grinned.

Sandy smiled too and lowered her eyes. He was so easy and friendly, and though she felt hugely out of her depth she wished he would go on talking. 'Where are you from?' she asked. 'I mean, where were you born?'

'Ireland,' he said, when he'd finished chewing. 'My sister Colleen and I were born there and moved to Liverpool when I was four and she was three. My dad worked on the docks, had too much to drink one day and fell off a crane. I was six when he died, Colleen was five. My mother married again a few years later and Cavan, my brother, came along not too long after.' The way he was smiling suggested that his mother was pregnant when she married. 'My stepdad died a couple of years ago from cancer,' he went on, 'and Clodagh, my mother, God bless her, lives most of the year with Colleen in Putney and the rest boasting about us all to her sister in Tralee.'

Sandy was smiling. 'You sound like a very close family,' she said, realizing she'd made the same remark to Jodi.

'Sometimes too close,' he said with raised eyebrows. 'Now, what about you? Do you have any family now that your father's passed on?'

Sandy shook her head. 'No, I was an only child,' she said.

'But you have a cousin here in London, right?'

'Oh! Yes!' she replied, realizing he must have already done some homework on her. 'Well, she's only a second cousin and we don't really get on. She said I could live with her when I got here, but I only stayed a couple of nights, then moved into my own place.'

Michael's eyes showed his interest. 'What happened to your mother?' he asked.

'She died when I was six. Cancer. Of the brain.'

'I'm sorry,' he responded softly as Jodi came back in the door. 'Zelda asleep yet?' he asked.

'She's chanting,' Jodi answered as he got up from her chair.

Michael chuckled. 'She's probably asking for strength after this morning,' he said. 'Has she heard back from Gloria yet?'

Jodi grinned. 'That's why she's chanting. Gloria is still refusing to take off her top and the whole shoot is at a standstill. Zelda just spoke to her and reminded her that the contract she signed stipulates that she'll bare her tits, but Gloria has gone shy. She wants Zelda to go down there and sort it out, but Zelda thinks you should handle it because you probably stand more chance of persuading Gloria to get her tits out than anyone else on the planet, I quote.'

Michael gave a shout of laughter. 'Leave Zelda to me,' he said, picking up his coffee.

The fax rang and Sandy turned to watch the message come through, so dazzled by all the attention Michael had just given her that there was just no way she could see anything on the page. Nor, as she kept her back turned for fear of showing her feelings, did she see the quick look that passed between Jodi and Michael as he walked out of the door.

Chapter 4

The afternoon turned out to be even more hectic than the morning as Sandy ran around the office delivering faxes and phone messages, collected the outgoing mail and tried to keep on top of everything else. The chat with Michael had buoyed her confidence so much that she was having no problem talking to anyone else now, not even Bertie, whom she'd found quite intimidating at first. But she had few thoughts for anyone other than Michael. She was totally entranced, for she'd never dreamed she'd find it so easy to chat with someone like him. He wasn't like a boss at all, in fact none of the agents were, but there was something different about Michael, something even more down to earth and easier to deal with than the others. She suspected that it was to do with him being working class too, like her, even though he had gone to Oxford later.

But no, it went deeper than that. She didn't want to start kidding herself here, but she hadn't been able to help noticing the way he looked at her, nor how keen he had been to talk to her. Blimey, he had asked her enough times, had even ended up coming in to see her, which couldn't be normal for a man in his position. No, she definitely reckoned he fancied her and God knew she fancied him. After all, looking like him, how could anyone not?

She was so engrossed in her fantasy world that, had

the lift doors not opened around five o'clock to deliver one of the most beautiful women she had ever laid eyes on, she might actually have ended up persuading herself it was all an attainable dream. But just one look at the stunning creature who was at least six feet tall, with the most gorgeous long blonde hair, exquisite slanting eyes and a smile that was just too lovely for words, was enough to crush Sandy's hopes to dust and make her want to dash across the office to shove the woman back in the lift before Michael ever set eyes on her. Then, realizing it was Michael the woman was smiling at, she felt sick inside, and watched miserably from her office as he slipped an arm around the woman's shoulders and walked with her down the steps into the well.

'Ah, Janey!' Jodi cried jumping up from her chair and going to the door. 'Bobby Mack's been trying to get hold of you. Have you got your mobile turned off?'

'The battery's dead,' Janey answered. 'Did he say where I could reach him?'

By now Janey and Michael were coming up the steps towards Jodi's and Sandy's office. 'He's at Wembley,' Jodi said. 'Michael, the contracts guy at Vargo is holding on the line for you.'

'OK, I'll take it in my office,' he said. 'Don't forget to introduce Janey to Sandy.'

Sitting at her desk, Sandy's heart swelled to think he hadn't forgotten her, even though the last person she wanted to meet was his bloody girlfriend.

Her face was stiff and her voice stilted as Jodi introduced them, and not even when Jodi explained that Janey was one of the agents did Sandy feel herself thawing. She could sense Janey's confusion at her hostility and even knew the point at which Janey put her manner down to shyness, but all the time, deep down inside Sandy wanted to scratch the woman's eyes out because even if she was an agent she was probably still Michael's girlfriend.

'What, Janey?' Jodi laughed after Janey had gone and Sandy had asked point-blank if she was right. 'If she is then it's news to me,' Jodi said. 'It'll be news to Bobby Mack too, who Janey's been living with for the past eight and a half years.'

Sandy lowered her eyes. To be told that Janey was living with someone else made her feel better, but not much, for seeing her walk into the office like that, so willowy and elegant and heart-stoppingly lovely, had shown Sandy just how ridiculous she was even to be thinking the way she had about Michael.

'They've got a couple of kids,' Jodi was saying while sorting through the paperwork in front of her. 'Actually, they're Bobby's kids. Janey took them on when she and Bobby moved in together. Their mother died in a car crash. They were so young when it happened I don't expect they even remember her now. Sad, isn't it? But Janey's a great mum. She used to be a model. Did all the catwalks in Paris and Milan. Most of her clients are models who want to be actors. A couple have made it, actually, like Beena Fairbanks, she plays the sidekick in *Lampson PI*, I expect you've seen her, and Gary Bruce, he's just got a regular part on *The Bill*.'

'Does Michael have a girlfriend?' Sandy asked, the words coming before she could stop them.

Jodi's pause was momentary as her eyes flicked towards Sandy, then returned to what she was doing.

Embarrassed, Sandy looked out to where the two booking assistants were putting on their coats ready to go home. She forced herself to laugh in the hope of lightening her question. 'I'm sure someone like him must have lots of women after him,' she said.

'He does,' Jodi confirmed. 'All the time. The current one's name is Kate Feather. She's some kind of high roller with the European Parliament, but don't ask me what. Class, beauty and brains. The woman makes me sick, or she would if I didn't like her so much.' She grimaced, then, tucking her fluffy dark hair behind her ears she said, 'God knows how long she'll last, though I have to say it seems to be going pretty strong right now.' She glanced up as Shirley walked past the office, waved good-night, then went back to what she was doing.

'He'll drop her soon enough, though,' she continued, 'he always does.' She looked at Sandy and gave a rueful smile. 'You should see the state some of them get themselves into when he tells them it's over,' she said, 'makes you wonder if they ever heard of pride. He tells them right at the start that it's not going anywhere, the trouble is they never believe him. I mean, he goes out with them, you know takes them on dates and stuff; sometimes, if he's getting on particularly well with one, he might take her to the boat he keeps in Cannes or to his house in the Caribbean, but none of them ever last very long.' She sighed and shook her head.

'God, the times women have rung up here, or even turned up in the lift, in a right mess because he's not returning their calls or they've found out he's seeing someone else. You can't help feeling sorry for them, because every one of them thinks she's the one who's going to change him and make him settle down, and it comes as a real shock when they find out they're wrong.' She leaned forward and, resting her chin on her hand, gazed absently out at the darkening night.

'I sometimes wonder if he ever will settle down,' she said, almost to herself. 'It's been such a long time since Michelle, he must be over it by now, but ...' She shrugged and turned to Sandy. 'You might remember it,' she said. 'It was in all the papers at the time. Michelle Rowe? Do you remember her?'

Sandy was frowning. 'The name rings a bell,' she said. 'Oh, yes, I know, wasn't she in that series about

Bosnia? She played the mother who never found her kids.'

Jodi nodded. 'That was her. Michael bought the book and commissioned the series specially for her. They made a bundle on that, I can tell you. Everyone did, it was so successful.' She paused for a moment then went on, unprompted. 'She was fresh out of drama school when Michael first met her,' she said. 'He saw her in a Sam Sheppard play at the Latchmere and signed her up that night.' She chuckled. 'Listen to me, signed her up! What he did was fall smack, bang in love with her. She did with him too. They were inseparable the two of them. I think they'd only been together a couple of weeks when she moved in with him. Of course, having Michael as a lover she could hardly go wrong, could she? But she had real talent as an actress, I mean she was *good*. Everyone thought so, even the critics. Did you see her in that film, *Good-night to Ben Bower*? God, she was brilliant. I cried buckets when she walked up to that grave. She got a BAFTA for that. She was nominated for *Gone Without Trace*, the series about Bosnia, but someone else got it, Jessica Pollinger, but that was a political decision and everyone knows the award should have been Michelle's. Anyway, she and Michael were working together on a movie when she left. It was the first time Michael had gone into producing. It was something he'd always talked about doing, but he was so tied up with other things he just never got round to it. Then this script came up that was dead right for Michelle and she was so excited about it that Michael decided to go with it. He'd have been a brilliant producer, everyone says so. He still gets offers now, but he always turns them down.'

'Why?' Sandy asked.

Jodi's lips flattened as she shook her head. 'I don't know,' she said. 'It's not something he ever talks about.

All I know is when Michelle walked out he pulled the plug on the movie and has never mentioned it since.'

'Why did she walk out?' Sandy asked.

Jodi looked at her in surprise. 'It was in all the papers,' she said, 'don't you remember? She ended her relationship with Michael, gave up acting and went off to work for Save the Children, or some charity like that. It was the TV series that did it. She got so into the part and was so torn up by all the things that were happening to the women and children in Bosnia that she just had to do something to help. And her idea of doing something to help was to go over there and get right into it.'

Sandy was staring at her in amazement. Now that Jodi had reminded her she did remember the story, but what was having the biggest effect of all on her right now was the fact that she, Sandy Paull, was falling for the same man as Michelle Rowe – *the* Michelle Rowe – had gone out with. God, she could remember so well the way she and her sisters had devoured the story in the papers, and how everyone in the office had been talking about it too. It seemed so unreal, so beyond all her wildest dreams that she should be mixing with people like that. But she was, and now she had met Michael McCann Sandy couldn't even begin to imagine how Michelle Rowe had brought herself to leave him, especially not for the reason she had. Not that Sandy didn't care about children, but there were always envelopes to put money in, or pledges you could make on the telly, so why did anyone feel they had to give up a superstar career and the most fantastic man in the world to go and be an aid worker in some godforsaken part of the world? To Sandy it just didn't make any sense.

'How did Michael take it?' she asked.

Again Jodi shook her head. 'He was devastated,' she answered. 'Completely devastated. You see, they weren't only planning to do the film, they were planning to get married too.' She sighed. 'He really loved that woman,' she said softly. 'I mean *really* loved her. And they were so good together. Always laughing and fooling about, here in the office or at parties, wherever they were. They were just made for each other.' She paused as her mind wandered back through those times. 'We didn't see him for a month after she went,' she said in the end. 'He took off somewhere with Cavan, his brother. They went to his boat, I think. I never asked.'

'Does he ever hear from her now?' Sandy wondered.

'Not that I know of,' Jodi answered. 'She tried to keep in touch at first, I think, but he never answered her letters. God only knows where she is now. I think she left Bosnia and went on somewhere else, but I don't remember anyone ever saying where. We were all dead certain she'd come back once she'd got it out of her system, but it doesn't look like she's going to.'

They both looked round as a sudden commotion started up in the well and getting up went to see what was happening.

'They're mad,' Jodi laughed, when they saw Zelda in a matching midnight blue head band and track suit, trying to push Michael off an exercise bike. 'Completely mad.'

The others were all coming out of their offices and laughing as Zelda cuffed Michael round the ear and Craig launched into a hilarious Tour de France commentary to encourage Michael's exhausting uphill pedal. The bike was outside Zelda's office on the upper level, not far away, but Michael's back was turned so Sandy couldn't see his face.

Nevertheless, it felt strange to think of him as the man Jodi had just been talking about, the one who had been so broken up when his girlfriend left him that he'd never been seriously involved with anyone since.

He must be over it by now, though, because like Jodi said it had happened at least three, maybe even four, years ago. It was just that he hadn't met the right person since. That was all. Nothing to do with him still carrying a torch for Michelle Rowe.

'Oh, there goes the phone,' Jodi tutted, starting to turn back into the office.

'It's OK,' Sandy said, 'I'll get it.'

'Jodi, get the man a stretcher!' Harry shouted.

As Jodi skipped off to join in the fun, Sandy went to answer the phone. 'Hello, Michael McCann's office,' she said, reaching for her Post-its and pen.

'Hi. It's Kate,' the voice at the other end said. 'Is that Jodi?'

Sandy was silent for a moment as she realized this must be the Kate Jodi had mentioned, Michael's current girlfriend. 'Uh, no, it's Sandy,' she said.

'Oh, I don't think we've met,' Kate said. 'Are you new?'

'I started today,' Sandy answered.

'Really? Then I hope it works out well for you. Is Michael there? I'm in a taxi, so we could get cut off any minute.'

Sandy was quiet again. Then, looking towards the empty doorway and feeling herself start to perspire she said, 'No, I'm afraid Michael's not here. Can I take a message?'

'Yes. Tell him I'm pissed off he didn't call me before I left earlier, but he can reach me at the Hotel Miramar after seven o'clock.'

'If he rings in I'll pass the message on,' Sandy said and rang off just as Jodi came back through the door.

'Why don't you head off home now?' Jodi suggested. 'I've still got a few things to clear up here, but you must be shagged out by now, this being your first day and all.'

Sandy looked at her, then turned quickly away as her

throat suddenly tightened and the hunger pangs in her stomach intensifed to pain. Kate Feather, and what she had just done, was abruptly eclipsed by the terrible reality of her immediate plight. If only she could stay here for the night, at least then she wouldn't have to worry about how she was going to get back the next day – and maybe, just maybe, someone had left some biscuits or crisps in their desk . . .

Not seeing what else she could do, she reached for her coat and started to put it on. The desperation in her heart was making her light-headed and strange inside. In a way it was like it was happening to someone else. Maybe that was something she should hang on to, maybe she should pretend this wasn't her at all; if nothing else, it might help keep the horrible claws of hunger at bay. And it shouldn't be hard to pretend, not when almost nothing about today had seemed real anyway. It had all been so different from what she had expected, so exciting and exhilarating, and she hadn't ever felt so happy nor filled with eagerness and hope for the future. It was just too horrible to think that it was all over already, but if she didn't find some money for her fare in the morning it would be. It seemed so ludicrous and petty that she couldn't scrape enough together for a single, never mind a return ticket to Barking, but she couldn't. She'd tried all weekend to think of a way round this, but still she hadn't come up with any answers and time was running out. A voice inside her started to rage, though against what and at whom she didn't really know. All she knew was that she'd never been in a state like this before; there had always been a sister to borrow from, or a brother to cadge a lift from, and never in her life had she had to go without food.

She looked at Jodi who was busy now on the phone. If only she could find the courage to ask. Five pounds would be enough. It would get her a McDonald's tonight and a return ticket for tomorrow. But what did she do after that? Who was she going to borrow five pounds from next?

Her eyes fell to Jodi's bag sitting open on the floor beside her desk. It would be so easy to knock something over, go down to retrieve it and take the purse while she was there. She had never stolen anything in her life, but she had never been this desperate or hungry in her life.

Feeling sick with shame that she had even considered it, she tore her eyes from the bag, picked up her own and started for the door. She was going to have to think of something, though, because she just couldn't bear the idea of never coming back here now. She belonged here, it was where she was meant to be. These people were her new family and already she was making plans for how she was going to work her way up so she could become someone Michael would be proud to love.

She glanced along the upper circle and for a moment toyed with the idea of talking to Zelda, but Michael was probably with her and Sandy would rather die than have him know what a predicament she was in.

She rode down in the lift with Harry and Thea. They were asking how she had enjoyed her first day and if she thought she could put up with them any more. Sandy laughed and told them she would try, while wanting to cry. When they reached the lobby she got out while the others continued down to the car-park.

Her journey home passed in a blur of hunger and despair, as the crowds whizzed by on their way home to families and hot food on the table. They would probably be shocked if they knew what a state she was in, because she certainly didn't look destitute – not yet, anyway. Those she noticed the most were the lonely, bedraggled figures on station platforms or sitting huddled in shop doorways, begging. At least she had a roof over her head, but that still didn't provide her with something to eat and how long was the roof going to last if she couldn't keep up with her job?

It was just before eight when finally she let herself into the cold, cheerless little room on the first floor of what might once have been a fairly grand house. There were four more doors on the landing, two to other bedsits, one to the toilet and another to a shower room with cracked and stained tiles and a mouldy plastic curtain.

Closing the door behind her she didn't bother to flick on the light as she covered her face with her hands and started to cry. She'd spent all weekend shut in this room crying, as she tried to think what to do – it had changed nothing then and it was going to change nothing now. But she couldn't stop. She was so hungry and lonely that she just didn't know what to do. She couldn't even go home because she didn't have the money for a ticket.

Tears streamed down her face as her breath caught on the terrible fear welling inside her. Her body was stiff with cold. Her head throbbed and her stomach was growling for food. She wondered if she was going to starve to death here in this horrid little room with its chipped sink and water heater in one corner, single bed with no sheets or blankets in another and a damp, musty old cupboard where her clothes were hanging in the other. She thought about Michael and her tears grew thick with shame at the way she had sat at her desk day-dreaming about a fairy-tale romance and story-book rise in her career, when *this* was the reality of her life. What a miserable, loathsome little fool she was to think that a man like Michael McCann would even consider having someone like her in his life. And what the hell had made her lie like that to his girlfriend, when she was sure to get found out and was probably never going to see him again anyway, so what was the point in trying to break up his relationship?

She pressed her hands to her face, seething and sobbing with fury and frustration. She hated it here; she hated the traffic that roared across the flyover outside her window; she hated the wallpaper that was peeling off the walls; she hated the stripes of light across the floor from the Venetian blinds, the electric rings caked with other people's food, the paint-stained carpet, the neighbours who ignored her and the mattress on which she had to lie huddled in her coat for warmth. But most of all she hated herself for being so stupid as to have thought she could come to London on seven hundred and fifty-three pounds and survive.

Hearing the main door downstairs slam closed, she sank to her knees and sobbed as though her heart would break. Another door slammed and she heard someone moving about in the room below. It was probably the woman she'd seen coming out of there on Saturday, the one who had said hello and smiled as she passed. The thought of a friendly face made her cry even harder. Why the hell hadn't she thought to share a flat with someone, rather than be here on her own like this? If she had flatmates she might have friends and someone to borrow money from. But it was too late even to go looking for somewhere to share now, for she'd given all her money to the landlord of this miserable dump.

By the time she finally dragged herself over to the bed her face was ravaged by despair and her whole body was juddering with the aftermath of tears. She felt weak and cold, and so hungry she couldn't bear it, but she was a little calmer now, too exhausted perhaps to care much any more. But she did care. She loved her job and the people who worked there, and she wanted to go back more than she had ever wanted anything in her life. So somehow she was going to have to find a way out of this mess, because if she didn't she really was going to end up begging in doorways or starving to death. And now she'd met Michael and seen what her life could be like, she just couldn't let that happen.

'God, is it that time already?' Michael said, looking at his watch as Zelda walked into his office and sank her ample body into the sofa.

'No, it was that time an hour ago,' she responded, dusting something out of her substantial cleavage and putting her feet up on the coffee table.

Michael dropped his pen and stretched. 'Jodi still here?' He yawned, only just noticing that it was pitch dark in the well.

Zelda nodded and enjoyed a yawn of her own. 'She's copying the final drafts for Vic and Ally,' she answered. 'We'll bike them over to the National first thing tomorrow. What was that?' she said cocking an ear. 'A gin? Och, laddie, you know what it takes to make an old lady happy.'

'Coming right up.' Michael laughed, getting to his feet. 'By the way, I spoke to Alex Drew just now,' he said, walking round his desk to the bar he kept in the bottom of the bookcase. 'Gloria's got one tit bigger than the other he tells me.'

Zelda bubbled with laughter. 'Oh dear,' she said, tucking a wisp of her cherry-red hair behind one ear. 'No wonder she didn't want to take off her top. Still, the main thing is she fulfilled her contract and I'm sure with the kind of technology they've got today they'll manage to straighten things out in the edit.'

Laughing, Michael passed her a drink, then turned back to fix one for himself. 'Brandy and coke?' he said to Jodi as she came in the door.

'Does the Queen fart?' she responded, collapsing beside Zelda on the sofa.

'Does she?' Zelda asked, turning to look at her.

'Is anyone else still here?' Michael said.

'Everyone else went home hours ago,' Jodi told him. 'God, my feet are killing me,' and kicking off her boots she put her feet up next to Zelda's. 'What's that perfume you're wearing, Zelda?' she said. 'It smells like a toilet.'

'Dettol,' Zelda answered. 'I cut my hand on that blasted exercise bike. I'm sending it back, by the way, it goes too fast. Michael, are you going to the screening of *Miraculous* tomorrow night?'

'I don't know, am I, Jodi?' he asked, handing her a drink.

'It's in the diary, but it's clashing with something else. Can't remember what, off the top of my head.'

'Well, if you are,' Zelda said as Michael carried a Scotch on the rocks back to his chair, 'can you take your mother? I promised I would, but I've got to fly up to Manchester tomorrow to see Pru Duffield.'

'No problem,' he said. 'Did Kate ring, by the way?' he said to Jodi.

Jodi shook her head. 'I told you, you had to call her before one o'clock or she was on her way to Brussells.'

'She's in Brussells?' he said.

Jodi nodded.

He grinned. 'An evening at home on my own,' he said. 'I can't remember the last time.'

Jodi looked at him in amazement. 'It's nearly nine o'clock, Michael,' she said. 'The evening's already over. So shall we get on with this?'

Michael leaned back in his chair and put his feet up on the desk. 'So,' he said, stifling a yawn, 'what did you think of Zelda's little lame duck?'

Zelda blinked and took a large mouthful of gin.

'Actually, I quite liked her,' Jodi answered.

'Why do you sound so surprised?' Zelda objected.

'Well you've got to admit, she's a bit weird,' Jodi responded.

'She's not weird at all. She's just shy.'

'Weird,' Jodi insisted. 'And OK, shy. But given a chance, she could probably turn out all right, despite the queer accent. She's certainly not as thick as some we've had. She's got a mega-crush on you, by the way.'

Michael's eyebrows went up.

Jodi chuckled. 'Look at him, pretending he didn't notice,' she said to Zelda. 'Honestly, Michael, you're easier to see through than Sharon Stone's knickers.'

Michael looked at Zelda. 'Where does she get this stuff?' he asked.

Zelda blinked. 'You, I expect,' she answered. 'And speaking of . . .'

'Before we get off the subject, there's something I should mention,' Jodi interrupted. 'I tried calling the numbers Sandy gave me earlier, you know, to check out if they were kosher . . .'

'Why did you do that?' Zelda protested. 'She's hardly a criminal . . .'

'Zelda, there was a time in her life when Myra Hindley was just the girl next door,' Jodi pointed out.

Zelda choked on her drink. 'Surely you're not suggesting . . .'

'No,' Jodi interrupted. 'All I'm saying is there's something about our Sandy that's not quite adding up, or isn't sitting quite right. So I just thought I'd try the numbers, see who answered.'

'And?' Michael prompted.

'One just rang and rang, the other was a greengrocer in Ealing.'

Zelda looked sheepishly at Michael, whose amusement at the interest in Sandy was fading fast. 'I told you, she was sent by the Lynne Masters agency,' Zelda said defensively. 'We've always had good people from them in the past.'

'Zelda, the last time we took in one of your waifs we almost ended up in court,' Michael reminded her.

'Ah, yes, but the last one didn't come through an agency,' Zelda pointed out. 'Sandy did, and I know Lynne Masters, she wouldn't send us anyone duff.'

Michael looked at Jodi. 'What do you think?' he said.

Jodi shrugged. 'I reckon we should give her a go,' she answered. 'I mean, she's here now, so we might as well.'

'OK,' Michael said. 'But the first sign of anything untoward, she's out.'

'God, he's so hard,' Jodi commented.

'Ruthless,' Zelda agreed.

'Can I go home now?' Jodi asked Michael.

'Just try that other number again,' he said. 'The one that rang and rang.'

Jodi padded obediently off to her office, rooted out the phone number and dialled it again. This time she got a reply.

'Well, it seems to be where she lives,' she said, carrying her coat into Michael's office where he and Zelda were by now talking about other things. 'Sandy,' she reminded them when they looked at her blankly.

'Did you speak to her?' Zelda asked.

Jodi shook her head. 'A woman answered and said yes, Sandy Paull lived there, but it wasn't convenient for her to come to the phone right now.'

Michael and Zelda looked at each other. 'He thinks that's sinister,' Zelda said to Jodi.

'Don't you?' he asked.

'She might have been in the bath,' Zelda pointed out.

Michael shrugged. 'Did you say it was you calling?' he asked Jodi.

'Yep,' she replied, 'and the message I got back was that Sandy might not be able to make it until lunch-time tomorrow, but that we weren't to worry she would definitely be coming.'

Michael looked from Zelda to Jodi and back again.

Jodi had seen that look before. 'Duck,' she advised Zelda.

Michael's face was deadly serious. 'If she turns out to be a plant from another agency,' he said, 'a thief, a stooge from the press, or God forbid someone from Ted Forgon, then I'm warning you now, heads will roll,' and getting to his feet, he took his coat from the stand, picked up his briefcase and walked out of the room.

Chapter 5

'Hey! Ellen! How're you doing? Where are you?'

'Hi, Joey.' Ellen laughed, switching the carphone on to the speaker. 'I'm in the car on my way to a new life. Want to come?'

'OK, you talked me into it,' he replied. 'But if I do, you got to do this commercial.'

Ellen laughed again. 'No way, Joey,' she said, spinning the wheel hard left as she pulled out of Riverside on to Laurel Canyon.

'Ellen, you're breaking my heart,' he warned. 'I got it all set up. I showed the client your picture, the guy's ready to roll. You're the face of America, Ellen. You're beautiful. You got it all!'

'Who is this guy?' Matty murmured, her eyes simmering with laughter as she sat in the passenger seat, listening.

'Joey Mancini,' Ellen answered. 'He's in advertising. Come to the point, Joey,' she said into the speaker.

'Hang on, someone's coming through on my other line,' he said. 'Don't go away.'

Matty leaned forward to centre the cool air on her face. 'What's the commercial?' she asked as Ellen slowed up for a red light.

'There is no commercial,' Ellen chuckled. 'This is just something we go through before he gets to the real reason for calling. Which, unless I'm greatly mistaken,

73

will be to try to get me to lean on Hal Gates for some home-loan commercial that Hal Gates doesn't want to do. So, we'll just waste each other's time for a while, then Joey'll go back to his client who'll probably come up with even more money for Hal Gates to turn down.'

Joey's voice came back over the speaker. 'Ellen! I love you,' he called.

Matty gurgled with laughter, then, leaning back into a comfy corner and putting her feet up on the dash, she listened as Ellen took the call which went pretty much the way Ellen had predicted. It took a while, though, and Matty couldn't help but be impressed at the way Ellen handled herself. Of course, she'd had a lot of practice by now, and plenty had been written about her unique mix of charm and ruthlessness, but it wasn't too often that Matty got to see her in action, and she had to confess that each time she did, her respect and admiration just grew. No one would ever know that beneath all that wit, beauty and confidence she had as many insecurities and vulnerabilities as any other woman on earth. In fact, there were times when even Matty wondered if they existed, Ellen was so good at hiding them.

As Ellen punched out a number to make another call, Matty rested her head on the chair back and studied her profile. With her coppery chestnut hair that was so thick and curly and cut bluntly around the collar, her rich, creamy skin, soft brown eyes and gorgeously full mouth, she was probably the most sensuously feminine woman Matty knew. What was more, everything about her was real, from the full, pert breasts to the slender curves of her hips and thighs, even the flat stomach and tastefully manicured fingernails.

'Did I hear you mention Ted Forgon just then?' Matty said as Ellen finished her call.

Ellen nodded.

'So how is he now?' Matty asked. 'When did he get out of the hospital?'

'A couple of weeks back,' Ellen answered. 'He's been recuperating with his sister in Florida.' She glanced quickly in the rear-view mirror, then slipped into the middle lane to avoid a line waiting to join the Freeway. 'Well done, Gene,' she murmured as Matty's boyfriend kept close on her tail in the jeep behind. As he was transporting most of her worldly possessions over to her new apartment, Ellen was particularly concerned he should keep up, especially as he had a tendency to forget where he was going.

'I didn't know Ted Forgon had a sister,' Matty said. Then, after a pause, 'It seems an age since he had that coronary. How long ago was it?'

'Three months,' Ellen answered. 'Did I tell you he fired the secretary he was screwing at the time?'

Matty laughed. 'Get out of here,' she said. 'Is she suing?'

'Not that I've heard,' Ellen replied. 'But Carleena, the secretary he fired a few years back, is still on his case, or so the rumour mill has it. I heard he already paid her fifty thousand bucks, some say it was five hundred thousand, but you know how these things get exaggerated.'

'I take it he was screwing her too?'

'Of course. It's what a secretary's for,' Ellen responded with a droll glance.

'So, are they saying he can return to a normal life now?'

'I've got no idea,' Ellen replied. 'All I know is he's flying back to LA tomorrow and wants to see me first thing Monday. Just like these last three months didn't happen.'

Matty unfolded the visor and studied her reflection in the mirror. Her long, shiny dark hair needed a wash, her attractive, olive-skinned face was pale and her usually vivid dark eyes were shadowed with tiredness. 'God, I look a mess,' she grumbled. 'Did I wake you when I came in this morning?'

'Didn't hear a thing,' Ellen replied. 'What time was it?'

'After three. I can't go on like this, it's killing me. What am I saying, tonight's my last night at the club, so as from tomorrow it'll just be the trusty old coffee bar.' She sucked in her cheeks, then let them go with a pop. 'So, when did you find out Forgon wanted to see you?'

'Julie, his secretary, told me on Tuesday. She also had a file delivered to my office so's I could get some background on the British guy I told you about. So that about confirms my worst fears, wouldn't you say? I've got to go headhunt Michael McCann, only in this case the meaning's more literal, because it's McCann's head on plate that Forgon's after. There's a supermarket up ahead,' she said, pointing. 'Let's go pick up some groceries to take over to the apartment.'

'Do you have a refrigerator?' Matty asked, as Ellen pulled into the parking lot.

Ellen laughed. 'Sure I have a refrigerator,' she answered. 'I told you, I had everything delivered on Thursday, so the place is pretty much in shape already.'

'Has Clay seen it?'

'Not yet. He's coming over tomorrow night when he gets back from San Diego.'

'San Diego?' Matty echoed. 'What's he doing there?'

'The kids are staying with Nola's mother,' Ellen answered, checking to make sure Gene was still with them.

'What news on the divorce?' Matty asked. 'Any idea yet when it's going to happen?'

Ellen shook her head. 'Nola's really dragging things out,' she answered, pulling up to wait for someone to vacate a space. 'It's really starting to get to him,' she said, gazing absently ahead. 'He doesn't care so much

76

for himself, it's what it's doing to his kids that upsets him. He's crazy about them and Nola just doesn't seem to care what she's doing – to any of them.'

Matty sighed. 'You know what gets me,' she said, 'is what the hell the woman's got to be so bitter about? I mean, she was the one who had the affair, she was the one who wanted out of the marriage and she's the god-damned superbitch who's dishing all that garbage out to the press about him being some kind of drunk and wife-beater and God knows what else. So what does she want, for Christ's sake?'

Ellen was shaking her head. 'Believe me, if he knew he'd give it to her. Anything, just to get this mess over with,' and putting her foot down hard she swung her gleaming white Pontiac into the empty space.

An hour later, after stocking up on everything from Windex to whisky, they returned to their cars and rejoined the traffic crawling up to Mulholland. It was an unseasonably hot day for January, even by California standards, and the Santa Ana winds which had torn through the night had cleared the sky of cloud and smog, leaving it a perfect, crystalline blue.

Matty rested an arm on the edge of the door and gazed up at the wooded hills ahead. 'I'm going to miss you,' she said.

'I'm going to miss you too,' Ellen said, pulling out around a mail truck, and smiling at Gene in the rear-view mirror as he came up behind her. 'It's really good of him to give up his Saturday like this,' she commented.

Matty looked bemused, then realizing who Ellen was talking about gave a dismissive wave of her hand. 'You know Gene,' she said, 'he was happy to help. Did he tell you he did an audition yesterday for the new Scorsese movie?'

Ellen nodded. 'The bystanding body-builder with a heart. I read the script. He should be good for it.'

Matty chuckled and adjusted the visor mirror so she could see him. 'I swear he's not just brawn,' she said. 'He's got brains too, it's just with a body like that he doesn't get much call to use them.'

The look Ellen threw her caused her eyes to dance.

'Hey listen, you didn't get back to me about the ex-con's script I gave you,' Matty said. 'Did you get chance to read it?'

'Oh, yeah,' Ellen answered. She threw Matty a glance. 'My honest opinion?'

Matty deflated. 'It stinks,' she said.

Ellen laughed. 'It's got no focus,' she said. 'The characters aren't defined and the story's just not there. You need to work on why he got involved with the other guys, where his motivation is. Take a look at his mother, his father, his kids, if he's got any. They'll tell you everything you need to know about him.'

'But his mother's not in the movie,' Matty protested.

'Whether you cast her or not, a mother's always in a movie,' Ellen told her. 'Did you see *Looking Up* yet?' she asked, nodding towards the five-screen cinema on the corner of Crescent and Sunset as they drove by.

'No. Should I?'

'If you want to see a good structure, then yes,' Ellen answered. 'It's not the best movie you'll ever see, but the characters are solid and the story is sound. How did you come across this ex-con guy, anyhow?'

'He's someone Gene met at voice class,' Matty answered. 'He reckons he's got a lot of interest in his story, he just needs some help with the dialogue.'

'So you and Gene offered? If you want my advice you'll tell him to find some other suckers to share his load, because getting involved in someone else's grudge against the government, which is what that script's really about, is never a good idea. And if he's got the kind of interest he says, why is he asking two actors to help him out, instead of two writers?'

Matty looked at Ellen, waited for Ellen to flash her a grin, which she did, then turned to look straight ahead. 'You didn't have to call me a sucker,' she grumbled.

Ellen laughed. 'OK, I take it back. But you get what I'm saying. The story's no good. It's not going to work and if you're asking me, you're crazy to get involved.'

Matty started to reply, then thought better of it. When it came to knowing what would and wouldn't work on the screen Ellen had a natural born instinct, which was how come she was one of the top agents at ATI with more big names on her list than was decent. God only knew how much she had made for the agency in the two years she'd been there, but whatever it was, more than half a dozen wannabes, who'd been waiting tables and tele-marketing two years ago, had her to thank for their sudden rise to international stardom and millionaires' row. There were also the dozen or so box-office big shots who'd debunked from other agencies to sign up with ATI once word started getting out that was where destiny's darling, in the guise of Ellen Shelby, was currently to be found. Everyone wanted to be on the bandwagon, even Forgon had put some of his bigger clients with Ellen when she'd started getting so many movie and TV packages off the ground. So, in Matty's book, Ellen was in a better position than most to give a judgement on this ex-con's story.

'They're throwing a party at the club when I get off tonight.' She yawned as Ellen's carphone rang again. 'Are you going to come?'

'It'll be too late for me,' Ellen answered, putting the call on the speaker. 'Hi, Ellen Shelby speaking,' she said.

By the time she got off the line they were crossing the city limits into Beverly Hills and Matty was wincing. 'Tell me that's not where I'm headed,' she implored, referring to Rita Norman, the old-timer actress who had just been begging Ellen not to let her career disappear down the can.

'If you keep off the booze, I'll guarantee it,' Ellen told her.

'It was the booze that ruined her?' Matty said, gazing out at the tree-lined avenues and million-dollar homes they were passing.

'Drink, divorce and crooked lawyers,' Ellen expanded.

Matty turned to look at her. 'You know, I remember her from when I was a kid,' she said, sounding and even feeling slightly offended that one of her most cherished icons had proved so depressingly mortal. 'To tell you the truth, I thought she was dead. So how come you're her agent?'

Ellen's smile was sardonic. 'I inherited her from Phil and Flynn. She never works, she's not capable of it, but she needs to speak to someone from time to time and having an agent to call at least gives her some dignity.'

'God,' Matty murmured, 'makes you wonder what those who don't have agents do, doesn't it?'

'They call radio shows,' Ellen responded.

Matty laughed. Then, remembering something she had read only recently about Ellen she said, 'So you really are the Hollywood Oxymoron?'

'What?' Ellen said, screwing up her nose.

'A decent agent?'

Ellen laughed. 'Don't believe everything you read,' she advised and turned into a neat, sloping courtyard that fronted two gleaming white villas. Running between the villas was a gated driveway where she pulled up to speak to a security guard.

'Hi,' she said, as he strolled out of his booth. 'I'm Ellen Shelby. Apartment fifteen. I'm moving in today.'

'Shelby. Apartment fifteen,' the guard repeated, squinting against the bright sunlight as he checked the clipboard he was holding. 'You got some ID?'

Ellen's driver's licence was already in her hand.

'OK,' he said, ticking off her name. 'You're the second floor, right? I'll have a couple of guys come over to help you up the stairs.'

'Thanks,' Ellen said, preparing to drive on. 'The guy behind's with me, by the way.'

The guard gave her the thumbs up and Ellen accelerated the car forward into a horseshoe-shaped inner courtyard where decorative fountains and a couple of Japanese-style gazebos were glistening brilliantly in the mid-winter sun. The two-storey complex of apartments with its simple, moorish-style arches, white-washed walls and occasional green-and-white-striped awning, lined the outer edge of the drive which dipped at the apex to the underground parking and because of the fountains either side gave the impression of sinking into a waterfall.

'You're kidding me,' Matty murmured as Ellen pointed out which apartments and duplexes certain movie stars or industry moguls occupied. 'How much is this costing you?'

'Four grand a month,' Ellen answered.

'I think I'm going to faint,' Matty responded as they descended into the parking lot.

With the help of the two porters, though slightly impeded by Ellen's non-stop phone calls, they finally unloaded both cars and opened up the apartment. The huge french windows, leading on to a veranda that ran the entire width of the apartment and overlooked the pool and tennis courts on the south side of the complex, were doubly secured by electronic blinds, and as Ellen pushed a button to remove them a flood of sunlight spilled across the ivory carpets and deep, creamy white sofas.

'Will you get a load of this!' Matty cried, when she saw the expensive drapes and furnishings. 'Where did you get all this stuff? It's so classy.'

'Great, isn't it?' Ellen answered, walking round the split-level counter top that divided the kitchen from the living-room. 'I bought most of it from the woman who lived here before. As you can see, she hardly ever used the place, so most of what's here is still brand-new. I think she got it from that store on Robertson, you know, where they do all the custom-made furniture. The one on the corner of Melrose.'

'I know it,' Matty nodded, going out on to the veranda and weaving through the expensive white cane furniture with its Mediterranean-blue seat pads and stylish parasol. To her left were a set of double sliding windows leading into the master bedroom; to her right were the arched doorway and curved windows that opened into the study and TV room. Ferns and yuccas were planted in large, hand-decorated pots and a crimson and pink bougainvillaea was twisting around the railing.

Ellen rushed to help as Gene came struggling in the door, a suitcase in each hand, a boxed mirror under one arm and a silk amaryllis under the other. 'Here, let me take that,' she said, easing the mirror carefully out of his grip.

Considering his size, he was surprisingly unclumsy, in fact, with his bulging muscles, tight little T-shirt and snug-fit denims, Ellen had no problem seeing his appeal, especially as he had a genuinely kind nature and virtually unshakeable good humour. It was just a shame he had such limited talent as an actor, for she'd love to sign him to ATI and do what she could to get him work. But there was only so much nepotism the agency would allow and having Matty on her books was probably considered the line. Fortunately, though, Matty had talent so Ellen never felt there was any justifying to be done there, she was just waiting for the right one to come along and Matty would be on her way.

'Where do you want this?' he asked Ellen, who was now retrieving the amaryllis. His tanned, clean-cut features were flushed with exertion, but his cheerful smile was still intact.

'Through there,' she answered, pointing to a door opposite the kitchen. 'That's the dressing-room,' she said as he pushed the door open. 'The bathroom's down the steps to the right, the bedroom's straight ahead. Leave the suitcases just there. Anyone for champagne?' she shouted, so Matty could hear too.

'Sounds good,' Gene answered, rubbing his hands together as he came out of the dressing-room. 'This is a hell of a place you got here, Ellen,' he commented, passing the fully equipped kitchen with its central island for cooking and handmade units with antique brass handles and Italian marble surfaces.

Ellen smiled as he descended the steps into the sitting room and paused to get a look at himself in the mirrored wall at the far end of the room. Directly in front of the mirror was an eight-seater dining-table with eight pale oak dining-chairs and a beautifully hand-painted silk screen partially obscuring the mirror.

'Gene! Come take a look at this pool,' Matty called from the veranda.

As Gene padded off across the carpet Ellen pressed a speed dial on her cellphone, planted it between her ear and shoulder and rummaged in the grocery bags for the chilled champagne they'd picked up at the market.

She was still talking to Rosa, another agent at ATI, when she carried the champagne out to the veranda and set it down on a glass-topped table. The agency was currently suing a Canadian production company for three clients' fees which amounted to over five million dollars, so there was no such thing as a weekend for the two agents concerned. Ellen was going over to the office in a couple of hours and would probably be there for most of the following day until Clay got back in the evening.

'Boy, it's hot,' she said, finally clicking off the phone and handing a glass each to Matty and Gene who were reluctantly tearing themselves from an embrace now she had joined them.

'Did you buy or are you renting?' Gene asked, taking the champagne.

'Just renting,' Ellen answered. Then, raising her glass, 'Shall we drink a toast? To my new home?'

Matty's eyebrows arched as their glasses touched. If Ellen had taken this apartment for the reasons Matty thought she had then there wasn't much chance of this being home for long, as Clay was almost bound to feel threatened by her independence and come up with the commitment Ellen was aiming for.

They chatted idly for a while, catching up on the industry gossip and hazarding guesses on who was most likely to take over at Universal now Charlie Roscoe had been fired. Though Ellen was as keen to know as anyone else and as willing to speculate, in truth she was finding it hard to get her mind off Clay. He had called her early that morning, sounding really fed up and angry because his wife was insisting that he stay at her mother's house with her and the kids while he was in San Diego, instead of a hotel. Considering how acrimonious things had been between them, this was a real one eighty for Nola, as she'd sworn publicly and viciously several times that she'd rather burn the house down than let him over her threshold again. Ellen wasn't sure what to make of this new turn of events, except every time she thought of it her heart contracted and her insides churned in a way that almost made her feel sick.

'You know, I'm so proud of you,' Matty said, leaning on the counter as she came back from seeing Gene to the door.

Ellen smiled and shook some pretzels into a dish for them to snack on.

'No, I mean it,' Matty said seriously. 'You're doing so well. It's like you were born to this life. You handle the stars like they were your best friends, the studio heads like they were your favourite uncles, assholes like they mattered, competition like it didn't exist, pressure like it's something to be enjoyed, egos like they were crown jewels, and everyone responds. You're a miracle, Ellen, I swear it. Nothing ever seems to faze you, not even all the paranoia that's going on out there. You just get on with it like it's some kind of game. You pull the rug right out from under some guy's feet and end up making him feel good about it. Getting rolled over by you is starting to acquire some kind of kudos, did you know that? You're no one 'til you been licked by Ellen Shelby.'

Ellen was shaking her head and laughing. 'Tell that to the guys who've been there,' she said. 'Grudge doesn't even come close to how some of them feel. And I've taken my share of being licked,' she added, 'make no mistake on that. Only last week one of the agents at CAA walked right over a deal I had going with Touchstone and I never knew a thing about it until the contract didn't show up on my desk next day.'

Matty was looking at her hard. 'A minor set-back,' she said. 'You're headed right up there with all the major players, I can see it now. I just hope it doesn't change you, that's all.'

Ellen's eyes widened in surprise. 'Why, are you seeing signs of it?' she said.

Matty shrugged. 'I don't know,' she answered.

Ellen was really taken aback by that. 'Yes you do,' she said. 'So say it, Matty. Whatever you're thinking, say it.'

'OK. I guess what I'm saying is here you are, with this fantastic apartment, a real high-powered job, a rock-star boyfriend who just happens to be a movie star too, more money than should be legal for one person and ...'

'And?' Ellen prompted.

Matty's tone was defensive. 'And nothing,' she stated.

Ellen's lovely eyes were dark with confusion. 'You're not making a lot of sense, Matty,' she told her.

Matty threw out her hands. 'OK,' she cried. 'You've got so much going on in your life that you seem to have forgotten about those of us who care for you. You know, like your family! Like me. You got all this together without so much as talking about it to me. You find the apartment, you say, hey Matty, come see the apartment I just rented. You'd been seeing Clay for over two months before you said anything to me. You're uptight about a meeting you're going to have with Ted Forgon, and I don't even know the guy is out of the hospital until some jerk calls up on the carphone and makes a joke about it. Do you hear what I'm saying? We've stopped communicating and it's scaring me. I hardly see you any more. It's like we're no longer a part of each other's lives and now you've moved out I'm wondering if I'm ever going to see you at all.'

'Matty, you've been working in the club every night and running a coffee shop during the day,' Ellen reminded her. 'It's you that's never at home. So why don't you tell me what this is really about?'

Matty's charcoal eyes flashed, then, inhaling deeply she leaned back against the wall and gazed sightlessly out of the window. 'OK,' she said in the end, 'if I tell you, do you promise not to get mad?'

'No promises,' Ellen responded. 'Just tell me.'

'Well,' Matty began, obviously finding it hard to force the words out, 'I want you to tell me ... I mean, you can be honest. You don't have to think that just because you're my cousin ...'

86

'Matty!' Ellen cried.

'Give me a break, will you? This isn't easy,' Matty shouted back. 'What I'm asking is, do you think I've got talent, or do you think I should give it up and find myself another career? I mean, is that why you're avoiding me, why you moved out of the apartment, because you want to distance yourself from a talentless hanger-on you're stuck with because she's family? Now, don't give me any bullshit. I can handle it. It'll hurt, but . . .' Her eyes fell to the floor. 'It'll hurt,' she said simply.

Ellen was walking round the counter to join her, barely able to suppress her laughter. 'OK, talentless hanger-on,' she said, circling an arm around Matty's shoulder, 'let me put it this way. They've just written a new love interest for one of the leads in *ER* and do you want to know who's going to be playing her? Matty Shelby, that's who. The great Matty Shelby is going to make a major guest appearance in *ER*. And shall I tell you how come I know that? Because the contract is sitting on my desk right now, for my extremely talented client and crazy, insecure cousin, to sign.'

Matty's eyes were wide with disbelief. 'I don't get it,' she said. 'I didn't even do an audition, so how can I have the part?'

'Because,' Ellen responded, 'I know one of the producers and he owes me a favour. It's just two episodes to begin, but if the character works there could be more. And before you say it, the producer knows I wouldn't hand him a lemon, it's more than my reputation's worth.'

Matty was speechless.

Ellen watched her and felt such pleasure surging inside her as Matty's euphoria started to break.

'Tell me I'm not dreaming this,' Matty groaned, 'please tell me this is for real.'

'It's for real.' Ellen laughed. 'The scripts are already

on their way to you. Someone'll be in touch in the next couple of weeks to talk about costume, dates, call times and all the other stuff you need to know.'

'I think I'm going to cry,' Matty said shakily. 'I can't believe it. *ER*! I mean anything would have been good, but *ER*!'

'That's why you have an agent,' Ellen reminded her, 'to make sure you don't end up doing "anything". *ER* is right for you and you're right for it, for now. It can only raise your profile and if the show should start to fade while you're still in it we'll get you out quicker than they can switch to a commericial break.'

'You're unbelievable, do you know that?' Matty laughed, hugging her. 'I just hope and pray that you make it to that producer's chair you've got your eye on, because you sure as hell deserve it. Hey! What am I saying here? If you become a producer I'm going to lose the best agent a girl ever had.'

'By then, you'll be so big you won't even notice,' Ellen assured her, leading her back out to the veranda. There was no point telling her now that both their careers were resting in the hands of a man neither of them had ever met, because the chances of Michael McCann actually even caring about that were probably only marginally higher than Ellen's chances of pulling off what three other agents, at the cost of their careers, had already failed to do. And when she added to that this latest twist in events between Clay and Nola she was seriously afraid that her age of Aquarius was right on the verge of yielding to another era.

'Are you crazy?' Clay laughed the following evening when he called to let Ellen know he was on his way. 'Nola and I getting together again? It's never going to happen. Just no way.'

'So what was staying at her mother's house all

about?' Ellen asked, hating herself for showing how unnerved she had been by it.

'Would you believe, the woman's developed a conscience about the kids at last?' he answered, turning down the music at his end so he could hear better. 'She thinks it's time we made friends and at least pretended to like each other, before we do some serious damage in areas we're both going to end up regretting.' He chuckled softly. 'If you ask me, what this is really about is she's found herself a new boyfriend.'

Ellen's heart gave a skip of hope. 'Do you think so?' she said, starting to run herself a bath.

'It looks pretty much that way. But enough about her, how's your weekend been?'

'Hectic, but I'm all moved in and the legal stuff at the office is more or less sorted. What time do you expect to get here?'

'Let me see,' he responded, 'I'm in Brentwood now, so I guess I . . .'

'Brentwood!' she cried. 'I thought you were just leaving San Diego.'

'I should be there in about ten minutes,' he laughed, 'and if you've got any clothes on now make sure they're gone by the time I walk in the door.'

Not even waiting to say goodbye, Ellen clicked off the phone, dashed into the bedroom, tearing the slides from her hair as she went, then pausing only to take a new silk mini-slip from a box on the bed, she sped back to the dressing-room and grabbed a hairbrush. Seconds later she was in the bathroom again, cleaning her teeth and turning the water to run faster.

'Candles,' she muttered. 'Where the hell did I put the candles?'

She found them in a kitchen drawer, carried them back to the bathroom, lit them and placed them around the tub. Then, turning down the lights she surveyed the scene, tidied up a couple of towels, sprinkled more

89

scented oil in the steaming water and went to straighten up the living-room.

Ten minutes later the telephone rang.

'Hi, it's me,' he said when she answered.

Her heart sank with disappointment and frustration. 'Where are you?' she demanded, failing to keep the gripe from her voice.

'There's no way I can come visit you,' he told her, 'not with those security guys on the gate. They're sure to recognize me and the next thing you know we're going to be all over the press.'

Furious with herself that she hadn't thought of that, it was all she could do to stop herself screaming and ranting and telling him how much she hated this secrecy, that she couldn't go on like it and that it had to change or she was getting out. But fear that he would let her go stopped her. Besides, he'd probably had a tough enough weekend already without her adding to it. So, in a voice that was hopefully more conciliatory than pleading, she said, 'Is it so bad to have your name linked with mine? Or are you going to keep me hidden away like this for ever?'

'I told you, Ellen,' he said, 'we've got to play it cool. I don't want any last-minute fuck-ups with Nola and we're close now to ending it, real close.'

'So what do you want me to do? Come over to your place?'

'How soon can you get there?' he asked, his voice taking on an intimate lilt.

'Give me an hour,' she replied and before he could say any more she slammed down the phone, seething with fury at herself for being so weak and at him for being so damned famous that they were forced to live like this. She picked up a magazine, hurled it across the room and storming into the bathroom, was about to sweep the candles into the tub when a knock on the door stopped her.

All she was wearing was the semi-transparent slip, so quickly grabbing a robe from the back of the door she went into the hall to ask who it was.

'Just the guy who's so crazy about you he doesn't care if some security guard calls the papers,' he answered.

Ellen blinked in surprise and starting to smile, she dropped the robe and pulled open the door.

'Hey,' he laughed, catching her as she threw herself into his arms.

'You were already here,' she accused. 'When you called just now, you must have been right outside to have got here so fast.'

'I was coming up the steps,' he confirmed. 'I just wanted to let you know what I was prepared to do for you. I slipped the guy a couple of big ones. I doubt it'll work, but who the hell cares? I don't want you thinking I'm not proud of you, 'cos that sure as hell isn't the case. God, you're beautiful,' he murmured.

Ellen was smiling up into his craggily handsome face, her heart pounding with joy at what he'd just said. His sleepy dark eyes were gazing into hers, the deeply ingrained laugh lines and jagged birthmark somehow making them all the more seductive. His smile, the smile that still set millions of hearts racing, widened as she pushed her fingers into his thick, silvery hair and ran her thumbs along his clean-shaven jaw to the tiny stud earrings in each of his ears. He was so tall and powerfully built that she felt deliciously swamped by his masculinity when he held her, especially when he was wearing his denims and she was either naked or near it.

Though her mouth was tilted towards his he didn't kiss her right away, but stood holding her and watching her eyes. 'You wearing anything under this?' he asked, splaying his fingers across her hips.

Ellen felt a piercing lust bite into her. 'I could if you wanted me to,' she said huskily.

He shook his head. 'Uh-uh, nothing is fine by me,' he said, slipping his hands under the hem and lifting it to her waist.

Ellen's knees almost buckled as holding her eyes with his, he slipped his fingers between her legs. Though they were still outside in the hall and a neighbour might come by at any moment, she did nothing to stop him as she knew how much it turned him on to dare her like this. So often he had made her stand naked in front of the windows of his mansion, displaying herself as though all the world could see, even though they both knew that the house wasn't visible from the street. He even got her to walk nude through the gardens, teasing her that the Mexican gardeners were watching, though she knew she was never allowed to come when any of the staff were around.

'Did you miss me?' he whispered.

'When I wasn't entertaining my other lovers,' she whispered back.

He smiled, then finally touched his mouth to hers and probed very gently with his tongue. Ellen's eyes fluttered closed as the sensuousness of his mouth swept through her like a flame. Her arms were circled around his neck, but she kept herself slightly apart so that his hands could roam freely over her body. Her breasts were aching for his touch, but when finally he found them it was merely to brush the backs of his fingers over the protruding hardness of her nipples.

'You feel good,' he murmured.

She opened her eyes. 'Can I fix you a drink?' she offered.

He gazed at her from under lowered lids, then nodded.

Turning back into the apartment, she walked over to

the ornate Japanese cabinet she had turned into a bar and took out a bottle of Scotch. Her legs were slightly shaky, her senses still raw from his touch. She put a tumbler on the counter but stopped as she felt him come up behind her. Her eyes closed and her pulses started to race, as taking her slip he pulled it up over her head and tossed it aside. The sensation of her own nudity burned through her as his fingers moved like feathers over her skin. Then she heard his zipper go down and felt a stinging desire as he turned her to face him.

'Don't ever think I'm ashamed of you,' he told her huskily, 'because this, you, mean more to me than anything.'

She looked up into his eyes and felt her emotions whirling as his hands moved to her shoulders and began to push gently down. Obediently she dropped to her knees and circling the base of his penis with her fingers she guided it to her lips. He rested his hands high on the wall behind her and looked down at what she was doing, breathing hard as she licked him, moistening him all over before drawing him into her mouth. From the corner of her eye she saw him turn to look at their reflection in the mirror, watching her mouth slide up and down his erection.

The tension in his body started to increase as she took him closer and closer to orgasm, until finally, with a strangled gasp, he buried his fingers in her hair and pulled her head tightly against him. He held her there, waiting for the brinking need for release to subside, then letting her go he withdrew from her mouth, still hard and ready now to move on.

Ellen stayed where she was, waiting to see what he wanted. Stooping, he took her by the elbows and raised her to her feet. Then, lowering his head, he took each of her nipples into his mouth and sucked hard. His fingers were sliding between her legs and finding her so ready

93

for him he lifted his head and looked intensely into her eyes. 'Soon,' he whispered.

Ellen's breath shuddered inside her as he led her to the couch and bent her over the back of it until her hands were resting on the cushions. Then parting her legs he stood to one side and stroked the velvety softness of her rear and inner thighs. Then quite suddenly he dealt a stinging blow to her buttocks. Ellen gasped and bit down on her lips as the blows continued to come, faster and harder, until at last he was standing behind her, lowering his jeans to his knees and burying himself so deep inside her her legs would have given out had he not been holding her up.

'Is this good for you, babe?' he panted, thrusting with all his might. 'Tell me this is good for you.'

'It's good for me,' she choked. 'Don't stop. Please, don't stop.'

'I'm there, honey,' he told her, banging brutally into her. 'I'm right there. Come with me. Come *now*! Christ Almighty,' he seethed. He was pumping so hard he was almost lifting her from the floor. Ellen struggled to raise her head, but he held her down and drove himself in deeper and harder until finally his seed began spurting fast and hot into her.

She turned to watch him in the mirror. His head was thrown back, his eyes were closed, his teeth bared and with one hand he was still holding her down. He was almost spent now and as his head fell forward he drew her up in his arms and crushed her against him.

'You're the best,' he said hoarsely. 'Do you know that? You're just the best.'

Ellen turned her head, searching for his mouth and found it. His breath was still laboured, but he kissed her softly and tenderly.

'We're so good together,' he told her, taking her breasts in his hands. 'So fucking good.'

Ellen waited until he had withdrawn, then turning,

94

she put her arms around him. 'Want to take a bath?' she offered, smiling into his eyes.

'Sounds good,' he murmured and hiking his jeans up he took the hand she was holding out and allowed her to lead him to the bathroom.

The candles were still flickering in the jasmine-scented steam and when he saw the giant tub with four seats carved into the marble and jacuzzi jets concentrated in all directions he started to laugh.

'This is one hell of a place you've got here,' he told her as she started to undress him.

Ellen smiled, kissed him briefly on the mouth, then pushed him back in a chair to take off his boots.

A few minutes later they were both stretched out, facing each other in the hot, steamy water. Slender, sharp jets of air were pummelling their bodies and as Ellen opened her legs so they could massage her there, she closed her eyes and allowed her imagination to take over. She could feel him watching her as the pulsating rhythm began carrying her towards climax. Her back arched and she ran a hand across her soap-covered breasts, pinching her nipples and starting to moan aloud.

Clay was smiling as he watched her. 'You going to come again?' he asked.

Ellen nodded, then her body began to jar as the first spasms of orgasm erupted inside her. Her legs opened wider, her head rolled from side to side and her hands reached out to grip the handles beside her. Knowing he was watching her was making it all the more powerful and when his hand slid along the inside of her thigh she gasped and cried out loud.

'Come here,' he whispered, when finally she relaxed and opened her eyes.

Ellen moved through the water and lay in his arms, her cheek resting on the wet, matted hair of his chest, one arm circled around his neck.

'Love you,' he said softly.

Ellen kissed his chest. 'Can you stay tonight?' she asked.

He laughed. 'Sure,' he said. 'Did you think I was going someplace else?'

She smiled. 'No, I guess not,' she answered.

Tilting her face up to his he said, 'I swear it won't be like this for much longer. Nola's about ready to settle and when she does we'll be just weeks away from making it all legal.'

'And then?' she said.

He kissed her. 'I'll take you out to dinner to celebrate.'

Laughing, Ellen reached for a towel and climbed out of the tub. 'Your turn to cook,' she told him. 'I got chicken breasts and a couple of different salads from the deli and there's some orange ice-cake for dessert.'

'Did I die and go to heaven?' he asked, smiling up at her. 'That comes later,' she promised. 'Now, I've got some last minute reading to do before I meet with Ted in the morning. Call me when dinner's ready.'

Much later they were sitting together at opposite ends of the couch, reading while Schubert's Eighth played softly on the stereo.

It was during the *andante con moto* that Clay turned over a page of the paper and said, 'You still reading up on that guy Forgon's after?'

'Mmm,' Ellen answered.

'So what's the big deal?' he asked. 'What's bugging Forgon that he's got to go after the man?'

Ellen grimaced. 'It's a long story,' she warned, turning to look at him. 'Are you sure you want to hear it?'

He shrugged. 'If it's bothering you as much as it seems to be, then sure I want to hear it,' he said. 'Remind me, what's the guy's name?'

'McCann. Michael McCann. He's British.'

'Lives here?'

'No. London. And that's what I've got to try to change, because Ted Forgon wants him here in Hollywood so, professionally at least, he can kill him. The problem is, McCann's not interested in coming.' She paused as her heart tightened with misgiving. 'Correction. The problem is, if I fail to get him to come I can kiss goodbye to everything I've worked for, because Forgon doesn't keep losers on his team, nor does he let them work again once he's kicked them off. He's already fired three agents for not delivering McCann, so I guess there's no confusion about where I'm headed if I don't pull this off.'

'So what did this guy do to make Forgon so mad?' Clay asked, turning to face her and resting a cheek on one hand.

Ellen sighed and lowered the file to her lap. 'A couple of years back McCann pulled off a deal, here in Hollywood, for some unknown British actor to play the lead in a movie that ended up winning six Oscars and making everyone involved a fortune at the box office. The movie was *Mainliner*.'

Clay looked impressed. 'I guess we're talking about Nick Quillan,' he said, naming the actor.

Ellen nodded. 'It made Quillan's career. At least here it did. From what I've heard he was already pretty well established in Europe. Anyway, that was great for Nick Quillan, but not for Dennis Simes.'

'Dennis Simes? *The Redneck Roadster*?' Clay cried. 'What the hell ever happened to him?'

'He couldn't get any work after the *Roadster*, is what happened to him,' Ellen answered. 'But then Forgon heard about *Mainliner*, told Simes it would make a great come-back movie for him, did a handshake deal with the producers and told Simes the part was his. Of course, the press got hold of it, I think someone from our office was told to tip them off, and the multi-million dollar deal Forgon had pulled off for Simes whose career was supposed to be finished, made headlines. So of course the whole town was talking about how the old Forgon magic was as hot as ever and parties and press conferences were laid on to celebrate Simes's return.' She shook her head as though she still couldn't quite believe what her boss had done. 'It was a really dumb thing to do,' she said, 'to start spreading the word like that before the ink was on the page. But it's what he did. And right off the bat Simes started calling up all his friends and telling them what a great guy Forgon was ... I'm surprised you don't remember any of this,' she said. 'It made most of the papers at the time.'

'I do now you're telling it,' Clay responded. 'So how did McCann manage to get the deal? I mean, Forgon must have been pretty sure of his ground to have done what he did. I mean the guy's not stupid.'

'Forgon *had* a deal,' Ellen reminded him. 'OK, it was just a handshake until the contract was typed up, but he knew Alistair Peeke, the exec. producer, pretty well, they'd done business together plenty of times in the past, so Forgon didn't see any reason not to trust him. I guess it's a mistake any of us could make, but being the old cynic he is it's a surprising one from Forgon. And I'm betting McCann knew nothing about that hand-shake and Peeke never told him. Peeke, by the way, is of Irish stock, just like McCann and Quillan.'

Clay's eyebrows went up. 'Sounds like Forgon never stood a chance,' he commented.

Ellen shrugged. 'Maybe, maybe not,' she said. 'It certainly seems Peeke was holding out for Quillan all along, but the studio boys were dragging their heels. No one had ever heard of Quillan so why the hell were they going to stake thirty million on a guy who could lead them all to their deaths at the box-office? So

McCann and Peeke went to work on convincing everyone who needed convincing, while Peeke carried on assuring Ted that his man was definitely up for the part. In the end, it looked like the studios just weren't going to buy it with Quillan, so Peeke closed the deal on a handshake with Forgon, only to be told at the eleventh hour that Quillan was in. So McCann got the contract firmed up, then flew to New York the next day where Quillan was playing off Broadway.

'Peeke double-crossed Forgon in a big way, there's no doubt about that,' she said, 'and Forgon's never forgiven him. But since Peeke died of a heart attack the day the movie was released, Forgon feels that he's gone some way towards paying for what he did. McCann, on the other hand, is still out there, rolling around the decks like a loose cannon and Forgon has decided that the only way to regain the face he lost and pay McCann back for making him look such a jerk in his own town, is to lure him under his wing, give him everything he wants, groom him, build him, get his name up in lights, then crush him. And just why the hell he thinks McCann is going to roll over and say hey, Ted, here I am, come tickle my tummy then kick me in the balls, I've got no idea.'

Clay seemed confused by that too. 'So McCann knows that's what's behind all Forgon's offers?' he said.

Ellen shrugged. 'The man's not stupid, he's got to have worked out that what Forgon's really after is revenge. And if he has worked it out, which all his refusals suggest he has, then I don't see any way of getting him to change his mind, do you?'

Clay was staring past her thoughtfully and though Ellen was extremely anxious about the way the meeting was going to go in the morning, at that moment she was far more involved in the concern and interest Clay was showing in her problem. Not that he ever seemed

99

bored by her work, it was just good to know that he cared enough to talk it all through with her.

'You know what I think,' he said in the end. 'I think you're going to pull this off.'

Ellen laughed and wanted to hug him for having such faith in her. Instead she said, 'Remember, three other agents are out there right now, either selling insurance in Missouri, playing the tables in Vegas or God only knows what the third is doing, but she's not working in Hollywood any more that's for sure.'

'So what you've got to ask yourself,' Clay said, 'is why did Forgon choose *you* to go after McCann, when there's no way in the world the man wants to lose you. You're bringing too much business his way.'

Ellen shrugged. 'I guess it either shows how bad this obsession with McCann has got, or maybe he really does think I can pull it off.'

'Or,' Clay said, 'he's going to work it so's you present McCann with an offer he *can't* refuse, then let *you* walk off with all the glory.'

Ellen laughed in surprise. 'Now *that*,' she said, 'is a scenario I could really go for.'

Clay yawned and stretched, then reached out for her to come sit with him. 'Listen to me,' he said, snuggling her into his arms, 'you're smart, you're classy, you're ambitious, you're tough and you're headed right for the top, so I just don't see this McCann guy getting in the way, nor Forgon letting him. Because whatever else Forgon is, he's too damned smart to let anyone get the better of his favourite girl.' He snatched up the phone that was ringing beside him. 'Hello?' he said.

Ellen looked at him in amazement. Obviously he'd forgotten where they were to have answered the phone like that.

'Sure, I'll pass you over. Matty,' he said, handing the receiver to Ellen.

Not wanting Clay's mind to wander, she didn't stay

long on the line with Matty. 'So what are you saying?' she repeated, passing him the receiver to hang up.

'What I'm saying,' he said, wrapping her back in his arms, 'is that Forgon's got to have something up his sleeve, 'cos he's not going to run the risk of losing you both, which is what it could end up costing him if you don't come home with the star prize. Did you read the script I left for you on Friday?' he said, abruptly changing the subject.

'The first few scenes,' she answered, adjusting quickly. 'I didn't get chance to finish it yet. What I read needs tightening, or maybe it needs extra scenes . . . I'm not sure. It's out of balance somewhere anyway. Are you serious about it? You really want to play this part?'

'I'm interested,' he countered. 'Why? Do you want to represent me?'

Ellen turned to look at him. Signing Clay Ingall would be such a major coup for her personally, as well as for the agency, that even if she did take a fall with McCann there was just no way Forgon would fire her. And even if he did, with Clay as her client she could probably start her own agency and Forgon wouldn't be able to do a god-damned thing to stop her. 'You don't mean that,' she whispered, knowing that his relationship with Zac Luberman was solid.

He laughed and pulled her mouth to his. 'Don't rule it out,' he told her, while kissing her. 'Now, I reckon it's time we had ourselves some more fun, don't you?'

'Whatever you say,' she murmured against his lips.

'How about,' he said, 'I put you in the car and take you out for a drive?'

Ellen frowned.

He chuckled. 'In the nude,' he said. 'That security guard you got yourself out there could be in for a treat when we go by.'

Though she felt her pulses quicken Ellen was already

protesting. 'Clay, no,' she said. 'I live here. I've got to pass that guy every day.'

'But the client wants to take his new agent for a test drive,' he joked, starting to unbelt her robe. 'Hey, you do want me to be your client, don't you?'

'Yes,' she said. 'Yes, but I really don't know if I'm comfortable with this, Clay.'

'We've done it plenty of times before,' he reminded her as he reached inside her robe and started stroking her breasts. 'But hey, if you're not comfortable then we just don't do it.'

She turned to look at him and felt her resolve weakening as his fingers tightened on her nipples.

'Of course, I could drive real fast,' he said, 'and the windows are tinted so the guard couldn't see in anyway. It'll only be me who knows you're naked right there in the seat next to me. And honey, I've got to tell you, it'll just about blow my mind.'

Chapter 6

The following morning, at seven thirty, Ellen was shown to a corner table in the busy restaurant of the Four Seasons Hotel on Doheny. The place was already crowded with industry people, there to see and be seen so the rest of the world would know they were still in business. As usual, the noise was cacophonous; cell-phones ringing, cutlery clashing, voices battling to make themselves heard. Ellen waved to those she knew, paused to chat to a few, then sat down at the table Ted Forgon's latest secretary had reserved.

After ordering some tea she took out the notes she had made and started to read. She knew it all by heart now, so her concentration was poor and by the time the waiter returned with her tea her mind was a long way from the problem facing her. Realizing it, she struggled to refocus on McCann and tried asking herself again why Forgon had switched the meeting from the office to the Four Seasons at the last minute. Probably, she told herself, because he wanted to let everyone know he was back in action and this was as effective a way of doing it as any. The fact that it seemed odd that he would hold this particular meeting in a public place wasn't something she was going to dwell on. If there were any sinister overtones or hidden agendas she would find out soon enough.

She looked back down at the page in front of her and

was about to start reading again when a director she knew stopped by to say hello. By the time he moved on, Ellen was burning hot and cold inside. Of course, she was being paranoid and she knew it, there were no double meanings to anything the man had said, and he looked at everyone that way, as though he couldn't quite believe they could speak. So there was nothing for her to worry about, no reason to feel so ashamed. Except the very idea that anyone should ever find out that Clay Ingall had driven her around Beverly Hills in the nude last night was too horrible for words.

She should never have given in, but the real truth of it was, it turned her on too to be sitting beside him naked and watching what it was doing to him. And even the fact that she would rather die than be caught like that didn't make much difference in the heat of the moment. Mercifully, the security guard had been attending to someone arriving when they'd left, so he hadn't seen her and by the time they returned she had managed to persuade Clay to get her coat from the trunk. Whether anyone had seen her while they were driving around or when they'd pulled up at stop lights, she had no idea, for she studiously avoided any eye contact other than with Clay. As usual, he had loved every minute of it, and, so he said, loved her even more for doing it. Certainly their love-making had been good when they'd returned, and again this morning before she'd left. But, she had to ask herself, was it worth what it would do to her parents were they ever to open a newspaper and see their only daughter exposed that way? The very idea of it made her feel sick inside, for not since she was a child had she undressed in front of her father and now, for him to see her like that, knowing the rest of the world was seeing her too . . . His shame would be so great he would never be able to hold up his head in public again. God knew, it would be bad enough if they were to learn about her

104

relationship with Clay that way, but that they should ever have to suffer the disgrace of knowing that she had actually gone out in public without her clothes was something she would almost rather die than subject them to.

And what about all these people here, her friends and colleagues? How the hell would she feel, sitting among them now, if her picture had been in the paper that morning, nude in Clay Ingall's car? It would probably mean nothing to them – after all this was LA – but for her it would be a nightmare of unlimited proportions, not only because of the embarrassment it would cause her, but because the carefully cultured image and rare credibility she had worked so hard to build up would be destroyed. Jesus Christ, the power of lust while it was burning was so incredible it defied understanding, for sitting here right now she couldn't imagine herself ever even considering taking such a risk, never mind going through with it.

Spotting Forgon talking to the vice-president of Sony, who was on his way out, she quickly pushed her personal life aside and forced herself to concentrate on McCann. She really had to have her wits about her for this meeting, because there was every chance her career could hang or fall by its outcome. She almost laughed, for this morning it seemed whichever way she turned she was on the brink of doom, either from a sex scandal or because of a failure for Forgon. For a moment she felt extremely uneasy and afraid. Then with a quick and forceful effort she reminded herself that she wasn't going to fail at all. She'd really done her homework on McCann and she was pretty sure she'd found his Achilles' heel. In fact, he had two and it was probably the second that intrigued her the most, for she had no answers yet to why an actress as successful and set for superstardom as Michelle Rowe had been had turned her back on McCann at such a crucial point in her career and gone off to save the world. Oh, she knew all the official reasons, being affected by the TV series, feeling some kind of divine calling, knowing she could make a difference, never being able to live with herself if she didn't go. But all those statements had been made by Rowe's agent. Nothing had been quoted from Rowe herself, nor from McCann. So what was really behind Rowe's astonishing change of heart, Ellen wondered. Whatever it was it might not, in the end, prove useful, but it was worth looking into, she felt, because there was just no telling what she might find.

McCann's other Achilles' heel was something she was very surprised had never been properly exposed or utilized before. It was there in every agent's file and in every newspaper report around the time of his break-up with Rowe, so it was well documented, but it had clearly never occurred to anyone before to use it. But she was about to put that to rights at this meeting because it could be the very thing that would end up not only safeguarding her job, but finally capturing McCann.

'Hi.' Ted Forgon grinned, pulling out a chair. 'How're you doing? You're looking great.'

'I'm fine,' Ellen said, feeling a bolt of nerves shoot through her stomach as he sat down. No matter how many times she told herself she wasn't unnerved by this man she still was. 'You're looking pretty good yourself,' she told him.

His unruly eyebrows flickered, as though telling her she'd have been a fool to expect anything else. And maybe, considering it was Ted Forgon, she was. At sixty-eight he was still considered a handsome man, though it was probably his height more than his looks that gave him such a presence, for his large, leathery brown face was ravaged by years of Lucky Strikes and vodka Martinis. His twenty-thousand-dollar hair transplant had proved a success, even though it meant he had a head of glossy brown hair that belonged to a man half his age. Whether there was anything that could be done about his trembling hands and odorous breath, however, Ellen didn't know, but they certainly hadn't lessened his appeal, for rumour had it that his latest, the one he had been screwing at the time of his attack, was just nineteen.

'How was Florida?' Ellen asked.

'Sure, it was OK,' he answered, waving to a waiter. 'Bring me some hot coffee, Eggs Benedict and a side order of smoked salmon,' he ordered, with blatant disregard for his recent coronary. 'Are you eating?' he asked Ellen.

'I'm fine with tea,' she replied, turning to see who was calling across the room to him. It was another executive from Sony.

'So how are you doing?' he repeated, as a server poured his coffee. 'Are we ready to do battle with the Canadians?'

Ellen nodded. 'We've got a good case,' she said. 'We should win.'

'Way to go,' he grinned, saluting her with his coffee. 'I heard you were with Clay Ingall last night.'

Ellen's blood ran cold.

Forgon grinned. 'Must be six months you guys been seeing each other,' he said.

Ellen's heart was thudding, her head was in turmoil. How did he know about last night? How did he know about Clay at all? Was he sitting there now, imagining her naked in a car? Her skin crawled at the thought of even his imagination touching her. But she had to get a grip on this. It should be no surprise that he knew, for it would be just like Forgon to have her watched. And the fact that he'd introduced the subject of Clay the way he had, as a friendly kind of *non sequitur*, should be giving her a clue to where this was leading.

His shrewd predator's eyes were locked on hers. She

met the gaze, trying by force of her own will-power to let him know that he didn't scare her. It wasn't easy, especially when she could feel the power of him as though it was crushing her mind, but she'd come here today determined to hold her own and she was damned if she was going to be felled at the first hurdle, even though it was one she definitely hadn't seen coming.

'Is it serious?' he asked, sitting back as his food was put on the table.

Ellen waited for the server to leave. 'If you know so much already, then I'm sure you know the answer to that too,' she responded.

A flicker of amusement passed through his eyes. He picked up his knife and fork, then looked at her again. 'He's been cheating on you,' he told her, chewing slowly.

Ellen didn't even flinch. 'Try again,' she said smoothly.

He grinned, loaded up his fork and ate. 'Michael McCann,' he said, swallowing.

Ellen waited.

He took another mouthful of food, then picked up his coffee. 'There are plenty of ways we can play this,' he said, 'but I want to hear what you've got in mind first.'

'OK,' Ellen said. 'But before I do that I think you should hear my terms.'

Forgon's cup stopped mid-air. 'Terms?' he repeated.

Ellen looked down at the page in front of her. 'They're negotiable,' she said, 'but only insofar as is reasonable.'

Forgon put his coffee down. 'I think we'd better get something straight here,' he said. 'I don't do deals with my staff. At least, not the kind of deal you're aiming to pull off.'

'There's always a first,' she replied, amazing herself by how firm she sounded.

Forgon was shaking his head.

Ellen's eyes flashed the challenge. 'How bad do you want McCann?' she demanded.

Forgon's eyes narrowed as he put his head to one side, assessing her. 'Maybe not as bad as you think,' he responded.

'Bullshit,' she said.

Forgon's exorbitant dentistry made a dazzling appearance. 'I've got to hand it to you, Ellen,' he said, 'no one in your position ever had the guts to say bullshit to me before.'

'Do you want to hear my terms?' she said.

'Sure. Why not? Just for the hell of it.'

Knowing he was mocking her Ellen inhaled deeply, then forced herself to continue. 'OK,' she said, 'but first I need to know how much you're prepared to offer McCann.'

He looked curious. 'Seven hundred and fifty,' he answered.

Ellen noted the figure down. 'I take it you mean thousand.'

Forgon didn't grace that with a reply.

'A month?' she asked.

Forgon choked.

Ellen's lucid eyes watched him. 'Then you must mean a year,' she said. 'I'm sorry, but I want to be absolutely clear on this, that way there won't be any mistakes. So seven fifty per annum plus what?'

'Car. House. Country Club. All the right introductions.'

'A piece of the action?'

Forgon's good humour was dying. 'What are you, this guy's agent all of a sudden?' he snapped.

'The question stands,' she said in reply.

'No deal.'

'You said it.' She closed her book. 'No action, no deal.

And if I were McCann now, I'd be out there with the car jockey waiting to leave.'

Forgon stared at her.

Ellen stared back. 'I just want you to be clear that if there's no piece of the action then there's no way McCann will deal,' she said.

Forgon's grin came back. 'Wrong, smartass,' he told her. 'The guy's already been offered some action and turned it down flat.'

'Then obviously it wasn't a big enough piece,' she responded.

Forgon sat back in his chair and folded his arms. 'OK, now let's do this another way,' he said. 'This time *I'm* going to tell *you* what I'm prepared to offer, then you're going to tell me how you're going to present it in a way McCann can't refuse.'

'Go on,' she said.

Forgon cleared his throat. 'This is how it goes,' he began. 'Seven fifty a year, twenty-five per cent annual bonus; a decent car, Mercedes, Lexus, Caddy, whatever lights his fire; a five grand a month housing allowance; full expense account; his own staff and first-class travel.'

Ellen looked at him, expecting him to go on. When he didn't, she rested her chin on one hand and said, 'You're forgetting the action,' she reminded him.

'OK, here's the deal,' he said, 'and this, Ellen Shelby, is going to be your trump card; I'm prepared to offer him the going market rate for his London agency – it can retain the name McCann Walsh and the staff he chooses – I will also redirect a full one hundred per cent share of all European deals that come out of this office to McCann's in London and he'll get no interference from me on the book he wants to start here. My only conditions are that he provides a turnover of at least three million a year for the first three years and that he bases himself right here in LA.' He reached for his coffee, looking extremely pleased with himself. 'So how's that for a package?' he said. 'Do you see him turning it down?'

Ellen had to admit she was impressed – and mildly shocked. The offer was so disproportionately generous that surely no one in his right mind would walk away from it. On the other hand, from all she'd read about McCann he seemed so fiercely independent and unaffected by Hollywood she was having a hard time seeing him signing away ownership of an agency he had created himself, at any price.

'What are you thinking?' Forgon asked, a trifle peeved that she hadn't gasped in admiration.

'If it were anyone else,' she said, 'you'd have yourself a deal. With this man . . . Well, I guess we'll just have to run it by him and see.' Her eyes lost focus for a moment as she chewed thoughtfully on her lower lip. 'I'd like to add one other bonus to the package,' she said after a while. 'We don't have to offer it, but I'd like to have it up my sleeve as an extra.'

'Well?' Forgon encouraged.

'I don't know if it'll do the trick,' she said, absently toying with her pen as she thought, 'but there is a chance the real carrot could be some kind of production deal.'

Forgon frowned. 'What kind of production deal?' he asked.

Ellen's lips pursed as she continued to think. 'There's evidence,' she said, 'that he's interested in producing. It could be where his weakness lies, I'm not sure. He got into it once with Michelle Rowe, the actress he was involved with, then let it drop when she walked out on him. I'm wondering,' she continued, 'if you offer to back him as an independent producer . . .'

'I want an agent, not a fucking producer,' Forgon growled.

Ellen ignored him. 'If you put a ceiling on his

111

contract, say three, OK, five years,' she continued, 'at the end of which you offer to back him as an independent producer, get him set up with MCA or Fox or one of the big studios . . .'

'Do I look like Santa Claus?' Forgon growled.

'. . . and leave his book at ATI,' she went on, 'then you get a stake in his production company as well as retaining all the clients he's brought in to the agency.'

She had his attention. She watched him, almost smiling at all that neural commotion as he attempted to ferret out the catch. 'So what you're saying,' he said after a while, 'is that if I do it your way I could buy right into McCann's personal ambition.'

'If producing's what he wants, yes.'

Forgon's sharp eyes were glinting. 'And if it's not what he wants?'

'Then you get him for five years, *if* he accepts the offer.'

'Draw it up,' he said, 'I want to put it in front of the lawyers.'

Ellen reached for her briefcase. 'I have it right here,' she said.

Forgon chuckled. 'I remember now why I hired you,' he told her, holding his hand out to take the document she'd prepared herself.

'My terms,' she reminded him, holding it back.

Forgon's face darkened.

Ellen forced herself to ignore it. 'I want a written contract guaranteeing I keep my job with ATI should I fail with McCann,' she said.

'Forget it,' he snapped. 'Apart from anything else there's no incentive in that.'

'There is in a fifty-thousand-dollar bonus if I succeed,' she countered.

Forgon's eyebrows jumped. 'Are you crazy?' he cried. 'You work for me, remember? You do what I tell you and feel happy to do it.'

112

'Those are my terms,' she replied.

Forgon looked about the room, obviously nervous someone might be overhearing this. 'You don't get it, do you?' he said. 'I'm your employer. You don't dictate terms to me. It's me who dictates terms to you.'

Ellen's eyes held fast to his as she resolutely ignored the crazy thudding of her heart. She knew he was expecting her to speak, but she forced herself not to. It was an intriguing and terrifying contest as the silent treatment was a known tactic of his, but she had no intention of backing down even though, beneath her implacable façade, there was a very real fear she had gone too far.

In the end he spoke first, his eyes blazing with suspicion, his voice edged with ire. 'Are you trying to stitch me up here?' he hissed.

'No. I'm just trying to stop you stitching me up,' she said frankly.

Forgon glanced about him again. 'Listen to me,' he said, leaning forward so no one could hear, 'I hired you because you're a smart operator who's got more balls than half the jackasses in this town put together. You're quick, you're cute and you're brave enough to stick it out even when you know you're beat. And this time you're beat. I didn't hire you to fuck me over, I hired you to fuck over all those other bastards out there. So get that cute little butt of yours out of here and go kick ass where I pay you to kick ass.'

Ellen's eyebrows flickered. 'I think I mentioned my terms were negotiable,' she said, placing the tea strainer over her cup and picking up the teapot. 'I'd settle for forty-five and a clause in the contract that stipulates payment in full the day McCann signs.'

Forgon gave a snort of incredulity. 'This is me you're dealing with, Ellen Shelby,' he reminded her, 'so don't come on like I'm some bozo who can't work out that you just handed me five grand with one hand and took it back with the other, because I been pulling it over guys out there with that one since before you were born.'

Ellen was grinning. 'The old ones are always the best,' she said cheerily.

Forgon looked at her for a long, hard time. 'OK. You got yourself a deal,' he said grudgingly. 'But only because I'm a sucker for a beautiful face and God knows at my age I'm allowed to be.'

Stunned, she watched him signal for the check and in an effort to disguise a sudden flood of relief took what was supposed to be a nonchalant sip of tea. The fact that her hand shook was a give-away and the euphoria she could barely keep suppressed was making it worse. She couldn't wait now to be alone, to get Clay and Matty and Rosa on the phone and tell them how cool she had been, how tough and relentless. She was so proud of herself she could almost explode with the joy of it, but true to form she kept herself quietly in check and gave nothing away.

It was only when Forgon turned back to her and she saw the look on his face that she realized her triumph was premature. She put down her cup and forced herself to meet the gleam in his glassy blue eyes. Already her skin was starting to prickle, for suddenly she knew that her triumph hadn't only been premature, but was now on the point of being annihilated altogether.

'So, you got yourself a contract,' he said benignly. 'Congratulations. Have your lawyer draw it up and see that it's on my desk by the end of the day.'

Ellen's eyes were steeped in caution, her heart was pounding. 'I'll do that,' she said.

'A one-off payment of twenty grand, non-negotiable,' he said, looking over the check while reaching inside his jacket for his wallet, 'and a guarantee you keep your job if you fail.'

Ellen waited. Though her eyes remained fixed on his, inside she was faltering too badly to argue the figure.

He flashed her a grin. 'But if you do fail,' he said, tossing an envelope across the table, 'these go straight to the papers.'

Ellen's heart stopped beating as she looked down at the envelope. She didn't have to look inside to know what it contained, nor did she have to see them to know what the photographs were of. All she wondered, as her head started to spin, was whether they included shots of last night or if those were still at the developers. Blackmail, the oldest and most obvious trick in the book.

'Now *that's* what you call incentive,' Forgon smiled getting to his feet and leaving her to pick up the tab, he strolled casually out of the room.

Chapter 7

'Sandy? Sandy? Are you OK?'

Sandy stirred and tried to open her eyes.

'Sandy. Come on, wake up.'

Through the cloying layers of sleep Sandy could feel a hand on her shoulder and the strangely comforting presence of someone standing over her. She murmured softly and her eyelids fluttered again.

'Sandy? Can you hear me?'

It took a moment, but when finally she recognized the voice her heart ground to a halt. His hand was still touching her, but she couldn't think where she was. Very slowly she opened her eyes, afraid now that this was only a dream.

'Are you OK?' Michael asked, concern showing in his deep-blue eyes.

There was such a stiffness in her body that it hurt to lift her head.

'Have you been here all night?' Zelda asked.

Sandy frowned, then blinked her eyes. She was in her office, with Michael and Zelda standing over her. She felt terrible, her head was throbbing, her limbs were like lead and there was a ghastly taste in her mouth.

'What time is it?' she said.

'Just after nine,' Zelda answered, glancing at

116

Michael. 'Did you come in early?' she asked. 'Or have you been here all night?'

Sandy was still bemused.

'She must have been here all night,' Michael said. 'The lamp's still on and look at all these scripts.'

Sandy ran her hands quickly over her face. 'I'm sorry,' she said hoarsely. 'I was working late and must have dropped off.' She laughed and shrugged self-consciously. 'Sorry,' she said again.

Michael's concern was still evident as his eyes searched her face. 'You're working too hard,' he told her. 'I'll call a taxi to take you home so you can get some proper sleep.'

'Oh no!' she cried. 'There's no need. I'll be fine once I've showered and changed. I can be back here by lunch-time.'

Michael looked at Zelda.

'Sandy,' Zelda said gently, 'we know how keen you are to get on and how hard you're prepared to work to show us what you can do, but you can't go on like this. You're going to make yourself ill.'

Sandy looked at her, then returned her gaze to Michael as he said, 'I want you to take the rest of the day off, then come and see me after the meeting tomorrow.'

Her eyes followed him as he left the room. His dark hair was still damp from the rain, his long leather coat had left a lingering aroma. Sandy turned her gaze to Zelda. 'Is he angry?' she asked, uncertainty and dishevelment making her look younger than her twenty-four years.

'No, of course not,' Zelda answered. 'He's concerned, like the rest of us.'

Sandy lowered her head, then, forcing a laugh she said, 'It was such a shock to wake up and find him there.' She stopped and blushing hard, brought her eyes back to Zelda's.

Zelda's smile was sardonic as turning to leave she said, 'I'll go downstairs and get you a coffee.'

'Why do you think he wants to see me?' Sandy asked, before the door closed.

'I'd only be guessing,' Zelda answered and left.

Sandy stared down at her cluttered desk and tried to stop her mind and heart racing. Zelda was right, she was working too hard and maybe she was going to make herself ill, but she didn't care. All that mattered was that she learned as much as she could about McCann Walsh and about becoming an agent.

By now she was a fair way along that road, for she had a good working knowledge of how most of the agents operated, she knew the name of every actor, writer, director and producer on their books; she knew who was working and who wasn't, whose prospects were good, how their talent was rated, she was even beginning to understand what made one actor stand out above another and what gave certain writers the edge that was needed to get his or her work on stage or screen. She watched, listened, helped out, enquired, researched and made notes constantly. She had gone out of her way to make herself popular with all the clients and had even been invited on to some film and TV sets or, on a couple of occasions, to rehearsals. The agents themselves were only too willing to give her as much advice as she wanted and she could but marvel at how generous they were with their knowledge and time. She had been to most of their homes now, had been taken along to business dinners and had even entertained once or twice herself. In fact, her life was so different now from what it had been six months ago when she'd started that she not only looked and behaved like a different person, she actually felt like one.

The grisly little bedsit in Barking was long gone, so were the second-hand clothes, the lingering Midlands accent and financial crisis. Now, thanks to her best friend, Nesta Haines, she lived in a smart, second-floor flat just off Sloane Avenue in Chelsea and shopped only in Harrods or Harvey Nichols for everything except food – for that she either went to Fortnums or phoned in her order and got them to deliver.

She'd met Nesta because Nesta's grandmother had occupied the flat below hers in Barking. Nesta had been there checking on the old lady that terrible night when Sandy had arrived home from work not knowing how she would ever get back in the morning, or even how she was going to find enough funds to eat. Had the old lady not run out of milk and had Nesta not found the twenty-four-hour Indian shop on the corner closed, Sandy and Nesta might never have met. As it was, Nesta, who was the same age as Sandy with large hazel eyes, wide cheek-bones and a delicately pointed chin, had knocked on Sandy's door to borrow some milk and finding Sandy in such a state of despair had immediately taken charge of the crisis.

It was Nesta who had answered the phone when Jodi had called that night and it was Nesta who had taken Sandy to the supermarket first thing the next morning, before going on to the station to purchase a three-month ticket. In less than a fortnight Sandy had been able to pay Nesta back, for by then she had been recruited by Isabelle Woodhurst, senior director of the exclusive service Nesta belonged to, which provided glamorous female escorts for out-of-town businessmen, politicians and all kinds of foreigners.

It was thanks to Maurice Trehearne, a property tycoon whom Sandy met through the agency and had become very good friends with, that she and Nesta, just before Christmas, had moved into a two-bedroomed flat in Chelsea, which had a wonderful art-deco entrance hall and stairway, and was furnished with the most elegant reproduction sofas, beds, bookcases, tables and desks. They never brought their official dates home and apart from the first couple of months when she had desperately needed the money, Sandy never slept with the men who paid to take her out. She only continued to date because she enjoyed the extra luxuries it provided and because she was learning so much from the men themselves, who had introduced her to a whole other world of top-class restaurants and hotels, exclusive night-clubs and a code of behaviour and dress that might otherwise have taken her years to learn. They were also easily persuaded to boast about the successful strategies and tactics they had employed to get to the top – a veritable wealth of information that was proving invaluable in her bid to get there herself and was almost unfailingly effective.

Nesta thought she was mad, turning down all the wildly extravagant incentives to get her into bed, but though she hadn't had a problem sleeping with a man for money when she'd had to, she wasn't a prostitute, nor was she going to allow them to turn her into one. In her heart she knew it was the way she felt about Michael that really kept her from going that route, for the temptation otherwise of shopping sprees in Paris, royal enclosures at Ascot or Henley, or luxury cruises on private yachts, would probably have been too great to resist. As it was, she slept only with Maurice, because she liked him, enjoyed her other dates, stored away her knowledge and devoted the rest of her time to furthering her career with McCann Walsh in the hope of one day showing Michael that she was worthy of someone like him.

Quite how well she was doing in that area was hard to tell, though she'd definitely been getting a few vibes lately. She didn't think she was the only one who'd noticed either, but apart from Jodi and Nesta she never talked about it to anyone. As far as the rest of the office was concerned, with the exception of Bertie, Janine and

Frances, she got along great with everyone, especially Craig, the gay literary agent, who spent many of his weekends sharing the benefit of his agenting expertise with Sandy because his lover was married and he had nothing else to do.

Sandy watched Craig now as he leaned over his assistant's shoulder to read the paper Bertie was holding. His thick, golden-blond hair and exquisite face had really got Nesta going the first time she'd met him, and Sandy had never failed to notice how many heads turned, both male and female, whenever she walked into a restaurant or wine bar on his arm. There was no question that with his looks Craig could get just about anyone he wanted, but not once had Sandy ever seen him show a single flicker of interest in anyone but the Under-Secretary of State with whom he was involved. They had been seeing each other for the past two and a half years, Craig had told her, and there was no doubt in Sandy's mind that Craig was as deeply in love with the twinkly eyed sixty-year-old as she was with Michael. She knew, too, that apart from Michael and the Under-Secretary himself, she was the only other person who knew about the affair – with the possible exception of Zelda, as Zelda had that uncanny knack of knowing everything without even being told.

Kicking around under the desk for her shoes, she heard the lift doors open and turned to watch two of the agents, Harry and Diana, stroll down the steps to the inner circle. They stopped, still chatting, to check the message board, which reminded Sandy, she'd taken a call for Michael last night from an old girlfriend who was in town for a couple of days, but it wasn't a message Sandy felt inclined to pass on, so she promptly dismissed it from her mind.

Catching Janine and Frances, the booking assistants, looking her way and making no attempt to hide the fact they were talking about her, Sandy smiled in the hope they might smile back. She'd tried hard to make friends with those two, but nothing she did ever seemed right and as far, as Bertie was concerned she got the impression she was hardly worth speaking to at all. Of course, she couldn't expect everyone to like her, but she was greatly looking forward to the day when she finally achieved her goal and became Michael's partner, because then she would take immense pleasure in firing every one of them.

Yawning, she picked up her Smythson's briefcase, stuffed a couple of scripts inside and rummaged around for her foolscap pad. Once she got home she'd probably sleep for the rest of the morning, then she wanted to get back to work on these scripts before going out to dinner at eight. A flicker of excitement suddenly lit up her heart as she recalled who she was having dinner with, and why. Marlene, Diana's assistant, was about to go off on maternity leave and had, unofficially, for the past few weeks been grooming Sandy to take over while she was away. Tonight, she was treating Marlene to dinner out, because Marlene's husband was in Manchester on business and Marlene got lonely without him. Though the woman herself was a bit of a bore, her knowledge and support were invaluable, so Sandy was more than willing to put up with her, as she would undoubtedly carry some sway when it came to recommending her replacement. In fact, Sandy thought with a sudden burst of elation, it could be what Michael wanted to talk to her about in the morning.

Hearing a bump behind her, she looked up to see Jodi struggling in through the door with a giant parcel.

'What on earth's that?' Sandy laughed.

'A birthday present for my niece,' Jodi answered, dumping the parcel on her chair. 'My God, you look like you've been here all night! Are you OK? Heavy date last night, was it?'

'I wish,' Sandy responded. 'Oh, Zelda, thanks, you're a life saver,' she added, as Zelda came in behind Jodi with a fresh cup of coffee.

Jodi's eyebrows went skywards. 'How come you never bring me a coffee when I've got a hangover?' she demanded of Zelda.

'I haven't got a hangover,' Sandy told her, flinching as she burnt her lips on the coffee. 'I fell asleep at my desk.'

Jodi gawped at her. 'You mean you really have been here all night?' she cried. 'I was only kidding. What happened, did you get kicked out of your flat or something?'

Zelda gave a choke of laughter.

'Why, are you offering to put me up?' Sandy challenged.

Jodi shrugged. 'You can have the sofa for a few nights if you're stuck,' she said generously.

Sandy was no longer listening. Michael was coming in the door behind Jodi. 'Taxi should be here any minute,' he said, looking at Zelda. Then turning to Sandy, 'How are you feeling?'

Sandy smiled and silently prayed that she didn't look as bad as she felt. 'I'm OK,' she said softly. 'Thanks for ordering the taxi.'

Jodi's head was swinging back and forth between Zelda and Michael. 'Coffee? Taxis?' she said. 'Would someone mind explaining what's going on here? I mean, what is she, Sleeping Beauty or something?'

Michael laughed. 'It didn't cross my mind to kiss her awake,' he said and Sandy's heart stopped beating as winking at her he added, 'Maybe next time,' and before she could respond he had gone.

Jodi's eyes bulged as she looked at Sandy, and Zelda had barely left the room before she hissed, 'Is there something going on here you've forgotten to tell me about?'

123

Sandy laughed, then laughed again as a surge of euphoria took her. 'I don't know,' she said. 'I mean, no there isn't, but it's not the first time he's said something like that. Oh God, Jodi,' she groaned, slumping into her chair, 'do you think he's actually starting to notice me at last?'

'Well, if that was anything to go by ...' Jodi responded. Sandy peered at her from under lowered lashes and wanted to hug her, for just those few short words had instilled such a sense of joy and hope in her she could quite happily have hugged the world.

'So why *did* you sleep here?' Jodi asked. 'Don't tell me you were poring over more of those scripts Craig keeps throwing your way. You don't have to read them, you know. I mean, it's not as if you're getting paid for it.'

'I want to do it,' Sandy told her. 'And Craig's got a meeting at Channel 4 on Friday, so he wants to make sure no little gems have been missed before he goes.'

Jodi tutted. 'Well, if just now is anything to go by,' she said, hooking her coat on the stand beside Sandy's, 'your hard work seems to be paying off.'

Sandy was on her feet. 'I'm going home,' she said. 'He wants to see me after the meeting tomorrow.'

Jodi's eyebrows went up. 'No kidding,' she said. 'What about, did he say?'

Sandy shook her head. 'I'm going to go insane thinking about it all day, but I can hardly ask, can I? I take it you don't know.'

'This is the first I've heard of it,' Jodi answered. 'But I'll lay money it's about Marlene's job. She goes next Friday.' Sandy's heart somersaulted. 'Jodi, you're speaking the language of my wildest dreams,' she said, quoting from one of the scripts she'd read the night before. 'But after just six months even I wouldn't hold out that much hope.'

'Sandy Paull! This is me you're talking to,' Jodi cried.

'It's exactly what you want and we both know it. What's more, you deserve it.'

Sandy was so touched that for a moment she didn't respond. In the end she said, 'You're a great friend, Jodi. Thanks.'

'Oh, get out of here,' Jodi chuckled, embarrassed but none the less pleased. 'Oh look, the Christmas fairy missed his cue again,' she said as Bertie, Craig's assistant, came waltzing into their office.

'I just had a call from security,' he said, running an affected finger to the corner of his mouth. 'They say there's a taxi waiting downstairs for Miss Paull. Going somewhere special, are we?' he asked, wrinkling his nose as he gave Sandy the once-over.

'Yes,' she answered.

Bertie waited, but Sandy merely picked up her bag and coat, said goodbye to Jodi and left.

'You should look out for that one,' Bertie warned as he and Jodi watched her walk over to the lift. 'She's got more bad news about her than ITN.'

'So you keep saying,' Jodi reminded him.

'I'm telling you, don't trust the woman.'

'Bertie,' Jodi said, smiling sweetly, 'whatever problem you have with Sandy is all yours. I don't want to know, OK?'

His top lip puckered as his nostrils flared. 'That's right, Jodi,' he said scathingly, 'stay on her good side, because with the way she's sucking up to the management around here there's every chance she'll end up your boss one of these days.'

'Really?' Jodi responded with mild interest. 'Do you know something I don't, by any chance?'

'What I know is what I see,' he replied. 'And if you've had your eyes open lately, Jodi Webb, you'll have seen the way our lord and master has been looking at Ms Paull, and if you ask me there's a whole

125

lot more interest going on behind those looks than merely the professional.'

'Then I guess you'd better start mending your ways, Bertie boy,' Jodi told him, tweaking his tie as she passed and before he could say any more she picked up the phone to take a call that turned out to be yet another attempt by the Hollywood agent, Ellen Shelby, to get through to Michael.

Jodi looked at her watch. It was past two in the morning LA time, so it seemed the woman was starting to lose sleep over this. And if what Jodi had heard was true, that Ted Forgon had fired the previous three agents who had failed to hook Michael, she had reason to. Jodi liked the sound of the woman and wished there were something she could do to help, but Michael's instructions had been clear: if anyone called from ATI, anyone at all, he didn't even want to know about it.

'I'm sorry,' Jodi said into the phone. 'If I could put you through, I would, but I can't.'

'OK,' Ellen answered. 'But just tell me, did he get my faxes?'

'Yes,' Jodi confirmed. 'He got them.'

'Did he read them?'

'I don't know,' Jodi answered. 'He didn't say.'

There was an exasperated silence at the other end before she said, 'Will you tell him I called? And give him my home number?'

'OK,' Jodi responded, knowing she probably wouldn't, but she didn't want to dash the woman's hopes altogether, even though common sense and charity told her it would probably be kinder if she did.

Later that day Zelda was in Michael's car as he drove them both up to the West End. For the moment he was speaking on the phone so Zelda waited until he had finished, then quickly said, 'Before you start dialling again there's something I want to say to you.'

Michael grinned. 'I was trying to avoid it,' he confessed, clicking off the phone and dropping it into his lap.

Zelda chuckled and popped a mint humbug in her mouth. 'So,' she said, her cheek bulging, 'what's the answer?'

'To what?' he countered, holding his hand out for a sweet.

'I know you've read the faxes, so have you given any thought to this latest offer from Forgon?' she said.

'Some,' he answered.

'Aaaand?' she prompted.

'And nothing. I read the faxes, I thought about the offer and nothing. It doesn't interest me.'

'Doubling, maybe tripling, the output of McCann Walsh doesn't interest you?' she said flatly.

'That always interests me, provided I'm the head of McCann Walsh,' he replied.

Zelda stuck out her bottom lip. 'Maybe you could add a few conditions of your own,' she suggested.

'Like?'

'Like, you get to buy McCann Walsh back after a period of, say, five years?'

'At its going market rate?' he scoffed. 'With all ATI's business coming this way, I'll never be able to buy the agency back. For Christ's sake, Zelda,' he said, 'can't you see where the man's coming from? All he wants is to destroy me. He doesn't give a flying fuck about the agency. OK, he'll probably make it four, five, even ten times bigger than it is now – he wants to make money, so why wouldn't he? But all he's really concerned about is settling a score that was only ever a big deal to him in the first place. Christ, that sort of thing goes on all the time in Hollywood.'

'Maybe, but the way he sees it, you cost him more face than a plastic surgeon trashes in a month,' Zelda responded.

Despite himself Michael laughed. 'And I'm supposed to give him my agency to say sorry?' he said.

Zelda sucked on her sweet and they drove on in silence until finally Michael said, 'If I didn't know better, I'd think you were trying to get me to consider this offer.'

Zelda foraged for another humbug. 'What I think is that you should know what you're turning down and why,' she said.

He seemed amused as he raised an eyebrow. 'And are you satisfied that I know the answer to both those questions?' he asked.

She nodded slowly. 'Yes, you probably do,' she said. 'I'm just surprised that you're so determined to hold out against Hollywood.'

'I don't see that I'm holding out,' he responded. 'We do plenty of business out there. You were there yourself a month ago doing a deal for Carro and Millman. Craig's got his contacts out there, so have Janey and Diana, and from what he tells me Harry's been talking to someone at Front Row about a twelve-month tie-up. So we're definitely not holding out against Hollywood. We're just spreading it around a bit, rather than putting all our talent in one show.'

'And you have no desire to base yourself there?'

'None whatsoever.'

'Not at any price?'

'Correct.'

Zelda popped her humbug, then sat with her hands resting on the top of her bag. 'Have you ever met Ellen Shelby?' she asked.

Michael frowned as he thought. 'Not that I know of,' he said. 'Have you?'

Zelda shook her head. 'I called someone at CAA last night. Seems she's pretty big news over there.'

'Everyone's big news in Hollywood,' Michael commented, 'or they like to think they are.'

'She's got a good reputation,' Zelda said. 'She's a genuine Forgon protégé, apparently. He took her on a couple of years ago and she's gone from strength to strength ever since.'

'Which means he's screwing her.'

Zelda rolled her eyes. 'I expected more of you, Michael,' she chided.

'We're talking Hollywood, Zelda,' he reminded her. 'OK, so she's a Forgon protégé,' he conceded, when she went silent on him.

'Mmm,' Zelda responded, moving her humbug from one cheek to the other, 'but probably not for much longer, if you're going to turn this offer down.'

Michael's surprise was expressed in a laugh. 'Zelda, I've got no intention of being held to account for these people's jobs,' he told her. He glanced over at her, then braked hard to avoid ramming the car in front.

Zelda stared straight ahead.

'OK, I feel bad about it,' he confessed, 'but if you think I'm going to put my soul and my integrity along with everything I've ever worked for into Ted Forgon's pocket just to save one person's job, a person I've never even met remember, then think again, because it's not going to happen.'

Zelda's fat, gentle face was alight with surprise. 'I didn't know you had a soul,' she said, sounding rather cheered by the idea.

'OK, I lied. But you get the general idea. Anyway, conversation over. This guy's not for sale.'

'And if Ellen Shelby flies over to London, which she undoubtedly will, are you going to see her?'

'What's the point? It'll be a waste of her time and mine.' He looked at his watch. 'Remind me where you're going now.'

'The Savoy,' she answered. She allowed a few seconds to pass, then said, 'So, it's no way, LA.'

Michael frowned. 'What is this, Zelda?' he

demanded. 'I'm beginning to think you actually want me to go.'

'It'd break my heart,' she told him frankly. 'But it's been over four years now, Michael. It's time to let go of the past and start working towards what you really want.'

'What's that supposed to mean?' he retorted. 'No, don't tell me, I don't want to hear it.' He let a few seconds pass, then, glancing at her he said, 'Is that what everyone thinks? That I haven't got over it yet?'

Zelda blinked mildly, then scratching her nose turned to gaze absently out at the peculiar King's Road fashions.

'But that's crazy,' he protested. 'It was so long ago I don't even think about her any more.'

'Who?' Zelda asked.

Confused, Michael glanced at her, then was forced to brake hard again as he turned back to the road.

They were approaching Sloane Square before he spoke again. 'Are you going to O'Malley's first night on Friday?' he asked.

Zelda's eyebrows rose. 'Does a drowning man yawn?' she answered.

Michael laughed. 'You know, for someone who professes to spread only good thoughts through the world you've got some corkers hidden away,' he told her.

'I save them all for you,' she confessed, looking off down Sloane Avenue as they headed towards Eton Square. 'Oh, that reminds me,' she said, wondering which of the grand Edwardian houses Sandy Paull's apartment was in, 'what are you going to do about Sandy?'

Michael looked surprised. 'What about her?' he said.

'You told her to come and see you after the meeting tomorrow.'

'Oh yes,' he responded.

Zelda waited, not entirely surprised by his silence, for she had long experience of his refusal to be drawn on subjects he wasn't keen to discuss, and she'd certainly noticed these past couple of months how reluctant he was to discuss Sandy. Even all the speculation going on around the office as to how Sandy could afford the kind of clothes she wore and the primely located flat she rented hadn't seemed to evoke any response from him. It was true he had once remarked on the change in her, though whether he had been referring to the distinct improvement in the way she looked, or the surprising confidence she'd acquired in so short a time, had been impossible to tell. And as for her crush on him, which was so obvious it bordered on the embarrassing at times, well, that was a subject he definitely didn't welcome, not even as a joke.

'What is it you've got against the girl?' Zelda asked bluntly.

'Who are we talking about now?' Michael wondered.

'Sandy Paull. And before you answer, remember I know you, Michael, so I know when you're going out of your way to be nice to someone to compensate for not liking them. God knows, I've seen you do it enough with the luvvies. Now you're doing it with Sandy. So why don't you like her?'

'I'm about to promote her,' he said, slowing for a pedestrian crossing.

'Which is what tomorrow is about? Good, she deserves it. But why, when you don't really want her around?'

'I don't have a problem with her being around,' he responded. 'Christ, if everyone put as much effort into the agency as she does we'd never have to worry again.'

Zelda looked at him. 'You're not going to give me an answer, are you?' she said.

He shook his head. 'My personal feelings towards

131

Sandy Paull aren't important enough to discuss,' he said.

'But you are going to promote her?'

'Probably. We've got a couple of things to straighten out first and if I'm satisfied with their outcome she'll get her promotion.'

'Blimey, what's going on here?' Nesta demanded, unbelting her raincoat as she wandered into Sandy's bedroom and found the contents of Sandy's wardrobe scattered all over the high mahogany bed. 'Are you moving out or something?'

Sandy didn't even turn round as she continued hunting through what was left in the reproduction armoire and pulled out a blush-pink Escada suit. 'I'm seeing Michael in the morning,' she answered, holding the suit up against herself in the mirror.

Nesta draped her coat across the dressing-table stool, kicked off her boots and climbed up on to the pillows. 'Don't you see him every morning?' she asked, crossing her legs and picking up a hand mirror from the dressing-table to study her large hazel eyes and luscious, heart-shaped lips. 'Do you think my hair needs a colour?' she asked, flicking it with her fingers.

'I think he's going to promote me,' Sandy said, feeling the excitement close around her heart as she said the words.

'You mean he's going to give you the job while what's-her-name's on maternity leave?'

Sandy nodded and gave a shudder of nerves. 'I think so,' she said. 'I expect I'll find out when I see him in the morning. Oh God, what am I going to wear? What do you think of this?' she asked, indicating the pink suit.

Nesta shrugged, then turned to look out of the window as a fire engine screamed past. 'Depends what you wear with it,' she said, glancing at her watch. 'Are you going out tonight?'

'Yes, later,' Sandy answered, dropping the suit on the bed and returning to the wardrobe.

'Go like that,' Nesta suggested, tossing the mirror aside and putting her hands behind her head.

Sandy laughed. As she was wearing only a black thong, black push-up bra and black hold-up stockings the suggestion wasn't serious, but the idea of the response it might provoke was definitely appealing.

'Aren't you going to ask where I've been?' Nesta yawned.

'Do you reckon this would work?' Sandy asked, taking a cream silk top from a drawer and matching it to the suit. 'No,' she said, answering her own question. 'Too Cherie Blair. Maybe black. What do you think? I've got that see-through stretch lacy top, remember? I could button the jacket up over it. Or no, the suit's wrong, isn't it? It's too dressy for the office. I wonder what colours he likes.'

'You're obsessed with that man,' Nesta grumbled. 'He's only flesh and blood, for God's sake, so do what I tell you, go in like that, he'll probably end up promoting you and screwing you over the desk at the same time.'

'Don't,' Sandy shivered. 'Just the thought of it makes me come over all funny. But it wouldn't surprise me, once I'm an assistant, if that kind of thing didn't start happening quite a bit after everyone goes home, because it's usually just me and him left working late, and I'm telling you, something's definitely starting to happen between us.' She giggled to herself. 'I bet he can't wait to promote me so we can hurry up and get on with it.'

Nesta looked at her incredulously as she whisked a short tartan kilt and red lycra top over to the mirror. 'You really think that getting this job is going to make a difference, don't you?' she said.

Sandy's head came up to look at her in the mirror.

Nesta looked back. 'I mean, you really believe he's going to fancy you just because he's made you an assistant to one of his agents,' she said.

'Well, I don't . . .' Sandy began, her eyes starting to fill with confusion. 'What are you saying?' she asked.

'I'm saying that if he fancied you, Sandy, he would have screwed you by now, no matter who you are.'

'No he wouldn't,' Sandy responded defensively. 'I'm only a clerk, remember? He can hardly be seen going out with a measly little clerk, can he?'

'I didn't say going out,' Nesta reminded her. 'I said screw. And believe me, Sandy, that's about the most you can hope for here, because men like him, they don't go out with women like you.'

Sandy's face was drawing tight with anger and hurt. 'What do you mean, women like me?' she demanded.

Nesta drew in a breath. 'Look, I don't want to hurt your feelings,' she said, 'but the Michael McCanns of this world only get serious about women of their own sort. In other words, women with class. Women like you they just screw.'

'For your information,' Sandy said, 'he comes from a working-class background too, so he's just the same as me.'

Nesta was shaking her head. 'He's nothing like you,' she said. 'To start with, the man is well-educated, he's got money, he's got more women than he knows what to do with, so what's he going to want with someone like you? I keep telling you, give it up. You don't want to be an agent, all you want is to impress him so's he'll think you're the greatest thing that's ever happened to him and fall madly in love with you and make you queen of the McCann court. Well, he's never going to do it, I promise you. What he'll do, *maybe*, is screw you a couple of times, then dump you. I'm sorry, I know it's not what you want to hear, but I don't want to see you go on kidding yourself like this. You should get out of that place and start having some fun. I mean, look at me, I've just flown back Concorde from New York where I was wined and dined, and stayed at the Plaza and got driven about in a stretch limousine, shopped on Fifth Avenue and saw two Broadway shows, best seats in the house, and do you know what I had to do for all that? Let him watch me put lipstick on my tits. I ask you, what could be easier? There was a whole gang of us, we had a great time. And what were you doing? Stuck here with gay Craig, I'll bet, going over some crappy writer's script that's got even less chance of making it to the screen than you've got of making it as Michael McCann's woman.'

Sandy's face was stricken. 'You're the one who's been telling me all this time that I *did* stand a chance,' she cried.

'Only of getting screwed,' Nesta cried back. 'I've never said anything about a long-term relationship, because I know it's not going to happen.'

'What are you?' Sandy shouted. 'Some kind of fortune-teller or something? You can't say what he's going to do, you don't know what's going on inside his head. You don't even know him!'

'I've seen that man on three separate occasions now,' Nesta shot back, 'and I'm telling you, Sandy, you're going to end up disappointed. You're attractive, you've got a good body and when you want to, you know how to use it, but even if you end up being the best fuck he's ever had, I promise you he's still never going to make you his partner, not in any way, shape or form, because men like him don't go out in public with girls like you.'

Sandy's face was white, her whole body was tense with fury. 'You mean like *you*,' she raged. 'You're the one who gets paid for it, not me. I *never* take money for sex and you know it. I only did it those few times at the beginning, because I didn't have a choice and no one will ever know about that unless you tell them.'

'Don't be daft, I'll never tell them,' Nesta said. 'But you're still going out on dates in a professional capacity and whether or not you're having sex at the end of the night is irrelevant. The fact is, you do have sex with some of them, at least you do with Maurice, you just don't take his money. OK, you like him, you get on well with him, but why do you think we pay such a low rent for this place? And the other men? I know you like to think those dates are respectable, but do you honestly think Michael McCann would see it that way? You're still meeting them through Isabelle Woodcroft, they're still paying for the privilege of taking you to dinner or a show or wherever you go ...'

'He's taking women out all the time,' Sandy protested.

'Oh God, Sandy,' Nesta groaned, 'it's not the same and you know it, so stop trying to fool yourself that it is.'

Sandy glared at her mutinously, not wanting to accept she was right, but unable to defend herself further.

'OK,' Nesta sighed, starting to regret how blunt she had been, 'go ahead and try to hook the man, do whatever you think it takes to make yourself his equal, just don't come crying to me when everything I've tried to warn you about starts coming true. Well, you can come crying to me, but why don't you save yourself the heartache and give up on it now?'

'Because you're wrong, Nesta,' Sandy replied fiercely. 'You're dead wrong. It will work out for me and Michael, I know it will.'

Nesta shook her head sadly. 'What about this actress he's been seeing?' she said. 'Is she still around?'

'She won't last,' Sandy answered, 'none of them ever do.'

'But you're different,' Nesta said flatly.

Sandy averted her head. 'You just don't understand,'

136

she mumbled. 'It's not something you can put into words.'

'Oh yes, you can,' Nesta corrected, sliding down from the bed, 'it's called blind obsession, that's what it's called, and the worst part of it is that you could be having such a good time with us if you just forgot about him and threw all that precious energy into doing what you do best. Who are you seeing tonight?'

Sandy's face was sour. 'Marlene, actually,' she answered.

'What about the duke? Don't you usually see him on Wednesdays?'

'I cancelled.'

Nesta rolled her eyes. 'That man would probably leave you his entire fortune if you gave him what he wanted and he's got to be worth millions. For God's sake, Sandy, he's in his eighties, he can't be much longer for this world, so why don't you just do it? No one would ever know ...'

'The whole world would know if he left me his fortune,' Sandy pointed out. 'And he's got two sons and three daughters who'd have plenty to say about it if he did. Besides, he doesn't want to do it. He's lonely. He wants to talk and reminisce and show me his mementoes from the war. That's why I go there and no matter what you say, I can't see anyone thinking there's anything wrong in that, especially not Michael ...'

'All right, all right,' Nesta said, holding up her hand. 'You do it your way. All I'm saying is stop making out you're whiter than white and butter wouldn't melt, when we both know the truth. And I'm not talking about being paid for dates now, I'm talking about all those little stunts you've been pulling over at that office that have got you to where you are now.'

Sandy's eyes flashed. 'I haven't done anything wrong,' she snapped.

'Maybe not to your way of thinking,' Nesta conceded, 'but there are others, if they knew about it, who might not agree,' and picking up her coat she started to walk out.

'The trouble with you, Nesta,' Sandy called after her, 'is that you don't understand ambition or office politics or any of the things that go with a normal job. What I'm doing to get on in the world is nothing in comparison to the things you do.'

'At least what I do is honest and up front,' Nesta responded, turning back. 'What you're doing is lying to yourself and cheating on people who trust you. And do you know who's going to end up getting hurt, Sandy? You, that's who. And I don't want to see that happen, because I know that deep down inside you're a decent, caring and honest person, who for some unknown reason seems hell bent on destroying herself over a man who just isn't worth it, because none of them ever are.'

Chapter 8

'Has anyone seen Michael?' Jodi said, putting her head round the door of the meeting room where four out of the seven McCann Walsh agents were seated around the conference table, with Sandy at the far end ready to take the minutes.

'We should be asking you that question,' Zelda responded, looking at her watch. 'Did you call his home?'

'About fifty times,' Jodi answered, avoiding Sandy's eyes as Sandy stared across the room at her. 'His mobile's not on either and I've got Grungehart, or whatever his name is, on the line from Budapest. The man's doing his nut.'

'What's the problem?' Zelda asked, letting her half-spectacles slide down her nose as she looked at Jodi.

'He says about six East European publishers are ready to do a deal on the *Crazy Cult* books, but he can't finalize until he clears the figures with Michael.'

Zelda glanced over at Craig who was engrossed in the latest edition of *Variety*. 'Did you hear that, duckie?' she said.

'What?' he asked, as Diana nudged him.

Zelda repeated what Jodi had said. 'So I thought,' she continued, 'as you claim to be our literary lunch ticket, that perhaps you might like to take the call.'

'Where's Michael?' he asked.

'Temporarily misplaced.'

'I handled the TV series,' Craig said. 'Michael's been dealing with the books.'

Zelda swivelled her chair back towards Jodi and peeled her spectacles from behind her ears. 'Tell Grungehart, or whatever his name is,' she said, 'to add a third to the offer, then do the best he can and sign.'

'Do I tell him the instruction came from you or Michael?' Jodi asked, tucking her hair behind one ear as she noticed Harry looking her way.

Zelda rotated her head slowly in Harry's direction, then, having got the measure of the subtext, said, 'From me. Any word from Janey, before you go?'

'Not that I know of,' Jodi responded, with a quick last glance at Harry.

'Was Michael at the Westlake party last night?' Diana asked of no one in particular.

'Didn't see him,' Craig answered.

'He was going to Clinton Day's preview, the last I heard,' Harry chipped in. 'Now, do you want to hear the rest of this joke, or don't you?'

'We've already heard it,' Zelda responded. 'Now, why don't we get this meeting under way? Michael and Janey can pick up when they get here. Sandy, you're taking the minutes?'

Sandy nodded and put a hand on the tape recorder ready to start it. She came to all the meetings now, not only to record what was said, but, because of the many extra duties she'd taken on of late, to contribute too.

This morning her sleek blonde hair was softly brushed into place behind her ears, with a full sweep across her forehead. Her shiny turquoise eyes were carefully circled in kohl and highlighted with a light Chanel shadow, her narrow cheeks were widened with blusher and her lips were darkly outlined with a fine bronze pencil. Her ear-rings and necklace were a matching Butler and Wilson set, and her Moschino tight-fitting black velvet suit contrived to be as sexy as it was businesslike. Beneath the table her slender, seam-stockinged legs were crossed at the ankles; beneath her impassive façade her heart was twisting with nerves. Michael had to come in today, he just had to. She'd gone to so much trouble to select her wardrobe and rehearse what she was going to say when he promoted her that she just couldn't bear it if it didn't happen now.

As the meeting got underway she returned her fingers to the keyboard of her lap-top, keeping her eyes lowered as the dread that he had overslept with a woman started wrenching at her heart. She swallowed hard and gazed blindly down at her crimson nails, thinking of all the things Nesta had said the night before. But then she forced herself past Nesta's warnings and thought instead of what he had said yesterday about kissing her. Slowly the warmth of hope stole back into her heart.

'Did Frank Rotter get back to you about the Christmas episodes of that terrible game show, whatever it's called, Sandy?' Zelda asked as the door opened and Janey McIntyre let herself apologetically into the room.

Sandy smiled as Janey edged past the others and laughed at their teasing. She hated Janey with a passion, for at five foot eleven she was at least seven inches taller than Sandy, and was so damned sexy and gorgeous it made Sandy want to puke. The woman had barely turned thirty and already she'd had three successful careers, as a photographic model, an actress and now as an agent. Her relationship with Bobby Mack, the musician, was supposed to be great, but if that were true then why did she flirt with Michael the way she did? And where had she been until now? Sandy's heart lurched violenty with the sudden fear that she might have been with Michael. It was bad enough that he'd had seven dates with the actress

Fiona Atkins, but were he to break his own rule of no office relationships with Janey, rather than with her, then Sandy didn't even want to think about what she would do.

'Sandy?' Zelda prompted, as Janey sat down in an empty chair and started to unpack her briefcase.

Sandy looked at Zelda. 'You mean *Hazard*?' she said. 'They're shooting fifteen episodes a week throughout November. I just need a list from everyone of the celebrities you've got who'll be willing to do it.' She glanced down at the pad beside her computer. 'They're paying two hundred and fifty an episode,' she said. 'No cars, no expenses, but make-up will be provided.'

'Craig, did Bertie tell you that George Gordon is interested in directing the McInerny script?' Diana said, noting down what Sandy had said and moving on.

'Yeah,' Craig answered. 'That's great news. I didn't think he was free.'

'If the BBC will agree to move it forward a month he will be,' Diana told him. 'Do you think there's a chance?'

'Talk to Michael,' he said. 'He's the only one who can move mountains around here. Do you think he's going to put in an appearance today? I need his thoughts on the rewrites Jill Allinson's just submitted.' He looked at Sandy and winked. 'I'll get you a copy,' he told her.

'Thanks,' Sandy smiled. 'I spoke to Jill yesterday, by the way. She's telling everyone that the rewrites are mostly down to you and that you're in the wrong job.'

Craig laughed, though he was obviously pleased by the compliment and Sandy knew that it would never even occur to him that she had just made it up.

'Uh, Sandy,' Janey said, slipping on a pair of Dior-framed glasses as she scanned the notes in front of her, 'I just popped in on the *EastEnders* set, and Theo Jacks asked me to pass on his thanks.' She looked up at Sandy and treated her to a dazzling smile. 'I didn't even know he was up for the part,' she said, 'so thanks from me too. When did you hear about it?'

'Two or three days ago,' Sandy answered. 'I just happened to be speaking to one of their casting people and she asked me if I had any news on Theo. She said a script had been sent over, marked for your attention, and the part was his if he wanted it and she was surprised no one had got back to her. It's only a couple of episodes I think, isn't it?'

Janey nodded. 'But he would have missed them if you hadn't been on the ball,' she said. 'I can't think what I must have done with that script. I don't even remember seeing it.'

Sandy shook her head. 'Me neither,' she said. 'But I got them to bike a copy straight to Theo, that way there was no more time wasted. The contract's on its way, apparently.'

'Well, thanks again,' Janey said. 'Further proof, I think, that I need to find myself an assistant.'

'Speaking of the BBC and contracts,' Freda, the contracts manager, piped up, 'I've found a problem with the royalty clause on Gillian Peachey's renewal. She's yours, isn't she, Diana? I'll speak to you about it after.'

'Next item,' Harry declared. 'The Cannes Film Festival. Seb Johnson's offering us his house for the duration, but he needs an answer by the end of next week. So anyone who needs to go should speak to my personal Rottweiler, Thea. Apparently, *Just Waiting* is being nominated so . . .' He stopped as the door opened and Michael walked in.

'Sorry I'm late,' he said, kicking the door to behind him. 'My mother arrived with breakfast and I don't have to tell you what she's like when her mind's made up.'

'Clodagh, God bless her,' Craig responded in an Irish accent.

Laughing and ruffling Craig's shock of fair hair as he passed, Michael edged his way round the room to the only empty chair left and sat down next to Sandy. He was wearing a dark Armani suit, white shirt and an unknotted burgundy tie. The gold watch he always wore hung loosely over the back of his hand, the keys to his Mercedes jangled as they hit the table in front of him.

'So where were we?' he asked, opening his briefcase and taking out a wad of papers.

Sandy rewound the tape and played back the meeting so far. It was amazing, she was thinking, how different the room suddenly felt now he was in it. It was as though the ubiquitous humour in his deep-blue eyes had brought a new light into their surroundings, upping the mood, increasing the pace and relaxing any hidden tensions.

Sensing her eyes on him, he glanced briefly in her direction. She smiled politely, then returned her gaze to the tape.

'OK,' he said when it had finished. He was scanning the documents in front of him. 'Janey, speak to me after about an assistant and Freda, have the Peachey contract on my desk by the end of the day. Now, Dan's just given me the figures for the second half of last year and you'll all be happy to hear next year's Christmas bonus is already looking safe. We're getting a touch heavy on the entertaining, though, so try to keep it down folks, eh? One bottle of champagne instead of two maybe; Joe Allen's occasionally, instead of the Ivy. Reece Hawthorne called me this morning,' he said, looking over at Craig. 'He read your guy's script, remind me of the name?'

'It's a woman,' Craig answered with a quick glance at Sandy. This was a script they'd done a lot of work on together. 'Molly Footman.'

'That's her. Hawthorne's interested to meet her. He's expecting your call to set up a time.'

Sandy was smiling as she looked at Craig. His pleasure, on behalf of his client, was both genuine and touching. And why shouldn't he feel proud? Reece Hawthorne was one of the country's leading film directors and one of the exclusive names whom Michael handled personally. And knowing Craig as well as she did now, Sandy was sure he would tell Michael how much she had contributed to the script. At least Craig thought she had, but all she'd done really was listen to his ideas, then field them back to him as though they were hers. It was a technique that was proving almost as effective as the system she had developed for rescuing situations that no one ever seemed to suspect she had created herself. In fact, some of them didn't even exist, but they were still just as successful in bringing her to the attention of the actors, or putting agents in her debt.

'Chantal Debussy's coming over from Paris next week,' Michael continued. 'She's sending a pile of the *Cherchez la femme* scripts over by courier . . .'

'They arrived this morning,' Zelda told him.

He nodded. 'OK. The producers and a couple of the directors are coming with Chantal for the British casting. We need to be lined up ready for auditions by next Tuesday. Sandy, you're co-ordinating it for us?'

'Yes,' Sandy answered. He was still looking at the notes in front of him, he could have spoken to anyone, but she understood that he would never flirt with her during a meeting like this.

'This is a twenty-six-part series,' he went on, sounding surprised. 'Did you know that?' he asked, looking up at Zelda.

'I knew there was talk of it,' she answered. 'Lysette Hopkins is interested in playing the mother, by the way.'

Michael pulled a face. 'They don't have that kind of budget,' he said. 'But talk to Chantal, maybe they can come to an agreement. Harry, did you get anywhere with Pete Dawes?' He looked up as the door opened and Jodi came in with his coffee.

'There's a call for you,' she said, as she set the cup down next to him. 'Do you want to take it in your office?'

Michael looked at her quizzically. He didn't normally take calls when he was in a meeting. Jodi stared back and a flash of impatience crossed Michael's face as her silence gave him a clue who was on the line. 'Tell them I'll get back to them,' he said tersely and returned his attention to Harry.

'They said to tell you it was urgent,' Jodi persisted.

Janey was laughing. 'Very discreet,' she told Jodi, 'but we're none of us fooled, honey. Michael, there's a woman on the line for you and it seems like she's pretty desperate, so do the decent thing for once in your life and go put her out of her misery.'

Sandy looked at her and hated her more than ever.

Michael was laughing. 'Wrong,' he told her. 'It's someone from *Esquire* who, while inspired by the benevolence of bourbon at some party last week, I half-promised to give an interview to.'

Now everyone was laughing as they all knew how much Michael hated publicity and how often he managed to get himself into these situations.

'The guy's obviously on some kind of deadline, if he's saying it's urgent,' Craig decided. 'So give him a break. Give him his interview.'

'I might if it were me he was interested in,' Michael protested.

Zelda chuckled. 'Fiona upstaging you, is she?' she said. Michael's eyebrows went up in a way that made them all laugh again.

'So, is it serious between you two?' Harry asked.

146

Sandy's tongue cleaved to the roof of her mouth as her insides turned hot.

'Zelda would never forgive me,' Michael responded.

'Clodagh would,' Zelda said with a grin.

'Michael, what are you going to do about this interview?' Jodi persisted.

'Tell him to call me mother,' Michael replied, in a broad Irish accent. 'She'll be happy to talk, so she will. She's an expert at it.'

Laughing and shaking her head in exasperation, Jodi left the room.

'Where were we?' Michael said, looking around for enlightenment.

'I think you were about to ask if I'd got anywhere with Pete Dawes,' Harry reminded him.

The meeting rumbled on for the rest of the morning, with items of business being tossed randomly into the arena, while the rain outside drizzled down the windows. It wasn't until everyone was getting up to leave that Michael addressed Sandy again.

'We have a meeting scheduled for now, don't we?' he said. Sandy's heart skipped and she kept her eyes lowered, not wanting anyone to see her reaction. 'Yes,' she answered. 'Shall I come straight in?'

He glanced at his watch. 'Give me half an hour,' he said, 'I should have cleared the more urgent calls by then.'

It was right on the tip of Sandy's tongue to suggest lunch, but she didn't quite have the nerve. She wasn't in that kind of position yet. Besides, he was bound to have a prior engagement, and even if he didn't she couldn't bear the idea of him turning her down in front of other people. Not only that, there was a chance she was jumping to conclusions about the promotion and her heart started to thud with unease as she thought of what else it could be. But surely he couldn't have found out about the conversations she'd had with some of the actors and writers out of the office. And even if he had, they could hardly be considered her fault. She never instigated them and what was she to do when there was nothing an artiste loved more than to bitch about his or her agent?

Walking into the ladies, she let the door swing to behind her and stood staring at herself in the full-length mirror. She looked good, and taking a deep breath she held it and waited for the fear and nerves to drain out of her. In half an hour she was going to go in there, smart and confident and ready to take on whatever challenge he threw her way. And after that ... Her eyes closed as she allowed herself to dream of the day when he would realize that the real great love of his life wasn't doing noble and dangerous things in far flung places of the world, but was sitting right here, under his very nose.

Michael had just finished his fourth call of the morning when Jodi's voice came back on the intercom. 'The High Fliers production office on line one,' she told him. 'Surprise on line two. And Sandy's still waiting.'

'What kind of surprise?' he said dubiously, while scanning a billings sheet and picking up a stale cup of coffee.

'Live dangerously,' she responded and promptly put the call through.

'Hello? Michael? Are you there?'

The voice was faint, but not to the point that Michael didn't know instantly who it was and snatching up the receiver, he pressed it firmly to his ear. 'Hey! Cavan!' he cried down the line to his younger brother. 'We were about to book the memorial.'

Cavan laughed. 'It's good to hear your voice,' he said. 'How's Ma?'

'Knitting – and dying to hear from her favourite son.'

'Knitting? Is our Colleen preggers again?'

148

'Cavan, it's due in a couple of weeks so don't for Christ's sake let on you forgot. Where are you?'

'Manaus.'

Michael's brow creased as he did a rapid tour of the world. 'Manaus, Brazil?' he said.

Cavan laughed. 'Is there anywhere on this godforsaken planet you've never heard of?' he said.

'Manaus is famous,' Michael responded. 'The Paris of the Tropics. So what are you doing there? How did you get there?'

'We sailed along the Amazon. You've got to do this trip, Michael, it's like nothing you've ever seen in your life. We got into Manaus a couple of days ago, but we've only just left the ship.'

'We? Ship? What happened to the *Lazy Lou*?'

'I left her in Tortola.'

'So what are you doing in Brazil, oh Cabral of the great discoveries?'

'Rescuing Indians.'

'Indians? Last time it was otters.'

'Seals.'

'How much are the Indians going to cost?'

'A question for your conscience.'

'I'll give you five hundred, and I want *my* name on the title deeds to a rain forest. It's tax deductible. Where does the ship come into it?'

'It's a cruise ship. I worked my passage here.'

'You're earning money?' Michael cried in amazement. 'Do you know what to do with it?'

'Sure, I drink it. I miss you.'

'We all miss you. Can you get back for your birthday? It would make Clodagh happy.'

'I'm aiming for it,' Cavan answered. 'I should be heading down to Rio in a couple of weeks. They've found a wreck, sixty miles or so off the coast. The experts are going down some time next week, but word is it dates back to the seventeenth century.'

'I thought you were rescuing Indians, now you're dredging up Conquistadors.'

'It's a busy life, Michael,' Cavan answered, the grin audible in his voice. 'Anyway, I've got to go. Send Clodagh my love. Tell her I'll call at the weekend if I can. And thanks for the donation. I've already given Jodi the address to send it to.'

'Now why doesn't that surprise me,' Michael said drolly. 'Take care of yourself. *Até a vista.*'

As the line went dead, Michael was smiling and shaking his head in exasperation. They were a close family by any standards, but Cavan held an extra-special place in all their hearts, possibly because he was so much younger than Michael and Colleen, but more probably because there was nothing about Cavan, from the top of his shambolic head to the soles of his oversized feet, that it was possible not to love.

The lad was going to be twenty-three in less than six weeks; it was hard to believe how fast the years had gone. Harder still, Michael found, was convincing himself that Cavan was old enough to take care of himself now, even if he did need a little financial back-up here and there. Actually, it wasn't Cavan who needed the back-up, it was Cavan's causes, as the fertile nature of his concerns was only matched by the cavernous hole in his coffers. Michael tried to imagine Cavan sitting behind a desk and almost laughed out loud. Since dropping out of university three years before, Cavan had either driven, walked, cycled, but more often than not sailed the globe in search of adventure. And he had found plenty, that was for sure. The *Lazy Lou*, a ten-year-old, thirty-foot catamaran, had been a gift from Michael in an effort to provide his wayward brother with something akin to a home. What it had also provided was an escape for the brothers as often as Michael could make it, when they would fish, or dive, or simply sail aimlessly off towards the horizon in pursuit of nothing more than each other's company.

'Michael?' Jodi's voice came over the intercom. 'The guy from *Esquire* is on the line again, what do you want me to tell him?'

Michael thought for a moment. 'Tell him how Zelda helps me deal with my Oedipus fixation, then call *Hello* and tell them to be there to curse the wedding.'

'Very funny.'

'Not really. Tell him I'll stick to the agreement if I get copy approval. If he goes for it I'll call him around four this afternoon.'

'OK. Sandy's wondering when she should come in?'

Michael's spirits instantly sank. 'Is she there?' he said.

'She's just popped to the loo.'

He thought for a moment, then, realizing it wasn't fair to put it off any longer he said, 'Send her in when she gets back. Meantime, get on to Interflora and have them deliver some flowers to Fiona. She's at rehearsals today, in Kensington. Make it a big bunch, I've got some making up to do.'

'And that's all you're giving her, flowers?' Jodi cried in feminine disgust.

Michael was stymied for a moment, then, with a wicked twinkle in his eyes he said, 'If I told you what else I had in mind, Jodi, they'd take us off the air. So you just see to the flowers, OK, and leave the rest to me.'

'Over and out,' she responded.

Michael was still smiling when Sandy came in a few minutes later, which was lucky, for there was something about Sandy Paull that made him want to do anything but smile.

'Hi,' she said, closing the door behind her. 'Oops!' she laughed as a sheaf of papers cascaded from a file she was carrying to the floor.

151

Despite his antipathy, Michael couldn't stop himself looking at her shapely rear as she bent to retrieve the papers. He wondered if she'd dropped them on purpose but decided not to pursue that, for he had no desire to go where it would inevitably lead.

'Sorry,' she said, straightening up and smiling straight into his eyes. 'I'm a real butter-fingers.'

Slightly disconcerted by the directness of her stare, Michael shifted in his seat and tried not to notice the swell of her breasts as she came towards him. He was sure they hadn't been so noticeable during the meeting, or maybe more buttons than she realized had popped open on her jacket. Whatever, for such a small and compact woman, there were times when she had a way of displaying herself that made her about as easy to ignore as a *Playboy* centrefold.

'I thought I'd take this opportunity,' she said, putting the file on his desk and spinning it round for him to see, 'to give you what I have so far on the *Cherchez* auditions.' As she leaned forward he received a generous view of a soft and pliable breast cradled by a black lace bra.

He lowered his eyes quickly, but knew she had seen him looking. 'I'll go over it later,' he said, closing the file and sliding it to one side. 'For the moment there's something else I need to discuss with you.' He gestured towards the chair she was standing next to. 'Please sit down,' he said.

Sandy smiled. 'Thank you,' she said. 'But I was wondering,' her voice faltered for a moment and a faint colour rose in her cheeks. 'Uh, as it's twelve thirty already, maybe you'd like to talk over lunch. My treat,' she added with a self-conscious laugh.

Despite his efforts to appear friendly, Michael felt his jaw tighten. 'Thank you,' he said politely, 'but I already have a lunch date.'

Though her smile remained, he saw the warmth seep

from it and half expected to see her thick, glossy pink lipstick start to run.

'I was talking to Fiona Atkins yesterday,' he said, as she sat down.

The pause in her movement was barely perceptible, but it was enough to tell him that, despite the innocent curiosity on her face, she knew exactly what he was coming to.

'She was extremely upset,' he continued.

Sandy's expression flooded with concern. 'Oh?' she said, putting her head to one side. 'I'm sorry to hear that. Nothing serious, I hope.'

Michael took a breath. 'She was upset for several reasons,' he said, 'the first being the way you had spoken to her on the phone when she called on Tuesday.'

Sandy's eyes widened and a small ringed hand moved to her cleavage. 'Whatever I said, I'm sorry,' she told him earnestly. 'But I think she must have misunderstood, because I'd never say anything to upset her. At least, not intentionally.'

'She claims you were rude when she asked you to give me a message.'

Sandy frowned. 'What message?' she said.

'That's what I was hoping you could tell me,' he replied, admiring her performance as much as he abhorred it. 'She claims you told her that I'd asked not to be interrupted, which I know was true, and you'd pass her message on if I wasn't too busy later.' He rested his chin on his bunched hands. 'Do you have the message?' he asked.

Sandy was looking perplexed. 'But she didn't leave a message,' she replied. 'All she said was to tell you she'd called, which I would have done if you hadn't already gone by the time I came in to tell you.'

Michael's bottom lip jutted forward. 'She says there was a message, a very specific one, in fact.' His manner

153

was mild, but underneath he was seething. 'Is she lying?' he asked.

Sandy's wide eyes moved around the room, as though hunting out a response. Then, with a small, uncomfortable laugh she said, 'Look, I know Fiona is a close friend of yours, so I'm in a very awkward position now, aren't I? I mean, on the one hand I don't want to call her a liar, but on the other I don't want to own up to not passing on a message I know nothing about.'

To his surprise, Michael felt suddenly sorry for her, though was at a loss to say why. The moment was only fleeting. 'You're aware, I'm sure,' he said, 'of how much trust I put in you because of how closely you work with Jodi. And I'm afraid, Sandy, that this isn't the first time a friend of mine has complained about your telephone manner, which is leading me to wonder how many other messages haven't got through. In Fiona's case she was left sitting in a restaurant for an hour and a half waiting for me to turn up, which of course I failed to do.'

He could see the heat colouring her cheeks as a convincing blend of hurt and confusion clouded her eyes. 'So you're calling me a liar?' she said, swallowing.

Michael sighed. 'What I'm calling you is stupid for thinking you could get away with it,' he said. 'So in future maybe you'll make sure that all messages are on my desk by the end of the day at the latest, and when we've finished here I'd appreciate it if you called Fiona yourself and apologized for the misunderstanding.'

'But . . .'

'Is that clear?' he barked.

'Yes,' she answered. 'But she didn't leave a message. At least not with me.'

For a moment he was sorely tempted to let rip, for getting angry with Sandy Paull held the promise of an extremely pleasurable experience. It was only when he

154

realized how deeply he wanted to let go, how tempting, almost irresistible, the prospect of hurting and humiliating her suddenly was, that he firmly reined in his control.

'Let's leave it there,' he said, picking up his cold coffee as though it were a barrier he could put between them. Then, making a supreme effort to lighten his mood he said, 'I imagine you probably know how many people have been in here banging the drum for you, so I'll spare your blushes and tell you that I'm prepared to let you take over as Diana's assistant until Marlene comes back after the baby.'

He watched her as she struggled to deal with the sudden move from misery to euphoria and felt rotten, for he'd known he would ruin her moment by bringing up the problem with Fiona first. He wondered if that was why he had done it, to get some kind of sadistic revenge in wrong-footing her the way her sexuality and shyness wrong-footed him.

'I'm sorry.' She laughed. 'It's just ... Well, I'm sure you know, I've been really hoping ... I won't let you down. I swear it.'

He forced a smile. 'That's a relief,' he said, making a joke that didn't quite come off. 'I should also tell you,' he went on, 'that if Janey's agreeable, which I know she will be, I'd like you to act as her assistant too. If you think it's too much to take on ...'

'No!' Sandy cried. 'I'd be happy to. I was going to ask, but I didn't quite know how to.'

Her uncertainty was as plain as her childlike eagerness to please him and, feeling he had been unnecessarily unkind in the way he had treated her, he found himself saying, 'You should think about building up a list of your own, once you get settled into assisting. Unless, of course, you want to go back to being a clerk at the end of the six months.'

Sandy's amazement showed. 'No, of course not,' she

said hurriedly. She looked down at her hands, bunched in her lap, then returned her eyes to his. 'I really don't know how to thank you for this,' she said simply.

Gone was the amateur vamp. In her place was a grateful, pretty young girl who looked more out of her depth than Michael had ever seen her before. 'Just prove you're as good as they say you are,' he responded. 'And don't be a stranger in the evenings. The job comes with a great social life, so make sure you take advantage. It's where most of the business gets done.'

Sandy looked at him. 'You can count on me,' she assured him. 'After work, the thing I love best is to . . . socialize.'

His expression was unreadable as he looked back at her, but the way she had turned socialize into a euphemism for something else had not passed him by. He wasn't sure, as he continued to stare, whether he was more repelled by the idea or surprised by her nerve. Her neck, he could see, was blotched with a tell-tale colour, her breasts were rising and falling like those of a woman about to make love.

'OK, you can go now,' he said, picking up his pen. 'Liaise with Diana and Marlene about a hand-over period and tell Jodi she can get on to an agency for a temp to cover your old job.'

To his relief she went without uttering another word, leaving her expensive scent lingering in the air and the promise of her body clear in his mind. He sat where he was, staring blankly at the script in front of him. His breath felt suddenly short, his throat was tight and the partial erection in his trousers appalled him. This certainly wasn't the first time he'd felt the urge to screw Sandy Paull, and he could only thank God for how swiftly and easily he managed to suppress it.

Pressing his fingers to his eyes, he took a deep and bewildered breath. He couldn't remember ever coming across a woman who affected him the way she did. He hoped to God he never let it show, for he despised her almost as much as he desired her. She felt like a sickness, an aberration; it was as though she walked the darker side of his instincts like some kind of she-devil, exposing his weaknesses and mirroring his depravity. Yet there was that other side of her, the one that appeared tender and vulnerable, so easily hurt and bemused by his cruelty. It was a side he tried hard not to see, for in his soul he feared it would be his undoing.

He looked across to the door, half expecting to see her, still standing there like some gaunt and ghostly image of Medusa. Then suddenly Jodi's voice burst into the office announcing an emergency on the set of *Invisible Difference*, and Sandy Paull and her almost naked breasts were, for the moment at least, forgotten.

Chapter Nine

'Ellen, I've got Patty Dreyfuss on the other line,' Felicia, Ellen's latest secretary, told her, popping her head round the door to find Ellen with a phone tucked into her shoulder as she verified a residual agreement on her computer. 'She's saying the movie's gone into turnaround.'

'Hold on, Bob,' Ellen said, sliding something into a pile of screenplays as she glanced at the secretary and wished she could remember the girl's name. '*Extravagance* has been shelved?' she said incredulously. 'When did she hear?'

'A couple of minutes ago,' Felicia responded. 'Shall I put her on.'

'No, I can't talk to her now,' Ellen replied. 'Put her on to Rob Weinberg in legal, he'll go through the detail with her. Did you hear anything from Clyde Russell on the *Manhattan* deal yet?'

'Not yet,' Felicia answered, looking down at her notepad. 'But Krissie Dicks called to say her shoot dates for *Madness* have been put back and they're clashing now with *Madame Bovary*.'

'Shit!' Ellen muttered. 'Bob, I'll get back to you,' she said into the phone and hung up. 'Get the *Madness* producer on the line and let's find out what's going on,' she instructed Felicia. 'Or no, you speak to him, ask him how many more times he's going to change the god-damned schedule and can he afford it? Did the money drop yet for John Gallin's movie? The bank was supposed to release today.'

'I'll find out,' Felicia responded. 'Check your E-mail, I think Ted Forgon wants to see you at the end of the day and Rosa said to cancel whatever ...'

'... you're doing for lunch,' Rosa picked up, sailing in through the door behind her, all blonde corkscrew curls and micro-mini couture, 'because I'm taking you to Kate's. *Extravagance* is gone into turnaround I hear?'

'News travels fast,' Ellen remarked, dashing a hand through her already dishevelled hair. 'I can't make lunch, Rosa,' she said, 'I've got too much to do here. Are you going down to the *Batman* set? Could you take Vinny Costello with you? He's coming here at two. His call's for four, so there's plenty of time. Felicia,' she called, remembering the girl's name as she started to walk away. 'How are you doing with those contracts? They've got to be finished before tonight.'

'No problem,' Felicia called back.

'She's a real find,' Ellen said, as Rosa took a screenplay from her desk and started flicking through. 'Why don't they stay more than six weeks is what I want to know?'

'Because they find other jobs – acting,' Rosa reminded her. 'What did you think of this?' she asked, meaning the screenplay.

'In a word, brilliant,' Ellen replied, going back to her computer. 'It's the fourth draft. Sam Coates took it over, apparently.'

'That's why it's brilliant,' Rosa declared, sauntering over to the window and looking down at the busy street below. 'I made some calls for you,' she went on, 'come see me when you get time and I'll go through who everyone is and what they do over there in good old London town. Boy, do I envy you. Are you flying first class?'

'I think so,' Ellen answered, tensing badly as Rosa returned to the pile of screenplays and made like she was going to start looking through. Please God, don't let her pick up any more, Ellen silently prayed.

'Let me know which hotel you're in, I'll tell you if it's any good,' Rosa said. 'You're going to love London, it's like New York but older and chicer.'

As she turned for the door, leaving the screenplays in place, Ellen breathed a sigh of relief and reached out for the phone as it rang.

It was a producer she was in negotiation with. She was trying desperately to tie up the deal before she left the office that day, but the man was stubborn and clearly had a problem with women. The call lasted for over ten minutes as they haggled and compromised, added clauses and disagreed over credits. It ended with him saying he'd get back to her and the minute she hung up the phone rang again.

'Your cousin, Matty,' Felicia announced. 'Shall I put her on?'

'Definitely,' Ellen cried.

There was a click on the line and Matty's voice came through.

'Ellen, you've got to do something about this fucking bitch!' Matty shouted. 'She's humiliating me every chance she gets, she's getting my lines cut, she's stealing my shots and the director's not doing a goddamned thing about it. Can you get down here?'

'Matty, I don't have time,' Ellen groaned. 'If you can get the director to call me I'll speak to him. Who is it?'

'Bob Wolf. He won't call, he doesn't have time. You're *her* agent too, speak to her.'

'And you're my cousin, so she'll think I'm taking sides.'

'It's why I asked you to come down here. You can see for yourself what's going on, then you can appear for the defence when I get cited for murder.'

'I'm going to London tomorrow,' Ellen reminded her, 'and I've got a million things to finish up before I leave. Can you come over tonight? Matty, I really need to talk. Please don't say no.'

There was a pause at the other end and Ellen felt her chest starting to tighten as she realized Matty was going to let her down. 'Gee, Ellen, I'm sorry,' Matty said softly. 'I got so carried away with what was happening here ... I saw it, honey, in the *Globe* this morning. Oh, Christ, I'm sorry. Sure I'll come over. What time?'

'I've got to see Forgon before I leave,' Ellen answered, swallowing hard. 'Come around eight?'

'I'll be there. How are you holding up?'

'OK. I'm real busy right now, which helps. I could do without this trip, though.'

'It could be a blessing,' Matty told her. 'Did you speak to Clay?'

'No.'

'What about Karen Delphi? Did you ever meet her?'

'No,' Ellen answered, pulling a copy of the *Globe* out from between the pile of screenplays. Emblazoned across the cover was a full-colour shot of Clay Ingall and the latest *Baywatch* babe, Karen Delphi. They were coming out of the Viper Room and Delphi, in a black diaphanous top that hugged her enormous breasts like a second skin and left nothing to the imagination, was gazing up into Clay's eyes under the headline, INGALL'S NEW ROMANCE REVEALED.

'They've been seeing each other in secret for the past four months,' Ellen said flatly. 'Or so it says here.'

'Honey, listen, I've got to go,' Matty said, 'but I'll be there tonight, I promise. Are you going to call him?'

'I don't know,' Ellen answered. 'I thought he might call me.'

'Maybe he will,' Matty said. 'Eight o'clock, OK? Hang on in there,' and the line went dead.

There was no respite for the next call came seconds later, from a First Assistant Director, complaining he had a 'corpse' who was only in one scene, for fuck's sake, and already they'd done twenty-four takes, because the sonofabitch wasn't happy with his performance.

'What do you want me to do?' Ellen asked, poring over the contract in front of her while silently cursing Yardley Aymiss for being such a pain in the butt.

'Get over here and sort it, or we're going to bury the schmuck right now,' the AD replied. 'Literally.'

'I'll be there as soon as I can,' Ellen responded and rang off. Quickly she dialled Rosa, whose office was just a couple of doors along, and fixed it with Rosa for her to go sort out Aymiss while she carried on with the problems that were piling up on her desk like wannabes at a public audition.

The relentless pace and pressure continued on throughout the day, as Felicia brought her tea and granola bars, fielded as many calls as she could, blocked idle gossipers and made herself so genuinely indispensible that in the brief pauses Ellen had time to, she wondered how she'd ever managed without her.

But despite how busy she was the struggle to keep her mind on the task in front of her, or to register the figures being yelled down the phone by some irate producer who was too mean to cough up but knew he had to, was getting harder all the time. But she kept on going. That morning's breakdowns were strewn across a table over by the window, listing all the new parts coming up for casting, and the journey back and forth between it and her desk was almost ceaseless. She was trying desperately to care, the way she always had before this nightmare had started, but as the days since her meeting with Forgon crept into weeks and McCann consistently refused to speak to her, her fear of what Forgon was going to do with the photographs was fast reaching the point of panic. And as if that wasn't bad enough, she had to find out now, through the god-damned *Globe* of all rags, that Clay, whose divorce had gone through three days ago, had been cheating on her for months with a pair of silicone implants that were happily exposed to man or lens at the mere drop of a publicity promise.

Of course, that was right up Clay's street, for few knew better than Ellen how he got off on treating the world to uncensored views of his women. Even Nola, his now ex-wife, had been a soft-porn actress before he'd married her, a fact Ellen hadn't known until a couple of months into their relationship when he'd invited her to watch one of Nola's movies. And like a fool, she had sat there, watching his wife cavort around the screen with a bunch of half-naked Germans in a beer house, because she adored him so much she was willing to do almost anything to please him.

And look where it had got her. Into the kind of position she had never, even in her worst nightmares, imagined she would ever find herself, for she simply wasn't like the Nolas or Karens of this world. To her the idea of displaying herself, even half-undressed, in public was so horrible it was torture even to think about it. It wasn't that she was a prude, for there was no question that the idea of it had turned her on – the reality, however, was nothing short of hell. So too was the fact that Clay had deceived her the way he had and made such a fool out of her that she was finding it hard to face herself in the mirror.

It didn't matter that no one else knew, except Forgon and Matty, of course, what mattered was that she had been so blind and so god-damned stupid. And now Forgon had shots of her walking nude in Clay's garden, and making love with him in the back of a car. But that wasn't all, because in the envelope he'd so casually tossed across the table that morning, were polaroid

163

shots that Clay himself had taken, which made the others Forgon had look about as explicit as a Victorian postcard. She didn't want to think about how Forgon had managed to get hold of the polaroids; she hadn't even known they were missing until they'd turned up in the envelope and now the very idea that Forgon had seen her that way was even worse than the fact that Clay had been turned on by it when she'd told him.

It was that, probably more than anything else, that had finally made her see how deeply into humiliation Clay was, which obviously made her some kind of masochist, because even knowing what she did about him, she had carried on seeing him and allowing him to treat her like a whore, while telling herself that all the things he wanted to do turned her on too. And now, just like she didn't even exist, he had got his divorce and come straight out in the open with Delphi.

By the time six thirty came round she was pretty much ready to leave. She'd have given anything to be able to go straight home, exhausted by her efforts to keep her mind off Clay. She took out a compact and seeing how pale she looked only made her feel worse. It was easy enough to put some colour back in her cheeks, but rekindling the sparkle in her eyes and the warmth in her smile was too much to ask. Nevertheless, she was going to try, for the last thing she wanted was Forgon to know that she was buckling under the pressure. She had to go in there now and try somehow to instil confidence in him that she would return from London with what he wanted, for if he thought her enthusiasm was flagging he'd no doubt take great pleasure in reminding her exactly why she needed to succeed.

The cacophony of phones and last-minute deals going down reverberated through the corridors as, dressed in a loose white shirt buttoned to the neck and an ankle-length woollen skirt, she carried her heavy briefcase to the elevator and rode up two floors of the Wilshire Boulevard office block to Forgon's penthouse suite. The fear that he might use the photographs to get her to perform personal favours for him was alive in her heart, dragging her spirits down. Other people had survived a lot worse, she knew that, but she just hated the fact that it was all because of her passion for a man who had never loved nor respected her, who wanted only to humiliate and fuck her.

'Ah, Ellen, come in,' Forgon said, as she pushed open the door and looked across to his desk. His secretary had already gone home and he was sitting in his huge, cowhide executive chair, feet up on the desk as he browsed through the *Hollywood Reporter*. 'Can I fix you a drink?' he offered, putting the magazine down and going over to the wet bar.

'No, thanks,' Ellen answered. Surrounded by windows as they were, she was feeling very much as a reporter had once described her, like an angelfish in a tank full of sharks. In this case just one shark, but it was the one from which she had the most to fear.

'Take a Martini,' Forgon instructed. 'It's the end of the day, you could probably use it.'

It was true, she could, so she didn't object.

As he poured she continued to stand in the middle of the room, clasping her briefcase in front of her as though to shield herself from his eyes, while looking at the numerous publicity shots of him with just about every major movie star of the past forty years. She'd seen them all before, but she'd rather study them now than look at Forgon and know what he was seeing as he looked back, through her briefcase, through her clothes, to the most private parts of her body.

'Here,' he said, waving her to one of the plush, tan leather couches and placing her Martini on the marble table in front of it. 'Cheers,' he said, saluting her with his own Martini as he sat on the couch opposite and rested an ankle on his knee.

'Cheers,' she said, picking up her glass and taking a sip. It must have been seven-eighths vodka, but it was good and feeling it revive her slightly she took another sip.

'Are you OK?' he asked, his pale blue eyes peering at her quizzically.

'Mmm, sure,' she nodded, fixing on his ludicrous wavy brown hair which usually helped her to smile. 'Looking forward to London. I've never been out of the States before.'

'You look tired,' he told her frankly, 'so I'm not going to keep you long. I just want to tell you that I'm sorry about what you learned from the *Globe* today. I know it must have hurt to find out that way, but the man's an asshole, Ellen, and take it from me, you're well shot of him.'

Ellen lowered her eyes to her drink.

'Georgie Henniker,' he said, naming the lead vocalist of the band Clay was currently working with. 'He gave me the polaroids. The sonofabitch thought I might like to take a look at one of my staff the way I wouldn't normally see her.'

Ellen's cheeks were burning. All she could think of now was how her stupidity was reaching new heights all the time, for it had never occurred to her that Clay would have shown those shots to anyone, never mind pass them round the band.

'They're yours now,' Forgon told her. 'I hope you destroyed them.'

'Would it do me any good if I did?' Ellen asked. 'You've probably got copies.'

'No,' he said, shaking his head. 'I don't imagine Ingall or the band do either. Now, I've rooted out some contacts of mine in London,' he continued with an abrupt change of subject as he got up and walked over

166

to his desk, 'and I hear Rosa Kleinberg's done the same, so you're not going to be short of company while you're over there. They'll make you welcome, show you around, catch a few of the sights, a couple of shows, eat well, they've got some great restaurants, but don't forget why you're there. Did you fix yourself a meeting with him yet?'

Ellen shook her head. 'He's still refusing to take my calls and he hasn't answered any of the faxes.'

'Sonofabitch,' Forgon muttered. 'But you'll get him, I know you will.' He dropped a sheet of contacts on the table in front of her. 'Call up some of these guys. If they don't already know him, they'll know someone who does. Corner him in the john if you have to, but see him. Speak to him, make him an offer he can't refuse.'

Ellen flinched, but quickly realized that it was only she who had caught the double meaning of that last remark. It was something she was doing a lot lately, imagining hidden agendas or lewd connotations in all kinds of otherwise innocent statements and she hated herself for it.

'It's like I'm possessed by some ugly little demon,' she said to Matty later that evening as they picked at popcorn in her bedroom while she packed. 'I can't seem to trust anything anyone says. I think everyone knows and is imagining me the way I am in those polaroids. I'm getting to the point where I can't even bear to see myself in the nude, because it just reminds me and makes me feel like such a slut I want to tear out my hair and slash up my body. Oh God, Matty,' she groaned, sinking on to the edge of the bed and burying her face in her hands, 'why did I ever do it?'

'Hey, come on,' Matty said, going to kneel in front of her, 'plenty of women have gone a lot further than that for men they're crazy about. A *lot* further.'

'I know,' Ellen said, 'but this is a really big deal to me, Matty. I mean, if Mom or Dad ...' She stopped to catch her breath. 'It would kill him, Matty. The shame, he just couldn't live with it, and he might die without me ever speaking to him again and I just couldn't bear it.'

'Hey, it's not going to come to that,' Matty assured her. 'Forgon's not going to publish those pictures, not any of them, I promise you.'

Ellen laughed bitterly. 'You don't know him,' she retorted. 'The man sits there calling Clay an asshole for showing around those polaroids, when all the time he's got other shots of me, *publishable* shots, not like the polaroids, stashed away as his security. So tell me, what kind of asshole does that make him?'

'About as big a one as most of the executives in this town,' Matty conceded. 'But look at the package he's put together for McCann, then ask yourself is any man in his right mind going to turn down an offer like that? Of course he's not and Forgon knows it. So, believe me when I tell you he's got no intention of doing anything with those photographs, they're just providing him with an excuse for not firing you if McCann does refuse. He'll just humiliate you instead. But it won't come to that,' she rushed on as Ellen started to speak. 'I mean, look at it sensibly. What the hell does Forgon have to gain by publishing those shots? Nothing. Not a solitary sou, not a dime, not a dollar. And he's just not the kind of guy to do anything unless he personally is going to gain from it.'

Ellen swallowed hard. Then, forcing a smile she gazed into Matty's beloved brown eyes and said, 'Why aren't you coming with me tomorrow?'

'Because,' Matty said, in her best long-suffering voice, 'some jerk of an agent, whom I happen to love very much by the way, got me a job on one of our nation's top-rated series and I'm kind of committed now for the next four weeks. Of course, if this jerk of an agent, whom I happen to love, could get me out of the series she would be doing me a very great favour, 'cos getting upstaged by Marcia Glass every fucking two minutes isn't my idea of fun, whereas London most definitely is. How long will you be gone?'

Ellen was laughing. 'Two, maybe three weeks,' she answered. 'Rosa's taking over for me while I'm gone. It's a shame we can't find someone to take over for you.'

'Next trip I'm there,' Matty promised, 'even if I have to beg the money from Uncle Frank.'

The idea of Ellen's father financing a fun trip for Matty was so absurd that they burst out laughing. At that moment the telephone rang.

Ellen's face instantly paled. 'What if it's Clay?' she said, tightening her grip on Matty's hands. 'What am I going to say?'

'Do you want me to answer?' Matty offered.

Ellen looked at her, clearly tempted. 'No,' she said in the end, 'I'd better deal with it,' and getting to her feet she walked to the bedside table and picked up the phone. 'Hello?' she said shakily. In her heart she was pleading with God for it to be him, even though she knew she was crazy even to think it.

'Put it on speaker,' Matty hissed.

Obediently Ellen pushed the button as the voice at the other end said, 'Hi, Ellen! It's Joey! I'm not calling too late, am I? I heard you were going out of town for a couple of weeks, are you coming to New York? Can I fix it for the commercial?'

Ellen turned to Matty. 'Another time, Joey,' she said. 'I'll call you,' and she hung up.

Matty watched her as she wandered back to the dressing-room to fetch more clothes from the closet. She took her time making a choice, then carried a couple of sweaters and a cocktail dress back to her suitcase.

Though she hadn't said so, Matty could sense her

terrible disappointment that it hadn't been Clay on the line. 'Ellen,' she said, catching her hand as she started to return to the closet.

Ellen stopped, but didn't look at her.

'Honey, you've got to let it go now,' Matty said as gently as she could. 'He's not worth it and in your heart you know it. So put it behind you and move on.'

Ellen laughed drily. 'Words are so easy,' she said.

'I know,' Matty replied. 'So are dreams. It's reality that's hard, but you can do it, Ellen. You can get past this. And look on the bright side, you're going to see London, you'll probably meet a whole bunch of people really worth getting to know and for a couple of weeks, at least, all this is going to seem like part of another world. So relax and go have yourself a good time. And who knows, you'll probably be calling me up in a week's time to tell me you've fallen madly in love with some English lord who you don't have to fake it with, the way you did with Clay.'

Ellen's eyes closed in dismay. 'Matty, I swear it, right now I wouldn't mind if I never had sex again in my life, never mind an orgasm.'

'Tell me that in a month and I might believe you.' Matty smiled, slanting her eyes towards a cutting of McCann that was lying loosely on the bed. 'There again,' she added, 'I might not.'

Chapter 10

'Hey, look at the champ,' Michael laughed, taking his sleepy, two-day-old nephew from his sister's arms and holding him at arm's length to get a good look.

Colleen stood beside him and resting her head on his shoulder gazed adoringly at her new son.

'He's just like me when I was his age,' Billy, her three-year-old, told Michael, looking earnestly up at his uncle from his little standpoint of two feet eight. 'Nana said. She said Charlie is like me, and I am like you and Daddy which can only mean trouble. Can I come up too?'

'Please,' Colleen reminded him.

'Please,' he repeated.

Laughing, Michael scooped him up in his other arm and carried both nephews through the jumble of toys, changing mats and casually dumped clothes, to the sofa. Dan, his brother-in-law and partner, was on the other sofa making sure Tierney, his five-year-old daughter, was getting her share of attention.

'So, are you pregnant again yet?' Michael asked Colleen, as he stretched out on the sofa with the two boys on top of him. 'Nice one, Charlie,' he remarked, as the baby threw up on his shoulder and Billy started to bounce dangerously close to his groin.

Colleen's vivid blue eyes were dancing with laughter as she swept her unruly black curls back from her face

171

while she sponged off Michael's sweater and Michael kept a firm hand on Billy. 'He says he's not up to it yet,' she told him, nodding towards Dan. 'Give me a break, he says, I've only just given birth. Oh, and it was a terrible time you had in the hospital, was it not, my darling?' she teased, going over to tweak Dan's nose. 'All those nurses making such a fuss of you.'

'It was hell,' Dan agreed with feeling. 'I swear I'm never going through it again.'

'Mummy, can I feed Charlie next time?' Tierney asked.

'What, with those little boobies?' Colleen laughed.

'Tell her you've got lovely boobies,' Dan said, wincing as Tierney twisted his sparse fair hair around her grandmother's curlers. 'It's why I'm going bald, or so your mother tells me,' he said to Michael. 'I didn't get enough of my mother's milk.'

'Clodagh said that?' Michael laughed, looking across the sitting-room and through the dining-room to the small flower garden at the back where his mother and Cavan, who'd jetted in the night before for a flying birthday visit, were in earnest reunion. Earnest reunion in Clodagh's language meant a serious ticking off for not respecting his mother sufficiently to stay in one place long enough for her to look it up in the atlas. Michael grinned when he saw the look on his brother's face, for as adult and independent as he'd become, there was no arguing with Clodagh and he knew it. Then, to Michael's great amusement, Cavan suddenly stopped his mother mid-sentence by sweeping her into his arms and treating her to a resounding kiss. It was a gesture so typical of Michael that he laughed out loud. Not only did Cavan, with his long, untidy dark hair, intense navy eyes and devastating smile, look like his older brother, he was starting to behave like him too.

'Uncle Michael?' Billy said from atop Michael's head.

'Yes Billy,' Michael replied.

'Can we play soldiers up in my bedroom?'

'You've got soldiers! In your bedroom!' Michael exclaimed.

Billy's face lit up. 'Can we go and play with them?' he said. 'Charlie can't come, he's too little.'

'Can I come?' Tierney cried, leaping down from her father's knee and tearing a curler from his hair as she went.

'Tierney, go steady,' Colleen told her, stretching her legs out in front of her as she relaxed in a giant armchair. 'Daddy doesn't have much as it is and you've just taken half of it.'

Tierney looked confused.

'Give Charlie to Mummy,' Billy instructed Michael, starting to push the baby away.

'Give Charlie to Daddy,' Colleen corrected. 'Are you cooking dinner, Michael? Clodagh said you were.'

'Clodagh's full of it today,' Michael commented, passing the baby over to Dan.

'Stay the night and have a drink,' Colleen said, as he swung Tierney in the air and made her laugh with delight.

'Daddy, I want you to play soldiers too,' Billy said, pulling his dad's arm.

'What about Charlie?' Dan replied. 'We can't leave him on his own with Mummy, she might take him back.'

'Can you put him back in your tummy?' Tierney asked, looking wide-eyed at her mother.

'Come and give your mummy a kiss,' Colleen said, holding out her arms.

Michael carried his niece over and depositing her on Colleen's lap, he allowed Billy to lead him out across the smart but cluttered entrance hall to the stairs.

'And where might you two be off to?' Clodagh demanded, coming in through the kitchen with Cavan behind her.

173

'Nana, Uncle Michael's going to play soldiers,' Billy told her eagerly. 'And then we might play Batman. I've got a Batman outfit now,' he said to Michael. 'Nana bought it for me, didn't you, Nana?'

'Spoiled rotten,' Clodagh responded, her clear blue eyes sparkling with love as she looked at her grandson. She was a small woman with neat white hair, a wrinkled face and a love for her family that was only matched by theirs for her.

'Do you think Nana would buy me one too?' Cavan asked Billy. 'If I'm a good boy.'

Billy laughed. 'You'd look silly in a Batman outfit, wouldn't he Nana?' he said.

'Darling, he doesn't need a Batman outfit to make him look silly,' Clodagh responded.

'He's got a mother instead,' Michael chipped in.

Clodagh laughed and cuffed Cavan round the ear because Michael was out of reach. 'I told our Colleen you were cooking dinner,' she said to Michael. 'Are you going to make your mother a liar?'

Cavan burst out laughing. 'She does it every time,' he said, putting an arm around her.

'You can help,' Clodagh told him, 'and I'll take the kids upstairs to give our Colleen and Dan a bit of time to themselves before we eat.'

'Are you angling for more grandchildren already?' Michael teased.

Clodagh fixed him with a look only Clodagh could give. 'Well, if I waited around for you I'd be having to rise up from me grave to come visit them,' she told him.

'Give me a chance,' he groaned, 'I've only just learned how to do it.'

'Do you think you could teach me?' Cavan asked. 'I seem to be having a bit of a problem with the condoms. I can't get the bubbles out.'

'Clodagh's an expert on bubbles,' Michael informed

174

him. 'It was her who showed me how to dress a banana when I was nineteen, am I right?'

'And you've never let me forget it,' she scolded, though her eyes, which were so like Michael's, were twinkling with laughter at the memory.

'What's a condom?' Billy asked, his upturned face looking from one to the other.

Clodagh and Cavan looked expectantly at Michael. Michael looked back. Then swinging Billy up into Clodagh's arms he said, 'I'm cooking dinner. Clodagh, I love you and if you weren't my mother I'd marry you.'

'He's been saying that since he was six,' Clodagh told Billy. 'You'd think he'd have found a new line by now, wouldn't you, after all that education? Come on, let's go and get that Tierney and Charlie. I expect Charlie would like to meet your soldiers, don't you?'

Michael and Cavan wandered into the kitchen and after pouring themselves a large whisky each they set about preparing the evening meal. It wasn't unusual for them to take over Colleen's kitchen when the whole family were together, since Colleen loathed cooking and both Michael and Cavan were pretty good at it. As they began rummaging through the fridge, freezer and cupboards to sort out what to prepare, Cavan was filling Michael in on his time in Manaus. His plane had landed at ten the night before, to be met by a taxi Jodi had arranged to take him straight to Michael's. Michael had come in from dinner shortly after midnight to find his brother crashed out in the guest room, where he had stayed until Michael had turfed him out at midday to get himself ready to go and see Clodagh. So they'd had little time to catch up and though Cavan was obviously bursting with news, Michael's mind kept wandering along avenues he'd rather not go down.

He wasn't sure whether it was Cavan with his passion for lost causes that was making him think of Michelle, or if it was the new baby and what might have been had Michelle stayed. But she hadn't and now so much time had gone by it no longer mattered. Except during odd moments like this, when for some reason her absence was so strong it felt more like a presence.

'So there I was, scooting up this damn tree,' Cavan was saying as he set about peeling some potatoes, while Michael plucked a bulb of garlic from a rope to start stuffing a leg of lamb, 'when this bloody monkey drops on my head and we both hit the deck screaming. Whereupon the wolf, or whatever the bloody thing was, runs back off into the jungle in terror, maybe to get his mates, maybe not, I didn't hang around to find out. I was back in the landie and heading for camp, *with* the damned monkey that I couldn't get rid of. Stuck on me, it was, in every way. Made a right bloody fool of me too ...' He stopped and looked round as Dan came in.

'Colleen's about to feed Charlie,' Dan said, 'so we're going upstairs to lie on the bed. She wants her feet massaged while she does it and you know your sister's every wish is my command. Help yourselves to ... Ah, you've already got one. Did you pour me one too?'

'Coming right up,' Cavan said, walking round the breakfast bar to the dresser where the drinks were kept under lock and key, after Tierney and Billy had got drunk on sherry one day.

'Are you coming into the office this week?' Michael asked Dan, setting the lamb in a roasting tray, then searching out some rosemary in the fresh herb pots on the window sill.

'If you want me to,' Dan answered. 'Why? Is there a problem?'

'Not that I can think of.'

'I'm preparing some pension plans for the Delaney Group,' Dan said, referring to one of the other companies he was finance director of, 'so I'll be tied up with

176

that for the next couple of weeks. Sheila's managing without me, I take it?'

'Where would we all be without Sheila?' Michael smiled. 'I promoted Sandy Paull, by the way. Did anyone tell you?'

'Clodagh mentioned it eighteen or nineteen times,' Dan answered, taking the drink Cavan was passing him. 'She's full of the girl lately, thinks she's the best thing since tights.'

Michael and Cavan looked at each other and laughed. 'Only Clodagh would think tights were a good thing,' Cavan remarked.

'And only Clodagh would think Sandy Paull was,' Michael responded. 'Actually, Clodagh and the best part of my staff.'

Dan's eyes were suddenly simmering with humour. 'Shit, I forgot, she's got a thing for you, hasn't she?'

'Show me a woman who hasn't,' Cavan chipped in, ducking as Michael threw a tea-towel at his head. 'So what's she like, this Sandy whatever her name is?'

'I'll tell you what she's like,' Dan jumped in, 'she's the only woman I've ever seen make Michael McCann blush.'

Cavan's eyes lit up. 'A bit of a goer, is she?' he said, warming to the idea of teasing his brother.

'I wouldn't know,' Michael replied. 'But she certainly behaves as though she is. Dan, is that Colleen calling?'

Dan listened. 'Ah, the honeyed tones of my very own Cruella DeVille,' he intoned as Colleen yelled for him again. 'What a happy man I've been since marrying into your family. Not only do I get your fair sister, but I get your fair mother too. Ah, and my very own little people,' he added, as the baby started to cry and Billy shouted down the stairs for him to come and play soldiers because Nana and Tierney kept shooting the wrong side.

An hour or so later they were all carrying piping hot

dishes to the big round dining-table, their mouths watering as Cavan set down the delicious garlic-and-rosemary scented lamb, while Tierney complained she couldn't see as her father lit the candles and lowered the lights. Then all the usual arguments started as to whom the children were going to sit next to, so Michael ended up with Billy one side of him and Clodagh the other, while Tierney sulked between her parents because she couldn't sit next to Michael too, because Nana wanted to sit between her sons. It was a warm May evening so the French windows were open and the lights were on in the toy-cluttered garden. It was such a perfect family scene that the poignancy of it seemed to reach them all for a moment, even the children, who sat quietly looking at the grown-ups as though awaiting permission to speak.

Michael's eyes were sparkling with humour as he picked up a bottle of Cabernet Sauvignon and winked at Tierney. 'Clodagh, are you going to have some wine?' he offered, holding the bottle over his mother's glass.

'Is the Pope a Catholic?' Cavan responded.

'There he goes, blaspheming again,' Clodagh chided. 'Pour me a little drop, Michael. I'll see if I like it.'

Tierney gave a shout of laughter, though it was clear she didn't really know what at, but it provided everyone else with an excuse to do the same.

'So, Cavan, tell us more about Rio,' Colleen said, as they began to eat. 'Is it as dangerous as they say?'

Cavan nodded as he took a mouthful of lamb. 'In parts,' he answered when he could. 'It's a beautiful place, though. And wild. There's so much going on, you have to see it to believe it. The beaches are heaving with people and everything stays open right through the night. The music never stops, everyone's dancing and singing, it's like a carnival every night, so God knows what the real thing is like when it comes time

178

for Mardi Gras. And the girls! I've never seen bodies like it. I thought I'd died and gone to heaven, so I did.'

'I expect that's what they thought when they saw you,' Clodagh told him.

Dan and Michael laughed as Colleen teased him about borrowing Michael's razors, while Cavan studiously ignored them and said, 'You know, Ma, you could be right.'

'What about the wreck?' Michael asked. 'Did you get down to see it?'

'Twice,' Cavan answered. 'They reckon it could date back to the Conquistadors, which would make it a pretty important find. They've got a team of experts working on it already, researching the stuff they're bringing up.'

'Any treasure?' Colleen asked.

'Only in the historical sense,' he answered.

'So where are you staying there?' Clodagh asked.

'I've borrowed someone's apartment in Leme, which is almost on the Copacabana beach,' he said, picking up his wineglass. 'You should think about coming back with me for a holiday. There's someone there you know.'

Everyone expressed surprise as they looked at Cavan and from just the look on his brother's face Michael's insides started to tighten.

'Someone she knows? In Rio?' Colleen said, incredulously. Already Cavan was looking uncomfortable, almost as though he regretted saying anything, which made his sister more curious than ever.

'Who is it?' she asked.

'She's got friends all over the world, has Clodagh,' Dan informed them. 'She's a secret agent really for the IKA, the Irish Knitting Army.'

Colleen nudged him as Cavan laughed. Then to her surprise Cavan threw her a warning look and half nodded towards Michael.

179

'Cavan?' Colleen said, glancing at Michael. 'Who does Ma know in Rio? Is this some secret admirer we're about to discover?'

Cavan stared at her hard, as though telling her to shut up.

'I think,' Michael interrupted, 'what Cavan is having a problem telling you is that Michelle is in Rio. Am I right?' he added, looking at Cavan.

Cavan's colour was answer enough.

'Michelle?' Clodagh cried. 'You mean *our* Michelle? Well, how is she? I didn't know she was in Brazil, she never said. But I haven't received a letter for a while. Did you send her my love, Cavan?'

'Of course I did,' he assured her.

'What is she doing there?' Colleen asked.

'Working with the street children,' Cavan answered. 'She's got . . .'

He broke off abruptly and everyone but Michael, looked at him again. 'She's got what?' Clodagh prompted.

Cavan shook his head. 'It doesn't matter,' he said. Then turning to Michael. 'How did you know she was in Rio?' he asked.

'A lucky guess,' Michael smiled.

'Are you in touch with her again?' Clodagh wanted to know.

Michael shook his head. 'I told you, it was a lucky guess,' he repeated. 'But the way this family clams up whenever her name's about to be mentioned is always a give-away.'

'I don't know why you ever let her go, Michael,' Clodagh sighed. 'She was a lovely girl. And you two were made for each other, anyone could see that.'

'Let's leave it there,' Michael said. 'It was a long time ago and we've been over it enough times since.'

'But you should listen to your mother,' Clodagh

180

persisted. 'Swallow that pride of yours and go after her. She'll forgive you, Michael. I know she will.'

Michael started to laugh. 'Who said there was anything to forgive?' he asked. 'She did the leaving, not me. It was her choice.'

'But you've got to fight for a woman,' Clodagh told him. 'Especially if she's a woman like Michelle, because they don't come along with the number fourteen bus, you know. You let her slip through your fingers, Michael, and you've regretted it ever since. Now don't deny it,' she said, putting a hand over his as he started to speak. 'I'm your mother, I know these things. You haven't settled down to another relationship since and the Good Lord knows you've met enough women. So now you know where she is, why don't you drop her a line and tell her you forgive her.'

Michael's expression showed only humour. 'So it's me who has the forgiving to do now, is it?' he said.

'It doesn't matter,' Clodagh responded. 'What's important is that you two get back together, the way you belong. Or get yourself out there, son, and find yourself someone else. Just stop all this playboying around, because it doesn't suit you.'

'No, it doesn't, does it?' Dan agreed, evidently enjoying himself. 'And there's Sandy right there in the office, who'd make him a perfect wife and he ...'

Clodagh was swallowing fast. 'A lovely girl,' she said, taking up the theme warmly. 'Pretty, too, and she's very fond of you, Michael, she told me. And she's been working for you six months or more and you never said a thing.'

'You knew she was there, you were speaking to her on the phone every week.'

'But I didn't meet her until recently, so I had no idea she was so lovely.' Looking at Cavan, she said, 'She took me to one of those press screenings, you know where the stars and the newspaper people go. We had

181

a marvellous time, the two of us. Took me in a taxi, she did, then saw me home after. I don't know where you were, Michael, but you missed a very good film.'

'I expect he was with Fiona,' Colleen remarked. 'Or am I out of date?'

Michael rolled his eyes. 'Shall we change the subject?' he suggested.

'Yes, tell us more about Michelle, Cavan,' Colleen said, helping Billy help himself to more carrots. 'How long's she been in Rio?'

'Only a few weeks,' Cavan answered, pouring more wine into Clodagh's glass and waiting for her to stay stop. When she didn't he winked at Dan and carried on filling it right to the brim.

'Oh, look what you've done now, you silly boy,' Clodagh complained.

'I'll finish what you can't manage,' Colleen assured her.

'You can't be drinking now, when you're feeding a baby,' Clodagh reminded her.

'Precisely,' Colleen smiled. 'So she's working with street kids,' she said, turning back to Cavan.

'Is she working with the church?' Clodagh asked.

'Not exactly. Well, yes, she probably is,' he corrected himself, 'but it's more like an undercover operation she's involved in, with this American journalist. I don't know too much about it yet, but I'm considering going in with them, because if you saw the kinds of things the police get away with over there, take it from me, you'd get involved too.'

Clodagh was frowning. 'That sounds dangerous to me,' she decided. 'What do you think, Michael? Does it sound dangerous to you?'

Michael nodded. 'I imagine it could be,' he said in a voice that gave no indication of what he might be either thinking or feeling.

'Mummy, can I watch *Beauty and the Beast* after dinner?' Tierney asked, turning to Colleen.

'It's going to be time for bed after dinner,' Colleen told her, tapping her plate for her to carry on eating.

Tierney's lovely blue eyes filled up with hardship. 'If I eat all my cabbage, can I watch it then?' she asked.

'How about I read you a story instead?' Michael offered. 'We haven't had a story for a long time, have we?'

Tierney's excitement was so great she could barely get her words out. 'I've got three new books,' she exploded, 'and I can read them all. But Billy drew in one of them, didn't you, Billy?' she said, reaching around her mother to thump him.

'Ah, it's like watching meself thirty years ago,' Clodagh remarked as Colleen sorted them out. 'I remember when she poured gravy over your head, Michael, and you put spiders in her bed to pay her back.'

'Ma, they don't need any more ideas,' Colleen reminded her, as Dan whisked Billy away before he could grab the gravy. 'Is that the baby crying?'

'I'll see to him,' Dan said, pushing her back down. 'You finish your dinner.'

'Have those two had a bath yet?' Michael asked, eyeing Tierney and Billy.

'No!' they chorused.

Michael looked at them in amazement. 'Did you think that was me offering to give you one?' he cried.

'Yes,' they laughed.

'No way,' he said. 'I'm not giving you two a bath, I always end up wetter than you. Besides, you haven't seen what we've got for dessert yet.'

Their eyes grew round with anticipation and Clodagh chuckled.

'What is it?' Tierney asked.

Michael looked at Colleen, hoping she might give

him a clue as to what he could offer, but Colleen, her eyes dancing with mischief for she could see the hole he was about to fall into, merely shrugged.

'What is it?' Billy asked, leaning against his mother.

'Cavan, you tell them,' Michael said, turning to his brother.

'Oh no, I don't want to spoil your surprise,' Cavan responded. 'You tell them.'

'I expect Nana knows,' Michael said.

Clodagh was shaking her head. 'No, Nana doesn't,' she said, 'and we're dying to find out, aren't we?'

Two little heads nodded as they turned back to Michael.

'I guess this serves me right for trying to change the subject,' he said, giving up.

The others laughed and Colleen said, 'Uncle Michael's brought us some chocolate chip ice-cream all the way from Sainsbury's.'

The children cheered as throwing down his napkin Michael went off to get it. He was just taking it from the freezer when Clodagh came into the kitchen behind him and putting a hand on his arm looked up into his eyes.

'It's time you brought her back, Michael,' she said softly. 'All this running around, looking after strange children . . . I'm not saying it's not good work, because it is, but she's got . . .'

'Mum, let it go, will you?' he said.

'No, I can't,' she said firmly, 'and nor can you. Oh, you put on a good show, but I'm your mother, Michael, I know what's going on in your heart and I don't care what you say, you still love her.'

'Even if that were true, which it isn't,' he responded, 'I'm in no more of a position to tell her to come back than you are. She made her decision, I tried to change her mind, but . . .'

'Maybe you didn't try hard enough,' Clodagh interrupted. 'No, that's not a criticism,' she said, when he looked about to protest. 'It was a very difficult time for you both and you've borne this well, son, better than most men would have considering the truth of the . . .'

'Enough,' Michael said. 'We agreed a long time ago not to discuss it any more, now let's stick to that agreement before we end up falling out,' and taking a handful of dishes from a cupboard he carried them and the ice-cream back to the dining-room, leaving Clodagh looking after him with the pain she knew was buried deep in his heart shining brightly in her eyes.

It was way past midnight by the time Michael returned to his top-floor apartment in the eight-storey Edwardian mansion block on the south side of the river. Before he'd left Dan's and Colleen's he and Dan had put Cavan to bed in the guest room that had been prepared for both brothers to stay over. Cavan, well into his cups, had tried to insist on coming home with Michael, but fortunately the whisky had rendered him incapable of putting up too much of a fight and by the time Dan threw the duvet over him he was already snoring.

Michael had then had a small battle of his own, trying to convince Dan that the now empty bottle of Glenfiddich had been consumed almost entirely by Dan and Cavan, so he was OK to drive. Mercifully Clodagh and Colleen had gone to bed hours before, or there would have been no arguments at all, and in the end Dan hadn't pressed the matter too hard, for despite the amount of Scotch he had consumed he had seemed to sense Michael's need to get away.

Letting the front door swing closed behind him, Michael threw his keys on to the hall table and, ignoring the flashing light on the answerphone, pushed open the sitting-room door and walked through the

185

pooling moonlight over to the bar. The huge sliding windows that ran the full width of the room and opened on to a long narrow balcony outside gave an uninterrupted view of the river below and the exclusive town houses and apartments of Cheyne Walk on the opposite bank. From where he was standing, as he poured two shots of whisky into a tumbler, he could look down river and see the ornate white lights of Albert Bridge; in the other direction, beyond Battersea Bridge, was the towering office block that contained McCann Walsh.

Carrying his tumbler through to the stainless-steel and black marble kitchen that was kept pristine and orderly by a diligent Mrs Friend who came in twice a week, he dispensed two cubes of ice from the refrigerator, then, still wearing his coat, returned to the sitting-room and went to stand at the window. Though he was gazing down at the moonlight reflected on the river, he was neither admiring nor registering it; for his thoughts were so far from where he was now it was as though they had roamed beyond the normal pastures of comprehension. For a while his eyes tracked the progress of a barge as it chugged quietly upstream, then, letting it go, he looked out at the lamplit streets and occasional traffic over on the Embankment. Minute after minute ticked by, until finally, taking a large sip of his drink, he turned back into the room and went to sit on one of the sumptuous black leather sofas.

It wasn't often that he thought about the interior décor of his flat, the Noguchi glass coffee tables, figurative artwork, pale Berber carpet and expensive kelim rugs, but tonight he was acutely aware of it, for just about everything from the Clarice Cliff wall plates to the Berschwiz chrome-and-glass dining set had been chosen by him and Michelle together. Even the king-size Japanese-style bed, with its hand-carved deco reliefs and wide-edged frame that held the mattress like a work of art, had been designed by them. The place seemed much more austere now, for there were no photographs scattered around, nor flowers to lend colour. The femininity had vanished with Michelle, yet there was still nowhere he could go in the huge five-roomed apartment to get away from her.

He smiled wryly to himself. Apart from the early days, when she'd first left, he had felt no need to get away, but now, tonight, he was as uncomfortable with her presence as he was with her absence. It wasn't that he harboured any lingering desire for her to come back; she had taken her decision a long time ago, and in the months – years – to follow, they had both learned to live with it. She had only ever contacted him once, about six months after she left, when she had written from somewhere in Sarajevo to let him know how and where she was. He hadn't written back, but he had wired a great deal of money to make sure that whatever she did or wherever she went she would always be taken care of. She hadn't thanked him for it, nor had he expected her to. Some might have called it guilt money and he wasn't going to argue.

Sighing, he downed the rest of the whisky and held the empty glass on the arm of the sofa. Even if they were to meet, it would never work between them now; too much time had gone by and there were still too many scars that would probably never heal. He often wondered if she had met someone else, or like him, had just drifted from one relationship to the next, never experiencing the same depth of feeling they had shared, nor really wanting to. The real pain had been gone for so long that he'd forgotten what it felt like now, all he knew now was the unbridgeable void she had left and the terrible anguish of not knowing, maybe never knowing, if he had made the right choice.

Getting up to pour himself another drink, he caught the distant sound of a baby crying. He thought of his sister and of how cut off he sometimes felt from his family. He loved them all so much and knew that would never change, but since Michelle had gone he had felt like a stranger in their midst, or like someone who no longer belonged. He'd discussed it once with Clodagh and to his surprise she'd understood far better than he'd expected. She'd talk it through with him again if he were willing, but he saw no point in analysing a problem he recognized, but had no way of dealing with.

He grimaced, then almost laughed, as he thought of Sandy Paull and Clodagh's hopes in that direction. Nothing would ever happen there, of that he was certain, and he hoped to God that Sandy didn't think she could get to him through his family, for he'd never countenance having them used that way, nor would he ever accept the intrusion. He couldn't say what it was he disliked about her, nor did he want to, for exploring his feelings towards Sandy Paull was a pointless exercise that generally ended up annoying him. Besides, he didn't really dislike her, he was just uncomfortable with the way he responded to her overt sexuality. He'd known plenty of women like her before, though perhaps they'd been slightly more subtle in their approach and were a lot less vulnerable than he suspected Sandy to be, but in the end it still came down to the same thing, all they wanted was to entangle him in a relationship that he couldn't have wanted less. But he wasn't made of steel, and occasionally he had ended up in bed with one of these women. It was always a mistake and he sensed that with Sandy it wouldn't only be a mistake, it would very probably be a disaster. So maybe he'd better have a quiet word with Clodagh and get her to back off a little, or, God forbid, the next thing he knew he'd turn up at Colleen's and Dan's to find Sandy cosily ensconced at the table.

Carrying his drink back to the window and watching

the dancing ripples of moonlight on the river, he began toying with the idea of introducing Sandy to Cavan. Then suddenly realizing what he was doing, he cut the thought dead. A good many women on a good many occasions had accused him of being a bastard and maybe they were right, but he was never intentionally so and he sure as hell wasn't going to start now with Sandy Paull by baiting her as a potential screw for his brother while Cavan was in town. In fact, he felt bad for even thinking it, when it would be like treating Sandy as though she were some kind of whore and no matter how strong his antipathy towards her might be, nor how tartily she sometimes dressed or behaved, that was an insult she certainly didn't deserve. And there was Clodagh again, back in his mind and making him smile, for whatever else she had done in her chequered career, she had managed to instil a reasonable, if not entirely dependable, sense of honour and morality in her first-born son.

He wondered what Clodagh would say were he to tell her about Ted Forgon's offer. He'd been tempted several times to discuss it with her, but knowing his mother he guessed that though she would try hard to hide it, she would be as horrified by the idea of him going so far away as he was sometimes anxious to go. Not that she would ever try to stand in his way, for that simply wasn't Clodagh's style, nor would he allow it, but he had no desire to upset her when, despite the appeal of a new life in a new place, he had no intention of making that place Hollywood or of selling his life to Ted Forgon.

He glanced at his watch to check the date. According to the fax he'd received, Ellen Shelby had arrived in London almost a week ago. He was surprised she hadn't contacted him yet, though maybe she had and Jodi hadn't bothered to tell him. If that were the case then the woman, if she had any intelligence, should

189

have worked out by now that she was on as wasted a mission as her colleagues before her. Perhaps even more so, for he had agreed to see the others; this one, though, he had decided not to.

A few short miles across London, Ellen was sitting at her hotel room window, gazing down at the shadowy emptiness of Hyde Park. She'd just returned from an enjoyable dinner with one of Rosa's friends, but now, sitting here alone, she was feeling sad and worried, and extremely frustrated with Michael McCann. Were it not for him and the way he and his secretary were blocking her, there was every chance she'd be falling freely and happily in love with London, but his refusal to see her, or even speak to her on the phone, was starting to feel like a personal rejection and after what she had just been through with Clay, that was something she really didn't need.

The problem was, short of throwing herself in front of his car or riding up to his office in a window cleaner's cradle, she just couldn't think how to get to him. Both Rosa's and Forgon's contacts had tried to set things up, but so far nothing had worked. And she felt god-dammed furious with McCann, for he could at least pay her the courtesy of hearing her out, even if he did already know what she was going to say. She had never come across anyone so blatantly unresponsive and were it not for the fact that she had so much hanging on this personally, she would quite happily have left town never having met him. Well maybe not happily, for the craziest part of it was that having read so much about him, she actually wanted to meet him. But she was going to have to get her act together soon, or Forgon would start getting impatient and though in her heart of hearts she didn't believe he'd go to print with those photographs, she definitely didn't want to try calling his bluff, any more than she wanted to return to LA with the embarrassment of never having made contact with Michael McCann.

Chapter 11

Zelda whooped with laughter, bringing most eyes in the restaurant to their table. Michael, Craig and Sandy were laughing too, as Stephen 'Slim' Sutton, the celebrated British author, paused in his hilarious story about searching for an agent in LA.

'I don't believe it!' Zelda gasped, grabbing a napkin to wipe her eyes.

'I swear it,' Sutton promised, his round, polished face beaming with mischief as he downed another brandy. 'This guy was actually dressed as a cowboy. Hat, boots, spurs, the works. But you've got to remember we're talking Hollywood here, where everyone dresses the part. And we all know agents are cowboys so I don't know why I was so surprised. Anyway, I walk into his office, take one look at him and say to myself, Slim, this guy's telling you everything you need to know with the way he's dressed. You don't need to go any further, man, just get out now. But he was too quick on the draw for me; he had me sat down in his office and plied with coffee quicker than I could go for my gun. He then spends the next hour and a half telling me everything I never wanted to know about his god-damned agency, and how come it's located where it is and not up there in Beverly Hills with the big boys. I didn't know how to shut the fucker up. He was full of shit and obviously thought I was fresh off the boat, so couldn't see through all his crap. "So, you want to be a writer," he says, like maybe I've never even read a fucking book, never mind written one, "well what I want you to do is call up all these producers" – he's got a list as long as a toilet roll right there in his holster – "and tell them you're a best-selling British author and you see they're making the same kind of stuff " – *stuff* – "you write so can you have your agent send over a couple of your books." ' His face was a picture as he looked around the table, evidently enjoying the appalled amusement his story was evoking.

'So what's he supposed to be doing while you're making all these calls?' Craig asked, picking up his brandy. 'I mean, that is his job, isn't it? Or is it different in Hollywood?'

'I guess it must be,' Sutton responded with sublime sarcasm as he summoned the waiter to bring more brandies. 'Or in this boy's Hollywood it obviously is. And who can blame him when he's "doggone fed up with doing all the work while all those chicken-shit clients sit at home on their butts whistling dixie." '

'He actually said that?' Zelda chuckled.

'As true as I'm sat here,' Sutton replied. 'But wait, it gets better. He then tells me he wants me to forget my books, because no one in Hollywood can read, and come up with a new concept on *Rambo*. Or *Braveheart*. Or *Hamlet*. Or *Babe*. Whatever. So I say, what you're telling me is you want me to clone everyone else's ideas? "Absolutely!" he says. "If it works, do it again!" '

Michael was laughing and cringing, while Zelda dried more tears. 'So what happened in the end?' she asked.

'What happened in the end was that I, eager little writer that I am, ask if he's got a screenplay I can look at, just to get an idea of the layout. You know, they're real sticklers for layout in Hollywood. It's like they can't read anything unless it's put in a format they've been taught how to deal with. So I ask if he's got a script I can look at and he says, "Oh no, no, no. I'm not in the business of teaching you how to write." So I got up, punched him off his chair and walked out the door.'

Zelda whooped again and it was a while before they all finished laughing.

'So you've given up on Hollywood?' Sandy asked, glancing at Michael from the corner of her eye as he looked past Craig towards the far end of the restaurant. Something had been attracting his attention over there for a while and she still hadn't managed to work out what.

'Not on Hollywood,' Sutton answered, 'just on jerks like that, who are a lot thicker on the ground than guys with talent. In other words, it seems to me you've got to eat a bellyful of crow before you get to fly in LA. And anything you ever did before you got to the States rates a big fat zero, because you're no one until you've been on *Oprah* or killed your wife and got away with it. Do you know what they call actors' agents out there?' His eyes came to rest on Michael.

Michael nodded. 'Talent agents,' he answered.

Sutton's eyes grew wide. 'So actors have the exclusivity on talent?' he cried incredulously. 'Can you believe it? Writers count for less than nothing.'

'So are you going back?' Craig asked.

'Sure. It's a great place, just as long as you don't take it too seriously and you don't need it.'

'Did you write a screenplay?' Michael asked.

'Not yet. But I will. And I'll give it straight to you guys. Who do you deal with out there? CAA? ICM?'

'Both,' Craig answered. 'But Michael's got a lot of contacts here in England and Europe, so we could probably get finance without even going to Hollywood.'

194

'My books are expensive,' Sutton warned. 'Plenty of locations and period.'

'If the material's good enough we can raise the money,' Michael told him, glancing across the room again as an explosion of laughter erupted at a far table. 'And I've read your books, so I know already there's no problem with the material. The question still stands, though, can you write a screenplay? They're totally different media and you might not have the objectivity on your own work a screenwriter could bring.'

'You're beginning to sound like Hollywood,' Sutton commented. 'But it's a fair point and from you I'll take it. So, I'll write the screenplay, then you can tell me what you think.'

Michael nodded. 'How long are you in town?' he asked, feeling Sandy's thigh brush against his.

Sutton looked at Sandy, who didn't even flinch as his hand found her knee and squeezed. 'Could be a while longer than I intended,' he answered.

To Sandy's relief he didn't actually wink, though he might just as well have, for the leer didn't leave much room for doubt on his intentions. Fortunately Michael's attention had wandered again, so he probably hadn't noticed, and Zelda and Craig just seemed to find his lechery amusing.

Sandy had met him two nights before at Tramp, where one of her dates had introduced them. She'd recognized his name as soon as she'd heard it, though she'd never read his books, nor did she quite remember at the time just how important a writer he was. But fortunately he'd given her his card and when she'd mentioned it to Craig the next morning he had got her to follow up on it right away.

So here they all were now, dining at the Canteen in Chelsea Harbour, where despite being a regular customer Michael still refused to be seated at one of the tables on the podium where Michael Caine was currently sitting with his wife and guests and Viscount Linley and company were just leaving. There were probably other names and faces up there that Sandy knew or had heard of, but tonight she was much more interested in what was catching Michael's attention at the other end of the room.

'Where are you staying?' Zelda asked Sutton as she picked up a candle to light a cigarillo.

Sutton's hand climbed a little higher on Sandy's thigh. 'The Savoy,' he answered.

Sandy couldn't now be in any doubt about how much her date the other night had told Sutton about her, for the way his fingers were playing around the tops of her stockings and the right he seemed to feel at them being there told all. And she was in no position to disillusion him, for the last thing she needed was for him to take umbrage, when he could prove such a major coup for McCann's.

The table next to them got up to leave and as they cleared the area Sandy could at last see through to the other end of the room. She still wasn't quite sure where Michael was looking and as he was talking now, she returned her attention to what he was saying.

'I'd like to put you together with Neil Osgood,' he was telling Sutton. 'Do you know him?'

'You mean the director, Neil Osgood?' Sutton said. 'The one who did *Falls the Shade* and *Deep Valley Black*?'

'Among others,' Michael smiled. 'We've talked about your books before, but they've always been under option when we approached your publishing agent. How are they standing now?'

'All options have expired except on *Forest Gods*,' Sutton answered. 'I told you, they're expensive to do.'

'And not easily adaptable,' Michael said frankly. 'But Osgood's interested and he's going to be in London for the next couple of weeks so I think it would be a good

196

idea for the two of you to meet up. I'll call him in the morning and find out what his schedule's like. He's in pre-production right now so he should be able to fit something in.'

'Sounds good to me,' Sutton beamed, removing his hand from Sandy's thigh and getting up from the table. 'Back in two shakes,' he promised.

As soon as he'd gone Craig began to talk excitedly about the prospect of getting him and Osgood together, declaring it was a stroke of genius on Michael's part, while Michael insisted that it had been Osgood who had brought Sutton's work to his attention. All the time they were talking, Sandy was watching Michael closely until finally she became aware of what, or who, kept claiming his attention over in the far corner beside the window. And just one look at the woman was enough to turn Sandy's blood to ice, for she was so unconscionably beautiful, with her crystal-clear complexion, glorious wavy hair and sparkling eyes, that Sandy instantly felt like a showgirl by comparison. And the way the woman laughed with such ease and enjoyment, and seemed so unaware of the way men all over the restaurant were watching her, seemed to add a galling kind of mystique to her incredible appeal.

Sutton came back and almost immediately returned his hand to Sandy's thigh. Sandy was furious, for though he knew she'd been on an official date the other night, he also knew that she was a part of the McCann agency and as such should be treated with respect. OK, it was her own fault she was having to suffer this, for she had promised herself she would give up dating once she received her promotion, but she hadn't managed to get round to it yet. And besides, look at the kind of contacts she was making. However, being caught in a dual role like this where Sutton, the balding, overweight, old lecher – yet a genius, was seeing her as his sport for the evening, while Michael was sitting there apparently entranced by another woman whose allure and elegance seemed to ooze from every pore, only served to remind Sandy of the time Nesta had tried to warn her that Michael would never entertain the idea of a serious relationship with someone like her.

Feeling more wretched than ever, she fought to maintain her smile as she leaned back for Sutton to speak across her to Michael. 'You know who that is, don't you?' Sutton whispered, though the whole table could hear.

Michael frowned. 'Who?' he said.

'The woman over there,' Sutton answered, nodding. 'The one you keep looking at. It's Ellen Shelby. Maybe you've never heard of her. She works for American Talent in LA. Now *that's* an agent with class.'

Michael's eyes moved instantly to Zelda.

Zelda was already laughing. 'Oh, he's heard of her all right,' she said. 'He just hadn't seen her until now.'

Sutton's eyebrows were raised, as though sensing he might have hit on something here.

Craig was looking at Sandy, watching the tightness around her mouth as she tried to hold on to her smile.

'Shame she doesn't deal with writers,' Sutton was saying, 'because I'd be beating a path to her door right now, if only to get a closer look. Or maybe she does. Is that Kit Ringwood she's with?' he added, straining to get a better look.

'Yes,' Michael answered. 'And Bob Mansion and his wife.' He looked at Zelda again, then turned back to Sutton. 'Maybe you and your publishing agent can get together with Craig some time in the next week,' he said as though the last couple of minutes had never happened. 'It'll be mainly him you'll be dealing with while we work on getting something off the ground ...' His eyes shot to Sandy as he suddenly remembered that she had been the one to introduce them to Sutton and though she was primarily working for Diana and Janey, Sutton was still her find.

'Maybe Sandy should be at the meeting too,' Craig said, coming to the rescue.

Michael nodded and smiled as he turned his eyes to Sandy.

Sandy smiled back and felt her heart falter as their gaze locked. She wondered why, then, she was so worried about Ellen Shelby, for when he looked at her that way she just knew that it could only be a matter of time before he dropped his rule of no relationships in the office and gave in to his feelings. She had seen the way he looked at her breasts whenever she leaned over his desk and because of it she was becoming more daring than ever with what she wore. Not that the others were aware of it, for she always chose something with buttons that could be undone, or with a semi-transparent top that could be easily covered or uncovered by a jacket. She had even, on a couple of occasions, removed her panties before going to see him, but hadn't quite plucked up the courage yet to let him know that. However, if things carried on the way they were going there was every chance he was going to find out for himself.

As Sutton carried on talking, both she and Michael turned to look at him, but Sandy could sense how aware Michael was of her now, for she could almost feel it burning between them. In fact, she was so absorbed by the intensity of it that she didn't notice Ellen Shelby and her party coming towards their table until they were almost upon them.

'Michael, how are you?' Bob Mansion cried, grabbing Michael's hand as he rose from the table.

'Pretty good,' Michael responded. 'How are you, Jenny?' he said to Mansion's wife, while kissing her cheek.

'We were just talking about you,' Jenny Mansion told

him while giving Zelda's shoulder a squeeze. 'You've met Kit, haven't you?' she said to Michael.

Michael shook the other man's hand. 'Several times,' he smiled.

'And this is Ellen,' Jenny said proudly. 'Ellen Shelby.'

Ellen stepped forward, a cream silk crocheted shawl covering her shoulders, yet managing to reveal the gold chain straps of her elegant bronze satin dress. Her dark, lustrous eyes were firmly on Michael's as taking his hand, she smiled and said, 'You've been going to such pains to avoid me I was beginning to think we'd never meet up.'

Michael's surprise at her frankness showed, though he seemed more amused than put out by it. 'That would have been a shame,' he remarked, holding her gaze and feeling a faint stirring inside him as her head went to one side.

'Then perhaps we can put it to rights,' she said. 'Would you have lunch with me one day this week? Any day will suit me.'

'I'm sorry,' he said, 'you'll have to call my secretary, she keeps my diary.'

Ellen's eyes widened. 'What are you so afraid of, Mr McCann?' she asked, smiling the challenge.

Michael was momentarily taken aback, then he too started to smile. 'I won't be free for lunch,' he said smoothly, 'but do send my regards to Ted Forgon and tell him the packaging for his gift is certainly improving.'

Ellen's smile remained, though the way her eyes dimmed showed that the insult had hit home. 'That kind of comment doesn't only demean me, Mr McCann,' she said softly, 'it demeans you too for making it.'

Michael's eyebrows flew up and she could see she had rattled him. 'It was intended as a compliment,' he told her, 'but I can see it was misleading. Please accept my apologies. And I truly am all booked out for lunch this week.'

'Then dinner,' she said without hesitation. 'I'm free on Thursday, so I'll meet you here at eight o'clock. I'll make the reservation. Good-night everyone,' and allowing no time for a response she moved on past.

After saying goodbye to the others in her party Michael sat back down and looked at Zelda, who was grinning all over her face. 'Did I miss the joke?' he enquired. 'Or am I it?'

'I think you just met your match, Mr McCann,' she told him.

'You do?' he said mildly.

Zelda nodded and continued to grin.

'Let me tell you something, Zelda,' he said, 'it makes no difference to me what the woman looks like, the answer's still going to be no.'

'Oh, you mean like it was for dinner?' Zelda suggested.

'If I didn't want to go for dinner, you know very well I wouldn't,' he responded.

'So you do want to go?'

'She's come a long way, it would seem churlish not to.'

Zelda seemed to find that more amusing than ever. 'Now let me tell *you* something,' she said, leaning towards him and whispering, 'if you think she's going to prove one of your easy conquests, then I'm going to lay money right now that says you're wrong.'

Michael's eyebrows rose in surprise. 'If I'm not,' he told her, 'it won't be at all disappointing,' and it was his turn to laugh at the way Zelda's eyes crossed as she tried to work that one out.

Sandy sat huddled in the corner of the sofa, a voluminous towelling robe encompassing her as she gazed at the slumbering figure on the bed. The room was in

201

darkness, but the moon cast a silvery glow over the tousled sheets and pale, balding head resting on a rucked-up pillow. She felt so unbearably sad about what she had just done that even the resentment that had driven her to do it had collapsed under the weight of her sorrow.

It would be easy to tell herself she had done it for Michael, to secure Slim Sutton's commitment to McCann's and to stop Sutton telling what he knew about her. But in her heart she knew she had done it to punish Michael for the way he had looked at Ellen Shelby tonight. Or maybe she had done it to punish herself. That was more how it felt, but she had no idea what she needed to punish herself for, except being so lacking next to someone like Ellen Shelby.

From the moment Ellen had walked up to their table and Michael had got to his feet, Sandy had felt sickened by herself and now she hated Sutton for making her feel so much worse. But it wasn't his fault that she had been another man's paid date for the night when they had met. And Sutton hadn't actually threatened to tell anyone her secret, so it was she who had turned herself into a whore tonight, not him. It was true she had done it out of anger and resentment, but the fire of her passion had only turned him on all the more, and now her body and her heart ached with regret and self-loathing.

Her eyes were still fixed on the bed. She didn't think he would ever tell, but she was going to have to ask him not to and he would probably want to have sex with her again as payment for his silence. It wasn't that she really minded the sex, for she would simply pretend it was Michael she was with – in fact she had become so good at that now that she sometimes had to remind herself that they hadn't shared even a moment of intimacy, unless looks and smiles and the occasional comment could be interpreted as such, which of course they couldn't.

Getting up from the sofa she walked to the window and sliding her hands into the sleeves of the robe she gazed up at the stars. Her life had changed so completely in so short a time that she had almost forgotten now who she was. It was true, she could still feel the gauche young girl from Fairweather Street lurking somewhere beneath the façade of the slightly sophisticated, totally bewildered young woman, whose morals were as confused as her ambitions, but she wanted only to be rid of that ghost, not to be haunted and humiliated by her, as she was right now. She sighed deeply and felt a surge of self-pity as she wondered if all she really wanted was to be loved? She'd searched for it often enough, but even if she found it would she recognize it? She knew that men liked to have sex, so she had tried to win Michael by letting him know he could have sex with her any time, but maybe that wasn't what he wanted, a woman who was easy. Maybe what he wanted was someone who was aloof and unobtainable; a woman with class and refinement; dignity and self-respect.

Her eyes dropped to the floor as her heart contracted. What he wanted, she was thinking, was a woman like Ellen Shelby. Tears were stinging her eyes and her throat was locking with misery, for just the image of Ellen Shelby, burnt so cruelly and beautifully into her mind's eye, was enough to make her see how unattractive, maybe even sordid, she was to a man like Michael. To any man, maybe, except those prepared to pay.

She thought of Ellen again and saw those wonderful clear eyes, the elegance, the poise, the self-confidence and modesty that made her Michael's kind of woman, while she, Sandy, was just any man's woman. Ellen Shelby would never do the kinds of things she had done to make her way in the world; she would have no shameful secrets to hide or fears that her weaknesses would be uncovered or exploited.

Hearing Sutton stir in the bed behind her, she turned and watched him until finally his eyes opened and he saw her standing at the window. She smiled as he held out a hand towards her and felt a strange kind of affection for him, or maybe it was simple gratitude that someone wanted her. She would have to ask him now if he would keep her secret.

She walked to the bed and letting the robe pool at her feet, she lay down beside him. He began to caress her breasts gently, almost lovingly. The Ellen Shelbys of this world would never have to do what she was doing now, for they would never have got themselves into the kind of fix where they would have to. The Ellen Shelbys just came along to enchant men like Michael, who then loved them and took care of them and never had to worry about where they had been before or what they might have done.

Sandy's eyes were sightless as Slim rolled on a condom, then lay on top of her and entered her. She hadn't asked him to keep her secret, she was just letting him make love to her anyway. She didn't want to be paid for it, whether it be with money, jewels, weekends in New York or silence. She wanted to have sex because she liked it and because whoever the man was liked it too. OK, in an ideal world she might not have chosen Slim, but it wasn't an ideal world and they were here together now, so why not at least pretend that it was where she wanted to be?

But starting tomorrow she was going to change. She was going to give up her other life and stop fooling herself about Michael, for it was time she accepted that no matter what she did, how far she got, or how hard she tried, she was never going to be good enough for him. What she was going to be, though, was a normal, decent, young woman seeking her way in the world by means of hard work and merit. There would be no more paid dates, no more blinding herself to the realities of her life; and maybe one day she would see a man just like Michael look at her the way Michael had looked at Ellen tonight.

A single tear rolled from the corner of her eye as she wondered how long it would be before Michael sold out to Forgon and left for LA. She was terrified he would and what hurt most about it was the fact that in the end it wouldn't be Forgon's offer that would change his mind about Hollywood, it would be Ellen Shelby. She'd like to *kill* Ellen Shelby, tear that lovely face to ribbons and get her out of the way, so that she never bothered their lives again. Except lying here now, in one of London's most exclusive hotels with a strange man working his way to climax on top of her, she felt so depleted and defeated that all she could really think about was why life was so mean to her when it seemed to have lavished so many blessings on others.

Chapter 12

It was just a few minutes after eight when Ellen arrived at the Canteen restaurant in Chelsea Harbour. Though she was nervous about this meeting there was nothing in her appearance to show it as she stepped out of the taxi and handed the driver a ten-pound note. It was a cold, clear night and there was almost no one around. At the end of the road she could see a pool of moonlight rippling across the harbour waters where yacht masts clanked in the wind and the tide lapped against polished hulls and moss-covered walls. All around her, apartment and office blocks soared silently into the night sky with occasional lights signalling a world behind the façade. She gazed up at them and wondered which were the McCann Walsh offices.

Hooking her bag on her shoulder, she walked into the brightly lit foyer of Harbour Yard and headed towards the Canteen. The *maître d'* saw her coming, and was waiting with the door open to greet her with a warmth that startled her, until he showed her to 'Mr McCann's table' and conveyed 'Mr McCann's apologies' that he was running late. Apparently she had become Mr McCann's guest, rather than the other way around, but though this irked her, she said nothing to the waiter as she was seated and served a complimentary glass of house champagne with a small plate of mouthwatering *amuses-bouches* to get her 'tastebuds in the mood'.

When the waiter had gone she took out a book and opened it. It was simply a prop, for she was too anxious to concentrate on anything more than the task ahead. Three days had passed since coincidence had out-classed contrivance and brought her and McCann together here, at this restaurant, and most of that time had been spent going over the fine detail of Forgon's offer and her own strategy on how she was going to present it. The fact that McCann was now no longer an imaginary target drawn from the pages of Forgon's research, but a real flesh-and-blood man with all the disturbing elements that entailed, was a distraction she had already striven to confront and eliminate. Yes, he was exceptionally attractive, but that was no surprise, for she'd seen enough photographs of him to know that already. What the photographs hadn't prepared her for, though, was how annoyingly composed he seemed and apparently indifferent to her pursuit of him. In fact, he was so god-damned condescending that it had been a real struggle to stop herself getting mad just thinking about him. But she had that under control now and the desire she had to slap his face was one she would save for a time she was in a position to do so.

She turned a page and ran her eyes over the lines. Just no way was she going to allow him to rattle her by showing up late. She had all the time in the world and if he thought that she couldn't see through this tired old tactic of putting her at a disadvantage by keeping her waiting then he was in for a surprise. Too many men had underrated her in the past and it seemed McCann was about to make the same mistake. Well, he'd learn soon enough and she was going to have a good time showing him that she was no more fazed by his tardiness than she was moved by his charm.

'Hi, am I interrupting?' Michael said, pulling out a chair to sit down.

Starting, Ellen looked up from her book. 'Not at all,' she replied, covering the jolt to her heart with a smile. 'Is this what the English call fashionably late?'

Michael's eyes narrowed with humour. 'No,' he said. 'It's what we call unavoidably delayed. Please excuse me. Were you given a drink?'

She nodded and raised her still full champagne glass. His blue eyes were even more compelling than she remembered and as they focused somewhat curiously on hers, to her dismay she felt the indifference she had carefully nurtured these past few days starting to desert her.

'Good book?' he asked, raising a hand to summon a waiter while seeming to give her some kind of appraisal.

'Very,' she replied, hoping he didn't think she had made a special effort for him tonight, when she most certainly hadn't. In fact, she had resolutely not even thought about what she was going to wear until it had been time to dress after her shower.

'Your hair suits you like that,' he told her, referring to the way she had clasped it with artful carelessness on to the top of her head and left a few curls dangling around her neck.

Ellen's eyes showed her disapproval. If he thought he was going to win her over with compliments as bland as that he could think again. She'd already taken a breath to tell him so when she suddenly remembered that it was she who was supposed to be winning him over. 'Thank you,' she said.

His amusement at such a simple statement coming from such a large breath was reflected in his eyes as he turned to the waiter and ordered another glass of champagne. 'So how are you enjoying London?' he asked, when the waiter had gone.

'Very much,' she answered. 'It's a fascinating city.'

'Is it your first time?'

She nodded. 'Yes.'

'Then I hope you're being taken good care of.'

'I think so,' she said, sounding more defensive than she intended. 'Are you from London?'

He laughed. 'Forgon's got a file on me as thick as his new hair, so don't tell me you don't know the answer to that.'

Ellen's eyes moved to one side as she struggled to hide her smile at the remark about Forgon. 'OK, you're from Ireland,' she told him.

'And Liverpool,' he added. 'And you?'

She looked baffled.

'I've yet to meet an American who doesn't know their roots,' he explained. 'So from whence does your family hail?'

Ellen's eyes narrowed, showing her uncertain understanding of the question. 'Ireland?' she said hesitantly.

He laughed again. 'Well done, you've obviously picked up some old English while you've been here. Where in Ireland?'

'I think Galway,' she answered. 'We're going back several generations so I'd have to ask my father to be sure. Are you Catholic? Why are you laughing?'

'Sure I'm Catholic,' he answered. 'And I'm laughing because I'm enjoying myself.'

Ellen's smile fled. 'Please don't flirt with me, Mr McCann,' she told him sharply. 'That's not why I'm here and you know it.'

Michael's champagne arrived at that moment, so his only response to the rebuke was to look highly amused. Ellen's annoyance coloured her cheeks and she turned swiftly away.

'So, do you want to get down to why you are here?' he invited, saluting her with his drink as the waiter left.

'Maybe we should order something to eat first?' she

suggested, still smarting at how ludicrous she had obviously sounded a moment ago.

He nodded and turned compliantly to his menu.

As Ellen scanned hers she was frantically searching her mind for a way to regain control of the situation. The trouble was, she couldn't quite work out how she'd lost it, or in fact if she'd ever had it, and the careful strategy she had so painstakingly pieced together seemed to be falling apart by the second. She was sure he was using his looks to disarm her, which she had guessed he probably would, so it would no doubt surprise him to learn that in fact, she wasn't the slightest bit impressed by them. But she could hardly tell him that when it was neither relevant nor polite. Besides, she seemed to keep forgetting he had no reason to come here and impress her; she was the one supposed to be impressing him and if it weren't for recent experiences she would probably be handling that side of things very well. As it stood, she appeared totally hung up on the male–female element of their meeting, which appalled her, for it was something she had never allowed to get in the way before and the very thought that he might be considering her some kind of bonus in Ten Forgon's package was too horrible for words.

'Are you ready?' he asked, closing his menu.

Ellen quickly selected the macaroni of lobster and closed hers too. She had to get past this personal business, for it had no place here and the last thing she wanted was for her hang-ups to start affecting her professional ability.

'So where are you from in the States?' he asked, after a waiter had taken their order.

'Nebraska,' she answered. 'Tell me, is it your usual practice to ignore phone calls and faxes, or was it just mine you were having a problem with?' The instant the words were out she regretted them, not only because they had sounded so petty, but because of the amusement that had returned to his eyes.

'Believe me, Ellen,' he said, taking the wine list that was being handed to him, 'were I not sick and tired of Forgon's efforts to ransack my life I'd have been more than happy to take your calls. And just in case you misinterpret that as more flirting,' he added, 'I'm afraid it's a mere truth.'

Despite being disconcerted by the use of her first name, Ellen laughed. 'You're a hard man to stay mad at, Mr McCann,' she told him.

'Michael,' he said, 'and why would you want to stay mad at me?'

Ignoring the question she said, 'I take it you read the faxes detailing ATI's offer?'

He nodded and opened the wine list. 'Do you have any preference?' he asked. 'There's not much of a California selection, I'm afraid.'

Ellen narrowed her eyes. 'Do I look so parochial?' she challenged. 'French will be fine. Do they have a Puligny-Montrachet?'

Michael didn't need to check. 'Yes, they do,' he said, closing the list and handing it back to the wine waiter who had already registered the order. 'So, when do you return to the States?' he asked.

'I'm scheduled for a flight next Monday,' she answered. 'If I don't have an answer from you by then, I can always stay until you're ready to sign.'

Michael grinned. 'Do you feel so sure I will?' he enquired.

'I think you would be wise to,' she responded. 'The offer is exceptional and I don't imagine you'll ever get another like it, do you?'

He shook his head. 'No,' he answered, 'I don't imagine I will.'

He was looking at her so intently that she was suddenly finding it uncomfortable meeting his eyes.

She was sure he wasn't intending to be intrusive, but that was how it felt and she wished he would stop. Reaching for her champagne as an excuse to look elsewhere she said, 'Is it just Ted Forgon you have a problem with, or is it Hollywood too?'

His eyebrows went up. 'Both, for different reasons,' he replied and she noticed the luxuriance of his lashes and darkening shadow around his jaw as he lowered his eyes to his drink.

To her amazement she felt a sudden impulse to touch the hand that was idling on the stem of his glass. She stared at it, dumbfounded by the feelings it was stirring inside her.

'If you like,' he said, nodding as the waiter showed him the wine label, 'I can give you an answer for Forgon right now.'

Ellen's mouth went dry. He was obviously going to turn down the offer and though it was no surprise she realized with a jolt just how disappointed she was going to be by his rejection. 'I'm not sure I want to spoil a good meal,' she said softly.

He smiled. 'So you're not so sure I'll accept?' he replied.   She shook her head. 'Frankly, no.'

He looked away for a moment as he tasted the wine, then signalled for the waiter to pour. 'So why don't we turn this around and talk about you coming to work for me?' he suggested.

Ellen's eyes flew open.

Michael watched her, looking very much as though he was about to laugh.

Then, realizing what was happening, Ellen's lovely brown eyes started to shine.

'That's your answer?' she asked. 'That's what you want me to tell Forgon? That instead of accepting our offer, you're making one of your own?'

Michael nodded. 'My only concern,' he said, 'is that

losing one of his best agents to the other side might give him another coronary.'

Ellen's expression was caught between suspicion and laughter as she tried to work out if he was serious. 'It probably would if I accepted,' she said. 'Not because he'd be sorry to lose me, but because you'd outsmarted him again.'

Michael's eyebrows rose. 'He's sure to have good medical cover,' he said.

Ellen choked back a laugh. Then, deciding she was enjoying this line of patter, she pursued it by saying, 'I guess it would mean me moving over here to London?'

'I guess it would,' he confirmed.

Her humour began to retreat as the possibility that he might mean it started to root. 'Are you serious?' she said after a while. 'I mean I'm still having problems with British irony, so you're going to have to help me out here . . .'

'I'm serious,' he told her.

Her heart was suddenly unsteady. 'But why?' she said.

'Because I hear you're good and I'd hate to think of you losing your job because I won't play ball with Forgon.'

As his eyes remained on hers, Ellen was aware of a slow heat spreading through the more sensitive areas of her body, but was trying to ignore it. 'Actually,' she said, 'there isn't a danger of me losing my job. I got that sorted before I left. In fact, if you did accept I'd be twenty thousand dollars richer and minus a very big problem.'

Michael's head went to one side and the smile on his lips reflected darkly in his eyes. 'Well, at least I won't have your employment on my conscience,' he said. 'But my offer still stands.'

She smiled deep into his eyes and felt a warmth pull through her heart as he smiled back. 'I can't accept, of course,' she said, 'but I'll enjoy telling Ted Forgon you offered.'

Michael laughed. 'I wish I could be there,' he told her, leaning back as their food was set down on the table. When the waiter had gone he picked up his wine and touched his glass to hers. 'Let's drink to us agreeing on something before the evening's over,' he said.

Feeling herself respond to the possibilities that offered she said, 'I haven't given up hope of persuading you to come to LA.'

Michael put down his glass and picked up his knife and fork. 'Is that good?' he said as she took a mouthful of lobster.

'Mmm, delicious,' she replied. 'How's yours?'

'Better than that,' he answered. 'Do you want to try?'

'What is it?'

'Monkfish.'

Ellen leaned over with her fork, but he had already selected her a portion, so opening her mouth she allowed him to feed her. 'Mmm, you're right,' she told him, trying not to be so mindful of the intimacy, 'it's good.'

Seeing him watch her as she ate and feeling suddenly very self-conscious, she lowered her eyes to her plate. He was getting to her in a way she would rather not think about, especially after all the business with Clay. In fact, considering the horrors of the past few weeks and the terrible shame she felt whenever she thought about it, she was amazed at the way she was responding to this man when she hardly even knew him. But even if she wanted to, and she had to confess she did, there was simply no way she was going to fall into bed with him at the end of the evening, for it just wasn't something she did, sleep with a man on the first night. She looked at him again and wondered if that was what he was expecting. It was impossible to tell, for

214

despite the lingering scrutiny of his eyes the thoughts behind them were as unreachable as the answers to why she was feeling this way.

'Would it be rude to ask what the problem is?' he asked, watching her put down her wine.

Ellen looked at him in surprise.

'You mentioned earlier that if I came to LA you'd be twenty thousand dollars richer and minus a very big problem,' he reminded her.

'Oh, yes,' Ellen responded with a mirthless laugh. 'Actually, it's nothing worth talking about. Do you go to LA much?'

He nodded and took another mouthful of food. 'From time to time,' he answered. 'The other agents go more frequently. Most of my business is here in Europe. What about you, do you travel?'

'Back and forth to New York now and again,' she said, aware of how she was barely connecting with what she was saying. This was crazy, for all she seemed able to think about now was what it would be like to make love with him. Perhaps the wisest thing to do would be to get away from him for a while, as she was in grave danger of forgetting why she was there. 'Will you excuse me?' she said, getting to her feet.

On reaching the ladies' she walked to the mirror and stared at her reflection. Her cheeks were flushed, her eyes too bright and her mouth was cherry red and moist. She couldn't help wondering if she was having a similar effect on him, as without even looking she knew her nipples were hard and the attraction she was feeling was leading her thoughts in quite another direction from the one she should be pursuing. She wanted to laugh, but found she couldn't. It was incredible to be this drawn to a man whose only act of intimacy was to look deep into her eyes and feed her a single morsel of fish. She wished Matty were there to help her to see the funny side, for that was the only way she was going to be able to deal with the rest of the evening, she was sure of it. Except that was nonsense. She was a grown woman and perfectly in control of her senses.

'Are you OK?' he asked, getting up as she returned to the table a few minutes later.

'Yes, fine,' she smiled. Her quick escape seemed to have helped as she felt much more in control now. 'I'm sorry, what were we saying?'

'What are you doing at the weekend?' he asked.

Ellen's heart immediately contracted and once again she was in turmoil. 'Um, uh, I'm busy this weekend,' she answered, totally forgetting he was the sole reason she was in London, thinking only that she didn't want to appear too keen.

He seemed surprised, but said nothing.

'Why?' she ventured, sounding suitably casual.

'Victor Warren has invited about twenty people to his place in Scotland for the weekend,' he told her. 'I thought you might like to come too.'

Ellen's eyes were round. 'You mean Victor Warren the American director?' she said, actually more impressed by Scotland and the castle she knew Warren owned.

Michael nodded. 'There'll be hunting and shooting and fishing, all the normal things that go with a weekend in Scotland. I think he's holding some kind of ball too, I can't remember. But if you're not free ...'

Though Ellen looked crestfallen, she actually felt much closer to bereft. But there was no way she could go, not with him, for there was no doubt where it would end up and she just couldn't let that happen. 'I'm sorry,' she said. 'It sounds like fun and I'd love to see Scotland.' Forgon was going to hang her out to dry for this, but she couldn't run the risk of Michael thinking she was one of the perks in the package.

He shrugged. 'Another time maybe.'

216

They ate on in silence for a while, until Ellen finally managed to wrench herself from the disappointment of not going to Scotland and the fact that he hadn't tried to persuade her either and returned to the real reason she was here. 'When I was reading about you,' she said, 'I noticed that you once went into producing, but you didn't follow it up.'

His easy humour and attentive blue eyes were suddenly masked by caution, telling her she was on very delicate ground now.

'Have you ever considered resurrecting the movie?' she said. 'Or maybe producing something else?'

He looked at her closely, as though deciding whether or not he wanted to go any further. 'I think about it from time to time,' he said in the end, 'but the right project's never come along.'

'If it did, would you?'

'I might.'

Bracing herself and wishing desperately she didn't have to bring his name back into the conversation she said, 'Ted Forgon's willing to back you, give you as many contacts as you need to get your own production company started after a five-year period at ATI.'

Michael's eyebrows were in the air and his smile already growing before she'd even finished. 'Does Forgon seriously think I couldn't do that for myself?' he said.

'Here you probably could, in LA it might prove more difficult and Forgon holds a lot of sway with a lot of . . .'

'Ellen,' he interrupted gently, 'the answer's no.'

Ellen's eyes remained on his as she felt the consequences of her failure begin to fill her heart, with so many emotions she could find no voice through the chaos. But once past the personal loss she felt at his refusal, all she could see was the harsh reality of what it was going to mean – stuffed racks of cheap, smutty

217

journals cluttering every supermarket check-out from Washington State to Florida Keys, all of them glorying in the full frontal nudity of one of Hollywood's shyest and most respectable agents. Everyone she knew, when they went to get their groceries, was going to see her exposed in a way that would shock them as much as it would excite them with its potential for new gossip. Just like Clay's *Baywatch* Babe, a headline would be stamped over her nipples and pubic hair, but everyone would know she was naked and because the photographer had been Clay, other papers would pick up on it fast and some eager early bird would probably go straight to Nebraska to try talking to her folks. The TV would follow up with their own spin on the story and then, after the entire nation had been fed a full diet of titillating shots of Clay Ingall's secret love, and all her friends and colleagues had finished sniggering behind their hands and seeing straight through her clothes whenever she walked into a room, the heavyweights like *Playboy* and *Penthouse* would probably publish the whole damned lot, which left nothing, no single part of her, to the imagination. She tried to console herself with Forgon's assurance that she had the only set of polaroids, but it was no good, she knew Ted Forgon and there was just no way he would hand back ammunition like that when he might still make use of it.

Realizing Michael was watching her, she quickly forced a smile and, without really thinking about what she was saying, said, 'It's my ambition to become a producer. At least it was.'

'Was?' he said.

She shrugged. 'Still is, I guess, but . . .' She broke off, but before he could speak again she said, 'I've been looking at some of your tabloid papers while I've been here, they're much more explicit than anything we have in the States.'

Clay was so famous that there was simply no way the British press would pass up on the story, so Michael would get to see the whole god-damned carnival and for some reason knowing that seemed to make it all so much worse. The irony of it was that he was the only one who could rescue her, but she would never tell him that, because there was just no way he was going to sell up his life to save her reputation and her parents' shame. And why should he? He barely even knew her, and probably to him the idea of a few nude shots in tens of millions of newspapers and magazines wasn't a particularly big deal, at least certainly not big enough to persuade him to hand himself over to Forgon and Hollywood.

Wanting now only to get her mind off the horrors that lay ahead, she asked the question almost before it had chance to form in her mind. 'Why did Michelle really leave?'

Michael blinked in surprise and though his good humour seemed still to be there she could tell that he didn't want to answer.

'I'm sorry,' she said, putting down her fork.

'It's OK,' he said. 'You're not the first to ask.'

She looked at him, wondering if he was going to enlarge, but he just let the silence lie between them.

'I read about the charity work,' she said, wishing she hadn't got on to the subject, but seeming unable to get off it.

His eyebrows flickered. 'Then you know the reason for her going,' he said, finishing his meal too.

'That was all?' she said incredulously. 'I mean, she walked out on you, the movie, her life here and everything to go and work with the women and children of Sarajevo?'

He smiled. 'A worthy cause,' he reminded her, 'but I'm flattered you find it so hard to believe.'

'Frankly I do,' she told him.

219

'Well, it's why she went. It was something she felt she had to do and I wasn't going to try standing in her way.'

'But you loved her.'

'Yes.'

'Didn't you at least try to talk her out of it?'

'Of course. But she needed to go. It was a passion with her.'

As Ellen looked at him her disbelief was growing, for she simply couldn't imagine leaving a man she loved so much so easily. Except it probably hadn't been easy, it had probably been one of the most difficult and painful things Michelle Rowe had ever done in her life, but that kind of detail rarely found its way through to the press.

'Do you still love her?' she asked.

Michael smiled. 'After all this time? No, I don't think so,' he answered.

Ellen remembered thinking, when she'd first read about their break-up, that there must surely be something more sinister behind Michelle's reasons for going, but sitting here now with Michael she found that hard to believe, for he just didn't seem the kind of man to cause such devastation in someone's life that they would go to such extremes to get away. But then she had only to recall how wrong she had been about Clay to recognize what a poor judge she was of men.

Michael changed the subject and started asking her more about her life in LA, how she had come to be an agent, why she had chosen it as a profession and listened sympathetically when she told him about her father and how he couldn't forgive her for leaving. They discussed movies and theatre, books and music, politics and history; then he told her about his family, making her laugh as he recounted tales of Clodagh's eccentricities and efforts to marry him off. Their dessert arrived and the effortless move from one subject to another continued to surprise and intrigue Ellen until finally she began to wonder how she could ever have imagined she loved Clay when they had never known anything like this kind of rapport the entire time they were together.

Coffee came and though Ellen desperately didn't want to leave she knew she had to, for she had drunk too much wine and the way he had made her laugh and had drawn her so deeply into the disconcerting aura of his charm was making her feel much more vulnerable than she could deal with.

She wondered now, as she sipped her coffee and watched him unwrap a chocolate for her to eat, if he had any idea how very much she wanted him to make love to her. It was as though her entire body was coming alive to the mere suggestion of his touch and she had only to think of the way his eyes would close when he kissed her and how he would become hard as her fingers found him, to know how very close she was to going home with him. In fact, if he asked she knew she would, for just the sensation of his fingers on her lips as he fed her the chocolate, and the look in his eyes as he watched her take it, pushed her desire to a point where she no longer had the will to resist.

His eyes held hers as their hands touched on the table and a shock of desire surged between them with a force so strong it edged her lust with pain. Her lips were parted, her chest rose and fell with each breath as she watched his eyes darken and almost felt his mouth on hers. The pressure of his fingers increased and her eyelids fluttered as her need intensified to a point she could barely endure.

'Look at me,' he whispered.

Obediently she returned her eyes to his.

'There's nothing I want more than to make love to you right now,' he told her, 'but I can't . . .'

'It's OK,' she cut in quickly, snatching her hand

221

away, 'you don't have to make excuses. In fact, I really should be going. I mean, that wasn't meant to be rude, but it's getting late and ... Thank you for a lovely evening. I hope ...' She was fumbling for her bag and finding it she got abruptly to her feet, having forgotten what she was saying.

'Ellen, listen to me,' he said.

'I'm sorry,' she responded, knowing she was behaving stupidly but unable to stop, 'I really must be going. Thank you again,' and before he could say any more she was almost running across the restaurant on her way to the door.

It was only when she reached the foyer that she remembered she had intended to pick up the check. She groaned out loud, as she'd already made a big enough fool of herself without having to go back for more. So she left it and rushed on out into the night.

She'd known even as she was doing it that she was overreacting, but she had been so mortified when he'd started making an excuse not to sleep with her that she hadn't given herself time to think. Besides, he'd done her a favour, as she would have slept with him, there was no question about that, and she didn't even want to think about how that would have made her feel in the morning.

A wave of despair washed over her as she looked around at the bleak, windy night. She had never known a desire so intense as the one she'd experienced this evening and it was scaring her. After what she had been through with Clay, surely she should be experiencing a curb on her sexual needs, not an uncontrollable surge. So maybe there was something wrong with her, maybe she got off on being exposed and humiliated, which is what it would have meant had she allowed herself to do what both Forgon and McCann, in their own different ways, no doubt wanted her to.

Seeing a cab come round the corner she waited for it

to drop some people off, then ran across to get in. As she closed the door she looked back towards the restaurant and saw with a terrible disappointment that he hadn't bothered to come after her.

After settling the bill, Michael left the restaurant and headed back to the office. As he rode up in the lift his expression was grim and his temper was becoming blacker by the minute. OK, he could have gone after her, maybe he should have, but what would it have proved? That he could get her into bed with a few well-placed smiles and a couple of looks calculated to provoke the kind of response they had? He'd done it a thousand times and had known almost from the moment he arrived how easy it was going to be. Not that he'd had any intention of going through with it, he'd just wanted to find out how far she was prepared to go to get him to accept the offer. The problem was, somewhere along the line it had stopped being about Forgon and had started being about them. More accurately, it had been about her and the fact that she'd turned out to be so much more than he'd expected.

The lift doors opened and flicking on the inner-circle lights he walked across to his office and poured himself another drink. The intensity of his anger wasn't rational considering what had happened, but it was building to such a pitch that he slammed his fist hard into the wall in an effort to release some of the tension. Dear God, why had Forgon sent her, when she was so obviously a decent woman who probably had no idea she was being used as some kind of sexual offering in a sick man's game? But damn the man's eyes, he had chosen his weapon well, for Michael was still hard for her now and it was driving him crazy. He could see her mouth, so soft and full and red that he'd wanted to kiss her all night. He wanted to feel her skin next to his and watch her face as he entered her. He wanted to hear her moaning with the pent-up desire he had seen in her eyes and feel her hands and legs on his back as he carried them both to a place . . .

He stopped and closed his eyes. He was so damned hard now he hardly dared move. He had no idea why he should want her so badly, he just did. Or maybe it wasn't her he wanted, maybe it was just the release. And as though his prayers had suddenly been answered he heard a knock on the door and looked up to see Sandy Paull standing there watching him.

'Are you all right?' she asked, looking confused and concerned.

'Sandy,' he said, his voice sounding strained even to him. 'What are you doing here? It's past ten o'clock.'

'I had a lot to catch up on,' she answered. 'I just went to the ladies, then came back and saw the lights . . .' She laughed awkwardly. 'It frightened me, actually, so I'm glad it was you.'

Michael looked at her and though he started telling himself no, he knew already he was going to do it. He was vaguely aware of how different she had been lately, keeping herself more covered up and giving him much less of the come-on. The strange part of it was, now he came to think about it, it had made her seem more appealing.

'Do you feel like a nightcap?' he offered.

Sandy's eyes moved to the fridge, then back to him.

'Not here,' he said.

The speed with which she read what he was saying was awesome, though for one terrible moment he thought she was going to turn him down.

'Where would you like to go?' she asked.

'How about my place?'

Her eyes were locked on his and several seconds ticked by before she said, 'I'll get my coat.'

By the time they reached his car he knew he was making a big mistake, but he didn't know how to back out now and even if he did he knew he wouldn't. He was grateful to her for not speaking, though he was asking himself how the hell he had managed to resist Ellen when he was suddenly finding it so damned impossible with her?

They got into his car and suddenly they were kissing so urgently he could have screwed her right there and not cared who came by. Their breath was harsh, their tongues fast and demanding, their hands clawing at each other's clothes. He wished she was wearing the stockings she had always worn before, if she were he'd already be in her knickers. As it was, he was pressing his thumb hard against her crotch, while she gave the same pressure to his cock.

'Let's get out of here,' he said breathlessly.

She nodded and straightened her clothes as he started the car.

It took less than fifteen minutes to get to his apartment. She talked a little and he responded, but nothing was registering. He knew he was going to regret this in the morning, but right now he was past caring.

She walked on ahead as he closed the apartment door behind them and stopped to take off his coat. He watched her push open the sitting-room door, fumble for the lights, then saw the stunned expression on her face when she saw the size of the room and the view. He felt suddenly guilty and wanted to say something to make her feel welcome and let her know that he appreciated her being here. There were no words to say that, though, so he merely followed her into the room and instead of doing what he most wanted to do, which was fuck her right where she stood, he offered her a drink.

As he poured, she went to stand at the window and looked out.

'Are you going to take off your coat?' he asked.

She turned to him and smiled. Then unfastening the single button she removed her coat and laid it on the nearest chair. She was wearing a loose wool sweater and a pleated knee-length skirt.

'I knew this would happen one day,' she said, looking up into his face as he handed her a drink. 'Did you?'

He nodded and watched the uncertainty in her eyes turn to relief as she smiled. He knew he was being a bastard, but there was no way he could stop himself and running a hand over the front of her sweater, he said, 'God, you turn me on, do you know that?'

She smiled again and looked oddly bashful. 'I hoped I did,' she said, 'but sometimes I wondered.'

'Do you want me to fuck you?' he murmured, pushing a hand between her legs.

'Yes,' she whispered.

'Are you wet?'

She nodded and he heard her breath start to quicken.

'Take off your clothes,' he said.

She put down her glass and turning to look at him, she pulled her sweater over her head. Her breasts were crammed into her bra, bulging over the top, nipples squashed by the gossamer-thin gauze. Grabbing the front of it, he pulled her towards him, put his mouth over hers and tore the bra apart. His hands cupped her, squeezing her hard, pinching her, pulling her, licking her, sucking her, as she stripped off her skirt and panties, then ripped open his fly.

They pulled and tugged at his clothes until he was as naked as she was, then he was plunging into her and fucking her like a madman. There was a rage possessing him, driving his cock, twisting her body, violating her mouth, delving into every part of her, as she trapped him with her legs, pushed her breasts to his face and tore at his skin. Her frenzy was as great as his, as he screwed her on the floor, against the wall, on the

226

sofa, over the table. Her tongue was all over his cock, on his balls, in his arse.

He lifted her up, sat her on him and fucked her through to the bedroom, his hands squeezing her breasts, his tongue probing her mouth. The violence was making him so hard it was as though his cock might explode. He threw her on the bed, rolled her over and rammed into her from behind. It was as though all the fury locked inside him was rushing out from the shadows, urging him to excesses even greater than he knew. He wanted to hurt her, hear her scream and beg for mercy. She was gasping his name, pushing his fingers between her legs and sticking her arse out for more. He gave it to her, harder and faster than ever. He pulled out, spun her over and sat her on him. She pumped up and down, breasts bouncing, hair flying, skin soaking. He pressed on her clitoris, rubbing it and crushing it, then grabbing her head he pulled her mouth to his and buried his tongue inside. He could feel her coming, clenching him with her muscles and fighting for breath.

He held on to her tightly, banging his hips up and down as the semen rushed along the stem of his penis and exploded into her in long, excruciating spasms of relief. He kept on coming, kept on holding her, as the ghouls in his mind taunted him with all that possessed him. He went to the threshold of pain and beyond. The torment was total, the shame, the guilt, the anger, the pain. He hated her for being the one to release it and wanted to smash her away, but he held her and touched her and let her think that he loved her. He embraced her and wondered if maybe he did love her, as it seemed like his orgasm was going on for ever as pulse after pulse quivered through him.

It left him so spent and exhausted that when it was over, all he could do was lie there and let his limbs go weak and wait for his heartbeat to steady. She lay over him, panting and sweating, and smelling sweetly of scent and crudely of sex. He thought of Ellen and felt a need go through him, so pure, it almost tore him in two.

Pushing Sandy gently off him, he lay with his eyes closed, feigning sleep. He didn't want to think about her, he didn't even want to acknowledge she was still there, for he knew he was going to hurt her now in a way he had sworn he would never hurt another woman. Except, what he was going to do to Sandy couldn't even begin to compare with what he had done to Michelle.

Chapter 13

When Sandy finally opened her eyes from a strange and unrecognizable dreamscape, she wondered for a moment where she was. Then, remembering, her heart quietly erupted with joy and turning to the empty space beside her she ran a hand over the crumpled sheet where he had lain. It was still warm, and pushing her face into his pillow she inhaled deeply and felt the scent of him move through her like the lingering memory of a caress. It had happened at last! She had spent the night with Michael and as she recalled the passion with which he had made love to her, the way he'd lost control almost from the beginning, then had held her so close at the end, she knew in her heart that there were going to be many, many more nights like it to come.

For a while she lay where she was, amused by how small she felt in the enormous bed. She listened to the silence of the flat and wondered where he was. She guessed he hadn't wanted to wake her, so had slipped away quietly, but despite the ache in her limbs and soreness in her body she was ready to make love again and felt sure he would be too.

Sitting up, she hugged her knees to her chest and gazed around the room. The tall, arched windows that occupied two entire walls were like great columns of sunlight beaming long, silvery rays across the carpet and black lacquer furniture. From where she was sitting, dazzled though she was, she could make out the top of the balcony railings outside and the dense, blue sky with not a single cloud in sight. She knew that the door in the far corner opened out to the hall, so guessed that the other, recessed between the twin, hand-painted closets, would probably lead to the bathroom. Imagining and hoping that was where she would find him, she got up from the bed to go and look.

She was right, it was a bathroom and it almost took her breath away, for she had never, not even in books or magazines, seen one like it. Had she been familiar with Robsjohn-Gibbings she'd have known it was an adaptation of his American-deco style, but she had never heard of the designer, nor did she need to to appreciate the sheer magnificence of the high, oval room with its central dais into which an enormous black marble bath was sunk. The cream marble floor and walls with classical black pilasters, fan lights and mirrored shelving were all of the same thirties' design, and the chrome and brass fixtures gleamed in a jigsaw of colourful sunlight streaming through the stained-glass window overhead.

There was no sign of Michael and catching sight of herself in a mirror she could only feel glad, for her eyes were smudged with mascara and the hair that wasn't stuck to her head was sticking out at angles. Quickly grabbing a robe from the back of the door, she slipped it on and set about repairing the damage.

To her relief, as she searched for a comb and toothbrush, she found no signs of another woman, though it might have helped if there had been something to clean off her make-up. Settling for soap and water, she sponged her face, then dried her eyes with tissues. Most of the mascara came off and though she didn't look anywhere near as glamorous as she'd have liked, it was certainly an improvement on a few minutes ago. Her skin was fresh and shining, and though her eyes were slightly bloodshot from the soap, they looked young and sparkly and full of joy.

A few minutes later, as she sponge-washed the rest of her body, she heard him moving about in the bedroom and wasn't sure whether she should go to him wearing the robe, which was now on the floor, or as she was, in nothing at all. Standing back to get a good look at herself in a long, panelled mirror, she noticed a brass handle on the frame and turning it, found that it led into a spacious marble shower with five brass shower heads and a wall-to-wall bench. Chuckling to herself at the amazing splendour of the place and feeling a wonderful burst of euphoria at the idea that it was all going to become so familiar, she closed the door quietly and, deciding to put the robe back on, she walked over to the other door and let herself into the bedroom.

He had disappeared again, but she smiled as she saw a cup of coffee steaming beside the bed, obviously put there for her. Then, spotting one of the closet doors half open, she realized how much sexier she would look in one of his shirts rather than his robe, which all but drowned her.

As she sauntered into the sitting room she found the french windows open, allowing a crisp early morning breeze to flow in from outside, and feeling it touch her skin she was glad she had fastened only one button of the shirt.

He was standing at the dividing counter between the living-room and kitchen, dressed in a robe like the one she had just discarded. He was looking down at the paper and appeared not to have heard her come in. His hair was still tousled from sleep and he was in need of a shave, but to her he had never looked more attractive. Smiling to herself, she walked towards him, waiting for him to look up. She had almost reached him by the time he did and seeing the way his eyes moved instantly to the open front of the shirt her pulses began to quicken.

'Good-morning,' she whispered shyly.

His eyes rose to hers and he reached for his coffee. 'Good morning,' he answered, his smile seeming as uncertain as hers. 'Do you ... ? Would you ... like some breakfast?' He made an awkward gesture towards the kitchen behind him.

'I'm not hungry,' she said, realizing that he was as nervous as she was. She found it helped her to know that and, perching on one of the bar stools as he returned to the paper, she said, 'I hope you don't mind, I used your toothbrush.'

He shook his head and turned over a page. 'No, that's OK,' he said. 'Help yourself to anything. Did you find the shower?'

She nodded, even though he wasn't looking. She imagined that from where he was standing he could see along her thighs to her pubic hair and wondered if he had noticed yet. Maybe she should take the shirt off altogether, or tell him she was wet – he had seemed to like that the night before. For some reason, though, it didn't seem quite right this morning, so taking another sip of coffee she asked if there was anything interesting in the news.

'Not really,' he said, shaking his head. 'Another attack on the government over education and a train derailment somewhere in Cornwall.'

'Oh,' she said.

He continued to read and though she tried hard not to, in the end there was no way she could deny the awkwardness he seemed to be feeling. She felt her heart turning cold and a quick panic fired her fear. Please God, he wasn't regretting what had happened last night. He had seemed to want it so much at the

232

time and the way he had looked at her when he kissed her and held her while he slept . . .

'Are you sure you don't want any breakfast?' he said, looking up at her and raising his eyebrows in a self-mocking sort of way.

She smiled and felt herself turn weak with relief at the attempted humour. She realized then that he probably wasn't a morning person, but out of consideration for her was trying to be. 'I'm sure,' she said and sliding off the stool, she walked round the counter to join him. 'I wouldn't mind a kiss,' she said, tilting her face up to his.

His eyes were trained somewhere over her head as he touched his lips to hers, then, smiling and patting her bottom he said, 'I expect you'll want to go home to change before going into the office.'

She laughed and grimaced, knowing that was exactly what she'd have to do, for she had nothing here and though she could do without underwear for the day, she certainly couldn't go without make-up. The real pity of it, though, was that she wasn't going to get to walk in with him, but there was time enough for that, after she'd moved a few things over from her flat to take care of occasions just like this.

'It's only seven o'clock,' she said, turning his wrist to look at his watch. 'Do you have a breakfast meeting?'

'Uh, yes. Yes,' he said as she started to untie the belt of his robe. 'In fact, I'd better get in the shower,' he said, clasping a hand over the knot to stop her.

Laughing and turning his reluctance into a game, she pushed his hand aside and started tugging at the belt.

'Sandy, listen,' he said, grabbing her wrists in one hand while holding his robe together with the other.

'Yes Michael?' She grinned, letting her head drop back as she looked up at him. 'I'm listening.'

He looked down at her, then, taking a breath he said, 'Look, I don't want to . . . I mean, last night was last

233

night and ... it was great and you're great ... Oh Christ,' he groaned, as she broke one of her hands free and found his erection.

'Do you want to feel where I'm wet,' she murmured, taking his hand and putting it between her legs.

'Sandy, look, I don't think we should be doing this,' he said.

She laughed as despite his words he made no attempt to remove his hand from her, nor hers from him. 'Why?' she said, opening his robe wide and looking down at the solid stem of his penis as she rubbed her hand up and down it. 'Because we're going in to the office later? Don't worry, I won't let on to anyone what we were doing after supper and before breakfast.'

'It's not that,' he said, his voice faltering as she squeezed him hard. 'I just don't want you to think ...' His eyes closed as she touched the tip of his penis to her clitoris. 'I don't want you to think ...'

'That you're just using me for sex?' she finished, looking up into his face, her eyes twinkling with laughter.

He looked down at her and as her words registered through the distraction of what she was doing he wondered if she was telling him it was OK, that he could use her for sex, if that was what he wanted.

His eyes remained on hers and as she smiled he had the same terrible urge to take her as he'd felt last night. It was less violent this morning, less spiked with anger, but still too pressing to deny. She looked up at him as she carried on stroking herself with his penis and, forcing a tenderness to his eyes, he said, 'Is this good for you too?'

'Yes,' she whispered.

His eyes dropped to where their bodies were touching and despising himself for his inability to stop, he unfastened the button on her shirt and pushed it down

234

over her shoulders. Then, shrugging off his robe, he lifted her onto the kitchen table and laid her down on her back.

As he entered her she gasped and reached for his hands. His fingers closed around hers, squeezing them tight as he pressed them to her hips and held her as he began to pump in and out of her. She watched his face and gave a bashful smile when at last his eyes came to hers. His expression suddenly darkened and his strokes became longer and more rapid. He threw out her hands and dragged her buttocks from the table, holding her up so he could penetrate her deeper and harder. Then quite suddenly it was over and as he ejaculated into her and swore violently under his breath she was exultant to think that she had turned him on so much that he had been unable to stop himself coming so fast.

When finally he withdrew he helped her from the table and held her loosely round the waist as she circled her arms around his neck. 'I'm sorry,' he said.

She looked surprised. 'Sorry? What for?' She laughed.

He seemed embarrassed, then, stooping to pick up the shirt he handed it to her. 'It wasn't any good for you,' he said.

She laughed again. 'It was fantastic,' she told him.

He still looked doubtful, so she went up on tiptoe to kiss him and assured him that after last night, it was the best she had ever known. And it was true, it was, for even though she hadn't come herself, all that mattered was that he cared. And if she needed any further proof of that she got it when he joined her in the shower and washed himself in front of her as though they had been this comfortable together for years. He even, as she told Nesta when she returned to their flat later, offered to let her have the day off work if she wanted to.

'How very generous of him,' Nesta commented, her

large, hazel eyes still slightly clouded with sleep and looking decidedly uncertain about all this. 'Did he kiss you when you left?' she asked.

Sandy looked surprised at the question. 'Of course he did.' She laughed, digging a spoon into a giant bowl of cornflakes. 'What did you think, he shook my hand?' She ate the cereal, and winked at Nesta. 'It was only a quick kiss, though,' she said, when she'd swallowed, 'because the phone rang and I didn't hang around because the cab was waiting and I think he'd probably seen enough of me without make-up at this stage of our relationship.' She laughed and downed another spoonful of cornflakes.

Nesta breathed in deeply and glanced over to the radio, where a traffic report was giving way to the latest sound from Arrowsmith. She was still in her nightie, having been turfed out of bed by a jubilant Sandy some twenty minutes ago to hear all about the earth-shattering start to this long-awaited affair.

The tea in the mug she was holding was turning cold, so getting up from the table she poured what was left down the sink and replugged the kettle. 'So when are you seeing him again?' she asked, leaning against the draining board and watching Sandy as she lifted the breakfast bowl and drank the remains of her cereal.

As she finished Sandy laughed and, using her fingers to wipe away a milky moustache, she said, 'In about an hour.'

Nesta frowned, then remembered that of course she would see him at the office. 'I meant, do you have another date?' she said.

Sandy shrugged. 'I expect I'll go over there tonight,' she answered, carrying her bowl to the dishwasher. 'Unless he's got some party or other to go to.' She stopped for a moment as she thought about that, then said, 'If he does, I wonder if he'll invite me.'

'Yes, I wonder,' Nesta responded dubiously.

236

Sandy glanced at her, then, depositing her bowl in the machine she took a loaf of bread from the wooden container and cut herself a slice. 'He might not want to go public yet,' she explained. 'Anyway, I thought you might have been a bit more pleased for me than this.'

Nesta shrugged. 'I am,' she said. 'It's just a bit early in the morning, that's all. So tell me again, how did you come to go back to his place?'

'He invited me,' Sandy answered, slotting two pieces of bread into the toaster. 'He came into the office around ten last night, while I was still working, and I suppose he just thought there was no point holding back any more. Actually, he probably made the decision before that, because he must have known I was there, otherwise why come back?'

Nesta shook her head, at a loss for another explanation. 'Where had he been until ten?' she asked. 'Did he say?'

'He was having dinner with that LA agent I told you about, the one who was at the restaurant the other night. You should have seen her. Honestly, talk about fancying herself. I mean, she's not bad looking, but the way she spoke to Michael it was guaranteed to get his back up and it did, anyone could see that. I think I told you about it, didn't I?'

Nesta nodded.

'Yes, well, I expect she managed it again last night, seeing how early he left the restaurant.' She was quiet for a moment and turning to look at Nesta she started to grin and her young, shining eyes filled with elation as Michael's dinner date of the night before was forgotten and the memory of all that had happened after came flooding back. 'Did I tell you about the way he said he didn't want me just for sex?' she said, not entirely sure those were his exact words, even though it was what he had meant.

Nesta nodded.

Sandy giggled. 'I'm telling you, he's that good I almost wouldn't mind if he did,' she said. Then, laughing, she went on: 'You should have seen him before he said it. I mean, I was starting to get worried, because it was like he didn't want to do it again or something. But then, when he said that, I realized he was just afraid I might think he was using me. God, he's so romantic.'

'Did he kiss you much?' Nesta asked, turning to pour boiling water on a fresh tea-bag.

Sandy's head went to one side as she thought about that. 'Yeah, quite a bit,' she said. 'He's got a fantastic body. You should see it. And he's pretty well-endowed, let me tell you.'

'You already did,' Nesta reminded her. 'So what are you going to do,' she asked, returning to the table with her tea, 'if he doesn't invite you to the party or over to his place tonight?'

Sandy frowned and instead of answering the question, she said, 'Why are you saying that? Why do you think he wouldn't invite me? I told you, it's really happening between us now, so why can't you accept that?'

'I can if it's true,' Nesta told her.

'Well it is,' Sandy assured her. 'It's why he waited so long. I mean, if all he'd wanted was to screw me he'd have done it ages ago, wouldn't he?'

'I don't know, would he?' Nesta countered. Then, sighing, she said, 'I'm sorry, I don't mean to be so cynical, but it just doesn't feel right somehow.'

'What doesn't?' Sandy asked churlishly.

'I don't know. The fact that he didn't take you out first, I suppose. Did you call Isabelle back, by the way? She wants to talk you into staying with your regulars.'

'No way!' Sandy cried. 'I told you, I told her, that's all behind me now. I don't want to be paid for dates any more, I want to go on real ones, the way other

238

women do. Besides, if it really does get going with me and Michael I can hardly two-time him with strangers, can I?'

Nesta's surprise showed. 'If?' she repeated. 'You sounded a hundred per cent a moment ago, now it's "if".'

'You know what I mean,' Sandy said irritably.

'What I know is that there's every chance you're jumping the gun here,' Nesta said frankly, 'and if you are, you're going to end up ...'

'Stop being so bloody negative, will you?' Sandy broke in angrily. 'If you'd been there, if you'd seen the way he was with me you'd know that it means something to him too. OK, he's still fighting it, but not as much as he was, and I expect by now he's already come to the conclusion that his rule about no relationships in the office is just a waste of time when he's the only one who sticks to it.'

'So everyone else is having an affair, are they?' Nesta said.

'No, not everyone. Just Jodi and Harry, though no one's supposed to know about that, because his wife's pregnant and due in a couple of weeks.'

'The bastard,' Nesta retorted, screwing up her nose in disgust. 'Give me the escort business any day, at least it's honest.'

Sandy threw her a look loaded with cynicism.

'I don't set out to deceive anyone,' Nesta reminded her. 'It's a business arrangement, we have some fun and no one gets hurt. What Jodi and Harry are doing is shameful.'

Sandy laughed mockingly. 'Oh, look at you on the moral high ground,' she sneered. ' "We have some fun and no one gets hurt." What do you think all those wives would say if they found out their husbands were paying to sleep with another woman every time they came to London?'

239

'There's no reason for them ever to find out,' Nesta said. 'And if they did at least they wouldn't have the fear of me trying to break up their families. Anyway, I'm not getting into defending myself here,' she said. 'My conscience is clear about what I do. I don't lie to myself and pretend things are the way I want them to be just because I don't like the way they are.'

Sandy's eyes sparked. 'Meaning I do?' she challenged.

'You said it,' Nesta responded. 'Not that it makes any difference to me. If you want to go around kidding yourself some man is crazy about you when all he did was screw you for a night, then you go right ahead and do it. Just don't be surprised when he doesn't invite you to parties or first nights or wherever else you're hoping to go with him, because you can take it from me, it's not going to happen.'

'What's the matter with you!' Sandy shouted. 'Anyone would think you were jealous, the way you're carrying on.'

'What's there to be jealous of?' Nesta cried, throwing out her hands. 'If the man had told you he'd been wanting this for months . . . If he was on the phone now telling you how he can't wait to see you again . . .'

'He did,' Sandy cried.

Nesta stopped and wrinkled her nose. 'Did what?' she said.

Sandy was racking her brains, trying to remember exactly what had been said about wanting to do it for ages, or always knowing it would happen, or something like that. She couldn't quite recall it now, but it had certainly come up. 'He did say he'd been wanting it for months,' she said. 'OK, not in those words, but we both knew it was something we'd wanted almost since we met.'

Nesta's eyes remained on hers, simmering with all the things she wanted to say, but didn't quite have the

240

heart to. In the end she simply sighed and shook her head. 'OK, have it your way,' she said flatly. 'The man's nuts about you.'

'Don't say it like that!' Sandy protested.

Nesta shrugged. 'Did you tell him you've got your engagement ring all picked out?' she said. 'Or are you saving that for the second date?'

'Very funny,' Sandy snapped, and turning away she snatched the bread from the toaster and yanked open the fridge for the butter. By the time the toast was ready to eat her eyes were so full of tears she could barely see. 'You bitch!' she suddenly seethed, slamming a hand on the counter. 'Why do you have to go and spoil it all?'

Her back was still turned, but it was more than evident she was crying. 'Oh God,' Nesta groaned, getting to her feet and going to her. 'I'm sorry. Look, I'm sure I've got it all wrong . . .'

'No! Don't!' Sandy snapped, shoving Nesta's arm away and rounding on her furiously. 'It's too late to take it back now. And why should you? You've never thought I was good enough for him, so don't start pretending now.'

'Look, all I'm saying is, you've only spent one night with the man and as far as I can make out he didn't mention anything about any feelings, which is normal for a first date,' she said, raising her voice as Sandy tried to interrupt, 'so do yourself a favour and try slowing up a bit. I know you think you're in love with him, but you've never had a relationship with him and he might turn out to be a complete bastard who you can't stand the sight of after a couple of months . . .'

'I don't want to discuss it any more,' Sandy cut in. 'You don't know him, so you don't know what you're talking about. And I can't expect you to understand the way I feel when all you want out of men is money.'

'I notice you haven't chosen one who's exactly poor,' Nesta shot back.

241

'It's got nothing to do with money,' Sandy raged.

Nesta was shaking her head. 'You're still lying to yourself, Sandy,' she said. 'It's got everything to do with money and status and power, and all those things you think he's going to give you to make you feel like someone instead of no one. You're using him, for God's sake. Or at least you're trying to and even if you succeed and he does fall in love with you, I'm telling you now, the only way you're ever going to be someone is when you do it for yourself. He can't do it for you, nor can I, nor can anyone else. It has to come from you, from *here*!' she cried, banging a hand against Sandy's heart. 'You've got to start believing in yourself and stop trying to climb on his ladder to get to the top, because it doesn't work that way. You don't want to be an agent any more than you want to be an actress. All you want is to impress Michael McCann because you've made up your mind he's the answer to all your prayers when you don't even know what you're praying for. So get a life, Sandy. Your *own* life. Not the one you think he wants you to have, because he's no different from any other man on this planet: he'll only start respecting you when you start respecting yourself.'

Sandy's face was pale as she stared blindly at the watercress on the window-sill. Though she could hear what Nesta was saying she was blocking it from her mind, for Nesta had to be out of her head, saying she should try to find a life without Michael when they'd only just started seeing each other. They had everything in front of them now, and there was just no way she was giving up her career when she'd just been promoted to Diana's and Janey's assistant. Nesta didn't know what she was talking about, saying she didn't want to be an agent. Of course she wanted to be an agent, it was why she'd applied herself to it the way she had these past eight months and she was damned

242

well going to carry on applying herself, because it was absolutely what she wanted, to become an agent and be as important to Michael as he was to her. And everyone, except Nesta it seemed, knew that if you wanted something badly enough you had to go out there and fight for it. Which was exactly what she was doing.

'I'm going to get changed for work now,' she said, and without even glancing at Nesta she turned and walked off to her bedroom.

Michael was at his desk going over a pile of new contracts that Freda had left for him to sign. It was almost midday and mercifully Sandy hadn't shown up yet, though the fact that she was likely to at any minute and maybe carry on like they were an item was putting an edge on his nerves that was ruining his concentration. The real irony of the day, though, was that a call should have come from Rio just as she was leaving the apartment.

Sighing, he dropped his pen and rested his forehead on the heel of his hand. What a god-damned mess, and right now he didn't know what the hell he was going to do to change it.

'Michael,' Jodi's voice came over the intercom. 'I know you said you didn't want to take any calls, but Ellen Shelby's on the line and I wasn't sure . . .'

'Put her on,' Michael said and picking up the receiver he put it to his ear and turned his chair to look out of the window. 'Hi. How are you?' he said, using the sonorous lilt of his voice to close out everything but her.

'Embarrassed,' she answered, matching his tone. 'And sorry I walked out like that. I meant to pick up the tab.'

As she spoke he was picturing her face, her soft brown eyes, the flawless complexion, the ripeness of her mouth, the amazing allure of her smile. He felt a pull on his heart and wasn't surprised by how much he wanted to see her again. 'Did you get back all right?' he asked. 'I should have come after you.'

'I was OK, thanks,' she responded. 'I found a taxi.' She paused, then said, 'I had a lovely evening, I just wish it hadn't ended the way it did.'

Michael smiled and was unable to keep the irony from his voice as he said, 'You and me both. Where are you now?'

'At my hotel.'

He was on the point of suggesting lunch, when he spotted Sandy outside and with a terrible sinking sensation he reminded himself that misleading one woman was bad enough, to do it to Ellen too would be unforgivable when he had no intention of selling out to Forgon. Except lunch wouldn't be about Forgon, would it? It would be about them, which was perhaps an even better reason to avoid it, as the last thing he wanted was to entangle himself in a relationship with Ellen when there was little doubt in his mind that the road they would travel would be much more serious than he wanted.

'When do you go back to the States?' he asked, already knowing the answer.

'Next Monday,' she said. There was a moment's hesitation before she said, 'Unless . . .'

'Don't do it,' he interrupted. 'Don't ask, because the answer's the same now as it was last night and it's not going to change by Monday.'

'Will it ever change?' she said and the ambiguity affected him more than he wanted to think about.

'No,' he answered.

They were quiet for a moment and as he watched a flock of birds soar through the sky he could only wonder at the amazing timing of it all, that she should come into his life now . . . But there was no point going any further with that so he let it go.

'I'm sorry about the twenty grand,' he said, 'but at least you get to keep your job.'

'Yes, I get to keep that,' she confirmed.

He would have given anything to be with her right now, for he could almost see the hurt in her eyes at the way he was rejecting her. 'What about the problem?' he asked.

'It's mine,' she answered. 'Nothing you need worry yourself about.'

'If Forgon reneges on the job, you know there's one here,' he told her.

'Thank you,' she said softly.

He knew instinctively that even if Forgon did double-cross her, she'd never come to London and as he'd never move to LA he could only consider it a good thing that they were ending this now, before it even began. But even as he thought it he was forming the words to ask her to the opera that night, or wherever he was going. It didn't matter as long as he saw her. Instead he said, 'You take care of yourself, OK?'

'You too,' she said. 'And if you're ever in LA, remember I owe you a dinner.'

He didn't reply and after a few seconds the line went dead.

It was a while before he turned back to his desk and hung up. He wondered what she was thinking now, if she was feeling as bad as he was, but it was better this way, less hurt, less complications. He suspected she'd go back to the States earlier than scheduled, now she knew there was no chance of persuading him to sign. In a way he hoped she would, as he knew the temptation to call her over the next few days was only going to get stronger.

Swivelling his chair back to the window, he got up and sliding his hands in his pockets, stared down at the river below. Minute after minute ticked by as he stood there reflecting on the past twenty-four hours and how he was going to handle the next. He felt so bad about Sandy and the way he had treated her that he wondered if he should take her out tonight in an effort to make up for it. But then he reminded himself that he had already put her in Ellen's place once and look where it had got him, so he'd be crazy to do it again. And cruel, for he knew how much it would mean to her, while all it would be to him was some kind of penance.

He was sorry for his antipathy, but there was no point pretending he felt anything for her when the truth of it was he'd fire her right now if he could, just to get her out of his life. Not that it would get her off his conscience, of course, if anything she'd probably weigh even heavier, but it might be better than having to see her and deal with her every day. God-damn it, it was why he had the rule about no relationships in the office, to avoid exactly this kind of mess. And OK, he was a coward too, he didn't want to face her, but what the hell kind of a bastard would he be if he were actually looking forward to telling her that all she had been was a one-night stand?

'Confucius, he say, when man look out of window he run out of luck.'

Laughing, Michael turned to Zelda who was closing the door behind her. 'But not out of gin,' he said.

Zelda looked amazed. 'Did you just read my mind?' she exclaimed.

Michael was still grinning. 'No, but I think you read mine,' he responded.

Zelda's eyebrows made a sardonic arch. 'Not difficult when I see you standing there like that,' she told him. 'Is it personal or professional? No, don't tell me, it has to be personal, because personal always gets you to the window. Professional just gets you mad. So let me

246

see, where does that lead me? To last night and Ellen Shelby? Don't tell me she turned you down.'

'You're right, she did,' he answered, not wanting to do Ellen the disservice of telling anyone it was more the other way round. 'But it's not about Ellen,' he said. 'It's about Michelle.'

'Oh.' Zelda's expression was instantly grave, for she knew that he never mentioned Michelle unless it was serious and only then if he had to. 'Have you heard from her?' she asked, sitting in a visitor's chair as he leant back against the window-sill.

He shook his head. 'Not from her, from Cavan,' he answered. 'He called this morning, from Rio.'

'Where Michelle is,' Zelda added unnecessarily.

Michael nodded.

'So what did he say?' Zelda prompted, when he showed no sign of enlarging.

Michael's eyes came back to hers. 'As a matter of fact he didn't mention her,' he responded. 'But I know Cavan and I know when he's holding back.'

'And you think it's Michelle he's holding back about?'

'I know it is,' he answered, 'because there's nothing else he'd have a problem mentioning. And he was definitely trying to tell me something.'

Zelda looked perplexed. 'So what was he saying, exactly?' she asked.

Michael shrugged. 'He just kept telling me it was all right, he's taking care of things and he thinks I ought to know but isn't sure he's the one who should tell me.'

'But he doesn't say what it is?'

'No. I asked, obviously, but all he says is that I probably already know and he's just making a mountain out of a molehill.'

'Do you think he's trying to tell you Michelle's involved with another man?' Zelda asked bluntly.

247

Michael laughed. 'I hope she is by now,' he answered. 'It's been a long time.'

Zelda's expression showed how unconvinced she was by that, but she passed no comment. 'So what are you going to do?' she asked.

'I don't see there's anything I can do,' he responded.

Zelda didn't even hesitate. 'Except call Michelle and ask her what's going on.'

His eyes were suddenly harsh and Zelda's heart went out to him, for she of all people knew what it would cost him to do that.

'It's been a long time for you too, Michael,' she said gently.

'She knows where I am.'

'So do you know where she is.'

Michael's eyes dropped to the floor and Zelda knew she'd hit home. But she'd done it many times in the past and he had yet to act on it, so she had no faith that he would now. She wished to God he would, though, for the pain and guilt he'd carried with him these past few years had to come to an end one day. If it didn't, then Zelda just couldn't see how he was going to get on with his life, for no matter how many women he met, she knew he was never going to let any one of them come close. The sad thing was that for a while there she had thought maybe Ellen Shelby could be the one, but obviously she wasn't, which was a great shame, for a new life in another country could be just what Michael needed. Not with Ted Forgon as the puppetmaster, though, Zelda had to agree that, but to fall in love and let go of the past was very definitely something Michael needed to do. Although, were she in his position, she wondered if she'd be any better at moving on than he was. She doubted it, in fact she imagined she'd be a whole lot worse.

'I was thinking about asking Sandy to join us at the opera tonight,' he said.

Zelda's astonishment couldn't have been greater. 'You were?' she said.

Michael laughed wryly. 'You can invite her,' he said, 'as a reward for getting off to a great start as an assistant. Have you seen Janey's and Diana's turnover for this month?'

'No,' Zelda said warily, 'but it's obviously impressive if you're inviting Sandy to the opera.'

'I'm not, you are,' he reminded her.

Zelda was watching him closely. 'If I didn't know better,' she said, 'I'd say there's more to this than a simple reward.'

'But you do know better,' he told her, and pushing himself away from the window ledge he took his coat from the stand and started out of the office.

At that moment he had no real idea of where he was going, though the name of Ellen's hotel was emblazoned on his mind, as was the mistake he had just made about Sandy and the opera. But he knew he wouldn't go to Ellen, any more than he'd go to Sandy. And right now it was hard to care about either of them when the memory of Michelle and what they had together had been brought so painfully back into focus. What he needed to know, however, was whether Cavan really was trying to tell him something, or if he was just using that as an excuse to be back in touch with her?

He drove and didn't stop until finally he reached the south coast, where the wind was chopping at the waves and the sun was beating down on the barren cliffs. It was no real surprise to find himself there, for it was where he and Michelle had said their final goodbye. But coming back to the place wasn't going to turn back the clock, nor was it going to eliminate the guilt that time had only intensified rather than lessened. Through the sough of the waves and the cry of the wind he could hear her voice echoing softly in his ears, telling him she was going, and as the pain flooded his heart he wondered bitterly why he was searching for an excuse to call her, when he already had one that not only gave him the right to speak to her morning, noon and night should he care to, but to force her to come back to England too.

He wouldn't use it, though, for the sin was as much his as it was hers and no matter how much love there was between them they had chosen their paths and it was too late now to turn back, or to forgive. But Cavan's call had unnerved him and he just hoped to God that she was all right, because Rio was a dangerous place and ... He stopped, knowing that if he wanted to keep his sanity then he mustn't even begin to go down that road, for there were times, like now, when her death seemed like it might be the only way out of this hell.

Chapter 14

The drums, just like the city traffic outside, were getting louder and increasingly frantic, as Michelle crossed the crowded play yard of the São Martinho Shelter for Street Children towards the main gates. Locked deep in the heart of downtown Rio, at the foot of the high white Lapa Arches, the shelter wasn't only a refuge for the starving and homeless, but a centre for culture, dance and education. As usual her progress was slow, for she was constantly assailed by children wanting to show or tell something, or draw her into the game they were playing. She stopped for a while to admire the painting three eight-year-olds were daubing on the high grey stone wall surrounding the yard. Then, hearing shrieks of laughter behind her she turned and burst out laughing too as Cavan, who was attempting to take part in the *capoeira* workshop, began cart-wheeling around the yard, back-flipping and swinging his legs in dangerously high arcs in imitation of the twelve- and thirteen-year-old experts. Actually, he wasn't too bad, though he certainly lacked the grace most of them were blessed with and, as Michelle took the *pandeiro* – tambourine – from little Maria and began banging it wildly, the entire yard rang out with laughter at the way Cavan launched into a hectic routine all his own.

Loving him for the way he had become so involved with the children and gave them such pleasure with his craziness and kindness, Michelle caught him as he rotated clumsily into her arms, then delighted them all by planting a kiss on his lips, before handing the *pandeiro* back to Maria and continuing on to the reception hut that was just inside the gates. It was the recreation hour, just before lunch, when the children got to do whatever they wanted, before returning to lessons or craft shops or the various tasks they had been assigned by Sister Lydia and Senhor Roberto.

She was on the point of entering the hut when she noticed Tania, the thirteen-year-old mother of a mentally retarded baby, standing alone behind the fraying goal net gazing up at the arches that crossed the busy street outside. The doctor who held surgeries at the shelter four times a week had informed Sister Lydia just that morning that both Tania and her baby were HIV positive. Michelle wondered if anyone had broken the news to Tania yet. It was possible, given the way the girl was swaying from side to side and hugging her frail little body. But it wasn't unusual to find her like this, standing slightly apart from the others and seeming to be reaching out for something only she knew was there.

As Michelle walked up to her, she turned her lovely young face from the sun and smiled into Michelle's eyes. '*Bonita*,' she said, reaching up to touch Michelle's face.

Michelle smiled, took her hand and held it. '*Tudo bem?*' she said softly. Are you all right?

Tania's liquid dark eyes dilated slightly and seemed to be filling with an emotion Michelle doubted she would ever understand.

'Where's the baby?' Michelle asked in Portuguese.

Tania pointed towards the three-storey building that housed the shelter's workrooms, canteen, surgery and offices. The dormitories were scattered about the district in decrepit old houses that were kept as comfortable and clean as their meagre funds allowed. '*Con doutar*,' she answered. With the doctor. 'We have AIDS,' she added in Portuguese. 'Does that mean we are going to die? Alfonso said it does.'

Michelle's heart contracted, for in the eyes of this child mother was an uncertain intelligence and a need for understanding that circumstances could only deny. She had been abandoned by her own family when she was only seven years old, had lived on the streets since then, stealing, begging, running drugs and prostituting herself until Antônio, one of the street educators from São Martinho, had found her, eight months pregnant, barely clothed, unfed for days, unwashed for weeks and sleeping under a lorry.

Michelle's Portuguese wasn't up to dealing with this, but nevertheless she tried, until finally Tania grew bored and drifted back across the yard to go and find her baby. All that really mattered to the child now was that she had something to eat, somewhere to sleep and people around her who would care for her to the end. After all, what was the sense in wanting to go on living when all life was ever going to offer her was more of the misery and terror she had known out there on the streets?

With those words still echoing in her mind, Michelle turned back to the hut and let herself quietly inside. The room was small, but light and airy, and the large open window looked out on to the yard where the Afro-Brazilian dancing continued, though Cavan was now undergoing football instruction from a group of ten-year-old fanatics. As Michelle went to sit at the table Andréa, a beautiful and dedicated Brazilian lawyer, looked up and smiled a greeting. With Andréa was Márcio, a lanky, fifteen-year-old boy who had sought refuge at the shelter two nights ago and young

Antônio, one of the shelter's most popular educators, who had grown up on the streets himself. Right now Antônio and Andréa were in the process of persuading Márcio to stay a while longer at the shelter – it was an argument they were likely to win, for as uncool as it might seem to the teenager to be in here hanging out with a bunch of dumb kids, the alternative, Antônio had discovered, was to go back out there and face almost certain death from the drug dealers who had declared him past his prime.

Michelle listened quietly, her blonde head bent in concentration, her exquisite features drawn as she struggled to understand the language. She was learning fast, but was still no match for Tom Chambers, the American journalist she had met in Sarajevo who had talked her into coming here. It hadn't been a hard decision to make, for she'd heard a great deal about the atrocities in Brazil, the children who were terrorized, tortured and executed by death squads who were paid by wealthy Brazilians to clean up the streets and make the city safe for people to live in. As if the children themselves didn't qualify as people. No one knew for sure how many death squads there were, but that they were military policemen acting both on- and off-duty was a well-documented fact. And it was one death squad in particular that Chambers was aiming to expose, for it was an élite force of a dozen or more men, mostly active policemen, who were boosting their meagre incomes by working for Pedro Pastillano, an ex-army colonel. Pastillano was now one of Rio's most prominent businessmen and a self-publicizing philanthropist, who not only employed his own *grupo de extermínio*, but was reported to have a private prison known as the 'Inferno' somewhere outside the city where young boys were taken to be beaten, brutalized, sometimes raped and often killed. There was even,

254

some said, a graveyard nearby, where the dead bodies were dumped.

Had Pastillano not decided to run for state governor, he might never have come to Chambers's attention, but he had and now Chambers was out to get the man in much the same way he had gone for the murdering soldiers of the Serbian army. Thanks to him, more than three hundred men were now facing trial for the crimes they had committed during a war that had been so bloody and senseless that the world could still not comprehend it. He'd had to leave the country fast, for there was a price on his head and too many were eager to claim it. Michelle had been ready to go too, for her friend, Cara Rejisto, a young primary school teacher whom she had found being raped by a group of drunken soldiers in front of her class of eight-year-olds, had been desperate to get her own children away from the madness and terror that had already claimed her husband and torn their lives apart.

Rio de Janeiro, with all its poverty, crime and corruption, might not have been the perfect answer for Cara and her young family, but when Michelle had explained what she was going to do there, Cara hadn't even hesitated. Exposing a monster like Pastillano would be dangerous for Michelle, very dangerous indeed, for the reason Chambers wanted her with him was to help get as many depositions as they could from those who had managed to survive Pastillano's Inferno. Chambers had watched Michelle at work in Sarajevo; he had seen how men and women alike were ready to trust her, to give her information they would never even tell their confessors and Michelle had never let any one of them down. In every case he knew of she had got the family to safety, often at even greater risk to her own life than to theirs.

Now Chambers wanted her to do the same in Rio, for Pastillano had to be brought down, or the *favelas* –

slums – of Rio de Janeiro would almost certainly become the death camps of Latin America. As it was, armed police raided them nightly, firing randomly at the boarded-up windows and makeshift shelters that the dwellers pathetically called home. Many bullets found human targets, but few ever complained – in this town justice was for the rich, not the poor. Not even when small children were forced into canals of raw sewage and left there to drown, did anyone speak out – if they did, older children would mysteriously vanish and parents would be told that if they didn't pay six hundred *reais* by Friday 'something would happen'. It was impossible for a *favelado* to find so much money, unless he borrowed from the drug dealers, who would then use his son as an errand boy and probably end up killing him anyway.

There were so many terrible things going on in this city that even after five months of being here, Michelle was still learning of new and horrific methods of torture and killing. Already she knew of more than a hundred cases that had never come to trial and probably never would. The police acted with impunity, because they were tried by their own courts and because the rich still naively believed that the only way to deal with the poor was to kill them – especially if they were black.

Andréa Sabino, the Brazilian lawyer who was sitting at the table now, was a rare exception to the rule of rich ignorance and assumed supremacy, for not only did she come from one of the wealthiest families in Brazil, she had also married into another. Though neither her husband nor her father particularly approved of her work at the shelter, neither tried to stop her, nor did they object to the frequent and generous donations she made. They drew the line, however, at her becoming involved in any kind of legal action that would draw unwanted attention to the families. That didn't stop

Andréa giving out free legal advice to those who needed it, nor from directing the needy and oppressed to lawyers who could and would get involved.

It was thanks to Andréa that Michelle was now living in a spacious hillside villa overlooking the ocean at Barra da Tijuca, just ouside Rio centre. The exclusive, forested *domaine* in which the villa sat was part of a private community protected by security guards and cut off from the city's rampant crime and pollution, so was perfect for Cara and the children. It also provided Michelle with much the same kind of appearance as Andréa, that of a rich woman with too much time on her hands who had decided to meddle with the poor. Tom Chambers approved of the image, for the less attention Michelle attracted to herself the better it would be for them all, particularly as he was often away. His agenda entailed frequent visits to other cities in Brazil where a Human Rights Watch director was documenting the numerous nationwide atrocities, and Chambers was filing the stories to the domestic as well as international press. His interest in Pastillano took precedence, though, it was just that he was forced to earn a living whereas, being more or less financially independent, Michelle was able to stay put in Rio and act as his person on the ground there.

Now, Michelle watched and listened as Andréa and Antônio continued to sell Márcio on all the advantages of him staying here at the shelter. The boy's scrawny limbs were thrown loosely over his chair in a kind of two-fingered gesture. His arrogance was outmatched only by his disdain for the shelter and the people in it, but no one was fooled, for they had all, including Michelle, witnessed enough fear in this room to recognize the many defences it hid behind. Sweat was pouring down the boy's pale-brown face, hostility glittered in his jaundiced eyes and curled his cracked lips, but the desperation in his heart was as palpable as

257

the dense humidity in the air. He liked to think he was a man, but in truth he was still just a child.

A sudden commotion out in the yard caused them all to look round and going to the window Michelle called out to Alfonso, a mischievous and horribly scarred fourteen-year-old, to ask what all the laughing was about. His answer started Michelle, Andréa and Antônio laughing too, for Flávio, the monkey-faced boy whom Antônio a couple of months ago had caught stealing from a trader's stall, had just been allowed by Sister Lydia to choose his birthday. That obviously meant that no family or records had been traced for the boy. Not surprisingly, Flávio had chosen today, for everyone got a cake on their birthday and a trip to the movies with Antônio and a friend of their choosing.

'Obviously the results of his bone analysis have come back,' Andréa commented, tucking a few stray strands of her glorious ebony hair into the knot at the nape of her neck.

'So, how old are those old bones?' Antônio called out, as Flávio came grinning up to the window.

'Eleven,' Flávio announced proudly. 'Want to come to the movies?' he said to Márcio.

Márcio started, then his large brown eyes looked at the monkey face warily, before he shifted his gaze to Antônio and shrugged.

Antônio, who had once undergone the same bone analysis to find out his age, shrugged too.

'How old are you, Antônio?' a little pale-skinned girl with wiry pigtails and gappy teeth called out cheekily.

'The same age as you,' he answered with a wink.

'He's twenty,' someone informed her.

'No he's not, he's a hundred!' squealed a dusty-haired little boy whose mother had abandoned him on the street after his stepfather had started beating him.

With the constant roar of traffic outside, the incessant hooting of horns, squealing of breaks and excited chatter of children, it was hard to keep up with what was being said, though even before Andréa nudged her Michelle had spotted Cavan over by the shelter's Volkswagen Combi, trying to fend off the amorous attentions of a brazen Cristiana. The fourteen-year-old prostitute came in regularly each month, stayed for the duration of her period, then went back to the streets. It was the only way she got to eat for that week, as her pimp only fed her when she was earning.

Michelle and Andréa hooted with laughter at Cavan's desperate lunge towards an approaching Sister Lydia, and Michelle silently marvelled at out how happy and light-hearted everyone seemed, despite the untold tragedy of their lives. Watching them now, it would be hard to make an outsider believe the ordeals these children had been through, the hardships they still knew, the fear and despair that descended upon them as cruelly as the aspirations and dreams that stole in with the night and magicked them to far-away lands and fairy tale lives just like any other child in the world.

With Márcio's acceptance of Flávio's offer the meeting in the hut broke up, for it was the shelter's policy to tread as lightly and undemandingly as possible. The children were all free to come and go as they pleased, which in many cases meant they stayed. There were only three rules: no violence, no arms and no drugs. They were also greatly encouraged to take a bath before breakfast each morning and change their clothes at least every three days. Michelle often reflected how good it would be for people in richer countries to see the old clothing they sent being handed out to those who had none. If they could see it she was sure they would give more, for they would know then that their gifts really did get through.

After a rowdy lunch of black beans, chicken and rice she went off for her usual hilarious Portuguese lesson with Andréa and a group of eight-year-olds who were as bent on teaching her street slang as Andréa was on preparing them for school. Later they all went down to the yard, where Flávio was sharing out his cake and Sister Lydia was breaking the good news to Maria that someone in a place called Yorkshire in England had just 'adopted' her. Maria was ecstatic, mainly because Michelle and Cavan were English, so England was her favourite place in the entire world and where she was going to go when she was sixteen.

Much later that day, as she rested her arms on the scratched, wrought-iron balcony that hugged the window of Cavan's eighth-floor apartment in Leme, Michelle was still thinking about Maria. The child had been so happy to know that she had 'parents' now whom she might never meet, but it didn't matter. They might send her a Walkman, or some trainers, or things for her hair, the way other parents did for their 'adopted' kids. If only people knew how little it took to change a child's life, to really make a difference. Yet it was up to Brazil to change too, to get one of the world's most violent police forces under control and start sharing the country's enormous wealth and resources with those who needed it most. And maybe, just maybe, what she and Tom and Cavan were doing here was going to move the possibility of that change a little closer to reality.

Sighing to her herself, she gazed down at the narrow, busy street below. She stopped off here most afternoons on her way home to the villa, glad of an hour's respite from children and always in need of a refreshing *caipirinha* made with iced vodka and crushed limes. Occasionally Tom Chambers would meet her here, but most often it was a private time for her and Cavan.

Taking a generous sip of her drink, she watched the bustling activity below. As usual, yellow taxis were weaving and hooting a route through the clutter of market stalls which toted anything from great, huge slabs of beef to cheap T-shirts and dresses, to plastic toys and scarred fruit. The motion was constant, as crippled pedestrians, cyclists and stray dogs clogged up the street, while the insistent blare of heavy metal vibrated from the music shop half a block down. The cracked and decaying façades of the towering apartments confronted each other across the narrow, hot space where the air seemed never to move and in the distance, glimpsed through the dancing shimmer of heat, the teaming swell of the Atlantic threw itself wantonly over the Copacabana beach.

'What are you thinking about?' Cavan asked, from where he was lying on the bed.

Michelle inhaled deeply, gave a sleepy murmur and turned to look up at the mountains that rose in timeless splendour from the heart of the city's mayhem. 'Oh, lots of things,' she answered.

Cavan watched her, a single dark-blue sheet covering his nudity, a fast overhead fan cooling the sweat on his matted chest. She was wearing a long, diaphanous robe and her shining blonde hair hung loosely down her back. The late-afternoon sun was so bright he could see the willowy outline of her figure through the robe she was wearing and kept at his apartment. Her high, narrow hips, superb long legs and wide, angular shoulders all looked so perfect to him. She often claimed she looked better in clothes, but Cavan disagreed, for to him, besotted as he was, she could never be anything other than completely beautiful, no matter how she was dressed. Though it was the very beauty he adored and the kind of elusiveness he was being subjected to, that fed his insecurity and turned him from the crazy, try-anything *gringo* at the shelter into the nervous and angry young man he was now.

'Are you thinking about Michael?' he asked querulously.

Michelle glanced at him over her shoulder and he flushed. Her wide green eyes were laughing, seeming almost to mock him and remind him of his youth. She turned away again, leaving the imprint of her incredible mouth with its slender though shapely lips and perfect white teeth burning in his eyes, as the jealousy burned in his heart. He moved restlessly and bit down hard on his frustration. It didn't seem to make any sense, but he felt closer to her when they were at the shelter, dealing with the kids, or at her villa playing with the children there, than he did when they were alone. It was as though, when the sounds of childish laughter and tears receded and a veil was drawn over the unselfish love and commitment, another woman emerged – a woman whose spirit was locked somewhere beyond his reach.

'Are you?' he persisted, unable to stop himself.

Michelle sighed and leaving the balcony walked over to the cheap vinyl chest where he kept his clothes. Sitting on it, she crossed her legs and holding her glass out in front of her, said, 'I'm always thinking about Michael. Whether consciously or unconsciously, he is always in my mind. You know that.'

It wasn't the answer Cavan wanted and turning his head away he stared moodily at the wall.

After a while Michelle got up and returned to the balcony.

'I spoke to him. Yesterday,' Cavan told her.

Michelle looked down the street to where a rowdy game of dice was being played on the pavement. 'How is he?' she asked.

Cavan's heart thumped on the pain as ignoring the question he said, 'I wanted to tell him about us.'

Michelle turned to look at him, then, coming to sit on the edge of the bed she reached for his hand. 'Darling,' she said softly, 'Michael and I are linked in a way neither of us will ever be able to break. Nor will we ever try. You know that, so why torture yourself like this?'

'Because I love you,' he said angrily. 'I love you and I want you to stop.'

She waited a moment, then said, 'Stop what? Loving Michael, or doing what I'm doing here?'

'Both.'

She smiled and bringing his hand to her mouth she kissed it. 'I can't do either,' she told him, 'but what I can do is love you too.'

He stared up at her as her eyes roamed his dark, brooding expression, then came to rest on his mouth. 'Do you see Michael when you look at me?' he challenged. 'Is that why you avoid my eyes?'

Michelle laughed. 'It's impossible not to see Michael when I look at you,' she answered, 'but that doesn't mean I'm not seeing you too.'

'And when we make love? Are you with him, or are you with me?'

'I love you too much for that,' she said, the humour dying in her eyes. 'But you're Michael's brother and you love him as much as I do, so he'll always be with us, Cavan. You have to accept that, just as I have to accept that one day you'll leave me for a younger woman.'

'Never,' he swore.

She smiled, then laughed. 'I'll be thirty-seven next birthday,' she reminded him. 'That makes me fifteen years older than you.'

'And four years older than Michael.'

'Four is hardly fifteen,' she said wryly. 'But what we have is very special to me and though I'd like to think it could last I know . . .'

'Stop,' he cried, snatching at her wrist and bending her arm back. 'It *will* last. I'm staying with you and if you move on to somewhere else after this then I'm moving on with you. I told you, right at the beginning, that I want to become a part of what you do. It's in me too, you know that. I feel the same things you feel. I want to help these people too.'

'Then why did you call Michael?' she asked.

He looked long into her eyes and she could see, almost feel, the troubled depths of his mind.

'You think he can stop what I'm doing here, don't you?' she whispered, touching her fingers to his cheek.

'I'm afraid for you,' he confessed. 'What you do at the shelter, is one thing, but what you're planning with Tom ...'

'I thought you were with us,' she said.

'I am. At least I'm with Tom. I just don't think you should be involved. It's too dangerous. You've got too much to lose and if Michael were to find out ...'

'This isn't Michael's decision,' she interrupted.

He looked as though he wanted to argue that, but instead he said angrily, 'There was a shooting in the *favela* you were at yesterday. Did you know that? The police went in and shot two innocent people stone dead.'

Her eyes suddenly widened with understanding. 'And you think that it was someone being punished for talking to me and Tom,' she said.

His eyes bored into hers. 'Actually, what I was thinking,' he said, 'was that it could have been you. But OK, yes, what about the people you're talking to Have you thought about the danger you're putting them in? And how do you know that yesterday's shooting wasn't some kind of warning, letting them all know what'll happen to them if they talk?'

'The shooting yesterday happened before Tom and I got there, not after, so it had nothing to do with us. In fact, Antônio told me today that it was drug related. The dealers in that particular *favela* were refusing to give the police a cut. And as we already know, the

264

police really don't care who they kill to make their point.'

'But you shouldn't be going in there with Tom,' he reminded her. 'The deal was, you go in with Antônio, as a goodwill worker, or whatever you want to call it. Not as a journalist, or anything else that could pose some kind of threat to the police, or more importantly, Pedro Pastillano.'

'It was a one-off,' she answered, 'and Antônio was with us. And as for the danger we're putting people in, you know very well that no one is being forced to talk to us. In fact, you're as aware as I am that we don't have anything in writing yet, nor have we found anyone who's actually been arrested or imprisoned by Pastillano's private force. All we have for now is hearsay, but we're getting closer all the time. In fact, Tom might have an ex-member of the death squad who's prepared to talk; if he does then maybe that's all we'll need.'

Cavan looked away, angry that he had been deprived of the last word. Michelle turned his face back to hers and widened her eyes imploringly. But, determined not to be won over, Cavan said, 'Does Michael know what you're using his guilt money for?'

Michelle's eyes darkened. 'There are no conditions attached to that money,' she reminded him.

Cavan gave a snort of derision, but as he started to speak the buzzer sounded announcing Tom Chambers's arrival. By the time he travelled the eight floors to the apartment both Cavan and Michelle were dressed. It wasn't that Chambers didn't know about their affair, but the apartment was so small it didn't feel quite decent to flaunt it in his face with dressing gowns and hastily covered thighs.

As he came in through the front door Michelle felt her heart tighten – not with attraction, though God knew he was a good-looking man, but with apprehension for the troubled look in his deep-set grey eyes.

'Chavés has disappeared,' he declared, as Cavan handed him a Scotch.

Cavan looked at Michelle for clarification.

'Julio Chavés,' she explained. 'The ex-member of Pastillano's death squad.'

Cavan turned back to Chambers. 'Since when?' he asked.

'Since Pastillano sent for him this morning,' Chambers answered, dashing a hand through his dishevelled dark hair. His handsome, beard-roughened face was pale with exhaustion, his clothes were crumpled and his imposing physique was taut with frustration.

Michelle looked at him and knew that ordinarily she would have found this man irresistible. But the more she got to know him, the more, in his character if not in his looks, he reminded her of Michael. And she, so he had told her, was too much like Rachel, the woman he had loved and still longed for every day. So they had agreed a long time ago never to muddy their relationship with futile attempts to take more from the other than platonic love and friendship.

'Did you manage to get from him the whereabouts of the Inferno?' she asked.

Chambers shook his head. 'I spoke to him for all of two minutes on the phone last night,' he answered. 'All he said was he'd meet me today at three to tell me what I wanted to know, in exchange for safe passage for him and his wife out of Brazil. When he didn't show I called his wife and she told me Pastillano sent someone for him this morning.' He drained his glass, then looked at Michelle. 'We won't see him again,' he said bluntly, 'nor will his wife.'

'Is she safe?' Michelle asked.

He nodded. 'She knows nothing and even if she did, her husband disappearing the way he has is enough to keep her silent.' He looked at Cavan for a moment, then, lowering his head he pressed his fingers to his eyes, as though to rub out the blur of tiredness. 'There was a message,' he said, looking at them again.

Michelle frowned. 'Message?'

'For me,' he elaborated, 'from Senhor Pastillano himself. Oh, he didn't sign it, he didn't even lay claim to it, but it's from him all right,' he went on, when both Cavan and Michelle looked incredulous. 'He left word with Teresa Chavés, advising me to leave Rio by the end of the week and take you two with me. In other words no one is fooled by your charity work.'

Michelle's eyes flashed. 'We're British and United States citizens,' she declared. 'He can't threaten us.'

Cavan glanced at her.

'Our nationality provides only a certain protection,' Chambers informed her. 'You've got to remember, these men are experts at making executions look like accidents or shoot-outs. If they need to kill us they will, don't make any mistake about that.'

'You're surely not thinking of going,' Michelle demanded hotly.

'Me, no,' Chambers answered. 'But I want you to think hard about what we're up against here so you can make your own decisions whether you stay or go.'

'There's no question, we're staying,' Michelle declared.

Cavan looked at her again, but Chambers was already speaking. 'Then we're going to have to take certain precautions,' he said, 'starting with Cara and the children out at the villa.'

Ted Forgon looked up from the report in front of him and fixed Ellen with sharp, baleful eyes. 'What's this?' he said, gesturing to the half-page of typewritten notes. 'I send you over to London for two weeks and you come back with this! Is it some kind of joke?'

267

'No,' Ellen replied shortly. She was standing in front of his desk, her hands clenched loosely in front of her. She'd arrived back in LA three days ago while Forgon was out of town, so this was the first time she'd seen him and in truth she was glad to be getting it over with, for the suspense had been almost as bad as the embarrassment she still felt for the way she'd handled things in London. God only knew what Michael McCann thought of her now, all she knew was that she couldn't stop thinking about him.

'So you went out to dinner with the guy, repeated the offer and when he said no you left? Is that right?' Forgon asked. 'I mean, this is what it says here.' His incredulity was struggling with his anger and for the moment winning.

'That's what happened,' she answered.

Forgon dropped the report on his desk and, sitting back in his chair, he steepled his fingers and looked at her. 'I take it you're going to try again,' he said.

Ellen shook her head. 'It's a waste of time,' she replied frankly. 'He's not going to come, no matter what you offer him.'

Forgon's face tightened. 'If I'd taken no for an answer every time I got it I'd be out there picking strawberries on Knotts Berry Farm,' he said darkly.

Ellen didn't respond.

His temper suddenly broke. 'What the hell's gotten into you?' he demanded. 'You see the man once, he tells you no way and you get up and walk like the movie's over. Did you hear anything I said before you went?'

'I heard everything,' Ellen answered, her cheeks flushing as she dropped her eyes for a moment. God only knew if she had the nerve for this, but Matty was right, he stood to gain nothing from publishing those pictures and if there wasn't anything in it for him there didn't seem any reason to do it. So all she could do

268

now, providing her courage held out, was try calling his bluff.

'Then I suggest you get yourself back out there and work a bit harder,' he growled, "cos you haven't only lost twenty grand here, Ellen, you're fast losing my respect too. Jesus Christ! Call yourself an agent! When did you ever pull off a deal by walking out at the first hurdle?'

'But it isn't the first hurdle,' she reminded him. 'You've sent three other agents over there and the answer's always the same. And now I'm telling you even if you send fifty-three it's never going to change.'

'Then you get the fuck back over there and make it change!' he shouted.

'He won't work for *you*!' Ellen shouted back. 'And face it, would you, if you were him? You keep saying how smart he is, so why do you think he's going to be dumb enough to sell out to you when he knows all you're after is destroying him?'

'Jesus Christ! Did you tell him that?' Forgon blustered.

'Of course not. I didn't have to, he can work these things out for himself. So even if I went down on my knees and begged him, he'll never give you what you want.'

'Then maybe you should consider doing something else while you're down there on your knees,' he suggested, his eyes glittering with malice.

'Oh for God's sake!' she spat. 'If you think all it would take to change his mind is a blow job then you're losing it, Ted.'

'No! It's you who's losing it,' he told her. 'Because if I put those pictures to press you can kiss goodbye to all the credibility you built up in this town, 'cos Ingall doesn't screw clever women, everyone knows that.'

'Wrong, he did,' Ellen shot back.

Forgon laughed nastily. 'You're so smart you got

yourself photographed nuddy and didn't even know it,' he reminded her. 'Now, like I said, get yourself back over there to London and work on McCann until he gives us what we want.'

'Then I'll need to apply for British residency,' she said, her face drawn with anger, 'because a visa waiver won't be long enough.'

'Save the wisecracks for your folks when you try explaining how come their precious girl is getting poked by Clay Ingall in front of a camera,' he snarled.

Ellen paled. 'You said you didn't have any copies of the polaroids,' she said quietly.

Forgon's eyes narrowed as he smirked. 'Ellen,' he said, 'the gods have been smiling on you these past few years. You been out there swimming about with the sharks, like the little angelfish you are and you never even caught so much as a cold. My, have you been blessed. Now why do you think that is? Oh, you're smart – or at least you were – you know how to put a deal together and you know when to duck and when to dive. But you've never been out there when the waters get so rough you can't see who's coming at you any more. And that's just where you're heading when those pictures hit the news-stands and the results won't be pretty, let me tell you. So now, do as I say and start working on a new strategy to get McCann over here . . .'

'For God's sake, this is an obsession with you!' she cried. 'You're never going to get him! He doesn't trust you, he doesn't respect you and he sure as hell doesn't need you, so why don't you just let it go?'

Forgon's eyes bulged as his face turned purple with rage. 'I'm sorry,' Ellen jumped in quickly, fearing for his heart. 'I didn't mean to lose my temper, but I'm trying to make you understand that people are laughing at you out there, the way you keep going after McCann, then firing your best people when they don't come up with the goods. It's not him you're destroying, Ted, it's yourself. So please, before it's too late, let it go and get on with your life.'

Forgon's face was twitching as his fists clenched on the desk. 'If people are laughing at me out there,' he raged, 'then they're going to be laughing a whole lot louder at you when they see you ...'

'Then do it!' she shouted. 'Print them. I don't know what you'll gain from it, but I'm telling you it won't be McCann. In fact, as far as I can see the only thing you're going to get is an empty office on the third floor when I go.'

'Is that a threat?' he demanded.

'Of course it's not a threat!' she seethed. 'It's a fact. I can't stay here if you're going all out to humiliate me and ruin my reputation.'

He stared at her hard, watching her with his sharp, flinty eyes as his chest rose and fell with the exertion of his fury. She looked back, refusing to be cowed by a man whose obsession was making him as pathetic as his synthetic hair.

'You really don't think I'll do it, do you?' he said in the end.

Ignoring the question she said, 'I think you should know that McCann's offered me a job.'

Forgon's eyes opened wide with shock and for a moment, as his face turned purple again and saliva appeared at the corners of his mouth, Ellen was afraid she really had gone too far. 'So that's what all this is about,' he sneered. 'The bastard's done it again. I send you over there to screw him into coming and he screws you into staying.' He laughed bitterly. 'I had a bet with Manny that you and McCann would get it on ...'

'We didn't,' Ellen interrupted.

Forgon's surprise showed. 'So how come he offered you a job?' he said. 'No, no, don't tell me. He did it to piss me off. Well he's succeeded. And if you go, then

271

you better call up your folks now and warn 'em about the publicity coming their way.'

'I'm not going. I turned it down,' she answered. 'But not because I knew you'd threaten me, because I don't want to leave my country any more than McCann wants to leave his.'

'Well that's about the first sensible thing I've heard you say here today,' Forgon told her. 'Now I don't want to hear any more of this print-and-be-damned nonsense, 'cos in this game the dice never stop rolling and you'd do well to remember that. You got a great talent list, you're a name here in LA and when I finally vacate this seat it'll be to someone like you I'll be looking to take over. Yes,' he said, when he saw the shock register on her face, 'that's how highly I rate you. You still got a lot to learn, but you'll get there and when you do you'll be one of the most powerful women in Hollywood. That's what *I* can do for you. It's what I *want* to do for you.' He sat forward and fixed her with a look that made her skin prickle. 'But I can crush you too,' he said savagely. 'I can make it so that pretty butt of yours never hits another chair in this town or any other. Remember that, Ellen. Remember who gave you all the breaks, who got you the high-end talent and who keeps those waters still when the sharks start coming. You don't know the half of what this town's like, because you've never had to deal with the shit. I've made sure of that, just like I make sure you get all the good deals and the praise that goes with them. I've been there every step of the way for you, Ellen Shelby, and you didn't even know it. Well, I'm telling you now, so's you'll know better the next time you come in here telling me I'm a laughing-stock in my own town. I want McCann and I want him here in Hollywood. So you take yourself back to the drawing-board and get to work on a strategy that doesn't include walking out the first no you get. Do you hear me?'

Ellen's face was strained as the ignominy of his words fell like stones on her professional pride. 'I hear you,' she said tersely.

'Now get the hell out of here,' he grunted.

Five days later Ellen was preparing Sunday lunch for Matty, who had just returned from Mexico where she'd filmed a small part in an independent. It had come from an audition Ellen had set up before going to London and now, though she said nothing to Matty, Ellen couldn't help wondering whether it was Matty's talent that had got her the part, or if Ted Forgon had exercised his ubiquitous powers of persuasion. She despised him for the way he had claimed that she was nothing without him, that all her accomplishments had been nothing more than curtain calls while he staged the real performance somewhere behind the scenes. 'You know,' she said, stirring the gravy as Matty refilled their glasses with wine, 'if he didn't have those god-damned photographs I'd have told him there and then what he could do with his job and I'd be out there now, getting it together as a producer. Christ, I've got enough contacts and the man can't have a finger in every Hollywood pie. Can he?'

Matty pulled a face. 'When it comes to the power freaks running this town,' she said, 'anything's possible. A lot of them go back a long way and who ever knows who's done who a favour on the way up? But I just don't buy him being behind everything you do. OK, so he might have given you a few breaks, but there's just no way he's baby-stepping you through. Why would he, when there're dozens of people out there perfectly qualified to do your job? And besides, you don't need him to succeed when what you really want is to produce. If you wanted to be a hot-shot agent, then yeah, maybe you'd do well to stick with the

273

old goat, but if you ask me, I reckon it's time to get out of there and go for what you really want.'

'He's got copies of the polaroids,' Ellen reminded her.

'So he tells you,' Matty retorted. 'The truth is, the guy's running scared you're going to take up McCann's offer and make him look an even bigger jerk than he already does, hair notwithstanding. That's why he told you he's been cutting up the cake so's you get all the cream, so you'll start doubting yourself, the way you are now, when he knows damned well you're the best agent he's got. And sure, he'll probably put you in the chair at ATI when his heart finally gives out, but it's interesting he told you that after you told him about McCann's offer, don't you think? So see it for what it is, more incentive not to go to London, just like all that shit about sharks and angelfish and behind the scenes manoeuvring was meant to make you think you're incapable of pulling down a deal without him.' She shook her head incredulously. 'Talk about mind games, the sonofabitch makes Svengali look like Old Man Walton.'

Ellen laughed and reaching for a towel, lifted a crisp, sizzling chicken from the oven. 'OK, enough about Forgon,' she said, lowering the gas under the gravy. 'Tell me about Gene. How's it working out? Did he move in yet?'

Matty's lovely dark features melted into an exaggerated display of romance. 'Forsooth, he doth leave flowers on the pillow in the morn time so I'll find them when I get back at night,' she intoned soulfully. 'He writeth me poems and calleth me every day while I'm away. Can it be that the man is in love?'

Ellen's eyes were dancing with laughter. 'Are you serious?' she said. 'Does he really write you poems?'

'You can read them if you like,' Matty offered.

'And the flowers?'

'Red' roses, every day and I'm a sucker for it all. I mean, it works for me, this romance thing. I'm done with all that hard to get shit, or, "hey cookie, look at all this emotional baggage I'm bringing to our relationship and guess who's in the first suitcase: *my mother*!" Just give me a man who makes me feel like I'm the most special woman in the world and that there was never a life until he met me and honey, I'm there.'

Ellen was laughing. 'Is he working?' she asked.

'Yeah, as a matter of fact he's just got himself signed up as personal trainer to the cast of some bimbo-and-brawn movie they're shooting over at Paramount.'

'Good for him,' Ellen remarked. 'Does he get a part in it himself?'

'He might. Gee, that smells good, Ellen. Where are we eating, in here or out on the veranda?'

'I've put the parasol up, so we should be OK outside,' Ellen answered. 'If it gets too hot we'll just come back in. Did you bring your swim-suit so we can take a dip later?'

'Sure. Can I carry something through? Oh hell, does your phone never stop, even at weekends?'

'The machine's on,' Ellen informed her. 'I promised us a day together and I intend to honour the promise.'

Matty's eyes started to dance, but she said nothing until they were sitting down at the table ready to eat. 'Does the promise still stand if Michael McCann happens to call?' she asked nonchalantly.

Ellen's fork stopped in mid-air, then returned to her plate. 'There goes my appetite,' she said, waiting for her heart to settle.

'Sorry,' Matty apologized. 'So,' she said, taking a mouthful of food and starting to chew, 'did you call him yet?'

Ellen shook her head. 'There's no point,' she answered. 'He's not interested in the offer and I'll feel

275

such a god-damned idiot asking him again. It'll be like, does the woman have a hearing problem?'

'Would you be so reticent if you didn't fancy him?' Matty asked bluntly.

Ellen's eyes moved to hers. 'Maybe, maybe not,' she answered. 'It's hard to say. All I know is whatever happened that night we had dinner didn't get left behind when I walked out the door. It went back to the hotel with me and now it's come all the way home with me. I can't get him out of my mind and it's driving me nuts, especially when he couldn't have made it clearer that he wasn't interested in me. I mean, OK, he offered me a job, but when I turned it down, did he try to persuade me? Did he hell! Did he try to change my mind about going to Scotland? Did he come after me when I walked out? There was plenty of time for him to see me again before I left, but he didn't even call. And when I called him . . .' She stopped and shuddered. 'I don't even want to think about it I feel such a fool. I mean, he knew I was coming on to him, I'm sure of it, but he just told me to take care of myself and that was it. Or it should have been, but I had to go and tell him I'd buy him dinner if he was ever in LA and he didn't even answer. Oh God, I want to die.' She closed her eyes and groaned. 'It doesn't make any sense. Here I am, surrounded by the world's most gorgeous hunks and talented movie stars and I don't feel a thing. Five minutes with Michael McCann and I'm hotter than Sharon Stone on a good day, except I don't look that good. But you should have seen him, Matty. He's so gorgeous I swear you'd have thrown yourself at him too.'

'I did see him,' Matty reminded her. 'You had pictures of him all over this place before you went, so it beats me why you're so suprised you fancied him.'

'It went deeper than fancy,' Ellen said.

Matty's eyebrows rose.

'Don't mock me,' Ellen complained. 'You don't know how it feels to want someone that much and have him reject you.'

'There'll be a reason,' Matty assured her.

'Sure there's a reason, he didn't fancy me,' Ellen retorted.

'No? So why did he hold your hand and tell you there was nothing he wanted more than to make love to you?'

' "But",' Ellen reminded her. 'He added a but, which means he was probably only being polite because he could see I was on fire for him and he had to find some way of putting me out.'

Matty laughed. 'Well he wasn't very successful, was he?' she commented.

Ellen threw her a look, then, making an attempt on her meal she said, 'I wonder what he'd do if I called up and said I wanted to take the job?'

Matty's eyes flew open. 'Why, are you thinking about it?' she said.

Ellen shook her head. 'No, but I can fantasize, can't I?'

'Oh my God,' Matty murmured.

Ellen looked at her in surprise. 'What is it?' she said.

'You're going to London,' Matty stated. 'I can tell. You're working yourself up to leaving the States and going to London.'

'I am not,' Ellen laughed. 'I told you, it's just a fantasy.'

' "Nothing happens unless first a dream",' Matty quoted.

Ellen was sobered by that for a moment, but then, picking up her glass she stared down at the wine and began shaking her head. 'I could never leave the States,' she said. 'It would break my parents' hearts. And I'd miss you too much and all my friends and besides, I want to be a producer not an agent.'

'Couldn't you do that with him?'

Ellen scoffed. 'In England? You're kidding. Their entire film industry makes an independent here look bigger than Disney.'

'Exactly,' Matty said, not even trying to hide her relief. 'You belong here, not in London. So what you've got to do is precisely what Ted Forgon told you and work on how you're going to get him to Hollywood.'

Matty's words were still echoing in Ellen's ears when the following evening she sat staring down at that week's *Enquirer*. The headline read: ANOTHER NEW LOVE FOR CLAY? And the picture underneath was one of her, standing in an upstairs window at Clay's mansion wearing nothing more than the '*oops!*' the *Enquirer* had cleverly angled to cover her breasts and pubic hair. The shot was so badly focused that unless anyone already knew, it was impossible to tell it was her. But she knew, because Forgon had sent an E-mail to tell her that this was a warning not to doubt his word again.

'And if you're right,' his message had gone on to say, 'about everyone laughing at me out there, then I'm counting on you to go wipe the smile off their faces before the one on yours gets any clearer.'

'Oh Christ,' Matty murmured, clicking off Ellen's lap-top and going to sit at the dining-table with her. 'I swear I never thought he'd do it.'

'It's OK,' Ellen said. 'It's not your fault and to tell the truth I didn't really think he would either.'

'So what are you going to do now?' Matty asked after a pause.

Ellen shrugged. 'I've already put in a call to Michael McCann,' she said. 'His secretary tells me he's in France for a few days. Don't ask me if she's lying, because I don't have the faintest idea. She told me to call back at the end of the week if I haven't already heard from him.'

'Well that sounds quite positive,' Matty responded.

'In fact,' she added as the phone started to ring, 'that could be him now.'

Ellen laughed. 'It's four in the morning in France,' she said, walking over to the phone. 'Hello, this is Ellen Shelby,' she said into the receiver.

'*Bitch!*' a voice spat down the line.

Ellen started and looked at the phone.

'What is it?' Matty said, getting up as she saw Ellen's face pale.

'*Are you there, bitch!*' the voice demanded.

'Who is this?' Ellen stammered, her blood turning cold, for she was fairly certain she already knew.

'You know who it is,' Clay seethed, 'so quit the play-acting and tell me what the fuck all this is about in the paper?'

'Listen, I didn't know . . .'

'If this is your sick way of trying to bust up me and Karen,' he cut in, 'then you can forget it, right? We got something good going here and I'm not about to let you fuck it up by putting yourself out there like you're someone new in my life when all you are is fucking history. I don't know how you got that shot and I don't care, but if you got plans for any more to show up then I'm warning you now, I'll be coming after you,' and the line went dead.

Ellen's eyes were stricken as she turned them to Matty and replaced the receiver. 'I don't believe it,' she murmured. 'I don't believe what I just heard.'

'I take it that was Clay,' Matty said.

Ellen nodded as outrage along with a misguided hurt that he would protect Karen that way started to knot inside her. 'He's threatening to come after me if any more shots find their way into the papers,' she said, shaking her head in disbelief.

'You mean he thinks you were responsible?' Matty cried.

'That's what he said,' Ellen replied and covering her

face with her hands, she pushed her fingers hard back into her hair. 'This nightmare just goes on and on,' she said. 'First Forgon, now Clay. When is it ever going to end?'

'I wish I knew,' Matty answered, 'but what I do know is, the only person who can get you out of it is Michael McCann.'

Chapter 15

'OK! Aaaand, *action!*'

The First Assistant's arm swung down and as the camera started to track slowly along the street the strategically positioned extras began shopping or skateboarding or whatever else they had been directed to do. An instant later the two stars of the movie burst from a shop doorway, collided with a pair of stunt men, knocking one into the path of a speeding taxi, then raced on down the street. The whole thing took no more than a minute and as the director yelled cut everyone stopped where they were and waited to hear whether they were going again or moving on to the next shot.

Sandy and Nesta were standing at the edge of the set, behind the producers' and director's monitors, so were able to get a good look at the action, live as well as on screen. They hadn't been there long, but Nesta was already amazed by the way the cast and crew seemed to be making some sense out of the chaos. Between takes, jokes and insults were bandied about as freely as the coffees and cold drinks, and every time the camera stopped a clutch of make-up artists and dressers, grouped outside the costume trailers, took up their gossip where they'd left off.

Carl Roman, the lead actor who was making his big-screen début with this movie, was every bit as gorgeous in the flesh as he was in the BBC series that had made him famous. Starring with him was Libby Sherwood, one of Zelda's recent signings who had appeared in several successful features before. Nesta watched them as they strolled back down the street towards the director and wanted to pinch herself to make sure she wasn't dreaming.

'This is unbelievable,' she whispered to Sandy, her eyes riveted to Roman.

Receiving no reply, she turned to find Sandy in conversation with one of the producers and a friendly-looking woman dressed entirely in leather. To Nesta's surprise, Sandy seemed to be doing most of the talking while the others listened, nodded or shook their heads and genuinely appeared to be taking note of what she was saying. Nesta moved in closer to eavesdrop and blinked as she heard Sandy say, '. . . so I'm afraid there's just no way we can allow her to do that. It wasn't mentioned in the original script and even if she's prepared to do it I still can't give the go-ahead under the terms we negotiated.'

The producer glanced at the woman in leather, then said to Sandy, 'We're hoping to get the shot in the can today.'

'So let's talk,' Sandy said.

They appeared about to move off when someone called across the street, 'Hey! Sandy!'

Nesta turned and her mouth almost fell open when she saw Carl Roman heading their way. Sandy had told her that it was Roman himself who had issued the invitation to the set, but until now she hadn't really believed it. Harder still to credit was the way Sandy greeted him, as though he were any old friend she'd just happened to run into.

'Hi,' she said, going up on tiptoe to return Carl's embrace. 'How's it going?'

'Pretty good,' he answered, 'or so I'm told. I just

heard we're going in for close-ups so we've got time for a chat while they move the lights. Christ, it's hot out here,' he said, grabbing a glass of iced water from the tray a runner was passing with. 'Did you speak to Len Holton?' he said to Sandy. 'The guy who wrote the book we talked about?'

Sandy nodded. 'I called him yesterday. The rights are still available, so Craig's going to talk to his agent. I didn't mention anything about you, or the price will automatically skyrocket. By the way, you and Libby have invited Michael to dinner tonight, OK?'

Roman frowned. 'Have we?'

'Yes,' Sandy told him firmly. 'I left a message with Jodi earlier to tell him.'

Roman's eyes started to dance as he broke into a grin, but before he could say any more Sandy caught sight of Nesta and said, 'Listen, I need to sort something out with the producer. Can I introduce you to my friend Nesta Haines? She's a really *big* fan.'

Nesta threw Sandy a daggered look and blushed to the roots of her hair as Roman turned his famously sultry eyes in her direction and held out his hand. 'Hi, pleased to meet you Nesta,' he smiled.

'Pleased to meet you,' she replied faintly.

He appeared about to say more when to her combined relief and frustration his PA came running over with a mobile phone for him to take a call.

As he walked away Nesta looked around and saw Sandy standing apart from the mêlée, obviously discussing terms with the producer, while the director and the rest of the crew got things ready for the next shot.

They were at a quaint little shopping area somewhere in Wiltshire, with crowds gathering either end of the street, hoping to get a glimpse of Carl Roman and Libby Sherwood. Nesta was just loving being on the inside, even if she was only a visitor, and was beginning to understand now why Sandy was so taken with her job. It must feel really good having people like Carl Roman treat her like she was someone and be able to tell a producer what he could and couldn't do. In fact, if the truth be told, it was blowing Nesta's mind finding out what clout Sandy had and the way she handled it, with such confidence and efficiency, was forcing Nesta to see her with new eyes.

'Are you OK?' Sandy said, coming to join her again, a mobile phone pressed to her ear while an anxious-looking producer went in search of the director.

Nesta nodded. 'This is great,' she answered, unaware of how lovely and fresh she looked without her night-time make-up and costly designer clothes. In fact, she was dressed much like Sandy in faded denim jeans and sneakers, though whereas Sandy was wearing just a plain white T-shirt on top, Nesta had chosen a body-hugging number with a lace up-front and underwire cups. It had already earned her several appreciative glances from some of the crew, but as a couple of other women around the unit were dressed much the same way she didn't feel she was letting Sandy down. 'But did you have to tell Carl Roman I was such a *big* fan?' she hissed.

Sandy laughed and failing to make the connection, dialled the number again. 'Feed an actor's ego,' she said, 'it's the easy route to an easy life.' She winked. 'And who knows, maybe an easy lay.'

'Don't,' Nesta gasped, using a hand to fan herself. 'Anyway, I thought you said he was gay.'

'He is, but no one's supposed to know, so keep it under your hat. What do you think of the DOP? I saw him looking at you earlier.'

'DOP?' Nesta frowned.

'Director of Photography,' Sandy explained. 'The one in the red shirt and black shorts.'

Nesta looked over at the rank of shops opposite where the DOP was just emerging from the tailor's, a

284

couple of riggers and his operator in tow. 'Oh him,' she said. 'He's OK.'

Sandy laughed, for she had seen the way Nesta had responded to Dick earlier and unless she was mistaken Nesta had actually blushed. 'Different being a woman to being an escort, isn't it?' she said.

Nesta's eyes narrowed, letting her know she wasn't going to get into that. 'What are you doing now?' she asked. 'Who are you calling?'

Sandy glanced back over her shoulder. 'Sssh,' she said, putting a finger to her lips. 'I told the producer I had to check some details on Sophie's contract, but I'm actually calling my boss, Diana, to make sure the increase the producer's just offered for Sophie to do her own stunt is acceptable.'

Nesta screwed up her nose. 'Why don't you want the producer to know you're calling Diana?' she asked.

'Because it would weaken my position,' Sandy answered. 'He has to think I can take the decision myself or he won't treat me with the same respect.'

Nesta was impressed. 'You've really got this sussed, haven't you?' she remarked.

'Damn!' Sandy muttered as she got cut off again. She redialled, then, laughing she said, 'All I do is watch what the other agents do and copy it. And believe me, it's amazing the way people respond if you behave like you're the one in charge. No one wants to deal with the monkey, so you act like the organ-grinder and everyone's happy. Hi, Jodi?' she said into the phone. 'It's Sandy. Is Diana there?'

Nesta waited as Sandy was put on to her boss, then relayed the new deal she had just struck. She received an immediate go-ahead and asked to speak to Jodi again.

'Jodi, did you give Michael the message about dinner with Carl and Libby tonight?' she said, pushing a finger into her other ear as a nearby walkie-talkie squawked into life. 'What did he say?' she asked, glancing at Nesta and crossing her fingers. She listened for a moment, then her face fell. 'Well, is he going to call me?' she said. 'I mean, I have to give Carl and Libby an answer.' She paused, then, taking a breath she said, 'OK. I'll see you tomorrow.'

'So what's happening?' Nesta asked as she put the phone back in her shoulder bag and dug around for her sun-glasses. 'Is he coming?'

Sandy shook her head. 'I don't know,' she responded. 'Jodi gave him the message, but he didn't say anything.' She shrugged. 'He only got back from France last night so maybe it's a bit soon to be ... Oh hi, Sophie,' she said, as the leather woman came up behind Nesta. 'I spoke to the contracts department and everything's in order. I just need to get the increase in writing, then you'll be free to go and leap from a window on to a passing lorry.'

Laughing, Sophie said, 'I've done it a hundred times before, but never for this much loot. You're a genius, Sandy. Diana's got a real gem in you. We all have and Phillip's right, you should think about setting up your own list.' As she spoke she was wiping the perspiration from her face and Nesta looked at her, not even wanting to think about how hot she must be in all that kinky gear. 'Was that me?' she said, turning to see who had shouted her name.

'I think so,' Sandy answered, looking across to where the First Assistant was waving for Sophie to come and join the director and continuity girl.

'Who's Phillip?' Nesta asked as Sophie ran across the street.

'Phillip Waring, the writer,' Sandy answered. 'He's one of Craig's.'

'Blimey, is there anyone here who isn't part of McCann's?' Nesta laughed.

Sandy rolled her eyes. 'I told you, it's a project

286

Michael got involved in personally because he knows the executive producer,' she said, 'so we've supplied the writer, director, two line producers, both stars and a handful of support cast. If you remember, that's why we thought he'd come down here for dinner tonight. And stay over,' she added glumly.

Nesta's lips flattened as she looked at her. 'He might still come,' she said. 'I mean, he, hasn't said no, has he?'

'He hasn't called either,' Sandy reminded her.

'But he will if he thinks Carl Roman and Libby Sherwood have invited him.'

Sandy immediately brightened. 'You're right,' she said, feeling the anticipation coast through her heart, 'there's no way he'll ignore them and you're brilliant for coming up with the idea in the first place.'

Nesta laughed. 'Well I had to come up with something,' she responded, 'and since this particular situation includes a night in a hotel I think I can safely say I've surpassed myself.'

Sandy smiled ruefully and went off to find the producer, trying hard to ignore the terrible nerves she was experiencing at the mere thought of Michael arriving on set, never mind what she hoped might happen after.

More than three weeks had gone by since they'd spent the night together and though he'd been in Paris for the past eight days there had been plenty of opportunities for them to see each other before that and he hadn't taken a single one. He hadn't even turned up for the opera the night he'd told Zelda to invite her, nor had he returned any of the messages she'd left on his answerphone.

There was no point fooling herself any more, he was obviously avoiding her and though she knew why, it still hurt to realize that he was trying to stick to his rule of no relationships in the office. She wanted desperately to let him know that she'd never tell a soul, that she'd keep their affair secret for as long as he wanted, just as long as he saw her again, but short of sending him a letter there seemed no way she could get near him. She was sure he still wanted her, for it just couldn't be possible to feel this way about someone and them not feel something too. Besides, she saw the way he looked at her sometimes, in meetings or while she was talking on the phone, and he always smiled as though letting her know how much that night had meant to him too. Or maybe he was telling her how much he appreciated the effort she was putting into her career, knowing that it would make a real difference to their relationship once she became a fully fledged agent.

Actually, if she were being honest with herself, she had no idea what he was thinking, though he'd seemed much more withdrawn lately, not just with her, but with everyone. Nesta agreed that it could well be his dilemma over her that was causing it and though neither she nor Nesta considered it a good idea to corner him at work, her attempts to reach him at home had all so far failed. Not that he ignored her messages totally, he just waited until the next morning in the office to ask her what the call was about. Each time she'd told him she'd managed to sort the problem out herself, as Bertie or one of the booking assistants were invariably in earshot and though she longed to let them know that her relationship with Michael had developed into something beyond the professional, instinct told her that Michael wouldn't appreciate it if she did.

And now, here she was, waiting for him to call again. She wished she had the courage to call him herself, but she couldn't bear to hear him say he wasn't coming when she'd invested so much hope in this one night away. In her heart she just knew that if they were able to talk, everything would change: he'd see how right they were for each other and stop fighting it. Not that she blamed him for the way he was holding back, most men had a problem with commitment, everyone knew that, and after what had happened with Michelle it wasn't very surprising he was finding it so hard to let go again. She just wished there were a way to let him know she understood that and was prepared to wait however long it took for him to be ready to take that step again.

It was as the unit was wrapping that Carl Roman sought her out to tell her he'd just received a call from Michael saying he was sorry he couldn't make it tonight. To make up for it he'd invited Carl and Libby to join him for dinner the following Thursday when they got back to London. The news hit Sandy hard, but she was right in the middle of trying to sort out a problem with one of Janey's clients at the time. So there was nothing else she could do but thank Roman for letting her know and carry on flipping through the pages of her Filofax making endless calls and copious notes on what the actor in crisis should be saying to the rest of the press after the *Sun* exposed his prison record the next morning.

As she dealt with the problem Nesta sat on the street bench with her, watching the crew packing up their gear and marvelling at the way Sandy was coping so coolly and effectively with a matter that should have gone straight to Janey, but because of the particular friendship and trust Sandy had built up with the actor he had come to her instead. In fact, the more Nesta watched Sandy in action the more impressed she was becoming. It was clear to her now that she had seriously underrated Sandy, both professionally and intellectually, for if what she'd seen here today was anything to go by, she was much more cut out for her chosen career than Nesta had realized. And though Sandy might profess just to mimic her superiors, Nesta suspected that the shrewdness and cunning were all her own. Not that Nesta considered there to be anything wrong with the way Sandy manipulated people and situations to her own end; God knew no one ever got to the top without such skills and though Zelda might have given Sandy her first break, to the best of Nesta's knowledge, no one else could be accused of giving her a leg-up. Unless one counted Maurice Trehearne, the property tycoon from Sandy's escort days, whom she still saw quite regularly, though no longer in a professional capacity. That wasn't to say she didn't sleep with the old guy any more, because she did, but only because she was so fond of him and needed all the invaluable advice on business strategy and executive technique he'd have happily given her anyway.

'You know what I think,' she said to Sandy as they walked back to the car they'd hired for the day, 'I think Michael's still seeing you as the starry-eyed kid from the sticks who doesn't know her soliloquies from her sit-coms. I mean, you can't really blame him for that when he only promoted you a month ago ...'

'Six weeks,' Sandy interjected.

'... but what I reckon is that you just have to wait this out and let him see for himself what you're really about, because I'm telling you, you've really knocked my hat off today and that was just one day. Give him another month and he'll have forgotten all about the peculiar little clerk with a crush who used to sit in his outer office in fancy stockings and Wonderbras; he'll be seeing you for the ragamuffin businesswoman you're turning into.'

Though Sandy laughed at the reference to her casual attire, her eyes were shining with pleasure at the compliment. 'Well, if I can convince you, I should be able to convince anyone,' she quipped.

Nesta shrugged. 'You can make out it's all an act if you like,' she said, 'but I'm not fooled. You know what you're doing and you know where you're going. In fact, I can see now why you gave up the escort business. You've carved a real niche for yourself here and I have to tell you, if I wasn't happy doing what I'm doing I'd probably be asking you for a job.'

Sandy laughed. 'I'm a long way from that kind of position,' she reminded her.

'But you'll get there,' Nesta assured her. 'If you carry on the way you're going I don't see how you can fail. What's more, I'll lay money on it you'll end up with Michael too. I just hope the bastard's good enough for you, that's all.'

Sandy looked at her in confusion. 'Well, that's a change of heart if ever I heard one,' she commented.

'I mean it,' Nesta told her.

Sandy smiled. 'It's nice of you to say so,' she responded, 'but it's still whether *I'm* good enough for *him* that's the issue.'

Nesta was shaking her head. 'No, I promise you we've got this all round the wrong way,' she said. 'Isabelle gave me this book the other day on self-esteem. I think you should read it, because honest to God, Sandy, you're worth more than a one-night stand and by rights you should be getting as mad as hell about the way he's treated you by now, not standing here wondering if you're good enough for the bastard.'

Sandy inhaled deeply and pulled a face. 'But you just said I had to be patient,' she reminded her, 'and after what happened with Michelle – you know, the way she let him down and everything – who can blame him for being nervous it'll happen again?'

'But how do you know he feels that way? Did he tell you?'

'No, of course not. He never even mentioned her. But think how you'd feel if someone walked out on you publicly like that? It must have been terrible. So I think you're right, I just have to wait this out and give him time to get used to the idea of having someone else in his life.'

'I don't understand, what's this guy hoping to get out of it?' Michael asked, referring to the proposal Harry had just handed him.

Harry shrugged. 'Publicity, I guess,' he answered. 'And kudos. And gazillion bucks, eventually.'

Michael scanned the document again. 'An initial investment of two million's a lot of money,' he remarked, looking up. 'How serious do you think he is?'

Harry drew a hand over the gingery stubble on his chin, then picked up his coffee from Michael's desk. 'I told you, I met the guy at a party the other night,' he said, taking a slurp. 'He seemed serious at the time and now this,' he added, indicating the document.

'Whose party was it?' Michael wanted to know. 'Who introduced you?'

'Ed Baldwin.'

Michael's expression suggested he was OK with that. 'Have you spoken to Ed since?' he asked.

'He's in New York. I left a message for him to call.'

Michael pursed his lips thoughtfully and looked down at the proposal again. 'I'll speak to Ed when he calls,' he said, 'because if this guy is serious it could be something we want to get into. Do you know if he's given this to anyone else?' he asked, referring to the three page dossier outlining one of the most ambitious film–TV–theatre projects Michael had ever seen.

'He said not,' Harry replied, glancing over his shoulder as Jodi came into the office. 'He said he'd heard good things about this agency so he wanted to give us first refusal. In fact, so he claims, he was scheduled to have lunch with you early next week, but something came up that meant he was flying back to Australia the morning after the party. So when he

292

heard who I was he made a point of introducing himself and asking me to start the ball rolling.'

Michael's eyes narrowed. 'Mark Bergin?' he said. 'Did we have him down for lunch next week, Jodi?'

She nodded. 'Yeah, we did,' she answered.

'So what do we know about him?'

'He's Australian, into mining or something, and wants to get into showbiz.'

'Do we know anything else?'

'Never heard of him before the other night,' Harry responded, watching Jodi from the corner of his eye as she started updating the schedule boards on Michael's wall.

Michael hit three buttons on his intercom. 'Zelda, does the name Mark Bergin mean anything to you?' he said. 'He's an Aussie.'

Zelda was quiet as she thought. 'Can't say it does,' she answered finally. 'Why?'

Michael told her about the proposal.

'Is that two million pounds or dollars he's prepared to put up?' she asked.

Michael looked at the document. 'Pounds,' he replied.

'And he wants you to find someone here to match it?'

'That seems to be the general idea,' Michael answered. 'And you haven't bitten his hand off yet?' Zelda marvelled.

Michael laughed. 'I'll keep you posted,' he told her and clicking off the intercom he handed the proposal back to Harry. 'Get me a copy,' he said, looking at his watch. 'I'll make a few calls to Sydney and let you know what I come up with. Jodi, it's past eleven o'clock. Did Fitzwarren come back to us yet?'

'No,' she answered, watching Harry leave.

'Then he's missed the deadline,' Michael said. 'Get on to Sally Byrd at Fox and tell her she's got herself a deal with RTV on the media-mania project. Then call

Philomena at the National and ask her for an answer on the tickets tomorrow night.'

'How many people are you taking?' Jodi asked, her pen poised over her notebook.

'Six,' he answered. 'Seven if my mother wants to come. Call her and find out, will you? Did you hear back from Ellen Shelby?'

Jodi nodded and started to go through a pile of paperwork she'd left on his desk. 'She faxed last night. Here it is.'

Michael took it, read it quickly, then said, 'Fax her back and tell her I'll deal with Forgon.'

Jodi jotted it down, then looked at him. 'Anything else?' she asked as he started going through his mail.

Without looking up he shook his head and continued to read the letter in front of him.

'Sandy's replacement started while you were away,' she informed him. 'Would you like to meet her?'

'I already have,' he answered. 'I interviewed her, remember? How's she working out?'

'Let's put it this way,' she replied. 'I don't expect she'll be giving you any trouble in the crush department.'

Michael's eyebrows went up as he treated her to a dark, cautionary look.

Jodi flushed and closing up her notepad let herself quietly and swiftly out of the office.

Michael was still looking at the door as she closed it, then, sighing to himself he turned back to what he was doing. The fact that Jodi and Harry had gone past the flirtation stage was pretty evident in the way both were behaving, but that was the first time Michael had even hinted he knew anything about it. Whether he was going to take it any further he doubted, for he didn't want to lose either of them and now that Harry's baby had been born, Michael had every faith that the man would come to his senses and give it up before either of them got in any deeper. As it stood, Michael was pretty certain that Laura, Harry's wife, knew nothing about it; he just hoped it stayed that way for there couldn't be many betrayals a woman would find less forgivable than that of her husband sleeping with another woman while she was carrying his baby.

It was lucky for Harry, Michael couldn't stop himself thinking, that he'd chosen Jodi rather than Sandy for his illicit affair, as Michael couldn't see Jodi clinging on to Harry the way Sandy was clinging on to him. Mercifully, she wasn't too bad around the office, but all those messages on his answerphone at home and the way she used other people to set up drinks or dinners or even overnight stays was irritating him to hell. Surely she realized the reason he was avoiding her was so that he didn't have to put her through the ignominy of a direct rejection? For God's sake, he was trying to save her feelings, but the way she was carrying on was making it so damned difficult she was practically forcing him to tell her he wasn't interested. Maybe, in the end, it would be kinder to do that and were it anyone else he probably would, but with her he had a horrible feeling that no matter what he said she wasn't going to accept it. But he had to do something soon, because he'd just learned from his sister that she was angling her way in over there, calling up for friendly little chats, or dropping in with treats for the kids and Clodagh, God bless her, had invited her to join the family for lunch this Sunday.

As luck would have it he was going to Ireland at the weekend, but he still wanted his mother to withdraw the invitation, for the last thing he needed was Sandy carving herself a cosy little niche in the heart of his family. Getting Clodagh to agree wasn't going to be easy, though, as she'd taken quite a liking to Sandy and once Clodagh had made up her mind about something it was damned near impossible to shift her.

He ploughed on through his mail until he was back at the fax Ellen Shelby had sent while he was in France. He smiled wryly to himself, for here was a woman of whom Clodagh would certainly approve, with her Irish ancestry and good Catholic values. Indeed, there was a chance that someone like Ellen would surpass even Michelle in Clodagh's eyes which would be no mean feat at all. But he'd never been in the habit of doing what his mother wanted where women were concerned, as well she knew, which was probably why she couldn't stop herself interfering. Like any other mother she always assumed she knew best and though he'd never disagreed with her about Michelle, he knew already that if she didn't let up about Sandy they were heading for a serious falling out. But he didn't see any reason for it to come to that, not if he gave Clodagh what she really wanted, and with the way he'd been thinking lately there was a chance he might. He'd spoken to Cavan a couple of times while he was in France and though he was still pretty convinced Cavan was hiding something, he was much less concerned now than he had been. Or, to put it another way, he didn't see any reason to go rushing over there, at least not until he'd come to a firm decision on whether or not he really did want to try again with Michelle.

Pushing it out of his mind for now, he pressed the button on his intercom and got Jodi back in the office to take down a fax to Ted Forgon. 'Let's get it over with,' he said, as she pulled up a chair. 'Not that I expect the man to take any notice, but we can at least try to get Ellen Shelby off the hook.'

'I've already sent the fax telling her you're dealing with this direct,' Jodi informed him, leaning forward to pick up his phone. 'Hello, Michael McCann's office,' she said into the receiver. 'Oh, hi, Craig, how are you?' She paused, then looking at Michael she said, 'He's right here. I'll put you on.'

296

'He's in a fix at LWT,' she informed Michael, passing the receiver over.

Michael took it and covering the mouthpiece with his hand said, 'You can do the fax to Forgon. Just tell him that under no circumstances do I ever want to do business with him, either now or in the future, and could he please get his staff off my back or I'll come over there and tear all his hair out.'

Jodi burst out laughing and leaving him to speak to Craig she returned to her own office to find Sandy standing over Michael's diary – again.

Chapter 16

It had turned out to be a much more pleasurable evening than Michael had expected. In fact, he would probably go as far as to say that he'd not only enjoyed the play, but had found Sandy much easier to deal with at the small party after than he'd dared hope. She'd asked him not long after he'd returned from France if he would go with her to see a young actor in a play at the King's Head in Islington and though he'd spent the past six weeks trying to think up an excuse to get out of it, he had ended up going, because he hadn't been able to find the heart to turn her down again. In fact, if the truth be known, he'd started warming to her a little lately, for there was no mistaking the effort she was putting into her job and though she seemed unable to stop herself trying to manoeuvre him into situations where they would be thrown together, he could also see how much it hurt her each time he thwarted her.

Now, as he drove her back to her flat in Chelsea and listened to her enthusiasm for her new discovery, he found he was feeling much more relaxed with her than he had since that fateful night. Indeed, there had been only a couple of awkward moments these past few weeks, the worst being when she'd come into his office and apologized for having lunch with his family. He had been so startled by the apology and embarrassed, that he had heard himself telling her that he hoped she'd join them again one Sunday. Fortunately, she hadn't brought it up since and his mother was under threat of credit card removal if she as much as mentioned it.

'So you'd be happy for me to take on Stevie Brown?' she said, glancing over at him as they passed through the dark, empty streets of King's Cross.

Michael nodded. 'Very,' he replied. 'He's got a good stage presence and you're right about his looks, they probably will work well on camera. How old is he?'

'Eighteen,' she answered. 'Did he tell you he's got a part in a friend's film that they're making for film school? He's going to send a copy of some of the rushes so we can see how he works on screen. Would you like to see them when they come?'

'Sure,' he said, swinging the car into the left lane to allow a speeding police van to pass.

They were quiet for a while then, travelling swiftly along Euston Road then heading south towards Park Lane. It was Sandy who finally broke the silence. 'Jodi tells me you're going to Australia the week after next,' she said.

Michael nodded. 'That's right.'

She looked over at him as he stopped the car at a red light and in the silvery glow of a street lamp she could see the perfect profile of his face and the strength of his hands on the wheel. Inside, she was such a bundle of nerves she barely knew what she was saying, for all she could really think about was what was going to happen when they got to Chelsea. Would he drive on over the bridge to his place? Or would he just take her straight home to hers?

'Are you going to see Mark Bergin, the man you mentioned at the meeting the other day?' she asked.

'Yes,' he answered. 'Among others.'

'How long will you be gone?'

299

'A few weeks. I'm flying on to LA after. Victor Warren's new film, *United We Fall*, is premièring there.'

Sandy turned to look out of the window. Her heart was tight with misgiving, for his mention of LA had reminded her of Ellen Shelby and the fear that that particular threat might not have gone away. As hard as she tried she couldn't quite forget the way he had looked at Ellen that first night he saw her, and the fact that he had had dinner with her after weeks, months even, of swearing he'd never see Ted Forgon's messenger still sat very uneasily with Sandy. But she must remember that it was her he had spent the night with, not Ellen, and as far as she was aware he hadn't seen or even spoken to the woman again before she'd returned to LA. So there wasn't really anything to worry about there, she was just nervous about everything where Michael was concerned and until they really sorted out how they were going to play their relationship she didn't see that changing. 'Do you think you'll strike a deal with Mark Bergin?' she asked, pushing Ellen Shelby from her mind as she gazed out at the smart white houses of Belgrave Square.

'Mmm, there's a chance,' he responded, glancing over at her. He could see only the back of her blonde head, and thought how much better her hair looked since she had let it grow. Her hands were bunched together in her lap and the way her fingers were agitating each other told him how anxious she was. In an effort to put her at her ease he talked some more about Mark Bergin and what a major coup it would be for the agency if the investment programme came off.

'What does he do, this Mark Bergin?' she asked, knowing already as he'd told everyone at the meeting, but she needed something to say.

'He's an industrialist who wants to get into the arts,' he reminded her. 'And with the kind of money he's

300

offering to put up no one's going to deny him,' he added with a smile.

Sandy fell silent again and could feel her tension mounting as they drove towards Sloane Square, where he was going to need to turn right for her flat or left for his. Whichever direction he took she knew what she was going to do, for this was the first time she'd been alone with him since they'd slept together and there was just no way she could let the opportunity pass. She thought about him going to Australia and wished desperately that she could go with him. From the corner of her eye she looked down at his lap and had to fight the urge to touch him.

'We're going to talk about an LA and New York link-up,' he told her, braking as they approached Sloane Square.

Sandy was confused for a moment, then remembered they'd been talking about the Australian, Mark Bergin. 'So you're going to make it international?' she said, wondering if that sounded as stupid to him as it did to her.

'It's a possibility,' he replied. 'I'll be talking to a few people in LA, then I'll probably stop off in New York to see Chris Ruskin on the way back.'

'Chris Ruskin?' Sandy echoed, though she was barely listening as her heart flooded with disappointment and panic. He was turning right and in less than two minutes they would be outside her flat. She had to do something. She had to make him change his mind and take her home with him.

'Our associate in New York,' he reminded her, sounding surprised she hadn't remembered. 'Is it this one?' he asked, looking up at the terrace of red-brick houses.

'No, the next,' she answered.

He accelerated gently, then came to a stop behind her neighbour's car. 'Would you like to come in for a coffee?' she asked staring down at her hands as he turned to look at her.

'It's late, I'd better be getting back,' he replied, glancing at his watch.

'Will you take me with you?' she asked, turning to look at him.

His eyes moved instantly away. 'I don't think that would be a good idea,' he said awkwardly.

'We need to talk, Michael,' she said. 'We need to sort out what's going on between us.'

He took a breath, and after several seconds he looked at her again. 'Sandy, listen,' he said, 'I know this is going to be hard, but—'

'I know how you feel about me,' she interrupted, 'and I know you're fighting it. But that's OK. I don't mind waiting. I just want you to know that I'll keep our affair a secret for as long as you want.'

'Sandy, we're not having an affair,' he said gently. 'It happened once and . . .'

He was about to say it had been a mistake, but he didn't want to hurt her any more than he already was. 'Look I like you,' he said, knowing it wasn't strictly true. 'You're good at your job and you're great with the actors . . .'

'It can happen again,' she said, moving towards him. 'Any time you want it to.'

He caught her hand as it slid along his thigh. 'Sandy, you're making this very difficult,' he told her, grabbing her other hand as she tried to kiss him. He turned his face away. 'Sandy, stop.' he said.

'You can touch me,' she panted, pushing his hand down to her lap. 'I'm wet for you, Michael. Its the way you like it. Remember?'

To his dismay she wasn't wearing underwear and yanking his hand away, he caught her hard by the arms and pressed her back into her seat. She pulled him with her and tried kissing him again.

'If you like, we can do it here,' she whispered. 'I don't mind.'

'Sandy, for God's sake, let go!' he seethed, trying to unlock her arms from his neck.

'Why are you pretending!' she cried desperately. 'I know you want it too. I see the way you look at me in the office. I know what you're thinking, but you don't want anyone else to know. Well, no one's here now except you and me. You can do me and I'll never tell anyone.'

She had let go of his neck, but as he drew back she began fumbling with his fly. Clutching her hands he pushed her hard back into the seat. 'Listen to me,' he snapped. 'There's no pretence going on here, except inside your head. I'm not going to make love to you tonight, or any other night. Do you hear me? What happened before, well, it shouldn't have happened. It was my fault and I'm sorry if I led you to think there would be any more between us than that. Now please, pull your clothes down and let's try to forget this ever happened.'

She lay back, looking at him, her breath ragged, tears of defeat standing brightly in her eyes. 'Please,' she whispered brokenly.

His eyes closed as frustration welled in him anew.

'Just once . . .'

'Sandy, no!' he shouted. 'Now, for God's sake, pull yourself together and get out of the car.'

Her head fell forward and he felt a tear drop on to his hand.

'I'm going to let you go now,' he told her a few minutes later.

She nodded and sniffed, and very gently he took his hands away, bracing himself in case she lunged at him again.

'I'm sorry,' she said, shaking her head. 'I tried to rush you and I promised myself I wouldn't. But I feel like I

303

just have to be with you and sometimes the feeling's so strong . . .' Her breath caught on a sob. 'I'm sorry,' she finished lamely.

'It's OK,' he told her, feeling the unsteady beat of his own heart. 'Like I said, let's just forget it happened.'

She lifted her face into the light. 'Will you kiss me, just once?' she asked.

He could see the tears glistening on her cheeks and as he looked at her he felt pity – and that same urge to violence he'd felt with her before. But there was no way he was going to touch her, either in tenderness or in fury.

'No,' he said softly. 'I'm not going to kiss you. I'm going to wait for you to get out of the car, then I'm going home.'

Her breath shuddered inside her and fresh tears appeared in her eyes. She could feel his eyes boring into her and though there was a part of her that was so deeply ashamed she wished she could die, there was still a very strong part that wanted to carry on begging him. 'Can I kiss you?' she said.

He shook his head.

Pain circled her heart. 'You do want me,' she said, pulling down her skirt. 'I know it. And I'll wait.'

He said nothing, as she picked up her bag and opened the car door.

'It doesn't matter how long,' she said.

He waited, watching her as she walked around the car and mounted the steps to her front door. He knew already that he hadn't been forceful enough, that he should have spelled out to her that there was just no way there would ever be anything between them. God only knew what was going on inside her head, but she had clearly convinced herself of something and pushing her away tonight didn't seem to have disabused her of anything. He groaned inwardly as he thought of how it was going to be from here, him constantly trying to avoid her and her never giving up on her quest. How long would it be, he wondered, before she caused a scene at the office? He had no evidence to say she would, but after what had happened here tonight anything was possible.

Starting the car, he pulled slowly away from the kerb and headed back towards the river. He was trying hard to come up with some grounds to fire her, something that wouldn't end up involving the agency in a law-suit or her in any more pain than she was already suffering. Off the top of his head he could think of nothing, but he wanted her out of his life before she became a serious liability to him as well as to herself.

He sighed as he thought of the young actor who'd been so excited tonight at the prospect of being taken on by McCann Walsh. The boy's hopes for the future were probably, even now, Oscar bound and who could blame him when Michael McCann himself had come along with the woman who was proposing to represent him. So what did he do now, assign the boy to someone else while he crushed Sandy's career? It hardly seemed fair to make her pay such a bitter price for the fact that he didn't care for her.

He accelerated hard, suddenly as angry with himself as he was with her. OK, he was to blame for sleeping with her in the first place, but God knew he'd done nothing to encourage the girl since. So there was no dilemma really, she had to go and she had to go soon, before she misinterpreted anything else he said and ended up even more desperate and pathetic than she already was.

'No! You're not serious!' Janine, one of the bookers, cried, her eyes glittering with delight as she clasped a hand over her mouth.

'Sssh,' Bertie warned, glancing over at Sandy and,

drawing Janine and Frances into a closer huddle, he went on with his gossip.

Sandy was at her desk the other side of the well marking up scripts for Janey and Diana. It wasn't unusual for Bertie to make out he was talking about her whether he was or wasn't, so ignoring his little performance she simply carried on with what she was doing, not wanting to give him the satisfaction of knowing she cared.

It was a laborious task she was undertaking and she doubted either Janey or Diana would look at the scripts when she'd finished, but she did it anyway so they could see, should they wish, which roles she was sending their clients up for. Already Janey had come to rely on her heavily, since about the time of Sandy's promotion one of Bobby Mack's kids had gone down with an illness no one seemed able to diagnose. It meant that Janey was rarely in the office, which suited Sandy perfectly, for not only did it allow her to act as an agent, it saved her from having to suffer the way Michael enjoyed Janey's company. As for Diana, she was more than happy for Sandy to take over her lower-profile actors while she concentrated on the bigger names.

All this meant that Sandy's hopes for further promotion were grounding themselves firmly in an expectation of being made up by the end of the year. At least, if she worked hard on developing her own list she might, but discovering new talent was one thing, finding productions to cast them in another altogether. But the way to remedy that was to put more effort into forging contacts with even more producers and directors than she was already on terms with. She'd give almost anything to find a way in with the directors Michael represented, but they were all such big names and worked so consistently that short of asking Michael to introduce her she knew there was little chance of making that breakthrough yet.

Hearing the others burst out laughing again, her insides turned hot, but without deigning to look up she opened another script and carried on with what she was doing. She'd seen Michael every day since that night in his car, and though she'd felt embarrassed and awkward at first, she still hadn't given up hope. To the contrary, in fact, for thinking about it after, she had realized that there was every chance he had rejected her because he wanted her to know that she mattered much more than a quick screw in the back of a car. So, by turning her down and telling her he liked her he had made her see that it wasn't how he wanted to treat her and that if she just gave it time the like would probably turn to love.

Drawing a thick yellow marker along the edge of a ruler, highlighting various names on a cast list, she kept her eyes lowered and tried not to hear the continued whispering and laughter going on over at Frances's and Janine's desks. Thea and Jodi had joined them now and knowing that Jodi was a part of it hurt a lot more than Sandy wanted to admit. But she would get her revenge one of these days, when she was an agent and in a position to make them pay.

After checking her watch, she picked up the phone and dialled Stevie Brown, her new protégé. 'Stevie,' she said when he answered, 'do you have the cassette yet?'

'I'm trying, Sandy,' he groaned. 'I swear it, but Todd's not calling me back.'

'Then let me ring him.'

'You can if you like, but his machine's on. He's up to his eyes trying to cut this film together. The last I heard he was wanting a reshoot for some of the scenes.'

Sandy sighed. That didn't bode well for Todd's film, but it was seeing Stevie on camera she was after. 'So when do you think he's going to get a tape to you?' she asked.

'It's hard to say, but I'll keep on it,' he promised. 'It's not going to affect me joining McCann's, is it? This not getting the tape.'

'No. You're already my client,' she assured him. 'It's just that I want Michael to see you on screen before he leaves for Australia.'

'When does he go?'

'The day after tomorrow.'

Stevie swore under his breath. 'Would it be too late when he gets back?' he asked.

Sandy's heart sank, for she was intending to use the tape as an excuse to see Michael before he went. She'd love to think he might seek her out instead, but she doubted it, so it was up to her to give them a few precious moments together to carry them over the time he was away. 'No, I suppose not,' she replied, already trying to think of another way through. 'But if you do get it before Friday call me. I'll send someone over for it.'

As she rang off the lift doors opened and Michael came in with Zelda and Dan. The instant she saw him Sandy's heart turned over and unable to stop herself she watched him walk around the upper circle to his office. He didn't look at her, but she felt sure he knew she was there. He had been to Chutney Mary's over on the King's Road with Zelda and Dan, where Craig would have joined them had he not stolen a rare few days away with his lover. Sandy wondered if Michael knew where Craig was. If he did she knew he would never say, any more than she would, for were anyone ever to get wind of the affair it would mean an end to the Cabinet Minister's career, if not his marriage, and probably Craig too.

Looking across to where Bertie was still perched on the edge of Janine's desk, Sandy found them all looking in her direction. Before she turned away she saw that Jodi at least had the decency to blush. Indeed, she got up and went back to her office and Sandy was so deeply engrossed on the phone by the time she emerged again that she didn't see her go into Michael's office, then come out a few minutes later – nor did she see the signal Jodi gave Bertie to tell him he could go in and see Michael now.

'. . . so I told him,' Bertie was saying to Michael, 'that since Craig's away until Tuesday he'd better speak to you.'

Michael was looking hard at Bertie's long, pinched face. 'Does Craig know anything about this?' he demanded.

Bertie shook his head. 'Not as far as I'm aware,' he replied.

'And you're sure you didn't misunderstand what Slim Sutton was saying?'

Bertie shrugged. 'He was pretty specific,' he answered.

'So run me through it again,' Michael said.

Bertie shifted his weight on to the other foot and folded his arms. 'Well, he called to say that he'd written to his agent at Sackville and Peters to tell him he was transferring here, to Craig. Then he said he was coming to London next Thursday to spend the weekend with a couple of other writers he knows and that he wanted Craig to set up a few more sessions like the one he'd had the last time he was in town. I asked him what kind of sessions they were, and he sort of chuckled and said, "you know, the kind the girl Sandy provides. And if she's got a couple of friends . . ." '

'All right,' Michael interrupted. His face was inscrutable. 'Do you know where Sutton is now?' he said.

'At home in Wales, I imagine,' Bertie responded.

Michael nodded and was about to tell Bertie to keep

this under his hat, when he remembered who he was talking to. So merely telling him he could go, he sat for a moment going over what he'd just heard. He toyed with the idea of speaking to Zelda, but decided to call Sutton first.

'Slim? It's Michael McCann,' he said when Sutton answered his phone.

'Michael!' Sutton cried. 'How are you?'

'Very well,' Michael said. 'Bertie tells me there's something you want to talk about.'

'Yes,' Sutton laughed. 'I certainly do. It's that girl of yours, Sandy. I'm coming down to London next week to stay with a couple of mates – they're writers too – and I was hoping you could see your way into lending her out for a couple of days. And if she's got any friends, all the better. I don't know if there's a going rate, but we're willing to pay, obviously. Providing they're not too dear, of course.'

'I think there must be some misunderstanding,' Michael responded, feeling the tension building inside him. 'We don't lend our staff out ...'

'Hire, then,' Sutton cut in. 'Or whatever else you want to call it. A mate of mine had her just before I did, that was how I came to meet her, as a matter of fact. He tells me he paid fifty quid for the evening. That was without sex, he said. I guess I got it as a courtesy, or an incentive to come over to McCann's maybe?' He chuckled.

Michael's face was white. 'We don't give those kinds of incentives,' he said tightly. 'Whatever happened between you and Sandy was between you two and had nothing to do with this agency. Is that clear?'

'Oh, well, sure,' Sutton replied, obviously smarting under the whiplash of Michael's tongue. 'I just thought ...'

'You thought wrong. I'm not a pimp, Sutton, and if

310

you repeat anything you just told me you better have a good lawyer ...'

'OK, OK,' Sutton grumbled. 'I obviously misundertood. Sorry if I caused any offence. It wasn't intended.'

'I'm sure,' Michael said and with no goodbyes he clicked off the line and buzzed through to Jodi. 'Tell Sandy to come in,' he said.

By the time she closed the door he was so angry it was all he could do to keep his voice level. 'Sit down,' he said shortly.

Sandy looked at the chair, then at him. 'Is something the matter?' she asked shakily.

Michael stared at her small, anxious face and the compact, curvaceous body that no matter how it was dressed contrived never to look anything but sexy. He thought of that terrible scene in the car and the night he had spent with her, and felt his anger build. He wished to God he could just spin her round and physically throw her out the door, for the position she had now put the agency in was so outrageous he could barely speak to her civilly. 'I've just spoken to Slim Sutton,' he told her.

Sandy's cheeks coloured, though her show of confusion was almost convincing.

'He told me how you graced him with your favours,' he went on bluntly. 'He also told me how he met you and what you were doing at the time.'

Sandy's face paled. 'What do you mean?' she said, her chest tightening as her mind started to reel.

'Fifty pounds for an evening, without sex,' he stated.

Her heart stopped beating and as she looked into his cold, accusing eyes she felt her world starting to fall apart. 'I'm sorry,' she whispered, 'I don't understand.'

'I think you do,' he said harshly.

She swallowed hard and struggled to keep the panic at bay. 'I was ...' She took another breath. 'I – I can explain,' she said.

311

Michael's eyes were like steel. 'I don't need an explanation,' he said bitingly. 'What I need is you out of here.'

'No!' she cried, clutching the back of the chair. 'Please, just let me explain.'

'Slim Sutton thinks I'm employing you to entice potential clients into this agency,' he raged. 'So how many more . . . ?'

'There aren't any more!' she shouted. 'You've got it wrong. I didn't . . .'

'Fifty pounds without sex!' he reminded her. 'Sutton wanted to know how much it was with, since he got his first session free, courtesy of me, or so he thought. So how many others have you tried doing this with?'

Her legs had turned weak and her mouth so dry she could barely speak. 'No one, except Slim,' she croaked. 'And I didn't do it to get him to come here . . .'

'He thinks you did, and I'm not prepared to have anyone working for me who's going to damage our reputation to the point where we get known as some kind of brothel. Jesus Christ, what were you thinking? Surely you . . .'

'Please, just listen,' she cried, hysteria building fast. 'It's not what you think. I did it because I had to. Because when I got to London I didn't have any money. So I joined an escort service. It was the only way I was going to survive. I never slept with the men. I just went on dates.'

'You slept with Slim Sutton.'

'He didn't pay me! I'm not what you're trying to say I am.'

He was shaking his head. 'I'm sorry, you have to go,' he said. 'I'll give you six months severance pay and you can choose whether you leave now or at the end of the month. But I want you gone by the time I return.'

'No, you can't,' she cried, tears starting in her eyes as desperation surged through her. 'Michael, please! I'm begging you. Don't make me go. It was all a mistake, a misunderstanding ... Please, Michael, listen ...'

'It's too late,' he broke in. 'Already Sutton's out there thinking I'm behind what you did. God only knows how many more there are.'

'There aren't any more!' she shouted. 'I swear it! I only slept with Slim because I wanted you and you ...'

'That's enough,' he cut across her. 'My decision is final. Talk to Sheila, she'll ...'

'No!' she screamed. 'Michael, no! I've worked hard for you. I've done everything I could to make you like me. I even slept with you ...'

'For God's sake,' he hissed, glancing out into the well to see everyone staring in.

'I'll do anything,' she sobbed, 'anything,' and falling to her knees she clasped her hands together and gazed up at him with desperate eyes. 'I'm begging you,' she whispered. 'Please don't sack me. I love you, Michael. I ...'

'Get up,' he said through his teeth.

'No, not until you say I can stay.'

He looked at her and a part of him was almost ready to relent, if only to get her off her knees. But hardening his heart he said, 'I need to ask you ...' He broke off as the enormity of what he was about to say hit him, but he had no choice, he had to ask. 'Did you use any kind of protection with these other men? Do I need to get tested?'

'Oh no!' she gasped, her eyes closing against the pain as she sank back on her knees.

'Do I?' he persisted.

Unable to look up she merely shook her head. 'No,' she said. 'And I'm not pregnant either.' She raised her eyes to his. 'Do you really think I'd do that to you?'

He looked at her and said nothing.

'I would never do anything to hurt you,' she cried. 'You and this agency are my life. You know that.'

His eyes fell away. 'I'm sorry,' he said quietly.

'No, don't say that! Please let me keep my job. *Please!*'

As she spoke he got to his feet and walked round the desk. 'I'll give you a good reference,' he said, heading past her towards the door. 'This needn't go any further.'

'No, no, no!' she screamed, clutching his legs. 'I'm not going. I'm staying here, where I belong. You can't make me go. Please, don't make me.'

'Sandy, let go,' he said firmly and wresting her arms apart he pulled her to her feet. He saw at once the terrible devastation in her eyes and for an instant he was transported to another place and time when Michelle had begged and pleaded with him too, and he had stood there, watching her, just like now, allowing himself neither pity nor mercy. But the circumstances with Michelle had been very different from these, so different they didn't even stand comparison.

'Don't make this any harder for yourself,' he said. 'You don't need . . .' He stopped, suddenly not wanting to hurt her any more than he already had. He turned and was starting for the door again when she grabbed his shirt and forced him to look at her.

'I know what's going on here,' she cried, her eyes glinting with hopelessness and pain. 'You screwed me then you wanted to get rid of me, and this is a nice, convenient excuse.'

He looked down at her and as she gazed up into his troubled blue eyes she could feel her heart breaking under the strain of anger and despair. 'I'm right, aren't I?' she insisted.

Still he said nothing, but his silence was answer enough and as the frustration erupted inside her her fists clenched and she began beating his chest in fury. 'You bastard!' she cried. 'I'm not going to let you do this. You can't just fuck me, then throw me out. You can't . . .'

'People can hear you ...' he said, grabbing her hands.

'Let them!' she shouted. 'Do you think I'm ashamed of sleeping with you, the way you are with me? I'm proud of sleeping with you. I want the whole world to know how you took me back to your flat and made love to me and let me think you loved me too ...'

'Sandy,' he cut in quietly. 'It was one night ...'

Her hand caught him so sharply across the face it cut off his words. 'You bastard!' she yelled. 'It was more than one night and you know it. So say it! Go on, say it, or I'm going to tell everyone how you made me go out there and and fuck every Tom, Dick and Harry to get them to sign up with you ...'

'Sandy!' Zelda's voice cut across hers like a knife.

Sandy rounded on her. 'Did you know?' she sneered. 'Did he tell you how he got me to fuck Slim Sutton ...?'

'That's enough!' Zelda barked. 'Go and pick up your things, I'll take you home.'

Sandy instantly turned back to Michael. 'You said I could stay until the end of the month,' she reminded him, looking so lost and bewildered for a moment it was hard to credit the change.

'Do you really want to – now?' he said softly.

She looked down at her hands and watched her fingers twisting and writhing, then lifting her eyes back to his she said, 'If I leave now will you take me home?'

He looked at Zelda.

'I'll take you,' Zelda said.

'No!' she shrieked, spinning round again. 'He loves me, don't you know that? You've seen the way he looks at me, everyone has, and this is all an act, because he doesn't want any of you to know how he feels, when everyone knows already ...'

'I'll take her home,' Michael said.

' ... he loves me as much as I love him. He wants to

315

marry me, but he's afraid to ask in case I do what Michelle did and walk out, but I'll never do that. I swear it, Michael. I'll never leave you, or hurt you the way she did . . .'

As she ranted and raved on, Zelda moved forward and began to lead her away. At first Michael tried to help, but Zelda gestured for him to leave it and realizing that to go with her now would probably only make things worse, he stepped back and watched them go.

The scene was excruciating and seemed to go on for ever as Zelda and Dan manhandled her across the office and tried not to get hurt as she yelled and kicked all the way to the lift. The last thing he heard before the doors closed behind her was her screaming, 'You'll pay for this, Michael McCann! I swear I'm going to make you pay.'

He knew she was hysterical, which was why the threat didn't bother him. But later, as he thought back over the whole hideous display he found himself unsettled by the extent of her self-delusion and couldn't help wondering how many more lies might come from it in the weeks and months ahead. But it wasn't so much her lies that were going to cause him any loss of sleep as his own guilt at seizing an excuse to get rid of her because he didn't want to go on facing her day after day. Even so, if she was as obsessed with him as she appeared, then firing her probably was for the best.

Once again her parting words resounded through his head, and suddenly it was Michelle's face he was seeing, reminding him of the day he had hurt her so badly it was hard to think of it even now. He had thought what he was doing then would be for the best, but he had paid so bitterly for what he had done in the years since that never a day went by when he didn't regret it and want more than anything to put it right. But too much time had passed now and no matter how hard it was living like this, it was the way he had chosen and despite his recent speculations about whether maybe they could repair it, he knew it would cause too much heartache and pain to turn back now.

Chapter 17

Michelle was sitting beside one of the colourful cabanas that edged the shimmering expanse of Ipanema beach. A few feet away a cluster of palms swayed in the breeze, while a hopeful young merchant struggled to lay his collection of vivid red sarongs out on the sand. Michelle watched for a while, her sandalled feet resting on an opposite chair, her long, tanned legs exposed to the blistering sun. On the table in front of her was an ice-cold glass of *chopp*, the local beer, and the latest report from America's Human Rights Watch.

She'd finished reading a few minutes ago and was now digesting the gruesome facts, while trying to equate all she'd learned with the sublime spectacle around her. It seemed so odd that nature should be at its most lovely in a place where humanity was at its most ugly, for in just the past six months the military police of this city had cold-bloodedly executed over four hundred people. Of course, they weren't people who could fend for themselves, or could afford lawyers or who could even report the crimes committed against them. They were the poor and hungry, black and jobless, and in many cases petty thieves or drug dealers. But as the report outlined very clearly, the reason they were driven to commit the crimes was either to eat, or to satisfy the extortion of the police.

The figures for the rest of the country were almost as

bad and it always had to be borne in mind that these numbers were an official toll. So God only knew how many more had been 'disappeared', for the failure of families to come forward was as understandable as it was regrettable. No one wanted to talk, for fear of losing another son, brother, husband or grandson. In other words the reign of terror was becoming more effective by the day and according to the report Pastillano's private death squad was thought to be behind more than sixty per cent of killings and illegal imprisonments.

Squinting against the sun, Michelle gazed thoughtfully along the street where the traffic honked, roared and squealed in a frantic bid to get from one set of lights to the next. At the very end of the beach, probably two miles from where she was sitting, a mountain rose towards the heavens, its peak shrouded in mist, its slopes bearing the burden of the world's largest slum. It was incongruous, really, and almost laughable that the poor should have such stupendous views of the ocean, while the rich strutted about the polluted city streets like silly peacocks in a maze of grime and concrete.

Turning to look down to the water's edge, she broke into a smile and waved at Cara and the children who were romping about in the surf. The beach was crowded today, for it was the weekend and it was here and at the Copacabana beach where all of Rio gathered, rich or poor, young or old, *carioca* or *mulatto*, parading their glorious sun-bronzed flesh in a spectacular orgy of sensuality and vitality. Despite the hundred-degree heat, scores of *cariocas* were leaping up and down with volleyballs or chasing footballs, or dancing wild sambas and reggae on the scorched white sands – or thieving from unsuspecting tourists who were sizzling like steaks in the cruel rays of the sun. In places the crowds were so thick it was easy for the kids to trip and fall on to a watch or wallet, or some other prized booty and no one ever seemed to know until it was too late. Barefoot hawkers turned a blind eye to the theft as they ambled about selling T-shirts, flags, cigarettes or vibrant string bikinis for some of the world's most beautiful women.

Sipping her drink, Michelle watched as the boy inside the cabana cleaved open a coconut and passed it to a fat German tourist. Then, looking on down the neatly mosaiced sidewalk, she spotted Tom Chambers coming towards her and broke into a smile.

'*Dois chopps*,' she said to the boy in the cabana, as she noticed Antônio from the shelter, was with him. She was very fond of Antônio and would always be grateful to him for the way he had so eagerly offered Cavan his apartment for the time Cavan was in Rio. Secretly Michelle suspected that Antônio was happier sleeping at the dormitories along with the homeless boys he knew so well. He probably got lonely at the apartment, for it certainly wasn't an environment he was used to. And providing Cavan with somewhere to live was helping her out too, for Michael would have to have a number for Cavan and though a part of her yearned for it to happen, another part of her dreaded picking up the phone one day and hearing his voice.

'How did it go?' she asked, as Tom sat down in the shade of the red and white *Brahma* umbrella while Antônio went over to talk to one of the deck-chair vendors.

'Good and bad,' Chambers replied. 'Where's Cavan?'

'He should be here any minute,' she answered.

Chambers took out a mobile phone and started to dial. 'Did you read that?' he asked, indicating the report on the table.

She nodded.

Chambers pursed the corner of his mouth, then making the connection he started to speak in rapid Portuguese.

As Michelle listened, she wondered what it was about him that always made her think of Michael. It had to be something in his manner, she thought, for his warm grey eyes, which relayed the only humour or gentleness in his otherwise hard and rugged face, and his large, muscular body were nothing like Michael's. Michael was taller and leaner, much more clean-cut and better looking. Yet there was a similarity in the two men which she found as disturbing as she did intriguing. She thought it probably came from a shared confidence and inner strength that was as reassuring to be around as it was sometimes maddening. Or maybe it was simply that she was thinking about Michael a lot lately, so no matter who it was, his brother or a virtual stranger, she was going to be reminded of him.

Chambers was still on the phone when Antônio came back and sat down. He had such a cheeky and happy look about him that it was almost impossible to credit the terrible life he had led – the imprisonment he had survived and torture he had endured – for his sunny, chocolate brown eyes were never far from mischief and his smooth, dark-skinned face bore none of the scars of his suffering. His body was a different story altogether, though, for thanks to the acid bath he had been forced to sit in while in police custody at fifteen years old he would never bear any children of his own.

'Tom said good and bad,' she told him as he picked up his beer. 'Did you see the public prosecutor?'

Antônio nodded and drank.

'Is he really on our side?'

Antônio nodded again. 'He doesn't want us going to his office,' he said. 'He thinks it's too dangerous – for everyone. It's best if he at least appears to be towing the line of corruption, so no one will look at him too closely.'

'And if we manage to get some evidence against Pastillano,' Michelle said, 'where can we reach him?'

321

'He's given us a number where we can leave a message,' Antônio replied. He glanced at Tom who was still engrosed in his call, then turned back to Michelle. 'Did Tom tell you about Márcio, the boy we took in a few weeks back? The one who turned out to be a member of the *Estrela* street gang?'

Michelle shook her head and frowned. 'What about him?' she said. 'I thought he went back to the streets.'

'He did. He was shot and killed by the police late yesterday afternoon.'

'Oh no,' Michelle murmured, remembering the boy's fear and arrogance, and the terrible sense of futility she had felt when he had chosen not to stay. 'What happened?'

'We found his brother outside the shelter last night,' Antônio answered. 'He'd been shot too. A couple of gang members carried him to us and dumped him. He's at the hospital now. Sister Lydia's with him.'

'Is he going to be all right?' Michelle asked.

He nodded. 'He should be. He's conscious, anyway.'

Michelle glanced at Chambers as he ended his call, then turned back to Antônio.

'Tom made some official enquiries this morning,' Antônio continued, 'and the police are claiming there was an incident with drug dealers in the Guararapes *favela*, where the *Estrela* gang usually hang out. For incident read shoot out, which is probably not too far from the truth, except once again we have no police injuries, while three teenage boys are dead and one is seriously wounded. So it doesn't look very likely that the boys were armed.'

'I take it the dead bodies were removed from the scene of the crime before the civil police had a chance to get there,' Michelle said.

Antônio nodded. 'I went over to the *favela* a couple of hours ago,' he said. 'According to the neighbours one officer stood over Márcio, who was lying on the ground already wounded, and shot him three times in the face.'

'Oh my God,' Michelle murmured. 'Is anyone prepared to come forward and say that?'

'Not that I could find,' Antônio answered.

'The real problem,' Chambers said, 'is the police being allowed to carry a second gun without having to register it. So all they have to do is open fire with their legitimate weapon, fire a couple of shots into the ground from the other and plant it on the body. *Et voilà!* A shoot out. And no one's ever going to look too deeply into it, because after all, armed or not, these boys are known criminals. Forced into it maybe, but there's no forum for mitigation here.'

Michelle looked at him. No matter how many times she heard these stories she never failed to be affected by the tragic loss of life, nor appalled by the terrible injustice that was meted out to these people.

'There's something else that might interest you about Márcio,' Antônio said. 'He has a baby son,'.

Michelle looked at him in astonishment. 'A son?' she echoed.

Antônio nodded. 'His name's Enéas. He's ten months old. I met him this morning.'

'But . . .' She shook her head, trying to make herself think. At fifteen Márcio was certainly old enough to father a child, in fact it wasn't so unusual here, but she just hadn't expected it. 'Where's the mother?' she asked.

'Dead from a drug overdose,' Antônio answered.

Michelle groaned with pity. 'So what's going to happen to the little boy now?' she asked. 'Did you take him to the shelter?'

Antônio glanced at Chambers.

Michelle watched them and seeing the way Chambers was looking at her she started to frown. 'What?' she said.

323

Chambers took a breath, then said, 'It would appear Márcio told his brother about Cavan and you, the fact that you're American – that's what he thought – and that you might take care of the child should anything happen to him.'

Michelle's eyes opened wide with shock. 'You mean he wants us to adopt the boy?' she said.

Chambers shrugged. 'I can't say for sure what he meant,' he answered.

Turning away, Michelle stared down the beach to where Cara and the children were still splashing about in the waves and seeing little Robbie and Larisa paddling frantically in to the shore she felt a very strange sensation passing through her. 'Where's the baby now?' she repeated, turning back to Antônio.

'With a woman in the *favela*,' Antônio answered. Then, laughing he said, 'Don't look so shocked. This kind of thing happens all the time with people who come here to help.'

'I know,' Michelle answered. 'But it's a first for me.' Then a sudden suspicion hit her and her eyes shot back to Chambers. 'Don't tell me this is the good news,' she said. 'That I'm about to add another child to that brood out there.'

Laughing, Chambers shook his head. 'That's for you to decide,' he replied. 'As far as I'm concerned the good news is that Antônio found out about someone this morning who spent some time at Pastillano's Inferno.'

Michelle's attention was instantly focused. 'And he got out?' she said.

'Some do,' he reminded her.

She turned to Antônio. 'Who is he?' she asked. 'One of the *Estrela* gang?'

Antônio nodded.

'Will he talk?' she said.

'I'm working on it,' Antônio answered. 'After what happened yesterday, there's a chance. But it'll probably mean going against the rest of the gang and they're not going to want any more trouble than they've already got, so don't hold out too much hope.'

'Will he at least *speak* to us?' she said. 'Even if we don't take anything down in writing, it'll be a start.'

Chambers raised a cautionary hand. 'This is the best lead we've had so far,' he reminded her, 'we can't rush it.' As he finished he was looking past her and starting to grin.

Michelle turned round and seeing Cavan paying for a taxi she got to her feet. 'Darling,' she said, putting her hands on his shoulders as he reached her. 'I was starting to worry.'

'And so you should,' he responded, his blue eyes shining with mirth as he looked over her shoulder to Antônio. 'You set me up,' he accused.

Michelle turned to Antônio and saw a picture of unabashed guilt. 'Not me,' he protested, holding up his hands.

'The hell it wasn't you,' Cavan laughed, pulling out a chair to sit down. 'He roped me in to giving the sex education class this morning,' Cavan explained, 'and who was there but Cristiana and all her chums from the night shift.'

Chambers burst out laughing and slapped Antônio on the back.

'So I take it you know how to do it now?' Michelle remarked as they sat down.

Antônio howled with laughter, while Chambers signalled for another round of beers.

'I wouldn't have minded,' Cavan protested, 'but Sister Teresa was sitting guard outside the door to make sure no one left without proper education and condoms.'

Michelle grinned. Sister Teresa might be a Catholic, but she was also a realist.

Having spotted Tom and Cavan sitting with

Michelle, the children were racing up the beach to see who could get there first. As they tumbled on to the pavement, Cavan swung Robbie and Larisa up in his arms, while six-year-old Tomasz, the eldest of the three, attempted to look too grown-up to care that he'd been left out. Noticing, Chambers immediately scooped the boy on to his lap and offered him some beer.

Michelle watched them, loving the way the men were so at ease with the children and smiling at the way Robbie in particular took such delight in their attention. He was a handsome little boy, with a strong, independent spirit and such a hopelessly mischievous nature that it wasn't really any surprise that he and Cavan had bonded so well. Catching Cavan's eye, she felt an unexpected tremor in her heart and had to quash a sudden desire to touch him. Lately, he had begun to talk of putting their relationship on a more permanent basis and though she'd never asked precisely what he meant by that, she knew that the time would soon come when she would have to make a decision one way or the other and it was a day she was dreading almost as much as the one when she and Michael would have to meet again.

But Cavan wasn't Michael. He was different in so many ways that were it not for the looks she could almost doubt their connection. She never felt threatened or overwhelmed by Cavan. With him she could be her own person and not feel railroaded into a life and ambition she'd never even been sure was her own. But she had loved Michael so much that for a long time she had believed that everything he wanted she wanted too. She'd have done anything to make him happy and even now, with so much distance and so many years between them, she still thought about him all the time and longed for him in ways he would probably never know. But what they had ended up doing to each other could never be repaired now, perhaps never forgiven

326

either. Lowering her eyes to Robbie, she wondered if her affair with Cavan was to punish Michael for what he had done. Or maybe it was to try and make him take her back, even though she was the one who'd left.

Finding her thoughts too painful to pursue she quickly put them aside and turned to Antônio. 'The woman who's looking after Márcio's son,' she said quietly. 'Is she a relative of Márcio's?'

Antônio's eyebrows went up as he nodded, giving Michelle the impression he'd been waiting for her to ask.

'Mother? Aunt? Grandmother?' she said.

'Aunt,' he answered.

'Did she see what happened yesterday?'

'So she says.'

'Do you think she'll talk to me if you arrange it?'

Antônio had no chance to answer before Chambers cut in. 'Forget it,' he said.

Michelle turned to look at him, surprised he'd heard and irritated by his tone.

'Don't even think about it,' Chambers told her, dodging Tomasz's head as he swung back to avoid Larisa's punch.

Michelle's expression darkened as sitting back, she made room for Robbie on her lap. 'I thought the point of us being here was to gather evidence,' she challenged.

'It is,' he confirmed, glancing at Cavan who had just become aware of the conversation, 'but if anyone's going in there to interview it'll be me. Especially after yesterday's shootings.'

'The women might feel more comfortable speaking to me,' she said, trying to keep the edge from her voice.

'You're here as a back-up,' he reminded her. 'If they won't speak to me, that's when we bring you in.'

'And by then they might not want to speak to anyone

at all,' she responded tightly. 'If they're even alive to do so. And what about the baby?'

'The baby's a different issue.'

'What baby?' Cavan asked.

Michelle glanced at him. 'I'll explain later,' she answered. 'I'd like to see it,' she said to Chambers.

'We'll arrange for it to be taken to the shelter,' he responded and raised his glass to his lips as though pronouncing an end to the subject.

Though Michelle was still bristling, she'd had enough experience of him to know when to back down. If she didn't he'd probably end up organizing her ticket out of Brazil and after coming this far there was just no way she was going to be forced out now. In fact, angry as she was, she understood his caution, for he had already lost one woman in the course of his work, so there was just no way he was going to risk losing another.

Hugging Robbie closer while Cara put sodas on the table, Michelle watched Chambers as he and Cavan, in a way that was so typical of men, managed to put aside the vital matters of the moment and launched into a heated debate on the football game they had attended at the Maracanã stadium two nights ago. Wanting to join in, Robbie scrambled from her lap, hesitated a moment as Cara told him to slow down, then climbed back on to Cavan's knee. Tomasz was still with Chambers and as the two little boys began echoing the men Michelle and Cara set about ordering hot dogs.

Though Chambers never talked about Rachel, nor gave any sign of the terrible guilt he had suffered following her death, Michelle knew how often he thought about her and how hard it had been for him to come to terms with her kidnap and murder. As a journalist herself, Rachel had been with Tom in Colombia reporting on the latest shock statistics to come out of the country – that street children were being exterminated at the rate of two thousand a year. Sadly, it was Rachel's kidnapping that had made headlines all over the world, rather than what was happening to the children, as had the discovery of her murdered body in the coastal town of Cartagena. But it wasn't her bold and impassioned reports on the plight of the children that the Colombians had objected to, it was Chambers's investigation into the infamous Condoza drug cartel. Had Rachel not been Tom's lover she would probably never have been a target; as it was, they had snatched her as a warning to Tom to back off, now! Had he done that, then what had followed might never have happened, but he hadn't, and it was for that mistake that he'd never stopped paying.

Though he'd wanted to go in search of the killers, a friend and senior editor at the Washington *Post* had sent a couple of ex-paras to force him out of the country before he got himself killed too. The *Post* along with *New York Times* and the *Times Picayune* in New Orleans, had then taken up the story of Rachel's murder, which triggered a long and bitter dispute between the US and Colombia, as Washington demanded the immediate arrest of those responsible for the killing and the Colombian government, who were all but controlled by the Condoza family, consistently failed to comply. It was only after more than a million people took to the streets of the Southern States, most particularly in New Orleans, Rachel's home town, to protest against what had happened and try to force the government to take stronger action, that the Colombians finally named the killers. The fact that at least one of them had been shot and killed by a rival cartel two weeks *before* Rachel was taken was a detail that Washington had very neatly overlooked in its bid to re-establish relations and calm the civil unrest that was starting to spread to the Northern States.

Had Chambers not taken himself off to Sarajevo by

then, in an effort to put it all behind him, the story might not have slipped from the spotlight when it did and the chicanery and deceit would have been exposed. As it was, he had been so disgusted with the performance of his own government, never mind the Colombians, that he had left before the killers were named. And by the time the news reached him he was too caught up in the war in Europe to do anything about it. Indeed, it was his failure to act at that time that he found so hard to live with now, for not only did he hold himself responsible for Rachel's death, he couldn't forgive himself either for allowing her killers to go unpunished.

It was because of his past and the grief he still bore that Michelle was prepared to bite her tongue now and allow him to take the decisions. After all, they'd already received one warning from Pastillano which no one had so far heeded, so there wasn't much doubt that they were being watched and the moment they appeared to be getting close to anything that might in any way cause Pastillano even the slightest embarrassment or anxiety, the danger they were in would increase to proportions it was probably best not to dwell on.

Michelle looked at the children again and watched young Larisa flashing her lovely blue eyes at Antônio. Though it was highly doubtful Pastillano would risk an international scandal by threatening the lives of three European children, arrangements had nevertheless been made for them to be whisked into hiding the very second anything untoward occurred. But without a single deposition in hand, or the guarantee of one in the near future, they were a long way from having to implement the plans yet. Unless, of course, Márcio's aunt and the Estrela gang member really did have some information worth pursuing.

Finding Cavan watching her again she smiled and

realized that the next time she spoke to Antônio she would have to make sure that neither Tom nor Cavan were around. It could be that Antônio, having just witnessed Tom's reaction to her getting involved without him, would block it too. But she had at least to try, for the elections were alarmingly close now and once Pastillano was in power the horrors the *favelados* would be subjected to then were going to make what was happening now look like a day on the beach by comparison.

Chapter 18

Ellen's concentration on the notes she was making appeared total. It was as though she were the only one in the room, she was so caught up in what she was doing. On the table in front of her was her leather writing case, a yellow legal pad inserted inside it, a couple of pencils with erasers and the silver pen she was using. She reached for her glass of water, took a sip, then resumed the industrious annotations she was making on a contract that had nothing to do with the one she was in the process of negotiating.

It was all an act, but she had to do something while the three studio executives, two producers, three accountants and two lawyers did the figure work on the final detail of the five-million-dollar-plus package they had been discussing for the past three weeks. It wasn't only the fee that was causing them a problem, it was the terms of the residual agreement and three and a half per cent share of international sales that she had thrown in just prior to this meeting. Added to that, she was now asking for a five per cent cut of any merchandise deal arising from the movie, should her client's voice or anatomy, in whole or in part, feature in the design or promotion of said merchandise, and a guaranteed casting and seven-million-dollar fee for a sequel with a basically one-sided option to renegotiate should the original movie gross more than eighty million in its first week at the domestic box-office.

The astonishment and discomfort that had followed her surprise clauses had turned quickly to anger, then to a flat-out refusal on the part of Butch Sommers, one of the producers, to continue doing business with her. Sommers was out on a limb, for he was the only one of his team who was against Walker Nicolas taking on the role of *The Traveller*, the new multi-million-selling sci-fi book that had broken all records in the publishing and magazine worlds. While Sommers ranted and raved, and demanded countless withdrawals to persuade his colleagues to drop Walker Nicolas, Ellen's client, Ellen had sat out the storm, remaining as unruffled and implacable as Foster McKenzie, the studio head who was watching her and the proceedings as carefully as his lawyers were scrutinizing the new terms and conditions she had so audaciously presented.

Until now there hadn't been much time for her to wonder why she was taking such a gamble with her career, except she was furious at Forgon for the impossible and often idiotic tests he was throwing her way lately. It was as though he wanted to see how far he could push her before the pressure became too much and forced her to self-destruct. And she guessed, considering what she had brought to the table today, she was pretty close to it now, for even Rosa and Kip, who had come along with her, had no idea that she hadn't discussed the last minute changes with Forgon or Nicolas, in fact they probably imagined them to be instructions rather than free-hand additions.

In truth, the fear of what she had done was making her light-headed, as adrenalin pulsed through her with a life force of its own and the reckless anger that had fuelled most of her decisions since Forgon had printed the picture of her at Clay's house was like a whip

333

lashing at her reason and blinding her to care or consequence.

Yet she showed none of what was going on inside her, as she sat there at the table, laboriously marking up an old contract, while the accountants and producers went outside to talk and Foster McKenzie finally got up and followed them. Ellen's skin felt as though a thousand red-hot needles were trying to break their way through, for it was a well-known fact that if McKenzie left the room *after* the lawyers, rather than *with* the lawyers, the show was all but over.

However, just under an hour later Ellen, Rosa and Kip were on their feet reaching across the table to shake hands with the opposing team. Foster McKenzie hadn't come back with them, but for the moment Ellen was too dazed to work out what it might mean. In fact, a part of her was convinced she must still be in bed dreaming, for as she received the congratulations and good-natured teasing of her colleagues and even a grudging admiration from Sommers, she realized how convinced she had been she would fail. Indeed, she even wondered if it hadn't been what she wanted, for she felt strangely empty now it was over, unable to connect with what was being said, even though she was responding to it fully and even joining in with the laughter and relief that all that was needed now was Nicolas's signature on the second-to-last page.

'I've got to tell you,' Rosa said as she, Ellen and Kip, ATI's chief legal officer, walked back to the parking lot, 'I never thought you'd pull it off, not with that one-sided option thrown in. Geez, whatever made them buy it is what I want to know?'

'I just knew, the minute McKenzie got up and walked out, we were sunk,' Kip declared. 'In fact, someone pinch me and tell me again we just got ourselves a deal, because in all my fifteen years of dealing with McKenzie I've never known him walk out of a meeting last without it meaning the deal was off.'

'Did you see the way he was looking at you?' Rosa said to Ellen. 'I swear he was waiting for you to break. Christ, the way you held out over that three and a half per cent . . . I've never seen anything like it. It put the fear of God into me. I really thought you were going to blow it. I'm telling you, McKenzie might not show it, but he was mad as hell when you stood your ground and I for one was convinced he was going to walk then.'

'Me too,' Ellen confessed.

Rosa turned to look at her, saw the humour shining in her eyes, then started to laugh. 'It's no wonder Forgon put you in to seal this one up. You're so damned cool you make Zen look like a neurosis. Or does Forgon know Foster McKenzie's got the hots for you?'

'He does not have the hots for me either,' Ellen laughed, digging into her purse for her keys.

'Oh, excuse me, just three invitations to dinner and no doubt a personal request to Forgon that you handle the negotiations on this deal.'

'Wrong way round,' Ellen informed her. 'McKenzie was livid when he heard I was taking over.'

Kip was laughing. 'Because Forgon had just dealt from the bottom of the pack,' he declared. 'Anyway, my car's up on the next level. I'll catch you two back at the office.'

Rosa and Ellen got into Ellen's car and as she drove them out on to Lankershim Boulevard Ellen was speaking on the phone to Walker Nicolas's manager, letting him in on the good news. By the time she finished they had left the Valley and were crossing the lights on Sunset, heading towards the next major junction at Santa Monica.

'We're invited to Walker's for a party tonight,' Ellen

said, dropping the phone in her lap. She glanced over at Rosa. 'Interested?'

'Are you kidding?' Rosa laughed. 'I'd lie on my back and catch peanuts with my chuff for that man. Is he still with Samara Vito?'

Ellen was laughing. 'I'm afraid so,' she confirmed.

'No taste,' Rosa muttered. 'So, what about Foster McKenzie?' she went on, folding her arms and crossing her long, skinny legs.

'What about him?'

Rosa rolled her eyes. 'Ellen, the man is head of one of the biggest movie studios in the world, he's currently getting divorced, he's not half bad looking and he's asked you out three times already. So when are you going to quit the aloof act and do what any right-minded woman in your position would do and offer up your tarnished virtue in exchange for the endless privileges this man can bestow?'

'Who says I'm going to?' Ellen countered.

'Sure you are. No one turns a man like McKenzie down for long. Unless they've got something seriously wrong with them, of course.' Her head came round. 'Do you have something seriously wrong with you?' she asked.

Ellen grinned. 'He doesn't do anything for me,' she said.

'What!' Rosa cried in disgust. 'All that power and he doesn't do anything for you! Jesus Christ, Ellen, did you get an imagination bypass, or something?'

'His eyes are too close together,' Ellen responded.

Rosa looked genuinely perplexed. 'What's that got to do with anything?' she demanded.

Ellen shrugged.

'Listen to me, honey,' Rosa said. 'Foster McKenzie's eyes might be too close together, but yours have got to be in your butt if you can't see where it could land you, getting involved with him. Christ, you could kiss

336

goodbye to Forgon right now and set up your production company with offices on the lot and projects coming in so fast you'll be hotter than Spielberg.'

Ellen smiled. 'Put like that, I could be tempted,' she remarked.

'So?' Rosa prompted.

'So what?'

'So, what's stopping you?'

Ellen glanced over at her, then, spinning the wheel hard to the right she turned on to Santa Monica and drove on towards the office.

Rosa was still waiting, but it soon became clear that Ellen wasn't going to answer, though she probably didn't have to for the glance had told Rosa enough. 'Listen, honey,' she said, bringing all the wisdom of her thirty-eight years and three disastrous marriages to bear, 'you've got to get past all that business with Clay. I know he let you down real bad and he didn't have to do it the way he did, but it's in the past now, you can't change it, so you've got to find it in you to move on.'

'I know,' Ellen said, keeping her eyes on the road ahead.

'Foster McKenzie's nothing like Clay,' Rosa said warmly. 'OK, he's had his share of women and I don't doubt there are some out there who'd cut off his balls as soon as look at him, but you haven't been out on a date in months, Ellen, and he surely can't be a bad place to start.'

Ellen inhaled deeply, but was saved from answering by Rosa's cellphone ringing.

'Hi, this is Rosa,' she said into the handset. 'Oh, Pollard, hi, how are you? Sure, I'm doing fine. What can I do for you?' She paused for a moment, then her eyes suddenly lit up and she turned to look at Ellen as she gasped, 'No kidding! You did! Pollard, you can raid my wardrobe any time. I really owe you for this.'

Ellen looked at her.

'He's got invites to the première of *United We Fall*,' Rosa told her.

Ellen looked impressed. There hadn't been so much fuss over a première since *Evita* and the tickets to *United We Fall* were just as hard to come by. In fact, exactly like with *Evita*, actors, agents, producers, directors, indeed just about anyone involved in the industry had been begging, stealing, dealing, bribing and God only knew what else, for weeks now in an effort to get themselves invited to the world première of Victor Warren's much talked about adaptation of the modern classic. It was a very definite arbiter of who was and wasn't on the Hollywood A list.

'You bet,' Rosa was saying. 'Sure I'll pay for the limo. I'll have it come pick you up first unless you want to meet up at my place. OK. Whatever you say. . . . Are you kidding? Pollard, I'll get you a whole bunch of Epicuran facials for Christmas, if that's what you want. I'll even pluck the hair from your nostrils.'

As she rang off, both she and Ellen were laughing. 'The man's a genius,' Rosa declared. 'If he weren't gay I'd marry him. I'm afraid his friend's gay as well, but who cares, at least we get to go to the movie. What the hell are we going to wear? Shall we go shopping tomorrow? What better excuse do we get?'

'You mean he's got me a ticket too?' Ellen said.

'Of course.'

They were stopped at red lights and Rosa could hardly believe her eyes as Ellen turned to her with a look Rosa didn't want to understand. 'Christ, don't tell me you don't want to go,' she said.

'It's not that,' Ellen responded. 'It's just . . .' As she finished what she was saying Rosa spoke over her, so didn't immediately hear.

'Now this I've got to hear,' Rosa was muttering, 'because no way in the world can I think of a good enough excuse not to go to this première. What did you just say?' she cried, her head swinging round as Ellen's words finally registered.

Ellen's soft brown eyes were twinkling with laughter. 'I said, I'm already going,' she replied.

Rosa gaped at her, struck dumb with amazement. 'You're going to the première of *United* and you never told me,' she cried.

'I'm sorry,' Ellen said, pulling down the corners of her mouth. 'I only found out last night and we've had other things on the agenda today.'

'So who are you going with?' Rosa demanded, obviously not sure whether or not to be pissed.

'Michael McCann,' Ellen answered and had the great satisfaction of watching Rosa's jaw drop.

'You mean the British guy Forgon sent you over to London to make an offer he managed to refuse?' she said.

Ellen laughed and nodded.

'Well how do you like that?' Rosa muttered to herself. 'Is he here then? In LA?' she asked. 'And how come he, a Britisher, gets an invite, when the rest of us red-blooded Americans have to practically sell our bodies just to get on the waiting list?'

Ellen was still smiling. 'He's Victor Warren's agent,' she said.

'No shit,' Rosa commented. 'And so what, he called you up and asked if you'd like to go along to the première with him?' she said, clearly having a hard time taking it in.

'And Victor Warren and his wife,' Ellen added.

'My God, I don't believe this,' Rosa said. 'I mean, what happened between you guys in London? Did you get it on, or something? I don't blame you if you did, he's good-looking enough to charm the pants off the Queen, should he ever be into acts of mercy, but why did you never tell me?'

'There was nothing to tell,' Ellen laughed, glad that

Rosa had no way of knowing what a turmoil she was really in over the invitation that had come completely out of the blue. She hadn't even known he was in LA when he called, in fact, she'd assumed he was in London, but he'd given her an LA number at which she could contact him should she need to, and unable to stop herself she'd tried it out that morning and found that he'd checked in to the Four Seasons Hotel on Doheny the day before. So he hadn't wasted much time in calling her when he got here, which surely meant he was as keen to see her as she was to see him. Well, perhaps not that keen, as the première was still an entire week away and already she was beginning to wonder if she could stand to wait so long.

'So, throw a party and invite him along,' Matty said, in the kind of voice that bespoke the obvious solution.

'I can't do that,' Ellen protested, almost losing her voice in a shudder of nerves.

'Why not? All you've got to say is that you already had it fixed and forgot to mention it when he called, but you thought he might like to come along too.'

'What if he says no? I'll have to throw a party I don't want.'

Matty threw up her hands in exasperation. 'Ask him first,' she said.

'What if he's not free on the night I choose? I can hardly say, oh sorry, I didn't mean Wednesday, I meant Thursday?'

Matty's darkly attractive face was incredulous. 'That's the whole point of asking him first,' she pointed out. 'And if he's not free on the night you pick, you'll just have to wait for the première.'

'So which night do I choose?'

Matty rolled her eyes. 'It's a good job you don't manage your career the way you manage your love life,' she chided, 'or we'd all be out of work. Friday or Saturday. If it were me I'd opt for Friday.'

'Why?'

'Because it's sooner and you can't wait to see him.'

'Actually, I can,' Ellen responded.

'OK, then Saturday.'

'Why not wait 'til the première?' Ellen suggested.

Matty shrugged. 'OK.'

Ellen signalled for the waiter to bring her another glass of wine. 'I could do Friday,' she said.

'Do you have your phone?' Matty asked. 'Stupid question, when do you ever not have your phone? So, call the hotel now and ask him if he's free on Friday.'

Ellen felt the bottom fall out of her stomach.

Matty's eyes narrowed. She knew that expression well. 'OK, I'll do it and pretend I'm your secretary,' she said.

Ellen passed her the phone.

Seconds later Matty was connected to the Four Seasons. 'Michael McCann's room, please,' she said. While she was waiting Ellen held out her hand for the phone.

'If he's there I'll speak to him,' she said, taking it.

As she put the phone to her ear she heard him say, 'Hello?'

Her heart did a series of somersaults, a sudden panic fried her nerve and she very nearly disconnected the call. 'Hi, it's Ellen Shelby,' she said shakily. 'Uh, how are you?'

'OK,' he answered, sounding surprised. 'Where are you? What's all the noise?'

'I'm in a Chinese on Sunset with my cousin Matty,' she answered. 'I was wondering . . . I mean, I forgot to say when you called last night that I'm throwing a small party on Friday and I was wondering if you'd like to come.'

'You mean this Friday?' he asked.

Ellen tensed. He had other arrangements, he was going to say no and she wished to God already that she'd never picked up the phone. 'Yes, this Friday,' she answered dully.

'What time?'

Ellen looked at Matty. 'What time?' she mouthed.

'Any time he can get there,' Matty provided.

'Around seven,' Ellen said, scowling at Matty. 'It's just drinks until nine or so.'

'I probably won't make it until eight,' he answered, 'but sure, I'd love to come. Do you want to give me your address?'

Ellen was about to go through the spelling of the elaborate Spanish name of the apartment complex when she said, 'I'll fax it over to you in the morning along with the directions.'

'OK,' he responded. 'I'll look forward to seeing you.'

'Me too,' she said and as she rang off and looked at Matty she muttered, 'I don't know if I can wait 'til Friday.'

By Friday Ellen was getting pretty close to calling the whole thing off. She couldn't remember ever feeling so apprehensive about anything, not a deal, a date, not even a diagnosis. It was crazy to be so uptight, she knew that, especially when she spent at least fifty per cent of her time with some of the world's most desirable movie stars, men who would turn most women to jello with a single glance. Yet here she was, a thirty-year-old highly successful woman, totally unable to hold it together over a man she barely knew, who was just an agent the same as her, with probably less clients than she had and virtually no Hollywood cred.

But what the hell did she care how many clients he had, or where he might rate on the Hollywood scale of who was pulling in the most bucks for whom? If anything, it only made him more attractive, as he was nothing like the Hollywood power-freaks and egomaniacs she spent so much time trying to avoid, in fact he was so different that she honestly couldn't see a single reason for him to want to move here. Not that that was on the agenda any more, at least not so far as she was concerned. Ted Forgon, of course, would be sure to disagree, but tonight's party wasn't about Ted Forgon, nor was what might come after. But she couldn't allow herself to think that far ahead. Even though the possibilities for him in Hollywood were endless and as he was anything but stupid, he had to know already that there were a lot more people in this town with real integrity and genuine artistic ability than the publicity machine ever gave credit for. In truth, he could be working with some of the most well-respected and highly paid talent in the world if he were to give up London and come here. There was nothing he couldn't achieve if he set his mind to it, for she just knew that it would take him no time at all to sort through all the flakes and phoneys and get himself into a position where he could make a real difference to what was going on in this élitist little oligarchy that had so much influence on the rest of the world.

Groaning inwardly as she realized her thoughts were coming dangerously close to some kind of sales pitch for Forgon, she hit several buttons on her keyboard and made an attempt to carry on with her work. But the thoughts just kept chasing each other around in her head and as her emotions shifted from anger to indignance to excitement back to nervousness, and on to a wild and embarrassing hope of where tonight might end, she could almost hear the panic chanting through her head. What am I going to wear? Where do I get my nails fixed? Is there time for surgery? Will it be painful?

'But you've never had your nails done before,' Matty cried when she called to ask Matty's advice.

343

'Maybe it's time I did,' Ellen responded, putting a script over the flashing lights on her phone pad so she didn't have to look at the incoming calls. 'Did you do the shopping? Did you get good wine? He knows about wines.'

'We got good wine.'

'Should we set up the drinks in the kitchen or on the veranda? You know, I'm not sure about that top I bought. What do you think?'

'Ellen, pull yourself together,' Matty laughed. 'Everything's in hand. Gene's here at the apartment with me now sorting out the music, we'll set up the snacks and wine where we think best and all you have to do is come home and get yourself ready. And forget about the acrylic nails, you don't need them and being no expert in these things you'll probably end up doing yourself, or him, a lasting injury if you do get them.'

'What about the top?' Ellen asked.

'It's terrific. You'll blow his mind.'

'You don't think it's too revealing?'

'It's perfect. Now get off the line will you, I've got a party to organize here.'

Ellen hit a couple of buttons and took another call. She had so much to get through before she could leave there was every chance she was going to show up late for her own party. Actually, it wouldn't be the first time, but tonight there was just no way she was going to allow her job to come first. She'd almost rather die than admit it, but she had two sets of new underwear in her cupboard, a three-hundred-dollar Moschino bustier still in its tissue and had earlier rushed out to buy a bottle of Hermès Vingt Quatre Faubourg, probably the most sensuous perfume in the world.

As she continued through meetings and phone calls and a ceaseless barrage of interruptions, she was persistently assailed by the dread of him calling to say he couldn't make it. But then she reminded herself that there was still the première and God only knew what state she was going to get herself into during the build-up to that. She guessed she just had to be thankful that because of her job she was by now pretty skilled at putting on a front, so no one but Matty knew what a pathetic mess she was inside.

'Rubbish!' Matty declared later. 'You look so terrible you're giving me the jitters. *It was a joke!*' she cried as Ellen's face paled. 'A joke. Remember them?' As Ellen's expression relaxed Matty turned back to the mirror and continued applying her mascara. 'Anyway,' she went on, 'who are you trying to convince about Hollywood? I thought you said there was no way he'd ever base himself here.'

She carried on with her mascara until realizing she hadn't received a reply, she looked down at Ellen in the bath tub and seeing the shy mischief in Ellen's eyes she started to grin. 'Except you're hoping he might change his mind for you,' she declared.

Ellen's cheeks coloured as she said, 'OK, I confess it. I want him to fall madly in love with me and come here and spend the rest of his life with me. There, I've killed it now by speaking it aloud.'

Matty's carefully shaped eyebrows were raised. 'Are you sure you only ever had dinner with this man?' she asked.

Ellen sighed and dipped down in the water. 'I've made love with him so many times in my imagination,' she said, after resurfacing, 'I already know what it's going to be like, I mean, should we ever get around to it. And there's something about him, you know, something I can't quite put my finger on that just works for me. It's like . . .' Her eyes moved back to Matty's and she started to laugh. 'Get out of here,' she cried, throwing a sponge at Matty who was gazing at her with love-struck, starry eyes.

'You could always go live in London,' Matty pointed out, turning back to her make-up.

Ellen pulled a face. 'Not really,' she said. 'There's not enough going on over there.'

'He's there,' Matty reminded her.

Ellen gazed absently down at her outstretched legs. 'You know, I really want him to come here,' she said after a while. 'Not necessarily because of me, but because I think this town could really work for him. And I want him to see that we're not all vanity freaks or power junkies the way everyone seems to think.'

Matty looked surprised. 'We're not?' she responded.

Ellen rolled her eyes, then, reaching for a thick, fluffy blue towel she stepped out of the tub. 'Did anyone call to cancel?' she asked, starting to dry herself.

'Only Karla, but you expected that,' Matty answered. 'Did you make any bruschetta?'

'Not yet, I'll do it just before everyone arrives. And unless you want to greet your guests like that I suggest you get a move on.'

As Matty left the bathroom Ellen turned to the full-length mirror and looked at her damp, naked body with its glistening, creamy skin, taut red nipples and thatch of curled chestnut hair at the join of her long legs. She tried to see herself through Michael's eyes and found that the mere thought of being naked with him was causing her pulses to quicken and a sharp bite of lust to tighten her loins. She was in no doubt now that the desire she felt for him had only increased since that night in the restaurant, indeed there were moments when she thought she might go crazy with the sheer power of it. And right now she was very close to believing that the reason he had called her virtually the minute he'd arrived in LA was because he felt the same way. Except she hadn't forgotten the way he'd turned her down last time and it was the horror of it

346

happening again that would make certain she kept herself well and truly in check tonight.

It was a quarter to ten by the time Michael finally knocked on the door of Ellen's apartment. The party was obviously over for there was no sound coming from within, though he knew she was there because the security guard had called up to announce his arrival. As he'd driven through the complex to the underground parking he'd wondered if she was angry that he hadn't called to say he'd be late. He probably should have, but the meeting with Victor Warren had gone on much longer than he'd expected and in the end it had just seemed more sensible to get in the car and come.

He was on the point of knocking again, or kicking himself for coming empty-handed, when the door suddenly opened.

'Hi, I'm Matty, Ellen's cousin,' the tall, attractive brunette told him. 'You must be Michael. Come along in. You're too late for some, not late enough for others.'

Laughing, Michael followed her inside. The lights were low and the debris of a finished party was still cluttering the room. He noticed a few people sitting out on the veranda, but for the moment there was no sign of Ellen.

'Can I get you a drink?' Matty offered. 'We've got just about everything.'

'Scotch,' Michael said and was about to ask where Ellen was when he noticed her sitting separately on the veranda with a couple of others. She looked so lovely, so much more beautiful than he remembered, that all the tiredness and jet-lag he had brought from Australia was fused into a single desire to hold her.

'Hi,' he said as she walked in to greet him.

She looked at him and as her lovely dark eyes gazed into his it was all he could do to stop himself reaching for her.

'Am I too late?' he asked.

Her eyes held his a moment or two longer, then, smiling she said, 'I hope not.'

It was hard to tell if she was mad at him, but he didn't think she was.

'Your drink,' she said, as Matty came up behind them.

He took it, then, as Matty went to rejoin the others he said, 'Next time it's your turn.'

She frowned, obviously not understanding.

'To be late,' he explained. 'This is the second time I've done it to you.'

She smiled. 'Everyone's gone for dinner at the Mirabelle,' she said. 'We were just about to go too.' She paused, then said, 'Would you like to come?'

He looked at her, holding her eyes with his and wanting only to touch her. 'If that's what you want,' he said.

Her lower lip trembled as she caught it between her teeth. She was still looking at him and neither of them seemed to hear the explosion of laughter on the terrace.

His eyes were roaming freely over her face and neck, taking in the lush, coppery hair tumbling around her bare shoulders and exquisite honeyed skin that was so soft and inviting. The gentle slope of her breasts was rising and falling with each breath she took and the light in her eyes was reflecting the emotions in his own.

She gave a small, self-conscious laugh, then, with an absent wave towards the others she said, 'You met Matty. The others are Gene, Matty's boyfriend, Rosa, who I work with and Rosa's date, Ernest. The two sitting in the corner, who I was talking to when you came in, are Joseph and Ally, they've just become Scientologists.'

He turned to look, then, taking a sip of his drink he said, 'Shall we join them?'

Ellen smiled. 'If that's what you want.'

A flicker of laughter shot to his eyes and following her outside into the quiet, balmy night, he shook hands with everyone and apologized again for turning up so late. Almost before he knew it he was drawn into a light-hearted banter with Rosa and Matty, and though he held his own well, he was distracted by how closely Ellen was watching him. She had gone to sit the other side of the table, next to Gene, and each time she laughed he felt something deep down inside him start to respond.

Aware of the chemistry between them, Ellen watched the intensity of his expression and felt the heat burn through her. She had been hurt and angry that he had turned up so late and so afraid that he wasn't going to show at all, that it had virtually ruined the evening. But now he was here and as the others laughed and joked around them, all she really knew was the commanding power of his eyes and a deep, inexpressible longing to touch him.

'I guess we should be going,' Matty said, putting her empty glass on the table. 'The others will be wondering where we are. Are you joining us, Michael?' she asked.

Michael looked at Ellen and as her eyes met his she heard herself say, 'You go on ahead, we'll catch you up later.'

Everyone got up to go. Ellen walked with them to the door and after saying goodbye, she turned back to find Michael sitting on the far balustrade of the veranda, watching her. She remained where she was, at the centre of the room, and as they continued to look at each other she could feel the strength of her need turning her body weak.

She started to speak, but her breath wouldn't come and her heart faltered as he got to his feet and walked into the room. He stopped in front of her and when she raised her eyes to his, he leaned towards her and kissed her on the mouth. It was the most sensational and erotic kiss she had ever known and as the scent of him coasted through her senses, the taste of him and the feel of him carried her to a point of insane desire. Releasing her, he gazed down into her eyes, then lifting her hand to take her fingertips into his mouth in a way that was letting her know what he was going to do to her nipples. By now the ache in them was so fierce she could barely stand it and the harder he sucked on her fingers the closer she got to losing control.

He dropped her hand and began to circle her lips with his finger. She drew the finger deep into her mouth and sucked it hard. Then her eyes closed and her lips parted as the sensation of his other hand moving down over her neck and across the tops of her breasts stole through her with a soft, insistent command for more. He continued to stroke her, watching her face as she became so aroused she could barely breathe. She wanted his mouth on her breasts so badly she was on the verge of begging. Reaching behind her she unfastened the hooks and eyes of her top, and peeling it away from her skin she let it fall to the floor. His eyes remained on hers, but she could feel the sudden tension in his body, and when finally he lowered his gaze to her breasts she felt them burn into her skin like the most ardent caress.

He was standing so close she could feel his breath on her face and seeing the strain of desire around his mouth she almost fell against him. As though sensing it, he put his hands on her shoulders and holding her there, lowered his lips to her breasts and took first one, then the other nipple tightly into his mouth. Her head fell back as her legs turned weak and the urgency of her desire soared to new heights. He kept going, a relentless assault with his tongue, biting her and sucking until she knew beyond any doubt he could make her come this way. Then suddenly his mouth was on hers, his tongue moving deeply and sensuously inside as he slid his hands to her buttocks and pulled her to his hardness. Feeling him so ready for her she pressed herself in closer, then unfastening the buttons of her wrapover skirt she let it slide to the floor. All she wore now was a tiny pair of lace panties and gold, high-heeled sandals

The kiss went on and on, their lips moulding together, their tongues entwining, their need of each other sounding in the quickening of their breaths and soft moans of desire. Then he was easing her panties over her hips, drawing them down over her thighs and dropping to his knees as he removed them altogether. She looked down at him as taking her buttocks in his hands he pulled her to him and began to kiss the most intimate part of her until she no longer knew how she was standing.

It was just as her climax was about to break that he reached for her hands and pulled her down with him. Gazing into her eyes once more, he began unbuttoning his shirt while she unfastened his trousers until at last he was naked too. She touched him and felt him so big in her hand, so hard and unyielding that she lay down on the carpet and pulled him down with her.

He groaned aloud as her hand tightened around him. Then suddenly his mouth was hard on hers and he was between her legs, moving right up inside her, stretching her with the enormity of his erection and holding her with the intensity of his desire. Her legs circled his waist and her fingers dug into his shoulders as he pounded her with the full might of his passion and looked down at her with a fierceness that pushed her so close to the edge. Then his mouth covered hers and the sudden change in his rhythm pushed her right out to oblivion.

She screamed and her whole body turned rigid as he raised himself up and looked down to where they were joined. The harsh, pounding break of her orgasm was

351

clenching his cock and ricocheting through him like the commanding pulse of a storm. He could feel her limbs turning weak as her inner muscles gripped him anew. Her arms sank to the floor, but her legs clung to him tightly and her breasts shook with the power of his pounding hips. Then suddenly his own climax exploded, and as the force of it rushed into her he grew so hard and pressed himself so deeply inside her she moaned aloud with the ecstacy and pain.

He held her close, feeling her body meld into his as the thrashing rhythm of their hearts began slowly to subside and the desperate gasping for air became a normal quest for breath. His hand moved up into her hair and as he finally rolled on to his back, she rested her head on his shoulder and eased one leg gently between his.

It was some time before she realized he'd fallen asleep. Smiling to herself she drew herself up to her knees and looked down at him. He was so incredibly beautiful in a wholly masculine way that she felt a quiet surge in her heart as her eyes moved over his body and back to his face. Then, very gently, she shook him awake.

His eyes opened and he seemed confused for a moment. Then, lifting a hand to her face he said, 'You're beautiful.'

Smiling, she said, 'So are you. And you're very tired too, so why don't you get into bed?'

He cocked a comical eyebrow and she guessed that had he been able he'd have treated her to some of his more droll English humour. As it was, all he managed was a mere, 'Only if you come with me,' and minutes later he was fast asleep again with a single sheet covering their loosely entwined bodies.

Chapter 19

Three days had gone by since Michael had spent the night at Ellen's apartment and she hadn't heard from him once. It was so incredible she could hardly make herself accept that the silence was real. It just didn't seem possible after the way they had made love that he could have left so abruptly the next morning, already an hour late for a meeting, and made no attempt to get in touch after. There had been no time for breakfast, not even a shower, as he'd pulled on his clothes, kissed her briefly on the cheek and run out the door. She was sure he'd said something about calling her later, but whether she'd imagined that or not was irrelevant now, as there had been no word from him at all and were it not for the anger and hurt she was feeling she might have believed she'd made the whole night up. Indeed, she almost wished she had, for the memory of the way she had shed her clothes at a mere touch of his lips was almost too excruciating to bear. But it had felt so right at the time, so very much what she wanted and what he wanted too. It was probably crazy to think it, but it had felt like the coming together of two people who had already waited too long for something that was quite simply meant to be. Such was the power of self-delusion.

It was now the night before the première of *United We Fall* and whether she was still supposed to be going with him she had no idea. In truth she didn't really know if he was still in town, for nothing in the world would induce her to call his hotel to find out. OK, she only had to speak to the telephone clerk, but her pride wouldn't even allow her to do that. Or perhaps it wasn't pride as much as fear, for she didn't know which was worse: that he might still be here and ignoring her, or that he had left without as much as a goodbye. Of course he had to be here because of the première and he was no doubt rushed off his feet, dashing from one meeting to the next, wining and dining producers, actors, directors, distributors, newspaper editors, talk show hosts, you name it, but she didn't see how any of it prevented him picking up a phone, so unless he was hospitalized or dead, no excuse was going to be good enough to get her to forgive him for treating her like this. At least it wouldn't have been until this evening, but now, as the countdown to the première began, she could feel her resolve starting to waver in a way she just knew she was going to end up regretting.

She hated herself for it, but having spent the entire weekend smarting with fury, she was now so dangerously close to tears that it was all that was stopping her picking up the phone. The last thing she wanted was for him to hear the hurt and apprehension in her voice and besides, if he did still want her to go to the première he'd have called by now. So she had her answer already. She'd give anything to be able to speak to Matty, but Ted Forgon had called her into his office today and told her he wanted to let Matty go. That had been the opener for what had turned out to be the day from hell. Threatening to drop Matty was another test of her mettle, Ellen was sure of that, but coming out of the blue the way it had, when she'd been convinced Forgon was calling her in to discuss Michael, had thrown her completely. In fact, she was so shocked by his failure to mention Michael at all, when he must have known Michael was in town, that the fight she'd put up to protect Matty was so shaming she wasn't sure she could face her cousin until she'd managed to put it right. Which she would, for there was just no way she was firing Matty from the agency, unless she herself walked, of course, which she was getting closer to every day.

After the blow about Matty and the disappointment of not being instructed to get to work on Michael, which, if nothing else, would have provided her with an excuse to contact him, she had received a call from Foster McKenzie that had left her in no doubt what he was expecting as gratitude for allowing her to bring off the deal for Walker Nicolas. Incensed by his assumption and outraged that he rated her along with the airheads of the industry, she'd ended up putting the phone down on him, which might not have been the wisest move she'd ever made, but it was definitely one of the more satisfying. At lunch-time some uninsured maniac had rammed her precious Pontiac while she was on her way to a meeting with Mel Gibson's managers, making her an hour late and liable to pay the two thousand dollars of damage out of her own pocket. She'd failed to get one of her more celebrated clients the lead in a new Levinson movie, her secretary had announced she was leaving and her mother had called to say her father was unwell. It was probably no more than a bad case of flu, but with the way things were between her and her father it was a constant fear of Ellen's that something would happen to him before they repaired things.

So now, here she was, having backed out of the cocktails she was supposed to be at, sitting in a corner of the sofa hugging a cushion to her chest and wishing the whole damned world would go away. Better still, she wished the god-damned phone would ring and

Michael McCann would be at the other end. She liked to think she would tell him where to go, but feeling as bruised by the day as she did, his shoulder to cry on would have been more than welcome. But it obviously wasn't going to happen and as the minutes ticked by and the phone remained obdurately silent the disappointment became more crushing than ever.

A jolt of impatience suddenly jerked her to her feet and snatching up the phone she carried it out to the veranda. Her heart was pounding as anger eclipsed her self-pity and drove her into action. She was done mooning around here like some faint-hearted Freda, wallowing in all the reasons she couldn't get on with her life. Michael McCann was obviously already history, so if sleeping with Foster McKenzie was her only way out of ATI then she was damned well going to get things moving. Like Rosa said, he wasn't so bad and when it came to the giants in this town they didn't come much bigger than McKenzie. So, give the man what he wants and in exchange take his protection from Forgon. For God's sake, she wouldn't be the first woman to get to the top this way, and who could say, if she played it real smart she might just end up the next Mrs Foster McKenzie with the private jet, half dozen homes, luxury yachts and unlimited kudos that went with it.

She had just connected with McKenzie's private number when there was a knock on the door. Irritated beyond measure at being interrupted, she threw down the phone and went back inside. It would either be Matty, whom security had been instructed to let through without calling up first, or one of her neighbours wanting to know if she could make the next residents' meeting. Either way, it wasn't going to be anyone she wanted to see right now and God damn to oblivion the vain and pathetic hope that had just entered her head that it might actually be Michael McCann.

Pulling open the door, she was on the point of claiming an untenable workload when the words dried on her lips and her jaw dropped open.

'Surprise!' Clay cried, a bottle of champagne in one hand a half-dozen roses in the other. His silvery hair was pulled back in a pony tail and his slender, handsome face was beaming with pleasure. 'How're you doing, babe? I missed you,' he said.

Ellen was too dumfounded to speak, or even to think.

He laughed. 'So, you going to invite me in?' he said. 'Or,' he added with a wink, 'we going to give the neighbours a show?'

Ellen's eyes widened in disbelief. 'What are you doing here?' she finally managed. 'How did you get in?'

His famously sensuous eyes were steeped in mischief. 'Hey, I'm Clay Ingall,' he reminded her. 'Why would they stop me?'

Ellen's face immediately showed her anger, but he appeared oblivious.

'You're looking great,' he told her and dropped his eyes pointedly to her bare midriff. 'Better than ever.'

'Clay, you're not welcome,' she told him bluntly.

'Oh come on,' he grinned. 'I got champagne here. You know how you love champagne.'

'Not your champagne,' she retorted.

He looked injured. 'Honey, I came to say I was sorry,' he said, the vaguest hint of rebuke in his voice.

'Apology accepted. Goodbye.'

She made to slam the door but he jammed it open with his foot, and pushing past her, sailed right on into the kitchen.

'Clay. Didn't you hear me?' she snapped, leaving the door open as she followed him. 'I don't want you here.

We're through, remember? You're the one who ended it.'

'Big mistake,' he told her, opening and closing the cupboard doors as he hunted for glasses. 'Yep, it sure was a big mistake. But I'm back now, honey, and boy have we got some making up for lost time to do.'

Ellen was speechless. 'Did you lose your mind?' she cried finally. 'There's no lost time to be made up for here. It's over.'

'Uh, uh,' he said, shaking his head. 'You and me, we can't be over. We got something going, something real good, you know that.'

Ellen suddenly saw red. 'Did you forget the way you spoke to me the last time you called?' she shouted. 'You threatened me, Clay. You do remember that, don't you?'

'Oh hell, it was a misunderstanding,' he told her, finding the glasses and setting two on the counter beside the roses. As he took hold of the cork he gazed around the apartment, drinking it all in. 'Shit, it's good to be here,' he smiled. 'I really did miss you, d'you know that? Life just wasn't the same without you.'

Ellen's hand went to her head as she struggled to deal with the mind-blowing madness of it. She heard the cork pop and watched in dismay as, filling the glasses, he continued as though they really did have something to celebrate. 'You look sensational,' he said, looking at her midriff again as he passed her a glass. 'But then, you always did.' He laughed. 'I got photos to prove it. Remember?'

Fury instantly flashed in her eyes. 'Photos that ended up on Ted Forgon's desk,' she seethed and slapped the glass right out of his hand. 'Now take your god-damned champagne and get the hell out of here.'

'Oh, come on, you don't mean that,' he said, looking pained as he put down the other glass and turned back towards her.

'Clay, just go,' she said, holding up a hand as she started to back off. There was something inherently unpleasant about the way he was looking at her now and a beat of unease was shaking her heart. 'You told me I was history, remember?' she faltered. 'You said you were in love with Karen. What happened to Karen?'

He waved a dismissive hand. 'You don't need to worry about her,' he assured her. 'We never had the kind of thing going you and me had.' He laughed. 'You know, you're so smart I guess you always knew I'd come back, didn't you? And hell, I don't blame you for putting that shot in the papers to try and break up me and Karen. I'd probably have done the same if I were you. But I got to tell you, you look a whole lot better in the flesh than you did in that picture and I should know.'

'I didn't put the god-damned shot in the paper,' Ellen spat. 'Ted Forgon put it there. He's using them to blackmail me, so how did he come by them, Clay? Did you give him the polaroids? Did you know he had someone staking out your house? Is that how much you thought of me, that you'd do something like that to me?'

'Hey,' he cried, 'I didn't know he had some snoop photographer going about the place until he told me. And I got to tell you when I found out, I threatened to sue the bastard.'

'But instead you gave him the polaroids.'

His large, handsome face with its three-day stubble and dark, liquid eyes was a picture of unconcern. 'Honey, I don't know what you're getting so uptight about,' he said. 'You look fan-fucking-tastic in those shots and you know it. Besides, you're the one who liked showing it off in public, so I didn't think you'd mind if a couple of the lads took a look . . .'

'What the hell are you talking about?' she raged. 'It

359

was you who wanted me to do all those things and I went along with it because I loved you.'

He grinned.

'Jesus, what a fool,' she muttered, dashing a hand through her hair. 'Just go, will you?' she said, looking back at him. 'Take your champagne and get out of my life.'

He put his hands on his hips and cocking his head to one side smiled at her. 'Now, if I thought you meant that,' he said, 'I'd probably take offence, you know what I mean? But I know you better, so I know how you like it kind of rough sometimes, so I understand what you're telling me here.'

Ellen's heart jarred with fear as he took a step towards her and laid a hand on her midriff. 'Clay, I mean it,' she warned, pressing herself into the wall. 'I don't want you to touch me. I just want you to leave and . . .'

'You got anything on under this top?' he interrupted, lifting it up to take a look.

'For Christ's sake, didn't you hear me?' she yelled, thumping his hand away. 'I don't want you to touch me. This isn't an act, Clay. This is real.'

'You want to do it in front of the window so everyone can take a look?' he offered, closing in on her and pressing his groin to hers.

'Clay, let me go,' she cried, as he began rubbing himself against her. 'Just let me go!' she shouted. But he had pinned her arms to the wall and with the rest of his body thrust so hard against hers she couldn't move. 'No!' she choked, jerking her head away as he tried to kiss her. 'Clay, please, don't do this.'

'Hey, come on, you're not fooling anyone here,' he sneered. 'You always want it.'

'No, Clay, stop,' she begged, twisting her head from side to side as he attempted to kiss her again.

'Hey, this is me, remember?' He laughed, pressing

harder on her wrists as she struggled to force them free of the wall. 'All I ever had to do was touch you and your clothes were off and you were reaching for my cock. Well here it is, babe. Come get it. It's all yours.'

Even as she fought, Ellen was painfully aware of how his words had struck a truth she hardly wanted to think about, for it was the way she had been with him and it was the way she had been with Michael too. One kiss and she had stripped off her clothes like she was some rampant, sex-starved nympho. So was that why Michael hadn't been in touch? Had she put him off by being too easy? Did he think she behaved that way with everyone? 'Clay, no!' she screamed, as his hand plunged into the elastic waist of her trousers. 'Let me go! For God's sake . . .' She was pummelling him with her fists and trying desperately to get his legs out from between hers, but while he held her that way, with her feet barely touching the floor, she was virtually powerless to stop him.'

'Oh God, no,' she cried as he dragged her trousers down over her hips and began fumbling with his fly. 'Clay, please, don't do this.'

But he wasn't listening. He was too intent now on getting her trousers off and with terrifying ease he pinned her arms behind her back, tore at the flimsy fabric and pushed his hand inside her panties.

Ellen was screaming and fighting, trying to bite and kick him, until finally she wrested a hand out of his grip and snatching up the lamp beside her she brought it crashing down on his head.

'What the hell's going on here?' Matty shouted from the doorway as Clay slumped to the floor.

'Oh God,' Ellen sobbed, clutching her arms about herself as she struggled to breathe.

'Are you all right?' Matty said, going to her as she slid down the wall. 'What happened? My God, is that Clay?'

361

'He tried to rape me,' Ellen groaned.

'She was asking for it,' Clay sneered, wiping the blood from his forehead as he struggled to sit up. 'And what the fuck did you have to go and hit me like that for? We were just having some fun.'

'You were raping me, you god-damned sonofabitch!' Ellen shouted. 'Now get the hell out of here before I call the police.'

'You want to get yourself some treatment,' he snarled, ''cos you come on to a guy the way you came on to me . . .'

'I didn't ask you to come here!' Ellen yelled as he got to his feet. 'You just turned up, you bastard. And I never did one god-damned thing to give you the come on. It's all in your head, you mother-fucking egomaniac. I'm suing you, do you hear me! I'm charging you with assault . . .'

'This is me you're talking to,' he reminded her, his eyes glittering with contempt as he wiped saliva from his lips. 'I don't need to assault women to get what I want. The real story here is you just like cutting up rough and the minute your cousin turned up you backed off, shouted rape . . . Well get this into your head, bitch, I don't want you phoning me up and begging me to come over no more, 'cos I don't like the way you do things. Did you get that? Did you hear what I said? We're through . . .'

'Get him out of here,' Ellen implored, turning to Matty. 'Please, just make him go, or I swear to God I'll kill him.'

'Hey, I'm out of here,' he replied. 'No way am I staying after this. You're sick, do you know that?' he spat, prodding his head with a finger. 'You're a fucking screwball. You ought to be locked up. Hey, maybe *I* might bring charges, do society a favour.'

'*Get out!*' Ellen screamed, and picking up the nearest

362

object she flung it at him. It missed, but he was already across the room.

'See, she's crazy,' he said to Matty. 'Get her some help,' and before either of them could respond he slammed out of the door.

'Jesus Christ Almighty!' Matty murmured, still staring at the door. 'What the hell happened? How did he get in here?'

Ellen was shaking her head. 'Security let him in,' she answered. 'I guess they figured because he's famous, he's harmless.' She gave a bitter laugh, then winced as she tried to get up.

'Are you OK?' Matty said, attempting to help her. 'Did he hurt you?'

Ellen shook her head. 'Not really,' she answered. 'He scared the hell out of me, though.' She sighed and shook her head again. 'Can you believe that? He just turned up here like we were still an item and started coming on to me. Oh God, it was horrible,' she gasped, screwing up her eyes. 'Get me a drink, will you? And not his champagne. I'll go change into something else.'

A few minutes later she was hunched in a corner of the sofa wrapped in a dressing gown and sipping a Scotch, while Matty cleared up the broken glass.

'Did you call him?' Matty asked, after a difficult silence.

'For God's sake, no!' Ellen cried. Then, banging down her glass she said, 'You don't seriously believe what he was saying, do you?'

Matty shook her head. 'Not really,' she answered. 'I mean, I know he was trying to rape you because I heard you right along the hall. I just can't figure out what brought him here, that's all.'

'He's broken up with Karen,' Ellen answered, 'and was obviously short of a screw for the night so thought he could get it on with me again. And who can blame him when I've got a history of giving it to a guy on the first date and ripping off my clothes on the first kiss.'

Matty wrinkled her nose in confusion. 'What are you talking about?' she said. 'Since when did you give it to a guy on the first date?'

'Since I met Clay,' Ellen answered. 'And since last Friday when I was so keen for Michael to screw me I tore off my own clothes before the rest of you had time to get down the hall.'

Matty blinked. 'So?' she said. 'It was what you both wanted, wasn't it? I mean, did you force him?'

'Of course I didn't.'

'Then why are you giving yourself such a hard time?'

'Because he hasn't damned well called me,' Ellen shouted, 'that's why. He got what he came here for and he obviously hasn't felt like it again since. Or maybe he's sleeping with someone else already. Someone who doesn't give it to him on a plate, who makes him feel like what he's getting is worth having.'

'Wow, this is some self-pity trip you're on here,' Matty commented.

Ellen glared at her.

Matty shrugged. 'Go ahead,' she invited, 'don't stop the train for me.'

Ellen slammed her eyes and turned to look out at the twilight. 'I almost got raped,' she said a moment or two later.

'Are we talking about Michael or Clay now?' Matty asked.

'It's not a god-damned joke,' Ellen snapped. 'You should try it some time, see how it feels.'

'I'm sorry,' Matty said, 'I guess it was uncalled for. But honestly, Ellen, I don't know what you're trying to deal with here, the fact that Clay came on to you like that, or that Michael hasn't called you.'

'Or that I'm thinking of quitting my job,' Ellen added. 'Or that some asshole ran into my car today. Or that I just screwed up on a major deal. Or that I was on the point of inviting Foster McKenzie to come screw me, before Clay turned up and beat him to it. Or that my dad's not well and I'm scared out my mind he'll die before he ever speaks to me again. Take your pick, there's a lot going on here today.'

Matty took a breath. 'OK, which of them do you want to deal with first?' she said.

'I told you, it's your call,' Ellen responded.

Matty nodded and leaning back against an armchair she hugged her knees to her chest. 'Is it serious with Uncle Frank?' she asked.

Ellen shook her head. 'Mom says not. Just the flu, but one day it's going to be more serious than that and before we know it . . .'

Matty lowered her eyes to the floor. 'I know,' she said softly. Then, after a lengthy pause, 'Did you mean it about sleeping with Foster McKenzie?'

Ellen shrugged and sighed. 'I don't know,' she answered. 'Not now, no. But earlier, when I picked up the phone, I was prepared to do whatever it took to get me out of Ted Forgon's clutches. And I suppose I was seeing it as some perverse kind of payback to Michael as well.'

'Has Forgon been at you about Michael again?' Matty asked.

Ellen laughed drily. 'I saw him today and he didn't even mention him,' she answered. 'But don't let that mislead you into thinking he's given up on Michael, or that he doesn't know Michael's in town. All that means is he's playing this a different way now and I don't even want to think about where it's going to leave me, because the sadistic old bastard is bound to find a way of making me pay for something that's not even in my control. That's what he's like. It's the way he operates with everyone, except I, Ellen Shelby, the biggest sucker of all time, was dumb enough to think he had

365

me starred for great things, when all he's really got me starred for is as many hoops as he can make me jump through before he gets bored and moves on to the next.'

Matty was quiet as she mulled it all over in her mind and wondered, not for the first time lately, if Ellen was starting to outgrow LA.

'I don't know,' Ellen answered, when Matty put the question to her. 'Sometimes I think so, but other times, well, I just don't know. You know what I heard someone say the other day, "Hell's kitchen might be in New York, but the boudoir is right here in LA." '

Matty smiled. 'Not bad,' she said. Then, after taking a sip of her drink, 'What about the job Michael offered you in London? Would you be interested in that?'

Ellen shook her head, then laughed. 'I don't expect it's on offer any more,' she said. 'And besides, I might be going through a tough patch here right now, but it'll get better and you know as well as I do that the time to quit is when you're ahead, not when you're down.'

Matty nodded. 'I guess you're right,' she said. 'So, what are you going to do about Michael? Will you call him?'

'No. It's the première tomorrow night, he knows he's invited me, so he either calls to say it's still on, or he doesn't. Whichever way, it's up to him.'

It was Hollywood doing what Hollywood did best – an all-star, glittering extravaganza to mark the première of Victor Warren's much hyped movie, *United We Fall*. The film's stars ranked among the industry's biggest box-office attractions and the support roles had brought together an international cast of easily recognizable as well as highly respected talent. The crowds outside The Shrine, in downtown LA, were going crazy, tossing rice and handkerchiefs, ribbons and flags in the air, as one star after another after another alighted from the endless stream of limousines and strode in all their chic designer splendour along the gilt-edged red carpet, towards the magnificent auditorium. Thousands upon thousands of flash bulbs lit up the night, while reporters from all over the world jostled aggressively for position and yelled out for Sandra, or Mel, or Arnie, or Julie, to look their way. Some stars were willing, others not, but the main cast of *United We Fall* were the prime targets this evening and each of them was as ready for the cameras as they were hungry for acclaim.

Laughing as some hack from London recognized him, Michael declined an interview, for he never sought or particularly welcomed publicity. The woman he was with, however, was smiling at every lens, waving at the crowds and doing her very best to give as many interviews as she could. As the star of the movie it was expected of her, as the niece of Victor Warren and daughter of one of the world's leading playwrights it came naturally to her.

Her arm was linked comfortably through Michael's as they made their way slowly through the crowd, he in his tuxedo, she in a stunning pink sequinned dress that revealed a great deal more than it concealed of the flawless, tanned body beneath.

'Justine! It's the BBC from London,' a voice called out of the crowd.

Immediately Justine turned, still clinging to Michael's arm and smiled at the reporter.

'What do you think of the turn out here tonight?' the reporter asked.

'Exceptional and exciting,' Justine replied, her soft, girlish face alight with laughter. 'I had no idea my uncle knew so many people.'

Everyone around laughed and as Justine looked up into Michael's face the cameras went crazy.

'Who designed the dress, Justine?' the BBC guy asked. 'It's gorgeous, by the way.'

'Armani, who else?' she laughed. 'Who designed yours?'

'His poor cousin,' he answered. 'Michael, have you seen the movie?'

'Sure,' Michael replied. 'It's terrific.'

'Are you hoping for an Oscar, Justine?'

'Who me?' she cried, clasping a hand to her chest. 'Would I lie?'

And so it went on, moving from newspaper, to TV channel, to radio station to glossy magazine, until they finally disappeared inside the theatre and took their seats with Victor Warren and his wife.

As with all these occasions, each opening credit brought the person concerned to their feet to accept the applause, whether actor, casting director, costume designer, cameras, sound, writers, producers or director. Victor Warren, a large, dour Scot, who was always taken for an American, was the last to rise but barely did so for the first scenes of the movie were already underway.

Having seen it three times in as many days, there was little Michael could do to stop his mind wandering and in relatively no time at all he was feeling as bad as he ought about Ellen. The way they'd made love the other night had confirmed what he'd suspected for some time, that she was a woman he wasn't going to find easy to resist, and his heart sank at the prospect of her turning on the TV and seeing him at the première with Justine Warren. He should have called her, he knew that, but he'd been so hectic since he'd seen her he'd barely had time to shave, never mind socialize. Except one phone call was all it would have taken and God knew he could have found time for that, had he tried. And he probably would have, were it not for the fact that he was so uneasy about his feelings for her. He wanted her, that much was clear, but he was pretty sure it went much deeper than that, and it just wouldn't be fair to pretend there could be anything between them when he still wasn't really clear what he was going to do about Michelle.

The film seemed endless as it moved ponderously from one scene to the next, building all the time to a climax that he knew wasn't going to disappoint. However, the prospect of sitting through another two hours, before moving on to a party that would no doubt rave through to dawn, was becoming increasingly unappealing. He glanced over at Justine and smiled as she looked back. The performance she was giving on screen was second only to the one she was giving tonight, for as yet only the family knew that her fiancé had chosen today of all days to inform her he was breaking off their engagement. Michael's heart went out to her, for he knew how devastated she was inside, which was why he hadn't been able to say no when she'd asked him to escort her tonight. And now, providing he didn't think of Ellen, he could only admire the courage Justine was showing in putting on a front for the world, and for her uncle, who had insisted he would understand if she wanted to back out.

At last the closing credits began to roll and as Michael looked at Justine again he knew that the tears on her cheeks were for her private pain, rather than that of the character she had portrayed. He wondered how she was going to get through the party now and not for the first time that day he felt a violent anger towards the man who had done this to her. Taking the handkerchief he was offering, she wiped away her tears and brought back her smile. The eyes of the world were on her again and she had too much pride to let any of them know that she was anything other than thrilled by their ecstatic reception of the film. From three seats away Linden Forsyth, her co-star, reached for her hand and drew her to her feet so that together they could accept the applause.

Victor Warren was the last to stand up and as he waved to the audience of his friends and colleagues Justine turned and held her exquisite diamond tiara in place, as she stooped to whisper to Michael. 'Let's just get through this, then if you don't mind, will you take me home?' she said. Her limpid green eyes were shining with tears, even though her smile was perfectly intact.

'Of course,' he answered.

An impish light made a fleeting appearance through her pain. 'I expect people will talk, both of us not being at the party. Will you mind?'

He smiled and shook his head.

It was past eleven o'clock by the time the limousine finally dropped them at Justine's Bel Air home, and after making sure she was all right and not about to do anything foolish, Michael got into the hire car he'd left there earlier and drove off towards Beverly Hills. This was against his better judgement and the chances of Ellen letting him in now were probably even slimmer than the chances of her forgiving him, but he was going to give it his best shot anyway and if that didn't work, well dammit, he'd just keep on trying until it did.

Twenty minutes later he pulled up at the security gates and told the guard which apartment he wanted.

She was a while answering the phone, so long, in fact, that he thought she was probably out. But then the guard started to speak, listened for a moment, then, replacing the receiver he wandered back out of his booth.

'Sorry man,' he said, 'she don't want to let you in.' Michael looked at him, looked away, took a ten-dollar bill from his wallet and said, 'Call her back and tell her I'll wait right here until she's ready to see me.'

The guard looked at the money, shrugged as he took it, then went back into his booth and picked up the phone. 'She says,' he said, coming back a couple of minutes later, 'that you're wasting your time, 'cos she ain't gonna change her mind.'

Michael pursed his lips and nodded. 'I don't suppose,' he said, 'you'd consider letting me in anyway.'

The guard shook his head. 'No can do, man,' he replied. 'Another guy did it just yesterday and it was a movie star he let in. Got fired all the same. Don't want to lose my job.'

'OK,' Michael said. 'So where's a good place to wait without blocking the entrance?'

The guard pointed him towards a couple of parking spaces in front of the entry villa. 'You can sit it out over there, if you like, but I got to tell you, man, she didn't sound to me like she was going to change her mind.'

Michael put the car into reverse. 'Just call her and tell her I meant what I said, I'll wait here until she's ready to see me.'

As the minutes ticked by and the warm, scented night became more and more still he asked himself over and over why he was doing this when he knew already that they were going nowhere and when the last thing he wanted was to hurt her again. Maybe it was just that he needed to explain, or perhaps he wanted to see her and hold her once more, or maybe it was something much less tangible and infinitely more perilous that was keeping him here. In truth, he had no real answers, all he knew was that he meant what he said, he was prepared to wait however long it took for her to let him come in, or even until she came out.

He'd been there more than an hour when the guard sauntered over and rapped on his window. 'She just called down wanting to know if you was still here,' the guard told him as he lowered the window.

'And you told her I was?'

'Sure I did.'

Michael waited.

371

'She says I can let you go up,' the guard finally informed him.

Michael looked into the guard's eyes. The guard looked back, then his handsome black face broke into a grin and holding out his hand he said, 'Hey man, give me five.'

Laughing, Michael slapped a hand against the other man's and reaching for the keys he started up the engine.

Minutes later he was standing in the smart, Andalusian-style hallway waiting for her to answer the door.

It didn't take long and just one look at her when she opened the door told him all he needed to know; that despite the fierceness of the pride in her eyes he had hurt her deeply. And without thinking any more he drew her into his arms. 'I'm sorry,' he murmured. 'I'm so sorry. I'll make it up to you. Somehow, I swear, I'll make it up to you.'

He pulled her more tightly to him and kissed her hair 'Did you see the première?' he asked.

She nodded.

'I can explain,' he said.

'It's OK, you don't need to,' she answered.

'I do and I will.'

'Oh God,' she laughed, rolling her eyes and trying to look away. 'I feel such a fool. I mean I know we . . . only once, but it meant so much to me and . . . I'm sorry, I know I probably shouldn't say that, but there's just been so much happening lately and . . . Oh God, I'm sorry, I'll have myself together in a minute.'

'It's OK,' he smiled, kissing her forehead, and keeping her close he took her back into the apartment.

She was wearing a thick towelling robe and he could see the thin cotton pyjamas beneath. Her hair was clipped on top of her head, with tiny wisps of curls escaping around her face and neck, and her soft, creamy skin was totally devoid of make-up. He felt a tightening in his chest as he wondered if he'd ever seen a woman look so lovely, for the colour of her cheeks, the moistness of her mouth and guileless clarity of her eyes were all as natural as the gentle aroma of her femininity.

'Can I get you something?' she offered. 'Would you like . . . ?'

'Nothing,' he interrupted and taking her hand he pulled her down on the sofa beside him. The only light came from the full moon outside and a small lamp at the other end of the room.

'OK?' he asked, as she brought her knees up on to his lap and rested her head on his shoulder.

'Mmm,' she answered and looked down as he took her hand and entwined her fingers in his. 'Tell me about the movie. Is it good?'

'Yes, it's good,' he answered. 'But I'd rather talk about what's been happening to you.'

'You mean apart from you not calling?' she said, only half teasing.

Putting his fingers under her chin, he lifted her face and looked right into her eyes. 'I'm sorry,' he whispered. 'It was a stupid thing to have done.'

'It's OK,' she said shakily. 'You're here now.'

He carried on looking at her, moving his eyes between hers, lowering them to her mouth, then bringing them back again to her eyes and gazing at her so seriously and intently she was almost afraid of what he was thinking. Then, very gently he touched his lips to hers and kissed her so tenderly and meaningfully that she felt her heart flood with so much emotion she could hardly bear it.

Later, she barely remembered how she began, all she knew was that she told him everything, from the way her father wouldn't speak to her to how afraid she was of leaving ATI; about the photographs Ted Forgon was blackmailing her with, the way Clay had tried to rape her the day before and the dread she had that he, Michael, hadn't called because she had slept with him so easily.

Only the last part made him smile, until, realizing how serious she was, he touched a finger to her lips and said, 'It wasn't easy, it was inevitable. You know that.'

Hearing that, Ellen felt her heart rise to her throat and as his hand tightened on hers her desire began to burn. His hand slid into her hair and she raised her mouth to his again, moaning softly as he kissed her.

'What are you doing for the next five days?' he asked, his mouth still very close to hers.

Ellen's eyes reflected her surprise and seeing the way he was looking at her she said, 'Why?'

'Because I want to spend some time with you and I can clear my schedule if you can clear yours.'

She looked away, looked back, then shaking her head she started to smile. 'OK,' she said.

He brought her mouth to his and a long time later he said softly, 'We'll get this sorted with Forgon, OK?'

She stared at him, not knowing what to say.

He kissed her nose. 'Does Ingall still have any more of those polaroids?' he asked.

She shook her head. 'I don't know. I thought I'd destroyed them all, but ... I don't know.'

'It's OK, there are ways of finding out.'

Ellen laughed. 'How do you do that?' she said.

'What?'

'Make everything seem so simple.'

He shrugged. 'I guess because everything generally is,' he answered. 'It's only complicated when you want it to be.'

Ellen frowned as she thought about that. 'I wouldn't say I want it to be complicated between us,' she said, 'but I feel that it is.'

He smiled and said nothing as his mouth closed over

hers again. And this time, as he kissed her, he pulled the top of her robe aside and unbuttoned her pyjamas until one breast was completely exposed to his touch. As he stroked her, her breath started to deepen, but they sat that way for a long time, watching the dark masculinity of his hand move over her skin, while occasionally looking at each other and kissing some more.

Finally he got to his feet and pulling her up into his arms he said, 'If you've got a problem with us making love . . .'

'No,' she said. 'I don't have a problem.'

His smile was so ironic she laughed and walking with him into the bedroom she said, 'I'm glad you came.'

'Me too,' he murmured and pulling her in front of him he began to undress her.

The next five days were the happiest and most romantic Ellen had ever known. She'd had no idea it was possible to laugh so much, nor to make love in so many different ways, nor to feel so alive and beautiful and mischievous and cared for, no matter what she did. She could see how enthralled he was by her and loved the way he teased her for how brazen and reckless and insatiable she was. In turn, she let him know how special he was too, though she was careful not to mention anything about him moving to LA, for the last thing she wanted was for him to think that she was trying to trap him, either for Forgon, or for herself.

They were rarely out of each other's sight as they roamed the canyons, relaxed in her apartment and drove along the coast to Big Sur. They talked endlessly about everything from existentialism to expressionism, from crime to passion and from the marvellous to the mundane. He watched her and listened as she spoke on the phone to her mother and was persuaded to say 'hi' himself. Then it was her turn to speak to his family, all three of the children, his sister and Clodagh. He confided how bad he felt about a girl from his office, Sandy, whom he had fired because of her crush on him, and confessed how he had slept with her the night he had so badly wanted to sleep with Ellen. Ellen's heart went out to the girl wherever she was now, for feeling the way she did about Michael herself it was all too easy for her to imagine how terrible Sandy must be feeling.

He told her about the deal he was trying to pull together with the Australian, Mark Bergin, and what it could do for the face of international co-production. She could sense how excited he was by it and understood why, for the project, if it came off, was bigger and more prestigious than any she'd ever heard of. Apparently Bergin had already upped his stake to six million sterling, while Michael's associate in New York was prepared to put up a further two million and Michael was committing McCann Walsh to an investment of three million, with a possible further three once he had spoken to the banks. They had yet to come up with a name in LA that all three trusted sufficiently to bring in on the deal, for the way Hollywood generally played was buy out, not buy in. Ellen desperately wanted to suggest herself as a partner, for she was certain she could raise the money – provided she got things sorted out with Forgon first – but the suggestion had to come from Michael and despite how close they seemed and how freely they discussed everything else, there was an unnerving silence regarding their relationship and where it might be headed.

She waited until their last night to bring up the subject, when they were having dinner at La Bohème, the Parisian music-hall-style restaurant on Santa Monica. It saddened her, and slightly panicked her too, that he went through the entire meal without once wondering when they might see each other again, or even mentioning how they felt about each other. In her heart she just knew that the past five days had meant as much to him as they had to her, but whether she could get him to admit it was another matter altogether, and even if she could, it still wasn't going to answer the question of where they went from here.

She watched as the waiter put two coffees down between them and asked if they would like a nightcap. Michael looked at her and she shook her head.

'Just the check,' he said and as the waiter walked away he picked up his coffee and looked into her eyes. 'Are you OK?' he asked.

Ellen nodded and picked up her coffee too.

'You seem quiet tonight,' he remarked.

She kept her eyes lowered, then, putting her cup down she looked up into his dark, candlelit face. 'I guess I'm just sad that you're going tomorrow,' she said.

Immediately he looked away and her heart ached with the need to hear him say that he would miss her too.

'Did you have a good time?' she asked.

'Sure,' he answered.

She tried to smile, but it didn't quite come off. She was right on the verge of saying what she wanted, but for some reason she couldn't make it come. 'Are you going to offer Sandy back her job?' she said.

He frowned.

'The girl you fired,' she reminded him. 'Will you take her back?'

He shook his head. 'I don't think so,' he said. 'I'll give her a good reference, so she shouldn't have much trouble finding another job.'

'What about the escort thing? Is that going to remain

a problem for her? I mean, will anyone else want to take her on once they know what her background is?'

'People are pretty broad-minded these days,' he replied.

'But not you?'

'I told you, it was an excuse to get rid of her,' he said bluntly, 'not a reason. It's why I feel so bad about it.' He sighed. 'But it's done now and I don't see there's anything to be gained in going back.'

Ellen fell silent again and wondered how many other things she was going to ask about before she got round to what she really wanted to say.

'Have you considered what you're going to do about ATI?' he asked.

Her mouth turned dry as her heart contracted hard. Was he going to ask her to go to London after all? Or was he just making idle chat?

'If you decide you want to leave,' he went on, 'then give Forgon a reminder from me that I know plenty of things about him he won't want made public, so if he doesn't get off your case I'll be on his.'

Ellen smiled and looked down at her coffee. 'My hero,' she murmured. It wasn't that she wasn't grateful, or that she wanted to go to London even, she just wanted to know that this wasn't the end.

'I was wondering,' she said, looking up at him, 'if we're going to see each other again after tomorrow.'

His eyes remained on hers until reaching for her hand, he held it between his and watched the slow entwining of their fingers.

Her heart was thudding painfully hard, for his silence was giving her the reply she dreaded and she just didn't know if she could bear to hear what he was going to say.

'Are you still in love with Michelle?' she asked, knowing instinctively that this was where her adversary lay.

She felt his sudden tension, though he didn't pull his hand away, instead he looked down to where it was joined with hers. 'It's not as simple as that,' he answered. Then, raising his eyes, 'If things were different ... If I didn't have ...' He stopped as the check arrived and reaching into his jacket for his wallet he dropped four twenty-dollar bills on the table. 'Come on, let's get out of here,' he said, starting to get up.

'No,' she answered, staying where she was.

He looked at her curiously.

'I can't do this, Michael,' she said, struggling to keep the emotion from her voice.

He sat down again.

'I can't go home with you tonight,' she continued, 'and know that you're going to leave tomorrow and I might never see you again. If it's going to be that way then we have to say goodbye here. I can put your things in a taxi and send them to the Four Seasons ...'

'Listen,' he said, reaching for her hand again, 'if you're thinking that these past five days haven't meant as much to me as they have to you, then you're wrong. I had a wonderful time, we both did, and if there were any way we could continue with this then believe me there would be no one happier than me. But you're here in LA and I'm in London, and no matter how much we might want to kid ourselves otherwise, that isn't going to change. So ask yourself, do you really want a relationship that only happens on the phone or during snatched vacations in one city or the other? Sure we could meet up for the weekend in New York from time to time, but whichever way you look at it, Ellen, in the long run it just can't work.'

'You told me once there would always be a job for me in London,' she reminded him, her eyes flashing with anger at her lost pride.

'But you don't want it.'

'You didn't ask.'

'OK. Do you want the job?'

She looked away.

'You see,' he said gently, 'you're as much a part of the States as I am of England ...'

'This isn't about geography,' she snapped, 'it's about two people who care for each other and want to spend more time together. At least this person does. What about you?'

He nodded.

'So what's wrong with trying it for vacations and weekends in New York?' she demanded. 'Do we have to throw everything away because it seems impossible now? No one ever knows what's going to happen in the future, how things might change, so unless you tell me that you're still in love with Michelle, because that's the real crux of things here, then I'm prepared to give it a go any way that might have a chance.'

'If I'm in love with anyone right now,' he said, 'it's with you.'

Ellen was already starting to speak when her breath was suddenly lost in an onrush of disbelief and elation. 'Do you mean that?' she whispered, trying to assimilate the shock.

'You know I do,' he answered. 'You've been there the whole time it's been happening so you've got to know.'

She stared at him, then, swallowing hard she said, 'Does that mean you know I'm in love with you too? I mean, you've been there the whole time for me.'

He grinned. 'I'd say you're pretty crazy about me,' he replied. 'We'll know you're in love when you decide to come to London.'

Ellen's heart skipped a beat. 'I could throw that one back at you,' she reminded him, 'and say we'll know when you come to LA.'

His eyebrows went up, but he made no comment as he got to his feet and stood to one side for her to lead them out of the restaurant.

380

'Could we do something now?' Ellen asked as he drove her newly repaired Pontiac back towards Beverly Hills.

He glanced at her in surprise. 'What do you have in mind?' he asked cautiously.

'Could we fly to Vegas and get married?'

'Jesus Christ!' he swore, swerving to avoid an oncoming car. 'Are you serious?' he asked a couple of minutes later.

'No,' she said happily, 'it was just a joke.'

He continued to drive, eyes riveted to the road ahead. 'You were serious,' he stated, when finally they turned into her apartment complex.

'No I wasn't,' she replied. 'You sounded so suspicious when I asked if we could do something that I didn't want to disappoint you.' She turned to look at him. 'What I wanted to do was make an arrangement for when we're next going to meet. Now, I know you might see that as still trying to tie you down, but you have to admit it's not as drastic as Vegas.'

Laughing as he circled the car into her parking spot he said, 'I'm going to miss you, Ellen Shelby.'

'You don't know how happy that makes me,' she responded.

Turning off the engine, they got out of the car and walked hand in hand to the apartment. 'What about New York, the weekend after next?' he said when they reached the door.

Ellen's eyes rounded with amazement. 'That soon?' she said.

'I have a meeting there on the twenty-fifth,' he answered, 'to do with the global tie-up.'

'Is that so?' she murmured, sliding her arms around his neck as he leaned back against the wall.

'Mmmmm,' he responded as she kissed him.

'Then I guess I'll just have to make sure I can be there too,' she said, and feeling pretty certain that somehow this international link-up was going to provide some kind of answer for them she led him into the apartment and poured him a nightcap.

'Tell me something,' she said, a while later as they were sitting quietly in the moonlight on the veranda, 'would you really have gone back to England tomorrow with no plans for us to see each other again?'

She was sitting on the floor in front of him and turned to rest her chin on his knee as she waited for him to answer. His eyes narrowed teasingly as looking down at her he contemplated the question. 'I guess,' he said finally, 'we'll never know now, will we?'

Chapter 20

Nesta was on the phone as Sandy walked into their Chelsea flat, shrugged off her raincoat and went through to the kitchen to drop her umbrella in the sink.

'If you can raise it to six we could be in business,' Nesta was saying. 'Yes, thousand. You surely didn't think I meant hundred.'

Hearing that, Sandy hurried into the sitting-room, kettle in hand, and looked over to where Nesta was sitting at one of the twin desks they'd rigged up in front of the window. 'Who's that?' she asked.

Nesta, looking very girlish in a high pony tail and pristine red bow, put a hand over the receiver. 'Vanessa Kerry,' she mouthed.

Sandy's eyes widened eagerly. 'Anything doing?' she asked.

Nesta held up a hand. 'Anything less than six and I'm afraid . . .' She paused, grinned across at Sandy, then sticking a thumb in the air said, 'OK, that's great. Sandy's just walked in so I'll put it to her and get back to you before the end of the day.'

Sandy descended into the opposite chair and leaned on the kettle. 'Well?' she said, as Nesta hung up.

'You know, I'm really getting to like this agenting lark,' Nesta responded, studying her fingernails. 'In fact, I reckon I'm developing quite a knack for it.'

'What did she say?' Sandy pressed. 'Are they offering Georgia the part?'

'Yep,' Nesta answered, 'for five grand. I'm trying to up it to six.'

'It's a real low-budget film,' Sandy cautioned.

Nesta shrugged. 'She said she was going to discuss some kind of deferred payment with the producer,' she said. 'If he agrees, and you agree too, then it looks like we might get six.'

Sandy's eyes were shining with joy. 'You're a genius,' she declared. 'Georgia Sands is going to be over the moon.'

'Shall I call and tell her?' Nesta offered, squinting as a rogue ray of sunlight suddenly splashed across the desk.

Sandy shook her head and started to get up. 'Let's wait until we've got it all firmed up, then you can tell her. Did anything else happen while I was out?'

'Just a couple of calls,' Nesta answered, looking at her pad. 'Someone from *The Bill* wanting to check on Miriam Flander's address and the source of all our non-existent misery, Slim Sutton.'

By now Sandy was dropping a couple of tea-bags into the pot, but at the mention of Slim Sutton's name she came back to the doorway. 'What did he say?' she asked.

'That he'll be in London the week after next and he'll be happy to meet up with you,' Nesta informed her with a triumphant smile. 'If you ask me, we've got him in the bag.'

Sandy threw her a look and as the phone started to ring again she returned to the kitchen, keeping an ear out for who was on the line. From Nesta's reception she guessed it was a friend, so she carried on with the tea and scanned the mail that Nesta had left in a pile on the dresser. There were two contracts ready to be signed for two of Janey's clients, a script for one of Diana's clients to read, a telephone bill and a letter from an independent producer she'd met at a party a week ago.

It was incredible how well things were going, for not much more than three months had passed since that dreadful day in Michael's office when he had fired her so callously and she had behaved in a manner she couldn't even bring herself to think about now. Actually, were it not for Nesta, she doubted she'd have come as far as she had, for it was Nesta who had picked her up and put the fight back in her, when all she'd really wanted was to crawl away somewhere and die.

'You can't let him get the better of you like this,' Nesta had shouted after finding her once again glued to a video of him at the première of *United We Fall*. 'He's just one man, for God's sake. There are thousands more out there worth a thousand times more than he is, so for God's sake pull yourself together and start showing him what you're made of.'

And the amazing thing was how easy that was proving, for, initally at least, all she'd needed was her contacts book, a computer, a telephone and an early-morning vigil on the mail at Chelsea Harbour. The vigil was no longer necessary, as by now she and Nesta had contacted most of the McCann Walsh clients Sandy had dealt with on a regular basis to tell them she was working at home for a while. She'd fully expected them to know she'd been fired, but by some astonishing good luck they either hadn't been informed, or simply didn't care. Either way, they seemed more than happy to continue with Sandy at her new address and number, probably because they'd had a great deal more attention paid to them since Sandy had become involved in their careers. She had also been in touch with the producers and casting directors she'd done regular business with while at McCann's to tell them the same story – that she was now working from home. It was quite staggering how smoothly she was cutting a slice out of McCann's without anyone noticing, for she'd not only started receiving contracts now and changing the agent's name from McCann Walsh to Sandy Paull, she'd actually banked several thousand pounds' worth of commissions. Of course it was generally only bureaucrats or accountants who saw the contracts after they were drawn up, so there wasn't really anyone to be curious about why the agent's name had changed; to them the name was irrelevant, all that counted were the terms and the figures. And when the clients asked, which very few did, she simply told them that it was a new system McCann's had introduced lately that was going through a trial period.

Of course, she knew what she was doing was illegal, but she had several good insurance policies that would ward off any threat of prosecution. In the first place, she could claim Michael had set her up to sleep with potential clients in order to entice them away from their current agents. Of course, he'd never done any such thing, but the fact that Slim Sutton thought he had was probably enough to make at least some of the mud stick. Secondly, there was the affair Craig was having with a member of Her Majesty's Government, which she could always threaten to reveal should Michael ever decide to bring charges against her. Craig's affair probably wouldn't do much harm to the agency, but Sandy was trusting to how loyal a friend Michael was to Craig and therefore how far he would go to protect him. And should all else fail she would either file a sexual harassment charge against Michael, or plant a considerable quantity of cocaine in his office and tip off the police. The last was a means of making sure that if she went down then he went down with her. So one way or another, she was pretty confident of making him pay for the way he had used her, then so cruelly discarded her when she became an embarrassment.

'So how did it go with Maurice today?' Nesta asked,

coming into the kitchen. 'Did he show you anything you liked?'

Sandy laughed. 'You're going to love this,' she answered. 'He almost took me to Chelsea Harbour.'

'No!' Nesta gasped. 'Oh, what a hoot that would be, setting up office right next door to Michael McCann.'

'It was underneath, actually,' Sandy corrected. 'And believe you me, I'd give anything to see his face if we did set up shop there, but we can't run the risk.'

'You'll have to make yourself official pretty soon, though,' Nesta pointed out.

'I know, but there are still a few things we need to get in place before we do. I'm seeing Jodi later, so we'll probably have a clearer picture after that. Maurice showed me some great premises just along the road from here, by the way. I've got to tell you I could quite fancy myself in the executive suite. Just wait 'til you see it.'

Nesta looked surprised. 'Have you taken it, then?' she asked.

'I'm considering it,' Sandy answered, passing her a cup of tea. 'Do you want a biscuit?'

'There's not a lot I wouldn't do for a biscuit,' Nesta groaned, 'but some of us have to watch our weight.'

Sandy shrugged and turned to the cupboard, while Nesta eyed her almost perfect figure with full-blooded envy. It was amazing how shapely such a small and slender body could be, Nesta was thinking, as munching on a digestive Sandy said, 'Are you going out tonight?'

'If you mean am I working tonight the answer's no,' Nesta answered, turning back into the sitting-room. 'But don't start thinking you're persuading me to give it up, because you're not. I just feel like a night in, that's all. Being your assistant takes it out of me, you know.'

Sandy laughed. 'I'll believe that when you really do

give up the night job,' she said. 'What are you doing there?'

'Typing this contract into the computer and changing the agent's name to yours,' Nesta answered.

Sandy stopped chewing, then, sitting down on the sofa she stared into her half-empty cup.

'You've gone quiet,' Nesta accused a few minutes later.

Sandy's lips were pursed as she thought. 'I was just thinking about something Jodi said on the phone earlier,' she responded. 'Michael's gone to New York again. That's the third time in eight weeks.'

'So?' Nesta responded.

Sandy's looked at her and Nesta rolled her eyes.

'Sandy, for God's sake, you've got to get a grip,' she scolded gently. 'The man screwed you over in a pretty bad way, remember? You can't let him get away . . .'

'I know, I know,' Sandy interrupted, sighing. 'And I'm not letting him get away with it, am I? But that doesn't stop me feeling the way I do. I mean, you can't just turn those feelings off when they don't suit you any more.'

'OK, that's true, but you're going to have to accept the fact that one of these days he will get involved with someone else.'

'He hasn't since he fired me,' Sandy pointed out.

'And you're thinking it's because it's still you he really wants?' Nesta responded.

Sandy shrugged.

'Oh, come on, get real, will you? Try making yourself accept that he probably *is* going to New York to see a woman, and deal with it. It's the only way you're going to get over him. And think what satisfaction you're going to get the day you're in a position to take over his agency, then decide whether or not you want to give him a job.'

Sandy laughed and felt a sudden thrill kick-start her

spirits the way it always did when she envisaged herself having more power than Michael. It was true, she still wanted him desperately and nothing, just nothing, was ever going to persuade her they weren't right for each other, but she could see now that it was never going to happen unless she made it happen. And she would, for she had too much ammunition on her side to fail.

'Actually, what I was really thinking,' she said, 'was that all these trips to New York are probably to do with the Australian tie-up thing I told you about. Michael told me himself he wanted to get Chris Ruskin, his associate in New York, involved in the deal. I'm just trying to work out a way of getting the low-down on what's going on there and somehow getting in on it too.' She looked at Nesta. 'Does that suit?'

Nesta was looking impressed. 'As long it's got nothing to do with you eating your heart out over him and another woman it suits,' she confirmed, and picking up the phone as it rang she said, 'Hello, Sandy Paull's office. Oh hi, Maurice. Yes, she's right here. I'll put you on.'

As Sandy spoke to her personal business guru, who was also the chief investor in her soon-to-be-official new agency, Nesta carried on doctoring the contract in front of her while listening to the conversation. She didn't know Maurice well herself, as he was a very private man, but there wasn't much question about his devotion to Sandy, without which they wouldn't be nearly as far down the road as they were. In fact, he and Sandy had spent the past couple of weeks going about London looking at possible venues for an office, and with the kind of contacts and indeed, ownership, Maurice could boast Nesta was pretty certain Sandy was going to end up in some penthouse suite in Belgravia or Mayfair. Or, if the current conversation was anything to go by, right here in Chelsea.

'Do I take it from all that,' Nesta said as Sandy hung up, 'that you've put in an offer?'

'He has,' Sandy confirmed, with a very satisfied wiggle of her eyebrows. 'We should know by the middle of next week whether or not it's ours. And if it is, are you going to come work with us?'

'Us?' Nesta echoed.

'Me and the other agents I'll be recruiting,' Sandy explained.

'My, we are thinking big already,' Nesta remarked. 'Is this more of Maurice's money that's going to pay for these agents?'

'In the very short term,' Sandy replied. 'But considering those I have in mind it shouldn't be long before they're paying handsome dividends on Maurice's very handsome investment.'

Nesta's eyes were alive with curiosity. 'Don't tell me you're going to start poaching already,' she said. Then, instinctively realizing she was heading down the wrong track she said, 'No, you're not going to other agencies, are you?'

Sandy was shaking her head. 'There's no need to,' she smiled. 'Not at this stage, anyway.'

Nesta's pleasure was widening her grin to a point that made Sandy laugh out loud. 'You know, sometimes I wonder if I don't underestimate you,' Nesta declared.

'I wonder if you do too,' Sandy responded.

Nesta gazed at her in amused admiration. 'I never thought you'd have the guts for it,' she said bluntly.

'To be honest, I wasn't sure myself until today,' Sandy confessed. 'Now, I can hardly wait to get started.'

Nesta gave a whoop of pure triumph. 'Yeehah!' she cried. 'I don't know what happened today, but whatever it was, hang on to your balls, Michael McCann, 'cos Sandy Paull's a-ridin' into town.'

The bar at the Collection, London's latest place to be seen at, was crowded with media types as Sandy pushed her way through to join Jodi.

'Hi, Sandy,' Jodi said, as Sandy struggled on to the bar stool next to her.

'How are you?' Sandy asked, trying to catch the barman's attention. 'Thanks for coming.'

'That's OK,' Jodi replied chirpily, watching Sandy as she quickly looked around to see who else was there. 'I wanted to see for myself how you're getting along. I can't believe how much time has gone by since you left. I wish I could have seen you before this, but we've been so busy . . . Well, you know how it is. It's good that you keep in touch, though.'

Sandy lowered her eyes from the gallery restaurant above and smiled. She was still the same old Jodi, dishevelled black hair, frank, pretty face and garish spandex clothes. For a moment Sandy felt as though she were the older of the two, when she was at least three years Jodi's junior.

'Are you OK?' Jodi asked, peering into Sandy's eyes as though to encourage a positive reply. 'You look good.'

Sandy laughed and held out her wrists. 'No scars,' she declared. 'Hope that doesn't disappoint you.'

Jodi flushed. 'Look, I know how it must have seemed,' she said, 'that I was taking sides with Bertie and everyone, but I swear I wasn't. And for what it's worth I think Michael treated you pretty shabbily when he fired you.'

Sandy's eyebrows went up. 'A gin and tonic please,' she said to the barman. 'Did you tell him that?' she asked Jodi.

'Are you kidding?' Jodi spluttered. 'No one's allowed to mention your name.'

Sandy's heart tightened. Was that because he was still angry with her, or because it hurt him to hear it?

'That must be a tough one on Bertie,' she commented, managing a smile.

Jodi looked miserable, for she never had found it easy to gossip behind other people's backs.

Sandy eyed her for a moment, then, digging into her bag for her purse she said, 'So Michael's been seeing Ellen Shelby in New York.' She had no idea how she managed to keep her voice so steady, when inside she was sick with rage. Indeed, it had taken very little to convince herself that Ellen Shelby was at the root of all the injustice she had suffered, for had she not come into their lives when she had, Sandy just knew that she would be the one Michael was seeing now.

'I shouldn't have told you that,' Jodi replied.

'You didn't, I guessed,' Sandy reminded her.

'All the same, I'd prefer it if you never mentioned I told you,' Jodi said.

Sandy laughed. 'Who would I mention it to?' she said. 'I don't work there any more, remember? And I certainly don't know anyone else who'd be interested.'

Jodi was saved from responding as Sandy paid for her gin and tonic, then touched her glass to Jodi's. 'Cheers,' she said. 'It's good to see you.'

'And to see you,' Jodi replied, brightening. 'So what have you been doing? Have you found another job yet?'

Sandy nodded. 'As a matter of fact that's what I wanted to talk to you about.'

'Oh? Well, Michael said he'd give you good references and if you don't want to speak to him yourself . . .'

'I don't need any references,' Sandy interrupted.

Jodi looked startled. 'Oh, then what?' she said.

Sandy smiled. 'Promise not to laugh?'

'Promise.'

'I want you to work for me.'

Jodi choked on her drink. 'What?' she gasped, wiping her mouth.

'I'm setting up my own agency and I want you to work for me,' Sandy repeated.

Jodi's eyes were steeped in amazement. 'How?' she finally managed. 'I mean, your own agency . . .'

Sandy was waving a dismissive hand. 'Oh, you don't want to hear all the boring details of how,' she replied. 'Just suffice it to say that we're quite a long way down the road now and should be moving into our new premises some time next month.'

'We?' Jodi echoed.

'Me and my partners.'

Jodi took more time to assimilate the news before saying, 'Does Michael know anything about this?'

Sandy shrugged. 'I shouldn't think so,' she answered. 'How could he, when no one's allowed to mention my name?'

'But how have you managed it?'

'I promise you, it wasn't hard. So, are you interested in joining our team?'

'To be honest,' Jodi answered after a moment, 'I'm amazed you're asking when you of all people know how fond I am of Michael. I mean, I might not agree with what he did to you, but I'm definitely not thinking of leaving him . . .'

Sandy was shaking her head. 'I'm not asking you to leave him,' she smiled. 'In fact, that's the last thing I'd ask you to do. No, what I want is for you to pass me information on what's going on in the office, you know like this Australian tie-up, or in Michael's personal life, or even in someone else's, if you think it might be of use.'

Jodi's mouth dropped open in shock.

Sandy smiled.

'Do you . . . ? Are you asking me, will I spy for you? Is that what you're saying?' Jodi said breathlessly.

Sandy nodded. 'Crude, but accurate,' she said.

'Then you've got to be out of your mind!' Jodi cried

angrily. 'For God's sake, what's got into you even to ask me something like that. You know how much my job means to me, so does Michael . . .' She broke off, too stunned to go on.

'You told me today that Michael was seeing Ellen Shelby in New York,' Sandy reminded her. 'It's as easy as that.'

'As a matter of fact that wasn't easy at all,' Jodi shot back. 'I've regretted it ever since.'

Sandy merely looked at her.

'Jesus Christ, Sandy!' Jodi cried. 'What's happening to you? Are you having some kind of breakdown or something?'

Sandy laughed. 'Believe it or not, this kind of thing goes on all the time in business,' she informed her. 'I'm just getting the hang of it. It's called utilizing your assets – and you, Jodi, are one of my assets.'

Jodi was shaking her head. 'No, sorry,' she said, 'count me out. I couldn't play that kind of game even if I wanted to, and I definitely *don't* want to. In any case, how do you know I'm not going to tell Michael about this conversation?'

'You probably think you are,' Sandy answered.

An instant wariness came into Jodi's eyes. 'What do you mean?' she said.

'Well, you would tell him, wouldn't you, you're so loyal to him,' Sandy pointed out. 'Except you won't, because I'm asking you not to. And because if you do then I'll just have to let Harry's wife know about the affair you were having with her husband the whole time she was pregnant.' She smiled and took a sip of her drink.

Jodi stared at her in horrified silence.

Sandy waited it out.

'Just like that,' Jodi said in the end. 'You're telling me just like that, that you're prepared to screw up I don't know how many people's lives in order to get me to tell you when Michael's seeing Ellen Shelby. You're sick, Sandy. You need help.'

'I'm not just talking about when he's seeing Ellen Shelby,' Sandy corrected. 'I'm talking about everything else as well. Most specifically, right now, anything you can find out about the Australia deal.'

'And if I don't, you're going to Harry's wife?' Jodi said, as if only by saying it herself could she believe it.

Sandy nodded.

Jodi shook her head. 'You'd never do it,' she said. 'You're not that evil. I know you're not.'

'Don't put me to the test,' Sandy said mildly. 'It'll only be the worse for you if you do.'

'And what about Harry? Why aren't you asking him to give you the information? He's a senior agent, he'll . . .'

'Obviously he hasn't told you yet,' Sandy smiled.

Jodi's face was showing her strain. 'Told me what?' she said.

'Harry's going to be leaving McCann's at the end of the month,' Sandy informed her. 'In time for the move into our new offices.'

Jodi looked as though she'd been slapped. 'You mean you're blackmailing him too?' she said finally.

Sandy laughed. 'Of course not,' she responded, taking a sip of her drink. 'I just offered him a better deal than he's got at McCann's. A full partnership, a generous profit share, the kind of room for manoeuvre that he's not getting now and a few other things besides.'

'And he accepted?' Jodi said, hardly able to believe it.

'Of course he did,' Sandy replied, obviously still amused. 'So would you, if you were in his shoes, because he won't get an offer like it anywhere else. Nor will Craig, which is why he's coming too.'

'Craig!' Jodi echoed.

'Oh come on, that surely doesn't surprise you,' Sandy

objected. 'You know how closely Craig and I have worked, right from when I joined McCann's.' She paused, then said, 'He won't be coming until a month or so after Harry joins, but he's already signed his new contract.'

Jodi eyed her suspiciously. 'You're blackmailing him,' she declared. 'You know something about him . . .'

'Jodi, even if I did, it would hardly be a good idea for me to employ him on that basis, now would it,' Sandy pointed out. 'I intend for my new agency to work, and I wouldn't stand much chance of that if I started out by forcing my new partners to come and join me. But if you don't believe me, ask Harry and Craig yourself, I'm sure they won't mind telling you the kind of deal I've worked out for them.'

'How come neither of them have told Michael yet?' Jodi wanted to know.

Sandy shrugged. 'Maybe they have and no one's told you,' she suggested.

Jodi flushed, obviously stung by the idea Michael might not have confided something so vital.

Sandy smiled and finishing her drink, started to get up from her chair. 'Think over my earlier proposal,' she said. 'I'll be in touch in few days.' She was already moving away when, as though suddenly remembering something she said, 'Maybe I'll see you at Harry's baby's Christening on Sunday.'

'I can't believe you're letting her get away with this,' Jodi said, as she and Michael stood in his office watching Craig saying goodbye to the others.

'The alternative isn't an option,' Michael responded as Zelda came in to join them.

'Makes you wonder if Hollywood haven't got it right, making their clients sign up, rather than trusting to a verbal agreement,' Zelda commented.

'Exactly,' Jodi agreed, 'at least then she'd only be able to take the agent instead of all the talent too. I don't mean to be disloyal to Harry, or anything, but we've got more of a chance recovering from him going than from Craig, 'cos Craig's got the best literary list in London, everyone knows that.'

'True, but with the way she's stripped Janey and Diana of half their clients too, we're not looking too healthy on any front, right now,' Zelda replied. 'Except Michael's of course.'

Michael laughed. 'Do you think she might try to poach me too?' he asked.

Jodi looked at him with something akin to pity. 'Doesn't any of this bother you?' she asked. 'I mean, it should, but it doesn't seem to the way you carry on.'

'Jodi, what would you have me do?' he said, starting to pour them all a drink.

'I don't know, match her offers, I suppose,' Jodi responded truculently.

Michael shook his head. 'It's already too late for that,' he answered, 'and with the commitments we've made to new projects, like the Australia deal, we just weren't in a position to counter-offer. Harry and Craig know that, and there's no bad feeling between us. Ah, Dan, great timing,' he said as his brother-in-law came in the door. 'What'll you have?'

'A small scotch,' Dan answered, patting his paunch. 'Colleen's at me to get rid of this. Hi, Zelda, how are you? Any grisly little secrets you want to tell us about before Sandy Paull comes in with an offer you can't refuse?'

'Och, to be sure, I'm feeling most left out,' she responded. 'What a dull life it is I've been leading all this time. And if only I'd known where my indiscretions might have taken me.'

Michael was grinning as he passed her a gin. 'Did you speak to Angela Siddall?' he asked.

Zelda coughed and nodded. 'I'm seeing her tomorrow,' she wheezed. 'Oh, heaven help me I can't shake this cold. I don't think,' she went on, 'she'll be able to join us right away, because she's on a year's contract with Shine Connell which isn't due to expire for at least six months.'

'OK, just get the low down and we'll take it from there,' Michael responded. 'And I've been considering getting Paul Patton out of the BBC to come and start up a new literary list here. What do you think?'

Zelda's eyes rounded with approval as she nodded over her gin. 'Great idea,' she agreed. Then, to Jodi, 'Don't look so aggrieved. It's not that we don't care about losing Harry and Craig, but life has to go on, hen, and there's just no way she's going to bring McCann Walsh to its knees, the way you seem to think she is, so stop worrying, will you?'

'But if I hadn't told you what was going on when Harry left,' Jodi said hotly, 'then none of you would be any the wiser now, would you?'

'Och, I think we'd have cottoned on in time,' Zelda assured her, 'what with Craig going as well. But it's true, we do have you to thank for telling us she wanted to know about the Australian tie-up.'

'How much have you told her about that?' Michael asked.

'Only the stuff you fed me,' Jodi answered. 'Why? You don't think I've been giving her anything else, do you?'

'Calm down,' Michael laughed. 'No, of course I don't. I just wondered how interested she still seemed, that was all.'

'Very,' Jodi stated. Then after thinking about it, 'Actually, less so lately, but then that's probably because I keep changing the subject and telling her about Ellen. That really bugs her, I can tell you.'

Zelda and Dan laughed, while Michael sat in his

chair and looked thoughtful. 'You know, it might not be a good thing to wind her up about Ellen,' he said. 'She's gunning for us as it is – not that she's going to succeed – but I just don't think it's wise to antagonize her any more than we already have.' Then, lifting his head and resuming his smile he said, 'Well, I think we've about exhausted that subject for now, so tell me, Dan, how long have we got before Clodagh and Colleen get here?'

'About half an hour,' Dan answered, perching on the window-sill and watching Bertie fussing around Craig's empty office opposite. 'What are you going to do about him?' he asked, nodding in Bertie's direction.

'Offer him to Sandy?' Michael suggested.

Zelda and Jodi laughed. 'They deserve each other,' Jodi commented.

Michael's eyebrows rose, then, after taking a sip of his drink he said, 'So, providing we're all in agreement that Jodi's to be trusted – all right, I'm sorry, that was uncalled for,' he apologized, when Jodi threw him a thunderous look, 'let's go over the latest developments with World Wide Entertainment, which is what we're now calling the international link-up. Chris Ruskin in New York is meeting up with an LA-based firm of headhunters some time in the next couple of weeks with a view to them searching out an agent to handle the West Coast operations.'

'Surely you must know someone?' Jodi piped up.

Michael shook his head. 'No one I'd feel happy trusting and Chris feels the same. Mark Bergin doesn't know anyone in showbiz except a couple of Australians, so he's relying on us.'

'What about Ellen?' Jodi said.

Michael shook his head. 'She works for ATI, remember, which would give her a real conflict of interests if we brought her in. So, for the moment we're going with the headhunters. They'll be given three months to come up with someone, which we're confident they will, since Ellen assures me not everyone in Hollywood is a crook.' He grinned to show he didn't really mean that, but no one was convinced. 'So,' he went on, 'as you know, we've already got an exchange programme worked out between three theatres in Sydney, three in London, four in New York and I've just found out today that we're including two in LA. I know LA isn't famous for theatre, but that's only because it's overshadowed by the screen world. They put on some damned good productions from time to time and it's another way of getting more shows into the US. All that should start early next month and in the meantime we're looking into financing a twenty-six-part series to be shot in Miami, Manchester, Perth and Singapore. It's an adaptation of the Shirley Whitfield novel, *Too Many Barriers*.

'Obviously, all this is costing a packet, but we've got some pretty strong support from a couple of banks in the US and Australia, as well as here. Am I right?' he said, looking at Dan.

Dan nodded. 'The Arts Council are interested too,' he said, 'and we're working on tapping the lottery for a few bob. I was in talking to our own bank manager today and though the balance sheets haven't looked too healthy the last couple of months – and probably won't for the next few either thanks to Harry and Craig going – no one sees any reason to worry. Incidently, it's now pretty evident that on top of the personnel she's availed herself of, Sandy's defrauded the company of some thirty-five grand or more, but Michael and I have discussed it and rather than bring any more unpleasantness to bear on the situation we feel the matter is best left as is.'

'You mean you're letting her get away with it!' Jodi cried indignantly, her eyes moving accusingly between Dan and Michael.

Dan looked at Michael.

'It was my decision,' Michael explained, 'which I took after the company lawyer contacted her and threatened to call in the police. She told the lawyer that if we did that she'd charge me with sexual harassment. So, all things considered, I think we'd do well to cut our losses and move past this. After all, we don't want that kind of publicity coming down on us and I sure as hell don't need it while we're getting World Wide up and going. Besides, I don't think she can hit us with much else now, can she? She's got Harry and Craig, which is tantamount to forty per cent of the company . . .'

'Don't forget all the clients she took from Diana and Janey,' Jodi butted in.

'I'm not. All in all, she's taken about fifty-five per cent of the company. But it's only temporary, because everyone's replaceable, even Craig, and unless Zelda succumbs to . . .'

'Och, no, not me,' Zelda cried, holding up a hand. 'I go down with the sinking ship. After all, it was me who employed the little madam, so I'm responsible for . . .'

'Let's not get into that again,' Michael stopped her. 'We'll get through this without too much trouble and when we do we're going to be even bigger and certainly more international than before. In fact, it could well be that without even realizing it Sandy's doing us a favour, because we could end up changing shape completely and with the way the industry's going that's probably no bad thing.'

'So in other words, everyone's dispensable, no matter who they are, or what they do, or how loyally they've worked for you?' Jodi's eyes were glittering with anger.

Michael inhaled deeply. 'Jodi, I know you think Sandy blackmailed them into joining her, but I promise you she didn't. They went of their own free will and we just have to accept that. So let's get back to World

401

Wide, shall we? We're putting just about everything we've got into this venture, which is a gamble by anyone's standards, so we need the whole team to pull together, which includes you, because if it works out it's going to turn us into more of a production house than an agency. Of course, we'll always be an agency, but as you know it was my intention a few years back to get into producing and I think the time has now come for me to take a look at it again. I've got a few projects in mind and if I manage to get any of them off the ground it's going to mean you running my part of the agency while I'm otherwise engaged.'

Jodi stared at him. 'But I'm not an agent,' she pointed out. 'I never even said I wanted to be one.'

'That's fine,' Michael replied. 'Zelda will be taking care of my clients. What we need you to do is get more involved in running the office.'

'What, you mean like a manager?' she said.

'Exactly like a manager,' he answered, 'if that's what you want to call yourself. The title's entirely up to you, the pay increase is up to us and we've voted you a twenty-five per cent rise effective from the first of next month. You'll also get a company car and an entertainment allowance.'

Jodi was boggle-eyed as she looked at Dan, then Zelda, then back to Michael. 'What about you?' she said. 'Will I still be your assistant?'

'Depends whether you want to be,' he replied.

'Well I'm certainly not handing over to anyone else,' she retorted. Then breaking into an enormous grin she ran across the room and hugged him.

'If I were you I'd keep this under your hat for a while,' he warned as she let him go, 'because the last thing we want is Sandy threatening to go to Harry's wife again in order to get you away too. So the best thing you can do is tell her we're already starting to struggle financially, which is more or less true as we've had to go into hock to the banks for a lot more than we intended thanks to Harry and Craig going, and tell her we haven't even managed to find a replacement for Harry or Craig yet either. Embellish it with as much gloom and doom as you like, and try to keep off the subject of Ellen. Have you told her Ellen's coming to London next week?'

Jodi shook her head. 'I was tempted, I must admit,' she said, 'but I had a feeling it might not be a good idea.'

'It wouldn't,' he confirmed.

Dan was frowning. 'You surely don't think she'd do anything to hurt Ellen, do you?' he said.

Michael shook his head. 'God knows what she'd do given half a chance,' he responded. 'I don't know how the woman's mind works, but if she starts delving deep enough into my personal life we all know what she's going to find and I for one would much rather she didn't.'

'Does Ellen know about that?' Zelda asked.

Michael shook his head.

'But I thought it was getting serious between you two.'

'We still live an ocean and continent apart,' Michael reminded her. 'Until we go at least some way towards closing that gap I don't see how you can describe us as serious.'

'He just calls her every day and goes over to New York twice a month to meet up with her,' Jodi pointed out. 'But that's not serious. Nor is taking a three-week holiday with her in the Caribbean.'

'All right, don't get smart,' Michael reprimanded. 'And nothing's been finalized on that yet.'

'Well Clodagh thinks it has,' Jodi informed him. 'In fact, she seems to think she's going too.'

'What?' He laughed. 'She'll be here any minute so we'll disabuse her of that notion straight away. And

403

speaking of my family, does any one know if Cavan called me back?'

'Oh, yes, sorry, he did,' Jodi answered. 'I forgot to tell you. He rang about an hour ago while you were talking to Craig. Sorry I didn't interrupt, but I thought . . .'

'It's OK, you did right,' Michael assured her, getting to his feet. 'I'll just go over to Dan's office and see if I can get through to him now.'

A few minutes later he was speaking to Cavan at his apartment in Leme.

'Hey, you're lucky to catch me,' Cavan called down the line, 'I was on my way out. How are you? How's Ma?'

'Everyone's great,' Michael answered. 'The question is how are you? When I spoke to you a couple of days ago you sounded like you had something on your mind and frankly it's not the first time you've left me with the impression you're holding back on me about something. So what is it?'

'There's nothing,' Cavan laughed. 'You're imagining things.' He laughed again. 'You've got to know by now that you'd be the first person I'd turn to if I was in any kind of trouble. So, take it from me, there's no trouble.'

'That's your word, not mine,' Michael pointed out.

'OK, call it what you like. Everything's coming up roses over here. How about over there? Colleen tells me there's a new woman. Is it serious?'

'We're not talking about me, we're talking about you,' Michael responded. 'Or should we be talking about Michelle? Is that who this is about?'

'Michelle's fine,' Cavan answered. 'Everything is.'

Michael knew he was lying, but short of coming right out and accusing him he didn't know how to get him to admit it. 'OK,' he said in the end, 'you're a big boy now, you can take care of yourself. If you find you can't, then you know where I am,' and he put the phone down.

As he started back to his own office he realized the call had made him much angrier than it should have and he couldn't quite fathom why. Except maybe it wasn't Cavan's reticence that was rattling him, maybe it was that Cavan knew what was going on with Michelle when he didn't that was giving him such a hard time. Whatever, something wasn't right over there, he just knew it.

Chapter 21

The smell of the *favela* was so overpoweringly noxious that it alone was enough to keep strangers out. The houses, if they could even be described as that, were put together from scraps of frayed and rotting wood, rusting sheets of corrugated iron, broken gates or fences, slabs of polystyrene and even cardboard. Some were made from the kind of brick that would crumble if crushed underfoot, while others were no more than makeshift tents put together from worn-out sheets and blankets that, like the rest of the materials, had been recycled from the rubbish dump at the foot of the hill.

The main street that Michelle and Antônio were now climbing, rose steeply into the heart of the *favela*. Either side of them, hidden alley-ways and tunnels snaked through the ghetto connecting one miserable ruin of a street to another. The gutters were clogged with rotting garbage, the air was so hot and humid that the stench of raw sewage clung to her nostrils and tainted her throat. Flies were everywhere, around the gutters, the garbage, the dogs and the children. The voice of Madonna singing 'Don't Cry for Me Argentina' blared from a radio; the traffic below was a fading roar, and when finally they turned from the main street and began to climb through a maze of dwellings that were stacked on the hillside like old lumber left to rot in the sun the views of Rio and the ocean disappeared.

All around them, faces were peering from broken shutters and doorways, while a small gang of children in ragged T-shirts and bare feet followed them up the precipitous steps. The guide, Aldo, had already warned them that the eyes and ears of the drug dealers were among the kids behind them, but no harm should come to them as long as they had no drugs or weapons themselves.

Feeling a tug on the hem of her shirt, Michelle turned round and smiled as the children ducked behind a wall.

'Are you all right?' Antônio asked, turning back to check.

'Fine,' she answered and took his hand as he helped her over a pile of twisted metal. The squalor and debris were so dense now that in some cases is was hard to tell the dwellings from the garbage, and the stench of human waste was so thick and putrid, as it oozed in a grey-brown sludge down the side of the steps, that it was becoming difficult to breathe.

At last, Aldo came to a halt near the top of the hill outside a crude brick house that had no door or shutters, just the ubiquitous graffiti that were all over the *favelas*. Its roof was fashioned from scraps of hardboard and lino, its backdrop was a rising forest of lush green vegetation.

Using an already sodden handkerchief to wipe the sweat from her face and still panting from the climb, Michelle looked up at Antonio who was standing in the dusty yard at the front of the house. Beside him was a free-standing stone sink where washing was soaking in grey soapy water, at his feet a handful of scrawny chickens was pecking the dirt among old plastic bottles and worn-out shoes.

'Cláudio!' their guide shouted. 'Antônio is here. The *gringa* is with him.'

An old man appeared in the doorway, his thin,

gnarled frame held as upright as he could manage. From where she was standing Michelle couldn't quite hear what he and Aldo were saying, but when, after greeting Antônio, his lucid brown eyes moved to hers and he held out his hand in welcome, she found herself moving towards him as though to greet someone she knew well. He reminded her, she realized, of her grandfather, such was the kindliness of his manner and ready warmth in his smile.

'You are very welcome to my house,' he told her in his tobacco-roughened voice. 'I thank you for coming.'

Michelle smiled and shook his hand warmly. 'Thank you for inviting me,' she replied.

A humorous light was glimmering in his eyes and chuckling, he said something she didn't quite understand. Looking to Antônio for translation into simpler Portuguese, she laughed too as she learnt what he'd said.

'I imagine plenty of beautiful women have accepted your invitations in the past,' she countered.

Appearing delighted with her answer he said, 'I am Cláudio Miguel, Márcio's uncle. You met my wife when she brought the baby to the shelter.'

Michelle nodded and hoped he wasn't going to ask if she'd agreed to adopt the baby, as the last thing she wanted was to have to tell him she couldn't.

'We have much to discuss,' he said, 'so, please, come inside.'

By *favela* standards his two-roomed house was surprisingly neat, by most other standards in the world it was a slum. Though the walls were constructed mainly of brick, there were several patches of wood and sheet polythene blocking up holes where the bricks had failed. The floor was black, compressed earth, cleanly swept and with a few pieces of threadbare carpet strewn about. The furniture consisted of a black vinyl three-piece suite with a faded pink-and-white pattern

408

and dull-yellow foam sprouting from the tears and against the far wall, as with most *favela* houses, there was a smart-looking cabinet containing a brand-new TV and video. It would probably take Cláudio the rest of his life to pay off the credit, for it was the only way he, and those like him, could ever afford such luxuries. The electricity had been appropriated from the street lighting below and was carried into the *favela* by a tangle of overhead wires and lethal junctions. Perhaps the real tragedy of it, though, was their addiction to the sumptuous Brazilian soap operas, in which they got to see everything they could ever aspire to and knew they would never have.

After inviting her and Antônio to sit down, Cláudio lit a cigarette, then, putting an overflowing ashtray on the arm of a chair he sat down too. 'I know what a risk you've taken in coming here,' he told Michelle. 'Indeed, it's a risk for us all. But my wife said you spoke to her at the shelter and told her you wanted to help.'

'That's right,' Michelle confirmed, refusing to think of Tom and Cavan, who were away in the north of the country right now, so had no idea she was here. Indeed, since they'd got wind that there was someone in this *favela* who might be willing to talk about Pastillano, Tom had actually forbidden her to go there. And she really wouldn't have defied him except for the fact that Márcio's aunt had sent word to Antônio to bring the woman and only the woman. Antônio hadn't been at all happy about that, as he was very aware of Chambers's insistence that Michelle be kept out of danger at all costs. So Michelle had lied and told Antônio that she had discussed it with Chambers on the phone and Chambers had agreed she should go. The consequence of that was something she would deal with later.

The old man blinked and looked down at his

cigarette. Then, bringing his gentle eyes back to hers he said, 'Are you taking care of the baby?'

Michelle's heart sank and swallowing before she spoke she said, 'Not personally, no. But he's in very good hands.'

Claudio nodded. 'We didn't expect you to take him as your own . . .'

'Only because I can't,' she interrupted. 'If I could, believe me, he's so adorable, I would. But we've registered him with an American agency and we've already heard of five couples who are interested.'

'Thank you,' Cláudio said. Then, getting to his feet, he gestured for Michelle to follow him.

Glancing at Antônio, who nodded for her to go ahead, she crossed to where the old man had disappeared through a doorway at the back of the room and found herself in a kind of lean-to kitchen, where a rusty iron stove, caked with old food and black spotted grime stood in a puddle of rank, greasy water. There was an old, slime-covered sink unit, dented metal pots soiled with burnt food and a pile of old bottles and canisters stacked up in a corner. Michelle was ashamed of the way her stomach reacted, but the smell and the filth were too overpowering for her to stop it.

Once out the other side, he took her further up the hill to where the beautiful Tijuca forest grew more densely and more colourfully than anywhere she'd seen, until they were on a small, elevated clearing looking down over the tragic chaos of the *favela*.

'Do you see the river?' he asked, pointing to a twisting black line way below them.

Michelle nodded. They had passed it on their way here, so she knew that it was about ten feet wide and four feet deep, and carried a foul, viscous flow of untreated sewage.

'Four nights ago,' Cláudio said, 'the police came and

made eight children jump into the canal. They did it for fun. One of the little girls almost died.'

From long experience Michelle knew that to try to respond to these situations in words was futile, and besides, she was so horrified by what he'd said she couldn't even find any words.

'You have saved Márcio's son from that,' he told her. 'And much worse,' then, taking her back to the house, he sat down again and was about to speak when several loud explosions echoed up over the hill.

'Isn't that a warning to say the police are on their way?' Michelle said, when no one else spoke.

Cláudio nodded.

Michelle looked at Antônio.

'Do you think they know we're here?' Antônio asked Cláudio.

'It is very possible,' Cláudio responded. 'You must remember, there are many in the *favelas* who are prepared to do anything to make a few *reais*, including spy for the people who torture and kill us. I expect someone sent word the moment you arrived.'

'So what do we do?' Michelle asked, feeling herself tense, despite her determination to stay.

Cláudio smiled. 'We keep calm,' he answered and, raising a hand, he shouted in a dialect Michelle didn't understand. Almost immediately his wife came into the room. She was a short woman, with a thin, angular body and a face that bore all the troubles of her fifty-five years. In her arms was a wide-eyed four-year-old boy who, the minute he saw Cláudio, held out his arms to go to him.

'My grandson, Paulo,' Claudio told them, taking the boy and shaking him playfully, before depositing him in the chair behind him. Michelle grinned as the little boy shoved his head under his grandfather's arm and peered out. Clearly amused, Cláudio swung the child on to his lap and treated him to a fond telling-off. From

411

the bottom of her heart Michelle wished that the so-called upper classes of Rio, who were so afraid of the poverty and crime they were perpetuating, could see this man with his grandson now, for surely they would have to realize then that the poor loved their families every bit as much as the rich; maybe, in some cases, even more.

'Will you take coffee?' Cláudio offered.

Michelle thought of the kitchen and longed to say no, but it would be a snub she could never forgive herself. The irony was she had no liking for the thick, sweet coffee they served here in Rio, but in this instance she was going to make herself drink it. Unless the police got there first, of course.

'Aren't you concerned about us being found here?' she said, addressing herself to both Antônio and Cláudio.

Cláudio's tranquil brown eyes watched her for a moment, then setting his grandson on the floor, he said, 'They won't come. They are just letting us know that they are aware of what is going on. In a few minutes we will no doubt hear the signal telling us they have gone.'

'But if they know you're speaking to me,' Michelle protested, 'doesn't that put you in danger?'

'Probably. But I am an old man, I shall die soon anyway. It is Luiz I am more concerned about.'

'Luiz?' Michelle repeated, feeling a beat of excitement in her heart. 'Do you mean the boy who was held at the Inferno? Is he here?'

Cláudio's expression was grave as he said, 'The police who have just entered the *favela* are almost certainly working for Pastillano. They are looking for Luiz. They know there's a chance he might talk and you being here is persuading them that he is hiding out here.'

'Is he?' Michelle asked.

Cláudio nodded. 'But only for the time you are here. You provide a certain security for him – they can't kill him while you're here, unless they kill you too. And they're not stupid enough to kill an American.'

'Actually, I'm British,' she told him.

'Same thing,' he said and, taking another cigarette from the pack he lit it and exhaled two lines of smoke from his nostrils. 'If it happens it won't be an act of stupidity,' he warned her, 'it will be an act of desperation, so beware.'

Michelle's eyes were on his as she registered his warning and waited for him to go on.

'We live in so much fear,' he said sadly, 'that even to pray has become a risk, because for that a man must close his eyes.'

The poignancy of his words sent a rush of emotion to Michelle's heart and her eyes wandered to the plastic crucifix stuck to the wall with candle wax. She thought of the thirty-metre statue on the peak of Corcovada, Jesus Christ the Redeemer, towering up there so far above the city, resplendent in its misery, superior in its aloofness as it stretched out its arms to the heavens and stared past the blighted flock at its feet.

Cláudio started to speak again and as she listened she was as surprised by his articulacy as she was moved by his words. 'The military régime is over,' he said, 'but I think someone has forgotten to tell the police and men like Pedro Pastillano, who wishes to become our new governor. If that happens, and it looks very possible, there will be nothing short of genocide on these hillsides, for the false imprisonment, torture and extermination of our young men will only become more widespread under a régime that is already allowed to act with impunity. I can give you many names of those in high places who not only approve of what Pedro Pastillano is doing, but who actually take part in the sadistic rituals at the private prison he has created. These are men you will see every day in the newspapers and on your TV screens. Businessmen, politicians, policemen, journalists, celebrities – people with influence and power. Have you ever asked yourself who supplies the traffickers in the *favelas* with their drugs?'

Michelle looked at him, already knowing the answer, but wanting to hear it from him.

'It is the men I have just told you about,' he said. 'The men who run our city. They control the police, they also control the crime. In other words, no one is safe and no one can be trusted. In the case of Pedro Pastillano, he puts on a very good show of donating thousands of *reais* to the poor, or giving us good terms for finance so we can shop in his stores and buy his televisions and VCRs and hi-fis. He brings us waste food from his restaurants and gives us many promises of good things for when he is governor; he will install sewers, increase the water supply, reduce bus fares, all things that will help the *favelados*. He does this because he wants our vote and there are many who are so desperate they are prepared to believe him, even though they know that behind the public image he is an evil man whose death squad has killed many of their friends and loved ones. This death squad, which is right now in the *favela* as a means of intimidation, is made up of policemen and security guards. Its main purpose is either to kill or torture, often both. To exterminate us is as necessary as to exterminate rats. They are almost never brought to justice, which is something, in his own circles, Pastillano laughs and boasts about, just like he laughs and boasts about his prison and the terrible things he does there. Luiz will tell you about that. You will not only find it inhuman, you will find it so repellent that you will not want to believe it.'

'But I will believe it,' Michelle assured him.

414

He smiled. 'It is why I am talking to you,' he said. 'Márcio believed in you enough to give you his son. My wife trusts you too. Have you found a prosecutor here in Rio who will help you?'

Michelle nodded. 'Carlos Camillo,' she answered. 'He's a decent and honest man who is prepared to do anything, including lay his own life on the line, to prevent Pastillano's reign of terror going any further than it already has.'

Cláudio nodded. 'I have heard of him,' he said, crushing his cigarette in the ashtray. 'He is a good man. Do you know of Judge da Silva?'

'I've met her on several occasions,' Michelle said, wishing she could tell him that da Silva was the judge Tom Chambers had singled out to be as fearless and incorruptible as a human being could get.

'She is a good person,' Cláudio said. 'In her court the poor receive justice and even mercy. In most other courts there is little chance of us receiving either. Now I will allow you to speak to Luiz. He has no mother and father, no family at all that we can find. All he knows is that his name is Luiz and that he is around fourteen years old. We know him through Márcio because they were of the same gang. There is not a very good chance of him living much longer, not now that he has spent some time at the Inferno, which is why we have persuaded him to talk to you. If he dies, you must take the truth to the world and see that his murderers are caught. People like you are our only hope.' He stopped as three more explosions resounded through the *favela*.

'The signal to say the police have gone,' he informed them. 'But they will be back, so I want you to give me your word that once Luiz has spoken to you you will do everything you can to protect him.'

Michelle's hand went to her heart. 'I swear it,' she promised.

'He can give you the names of at least two officers of

the death squad. He can tell you what happens at the prison and he can also tell you about other boys who have been held there and are still alive to tell the tale. It is doubtful those boys will talk to you, but some have given Luiz permission to tell you their stories.' He looked up as his wife came in with a tray of smeary glasses that contained an inch of sticky sweet coffee in each.

Michelle smiled as she was handed a glass, then looked down at the grandson who was watching her from between his grandfather's feet. Holding out a hand to encourage him closer, she listened as Antônio told the old lady what was happening to the baby she had taken to the shelter. Then her heart contracted with sadness as the old lady explained how much she'd wanted to keep the child, but with nine of them already living in the house, she'd really had little choice but to do as Márcio asked.

As she wiped a tear from the papery skin beneath her eyes, Michelle's throat tightened with emotion at the thought of one day having to say goodbye to a child she loved too. Indeed, with Cara's imminent departure that day was coming closer all the time, but now wasn't the time to start dealing with that.

'Come here, Luiz,' Cláudio said.

Michelle and Antônio turned in surprise as a tall, gangly figure emerged from the shadows of the adjoining room, where he must have been all the time, and limped awkwardly towards them. At first his injuries were difficult to see, as his T-shirt and jeans covered most, but as he drew closer and eased himself gingerly into the chair Cláudio had vacated, dark, livid weals and raw, ugly burns became visible on his face, neck and lower arms. His right eye was partially closed, an angry swelling around it, and his lips were badly cut and still bloody.

Michelle looked at him, her green eyes imbued with

416

horror and pity, and the resolve in her heart grew to make whoever had done this pay.

'I am lucky,' he told her, his voice rasping through the wounds on his lips. 'They didn't break my feet. Sometimes they break your feet.'

Wincing at the mere thought of it, Michelle glanced up at Cláudio, then, reaching into her purse she said, 'Do you mind if I record what you're saying?'

The boy's haunted, bloodshot eyes looked at the recorder, then turning to Cláudio, he said something Michelle didn't quite catch.

'He needs to know where you will hide him once he has told you his story,' Cláudio explained.

'We will take him to Carlos Camillo, the prosecutor,' she answered. Then, addressing Luiz she said, 'Seu Carlos and Judge da Silva have already arranged several safe houses for witness protection in and around Rio. Antônio and I can't tell you exactly where these houses are, because it isn't safe for us to know either, but I give you my word that if it comes to it, I will personally fly you out of the country to get you away from Pedro Pastillano and his death squad.'

Fear and uncertainty remained in Luiz's eyes as he looked at the recorder again and began to clench and unclench his hands.

'It's OK,' Michelle said gently, sliding the recorder back into her purse, 'we can just talk. There's no need to get anything on the record until you're ready.'

Luiz looked up at Cláudio's wife, as she perched on the arm of his chair and put a comforting arm around his shoulders. 'The *senhora* will keep you safe,' she told him in a whisper. 'You must trust her – and the man from the shelter. They will help you. They'll help us all, but you have to tell them what you know.'

'Why don't you start,' Michelle said, 'by telling me where the Inferno is.'

The boy's round, bruised eyes came back to her and

there was only a slight hesitation before he said, 'I don't know. No one knows. They take you there in a van with no windows. That's if you're conscious. Usually you're not. Sometimes they just use blindfolds. And if you get out alive, you come out that way too. No one ever escapes.'

Michelle nodded. Disappointing as the answer was, it was much what she'd expected. 'Could you hear anything while you were there?' she said. 'You know, noises from outside, like the ocean, or traffic, or planes.'

He thought for a moment, then said, 'I heard water. Not the ocean. More like a stream, a waterfall I think.'

Michelle smiled encouragement. 'So it could be in the mountains?' she said.

He blinked, obviously not understanding why she thought that.

Leaving it, she said, 'Do you have any idea what kind of building the Inferno is? Did you see it at all from the outside?'

He shook his head. 'All I know is that the tank where we were most of the time is underground. There are no lights, no air, no toilets. Just one door that is kept locked all the time.'

'Did they open the door to feed you?' she asked.

He shook his head. 'We didn't get food. Or maybe scraps and some water. They opened the door then – and to take us in and out. There were steps outside. You know, leading up to the open air, but the sunlight hurts your eyes so bad when you come out that you don't see anything and then you're back inside again, in a room where they ...' His eyes fell away and his hands began twitching again.

'What kind of room was it?' Michelle prompted gently.

'Stone,' he mumbled. 'Everything was stone. The walls, the ceiling, the floor. No windows. There were lots of rooms. One after the other. Not big. Bigger than this house, but not big.'

'Do you remember seeing anything in them?' she asked.

His chin was almost on his chest as he shook his head.

'Tell her,' Cláudio urged softly.

Luiz still didn't look up and reaching out for his hand Cláudio's wife gave it a comforting squeeze.

'The parrot's perch,' Luiz said so quietly Michelle didn't catch it.

She looked at Cláudio, but it was Antônio who spoke.

'The parrot's perch,' he repeated. 'It's a kind of swing. They make a boy hang by his knees, then they tie his hands behind his back, attach them to his ankles and make him hang there while they beat him.'

Michelle turned back to Luiz. 'Did they do that to you?' she asked, gently.

Luiz nodded.

'Why do they do it?' she asked Cláudio. 'Are they trying to get information?'

'Sometimes,' Cláudio answered. 'They want names of rival drug gangs, or they want to let the drug dealers know what will happen to them if they try to cheat the police out of their cut of the money.'

'Is that what you did?' Michelle asked Luiz. 'Try to cheat the police out of their cut?'

'Not me, Márcio,' Luiz answered. 'It was why they killed him.'

Michelle's eyes dropped for a moment as she recalled the fear she had seen in Márcio the day he had come to the shelter.

'Tell her what else happened while you were at the Inferno,' Cláudio prompted. 'Tell her about the . . .'

Michelle didn't understand the word he used, so looked at Antônio. Her eyes widened as she received

419

the translation and turning back to Luiz she said, 'They assaulted you sexually?'

Still Luiz couldn't meet her eyes.

'It's why it's so hard for him to walk,' Cláudio explained. 'They used their truncheons, as well as with their...' He gave a self-conscious gesture towards his genitals.

'They pulled Magno's teeth out and stuffed their pricks in his mouth,' Luiz said in a sudden burst.

Michelle's insides shrank from the horror. 'Magno?' she said.

'He's dead,' Luiz said flatly. 'They shot him.'

'Did you see them shoot him?' she asked.

He nodded. 'It was César. He fired the gun.'

'César?' she said.

Luiz nodded.

Cláudio said. 'Eduardo César. He was promoted from captain to major for bravery after he killed two men in a shoot out in the next *favela*.'

'So he's a policeman?' Michelle said.

Cláudio nodded.

Michelle glanced at Antônio, then, turning back to Luiz she said, 'While you were at the *Inferno*, did you see Pedro Pastillano?'

He shook his head. 'I don't know what he looks like,' he said. 'I only know his name.'

'Did you hear anyone using his name?' she asked.

'I think so. I don't know. But the others, Chico, Magno, José, they all said they saw him.'

'Chico and José,' she said, 'are they still in the tank, or did they get shot like Magno?'

'No, they were released with me,' Luiz answered. 'But they don't want to talk.'

Michelle nodded her understanding, then turned abruptly as a figure appeared in the open doorway casting the room into virtual darkness. For one awful moment she thought it was the police, then realizing it must be Aldo who was keeping guard outside she was about to speak when the room suddenly began to fill with men.

'What is it? What's happening?' she whispered to Antônio, as he pulled her to her feet and tried to shove her behind him.

'Marcelo,' Cláudio said, moving in front of Luiz as though to protect the boy from the menace that was boring out of the newcomer's eyes.

'I told you,' the man Marcelo snarled, 'the boy keeps his mouth shut. I warned you.' The men closing in behind him were all armed with machine-guns and Michelle's throat was turning dry with fear. She didn't need to ask who they were, for their tattoos, as well as instinct, told her they were members of the Estrela street gang.

Cláudio seemed unafraid as he began to shout in a dialect she couldn't understand, and wave his arms in a manner that was alarmingly contemptuous and dismissive. Behind him Luiz cowered in the chair, his fragile, injured body quaking with terror as Cláudio tried to prevent the gang leader from getting any closer to him.

Then, quite suddenly, Marcelo swung round and glaring at Michelle he hissed, 'We don't need your help. You just bring us more trouble. Now go! Leave the boy to us.'

Despite the dread thumping in her heart Michelle stepped forward, but before she could speak a volley of bullets tore into the wall behind her. The shock sent her back into Antônio, then a sudden, blinding pain shot through her head.

As she slumped to the floor she could hear men shouting, was aware of Cláudio trying to order the gang out, then suddenly she was jerked to her feet and Marcelo's face was right on hers. 'You brought the police,' he spat. 'They were here because of you.' He pointed behind him to Luiz. 'He's already dead,' he

421

seethed. 'He's marked and now you're marking us too. So get out of here and don't come back.'

His face was swimming in and out of focus as Michelle tried to stiffen her legs and free herself from his grip. 'You're a coward,' she muttered, barely knowing what she was saying. 'You're trying to scare . . .'

Grabbing her, Antônio rushed her to the door. 'Don't be a fool,' he hissed as he pushed her outside. 'They'll kill you. Or they'll kill the boy . . . Aldo! Why didn't you warn us?' he shouted at the guide. Then he saw the gun trained on Aldo's neck. 'We need him to get out,' Antônio told the gang member, his voice coming in short, frightened bursts. 'We don't know the way without him.'

'Let him go!' Marcelo barked.

Antônio spun round, then, grabbing Michelle again he dragged her across the yard after Aldo, down the treacherously uneven steps and got them as fast as he could out of the range of Marcelo's guns.

Two hours later Michelle was sitting with Antônio in the air-conditioned haven of Carlos Camillo's Copacabana apartment. Her head was throbbing from where she had been struck by one of Marcelo's men, while dust and grime from the *favela* clogged her pores and grazed her thorat. She was still shaken by what had happened, but had insisted on calling Camillo the minute they got to a payphone to tell him what they had heard. The prosecutor was now *en route* from his downtown office and Antônio was sitting across the study glaring at her in a way that was making her ashamed of the lie she had told him. He still wouldn't know, were it not for the fact that he had wanted to call Tom Chambers the minute they'd hung up from Camillo and the only excuse she could give for not doing so was to confess that Chambers had no idea she had gone to the *favela* without him.

'It's me he'll be furious with,' Michelle said, in an attempt to make Antônio feel better. 'Not you.'

'And if something had happened to you?' Antônio responded tightly. 'Who would have been blamed then?'

'But nothing did,' she said. 'OK, I got hit on the head. I've survived worse. What's bothering me more is what's going to happen to Luiz now.'

'Tom would have made them bring him out of the *favela* to talk to us,' Antônio stated. 'That way he would have lessened the danger to a point where it hardly existed.'

'You don't know that for certain,' she responded irritably. 'Nor do you know if they'd have agreed. As it stands, we now know that . . .'

'Carlos,' Antônio said, getting up as the prosecutor walked into the room.

He was a tall, heavy man with a long, handsome face and an overburdened demeanour. 'Sorry to have kept you,' he said, closing the door and tossing his crumpled jacket on a chair. 'The traffic was appalling. Did someone get you a drink?'

'Your wife,' Michelle told him. Then, smiling, 'When is the baby due?'

His tight, austere features softened for a moment. 'In two months,' he answered, setting his briefcase on the table. 'It'll be our first.'

'Congratulations,' Michelle said.

He nodded, then, waving for them to sit down again he took a pen and paper from his briefcase and asked Michelle to start from the beginning with what had happened at the *favela*. He sat silently throughout, occasionally jotting something down, but mostly his earnest face was turned in her direction, while his

423

piercing brown eyes concentrated almost exclusively on the Persian rug at her feet.

When at last she had finished he glanced at Antônio, then, looking straight at Michelle he said, 'I understand why you did this, but lying to Antônio the way you did was a very foolish and dangerous thing to do. It was also very stupid of Antônio to believe you when he knows how greatly Tom fears for your safety – and let me tell you, the risk you ran this afternoon was so high that it is nothing short of a miracle to find you sitting where you are now.' He raised a hand as she made to protest. 'You know very well how rife kidnapping is here, so to have put yourself in such a position as you did today, with no one outside the *favela* knowing where you were or who you were going to see, was an act of such bewildering irresponsibility that I am questioning my previously high opinion of your good sense.'

Though Michelle flushed with embarrassment, she was fighting back her annoyance that he should have focused on her lie when the issue at hand was so much more important. 'OK, I deserve that,' she said, keeping the edge from her voice, 'and I'm sorry I behaved so recklessly, but I'm here, I'm safe and surely what matters now is getting Luiz to a safe house where we can work on his statement and . . .'

'Michelle,' he interrupted, a note of surprise in his voice, 'I think you're going to have to face the fact now that the next time you see that boy will be when he turns up at the morgue.'

Michelle's dusty face turned pale.

'Marcelo Tinoco is one of the most notorious gang leaders in Rio,' he explained. 'He is a ruthless young man, a known drug dealer and a known killer. Yet still he walks the streets. So maybe you should ask yourself, where does he get his supply of drugs and how is he managing to avoid arrest?'

424

Michelle looked at him, a dawning realization turning her blood cold.

Camillo nodded. 'Yes, I think you are understanding me,' he said. 'Marcelo Tinoco is very probably in Pedro Pastillano's pay. Indeed, the fact that he happened to show up at the *favela* while you were there, collecting evidence from one of his "*kites*", is virtual confirmation that he is. Which can only lead us to wonder how long it will be now before we hear of Luiz's death.'

Michelle's eyes darted to Antônio as she struggled for a reason why Camillo might be wrong, but as desperately as she wanted to avoid it she could see only too clearly how inescapable his conclusion was. 'Oh God,' she groaned, covering her face with her hands. 'How could I have been so stupid? Why didn't I realize?' Her head came up and she fixed her eyes imploringly on Camillo. 'Is there nothing we can do?' she said. 'No way we can get the boy out?'

His expression was implacable. 'I'm afraid not,' he replied.

She looked around at the trailing plants and happy snaps of him and his wife, and knew that she had never felt so terrible.

'What you did,' Camillo said, his voice softening slightly, 'was certainly well-intentioned and even honourable, but it was very unwise. I don't know if it will help, but you aren't the first to have made this kind of mistake, some have even lost their lives in the attempt, so I suppose we must be grateful you were spared. Of course, we don't know how temporary that is, so for your own sake as well as those around you it would be best if you left Brazil right away.'

Michelle's eyes opened wide, as her heart gave a twist of dismay. 'Leave?' she said. 'But why?'

'Because you have put yourself in untenable danger just by letting it be known that you have spoken to the boy,' he answered. 'Were there any ambiguity in the matter, as there might have been if he'd been removed from the *favela* and installed in a safe house, the issue of your safety would be much the same as it has always been. In other words, no one would know for sure that we had the boy and the chances of them finding out for certain would be extremely slim. However, as it stands, Pastillano knows that you have obtained certain information and there is no knowing what he might do to try to ascertain exactly what that information is, or what you intend to do with it.'

Michelle's eyes went down as she realized the irrefutability of what he was saying. But no matter how ashamed and foolish she felt for trying to take matters into her own hands the way she had, it didn't even come close to how terrible she felt about the price Luiz would pay for her mistake.

'And I am sure,' Camillo said, evidently not yet finished, 'that you have no wish to put the rest of us in danger either, which is what you will do if you stay.'

Michelle's face was pinched with fatigue as his words drove mercilessly into her guilt and despair.

Reaching out to cover her hands Antônio said, 'Come on, I'll take you home.'

As Michelle followed him out to the lift she was still thinking about the danger she had left the boy in and how powerless she was to do anything about it. But there had to be something, some way of getting him out of the *favela* without endangering his life any further. She couldn't just stand by and do nothing, fly out of here and abandon him to a fate she had inflicted on him. No answers were presenting themselves right now, but there had to be a way of saving him and she had no intention of leaving Rio until she did.

Chapter 22

Ellen glanced up briefly as the waiter delivered a Bloody Mary to her table, then, telling him she would wait to order she went back to the book synopsis she was reading. She had a meeting the next day with one of New York's leading literary agents whose author had written this particular best-seller and she wanted to go in prepared. Elwin Little, one of her actors, was willing to pay a lot of money for an option on this book, but that was no reason for him to get stung – nor was there any particular reason for her to conduct the negotiations as this wasn't really her territory, but since she was in New York she had agreed to do it.

She could only be here for one night, as pressure of work in LA meant she had to fly back the following afternoon and now, considering how late Michael was, she was beginning to wonder if there was much point in her coming at all.

Struggling to contain her irritation, she stirred her drink, took a sip then attempted to carry on with the synopsis. It was a great story, one she wouldn't mind producing herself – in fact, she might just talk it over with Elwin when she got back to LA. She'd have liked to discuss it with Michael, but guessed by the time he got there he would be so full of what was happening with World Wide, and the changes taking place at McCann Walsh over in London, he'd forget to ask how she was, never mind what she was doing. Except that wasn't fair, for he'd never yet failed to show an interest in her life, or her family, or the day-to-day trivia and triumphs of her job; it was just their relationship and the future he had a problem with. Nothing was ever mentioned about that, except to work out when they could next be in New York together or how she was fixed for a couple of weeks' vacation in March.

Turning over a page she swept a hand through her hair and began to chew on a hangnail. They'd been going on like this for almost six months now, either meeting up here or in LA, snatching a few hectic days together, then parting for another three or four weeks until they could manage to squeeze a little more time from their schedules. When they were together – and not jet-lagged – everything was perfect, from their love-making, to their ability to make each other laugh, to the interest they took in each other's lives, to their frustration and sadness when it was time to leave. The trouble was the unsatisfactoriness of it all never seemed to bother him as much as it did her. In fact, she often wondered if he wouldn't be happy for things to continue the way they were for ever. And she could hardly be blamed for thinking that way when he rarely, if ever, mentioned anything about her going to London now, either for a visit or to live, and when he seemed so hell bent on finding another agent to represent World Wide in LA.

Despite her anger she could feel a horrible weight descending over her heart, for she was going to lose him and she knew it. She couldn't say how she knew, but at times the feeling was so strong it was as though they had already said goodbye. She didn't even want to think about what she would do when the time finally came, for he had become so much a part of her life now, was the source of so many of her hopes and dreams, that even as she sat there waiting for him she could feel herself becoming swamped by all the panic and pain she just knew was out there waiting.

She looked up as the door opened and her heart turned over as he came in from the freezing, windy night, his coat unbuttoned, his scarf wet from the rain and hanging loosely around his collar. He had obviously been running, knowing he was late and now, as his handsome face softened with typical, ironic humour at sight of her, despite her own smile, she almost wanted to cry. How, she wondered, as he weaved a path through the empty tables towards her, was she ever going to stop loving him?

'I'm sorry,' he said, leaning over and kissing her on the mouth. 'Have you been waiting long?'

'I got here early,' she answered. 'You're cold.'

'It's cold out,' he said, handing his coat and scarf to the waiter and sitting down opposite her. His blue eyes were curious as they scanned her face in a way she had come to love, then, reaching for her hand he said, 'I was thinking about you on the way over here. Shall I tell you what I was thinking?'

She nodded.

'I was thinking what a difference it makes to the day when I know I'm going to see you at the end of it.'

Her heart caught on his words and as she looked at him she was torn between hope and despair, for he had said so many things like it before and never yet had they been taken any further. 'I feel the same way,' she said softly.

He continued to gaze into her eyes and the pressure of his fingers on her palm began to kindle her desire. But she tried to fight it, knowing that if she didn't it would weaken her resolve and yet another opportunity to discuss their future would pass.

'You look lovely,' he told her. 'Is it for my benefit, or did you have a meeting before you came here?'

Ellen's eyes started to dance. 'I spoke to you from the

429

bath an hour ago,' she reminded him, 'so it's all for you.'

The waiter arrived and handing them a menu each, took Michael's order for a gin and tonic.

'So how was your day?' she asked, as they scanned the entrées.

'OK,' he answered. 'Pretty good, in fact. But the big news is over in London. Paul Patton, the script guy from the BBC I told you about?'

Ellen nodded.

'He's going to join us.'

Ellen managed to look pleased. 'That's great,' she said. 'As a partner?'

'Yep, so he and Zelda will be pretty much running the shop while I concentrate on World Wide. Did I tell you Sandy Paull got wind of him coming and tried to entice him away?'

'You're kidding,' Ellen cried. 'When did you hear that?'

'Patton told me himself a couple of hours ago on the phone. She was offering a damned good deal as well, so we can think ourselves lucky he turned her down.'

'But how did she find out you were after him?'

'Jodi told her,' he answered. 'I thought it would be as well for her to try to get him *before* he joined us, rather than after; that way, if he was going to go we wouldn't need to put ourselves to the bother of hiring him.'

'Or to the public ignominy of losing yet another agent to Sandy Paull,' Ellen added wryly.

'There's that too,' he grinned. 'Anyway, he joins us next month and Angela Siddall, the agent from Shine Connell whom Zelda wants, might be with us by June, meaning there's a chance we'll be up to strength again before summer. We need to be because we've got a small fortune staked in World Wide and it's going to be a while before it can take over its own debts. What are you having to eat?'

430

'The fish special, I think. What about you?'

'I'll have the duck.' He closed the menu and laid it to one side. 'So, what's been happening to you?' he said. 'You said on the phone you wanted to talk something over.'

She took a breath, but already a small hollow had opened up inside her, draining her courage away. She despised her own weakness, but she didn't want to see his expression change, or feel him withdraw from her or hear him tell her she had got it wrong about their level of commitment. So instead she said, 'I've got a meeting scheduled with Ted Forgon next week. I'm going to give him notice.'

Michael's eyes widened in surprise. 'Are you serious?' he said. 'When did you decide?'

She shrugged. 'A couple of days ago. I figured I'd been putting it off long enough and it's time I had enough faith in myself to go it alone. Of course, I've got no idea what he's going to do, you know, about the photographs and everything. I guess I'll just have to cross that bridge when I come to it.'

Michael's voice was dark as he said, 'If he threatens to publish any more,' he said, 'then remember, I know things about him that he very definitely won't want made public.'

Ellen's head went to one side. 'Like what?' she said.

'Another time,' he answered.

She considered pushing it, but knowing she probably wouldn't get anywhere, she waited until the waiter had taken their orders, then said, 'Did I tell you he's been warning me about you?'

Michael's hand stopped in mid-air and putting his drink back down he said, 'You've discussed me with Forgon?'

'Not exactly. But he knows we're seeing each other and he insists he doesn't want me to get hurt.'

Michael's face darkened. 'Well, that's rich, coming

431

from a man who's prepared to splash private photographs of you all over the press,' he declared. 'And besides, wasn't he the one who wanted you to seduce me into giving up London for LA?'

'Which I've obviously failed to do,' Ellen remarked, drily.

Michael looked at her, then, obviously deciding not to pursue that, said, 'What makes Forgon think you'll get hurt?'

Ellen shrugged. 'He didn't say.'

Michael's mood was changing. 'Then maybe you'd like to tell him to keep his damned nose out of our affairs,' he snapped.

'OK,' Ellen agreed, 'I'll tell him that the next time the subject comes up.'

Michael was silent for a while, obviously still angry at what Forgon had said, but not quite sure which way to handle it without getting himself into a conversation Ellen knew he was loath to have.

'You know what intrigues me,' she said, forcing herself past the frustration, 'is what's happened to his obsession with you? There was a time when he could hardly think about anything else except destroying you, yet now it's like he's mellowed out on it, like it's no big deal what you do or where you go and that's not the Ted Forgon I know.'

Michael shrugged. 'The man came face to face with his own mortality not so long ago,' he reminded her. 'That can have a sobering effect on a person.'

'True, but it was after his heart attack that he sent me over to London, so . . .'

'So?' Michael prompted.

'I was wondering if he hasn't found some other way of getting even with you, one that's going to come at you from the left side and . . . Well, I don't know what the effect might be, but you said yourself, McCann Walsh is in a pretty vulnerable state right now thanks to World Wide and if Forgon's managed to get ahold of that . . .'

Michael was looking thoughtful. 'Even if he has I don't see how he can do us much harm,' he said in the end, 'not unless he manages to sneak his way into World Wide by using some other agent as his Trojan Horse. But that's something we've already considered, which is why the LA agents we've been seeing go through such a thorough screening before the rest of us even get to hear about them.' He looked at her closely. 'Why, have you heard something?' he said.

'No, I was just curious that he doesn't show so much interest in you now, when you'd have expected him to be on my case daily, once he found out about us.' She sat back as the waiter brought their food and was about to speak again when her cellphone rang. 'Sorry, I meant to turn it off,' she said, digging around in her bag.

'Don't mind me,' Michael responded, reaching into his inside pocket, 'I've got a few faxes here I need to take a look at.'

'Hello, Ellen Shelby,' she said into the phone.

'Ellen, it's Nancy, your secretary,' the voice came down the line.

Ellen smiled. 'You might only have been with me for a week, Nancy,' she said, 'but I know who you are. What can I do for you?'

'OK, you ready for this?'

Ellen winced and it was ten minutes or more before she finished dealing with the day's crises as they were unfolding in LA. 'OK,' she said, as Nancy gave her the last problem, 'you'll have to take that one to Ted. Better still, talk to Rosa and let her take it to Ted. Anything else?'

'No, that's it. Oh, except there's a message here from someone called Sandy Paull. She wants you to call her back as soon as you can. She left a number where you can reach her.'

433

Ellen was looking at Michael. 'Is it an LA number?' she asked.

'Yeah. Shall I give it you?'

'No, it's OK, I'll get it tomorrow,' Ellen answered. 'Did she say what she was doing in LA?'

'No.'

'OK. I've got a meeting with the literary department at five tomorrow afternoon about the package we're putting together for one of Rosalie Marsh's books, could you have the file ready when I get in? I should be there around lunch-time.'

'OK,' Nancy responded cheerily and after saying goodbye she rang off.

'Sandy Paull's in LA and wants to speak to me,' Ellen told Michael as she tucked her phone back in her bag.

His eyes were wide with surprise as he looked up from the fax he was reading. Then he started to laugh. 'You don't suppose she's going to offer you a job, do you?' he said.

Ellen smiled. 'Who knows?' Then, unable to stop herself, 'If she is, then at least it'll be one person who wants me in London.'

Michael looked round as a rowdy group bustled in from the cold, then, turning back to Ellen he was about to speak when she said, 'It's OK, I know you don't want to deal with that, so let's change the subject, shall we? After all, that's what we usually do.'

Michael continued to look at her for a moment, then, sliding the faxes back into his pocket he said, 'You've got no interest in coming to London, and you know it.'

'So why don't I take on World Wide over in LA until you get to the investing stage,' she said, 'maybe then . . .'

'Listen,' he interrupted, 'before you go any further, we've had this conversation before and I told you then what kind of position it would put me in with Mark Bergin and Chris Ruskin if you come on board. They know who you are and neither of them have suggested their girlfriends or wives taking an active role in the company and I'm not prepared to either. So, OK, you're more qualified than they are, but the answer's still got to be no, Ellen, and not because of the reasons you're thinking. This isn't personal, it's entirely professional.'

Ellen looked down at her plate and fought back the temper that was egging her on to be as unreasonable as she could get. She was just so sick of the way he constantly avoided the subject of their future that she only wished she had it in her to tell him to go to hell and get up and walk out. Of course it was to do with Michelle, there was no question about that, but on the one and only occasion she had tried to make him talk about it he had told her quite bluntly that if she didn't let it go he would leave.

She watched as he tasted the wine and thought of the advice her father used to give her, 'deal with your fears before they deal with you.' And in just about every other walk of life she could do that, but where Michael was concerned she was so afraid of losing him she could hardly even think straight. Except, if it was going to happen then what was the point in delaying it? It had to be faced some time and she damned well wasn't going to go on like this, living in fear of when it would happen and panicking about how she was going to handle it when it did.

Putting her fork down, she moved her hand to her glass and circled the stem. Then, looking up at him she said, 'Michael, I want to know if there's ever going to be anything more for us than this.'

Briefly, he stopped chewing, then, reaching for his glass he took a mouthful of wine.

Her heart was beating so hard that her voice quavered as she said, 'Please don't change the subject. I want an answer. Should I continue to hope that one day

435

there might be something between us, or shall ...
Would it be better if we said goodbye now?'

He put his glass down and fixing her with sombre
blue eyes he said, 'Do you really want to do this when
you have to go back to LA tomorrow?'

She looked at him, feeling her resolve failing, but
fought to keep it.

'Why don't we wait until we're in Barbados,' he said.
'We'll have plenty of time to talk then. But the short
answer, if you're looking for one now, is no, I don't
think it would be better if we said goodbye.'

So much relief rushed into Ellen's heart that for a
moment it was hard to breathe.

'I think it would be better if I got the check now,
though,' he said.

Laughing, she said, 'But you haven't finished your
meal.'

'And you haven't started yours,' he pointed out. 'I
just think we need to be a little closer than this.'

It didn't take them long to reach their hotel and as
they rode up in the elevator he held her tight in his
arms, kissing her deeply. She kept wondering if she
had done the right thing in agreeing to postpone their
talk until they were in the Caribbean, but as she walked
into their room ahead of him and he pulled her back in
his arms she felt her insecurities starting to fade.

'No more talk of goodbyes, OK?' he said.

'OK,' she promised and raised her mouth to his as he
kissed her lingeringly and tenderly on the lips.

'Turn around,' he whispered.

Obediently she turned and found herself facing a
long cheval mirror where their reflections were bathed
in a soft, yellowy lamplight. He pulled her back against
him and gazing into her eyes in the mirror he said,
'You're so beautiful and I love you so damned much.'

'Harry, that's a great idea!' Sandy laughed, slapping

436

her hands on the desk in delight. 'You're a genius. Let's do it.'

'You're crazy,' Craig declared.

'Call him up! Call him up now,' Harry urged, his freckled face flushing with excitement.

Sandy looked at her watch. 'What time is it in LA?' she asked, losing a yawn in a laugh. 'I forgot to change my watch, so it's five in the morning. We can't call yet.'

'Then send a fax,' Harry said.

'Hang on, hang on,' Craig cautioned. 'Shouldn't we get in touch with the show's producers first, make sure they want an American in the lead?'

'They do,' Harry told him. 'I was on the phone to Eustace earlier, that's what gave me the idea.'

'But is their budget going to stretch to the likes of Marty Kernik? I mean, he's big time on Broadway, he'll be used to big bucks.'

Sandy looked from Craig's boyish face to Harry, then back again. What a formidable trio they were proving, and all because she'd had the common sense to offer them the kind of deal Michael never had. No threats, no blackmail, the way everyone thought, just more money, more perks and a generous share in the profits. 'So which way do we do it?' she said.

'I say we check out Kernik's availability first,' Craig answered, looking at Harry.

Harry nodded. 'Sounds cool,' he said.

Sandy's eyes were bright with excitement as she sucked in her bottom lip and looked at them. 'God, this is amazing, isn't it?' she said. 'I've only just done the deal with Prime Targets in Hollywood and already we're offering one of their clients the lead in a West End show.'

'Let's just hope they can come up with something equally as good for our chaps,' Harry commented.

'Precisely,' Sandy said, sobering for a moment. Then, clicking down her ball-point pen, she started to write.

'We need to check on the spelling of Kernik,' she said, 'it wouldn't look very professional if we got it wrong.'

'Where's Nesta,' Craig said. 'I thought she was coming in this afternoon.'

'She was supposed to,' Sandy answered, 'but she called an hour ago to say she couldn't make it. She had a heavy date last night that didn't finish until four this morning.' Sighing, she cupped her face in her hands. 'Do you think we should get another assistant? I mean, Nesta's good, but she's not very reliable and I honestly don't think we're going to persuade her to give up the night job.'

'What about another part-timer?' Harry suggested.

Sandy pursed her lips as she thought. 'We could,' she said, 'or,' she went on, looking at Craig, 'you could ask Bertie if he wants to join us.'

Craig spluttered with laughter. 'Are you serious?' he said. 'I thought you couldn't stand the guy.'

'I can't,' Sandy smiled, 'but he's good, and you're busier than the rest of us at the moment so it's you who gets to choose.'

Craig looked at Harry, who shrugged.

'Think it over,' Sandy said, getting to her feet, 'and let me know what you want to do. Now, I have to go home or I'm going to fall asleep where I'm standing. You were joking, weren't you, when you said it takes a week to get over jet lag?'

'Takes me ten days or more,' Harry informed her. 'But you'll survive. Just stay up as late as you can tonight.'

'Thanks,' Sandy responded, stifling another yawn and, leaving them in the grand octagonal room, with its wonderfully high ceiling, newly whitewashed walls and immense bay window, she went back to her own office to collect up her belongings.

In the end she hadn't gone with the premises Maurice had found in Chelsea, as he'd come up with these in Mayfair and though they consisted of almost twice the square footage, which was far too big at this stage of the agency, Sandy had been unable to resist one of the smartest addresses in London.

They were on the second floor of a magnificent Edwardian house which was just off Berkeley Square, not far from the Ritz, and boasted two blue plaques on its double-fronted facade, twin balustraded balconies that overlooked the elegant street below and a huge black front door with a shiny brass number ten, much like the prime minister's. When there was sun it streamed into the main office, making it a cheerful and welcoming place to work, which was why she had given it to Harry and Craig, taking the smaller, slightly darker ante-room for herself. She rarely worked there, though, for she preferred being outside with the others, not only because she didn't like being shut away on her own, but because she still had so much to learn and actually didn't have the first idea how to run an agency single-handed. Just thank God for Maurice, whose accountants were keeping an eye on the books, and for Craig and Harry, who were every bit as much in charge as she was.

As she went to retrieve the luggage she had brought straight from the airport her heart was swelling with pride and gratitude, and so many other emotions she could barely distinguish them all. She knew it was tiredness that was making her feel this way, but right now she'd love to throw her arms around Harry and Craig for all the support and enthusiasm they had brought to their jobs.

Sitting down at her desk, she started another quick check of her mail to make sure she hadn't missed anything vital. She ended up no further than a few letters down before she was staring absently at the two sash windows and doing one of her regular marvels at how far she had come in such a short space of time. In fact, it was incredible to think that she, Sandy Paull of fourteen Fairweather Street and West Green Comprehensive for Girls, could actually be sitting here in her own Mayfair offices, employer of two of the country's top agents, representative of some of the country's leading actors, actresses and writers, and the holder of a brand-new exchange representation deal with a big Hollywood agent. It would be so easy for it all to go to her head, but in truth she was as daunted as she was exhilarated by it and knew that were it not for Nesta and Maurice, she would never have had the courage to come this far. And were it not for Harry and Craig there would be virtually no chance at all of it working.

Looking down at where she had stopped in the mail, she picked up the fax she had already read once and started to read it again. *Cosmopolitan* had approached her a while ago, asking to do a feature on her and her meteoric rise to success, and this fax contained an outline of the way they saw the interview going. What a scream it was going to be, a photographer turning up on her mother's front doorstep asking to take shots of their shabby little terraced house, while her brothers and sisters strutted about in their Sunday best and tried to talk posh. It was almost worth going back just to see what prats they made of themselves – and, of course, to show them how it was really done. She wondered what they'd make of her being an escort girl, because that was going to come out in the article too, provided she was willing. Actually, she didn't much care what her family thought of that and rather than have anyone throw it in her face later, she reckoned it would probably be a good idea to get it out in the open now. After all, she'd never really done anything to be ashamed of and besides, it would probably add something to her cachet. She hadn't decided yet what she was going to say about Michael, she'd make up her mind about that later, and to answer the question what

440

was her proudest achievement so far, well, she supposed it had to be the deal she had just pulled off in LA, because it was one she had achieved all on her own.

Indeed, she almost had to pinch herself now to make herself believe that she had actually been on an aeroplane, never mind flown half way round the world to negotiate with some of the industry's toughest and most devious players. But it hadn't been so difficult when she'd done most of it by phone, and when Craig and Harry had given her stacks of advice and plenty of names to call up while she was there. In fact she had quite enjoyed the town and wouldn't have minded staying a bit longer, but she'd managed to get done everything she'd gone there to do – including lunch with Ellen Shelby – and judging by the amount of work that was piling up it really had been time to come back.

Smiling to herself, she wondered what Ellen had made of their lunch and almost laughed out loud as she pictured the confusion she must have sewn by discussing nothing more than the latest movie releases, the number of commercials on American TV and how brave Ellen was to drive on the freeways. Not a single mention of Michael had passed either of their lips, nor had they made even the slightest reference to the way Sandy had got her own business going. In fact, if Sandy had played this as well as she hoped, Ellen wouldn't have the faintest idea what the lunch was really about, nor was she going to find out until Sandy was ready for her to do so.

The feeling of malicious pleasure was soon swallowed into a vacuum of unease and tiredness. She thought of Ellen and how comfortable she had seemed in the shaded courtyard of the Café Roma with Schwarzenegger and his entourage in one corner and Pricilla Presley in another. There had been lots of other stars around whom Sandy had never heard of, whereas

Ellen had known them all and most had sought her out rather than the other way round, while Sandy had sat there trying, and no doubt failing, to look cool and unfazed. In fact, just to think of Ellen now, and the classy way she handled herself could make Sandy feel extremely violent towards the woman, especially because of the feelings of inferiority it invoked in her. But a good night's sleep would probably get her past that, there was just one last call she needed to make before she left which would determine whether or not she went straight home.

'Jodi?' she said into the receiver a few moments later.

'Sandy? Hi, how are you? I heard you were in LA.'

'I got back at lunch-time,' Sandy answered. 'How are you?'

'Fine, thanks.'

Sandy paused, as her heart began to flutter with nerves. 'Is Michael there?' she finally forced herself to say.

Jodi was silent, no doubt stunned by the question. 'Did you say Michael?' she asked in the end.

'Yes. I'd like to speak to him if I can,' Sandy replied.

Jodi's tone was truculent as she said, 'Hang on, I'll see if he's free.'

As Sandy waited her hands began to sweat and the terrible butterflies in her stomach were made a hundred times worse by the pounding of her heart. Unless he refused to let Jodi put her through, this would be the first time they had spoken since that dreadful scene in his office when she had disgraced herself beyond measure and he had hurt her so badly. But still not a day, not a single hour went by when she didn't think of him and want him more than anything else in the world. She understood that it wasn't going to happen yet, he still had a lot to forgive her for and if things carried on the way they were going there would be a whole lot more to add to that. But there was no reason

442

for her to go through with her plans; in fact, if this call went the way she hoped it would she would bring them to a stop right now, regardless of what anyone else thought, because this wasn't about success really, nor revenge, nor being famous in her little corner of the world. It was about loving a man whom she would happily give everything to when he finally realized how much he loved her.

Still she waited, seeing his face in her mind's eye frowning in the way she knew so well, as he asked Jodi what the call was about. She could see his office, hear his voice, even smell the mixed aroma of the wood, leather chairs and his cologne. For a moment she wished with all her heart that she could be back there now, working for him, seeing him all the time and living constantly with the hope that one of these days he would make love to her again. At the time, living like that had been hell, but it was better than the way she suffered now, never seeing him at all and always knowing that the path she had chosen since he had thrown her out was the very longest route back to him – unless she could manage to alter the course now.

'Hello? Sandy? Are you still there?'

Sandy's stomach fell away. It was Jodi, back again. 'Yes, I'm still here,' she answered.

'I'm just putting you through.'

Sandy barely had time to catch her breath before his voice came down the line: 'Sandy. What can I do for you?'

He sounded relaxed, not angry at all and the sudden urge she felt to see him almost overwhelmed her. 'Hello,' she said. 'How are you?'

'Pretty good. How about you?'

'Yes, I'm fine. I just wanted . . .' She hesitated as her courage started to fail, then forced herself to go on. '. . . to wish you a Happy Birthday.'

She could almost hear his surprise, even though there was nothing but silence at the other end.

'I've got a present for you,' she said. 'Can I see you, to give it to you?' As she spoke she was reaching into her holdall to take out a small, turquoise Tiffany bag.

'I don't think that would be a very good idea,' he said.

'I think you'll like it,' she told him. 'I mean, it's nothing much really, I just wanted you to know I hadn't forgotten.'

He was quiet again and pain seared through her heart as she wondered if he was thinking about Ellen.

'It won't take long,' she said. 'We can meet wherever you like.'

'Sandy,' he said, 'I really don't know how to say this without hurting your feelings, but . . .'

'Please, Michael, don't say no,' she implored.

'I have to, Sandy,' he responded. 'I'm not going to change my mind about us and I can't accept your present either.'

The Tiffany bag started to swim before her as her eyes filled with tears. 'That's not very gracious,' she said, attempting to laugh.

'I'm sorry,' he answered, 'but that's the way it is. Now, if you'll forgive me, I've got another call coming in,' and the line went dead.

It was a while before Sandy put the receiver back on the hook, the disappointment, the shame and the hurt were just too great for her to move. A single tear trickled down her cheek as she took a second Tiffany bag from her holdall and set it next to the other one. A silver paperweight each for Harry and Craig. And as soon as she could pull it off, a shock for Michael that was going to prove far greater than he, his agency, or Ellen Shelby could feasibly survive.

Chapter 23

Chambers's flinty grey eyes were shining with anger as he glared at Michelle across the wide, sunlit expanse of her sitting-room. 'I can't believe you would be so stupid,' he raged. 'Three weeks I'm gone, and I come back to find this! I've told you a thousand times you don't do anything without clearing it with me first. We're not trying to earn ourselves hero points here, it's not some kind of glory trip, we're trying to save lives and that includes our own.'

'I know that,' Michelle cried, 'and I'm sorry. But...'

He wasn't listening. 'Camillo told you to get out of here, he told you what danger you'd be putting everyone in if you stayed, so what do you do? You stay! For Christ's sake, you've got three kids out there, so what the hell are you thinking about?'

'They're there, aren't they?' she shouted back. 'Nothing's happened to them...'

'So, what are you doing, hanging around until something does?' he responded scathingly. '*Jesus Christ*! What's the matter with you? You've probably blown the whole damned thing now, do you realize that? I mean, I might just as well pack up and fly out with you, for all the good it's going to do me staying here after this.'

'Pastillano knew who you were and what you were

445

doing before I went into the *favela*,' Michelle reminded him hotly.

'He didn't know we were about to get a whole stack of evidence to help promote his demise,' he shouted back. 'But he sure as hell knows now, 'cos you went into the *favela* and advertised it for us. *Jesus*, how could you have done that? We were so god-damned close! We'd have got that boy out of there. He'd be in a safe house now and once the others saw the witness protection working they might have come forward too. But who the hell's going to speak to us now, when the kid's probably already dead and for all we know the old man and his wife too. And what's more, what's *more*, is no one's seen Antônio since he brought you back here that day, so where the hell is he, would you like to tell me?'

'OK, I fouled up!' she cried. 'You can't make me feel any worse than I already do.'

'You'll never feel as bad as the people you talked to are going to feel . . .'

'OK! OK!' Cavan butted in. 'Let's try and calm this down, shall we? The kids are out in the pool and they can probably hear what's going on.'

Chambers tore his eyes from Michelle, glared at Cavan then turned angrily away as Michelle looked out into the courtyard where Robbie and Larisa were paddling about the pool on a lilo while Tomasz and Cara attempted to light the barbecue. Noticing that the front door in the perimeter wall was ajar, she slid open the French windows and called out to Cara to close it. Then, after glancing up at the dense green foliage that overhung the courtyard from the street outside, she turned back into the room.

Chambers was now standing at one of the wide picture windows, almost lost in the early evening sunlight as he stared down the hillside to where the ocean was hurling itself against the rocks below.

Michelle looked at Cavan, who was perched on the arm of a sofa, and seeing how angry he was too, despite his attempt to cool things down, she turned to the bar and snatched a bottle from the shelf. 'Would anyone else like a drink?' she snapped.

Chambers looked round, then, sweeping his keys from the table he said, 'I'm out of here.'

As he passed her, Michelle longed to grab him and beg him not to go like this, but her own anger and pride wouldn't allow it. 'Cavan, why don't you go too?' she said tersely. 'It's been a long day and I'm sick of the way you're all twisting the knife in my guilt when you know damned well if I could turn back the clock I would. But I can't, so I'll book myself on a flight out of here tomorrow and you won't have to think about me again. Will that suit you? Will that make you happier, both of you?'

Chambers didn't answer as he stepped out of the French windows and headed across the courtyard.

'Don't drink too much of that,' Cavan warned as he started to follow. 'It won't help.'

'So you're going!' she demanded. 'You're walking out of here . . .'

'You just told me to,' he snapped.

'Then go! What the hell do I care?'

'I'll stay if you want me to,' he said.

She looked at his exquisite face, the incredible blue eyes, the beautiful mouth and inky dark hair. She wanted desperately to reach out to him and feel him with her in a way that needed no words. She longed to lose herself in his love and escape, if only for a while, the dreadful feelings she had inside. But she couldn't make herself say that and her eyes were suddenly bright with tears as her head filled with confusion and she cried, 'Why would I want you to stay? I've managed without you all this time. So why would I need you now?'

His face instantly hardened. 'You're talking to Michael,' he said and turning away, he stalked out of the room.

As the front door closed behind him she picked up her drink and downed it in one. Then, refusing to give in to the self-pity that was swamping her, or even to think about what he'd just said, she walked out into the shady courtyard and started to help Cara with the barbecue.

It was a difficult evening and the children, sensing the tension, were for once easily persuaded to go down to their room. Except Robbie hung back for a while and in his own four-year-old way tried to offer the comfort he seemed to sense she needed. She held him close, kissed his hair and smiled into his worried blue eyes, before taking him downstairs to the others and staying with them while Cara read a story. Later, she and Cara returned to the sitting-room and sat talking for a while, but Michelle was so dispirited and distracted that in the end they locked the doors, turned out the lights and descended the circular staircase to their own separate bedrooms.

It was in the very early hours of the morning, as Michelle lay awake on her tousled bed, that she first heard a strange noise somewhere outside. Though her heart jolted, she lay where she was, all her senses alert as she listened for it again. It was impossible to say what it had been, but there was something about it that had somehow jarred with the other night sounds.

Minutes ticked by and though she heard nothing unusual again her heart continued to thump as the ocean roared over the rocks fifty or so feet below her window. She turned her head to look at the moonlit blind and watched the shadow of an overhanging vine as it bobbed in the breeze. Suddenly a rogue dribble escaped the tap in the bathroom and her heart leapt to her throat. Her eyes moved to the open bathroom door and she could just make out the frosted glass of the shower and glinting brass frame of the towel rail. She wasn't sure why, but her heart was thudding so hard now it hurt. Then suddenly her head spun round as the quiet clatter of loose stones right outside her window lifted her from the bed and sent her racing down the hall to the nursery.

The door was open and in the generous moonlight she could see all three beds, the bunk where the boys slept and the divan where Larisa's soft toys were spilling on to the floor. Going to pick them up, she set them gently back on the pillow, then looked down at the child's peacefully sleeping face. Her eyes darted across the room as she heard another noise, and realizing it was Tomasz stirring in his sleep, she went to check on him too. Like his sister he was dead to the world, and after smoothing his hair she stooped to the bottom bunk where Robbie was sprawled out on his back, arms and legs akimbo, his little white undershorts appearing too big for his tiny tanned body. She stared at him for a while, still listening to the silence and trying to contain the emotion that was sweeping through her chest. Then, knowing nothing would wake him, she leaned over to kiss his cheek.

After checking on Cara and finding her sleeping too, she made her way back to her bedroom and sat down on the edge of the bed. Almost instantly she was back on her feet, spinning round to look at the window. Her heart was pounding, her entire body shaking. She could hear voices outside. A shadow moved across the blind and she opened her mouth to scream. No sound came. Her throat was dry. Her limbs were frozen.

'Michelle.' The voice was a shouted whisper.

A bleat of terror escaped her lips as she pressed a hand to her mouth and stared at the window.

'Michelle! It's Antônio.'

'Oh my God,' she sobbed, relief rushing so fast to her

veins she felt herself go dizzy. But why was he at the window, not the door? It didn't make any sense.

'Michelle,' he said again.

Her legs were almost too weak to move, as reaching for a robe she slipped her arms into the sleeves.

'Please, Michelle,' Antônio urged. 'I must speak with you. If you can hear me, don't be afraid. Just open the window.'

Michelle took a step forward, but she was shaking so hard she could move no further. Sweat was running down her sides, the sheer fabric of her nightgown clung to her skin.

'Michelle! Wake up!' Antônio called. A note of desperation had crept into his voice and as though spurred by it she crossed quickly to the window. But still she didn't raise the blind.

'Antônio?' she whispered. 'Why are you there? Why don't you use the door?'

'Because we'd have to go past the security guard and I have someone with me who mustn't be seen,' he answered.

'Who is it?' she asked, standing to one side of the window and trying to peer out through the edge of the blind.

'It's Chico, one of the boys Luiz told us about. Luiz is here too. He's down below in a boat, he couldn't make the climb.'

'Luiz is here? He's alive?' she said, the joy of it rushing like a drug through her veins, and without giving it a second thought she let up the blind and pushed open the window. 'How did you get him?' she said. 'Where did ...' She stopped suddenly and the blood drained from her face as she looked past Antônio to the man who was with him. 'Oh my God,' she breathed, unable to tear her eyes from Marcelo. 'Oh, Antônio, I can't believe you're doing this.'

'No, listen, I know what you're thinking,' he cried,

'but you're wrong. He wants to talk. He knows everything there is to know about Pastillano and he's prepared to tell us.'

Michelle continued to stare at the gang leader, whose mean, arrogant face was swathed in silvery moonlight, and whose presence was guarded by two gun-toting sidekicks. 'Why?' she said. 'Why would he tell us?'

'Because he's not in Pastillano's pay,' Antônio answered. 'And because Márcio was one of his.'

Michelle's eyes hadn't moved from Marcelo. 'Where's Luiz?' she asked.

'Down below,' Marcelo answered. 'If you like, I'll take you to him.'

Long minutes ticked by as Michelle's eyes bored right into him, while doubt and indecision raged through her mind. But if they were going to harm her they could have done so easily by now, and if Antônio trusted them maybe she could too.

'Just hear what he has to say,' Antônio urged, 'it can do no harm.'

In the end, as though acting with no will of her own, she stood back and allowed them to climb over the window-sill into the room. As they followed her quietly past the children's room and up the stairs to the sitting-room she was praying silently to God that she hadn't just made the very biggest mistake of her life.

To test it she turned on the lights, waited for them to assemble in the room, then, looking straight at Antônio she said, 'I'll have to call Tom,' and braced herself for the response.

'Michael! No! Michael!' Ellen squealed. 'Please, no. Stop. I swear I'll never do it again.'

'Are you sure about that?' He laughed, rolling her over and squirting more cream in her face.

'Yes!' she spluttered, catching a mouthful as she

451

gasped with laughter. 'Michael, I swear, I'll do anything, just don't ... *No!*' she screamed as he began tickling her again.

The struggle went on as they shrieked and laughed and rolled around the floor, trying to pin each other down and spray more cream in the other's face. It ended with Ellen sitting astride him, her hair matted and wet, her T-shirt soaked right through and her long, tanned legs gripping his waist.

'No more,' she gasped, holding his arms at a distance. 'I can't ... *No!*' she cried, as he pressed the nozzle again.

His face was alive with laughter as he looked up at her, his hair and two-day beard flecked with foam, his bare chest rising and falling as he panted for breath. 'Did I hear you say you'd do anything?' he challenged.

A new light shot to her eyes. 'Anything,' she vowed.

'Absolutely anything?'

Her smile was widening. 'Absolutely anything.'

'Are you sure?'

She hesitated. 'Almost,' she answered.

He shook his head. 'Uh, uh,' he said. 'I want unconditional surrender with amends on my terms or ...'

'Just a minute,' she interrupted, 'I'm the one on top here. OK, OK, OK,' she laughed, as he easily drew in his arms and started to get up. 'Anything, I swear it, just don't tickle me again.'

'Then get off me, woman,' he demanded.

'Do you promise you won't tickle me?' she said, keeping hold of his hands.

'Promise.'

She was laughing again and shaking her head. 'No, I don't trust you,' she said, then yelped, as quick as a flash he tipped her over and covered her body with his own.

'Ow! ow! ow!' she cried. 'Your buckle's digging into me.'

His eyebrows went up. 'Is that your way of getting me to undress?' he enquired drolly.

'Anything, just ... ah, that's better,' she said, as he adjusted his weight. His face was very close to hers now and she was simmering with laughter as she gazed up at him, waiting to see what he would do next.

'You know, there's still some cream left in that can,' he said, nodding to where it had rolled against the foot of a chair.

'Is there?' she said, looking from his eyes to his mouth and back again.

He nodded. 'And do you know where I'm going to spray that cream?' he asked.

She looked at him, ready to burst into laughter.

He nodded again. 'You're right,' he said. 'That's exactly where I'm going to spray it and guess what you're going to do?'

'No!' she cried.

'But you gave me your word, remember. Absolutely anything.'

She was laughing too hard now to answer, for she knew precisely what he was saying and knew too that she was perfectly happy to go along with it. So lying right where she was, she watched him as he rolled over and began to unfasten his shorts.

'Bring me the cream,' he commanded.

Obediently she reached out for the can and passed it over. Though she was still laughing, her pulses were quickening.

'OK, over to you,' he said, a few minutes later.

They were in the sitting-room of his Barbados home, a small, single-storey villa with quaint brick arches that separated each room from the other and huge picture windows that looked down over the hillside to the glorious sparkling-white beach below. A cluster of magnificent date palms soared over the red-tiled roof, while the soothing murmur of the sea drifted on the breeze into the cool, shadowy interior of the house. On the patio outside were the remains of their lunch, sheltered by a white canvas parasol and two thickly padded loungers, strewn with towels and stained with oil. There were only two other houses in the bay, neither of which were visible from the niche in which Michael's sat, so their privacy was total.

As their passions rose, fusing together like the waves in the bay below, Michael raised Ellen's T-shirt and lowered the skimpy bikini bottom. They had been here for almost two weeks by now, so their bodies were beautifully tanned and so blissfully attuned to each other that their love-making just got better all the time. The playful fight that had led to the urgency that was overwhelming them now had started with Ellen creeping up on him while he was asleep and decorating him with a beard of cream. That had been in retaliation for the ice-cold water he'd poured over her back while she was sunbathing earlier, which in turn had been a payback for something else. In fact the entire vacation had been such a madhouse of fun and laughter, relaxation and exploration that neither of them was ready to give it up in five days and return home.

They had yet to discuss the future, but she knew they would before they left and because of how close they had become these past couple of weeks she had little problem persuading herself that there was no reason to be afraid now. Though he hadn't told her again since that night in New York that he loved her, she knew from other things he said, from the way he looked at her, touched her and shared so much of himself with her, that he did. It was true she wouldn't mind hearing it again and maybe even have him look into her eyes when he said it, rather than at her reflection in a mirror. But he would when he was ready and though she had to confess to occasional tremors of unease if ever she thought of Michelle and how he never willingly mentioned her name, she had only to think of the way he held her and made love to her to realize how deeply he felt.

Much later that evening she was sitting alone at the edge of the sea, letting the gentle, translucent waves lap around her ankles as she sipped the last of a Martini and gazed contentedly out at the golden blaze of the sun. Michael was back at the house, throwing together some kind of concoction a beautiful, fat, ebony-faced woman had given him the recipe for at the market that morning. It amused Ellen no end the way he flirted with the locals and even took samples of his cuisine back to the market for them to taste. It had got so even the men were pleased to see him and the women's unabashed bawdiness, which was no less subtle than their huge, ripe melons and long, sturdy bananas, was so infectious that Ellen couldn't resist joining in and teasing him too. Every day they came away with cartons of luscious fresh fruit that they would never be able to eat themselves, so they invariably ended up stopping further along the road to give most of it away to a bunch of cute kids who had got wise to them by now.

Sighing softly she smiled to herself and took the olive from her drink and ate it. It was such a wonderful, balmy night and the tangy scent of the sea mixed exotically with the gentle aroma of the many shrubs and wild flowers on the hill. The high-pitched chafing of insect life chorused around the bay, while the hypnotic rhythm of an old jazz tune drifted lazily from the radio up at the house. She guessed that sooner or later one of them would bring up the subject of going home and what would happen after, but she had to admit that for once she was in no real hurry to get to it. She had already resigned from ATI and would be leaving at the end of next month, and from the way Michael was taking such delight in making jibes about her unemployed state she strongly suspected he was going to ask her to go to London.

She felt a small lurch in her heart at the thought of what she was going to say if he did, for though she'd more or less decided she would go, she didn't want to think about how her parents were going to take it. It was bad enough her being in LA, but London was probably going to kill any chance of her father ever speaking to her again. And as if that wasn't bad enough, what was she going to do about her career? She was in no doubt about how much she loved Michael, but he couldn't be her entire life and the entertainment industry in London was like a puppet show when compared with the panoramic stage of Hollywood.

'Hi,' Michael said, coming to sit down behind her and kissing the back of her neck as he wrapped his legs around her.

'It's so beautiful here,' she sighed, leaning her head on his shoulder and watching the sun's final, fiery rays fan across the horizon. 'I wish we could stay for ever.'

'Mmm,' he murmured, putting his drink to her lips as he noticed her glass was empty.

'Do you think we'd get bored?' she asked.

'Maybe, after a couple of years,' he answered.

She smiled and turned to kiss him. 'How's dinner coming along?'

'OK. Ready in about half an hour.'

They sat quietly then, listening to the eclectic sounds of the night as darkness spread through the cove and their thoughts moved peacefully through the contentment of being in each other's arms.

'I love you,' he whispered, staring out at the sea.

Ellen's heart swelled and putting her head back to look at him she said, 'Say that again.'

456

Though he smiled, his eyes remained serious as he gazed into hers and said, 'I love you.'

'I love you too,' she said softly.

He continued to look at her, his eyes searching her face, until finally he said, 'So what are we going to do?'

She shook her head. 'I don't know. I was hoping maybe you had the answer.'

'What do you *want* to do?' he asked.

'You mean, like if the choice were all mine?'

He nodded.

'Then I guess I would want you to come to the States.'

His eyes moved away and wandered to the dark, invisible distance. 'I thought that's what you might say,' he responded.

'But it's not going to happen, is it?' she said, feeling her insides starting to tighten.

It was a long time before he looked at her again, but before he could speak she said, 'I'll come to London. I've thought about it and ...'

He looked down at her and slowly shook his head. 'No,' he said. 'It won't work. And I don't want you to come.'

The shock of his words hit her so hard she couldn't speak. Then she started to break away.

'Ellen, listen,' he said, trying to pull her back.

'No, I don't want to listen,' she replied, getting to her feet. And staring down at him, her eyes bright with anger and pain, she said, 'I don't know what's happening with you. First you tell me you love me, then you say you don't want me ...'

'Just listen,' he said, getting up, 'I said I don't want you to come to London, that's not the same as saying I don't want you. I love you, for Christ's sake, and I don't want us to carry on the way we are either, meeting up for the odd days here and there, a vacation or two a year, but we've got to be realistic, Ellen, and try to find a solution that's going to work for us both. *Shit*,' he seethed as the phone started to ring inside the house. 'Can we ignore it?' he asked.

She shook her head. 'I asked my mom to call tonight, she'll worry if I don't answer.'

'OK,' he said and stooped to pick up the glasses as she started up the path to the house.

'Hello?' she said into the receiver when she got there.

'Hello. Can I speak to Michael please? It's his brother, Cavan?'

'Yes, yes, of course,' Ellen replied, a strange buzzing starting up in her head at the urgency in Cavan's tone. 'I'll get him,' and going to the door she called out to where Michael was, half-way up the path. 'It's your brother,' she told him, as he came on to the patio. 'He sounds upset.'

With a haste that surprised her he thrust the glasses into her hand and grabbed up the phone. 'Cavan?' he said. 'Is everything all right?'

'No. It's Michelle,' Cavan answered, panic shaking his voice.

'What about her?' Michael demanded.

'She's . . . she's been arrested.'

'What do you mean, arrested?' Michael cried. 'What for, for God's sake.'

'Drugs. But it's a set up. She's been working with some kids here, getting evidence against the police, I mean like really heavy stuff, and now they've arrested her. We've got to get her out, Michael. You don't know these guys . . . They can do anything. Tom Chambers, you know, the American I told you about, well he reckons the only chance we've got is to buy her out. But it's going to take a lot of money.'

Michael's face was so pale that Ellen couldn't bear to look at him. As she turned away, Michael turned too. 'What about . . .' he said quietly into the receiver.

'It's OK,' Cavan assured him, seeming to know what

he was saying. 'Everything else is taken care of. It's just Michelle we've got to worry about. Can you wire some money. We can take care of it, if you can just send . . .'

'How much?' Michael asked.

'I don't know. Twenty grand. Thirty.'

'Are you out of your mind!' Michael shouted.

'These guys are rich, Michael. We can't buy them off with a couple of hundred . . .'

'Just a minute, you're talking about bribing the police? Am I getting this right?'

'Yes,' Cavan answered in exasperation. 'But it's too complicated to go into now. Just send as much as you can, will you? Send it to Unibanco on Avenue Copacabana, Account 1515 in my name. You've got to help us with this Michael, or God knows what's going to happen to her.'

'I'll send the money,' he said, 'but I want you to ring me the minute anything changes. Do you hear me? I want you on this phone telling me everything's all right . . .'

'I'll call,' Cavan promised. 'First thing tomorrow. Can you remember the bank?'

'Yes, I remember it,' Michael answered and repeated it. 'Now tell me where . . .'

'I'll call you tomorrow,' Cavan cut in. 'I'll tell you everything then, but I've got to go now,' and he rang off.

'Damn,' Michael seethed, slamming the receiver back on the hook. 'Damn, damn and fucking damn.'

Ellen was standing in the doorway, her expression filled with unease as she felt the distance creep between them. 'What's happened?' she asked quietly.

He was standing with his back to her, staring at the wall. His anger and tension were so great she could almost feel it. At last he turned round to look at her. 'All I know is Michelle's been arrested for drugs,' he said, seeming to resent having to say even that much.

Ellen looked away, then jumped as he banged a fist into the wall.

'God-damnit, I should have known something like this would happen,' he raged. 'I should have damned well seen it coming.'

As Ellen looked at him she could feel herself breaking apart inside. 'I didn't realize you still cared so much,' she said.

His head came up and for a moment he glared at her, then, turning away, he walked out into the garden.

He didn't come to bed that night, nor did he eat any breakfast when Ellen prepared it in the morning. He simply paced up and down, waiting for the phone to ring. She'd heard him talking to his bank in the early hours of the morning organizing a twenty-thousand-pound transfer, but other than that he hadn't spoken at all. And now, as the minutes ticked by and his temper threatened to explode, Ellen knew that it would be pointless to approach him with anything more than coffee.

At last he reached the point where he could wait no longer and snatching up the phone he dialled Cavan's apartment. There was no reply.

It continued like that for the rest of the morning, pacing and phoning, pacing and phoning, until finally at around midday he got an answer.

'Cavan!' he shouted, his voice heavy with relief. 'Where the hell have you been?'

Ellen got up from the patio and came to the door.

'It's Tom Chambers,' a male voice at the other end told him.

'Where's Cavan?' Michael barked. 'I need to talk to him.'

'Is that his brother?'

'Yes.'

'I haven't seen Cavan since last night, just after he called you.'

460

'What do you mean?' Michael cried. 'What the hell's going on down there?'

'I wish I knew,' Chambers responded grimly.

'Oh Jesus Christ,' Michael muttered. 'I'm coming down there. I'll be there as soon as I can.'

'You can get a message to me through the concierge at the Rio Palace Hotel,' Chambers told him and the line went dead.

Michael hit the connectors, then quickly dialled again. 'Sam,' he said to the agent who took care of the house and garden, 'I need to get to Rio the fastest route possible. That's right, Rio de Janeiro. No, I'm not kidding. I'm on my way to the airport now, fix up what you can and I'll call you when I get there.'

'Michael,' Ellen said, as he started towards the bedroom.

He turned back.

'What about us?' she asked, knowing how inappropriate it was, but having to say it anyway.

'I'm sorry,' he said. 'Now's just not the time.'

Her head went down, then suddenly, surprising herself as much as him, she felt an anger rising in her that she just couldn't control. 'Well, I think that maybe it is,' she said tightly. 'In fact, it's the perfect time, because it's not about London and LA, is it? It's about me and Michelle. Or, more accurately, Michelle, because it's always been about her . . .'

'You don't understand,' he said.

'Then explain it.'

'There isn't time,' he answered, and walked off into the bedroom.

Ellen went after him. 'You still love her, don't you?' she challenged. 'That's why you're going . . .'

'For God's sake!' he cried, spinning round. 'She's got my son, OK? We've got a son and he's down there with her, and now Cavan's missing too. So what do you want, that I sit by and do nothing? Would it make you

461

feel better if I just ignored ... Oh Christ!' Seeing the stricken look on her face had stopped him and turning away, he dragged a suitcase from the closet and threw it on to the bed.

'Why didn't you tell me?' Ellen whispered, still so shaken she could barely find her voice.

'I don't want to discuss it,' he barked.

'But ...'

'Just leave it, OK.'

'Then tell me about Cavan,' she shouted. 'Has he been arrested too? I mean, what the hell is happening down there?'

'How the fuck am I supposed to know until I get there?' he shot back.

'OK, you don't have to take it out on me,' she shouted. 'I'm just the person you're leaving behind. The person you say you love, but couldn't even tell you had a child. I had to have it yelled at me as though it was my god-damned fault he's down there. And now you can't wait to get away from me because Michelle, the woman you really love, the mother of your son, needs you. Well, fuck you!' and she stormed out of the room.

'I'm taking the car to the airport,' he yelled after her, 'so if you want to come too, you'd better start getting yourself together.'

'I'll get a cab,' she yelled back. Then, returning to the bedroom, she said, 'And when all this is over, when you've done whatever the hell you're going down there to do, don't start thinking about us again, because as of now there is no us. Do you hear me? We're through. Finito. I've had it with you and your god-damned secrets. I don't want to see you ever again after ...'

'OK, you've made your point,' he cut in, snapping his suitcase shut and lifting it off the bed. 'Now, if you're not coming with me, would you mind getting out of the way.'

462

'No!' she cried through her teeth. 'I want you to tell me you're doing this for Cavan and your son. I want to hear you say you don't love her any more. At least tell me that.'

'We're through, remember,' he responded coldly.

'You bastard!' she seethed, her hand cutting him hard round the face.

'OK, now please, get out of the way,' he said.

With tears streaming down her face Ellen took a step back and allowed him to pass. She was so traumatized by her temper and the shock of finding out he had a son that all she could do was rest her head against the wall and sob.

She could hear him starting up the car and willed him to come back. But he didn't. And she knew, then, that the feeling she'd tried so hard to ignore that she was going to lose him had been right, because she just had and there wasn't a single damned thing she could do to change it.

Chapter 24

An impressive display of international flags flapped
smartly in the breeze as Michael got out of a taxi and
walked swiftly along the red carpet into the lobby of
the Rio Palace Hotel. It was just before midday. The sky
was as blue as polished sapphire, the sun as brilliant as
newly cut diamonds. Across the avenue the ocean
crashed on to the beach, spreading its waves like a
jealous embrace, while near-naked women with shiny
bronze flesh and exotic eyes strutted their beauty for
the world to admire.

Michael noticed none of it. He'd had a long wait at
Miami, he was tired, in need of a shower and was beset
by an unease that was fast getting the better of him.
He'd tried Cavan's apartment again as soon as he'd
landed and still there was no reply. Nor had he
managed to learn anything about Michelle. There had
been no mention of her arrest in the British papers he'd
tracked down in Miami, but they had been two-day-old
editions.

Finding the concierge's desk empty, he dropped his
bag on the floor and managed to restrain himself to one
hit on the bell. Immediately, a short, grey-suited man
with a pear-shaped face and a smile that squashed his
ruddy cheeks appeared from a rear office. 'Can I help
you, sir?' he said, in heavily accented English.

'My name is Michael McCann,' Michael said. 'I need to contact an American, Tom Chambers. He said you could get a message to him.'

'Ah yes, of course,' the concierge replied. 'Senhor Chambers informed me you would be arriving some time today. My name is Franco. I am happy to help in anyway I can. Senhor Chambers has already made you a reservation at the hotel. The General Manager has ordered the installation of an extra telephone line in your room and we have put a car and driver at your disposal. If there is anything else, you have only to let us know.'

As the man spoke, a fast-moving alarm was burying into Michael's chest. An extra telephone line, a car and driver ... Why? What the hell had been happening while he was on his way here?

'Senhor Chambers requested these things on your behalf,' Franco explained. Michael watched the man glance around the spacious reception. A couple of bell-hops and a group of linen-suited businessmen were the only people in sight. The check-in desk was deserted. Michael followed the concierge's eyes, then looked at him again, expecting him to speak, but the man only smiled.

Irritated by the theatricality, Michael's tone was brusquer than he'd have liked as he said, 'How can I get hold of Mr Chambers? I need to speak to him right away.'

Immediately Franco picked up a phone and dialled. A few seconds later he compressed his lips in disappointment. 'His mobile phone is switched off,' he said.

'What about his home?'

'He resides here, at the hotel, and I know he is out at the moment. Perhaps you would like to go to your room and I will let you know the instant I manage to contact him.'

Reining in his impatience, Michael followed a bellhop up to the seventh floor, tipped the boy in dollars, then closed the door behind him. Walking straight to the window he pulled back the billowing folds of muslin and stepped out on to the balcony. The air was so hot and humid it was hard to inhale. The sun was blinding. Slipping on his sun-glasses, he took in the magnificent sweep of the ocean and the long, elegant curve of the Avenue Atlantico, with Sugar Loaf mountain rising like a giant thumb at the far end of the bay. It couldn't have been more spectacular, nor the room, when he turned back inside, more accommodating, but again it wasn't the trappings that interested him, it was solely the whereabouts of his brother, and the son whose existence he had so long tried and failed to deny.

Going to the phone, he dialled Cavan's number again. Still no reply. Fighting the dread tightening in his gut he flicked open his suitcase, took out some fresh clothes and went to take a shower.

Half an hour later he was pacing the carpet. He'd tried Cavan's number several more times, but there was still no response. Franco had given him Chambers's mobile number, but the recorded message repeatedly informed him that the phone was disconnected. And the woman at the British Consulate had refused to give him any information on Michelle Rowe, as he was neither an accredited member of the press nor a relative. By now, his frustration was growing to such a pitch that when the phone finally rang and he heard Jodi's voice at the other end, he yelled at her that he didn't have time now and slammed the receiver down so hard he toppled the lamp on the nightstand.

In the end, unable to take any more, he snatched up the phone again, punched in Franco's number and told him he needed the car. The driver was waiting as he emerged from the hotel. Giving him Cavan's address, he got into the rear seat and tried to free his mind of all its encroaching trepidation as they headed off along the Avenue Atlantico towards Leme.

The driver weaved like a maniac through the deafening noise and choked up lanes of traffic, while Michael closed his eyes against the terror he was struggling to keep at bay. That Michelle could have got herself arrested was bad enough, but the danger she had inflicted on their son was unthinkable. God only knew what she'd been doing when they'd picked her up – Cavan had mentioned drugs, but he'd also said it was a set-up. Michael was ready to believe that, but he also knew how reckless she could sometimes be and heedless of the peril she was putting herself in. If it were just her he had to worry about then there was every chance he'd let her rot where the hell she damned well was, but it wasn't just her, and right now he was angrier with her and more afraid than he had ever been in his life.

When at last they came to a halt outside a towering apartment block that rose from the hub of a colourful market street, he told the driver to wait and ran inside the building, hoping to find a doorman or concierge who could help him. Spotting an old lady dusting a couple of cheap leather chairs, he put on his most charming smile and summoning the full extent of his Berlitz Portuguese he approached her with, '*Boa tarde, Senhora. Meu nome é Michael McCann. Eu sou . . .*' he stopped, realizing he didn't have the first idea how to say brother in Portuguese. '*Meu frero, Cavan,*' he said, giving it a shot.

For a moment the woman looked confused – obviously he'd missed the target – then to his relief a light started to dawn in her watery old eyes. '*Ah, Seu Cavan?*' she said.

'*Sim,*' Michael nodded, wanting to hug her for even trying to understand. 'Have you seen him? I'm looking for him.'

467

To his alarm her expression turned suddenly grave and she started to shake her head.

'Come,' she said in Englsh and, beckoning for him to follow, she took him into an iron-gated elevator, pressed a button for the eighth floor, then led him along a dull-yellow corridor to the furthest apartment. 'Here,' she said, looking up at him worriedly as she stopped at the open front door. 'I find like this. Seu Cavan, I no know he is.'

Michael's heart was thudding as he went past the woman into the chaos. Everything, from the chairs to the table to the mattress leaking feathers all over the wreckage, had been smashed, broken or totally ripped apart. Clothes had been torn from drawers and closets, books and papers had been slung across the floor and the drapes had been yanked from their rails. The shutters had been kicked open, the balcony was covered in broken pots; the guts of the phone were strewn across the floor and bright patches of wallpaper marked the spots where pictures had been wrenched from their hooks, then torn from their frames.

'Who did it, do you know?' Michael asked, going further into the room.

'I find this morning,' the old lady answered. 'I call police, but they no come yet.'

Michael looked down at a camera lying open at his feet. The film had been ripped out and lay entangled in the springs and stuffing of an old armchair. His throat closed over, for the camera had been a birthday present from him to Cavan the last time Cavan was in England.

Moving on, he pushed open a door and found a small kitchenette awash in food, smashed crockery and doors hanging from their hinges. The only other rooms were the bedroom and a shower room where the devastation was much the same. It was as he was leaving the bedroom that his foot knocked against something and bending down he picked up a wooden photograph frame. Turning it over he looked down at Michelle's lovely face smiling up at him from behind the fragments of splintered glass. It was as though she were looking at him through all the shattered pieces of their love. His chest started to tighten and for a moment the enormity of what he could be facing stole over him in a huge debilitating wave.

'I come this morning, it like this,' the old woman told him again. She seemed about to say more when she stopped at the sound of the elevator gates opening and someone walking down the hall towards the apartment. Her eyes were on Michael's, then, signalling for him to stay where he was she went to investigate. '*Ah, Seu Tom!*' Michael heard her exclaim as she reached the door, and as she launched into an unintelligible stream of Portuguese, he quickly put down the photograph and started across the room after her, assuming, in fact praying, that it was Tom Chambers.

The two men almost collided at the door.

'I guess you're Michael?' Chambers said, holding out a hand. 'Tom Chambers.'

'Glad to meet you,' Michael answered, shaking his hand. 'Any news? Do you know where Cavan is?'

Chambers's sharp, intelligent eyes were taking in the chaos. His expression was grim. 'I've got a pretty good idea,' he answered. 'Thanks for coming. I'm just sorry you had to walk into this. It wasn't like when we spoke yesterday. It's got to have happened overnight.'

'You said you know where Cavan is,' Michael reminded him.

Chambers nodded and walked further into the room. Then, lifting his head, he fixed Michael with a stare that drew a pause in Michael's heartbeat. 'Your brother's being held by a man called Pedro Pastillano,' he said bluntly. 'I got the call a couple of hours ago, informing me that if I don't hand over certain depositions by noon tomorrow, then Cavan won't be coming back.'

Michael's insides were turning to liquid. 'What depositions?' he said. 'Cavan said something about Michelle collecting some kind of evidence ...'

Chambers was nodding. 'She's been working with a bunch of teenage kids – street kids – detailing the kind of abuse and torture Pastillano goes in for at his private prison – they call it the Inferno, by the way – and the arbitrary executions his personal death squad are allowed to carry out with virtual impunity.'

Michael's astonishment was edged with horror as he registered the words abuse, torture, death squad and, almost worst of all, impunity. 'And he's holding Cavan?' he murmured. 'Who the hell is he?'

'Ex-military who's gone into business here in Rio and is about to run for governor. The elections are a couple of weeks away and with the way things stand he's likely to get in.'

Michael stared at him, then, mentally wresting himself from the shock he said, 'So what about these depositions? Where are they?'

Chambers's eyebrows went up. 'The sixty-four-thou-sand-dollar question,' he responded, looking around at the wreckage. 'Obviously they weren't here, or I wouldn't have got the call.'

Michael's eyes were wide with horror. 'Are you saying you don't know where they are?' he cried.

'I'm afraid that's exactly what I'm saying,' Chambers confirmed. 'I assumed Michelle had them, or would at least know where they were, but if she does, she's obviously not telling.'

Michael's confusion was inflaming his temper even further. 'Have you seen her?' he asked. 'Did you ask her?'

'She's still in jail,' Chambers replied, 'and so far they're refusing to let me see her. That should change pretty soon now though, because the New York Times and London Times ran the story I filed yesterday on her arrest, which is as big a guarantee as we're going to get that she'll be kept alive. Obviously they can't kill her while there's an international spotlight on her, especially not when both papers ran my allegations of a frame-up. As far as I know the Brits over at the Consulate are sorting her out a lawyer, so there's going to be some big-time pressure coming down any day now for the police to substantiate their charges, which, incidently, won't be hard for them to do. But provided we get our hands on the depositions there shouldn't be too much problem. Frankly, my concern is that she doesn't actually know where they are.'

'I don't believe this,' Michael muttered. 'Someone's got to know where they are, for Christ's sake.'

'Oh sure, someone does,' Chambers agreed. 'It's locating that person that could prove difficult. I've just come from the hospital where Carlos Camillo's wife is about to give birth. He's the public prosecutor who's been working with us. His office was torched last night and his apartment's in much the same state as this one. The guy's in bad shape. Always thought, as a public figure, he'd be safer than most, but I guess he's learning the hard way that no one is.'

'Well what about the kids who gave the depositions?' Michael said. 'Have you tried asking them?'

'Yeah, I asked them,' Chambers answered evenly, 'but they're all in witness protection and there's just no way the depositions would stay with them. Marcelo, their gang leader, is still out on the streets. I've put the word out I want to see him, but he hasn't shown up yet. Not that I'm expecting him to know where the statements are, but he might be able to help us with the whereabouts of the street educator who was working with Michelle. His name's Antônio. He disappeared within hours of Michelle's arrest. It could be he's taken himself and the statements into hiding, or – and we've got to hope this isn't the case – it could be that he's been arrested too and the police have neglected to inform us.'

'Jesus Christ,' Michael muttered. 'What kind of country is this?'

'You're about to find out,' Chambers responded, looking past Michael to the old woman as she started to speak.

When she'd finished Chambers translated. 'She says the cops could be here any minute,' he said. 'It'll probably turn out to be the same assholes as did the place over, so unless we want to start getting involved in a robbery charge I suggest we get ourselves out of here.'

Fifteen minutes later they were back at the Rio Palace Hotel, taking drinks from the minibar in Michael's room. Throughout the journey Chambers had been on his cellphone, speaking only in Portuguese, so Michael had been unable to understand what he was saying, or to discuss any more about the unholy mess Cavan and Michelle were in.

'Did you wire Cavan the money he called you about?' Chambers asked, flipping open a can of Pepsi.

Michael nodded.

'Then we'll stop by the bank later and see if we can pick it up.'

Michael's eyes were fixed on him hard as he tried to assimilate everything he had learned in the past hour. But it had come at him so fast he could barely comprehend it. Though he knew it was what else he had on his mind that was preventing him from getting a real grip on it all and though he dreaded asking the next question, there was just no way he could put it off any longer. So waiting for Chambers to finish drinking, he braced himself for the worst and said, 'When Michelle was arrested, what happened to ...?' He stopped as Chambers's head came up.

'Oh, shit, I'm sorry, man,' Chambers groaned. 'I was

forgetting. But listen, it's OK. You've got my word on it, the boy's safe.'

Michael just looked at him.

'I swear it,' Chambers said.

'So where is he?' Michael said.

'Still in Rio, with people who can make sure no harm comes to him. I took him there myself the minute I heard they'd picked up Michelle. Cara, the Sarajevan woman who was living with her, and her two kids are with him. And I swear, as soon as this is over I'll take you straight there.'

'Take me there now,' Michael said.

Chambers shook his head. 'I can't do that,' he said. 'As far as we know no one's aware he's Michelle's son, so if we go there and we're followed . . .'

Michael was so tense he felt his bones would snap. He knew what Chambers was saying made sense, but it was so damned hard to accept.

Chambers watched him and realizing that the only way to get him past this was to refocus his mind he said, 'Listen, right now our main concern is Cavan and working out how the hell we're going to lay our hands on the depositions.'

Michael remained silent.

'One of the calls I just made,' Chambers said, 'was to someone way up in the judiciary here. They told me there's a chance – not a good one, but still a chance – that one of us might get to see Michelle. If it comes through I think you should be the one to go. I'll arrange for someone to go with you, it'll probably be Jasper Klein from the *Herald Tribune*, or possibly Elaine Mayle from CNN. You'll need someone along to help with the language if nothing else.'

Michael nodded. 'And what if it turns out that Michelle doesn't know where the depositions are?' he asked.

Chambers was shaking his head. 'She has to,' he

responded. 'The more I think about it, the more I realize what's going down with her – she cares a lot about the kids who are risking their lives to give us what we need on Pastillano. They've put their trust in her and I've seen her in action before she'll put her own life on the line before she even thinks about doing anything that's in any way going to harm them.'

Michael's expression revealed very little of what he was thinking, even though the emotions simmering inside him were fierce. 'So what happens in the event we do get the depositions?' he said.

Chambers sighed. 'Good question,' he responded, 'but I guess we're not really going to know the answer to that until the time comes.'

Getting to his feet Michael walked over to the window and stared down at the beach. What was happening was so incredible, so beyond anything he'd ever experienced, or even expected to experience, he hardly knew what to say or do. In the end, turning back to Chambers he said, 'You mentioned this Pastillano character has some kind of prison. Do you suppose it's where they're holding Cavan?'

'Most likely,' Chambers replied. 'But if you're going to ask me where the prison is, then all I can say is I wish to God I knew. Marcelo, the gang leader, is still working on finding out, because the boys in witness protection don't have a clue.'

Michael didn't want to believe what he was hearing, but pushing himself on he said, 'At the risk of sounding foolish, I suppose going to the police is out of the question?'

'Totally,' Chambers confirmed. 'According to the information the boys have given us so far, Pastillano's death squad is staffed almost entirely by active police-men.'

'From all ranks?'

Chambers nodded.

Michael swallowed hard, then, forcing himself to voice the fear that was now uppermost in his mind he said, 'There's not much chance of us getting him back alive, is there?'

Chambers's steely grey eyes held firmly to his and as Michael's blood turned cold he tried not to think what this was going to do to his mother. 'You understand why, don't you?' Chambers said.

'I think so,' Michael responded. 'They'll have no way of knowing if we've made any copies of the statements before we hand them over and my guess is that's exactly what you intend to do – presuming we find them, of course.'

Chambers nodded.

'So framing this man is more important to you than Cavan's life?' Michael said coldly.

'If we hand them over, keeping nothing for ourselves,' Chambers responded, 'then everything, including the lives already lost, will have been for nothing. Pastillano will carry on the way he's going and all the kids who made those statements – and their families – will be dead inside a week. The other side of the coin is they could hold on to Cavan even after we hand the depositions over, as insurance against us ever going public.'

Michael's face was showing his strain. 'Do you think he's still alive?' he asked.

'I think there's a pretty good chance, yes,' Chambers answered.

'Then it seems to me we should be concentrating on finding out where that prison is, rather than where the statements are,' Michael said.

Chambers's eyes narrowed.

'Well, if neither of us has any faith the statements are going to get him back alive, then there doesn't seem much point in wasting our efforts trying to track them down, does there?' Michael snapped.

475

Chambers got to his feet, dropped his empty drink can in the bin and took his car keys from the table. 'I want you to sit tight,' he said, pulling aside a curtain and peering down into the street. 'Word is probably out by now that you're here in Rio, so someone might try to make contact.'

'You mean like Pastillano?'

'Never the man himself, but possibly someone who works for him. Or maybe someone giving the go-ahead for a visit to Michelle.' He turned back into the room. 'I know the people at the bank, so I'm going to try and pick up the money you wired over. Then I'm going to put in a call to the US Embassy in Brasilia. I've got a contact there who might come up with something useful.'

Michael watched him walk to the door, then, almost without thinking he said, 'I've never seen him, you know?'

Chambers turned back and the two men looked at each other across the room.

'He's a great kid,' Chambers said.

Michael swallowed. 'If anything happens to him . . .'

'It won't,' Chambers cut in firmly. 'I swear it. He's safe.'

Michael's eyes were glassy with all the pent-up pain. 'Does Michelle know where he is?' he asked.

'No,' Chambers answered. 'And take it from me, right now it's better she doesn't.' Then, realizing how rough this had to be for Michael he softened his tone. 'Don't be too hard on her,' he said, 'as mothers go, she's one of the better ones.'

Michael's answering laugh was bitter. 'And as fathers go, where would you put me?' he challenged. 'I told her I never wanted to see her again. When she was pregnant and she told me she was leaving, I told her if she went then she was never to think of the child as mine, because I sure as hell wouldn't. So what kind of father does that make me?'

'You're here, aren't you?' Chambers responded.

Michael looked at him.

'I think that answers the question,' Chambers said and pulling open the door, he walked out of the room.

As the door to the main office opened Sandy dropped her pen and spun round in her chair. 'Nesta!' she cried. 'Just the person.'

'That's me,' Nesta confirmed, hauling in half a dozen Harvey Nichols carrier bags.

Sandy grinned. 'Your timing's perfect,' she declared. 'Come and sit down, I've got something to tell you.'

'Where're Harry and Craig?' Nesta asked, dumping her bags on the floor.

'At lunch,' Sandy answered. 'And Michael's in Rio.'

Nesta screwed up her nose and sat down heavily in the chair opposite Sandy's. 'Rio?' she echoed. 'I thought he was in Barbados with Ellen.'

'He was. But he's now in Rio with Michelle.'

'How do you know?'

'How do you think I know?'

Nesta's eyes narrowed and her smile finally started to reflect the triumph in Sandy's. 'Jesus Christ, I can't believe how easily this is all coming together,' she said. 'I mean, it's like the man wants to give it all away. Where's Ellen, do you know?'

'Back in LA.'

Nesta laughed. 'I don't believe it!' she cried, clapping her hands together. 'It's so perfect it's scary. All we need now is for her to withdraw her resignation from ATI and I'm going to start believing you're doing deals with Him Up Above, or Him Down Below, because no one, just no one, gets this kind of luck on their own.'

Sandy's eyes moved to the Tiffany paperweights on Craig's and Harry's desks. They should have been one for her and one for Michael, but he had rejected her gift, just like he had rejected her.

'Well, you know who we call now,' Nesta said.

Instantly Sandy's eyes started to shine. 'I was just waiting for you to get here,' she said, looking at her watch – and picking up the phone she started to dial.

Chapter 25

Twenty-four hours had now passed since Michael had arrived in Rio, and though plenty had seemed to be happening they were still no closer to tracking down the depositions, or to locating the Inferno. Probably the most frustrating aspect of it all was not having the police to turn to, when that was something every British or American person took for granted. Two more calls had come from Cavan's kidnappers, Chambers had taken both and had negotiated a deadline of forty-eight hours for them to come up with the depositions. Now they were both back in Michael's hotel room waiting for news from a dozen different sources.

It had been a while since either of them had spoken, except for the brief phone call Michael had taken from London when he had told Zelda he needed the line free and would call her back when he could. Hearing Zelda's voice had, for some reason, made him think of Ellen and, with a horrible sinking sensation, the way he had walked out on her in Barbados. He guessed she would be back in LA by now, but when or even if he would be in touch with her again was impossible to say. If Michelle ever got out of this mess and he could persuade her to go home with him, then it would be all over for him and Ellen – according to her, it already was. The way that made him feel wasn't something he could deal with right now, so putting it aside he looked over at Chambers and fought the near overwhelming urge to ask more about his son.

He was right on the verge of speaking when Chambers, who had a stack of paperwork scattered across the bed, suddenly got to his feet. 'You know, I've been thinking,' he said. 'If we ...' He stopped as the phone started to ring.

Michael was there first. 'Hello?' he said into the receiver.

'Am I speaking to Senhor Michael McCann?' a soft, male voice enquired in accented English.

Michael's heart started to thud through his ears. 'Yes,' he answered. 'Who's this?'

'Tell me something about your brother no one else would know,' the voice responded.

Michael's eyes flew to Chambers. 'Who is this?' he repeated.

'Is there a certain birth mark on his left testicle?' the voice said.

Michael froze. 'Yes,' he replied.

'Not for long, there isn't,' the voice told him. 'Get those depositions by sundown tomorrow,' and the line went dead.

Michael put down the receiver and fought the nauseous fear churning in his gut. He'd tried everything he could to persuade himself that being British, Cavan wouldn't be subjected to the kind of brutality the street kids suffered, but the phone call had completely blown that.

'Don't go with it,' Chambers told him when Michael related the conversation. 'You'll drive yourself crazy and there's every chance they're bluffing.'

Michael walked over to the open French windows. His throat was dry, his hands were shaking and the terror burning in his heart was blotting out everything beyond the ordeal his brother was enduring.

Chambers stood watching him for a while, then took

480

a couple of beers from the minibar and opened them, handing one to Michael. 'Do you want to change your mind about going public on the kidnap?' he said.

Michael looked down at the bottle he was holding and took some time thinking. Finally, he shook his head. 'I don't see how it'll help,' he answered. 'It'll only antagonize them ...' He stopped as a horrible suspicion hit him and his eyes were suddenly blazing into Chambers's. 'Are you looking for a story?' he said bitterly. 'Is that what you're leading up to here?'

Chambers was unruffled. 'No, I'm just making sure you know what you're doing and why,' he answered, putting the beer to his lips.

Michael eyed him for a moment, then he drank too.

'I know this isn't going to make you feel any better,' Chambers said after a while, 'but I've been where you are now, so believe me I know how hard it is to make the right choices and I live every day of my life now knowing that I made a wrong one.'

Michael looked at him and waited for him to go on.

'You may recall the case of Rachel Carmedi, the American journalist who was kidnapped and killed in Colombia two years back,' Chambers said.

Michael's expression was unreadable, though his eyes widened slightly as a dawning recollection began stirring his memory. 'Of course,' he said, piecing it quickly together. 'And you must be the Tom Chambers who ...'

'... tried to call their bluff and got her killed,' Chambers cut in. 'So don't think I'm gonna try to push you one way or the other here, because I ...' He stopped as the telephone suddenly shrilled into the room again.

Michael looked at it, looked at Chambers, then went to pick it up. 'Hello,' he said, stealing himself for that same lyrical voice as before.

'May I speak with Senhor McCann?' a woman asked.

'You are,' Michael told her. 'Who're you?'

'I am calling to inform you that you will be able to visit Senhora Rowe at the prison tomorrow morning at nine o'clock. Please to take your passport or driver's licence for identification.'

Michael was looking at Chambers. 'I can see her tomorrow morning at nine,' he repeated for Chambers's benefit.

'Ask, will the visit be private?' Chambers told him.

Michael repeated the question.

'*Sim, senhor*,' came the reply. 'The visit will be private. Is there anything else you would like to ask, senhor?'

'Anything else?' Michael said to Chambers.

Chambers shook his head.

'Nothing else,' Michael told the woman and the call ended.

Chambers's fist tightened in a gesture of triumph. 'At last,' he said. 'I knew she'd come through, but I've got to tell you she had me worried there for a while.'

'Who is she?' Michael asked.

'Right now, one of the best friends you've got,' Chambers told him. 'She's also one of the most highly respected judges in Rio and probably the most cunning female you'll ever meet. But don't let that put you off, because Elena da Silva has more integrity than the Pope. She treads a real fine line here with the likes of Pastillano and the fact that she's managed to keep her position this long is testament enough to just how shrewd a cookie she is. Now, I suggest we go grab ourselves a bite to eat and start talking about what you're going to discuss with Michelle in the morning.'

Not for a single moment did either of them entertain the idea that Michelle might not know where the depositions were, for this was the biggest break they'd had so far and God knew they needed some hope. Not that they had exhausted all other channels, but their confidence in finding the Inferno was diminishing by the hour and even if they did, the likelihood of them being able to get in was less than zero. So finding the depositions was really the only chance of them getting Cavan back alive, and even then it was slimmer than either of them wanted to admit.

The women's penitentiary, on the far north side of the city, was as bleak and unwelcoming a place as Michael had ever seen. With its flat, unguttered roofs, narrow, barred windows, dun walls and desolate, sandy waste- land it was even more baleful and intimidating than the rugged mountains overlooking it. Knowing that Michelle was somewhere deep within its bowels was causing a sickness inside him that veered between outrage that any living person could be kept in such a place and a growing fear of what state he was going to find her in.

They'd learned yesterday, from the lawyer she had been appointed by the British Consulate, that having now been officially charged, her trial had been set to begin in seventy days. It was an unthinkable amount of time, during which Michael had no idea what he was going to do, for he just couldn't see how he could take their son and leave her here to face things alone. He guessed all he could do for now was take each day as it came. The lawyer was maintaining an optimism that he could get the charges dropped, but the man's prepos- terous bluster and nervous laughter did nothing to inspire any confidence. Indeed, he had taken fifteen thousand dollars from Michael that very morning to begin the process, which was why he wasn't accompa- nying Michael now and his wife, Mara, was.

As she brought the car to a stop outside the main gates, she told Michael to wait and walked over to the guards who charted her approach with combined insolence and suspicion. Michael watched as she spoke to them, her short, plump arms bobbing about like long balloons, her neatly crimped hair seeming as indignant as her manner. All the way there she had been regaling him with horror stories of the kind of conditions this particular prison was famous for, from the pitch-dark stinking cubicles with their squat pans and dripping water for washing and drinking, to the rats and roaches, the regular beatings and inmate attacks. Though he'd have liked nothing better than to gag the woman, he'd reminded himself that all he was having to do was imagine the nightmare, while Michelle was having to live it. It was why he was so concerned now about how well she might be holding up.

Seeing Mara beckoning him over, he got out of the car and went to join her outside the guards' hut. The sun was blisteringly hot and not a breath of air moved over the barren patch of land. There was no shade to shelter in as Mara explained in a crisp, busy tone, what he had to do. 'They're not going to allow me in with you,' she told him, 'but you should be all right. There won't be much need to speak to anyone, unless you're concealing a weapon about your person, or drugs. You aren't, are you?'

'No,' Michael answered.

'Good, because I'm afraid you're going to be subjected to a cavity search, which is only pleasant if you're the sado-masochistic type. Don't bother to object; if you do, you won't get in. I'm afraid they're doing it to humiliate you; it's their way of making sure you know who's in charge. My advice is, humour them.'

Fifteen minutes later, under the gloating eyes of two male guards and one female, Michael straightened up and put his clothes back on. He was inside the prison compound now, in a stark, sunlit room that was as claustrophobic as his rage. The sexual gratification that at least two of them had derived from the search was as

484

sickening as the process itself, but he gave no indication of his feelings as he was escorted out of the room, along a dank, shadowy corridor towards a strip of sunlight in the distance.

Before they got there they turned off, descended a steep flight of stairs and a few minutes later he was being led along a narrow, greasy walkway that separated two banks of crudely barred cells where dozens upon dozens of filthy and ragged women catcalled and jeered after him. The stench hit him right away. It was so noxious he started to gag. Clouds of flies buzzed around the rotting waste in the gutters, while the noise ricocheted off the walls in a terrible refrain. As he passed, their tormented, sneering faces seemed to loom from the depths of an apocalyptic nightmare. One woman managed to catch his arm and spin him round. A guard slammed her wrist with a truncheon and she howled like a cat, while one of her cellmates bared her large-nippled breasts and beckoned him forth. His eyes travelled from one grotesque, giggling face to the next, searching for Michelle and dreading he would find her.

At last he was shown into a long, bare room with high, rough stone walls, unreachable windows and a bench table running right down the centre. Above and below the bench were closely spaced iron bars, obviously there to prevent any physical contact between visitor and prisoner.

The guard barked at him in Portuguese and pointed at a chair. Assuming he was being told to sit, Michael did so and the guard, after scowling at him preposterously and uttering more unintelligible commands, left him alone.

Michael looked around and tried to get to grips with the reality of where he was and what he was doing there. It seemed so utterly incredible that this should be the setting in which he was at last going to see Michelle again, the woman he had loved so deeply and known so well, but who was now beginning to feel like a stranger. So many times he had imagined how it would happen, where it would be, what they would say, how they might feel. A thousand different scenarios had played themselves out in his mind, but none had ever been anything like this. He'd always imagined it would happen in England, for in his heart he had never really stopped hoping that one day she would come back to him and bring their son with her – the son he daily, hourly, thought of and longed to know, even though he'd never laid eyes on him.

As he sat there now, trying to make himself accept that she was going to walk through the door at any moment, he thought of how inseparable they had once been. It seemed so hard to credit now, but that was how it had been, right from the start, always together, never wanting to be apart. Everything had been so perfect, from the way they had created a home that was so uniquely theirs, to the certainty that each had found their soulmate. But maybe, in the end, it was the perfection that had ruined it, for it didn't take a cynic to know how ill at ease life was with perfection. Even so, nothing could have prepared him for the blow she had delivered the day she had told him she was leaving. He hadn't even known she was unhappy, hadn't sensed any restiveness or dissatisfaction with the way they were going, so to find out that she had hidden all this without him even noticing had shaken him right through to the core. But she wasn't unhappy, she had insisted, nor was she restless and dissatisfied, she was quite simply going to do what in her heart she knew she must – go to help the poor, abused and orphaned children of the world. The fact that she was carrying his child, or breaking his heart, had done nothing to change her mind; it was something she had to do and he must try to understand. They had argued for days, he had done everything he could to persuade her to stay, until, in the end, hurting more than he could bear, he had told her if she went, then he never wanted to see her or the child again. As far as he was concerned they would both be dead.

Now, more than five years had passed and in that time they had neither seen nor spoken to each other once. He wondered if he would ever be able to forgive himself for the foolish pride that had kept him from his son, or for the pain he must have caused Michelle by sending back her letters and the photographs he had guessed they contained. It was only because she had told his mother that he knew the baby was a boy, that he'd been born on 5 October and that his name was Robbie. More than that he had never tried to find out, nor had he wanted to know, for the need to have them with him was made so much worse by hearing their names. Now, he could only feel shame at how bitterly he had hurt them all by taking the stand he had – and whatever damage he had caused his son he could only pray he would soon get a chance to repair.

Hearing footsteps, he looked along the length of the room to the door they were approaching. He wondered how he was going to feel when he saw her and experienced a moment's dread of being suddenly possessed by the love he had kept buried for so long. A fleeting thought of Ellen came into his mind, then the door was opening and the guard was coming through.

He stood up and watched as two shadowy figures entered the glaring, misty bands of sunlight. Instinctively he knew that one of them was Michelle, though it was difficult to see in the blinding rays. He was so tense he could barely breathe. She started towards him, moving like a ghost at the other side of the bars. Still he couldn't make out her features, until finally she reached him and turned her back to the sun.

487

'Michael,' she whispered. 'Oh God, Michael,' and pushing a fist to her mouth she started to cry.

Her face was streaked with blood and dirt, her hair was tangled and matted to her head. There was a swollen cut on her lower lip and her left eye was circled by a livid purple bruise. He watched the tears drop on to her cheeks and more than anything else in the world he wanted to take her in his arms and carry her out of there. But he could barely touch her and his heart had been hardened against her for so long that even feeling as he did he could find no words.

She averted her head as the guard came up behind her and started to shout. It appeared he was telling her to sit, and after ordering Michael to do the same he turned abruptly on his heel and marched out of the room.

As the door closed, Michael started to speak, but she cut him off, 'Don't mention him,' she whispered. 'Not here. Just tell me, is he safe?'

Michael nodded and thought for a moment she was going to collapse.

She forced a smile and made a futile attempt to rearrange her hair.

'But it's over, you must know that,' he said.

She looked at him with wide, bloodshot eyes.

'You know what I'm saying,' he told her.

She looked down at the table, then back at him. 'Are you giving me an ultimatum?' she said softly. 'I either come home with you or you're going to leave me here?'

'For God's sake,' he responded angrily.

She shuddered and bunched her hands tightly on the table.

'What happened to your lip?' he asked.

She touched the cut with her fingers, then attempted to smile. 'You should see the other woman,' she said.

Michael forced a smile in return. It was so hard to know what to say, to step around all the surging emotions and find a place where they could communicate without hurting or accusing or wounding. 'We'll get you out of here,' he told her.

She nodded, but her head had fallen forward so he couldn't tell if she believed him.

'Listen,' he said, sitting in closer, 'I don't know how much time we've got, so I have to ask you now: where are the depositions?'

Her eyes were surprised as she brought them up to his. 'Do you honestly think I'd tell you just to get myself out of here?' she asked incredulously. 'Do you know how many children have died ... ?'

'Michelle, they've got Cavan,' he said, cutting her off.

Her face paled even further. 'You mean they've arrested him too? But he had nothing to do ...'

'They've kidnapped him. He's being held to ransom.'

'Oh my God,' she murmured, pressing her hands to her cheeks.

'So where are the statements?' Michael urged. 'You have to tell me, or God only knows what they'll do to him.'

She was shaking her head and tears were starting again in her eyes.

'You've got to tell me, damn you!' Michael seethed. 'It's probably our only chance of getting him back alive.'

Still she was shaking her head. 'No, listen, you don't understand,' she said. 'I don't know where they are. I swear it. If I did, for Cavan I would tell you. But Antônio took them. He was hiding them. I don't know where they are.'

Michael closed his eyes tightly as a bolt of anger and frustration rushed through him.

'There's a journalist here,' she told him quickly, as though afraid his temper would explode. 'His name's Tom Chambers ...'

'I know, I've met him,' he interrupted. 'And he doesn't know where Antônio is either.'

'But he has to,' she protested.

Michael merely looked at her.

Her eyes moved frantically in their sockets, then, looking at him again she said, 'There's a café in Santa Teresa . . .'

'We've already tried that,' he said, struggling to keep the anger from his voice. 'We've left a dozen messages and there's not been a single reply.'

Her eyes remained on his as her mouth started to tremble and tears blurred her vision. 'I'm sorry,' she said.

'You're sorry!' he snapped. 'What the fucking good is sorry going to do?'

She lowered her eyes and as he looked at her he was blind to the woman he had once loved. He saw instead the son he was so terrified he might never know. Then he saw Cavan and felt the unspeakable horror of his ordeal. She had caused him more pain than he could bear and now it was going to get so much worse. But venting his anger would do nothing to help Cavan, so struggling to control it he said, 'Was there anyone else? Someone you didn't tell Tom about who might know where the depositions are?'

She shook her head, then jumped as frustration brought his fist down hard on the table.

Forcing himself back in control he said, 'Is there *anything* you can tell me? Anything at all.'

She thought for some time and in the end she said, 'I expect you've already spoken to Sister Lydia at the shelter?'

Michael insides folded with despair. 'Yes, we tried her,' he answered.

'Maybe you should try her again,' she said. 'She's very fond of Antônio; she could be hiding him and not letting him know you're trying to find him.'

'OK,' he said. 'Give me the address, I'll go there on my way back.'

She did so quickly, then looked round as the guard came back into the room. She got to her feet and looked at Michael through the bars.

'Do you need anything?' he said. 'Is there something I can bring you?'

Her eyes were imbued with feeling as she looked at him and whispered, 'Have you seen him?'

He shook his head.

'Are you sure he's safe? Tom got him out?'

'Yes.'

Tears welled in her eyes again. 'I'm sorry about Cavan,' she said brokenly.

He looked at her and knew that if she were even half as afraid as he was then it was his strength she needed now, not his bitterness. So putting a hand to the bar he waited for her to do the same and linking their fingers together he said, 'He's going to be OK. I'll make sure of it.'

Those final words were still echoing through his ears as Mara drove him back through the town to the shelter. He just wished to God he had even a fraction of the confidence they had seemed to convey, for the fact that Michelle hadn't known where the depositions were was scaring the hell out of him. All he could hope for now was that Sister Lydia would come through, or he didn't even want to think about what it was going to mean to Cavan.

It was just after one o'clock when Michael got back to the hotel. Collecting his messages, two of which were from the office, the other from Chris Ruskin in New York, he went straight to his room and picked up the phone to call Chambers.

'By the time you get to the door,' Chambers told him, 'I should be right outside.'

491

Replacing the receiver, Michael unlatched the door, then went to take two beers from the fridge. As he opened them Chambers walked in, threw his cellphone and keys on the bed and went to stare out of the window as Michael told him about his visit with Michelle and the wasted trip to the shelter.

'Sister Lydia insists she doesn't know where Antônio is,' he said, 'and frankly I believe her. It was a long shot anyway, but I had to try it and now I don't know what the fuck we're going to do.'

'Take it easy,' Chambers said, turning back into the room. 'It's not as grim as it looks. Marcelo, the gang leader I told you about, made contact this morning.'

Michael's eyes widened. 'Does he know where the depositions are?' he said.

'No and I didn't expect him to. But he's pretty certain he knows where Antônio is.'

Michael choked on his beer. 'So what are we waiting for?' he cried.

Chambers put up a hand. 'Confirmation,' he replied. 'He's heard that they're holding Antônio over at the Leblon lock-up. He's checking to make sure and is going to get back to me some time in the next couple of hours. The other piece of good news is there's a chance Michelle might be out some time tomorrow.'

Michael stared at him in amazement. 'Are you serious?' he said. 'You mean that joke of a lawyer managed to pull it off?'

'Him – and the fifteen grand,' Chambers responded. 'And the fact that they're probably now taking the view that if they let her go, she might just be stupid enough to lead them to the depositions. Anyway, whatever they're thinking, our priority is still Cavan. Did Michelle know he'd been taken?'

Michael shook his head.

Chambers looked surprised. 'I thought they'd have used it as a means of persuasion,' he said, picking up

492

his cellphone as it started to ring, 'which just goes to show they're not as bright as they think they are. Tom Chambers,' he said into the phone.

As he listened to the voice at the other end Michael was about to turn away when Chambers's head suddenly came up, his eyes shining with excitement. 'OK,' he said, looking at Michael. 'I got it. Thanks for letting me know. Keep in touch,' and clicking off the phone he said, 'Antônio *was* at the Leblon lock-up. They released him ten minutes ago.'

Michael felt his adrenalin starting to thump. 'So where is he now? Can we talk to him?'

'Not yet. He'll be on his way to the shelter or the café, so he should get the messages we left any time in the next half-hour. If they didn't tell Michelle they were holding Cavan, it's doubtful they told Antônio, so he won't know the urgency of getting in touch until someone tells him. He will, though; in fact, there's a chance he could be on his way over here. We'll just have to sit it out and wait, which is no bad thing, because there's something I've got to discuss with you and the quicker we get to it, the quicker we can make some decisions. Did you eat yet today?'

Michael shook his head.

'Good,' Chambers responded and picking up the hotel phone, he ordered a *feijoada* for two.

'A what?' Michael asked when he rang off.

'*Feijoada*,' he repeated. 'It's tradition, everyone eats *feijoada* on Saturdays and I'm famished. Oh, it's kind of black beans and stewed beef and God knows what else they throw in. We'll skip on the *caipirinhas*, though, we need to keep a clear head.' As he finished, his phone started ringing again. 'Tom Chambers,' he barked into it. 'Yeah, I got a call from Marcelo,' he said. 'No, I didn't hear anything yet. You bet,' and he rang off. 'One of Marcelo's people checking to make sure we knew Antônio was released,' he explained. 'So, where were we?'

'There was something you had to discuss with me,' Michael reminded him.

Chambers's energy rush seemed to dip, as he moved his eyes to Michael and narrowed them thoughtfully. 'That's right,' he said, 'I just hope you're up to dealing with it.'

Michael's insides churned at the note of portent that had crept into Chambers's voice. 'If you've heard something about Cavan,' he said ...

'Nothing,' Chambers said, cutting him off. 'If I had, I'd have told you by now. But we've got to deal with reality here – there's just under five hours to go now before the deadline's up and so far we don't have the first idea whether we're going to be able to meet it. But say we can,' he continued forcefully as Michael made to interrupt. 'Say Antônio does come through with the depositions, there's still every chance Pastillano's going to try double-crossing us and take the stuff without handing Cavan over.'

Michael was staring at him hard. 'What are you getting to?' he said.

'What I'm getting to,' Chambers said, 'is that unless they give us some proof Cavan's alive, there's no point in us going to the trouble of handing the depositions over.'

Michael's jaw hardened as a bolt of fear dipped through his heart. The possibility that Cavan might already be dead was one he was living with every minute of the day and speaking it aloud made it no easier to handle. 'And just how are you proposing we get the proof?' he asked.

'They've got to call to set up a meet,' Chambers replied. 'We put it to them then.'

Michael took a moment with that, then said, 'I don't

494

know how they're going to do it, but if they do prove he's alive? What then?'

'We want him handed back at the exact same time as we give the documents over,' Chambers said. 'Of course, the problem with that is, they might well end up killing us all.'

'Holy Christ,' Michael murmured. 'Is there any way we're going to come out on top of this, because if there is, it's sure eluding me.'

'I've got to admit we still don't have much going for us,' Chamber confessed, 'but we could change that.'

Michael frowned, then felt his insides freeze as the phone suddenly rang. Picking it up he looked at Chambers as he said hello.

'Michael, it's Chris Ruskin here,' said the voice at the other end. 'Did you get my message?'

Biting down hard on his frustration, Michael said, 'Yeah, I'm sorry, things are getting complicated here and right now is a bad time, Chris.'

'Well, whatever's happening there,' Ruskin said, 'I think you should get yourself back here pretty pronto, because something very strange is going down with World Wide and ...'

'You'll have to handle it,' Michael broke in. 'There's no way I can leave here right now.'

Ruskin started to protest, but as the second line started to ring, Michael cut him off.

'Yeah, he's right here,' Chambers was saying into the other phone. 'I'll pass you over,' and blocking the mouthpiece with his palm he said, 'Now's your chance. Remember, we need proof.'

Michael's head started to spin and as he took the phone his insides turned hot with misgiving. He'd had no time to think this out, had not a single clue what he was going to say.

'Mr McCann?'

Michael's heart stopped beating. It was the same softly spoken voice as before. 'Yes,' he replied.

'Do you have the documents yet?' the voice asked.

Michael was thinking fast and praying he was going to come up with the right answers. 'Yes,' he lied. 'At least we know where they are.'

'That is good. I will call you again at six to give you instructions on where to take them.'

'No! No, hang on,' Michael shouted. 'I want some proof my brother's alive, or there's no deal.'

There was a brief silence at the other end, before the voice said, 'You are prepared to take that risk, Mr McCann?'

'There is no risk if he's already dead,' Michael replied. His head and heart were in such chaos now he barely knew what he was saying. He'd never been a gambler, but here he was, trying to bluff it out for his brother's life and not having the first idea what he had to call on next.

'Your brother is alive, you have my word on that,' he was
told.

'Not good enough,' Michael said. 'I want proof.'

'You want me to bring him to the phone?'

'You can do that, but what guarantee do I have that you won't kill him straight after? I want to see him.'

Chambers was staring at him hard.

'You will see him when you hand the papers over, Mr McCann,' the voice told him and the line went dead.

'Damn!' Michael muttered, as he slammed down the phone.

'You did good,' Chambers told him.

'Are you crazy?' Michael said angrily. 'I could have spoken to him! They offered that and I fucked it up by saying I wanted to see him. Jesus Christ,' he seethed, turning away. 'Why the hell did I do that?'

'If they offered to bring him to the phone, then we can be pretty certain he's still alive,' Chambers pointed out.

Michael's head was still bowed as finally he nodded. 'OK,' he said. 'But think about it. I just told them we've got the depositions which is an outright lie; and I've let them know we're not stupid enough to trust them to hand Cavan back as soon as they've got the papers. They could have been counting on our stupidity and now I've just alerted them into thinking their strategy through even further.'

'Or you've got them worried,' Chambers countered. 'Listen, they've got to have figured out for themselves by now that we're not just going to let those papers go without some kind of insurance ...'

'I don't see that we've got any choice,' Michael butted in. 'It's the only chance we have of getting him back ...'

'That's what I was trying to tell you just now,' Chambers said. 'It's not the only chance. The alternative isn't perfect, it's true, but right now it's the only alternative we've got. Are you ready to listen?'

Michael nodded.

'The guy I told you about at the US Embassy in Brasilia got back to me this morning. Apparently there's this couple, husband and wife, living right here in Rio, under the names Rita and Carmelo Ferrante. The Embassy didn't come right out and say so, but my reading of the situation is these guys are a couple of ex-federal agents who probably infiltrated the mafia or some whacko terrorist group or something and are living under assumed names now. I stopped by to see them on my way back here, and the bottom line is they've agreed to come in and help.'

Michael's face was white. 'Just exactly what are you saying?' he said.

'What I'm saying is the three of us discussed it and

we're all of the opinion that the only sure-fire way of getting Cavan out, depositions or no depositions, is to go in and get him.'

Michael stared at him as though he had lost his mind. 'You mean stage a raid like we were the marines or the SAS?' he responded scathingly. 'Because of course we've got the training, haven't we?'

'These guys do,' Chambers cut in.

'OK, but aren't you forgetting something? Like, we don't even know where the god-damned place is.'

'But we're going to find out,' Chambers responded. 'Whether it's today, tomorrow or a week from now, we're going to find out. And when we do, what then? Knock on the door and politely ask for his return? This is the only way, Michael. The Ferrantes have done this kind of thing before, plenty of times they tell me, and they're willing to come in and help us out, providing you're for it. He's your brother, so you get final say.'

Michael's eyes were trained on him hard as he did a rapid run-through of all the possible ramifications he could think of to this new proposal. In the end, as Chambers's cellphone rang, he said, 'OK, I'm for it.'

Putting a hand on his shoulder, Chambers picked up his phone. He listened for a few seconds, then, with a triumphant light in his eye as he looked at Michael he said, 'Good man. Can I speak to him? Sure, I'll be right there,' and clicking off the line he said to Michael, 'That was Roméro, at the café. Antônio just showed up.' He glanced at his watch. 'What time did that guy say he'd call back?'

'Six.'

'OK, that gives us four and a half hours. God knows if it's going to be enough, but we better start by getting the Ferrantes over here to talk to you, while I go pick up the depositions from Antônio. Just pray God he's got them, or knows where the hell they are.'

Michael looked at him and knowing how utterly

hamstrung he'd be without him, wished there were a way he could express his appreciation without embarrassing them both. But there wasn't, so instead he said, 'What's wrong with getting Antônio to bring the depositions here? *If* he's got them.'

'They're almost sure to be watching him,' Chambers responded, picking up his keys, 'which is probably why he didn't come straight here. Of course, I'm only guessing, but the boy's a long way from stupid and if he does have the depositions, or knows where they are, he'll be as mindful as anyone of just how god-damned precious they are.'

'So how are you going to get them? If he is being watched,' Michael asked.

'That's a good question,' Chambers replied. 'Why don't we put it to the experts?' and clicking on the phone he called the Ferrantes' Copacabana number.

'OK,' he said a few minutes later. 'Carmelo, the husband, is on his way over here to start getting detail from you, while I go over there to pick up Rita, the wife, who's coming with me to visit Antônio. So it looks pretty much like we're about to put this show on the road,' and with a wry tilt of his eyebrows, he pulled open the door and came face to face with a room service waiter and the *feijoada* he now had no time to eat.

From the instant Ferrante walked in the door Michael could feel his confidence level rising. He was a short, stocky man, with muscles like granite, skin like a lunarscape and a New York accent that was as rough as the streets he had come from. It was clear, as soon as he started talking, that he was as unfazed by the task ahead as he was serious about accomplishing it. And with his unnervingly direct eye and straightforward talk, he didn't leave much room for doubt that he would. He wasted no time in giving Michael a run-down on the information he'd been given, then set to work on getting whatever else Michael had to offer.

By the time an hour was up both men had a healthy respect for each other and an optimism that was as quietly understated as it was well-founded. Chambers had called from the café to inform them that they could be about to get the biggest break of all, as not only did Antônio know where the depositions were, but he had actually found himself in the lock-up with an ex-inmate of the Inferno, who knew an ex-member of a rival death squad who might just know the whereabouts of Pastillano's prison for a couple of hundred bucks.

'OK, it sounds a bit of a run-around,' Chambers had said, 'but when you consider how long we've been working on finding this place, which is months before you got here, then remember, this is the closest we've come. So conclude here that when needs must, life delivers. Or maybe it's when Pastillano panics, lieutenants fuck up, because he should have been told who Antônio was banged up with, but obviously wasn't. It could turn out to be the sonofabitch's Waterloo. Providing, of course, this ex-death squad low-life turns out to be on the level. We'll keep you posted.'

There had been no communication since, and with Michael's debriefing over there was nothing for him and Ferrante to do but sit and wait. Michael considered ringing Chris Ruskin in New York, but whatever problems Ruskin and World Wide were facing right now there was nothing he could do and besides, he really didn't need the distraction.

Each minute seemed endless as he and Ferrante took turns walking about the room, going out on to the balcony to take in the view, or just lie on the bed staring at CNN. It was during a sudden newsflash of how former British actress, Michelle Rowe, was expected to be released from prison in Brazil within the next couple of hours, with all charges against her dismissed, that the telephone rang again.

Still staring at the screen Michael picked it up.

'Hello? Seu Michael? Is Franco, the concierge. Your car is here.'

Michael frowned and looked at Ferrante. 'What car?' he asked.

'The car you order?' Franco answered uncertainly. 'Not car from hotel, different car. You not satisfied with car from hotel? We can change. Is no problem . . .'

'I didn't order a car,' Michael interrupted.

Franco's confusion was almost audible. 'Oh,' he said. 'I have message to say your car is here. You want that I send it away?'

'Hang on,' Michael replied and putting his hand over the receiver, he related the conversation to Ferrante.

Ferrante crossed to the balcony and looked down at the street below. The view to the reception was obstructed by the pool terrace. Turning back he said, 'Tell him you'll be right down,' then picking up the remote control he flicked off the TV and checked the gun in his waistband.

'It could be just a mistake,' he said, his pock-marked face and muscular body seeming to harden before Michael's eyes. 'I doubt it, though. What I reckon is it's a couple of Pastillano's operatives come to take you for a ride.'

Michael's heart gave a thump of alarm. 'You mean they're going to do as I asked and let me see Cavan?' he said.

Ferrante shrugged. 'Could be,' he responded.

'So what do I do?' Michael asked.

'Well, as we don't got any of the technology and back-up we usually got in these situations,' Ferrante answered, 'we go with what we got. Meaning, you give me enough time to get my car round to the front of the hotel, then you go down and find out what it's all about. If you get in the car they've got waiting, remember, there's no guarantees they're going to take you to your brother, nor of them letting you out alive. But the way I see it it's not in their interest to let anything happen to you yet. They want those depositions and they want them real bad. And Pastillano might have been dumb enough to lock Antônio up with an ex-inmate, but we can't count on him being that dumb again. Now, we don't have time to hang about here; if we do, they're going to start getting suspicious. So just remember, whatever you do, keep telling 'em we've got the depositions. If they ask where they are, say someone's bringing them to you just before the six o'clock deadline. OK?'

Michael nodded. 'OK,' he repeated.

Ferrante shook his head. 'This could turn out to be a smart move on their part,' he said, obviously not liking the situation too much. 'No advance warning a car's on its way, no setting up a meet, just, boom, the car's there, get in if you dare.'

Michael watched him leave and tried not to feel as though his lifeline was being reeled in. Though he knew there was no way he would back out, he still couldn't help wondering if he really had the courage to go through with this – after all, he was an entertainment agent, for God's sake, not James fucking Bond. He looked at the gun Ferrante had left for him and thought of Cavan and Michelle, and most of all Robbie. He had no reason to be so afraid for his son, but the spectre of never getting to see him was haunting him night and day. There was no clarity in his mind as to whether his fear was based on something happening to Robbie, or if it was to do with getting himself killed in the attempt to free Cavan. Probably it was both. All he knew for certain was that he was prepared to do whatever it took to get them all out of this alive, and with Michelle being freed at any moment and Robbie being kept in a safe place, the only one he had to concern himself with was Cavan.

The dark Mercedes saloon, with black-tinted windows, was waiting right outside the hotel entrance. As he approached it a doorman stepped forward, opened the rear door and from the darkness inside he was told to get in.

Fighting the urge to make sure Ferrante was in sight, he did as he was told. As he slammed the door closed he heard the click of the central locking cutting off his escape, then noticed the dividing screen between passenger and driver compartments sliding shut. Sitting adjacent to him, his back to the road ahead and a gun pointing straight at Michael's chest was a thick-set, cheap-suited man whose face, except for the limpid brown eyes, was hidden by a grey, woollen mask.

'The gun,' he said, pointing his own towards the one in Michael's pocket.

Michael's mouth was turning dry, as handing the weapon over he felt the car pulling away.

'Put this on,' the man commanded, tossing over a blindfold.

Michael took it, looked at it, then, hearing the click of the gun's hammer being pulled back he slipped it on, attempting to position it so that he could at least get a glimpse of where they were going.

The car was moving out on to the Avenue Atlantico and he knew it wouldn't be long before he lost his bearings completely. For some odd and unidentifiable reason he found himself thinking about Ellen and the things he'd been planning to say before Cavan's call had come and blown it all apart. Then, realizing why he was thinking about her now, his blood turned cold. A rogue instinct, that had come out of nowhere, was suddenly telling him that he was never going to see her again. Then it hit him why, and he could hardly believe what idiots he and Ferrante had been not to have seen through this straight away. Ferrante had said it could be a smart move on their part and now Michael was realizing just how smart. For by allowing no time to think, to plan, not even to second guess, they had lured Michael into what had to be the easiest kidnapping in history. And the only reason they'd need to do that was because they needed another hostage to take Cavan's place.

He tried to tell himself he was overreacting, but as he heard the crashing and grinding of metal behind him he knew instantly what it meant, that Ferrante had just been very effectively ambushed and he was now completely on his own, heading for God only knew where . . . or what.

Chapter 26

A dozen or so paparazzi were waiting outside the prison when Michelle was led across the dusty courtyard to a Volkswagen Santano. As she was driven away the press crowded about the car, eager for a shot of her pale, bruised face and shouting for a comment on how she had been treated and what she intended to do now. Within seconds the car was clear and speeding down the road towards the town, a smart Fiat Tempra close on its tail. The man in the rear passenger seat with Michelle had identified himself earlier as Walter Askew, a British Embassy official, and with his pompous manner and ill-disguised disapproval Michelle wasn't in much doubt of his honesty.

Just prior to her release Askew had informed her that a condition of them letting her go was that she leave Brazil by the end of the day, so a seat had been reserved for her on a flight to Miami at eight o'clock that night, where she would make the connection to London. Knowing that she was in no position to argue, she had accepted the condition, but now, as they travelled through the grimy, bustling streets of downtown Rio, she was bracing herself to ask for more time. If she didn't get it, then she knew she would have to find a way to escape her protection, for she simply wasn't leaving Rio without Robbie – or without knowing that Cavan was safe.

'I've been in Rio for a long time, Mr Askew,' she began, as they turned on to the main thoroughfare of Avenue Presidente Vargas and drove past the exquisite Candelaria Church, more famous now for the police massacre of eight street children than for society weddings.

Askew turned his lofty glance upon her as though enquiring of what possible interest that could be to him.

She looked at his lower lip which was puckered beneath his protruding teeth. His flaring nostrils reminded her of how she must smell. 'What I'm saying,' she continued, determined not to be put off by his hostility, 'is that I don't think I can be ready to leave in such a short time. There are things I have to do ...'

'Miss Rowe,' he interrupted, 'it was a condition of your ...'

'I know,' she cut in, 'and I went along with it because I knew they wouldn't let me out if I didn't. But, you see, there are things ... There are people ... at the shelter, I have to see. I've done a lot of work here. I can't just walk out on them.'

'You can write to them, Miss Rowe,' he told her stiffly.

Michelle looked at his implacable expression and knew that it was pointless to pursue this route. 'Listen,' she said, half turning in her seat to face him, 'I can't leave. Not yet. I mean, I will, but right now it's not just out of the question, it's impossible.'

His gingery eyebrows rose. 'And why would that be?' he asked coldly.

Michelle took a breath and crossing her fingers in the hope she was doing the right thing, said, 'Because my son is still here and I can't go without him.'

Askew's expression showed his surprise. 'Your son?' he repeated.

Michelle nodded. 'The children who were living with

me,' she explained, 'one of them is my son. He's four years old, so you see I can't leave without him.'

Askew's nostrils grew wider. 'I would hardly suggest you did, Miss Rowe,' he responded. 'But I don't see how taking him with you is going to stop you getting on the plane this evening.'

'Maybe it won't,' she said helpfully, 'but if I don't find him by then, you must understand I can't leave without him.'

'Find him?' Askew declared. 'What on earth do you mean by that?'

'Well, as soon as I was arrested a friend of mine took him and the other children into hiding,' she answered. 'For safety, you understand. If I can make contact with my friend I can find my son and we can leave.'

'Goodness me,' Askew grunted, clearly extremely put out by this awkward development.

Michelle was thinking fast, trying to work out where his thoughts might be leading him.

'Well, I can see you can't go without the boy,' he said finally, 'so I would suggest you try contacting your friend immediately.'

Michelle looked at the carphone he was handing her and tried to swallow her dismay. 'He won't give me the information over the phone,' she said. 'It's an agreement we have, just in case I am being forced to ask.'

'Goodness me,' Askew said again, obviously becoming more displeased by the minute.

'I could ask him to come to my house,' Michelle suggested. 'He'd probably tell me there.'

Askew pressed the phone into her hand. 'Tell him to bring your son to the house and we'll see you both on a flight this evening,' he said.

Michelle dialled quickly and within seconds had made the connection to Chambers's cellphone. 'Tom?' she said, experiencing such a surge of relief at the sound of his voice that her eyes filled with tears. 'It's Michelle.'

'Christ, where are you?' he demanded.

'They let me go,' she answered. 'I'm on my way back to the house. Can you meet me there? Can you bring Robbie?'

Chambers was silent.

Michelle was silent too and glanced from the corner of her eye at Askew.

'Who's with you?' Chambers asked.

'Someone from the Embassy,' she answered. 'They're saying I have to leave tonight and take Robbie with me.'

'You can't,' Chambers told her.

'Why?' she demanded, unsure whether she should be unnerved by this response or not. 'He's all right, isn't he? Tom, tell me he's all right.'

'He's all right,' Chambers assured her, 'but I can't bring him to the house. Not yet, it wouldn't be safe.'

'Why?'

'Trust me, OK? There's a lot going down over here right now and . . . hang on,' he was gone for a moment, then, coming back on the line he said, 'Michelle, I've got to go. I'll call you at the house as soon as I can.'

'Tom, wait!' she cried. 'Where's Michael?' But the line was already dead.

She could feel Askew watching her as clicking off her end, she handed the phone back to him. 'He's going to call me at home,' she told him quietly. Then, bringing her eyes up to his she said, 'I won't go without my son, Mr Askew, and there's no guarantee I'll get him back today.'

'You're putting me in a very difficult position, Miss Rowe,' he said crossly.

'I know and I'm sorry, but if I swear I won't leave the house until I have my son and we are ready to go, can you find it in your heart to give me some leeway?'

Askew stuck out his chin and fingered his collar. 'I'm not the one who set the condition,' he reminded her.

'But if I don't have my son, are you really going to make me go without him?' she asked.

Askew glanced at her quickly, then returned his eyes to the passing streets. When finally he answered they were slowing up to pass through the security gates of her *domaine*. 'I want your word that you won't leave the house,' he demanded.

'You have it,' she assured him.

He looked at her hard and she could see he didn't trust her. Then, glancing over his shoulder to check that the car following them was through the gates too he said, 'We have assigned someone to watch over you until it's time for you to leave. We've done this for your own safety. I'll instruct him to stay with you until midday tomorrow. By then you *must* be ready to go. Do you understand?'

Michelle nodded eagerly, and resisting the urge to clasp his hands, she got swiftly out of the car before he had a chance to change his mind.

As she unlocked the door to the courtyard the car began reversing. She turned to wave. Though he saw her, Askew didn't wave back. She looked down the shady cobbled street towards the security guard's booth and found the guard staring up at her. Then, glancing at the man in the Fiat Tempra she pushed the door open and disappeared inside the courtyard.

Remembering to lock up behind her, she ran around the pool and slid open the french windows that led into the lounge. She could feel herself starting to shake and wanted desperately to cry as relief and fear engulfed her – and the need for someone to be there opened like a void around her.

The place was so silent. She had expected it to be searched, but she hadn't been prepared for so much damage, nor for the terrible panic that was suddenly starting to seize her. But both Michael and Tom had said Robbie was safe and in her heart she knew he was, for Tom would have seen to it and if any harm had come to him Michael would have known. Or had they just been trying to spare her, not wanting her to fret any more than she already was? A terrible surge of fear cleaved through her chest as she looked at the broken toys and tried not to imagine what would have happened if he and the other children had been here when Pastillano's men came.

Forcing herself to take deep, steadying breaths, she made her way down to the bedroom and stripped off the foul-smelling clothes she'd been wearing for the past five days. She showered for a long time, allowing the hot, steaming jets to pummel her body and push through the tangled knots of her hair. She was trying so hard not to break down, to keep at bay the encroaching panic as she tormented herself with what was going to happen now. She had hoped Michael would be there when they'd released her, but there had been no sign of him and Walter Askew hadn't mentioned him. Maybe she should have asked, but she had no idea how Michael and Tom were playing things and she didn't want to the run the risk of messing things up. But she could see no harm in trying to find out where Michael was; after all, he had visited her in prison so Pastillano must know about him now.

By the time she stepped out of the shower the need to see him was coming over her in waves of such urgency and despair she could barely breathe. She had to find out what news there was of Cavan, but was almost too terrified to ask. It was all her fault, everything that was happening was totally down to her and if Cavan didn't get through this then she knew she would never be able to live with the guilt.

Snatching up fresh underwear from where it had been thrown on the floor, she quickly slipped it on and found a thin cotton dress to cover it. As she fastened the buttons her hands were shaking and the misgivings in her heart were growing all the time. She needed to speak to Michael. She had to know what was happening and whether there was anything she could do. She began searching around for the phone, throwing things aside and becoming increasingly more agitated, until finally she was on her knees hugging the torn photograph album she had used to tell Robbie stories about his daddy.

'Oh God, Michael,' she sobbed, as tears began streaming down her face. She'd always known how much she'd hurt him and now he was going to do the same to her. He was going to take Robbie away and give him the kind of life he should have, instead of the one she was forcing on him. 'It's over, you must know that,' he'd said when he'd come to see her that morning and though she'd pretended not to understand, she'd known exactly what he meant, because she'd always known that one day it would happen. It was why she had done everything she could to prepare Robbie for the time his daddy would come and take him to a place where he would have cousins and go to school with other children. She'd done all she could to prepare herself too, but now the time was here she knew she didn't have the strength to let go. He was so independent, so full of life and laughter and mischief, but he was just four and too small to go away with a stranger, even if the stranger was his daddy. Yet he talked about it all the time, was so excited for the day to come, so eager to see his real daddy instead of the photographs Mummy showed him. Never, she thought, had a child so longed to know his father as her son longed to know his, so how could she prevent it now, after all she had done to prepare for it?

She smiled, then, and sobbed again as she recalled the day he'd met Cavan and had thought he was his daddy. Cavan had never had such a greeting from a child and Robbie was so good-natured he had soon forgiven Cavan for being just an uncle. It was only later, when he was alone with Michelle, that he had let his disappointment show and it had been so hard to bear she had almost asked Cavan to take him with him to England when he'd returned for his birthday. But at the last she'd been unable to do it.

And now, here she was, not knowing where either of them was and so afraid she might not see them again that she could barely make herself think. Somewhere deep down inside she knew she wasn't being rational, that Michael was out there trying to find Cavan and Tom had made sure Robbie was safe, but guilt for all she had done was smothering her reason. She kept thinking about Cavan and imagining what they might be doing to him now. He was so young and undeserving of what she had brought upon him. But it wasn't only the kidnap, was it? It was the deception and the lies, the never knowing if it was him she loved, or if really it was Michael. They looked so painfully alike, smiled the same way, got angry the same way and almost loved the same way. He was Michael's flesh and blood, Michael's image, the brother Michael loved beyond life. So she had loved him too and through him had continued to love Michael, never really knowing where one ended and the other began.

But she knew now. After seeing Michael that morning there was no longer any doubt, all there was was a terrible fear that it might already be too late.

The car had come to a halt a few minutes ago, by which time Michael calculated they had been travelling for roughly an hour. He was pretty certain they had risen to some altitude, and from the frequent splashes of sunlight and shade and absence of traffic noise, he guessed they had come up through the vast, rambling

512

forest that climbed the hills behind Rio. Where they were now wasn't easy to gauge, though he was sure he had heard the motorized lifting of some kind of door, and after the car had turned around on what sounded like gravel it had reversed several feet back until there was virtually no light seeping through his blindfold at all.

After that, with the exception of the driver getting out of the car, nothing had happened. He knew his companion was still there, he could hear him breathing; the only other sound was that of frantic bird life and of rushing water, coming from a short distance away. At a guess, he would say they were in some kind of tunnel, or a garage, or perhaps a sort of heavy-duty container. He doubted it was the last, as the driver's footsteps had sounded as though they were on stone.

Several minutes ticked silently by. His mind was racing as he tried to fathom all the possible scenarios that could unfold from here. He liked not a single one of them, but each was dealable with, providing Cavan was still alive.

The sound of footsteps returning cut through his barrage of thought. All his senses were alert now, adrenalin was pumping through his veins as fear hammered in his heart. The electronic whirr of the car window going down preceded a short, angry exchange in Portuguese, then came the sound of metal, like a chain, being unravelled.

'Put arms behind back,' his companion instructed.

Michael did as he was told and was promptly dragged forward on to his knees.

'Arms behind back,' the man barked again.

Once again Michael did as he was told and felt the cold, hard bracelets of handcuffs being clasped round his wrists.

'OK, now you look,' the man said and wrenched off the blindfold.

513

Getting up from the floor, Michael sat back in the seat. It took a moment for his eyes to adjust. When they did, all he could see through the glass partition ahead was a small, sunlit clearing, surrounded by dense foliage. Either side of him were only drab, empty walls.

'Turn,' his companion barked.

Michael turned slowly, dragging his eyes from the man, then looked out through the rear window. There were three men standing several feet behind the car, all partially hidden by shadow. It was impossible to make out who any of them were, until the middle man's head was suddenly wrenched back and Cavan's brutally beaten face was exposed to the light. Michael spun round, ready to leap from the car, but the man beside him had a gun pointed right at him.

'See, he alive,' the man said. 'Now you look again.'

Michael turned back and as another figure stepped out of the shadows it was as though a silent explosion was tearing his senses apart. A terrible tightness closed around his skull, his heart was thudding, his ears were pounding, his vision was blurring and clearing. The shock was so great, the fear so intense that everything in him ceased to function. Though he'd never seen his son, he was in little doubt who the child now being held up to the light was, and with a sudden roar of denial and fury he lunged at the man in the car, knocking him senseless with a head blow to the face and almost managing to pick up the gun. But the car door was torn open and he was immediately halted by the frantic pressure of a barrel against his temple.

'You! You bring the depositions,' he was told. 'You bring them here, tonight, or you no see the boy again. You hear?'

Wanting only to kill, Michael somehow forced himself to nod.

'No tricks, you hear? You no make copies, because we keep your brother. OK? We keep him for good long

514

time. But you bring the depositions tonight, you get the boy.'

He was thrown back against the floor, while the other man's body was dragged free, then the door slammed shut and the engine started up. They were already pulling away when the door was wrenched open again and another man leapt in, gun in hand, and ordered him to put the blindfold back on. Remembering he was hancuffed, the man picked up the blindfold, wrapped it round Michael's eyes, then shouted for the driver to move.

The journey back seemed endless, until finally they stopped a few blocks from the Rio Palace, where he was untied and told he would be contacted in one hour. By then he'd better have the depositions.

The sun was starting to go down as he ran out on to the Avenue Atlantico and into the hotel.

'Seu Michael, Seu Michael,' Franco called out as he raced past.

Michael swung round.

'I have message for you,' Franco told him coming out from behind the desk. 'Seu Tom, he say you must call him right away.'

By the time Michael reached his room he was in a frenzy of panic. All he could think about was that brief glimpse of his son, with a wedge of thick black tape across his mouth and his small, fragile body clasped in the hulking arms of a madman.

He didn't have chance to pick up the phone before it rang and Chambers's voice came down the line.

'Where are you?' Michael barked.

'Where the hell are *you*?' Chambers barked back.

'At the hotel. I've got to see you. They've got Robbie. At least I think it's him . . .'

'It is,' Chambers confirmed grimly. 'I got a call from Judge da Silva. He was snatched from her car a couple of hours ago. Did you see him? Is he OK?'

For a moment Michael was unable to speak. Even though his every instinct had told him this child was Robbie, having it confirmed was almost impossible to deal with. 'They've got him gagged, but he looked OK,' he finally managed. Then anger took over. 'How did it happen?' he demanded. 'You gave me your word he was safe.'

'I'd have staked my life on it,' Chambers responded.

'Then you'd be fucking well dead!' Michael shouted, almost incoherent with rage.

'OK, get a grip,' Chambers said. 'There was a leak the judge's end. There's nothing we can do about it now. The boy's been snatched and we're going to get him back. Tell me about Cavan. Did you see him?'

'Cavan's there. He's badly beaten up, but alive.'

'Do you know where?'

'No. Have you got the depositions? They're calling me in an hour.'

'The depositions are here,' Chambers answered. 'The Ferrantes are with me too. We caught up with the ex-death squad guy. Unless he's lying we now know where the Inferno is.'

'Are you serious?' Michael cried, a sudden emotion tightening his throat. 'Did he say it was in the mountains? In the forest ...'

'You got it!' Chambers cried. 'Marcelo is here with half a dozen of his guys, we're just going over the map. Better still ... Listen, better still, this guy's drawing up a detailed plan of the prison, right down to where he reckons Cavan's being held. He wants ten grand for all this, by the way, I told him it was his.'

'Pay him whatever he wants,' Michael replied. Then, catching his breath he said, 'Christ, this is just the break we need.'

'Tell me about it,' Chambers responded. He went off the line for a moment, speaking to someone his end, then, coming back he said, 'Rita Ferrante's just leaving, she's on her way over to brief you.'

'Is she bringing the depositions?' Michael asked. 'I'm going to need them.'

'Yeah, she's got them. She'll go with you to hand them over. The rest of us are going to come separately. Did they take your gun away?'

'Yes,' Michael answered.

'She'll bring a spare. Marcelo's got a fucking arsenal over here.'

Alarm bells were starting to sound in Michael's head. 'Are you sure this is a good idea?' he said to Chambers. 'I mean, if we're all going in armed and it turns into some kind of shoot-out, which it's bound to, then Robbie and Cavan are going to get hit first.'

Chambers's reassurance wasn't good. 'By the time we get there we're going to know our way around that place pretty well,' he said. 'It's got to help. But if you can think of a better way I want to hear it, 'cos I'm no happier than you are going in like this.'

'We could try trusting them,' Michael answered. 'They said they'd hand Robbie back tonight if I give them the depositions.'

'What about Cavan?'

Michael's heart sank. 'They're planning to keep him,' he said.

Chambers's silence was brief. 'So as of right now we don't have much alternative?' he said.

'It doesn't look like it,' Michael conceded.

Chambers spoke to someone else for a moment, then, coming back, he said, 'I'm gonna have to cut this short now, but as soon as you hear anything call me. We need to know where you're making the exchange.'

'OK.'

'Hang on,' Chambers said. 'You heard about Michelle, did you? She's been released.'

'Oh shit!' Michael swore, his hand going to his head

as he closed his eyes in frustration. 'I'd forgotten. Do you know where she is? Does she know about Robbie?'

'I thought it best not to tell her,' Chambers answered. 'I think we should keep it that way.'

'Are you kidding?' Michael said drily. 'But I'll have to speak to her.'

'She was on her way home when she called,' Chambers answered. 'That was a couple of hours ago.'

'Do you have the number?' Michael asked.

Chambers gave it to him, then, telling him to get in touch the moment he heard anything he rang off.

Michael hit the connectors to get a new line, but after dialling Michelle's number he abruptly cut himself off. Everything was happening so fast now, things were getting so crazy that there was a very real danger they were going to get out of hand. He felt sick, shaken and so ludicrously hyped up it was dangerous. He needed to calm down, to think things through as rationally as he could and to prepare himself for the exchange. He could only be thankful Rita Ferrante was on her way, at least she had been through this kind of crisis before, whereas for him it was like he had stepped straight off the edge of reality into a nightmare of epic proportions.

He walked over to the balcony and began taking deep, controlling breaths. They barely helped. He was so caught up in the ordeal his son and brother were facing he couldn't let it go. But he had to. Somehow he had to find it in himself to cut out the emotion and go into this as level-headedly as possible. If he didn't, there was every chance he would lose his son before he ever got to hold him. The very thought of it caused a rage to gust through him like a storm, but he forced it back. To be angry with himself or Michelle right now would get him nowhere, for no amount of fury, accusations or recriminations was going to give him back the time he had lost with Robbie. He must concentrate on the future now and what he was going

518

to do to get him back – and where they would go from there. He just hoped to God he wasn't going to have to fight Michelle, but if it came to it he would, for there was just no way he was going to tolerate him being in this kind of danger again.

Glancing at his watch to check how much time was left, he started to pace the room. So what was the answer? That Michelle returned to England too? She was Robbie's mother, they should be together, but could they really go back to the way things had once been? Was it what either of them wanted? He thought of Ellen and his heart twisted inside him, for the idea of giving her up was suddenly as painful as knowing he had to.

An urgent knocking on the door brought an abrupt halt to his dilemma and moving swiftly across the room he went to answer it.

'Rita Ferrante,' the short, wiry woman with a stack of frizzy red hair announced.

As she entered the phone started to ring.

Michael ran back across the room and snatched it up.

'Michael! Oh, thank God,' Michelle gasped. 'I've been trying to call you for hours. I was so worried. I spoke to Tom and he said you might have gone to see Cavan.'

'I did,' Michael confirmed, shaking his head briefly at Rita to let her know it wasn't the call they were expecting.

'So what happened?' Michelle urged. 'Did they let you see him? Is he all right?'

'He's OK,' Michael lied.

'Are they going to hand him back in return for the depositions? Tom says you've got them.'

'Yes,' Michael said. 'I'm waiting for a call now to tell me where to take them, so I'll have to get off the line.'

'OK, I understand. But when this is over, Michael . . .'

'Not now,' he interrupted. 'I'll call you when there's any news,' and he rang off.

'OK?' Rita said, as he continued to stand there looking at the phone.

He nodded, then turned to look at her. 'Yes,' he said. 'Did you bring the depositions?'

She held up the envelope she was carrying. 'So let's get started on how we're going to handle this,' she said, dropping her linen jacket on a chair and sitting down cross-legged on the bed. 'We don't have a lot to go on right now, but there are a few basic rules I should familiarize you with, that could well end up saving your, and your son's, lives.'

Michael stared at her with wide, tormented eyes. 'And Cavan's?' he said.

Her eyelids dropped for an instant, then, looking at him again she said, 'Of course, Cavan's too.'

Chapter 27

The sun was disappearing fast as Tom Chambers and Carmelo Ferrante walked out on to the dusty veranda of an elegant old villa wedged into the hillside of Santa Teresa. In the shadowy room behind them Antônio, Marcelo, the ex-death squad bozo and half a dozen others were pouring over the map Marcelo and Ferrante had marked up to show the various routes they were to take to the Inferno. For the moment there was no more they could do; they were waiting on a call from Michael to tell them he was on his way to deliver the depositions.

As the warm evening air stirred the surrounding palms and the ocean glittered like burnt silver on the horizon, Ferrante began speaking to Chambers in low, casual tones. 'This isn't going to work,' he said, resting his hands on the wrought-iron balustrade and gazing out at the view.

Chambers leaned against a chalky pillar and folded his arms. The impression they were giving, should anyone inside look out, was of two men idly passing the time.

'Those guys in there are after a revenge killing,' Ferrante continued, 'which means, if we take them along, a lot of people are going to die. The hostages included.'

Chambers lowered his gaze to where a yellow

521

streetcar was trundling past below. 'Michael's thinking the same way,' he said. 'So what do we do? I don't see how we're gonna shake them now.'

Ferrante scratched his head and affected a yawn as someone came out on to the veranda behind them. 'So what's she like, this Michelle broad?' he asked.

Chambers frowned. 'What do you mean, what's she like?' he said as one of Marcelo's sidekicks planted himself a couple of feet away and began urinating over the railings into a window-box.

Ferrante shrugged. 'She good-looking or ... what's she like?' he said.

Chambers inhaled slowly as he considered his answer. 'She's as beautiful as any woman you'll ever see,' he said finally.

Ferrante's eyebrow was cocked as he looked at him. 'So you and her got something going?' he wanted to know.

'Me?' Chambers laughed incredulously.

'Why not? A good-looking guy like you ...'

'Hey, strictly solo,' Chambers cut in. 'Besides she's taken.'

Growing bored with the conversation, the slick-haired teenager, with tattoos up his arms and gold loops in his ears zipped himself up and wandered back inside.

'So what do we do?' Chambers repeated, picking up where they had left off.

'Well,' Ferrante responded, 'if their information's to be trusted – and I don't think we've got much choice but to go with it – then we're ahead on the Inferno's location, and we're pretty *au fait* with the layout of the place. So what we do is, you go back in there and tell them you just spoke to Michael on the phone – which you're gonna do the minute I finish speaking – to remind him of something that didn't occur to any one of us before now, which is there's every chance he's not

522

gonna know where he's being taken, because Pastillano will probably send a car, just like he did earlier. So we, you and me, are gonna take ourselves over there to watch the hotel and as soon as Michael and Rita hit the road we'll call these guys to give them the green light. Except of course we won't, because it's gonna be too dangerous having them around.'

Chambers was already taking out his phone and dialling the Rio Palace Hotel. Ferrante looked at him as he asked to be put through and covering the mouthpiece Chambers said, 'Let me get this straight. We *are* going over there, but as soon as Michael and Rita take off to deliver the depositions and pick up Robbie, we're heading straight for the mountains to get Cavan. Could be we're all going the same way, we'll find out when we get there.'

Ferrante nodded and picking a splinter of wood from the post beside him, began cleaning his teeth.

Chambers waited as the phone in Michael's room continued to ring. He looked at Ferrante and felt his adrenalin starting to pump. 'No reply,' he said.

Ferrante's eyes were instantly alert. 'Then something's wrong,' he said. 'They wouldn't have left without calling.'

Chambers disconnected the call and quickly dialled again.

'What are you doing?' Ferrante asked.

'Checking with Franco if he saw them leave.'

'*Sim, Seu Tom,*' Franco responded. 'He go out five minutes ago with one lady and two men. They go in big old car, like a Ford.'

Chambers thanked him, cut the call and put the phone back in his pocket while relaying the information to Ferrante.

'OK,' Ferrante replied, after taking a moment to think, 'go back in there and do like I said, then you and

I are heading straight for the mountains. We can call these guys when the party's over.'

Night was settling firmly over the city as the car that had come for Michael and Rita sped north along the Avenida Brasil towards Baixada Fluminense. The fact that they had forgotten to alert Chambers and Ferrante that they were on their way was a blunder neither could even guess the consequences to, but it had happened and there was no point fixating on it now. They just had to be thankful that they had reacted fast enough when the unexpected knock had come on the hotel room door so that Rita had taken the depositions and a loaded gun into the bathroom before Michael answered. If they hadn't, there was every chance the depositions would now be on their way to Pastillano with Michael's body lying bloodied and bullet-ridden on the hotel room floor.

The attempt at double-cross had unnerved them both, but it had also given them an advantage that they might not otherwise have had, as Rita's surprise entrance meant that she had been able to force Pastillano's emissary to drop his gun and at the same time it had enabled her and Michael to keep theirs. So now they were riding in the back of an old American car, their weapons close to hand and the depositions tucked inside Michael's shirt. The thug who had come up to the room was sitting sulkily beside the driver, in no position to make any demands of his passengers who were now calling all the shots.

They said very little, however, as they began travelling higher into the mountains and deeper into the luxuriant density of the forest. Michael was in the grip of an icy calmness that, for the moment at least, was glazing over a murderous rage at the way Pastillano had attempted to snatch the depositions and hang on to Robbie. It told him more than anything how slim their chances were of getting Robbie back and he knew now with absolute certainty that should it prove necessary he would kill Pastillano without thinking twice.

Feeling Rita's eyes on him he glanced at her briefly, then turned back to the passing darkness. With her flame-coloured hair, round, ruddy cheeks and rapidly blinking eyes, she wasn't anyone's idea of a trained killer, which was probably, Michael guessed, what had made her such a successful undercover agent. Certainly he was glad she was with him now, not only because of the way she had handled herself back at the hotel, but because he would have hated to be going into this alone.

'When we get wherever the hell we're going,' she said softly, 'I'm gonna keep this jerk who came into the hotel right here in the car. We'll have to hope he matters to Pastillano, because if he doesn't he's not going to be much use. It's a chance we'll have to take.'

Michael nodded and she continued: 'I don't see any way they're going to let you into the great man's presence armed, so don't even attempt it. Just hang on to the depositions and don't part with them until they've handed over your kid. We'll try making them bring him to the car. It could work, we don't know until we try. If you've got to go some place out of my sight, then you're on your own. It could be they'll shoot you dead the minute they get the chance, take the documents and hang on to Cavan and Robbie to make sure no copies start surfacing in places they don't want.'

Michael looked at her.

'That's the worst case scenario,' she confessed. Then, nodding towards the sullen figure in front she said, 'It all depends on him. If he's someone, it could be we're home and dry; if he's no one, we're history.'

Michael's eyes moved to the back of the man's squat, oily head.

'I know,' Rita whispered, 'he looks like a no one to me too, but let's try thinking positive.'

They'd been in the car almost an hour by the time they took an abrupt turn to the left and began winding down a steep, narrow road that offered an occasional glimpse through the trees of the glittering lights of a town below. Michael's tension started to increase, as though a sixth sense were warning him they were coming close to their destination. Rita must have sensed the same, for she picked up the gun beside her and touched it lightly to the wrinkled flesh at the base of the man's skull. He began to turn, but she prodded him harder and he gave up.

'How much longer?' she asked him.

'We there now,' he answered in a voice so dense with anger it was clear how badly he'd screwed up. Worse still, Michael thought as they approached a long, low, windowless building almost totally obscured by trees, was that he was now bringing two armed individuals on to Pastillano's territory, an eventuality Pastillano and his parasites were very probably unprepared for.

As they drew closer he noticed a waterfall cascading off to the right and felt his heart tighten. There was no doubt this was where he had been brought earlier. He turned at the recognition of another sound and saw two large garage doors at either end of the building, one of which was starting to glide open. The driver was moving towards it with the obvious intention of entering, until Rita barked at him to stop right where they were. Then, turning to Michael she glanced at his gun, indicating he should pick it up and put it to the back of the driver's neck. Michael did so and was suddenly aware of how hard his heart was beating.

'Does your friend here speak English?' she asked the man with oily hair.

He shook his head.

'Then you tell him to go inside and bring Pastillano and the boy out here,' she instructed.

'Who Pastillano?' he responded.

'Don't get smart,' she sneered, prodding him with the gun. 'Now tell him to do like I said and you and me, we're gonna wait right here. If he's not back in two minutes you'll be eating your brains? *Comprendo*?'

He turned his head slightly, presumably translated Rita's command, then watched the driver get gingerly from the car.

'Two minutes!' Rita reminded him, cocking the gun.

'*Dois minutos*!' he shouted.

The driver started to run, disappearing swiftly inside the garage, whose interior was as tenebrous as the pitch night sky.

Michael looked around at the towering black trees and tangled, impenetrable scrub. There was no movement, no sound beyond the high-pitched chafing of crickets, yet the sense of being watched was as eerie as the silent bunker before them. He looked at it, trapped in the headlights, and thought of the iniquity it housed.

'What's your name?' Rita demanded of the man in front.

No answer.

'Name,' Rita repeated, prodding him.

'Cardoza,' he answered.

'Oh, like you're the president,' she replied, smacking his head with the gun.

'Same name,' he cried. 'I got same name. Cardoza.'

'OK, Cardoza,' she said, lifting her watch into the light, 'looks like you're about to find out your value around here. And while we're waiting, you can tell us exactly where inside that summer camp over there we're gonna find this gentleman's relatives, should a search prove necessary.'

'I not know what you mean,' he answered.

'Oh, sure you do,' she replied. 'This is the Inferno, isn't it?'

'I not know what you mean, Inferno,' he said.

Rita glanced at Michael, then smashed the butt of her pistol down on Cardoza's head. 'The Inferno,' she repeated. 'You know, the place where Pastillano puts on his private shows. I expect you bring the players here for him, don't you, Cardoza? What is it you do? Break their feet? Is that your speciality? Or is it you who gets them to sit in acid, or pulls out their teeth? Maybe you get in on the rape too? Is that what lights your fire, Cardoza? Defenceless boys . . .'

'OK,' Michael broke in.

Rita looked at him, her face hard with anger.

'All we need to know is where Cavan and Robbie are likely to be,' Michael said, expecting an army of cohorts to come swarming out at any minute complete with masks, AK47s and enough ammunition to blow them all from here to life everlasting.

'Is impossible to say,' Cardozo spluttered as Rita pulled his head back and jammed the pistol under his jaw. 'Maybe they downstairs, in tank, or maybe they with the boss. Could be they not together. Is impossible to say.'

'How do you get to the tank?' Michael said.

'Through there,' Cardozo answered, pointing at the garage.

'Any other way?'

'I not know. I no think so.'

He squealed as Rita tightened her grip.

'Try harder,' she barked. 'Any other way?'

'Around back, I think. There is fire stair. Maybe there is door there, I not sure. I no remember.'

Rita was quiet for a moment, then said, 'You know what worries me about you, Cardoza, is how fast you're giving up this information. I mean, either you're a lily-livered slimeball, or there's something going down here you're not telling us about. So which is it?'

'No! No!' he cried, as she placed the flat of her hand under his nose, ready to chop it up into his skull. 'Is me. I lily-livered slimeball,' he choked.

Rita turned quickly to Michael as he nudged her, then followed his eyes to the garage. Two men were emerging, both carrying automatic pistols and neither weighing less than two hundred pounds.

As they approached, Michael's hand tightened on his own gun and as the blood began pounding through his head he heard Rita murmur, 'So, Cardoza, are you a Mr Big around here, or are you a Mr Nothing? I guess we're about to find out. Crack the window, then sit on your hands.'

Cardoza was shaking so hard he could barely move.

'The window,' she hissed, banging his head against it.

Michael's heart was in his throat. A Mr Big wouldn't be this scared. His eyes returned to the advancing figures. They were coming up on his side of the car.

'You will please come with us,' one of them said, as they reached him.

Fear cleaved through Michael's chest as he turned to Rita.

'So far so good,' she told him.

He looked at her.

'Well they didn't kill us yet, did they? Which could mean they want this sucker alive.'

Michael opened the car door and stepped out. The night was humid and airless, and alive with insect falsetto.

'I will take the gun,' he was told. 'Where are the depositions?'

'Where's my son?' Michael countered. 'The deal was, I bring the depositions, you give me my son.'

'The boy is inside. You will bring the depositions,' the man responded and turned towards the garage.

Michael stayed where he was. 'And my brother?' he demanded.

The man turned back. 'Your brother was not part of the deal.'

'Then make him a part of the deal,' Michael said.

'You are in no position to make demands. Remember, we have your son.'

Michael leaned back into the car and picked up the depositions. 'The chances are they're going to shoot me the minute I get inside,' he said to Rita. 'If they do, shoot him, then get the hell out of here.'

Rita's eyebrows were raised. 'You giving orders?' she joshed.

'For your own good,' he responded and straightened up.

The two men positioned themselves either side of him as they escorted him across to the garage, through a wide, heavy door at the back and into a large, brightly lit room where there were nothing but masked men in dark clothes, each brandishing an automatic pistol. They were standing absolutely still, feet uniformly apart, guns trained on Michael's head and heart. There was no furniture, nothing on the gnarled stone walls, nor on the white concrete floor. The room was a perfect square with no windows, two doors and nowhere to hide.

Michael looked from one concealed face to the next. There were half a dozen of them, without doubt all members of Pastillano's *grupo de extermínio*. He couldn't help wondering how many children these monsters had brutalized and killed between them, and knowing that they were very probably military policemen, so say protectors of the innocent, sickened him right through to his soul.

He waited motionlessly for someone to speak. Fear

530

thrummed in his chest and drove through his brain. His face was taut, every muscle in his body strained. The envelope containing the depositions was dangling from his right hand, his left fell loosely at his side.

A minute or more passed. Nobody moved. The only sound came from the hectic night forest, bursting in through the open door behind him. Sweat trickled from his temple and ran into his neck. Then, hearing footsteps approaching he moved his eyes to the other door.

As it opened the men in the room parted, creating a kind of aisle with Michael at one end and the man who was entering at the other. He was short, overweight, with a shining bald pate, pendulous cheeks and a pursed, fleshy mouth. His bulbous eyes glinted like newly minted coins, his hands and throat were weighted with gold.

'Mr McCann,' he said in accented English, 'you have brought the depositions I see.'

He was looking at the envelope in Michael's hand. Michael made no move. There was no doubt in his mind now that he was going to die, for the only reason Pastillano would have shown himself was because he had no intention of letting him out of there.

'Perhaps you would like to hand them over,' Pastillano suggested affably.

Michael's eyes were like steel. 'You've tried to escape your part of the bargain once already tonight,' he reminded him. 'Are you going to try again?'

Pastillano's thick black brows rose. 'Try?' he repeated in a curious drawl. 'Are you saying you are going to resist when you are surrounded by armed men?'

'What I am saying,' Michael corrected, 'is that you are a coward.'

Pastillano's eyes held steady as every gun in the room made ready to fire. 'Are you a fool, Mr McCann?' he enquired.

'Are you a murderer and a sodomite and all the other things you are accused of in these statements?' Michael replied.

Pastillano's nostrils flared. 'What you have there, Mr McCann,' he said tightly, 'is a pile of trash, false declarations made by the notorious Estrela gang whose drug activities are on the verge of being shut down by the Rio state police. They are prepared to go to any lengths to stop that happening.'

'Is that so?' Michael said sarcastically. 'Then perhaps you wouldn't mind explaining why you have abducted my son and my brother, and are holding them to ransom for these statements, if, as you say, they are false?'

'False though they are, they could still do me considerable harm,' Pastillano confessed.

'But surely a man in your position has no need to resort to kidnapping and torture in order to save his own skin,' Michael reminded him. 'Unless, of course, the charges against him are true.'

'I can assure you they are not,' Pastillano responded.

'Then you will have no problem in releasing my son and my brother,' Michael told him.

Pastillano stared at him hard, his narrowed, glinting eyes seeming to pierce right through his skull. Then, putting a hand out to one side he clicked his fingers. The door behind him was still open and Michael's insides began to solidify as a man came through carrying a small boy with a thick line of black tape across his mouth. The boy's deep-blue eyes were wide with fear as he looked around the room. As they came to rest on Michael, Michael felt his heart collapsing. Then a terrible rage suddenly seized him, almost plunging him into violence, as he struggled with the urge to annihilate every man in the room for ever laying a single hand on his son.

Pastillano was watching him closely, as though

532

waiting for the explosion until, realizing it wasn't going to come, he looked disappointed and said, 'Our arrangement was, the boy for the documents,' he reminded him and held out his hand.

Michael tore his eyes from Robbie and fixed them on Pastillano.

Pastillano smiled his encouragement. 'Come,' he said, 'the child is right here and I assure you I am a man of my word.'

Knowing he had no alternative, Michael started towards him. As he moved he felt strangely weighted, slowed by suspicion, distanced by fear. He wondered who the man was out in the car with Rita, for he surely was the only reason no one had yet opened fire. Pastillano's piercing eyes bored into his. He felt Robbie watching him and wished he could tell him it would be all right. But his throat was too tight, his senses too concentrated on what might happen at any moment.

At last he was face to face with Pastillano. Pastillano inclined his head politely and Michael passed him the envelope. The ex-army colonel slid the documents out and scanned them. Then, looking at Michael again, he said, 'Thank you, Mr McCann.'

Michael watched him and felt revulsion and terror slide through him as his smile started to widen. He heard, rather than saw, the click of fingers and before he could move a muscle a gun was pressing against his head.

Pastillano was still smiling. 'You see, Mr McCann,' he said, 'you are a fool. A fool to hand these over and a fool to think your son will be returned,' and nodding to the man holding Robbie he said, 'get him out of here.'

The man started to turn. Michael's eyes darted to him, then suddenly in one lightning move of madness and with a strength he never knew he possessed, he slammed an elbow into his captor's gut, spun round, grabbed the gun and hooking Pastillano around the neck jammed it right into his face.

It had happened so fast, and with such an insane precision and confusion of bodies, that not a single shot had been fired.

Michael glared over Pastillano's shoulder at the thwarted men. He was breathing too fast, his pulses were exploding. 'One move, any of you, and I'll blow his fucking head off,' he shouted, edging round so he had them all in his sight. He looked at the man holding Robbie. 'Put him down!' he barked.

The man didn't move.

'I said put him down!' Michael yelled and yanked Pastillano's head back so hard he heard his bones crack.

'*Ponha a criança no chão,*' Pastillano choked.

The man did as he was told, keeping his eyes fixed on Michael, as he lowered Robbie to the ground.

'Come here,' Michael said to his son, his voice roughened by adrenalin and terror.

Robbie ran to him.

'Get behind me,' Michael said, his eyes darting frantically about the room. He wished to God he knew what he was going to do now. 'You,' he said to one of the men who had brought him in, 'go back to the car and tell the woman to bring in Cardoza.'

The man looked uneasily at the others.

'Do it!' Pastillano seethed, his voice strangled by Michael's grip on his throat.

The man turned and hurried out of the room. Michael heard him running across the garage, then his muffled tread on gravel. He waited, his lungs pumping so hard he could barely keep up. Robbie was hanging on to him. He was here and alive. But where the hell was Cavan?

He looked at the others and realized they were still holding their guns. 'Drop your weapons,' he ordered.

No one moved.

534

'*I said drop them,*' he yelled in panic.

Six guns clattered to the floor.

They waited in silence until . Rita came in with Cardoza. Michael looked over at her, then gaped in horror, for the gun was on her, rather than the other way round.

'OK, let him go,' Cardoza barked, holding Rita by the hair and pressing her so hard with the gun that her head was forced to one side.

Michael stared at him.

'Did you hear what I said?' Cardoza shouted. 'Let him go or the lady here gets it.'

'You shoot her, I shoot him,' Michael responded, hardly able to believe what he was saying.

'You got to the count of three,' Cardoza warned, and from the way the others reacted Michael guessed this was some kind of signal. 'One,' Cardoza began.

Michael was confounded. He couldn't make himself think. Didn't know what to do. If he let Pastillano go they'd take Robbie, but how was he going to stand there and let them shoot Rita?

'Two.'

Michael stared at him and suddenly his eyes grew so wide that Cardoza started to look uneasy.

'Two,' he repeated forcefully.

'Three,' Carmelo Ferrante finished, as he stepped silently up behind Cardoza and planted the barrel of his gun in Cardoza's ear. 'Drop it, buster,' he said mildly.

As Cardoza's gun hit the floor, Michael continued to stare at Ferrante, still unable to believe his eyes. The timing was so unbelievable he just couldn't get a grip on it.

Then suddenly he was aware of some kind of commotion outside. Voices were shouting, guns were firing, men were running. All hell was about to break loose. Ferrante swung round, surprised; at the same instant Cardoza sprang for his gun. Rita kneed Cardoza in the face, then hit the ground herself as the first of Marcelo's gang burst into the room, guns blazing.

Without thinking, Michael shoved Pastillano into his men, scooped up Robbie and bolted for the adjoining room. Behind them bedlam broke out as gunfire echoed around the stone walls and injured men yelled out in fury and pain.

Robbie was clinging hard to his father, the tape still stuck to his mouth. Michael carried on running, moving from one stone room to the next, tripping over instruments of torture and trying not to gag on the smell. At last he reached the other garage and began fumbling frantically around the walls for some kind of mechanism to release the door. He didn't realize he was still holding the gun until someone came up behind him and spinning round, he almost fired. Rita banged the gun from his fist, then picked it up and handed it back.

'Carmelo's gone out the other way,' she told him, as they continued to search the walls. 'Here,' she cried, hitting a button, and the garage door started to open. 'Get back,' she hissed as Michael made to duck under.

Michael jerked back against the wall, waited for her to check the way, then followed her out.

'Make a run for the car,' she ordered.

'What about Cavan? We've got to find Cavan.'

'They've got him,' Rita said, dragging him behind a tree as someone ran out of the other garage into the clearing.

'Who?'

'Tom and Carmelo. They went in the back way. Now, make a run for the car.'

Grasping Robbie hard, Michael raced across the clearing and dived into the front passenger seat, just as Ferrante leapt in the driver's side.

'Where's Rita?' Ferrante demanded.

'Right here,' she answered, jumping in the back.

'Christ, there's Cavan,' Michael hissed, and passing Robbie to Ferrante, he dashed around the car to where Chambers was half-walking, half-carrying Cavan towards the car.

'We've got to get him to a hospital,' Chambers said, as Michael took Cavan's other arm.

'I'm OK,' Cavan croaked. 'Just get us the hell out of here.' Ferrante spun the car round and accelerated fast back up the track. 'They must have figured out we were planning on going without them,' he said, glancing in the rear-view mirror at Tom.

'Are you kidding? They had to have been right on our tails to have got here so fast,' Chambers responded.

'Who?' Cavan mumbled.

'Marcelo and his gang,' Chambers answered.

'They're gonna be mad,' Ferrante warned as the car leapt over a bump in the road.

Chambers winced with Cavan. 'If any of them lives through it,' he said.

'It wouldn't be wise to take any chances,' Ferrante told him. 'If I were you I'd be on the next plane out of here.'

'This boy needs a doctor,' Chambers reminded him.

Michael twisted round in his seat and gripped Cavan's hand. 'You're going to be OK,' he said firmly. 'We're going to get you some help just as fast as we can.'

'Michelle,' Cavan murmured. 'Did they ...'

'She's OK,' Michael told him. 'They released her this afternoon,' then turning back again his looked down into Robbie's big, staring eyes.

Making an attempt to wrest himself from the adrenalin pounding through his veins, he smiled and smoothed the boy's thick, dark hair. Carefully starting to peel the tape from his mouth, he tried to make himself grasp that this truly was his son, but right now

537

nothing seemed real – except perhaps the tightness in his throat and painful sting in his eyes. Then he grabbed for the dash as the car jack-knifed out on to the main road.

When the tape was off Robbie turned his face sharply into his father's shoulder. Michael hugged him hard and felt new and overpowering emotions flow copiously into his heart.

It was just after midnight when Michelle heard the outside bell ringing. Riddled with nerves as she was, she had to force herself to pick up the entryphone. The instant she heard Michael's voice she dropped the phone and raced across the courtyard to open the door. What she saw at first confused her, for there were people with him she didn't recognize and everyone seemed to be talking at once. Then, seeing a sleeping Robbie in Michael's arms, she cried out and stumbled forward to take him.

'Oh my God, my God,' she breathed, cradling him to her as he murmured drowsily. 'Where did you find him? How did you . . . ?'

'Michelle, please tell this man here who we are,' Michael interrupted.

Michelle looked up and recognized the man he was referring to as the one assigned to watch over her. The other two people she didn't know.

'This is my son,' she told the man. 'And this is his father. And these people here . . .' She looked helplessly at Michael.

'Are friends,' Michael supplied. 'Carmelo and Rita Ferrante. You can check them out with the US Embassy. Now, can we go inside?'

'It's been a busy night,' Rita said, putting a hand on his shoulder. 'We're going to head off home.'

Michael turned to look at her, then, hugging her he said, 'I don't know how to thank you.'

'You just did,' she told him and smiled at Michelle's bemusement.

'Will I see you again?' he asked, shaking hands with Carmelo.

'Could be,' Carmelo grinned, 'if you're unlucky.'

Michael smiled and looking up at the sky he said, 'I don't know that any of this has really sunk in. I mean, it's probably no big deal for you, but for us . . .'

'Believe me, it's a big deal,' Carmelo told him, 'and you're probably going to have some kind of delayed reaction, so prepare yourself and don't be too hard on yourself either. Not many men could have done what you did tonight and don't you forget it.'

'Would somebody mind . . .' Michelle began.

Carmelo put up a hand. 'Just give me a minute,' he said and sliding an arm about Michael's shoulders he walked him a few paces down the street. 'I don't want you to worry about this unduly,' he said quietly, 'but keep in mind that if Marcelo and his gang get out of there tonight there's every chance they're going to come looking for me and Tom. It could be their search will lead them here, so be on the look-out and call me if you need to. You've got my number?'

Michael nodded.

'Just get on a plane out of here as soon as you can,' Carmelo advised, as they turned back towards the apartment. 'They'll probably only keep Cavan in overnight, but if they want him any longer, leave him with Tom and get your boy home where he belongs.' They looked up to find Rita, Michelle and the British security agent all watching them. 'OK, Rita?' Carmelo said. 'Ready to hit the road?'

'I'll drive,' she said, catching the keys as he threw them in the air.

'I don't understand,' Michelle said as the Ferrantes got into the car and drove away. 'Who are they? What's been going on?'

Michael looked down at her pale, anxious face and Robbie's peacefully sleeping one, and felt suddenly so tired that all he wanted was to lie down with them and hold them for ever. But that wasn't going to happen, so slipping an arm around her he said, 'They're ex-federal agents who helped Tom and me get Cavan and Robbie back from Pastillano tonight.'

Michelle's eyes widened with horror and confusion. 'You mean ... ? Are you telling me Robbie ... ?'

'He's OK,' Michael assured her. 'Come on, let's go inside.'

'But how did they get him?' Michelle cried, as he closed the door behind them. 'I thought he was safe. You told me ...'

'When I spoke to you he was,' Michael cut in. 'But somehow Pastillano found out about him and managed to snatch him this afternoon. But we've got him back now and I've just had him checked over at the hospital and he's fine. Nothing happened to him, at least nothing physical. Cavan they're keeping for a while.'

'But how did they get Robbie?' she shouted. 'How? He was supposed ...'

'I don't know how they got him,' Michael answered through his teeth.

'But ...'

'Michelle, he's here, he's in one piece, now don't force me to say things we're both going to end up regretting.'

Her eyes flashed with fury. 'I see,' she seethed, 'so it's my fault, is it?'

'You said it,' he responded tightly, and taking Robbie from her, he carried him into the sitting-room and laid him down on the sofa.

Following him, Michelle went to sit on the floor beside her son and began stroking his hair. She took several moments to get herself back in control, then quietly said, 'What happened to Cavan?'

Michael was standing at the window, his heart so bound up with emotion he barely heard her.

Michelle turned round. 'What did they do to him?' she said.

Keeping his back turned, Michael said, 'He's got a broken arm, a couple of cracked ribs and some internal injuries.' He tensed as he thought of how Cavan had come by the injuries, but there was no need for Michelle to know about that – finding out Robbie had been taken was enough for her to deal with right now.

'Which hospital is he in?' she asked. 'Can we go there? Will they let us see him?'

'Tom Chambers is with him,' Michael told her. 'And no, we can't go there, at least not tonight. But he's going to be OK.'

Michelle turned back to Robbie. 'We have to be out of the country by midday tomorrow,' she said, gazing down at his sleep-flushed cheeks and thickly curling black lashes. He was such a perfect mix of her and Michael that it was sometimes hard to look at him and not feel the way she was feeling now – so full of love that it was binding her up in fear.

It was a while before she realized Michael hadn't spoken, so turning she looked up to find him staring down at her and Robbie. Her heart somersaulted at the look in his eyes and for a moment she found she couldn't speak either.

Becoming aware of the sudden intimacy, Michael started looking about the room.

'They searched it,' she said, explaining the mess. 'I've been trying to put it back together.'

He nodded, looked at her briefly again, then went to sit in a torn armchair. 'Do you have any Scotch?' he asked.

'If they didn't smash it,' she said, getting to her feet.

Going downstairs to the kitchen, she began searching for the bottle. She felt so nervous and afraid of what he

541

was going to say that her movements were jerky and her own words, when she spoke, felt as though they were falling from her lips in random, broken sentences that had no meaning until they were said. She wished desperately she could make herself think of what she really wanted to say, but she was so shaken by the enormity of all that had happened, so overwhelmed by the shock of him being there and the feelings he had rekindled deep down inside her, that her mind just wouldn't function.

Finding an undamaged bottle of brandy, she poured some into one of the children's plastic cups and carried it back to the sitting-room. When she reached the doorway her heart rose to her throat as she saw Michael was asleep in the chair.

Setting the brandy aside, she went to sit with Robbie, pulling him on to her lap as he started to wake up. 'Hello, sweetheart,' she said softly, as his eyes flickered open.

He rubbed his face, then turned it into her shoulder.

She smiled and swallowing the lump in her throat, waited to see if he would settle. A minute or so later he turned his head back and looked across to Michael.

'Do you know who that is?' Michelle whispered.

His lovely blue eyes came back to hers.

She nodded slowly. 'It's your daddy,' she said.

He looked at Michael again and Michelle's smile was twisted by the effort to hold back her tears. 'I told you he would come, didn't I?' she said.

Robbie continued to stare until finally, tired and still not too sure he was awake, he turned to Michelle and buried his face in her neck.

Hugging him to her, she rocked him gently back and forth until he had fallen asleep again. Then looking over at Michael she saw that his eyes were open.

'There was only brandy,' she told him. 'I put it over there, on the window-sill.'

Wiping a hand over his face, he got to his feet and walked over to the window. The sea outside was like ink, streaked with moonlight. He stood looking at it for some time, lulled by the rhythmic lapping of the waves, then, picking up the brandy he took a generous mouthful and relished the burn as it stole a path through his chest. He could feel Michelle watching him, but didn't turn round. This was hard, so damned hard he didn't know where to begin, but he knew she was waiting and knew too that she was every bit as afraid as he was.

At last he turned to face her and watched as she laid Robbie down again, then came to stand beside him. He passed her the brandy, waited while she drank, then walking away from her he said, 'I don't think now's the time to have this conversation. Too much has happened, we're still too shaken up and it wouldn't be fair to decide who's going to have him while we're feeling like this.'

Michelle's eyes were holding fast to his and he could see, almost feel, her pain. 'Is that how it's going to be?' she said softly. 'One or other of us must have him? Not both?'

Unprepared for that, Michael looked away. He had no idea how he wanted to answer the question, so avoiding it he said, 'He loves you, I'm aware of that. And he doesn't know me.'

'No,' she responded. 'But he needs you.'

Michael's eyes came back to hers. 'I don't want to hurt you,' he said, 'but I don't want him living this kind of life.'

There was a long and painful silence before finally she said, 'I think you should know, Cavan and I . . .'

Michael nodded. He hadn't known it for certain, but he realized now that subconsciously he had guessed it. He wondered how he felt about it, but for the moment there was nothing. 'Do you love him?' he asked.

She took a moment to think, then said, 'He's not you.'

His surprise showed. 'Did you think he would be?' he said.

She shrugged. 'I don't know. At first, yes, I suppose I did.'

'And now?'

'And now he's Cavan.'

She could see how taut his face was and could feel her own tension building as she tried to force herself to voice what was really in her heart. 'Robbie knows all about you,' she said instead. 'I show him pictures and tell him stories.' She laughed drily. 'He's really going to think you're his hero now, after this.'

Michael's expression showed only a flicker of humour.

Her eyes fell away, then looking at him again she heard herself speaking the words she most dreaded saying. 'Can I come back?' she whispered, her heart suddenly thudding so hard it hurt. Then she wanted only to die as he looked at her and allowed a terrible silence to pass.

Slowly he started to shake his head. 'I don't know,' he answered.

'Would you be willing to try? For Robbie?' she pleaded.

'I think, before I answer that,' he said, 'we should decide whether it's really for Robbie we'll be trying, or whether it's for ourselves.'

As his words registered in her heart her eyes began to shine with hope. 'Either way,' she said, 'don't you think it's time we were together, as a family?'

He smiled wryly. 'I always thought that,' he reminded her. 'It was only you who had other ideas.'

Chapter 28

After reading every last word of the article, Ellen put down the newspaper, picked up her coffee and walked on to her office. She was aware of the others watching her and wished now that she hadn't humiliated herself like that, by stopping in full view of everyone to read the latest news on the man they all knew she was in love with.

He was back with Michelle now, they had returned to London and were living as a family in Michael's Battersea apartment. According to the papers he was with the woman he had always loved, and the son they had created together and were now going to raise together. They had been turned into such a great love story, on both sides of the Atlantic, that it seemed the press just couldn't get enough of them. Nor of Robbie, who was a handsome little boy, looked just like his father and seemed to enjoy all the attention they were receiving.

Robbie's existence had explained so much, like Michael's reluctance to come to LA, his inability to commit to a relationship, his real reason for not wanting Ellen to go to London. He'd been waiting, hoping all this time that one day Michelle would return and bring their son with her.

And now she had, and in every picture Ellen had seen of them Michael seemed happy and relaxed, and

Michelle was every bit as beautiful as Ellen had imagined her to be. They looked so good together, the three of them, such a perfect little family, so how could she possibly wish him estranged from them any longer and still with her?

She didn't wish that. What she wished was that it didn't hurt so much, or that she could stop herself longing for him to call, when she knew he wouldn't. What reason would there be for him to? She'd ended the relationship while they were in Barbados. He owed her nothing. So she had to start working on putting them out of her mind and move past this before it tore her apart completely.

Pushing open the door to her office, she set her coffee down on the desk and leaned over to turn on her computer. Today was her last at ATI and she would rather die then let Ted Forgon know how much she was hurting. In truth, it would be much easier to withdraw her notice and stay in the protective sphere of the agency, for the thought of going it alone out there was so much more daunting now she was feeling like this. But she wasn't going to allow herself to do that. She wasn't a coward. She could find the strength to go ahead with her plans, so that was what she was going to do.

She just hoped that the reason Ted Forgon had summoned her to his office at the end of the day wasn't to gloat, or to treat her to his unique style of persuasion to get her to stay, because if it was, she was going to take great pleasure in slamming her fist right in his face, for she'd had enough public exposure these last few weeks to last her a lifetime – and it it if it weren't for Forgon and his ludicrous ego she would never have met Michael McCann in the first place.

Ted Forgon hadn't been in such a good mood since he'd made his first million. Or maybe it was since he got his first blow job. He couldn't really remember, both were so long ago, but there was no doubt that no ensuing millions, or blow jobs, had given him the same blood-rushing kick as the first. With the probable exception of those going down right now, for the deal he currently had cooking was bigger than any other he'd ever pulled off and the blow job in motion was like no other he could remember. She was sensational. In fact, she was so out-of-this-world sensational, he might just have to marry her to make sure no other sonofabitch got a piece of the action.

'Sure I heard about it,' he was saying into the phone as Kerry Jo's collagened lips worked his erection, 'it was on the Channel 9 news last night.' He looked up as the mail boy knocked and put his head round the half open door, indicating he had a package. Forgon waved him in and gestured for him to wait 'til he'd finished his call. Hidden beneath the desk, Kerry Jo didn't even pause in her task. 'What do you mean I don't sound very interested?' he said into the phone. 'I know we're talking about Michael McCann, but things change, Manny, life moves on. OK, so you win the bet – I didn't get him to come to Hollywood so I owe you a couple hundred bucks. OK, a couple thousand, who's counting? Did you get the script for Lucas's next movie? Sure, I'm changing the subject.' He slipped a hand under the desk and pressed down on Kerry Jo's head as a ball-breaking climax started to brink. 'I got to go now, Manny,' he said. 'I'll catch you later, OK? Where? Oh yeah, the Willises'. Sure, I'll be there,' and putting the receiver down he smiled at the mail boy.

'This package just came in from Warners,' the boy said, putting it on the desk. 'It says urgent, so I brought it right up.'

'You did good,' Forgon assured him, knowing he was going to lose it any second. 'Thanks, you can go now. Close the door on your way out.'

The boy left and Forgon fell back in his chair, grunting and puffing and starting to buck like a bronco. It went on – and on and on – until finally, after taking him to never-never land and dropping him there, Kerry Jo's mussed blonde head came up from under the desk.

'Well, we sure got a tune out of you today, honey pie,' she grinned, her baby blue eyes twinkling with laughter, her luscious ruby lips shining and wet. 'Now, did I hear something about a party at the Willises' tonight?'

Too spent to speak, Forgon watched her get to her feet and not for the first time wished he were a younger or fitter man, for what he didn't want to do to that body wouldn't be worth doing anyways. She was magnificent, standing there in her little white thong and four-inch high-heeled shoes, legs as long as Sigourney's, ass tighter than a fist and tits that made Pammie's look like po'boys. The surgery had cost him a fortune, but boy had it been worth it, and what the hell did he care that half the town was laughing at his fixation with an eighteen-year-old beauty queen from Texas, they weren't getting what he was getting, so let the suckers laugh.

'Now, honey, you know you should give me some warning about these things,' she chided, perching on the arm of his chair and twiddling his hair with her fingers. Her left nipple was right there, all big and juicy and just dying for attention, but he still wasn't recovered enough to try. 'It's not leaving me much time to go out and buy myself a new dress, now is it?' she pouted, leaning over to kiss the top of his head and squashing her breast in his face. 'So it looks like those itsy-bitsy little letters you wanted me to send out today are just gonna have to wait 'til tomorrow,' and giving his hair a playful little ruffle, she got up and walked over to the twin couches where she had left her microscopic miniskirt and lycra crop top.

'Now, would you be wanting me to go for a red dress or a white dress?' she said, dancing her skirt up over her thighs. 'I know those are your favourite colours ... Oh, look at you, honey, zip yourself up now, you got Ellen Shelby coming in any minute and you don't want her to see you like that, now do you?'

'No,' Forgon grunted, at last finding the strength to pull himself forward and sit up straight. 'Get a white dress,' he told her, 'and get them to charge it to me.'

She giggled. 'Oh you,' she cried, 'of course they're gonna charge it to you, you don't think I can afford Rodeo Drive on my little pittance of a salary, do you?' She pulled the top over her head, tugged it down over her breasts, then, fluffing out her hair she wiggled back towards him. 'OK, now let's take a look at you. Shirt all tucked in, zipper right up. Good boy. My, you're looking handsome today. Did I ever tell you what a looker you are?' She kissed him tenderly on the head. 'Now, what about those diamonds we saw the other day?' she murmured throatily. 'They'll go real well with the dress I've got in mind, shall I stop by Van Cleef's and pick them up?'

Forgon didn't even flinch. 'You do that,' he told her and putting a hand on her bottom, he turned her round and guided her over to the door. 'Now scoot,' he said. 'And be back at the house by seven. The party starts at eight. Oh, before you go, have someone come up from downstairs to sort out those letters.'

She saluted. 'Yes sir, anything you say, sir,' and pulling open the door she treated him to her best majorette strut over to her desk.

Smiling, Forgon turned back, muttering to himself that there was no fool like an old fool, while adoring her even more for reminding him what it was like to be in love. The last time had been with his wife, and she had gone to her maker more than twenty years ago now. They'd had a boy, just a couple of years after they got married, but he'd died too, before he reached six, and his wife had never wanted any more after that. He wondered how Kerry Jo would take to motherhood and reckoned, being the warm-hearted, flexible kind of girl she was, she'd take to it just fine.

As he sat back down he was thinking about McCann and the kid he'd just rescued in Rio. Must have been a tough call for him, that, wondering if the boy was going to make it. But there were just as tough times to come, because having a kid changed a person's life. Forgon grimaced as he thought about the little boy who had been dead for so long now that were it not for the sadness that stole up on him at times, he might have been just a dream. Then he started to grin as his mind returned to McCann, and after a while his grin became a chuckle and by the time Ellen knocked on the door he was writing a cheque for Manny and laughing out loud.

Ellen had assumed, because the door was closed and there was no sign of Kerry Jo, that Forgon's secretary would be in his office with him, but to her surprise, when he called out for her to come in she found him alone and in obviously high spirits.

'Ellen,' he cried, putting down his pen and getting up from his chair. 'Come in, come in. Can I fix you a drink? Martini? Marguerita? I make a mean Marguerita.'

'I'll take a soda,' she answered, watching him as he strode jauntily to the bar and started taking down bottles. He'd been doing well in the absurdity department lately, but today, in a Calvin Klein T-shirt, black leather pants and white stacked-heel shoes, he was excelling himself. Best of all, though, was the hair, which had undergone a serious henna job a couple of weeks back and was currently looking like a hedgehog on downers. Everyone knew that the new image was

Kerry Jo's handiwork and Ellen had to confess she was among those who couldn't help laughing at how ridiculous he was making himself. But he wasn't the only geriatric in Hollywood making that last desperate grab at youth, nor would he be the first to screw himself into an early grave as a result of it.

'So how are you doing?' Forgon asked, filling her glass from a shaker and spearing an olive with a cocktail stick. 'You all set to go, or did you come up here to tell me you changed your mind?'

Ellen's smile was remote as she took the Martini she hadn't asked for.

'I got to tell you it would make my day if you said you were staying,' he told her, spooning crushed ice into another glass and covering it with bourbon. 'You know I always had big plans for you. I wanted to get you right up here to this office, one of the most powerful in Hollywood.'

He looked so chuffed with himself Ellen almost laughed. Instead, she sat down on one of the sofas and took a sip of her drink. 'Don't think I'm not grateful,' she told him. 'It's just that I have other plans and they don't include staying an agent.'

'I know, I know,' he said, coming to sit opposite her, 'I just want to make sure you know you can stay. And if you want to come back, your job's always here.'

Ellen looked at him, trying to keep the suspicion from her eyes and wondering if it was love making him this agreeable, or if the hidden agenda was about to leap out and smack her in the face. For the moment she protected herself with a simple, 'Thank you.'

'You lost weight?' he asked bluntly, sipping his bourbon.

Ellen nodded.

'It doesn't suit you. Put it back on.'

Ellen's eyes dropped, as a sudden pain clawed at her heart, but bringing them quickly back to his she said, 'I doubt you asked me to come up here to discuss my weight.'

He nodded. 'You're right, I didn't. What I want is to persuade you to stay.' His hand went up as she started to object. 'It's OK, I know I'm not going to succeed, so I've accepted it, but I can't come to the party tonight and I wanted the chance to say goodbye and to give you something to take with you. It's valuable and it'll stand you in good stead for a long time to come.'

Ellen's surprise and embarrassment showed, which seemed to please him, though there was no sign of a gift or anything she could actually thank him for, and as he appeared to be waiting for something she gave a self-conscious shrug of her shoulders and said, 'I don't know what to say.'

'You don't have to say anything,' he told her. 'All you have to do is listen,' and sitting forward he set his drink on the table and resting his elbows on his knees, looked her directly in the eye. 'It's a big, tough world out there, as you're very well aware,' he said, 'and believe me it's not as easy getting started on your own as you might think. OK, you got a lot of contacts and you got yourself a reputation most women your age and in your position would kill for. People are going to be falling over themselves to work with you, Ellen, I expect they already are, but there are a lot of flakes out there, people who could do you a whole lot more harm than you know until it's too late. So I want you to remember where I am and know that my door is always open. I haven't got to where I am today without learning a thing or two, and I know this town. What's more, the greatest difference between me and you right now is that I know how to play the game and you're just learning. It's mean, it's tough, it draws blood and God knows it breaks hearts. But take it from me, making it in Hollywood is better than making it anywhere else in the god-damned world, because there is no place else like it and because it's so damned hard. And now, the best piece of advice I can give you is make damned sure you don't get yourself into any more fixes like the one you got into with Clay Ingall, because there'll always be someone out there, like me, who's looking for something on you they can use to their advantage. It's how this town operates and the quicker you get used to that the easier you're gonna find it. It's not nice, but it's a fact.'

He picked up his drink, then, walking over to his desk he opened a top drawer and took out an envelope. 'These here,' he said, coming back, 'are the remaining photographs and negatives of you and Ingall. Do what you want with them, just know that they're no longer in the hands of someone who can do you some harm. It was a tough lesson for you to learn and I want you to know that if I'd found it necessary I would have got them published. That's the kind of guy I am.'

Ellen looked at the envelope as he laid it on the table, then, not even attempting to hide her confusion she looked across at him and said, 'I don't understand why you're doing this. I mean, I'm grateful, but this is such a one eighty . . .' She shook her head, not sure how to continue.

'You've been through a tough time lately,' he said frankly. 'I don't see any reason to make it any tougher.'

Ellen swallowed hard, angry now that he was touching on her private pain. 'Do I take it you've given up on the idea of Michael coming to work for you?' she asked in a tone designed to show him she had no problem mentioning Michael's name, even if he did.

He laughed. 'I confess when you two started to get serious I thought there was a chance I might win,' he said. 'But now there's a kid . . .' He was shaking his head and looking absently into space. 'Just isn't any way he's going to up sticks now.' His eyes refocused on hers. 'Would you have gone to London if there wasn't this other woman?'

'No,' Ellen answered. Then, seeing the way Forgon was looking at her she realized that despite her efforts to hide it he knew how much she was hurting.

'You'll get over it,' he told her. 'It just takes time.'

Ellen's jaw tightened. If one more person told her that, she was likely to turn violent. After all, she was hardly weeping about the place, was she? She hadn't even discussed it with anyone but Matty, so what right did people have to assume that she was falling apart when she'd never said or done anything to make them think that? She was getting on with her life. She had things in place now, projects in hand; and very soon she was going to be too busy even to think about Michael McCann. Better still would be when the press finally got off her case, because as much as Michael and Michelle were receiving in England, she was receiving in the US. *The Gossip Show*, *Entertainment Tonight*, *Access Hollywood* and the myriad magazines focused on the industry were just lapping up her heartbreak, and leaping out of practically every doorway she passed to try and capture her distress. After all, they couldn't do anything about Michelle Rowe when no one in the US knew who she was, but most had heard of Ellen Shelby, agent to the stars and Hollywood leading light. So there it was, her own fame, such as it was, being held up to the world as a mirror to her pain, reflecting it out there to the public who then commented on it, analysed it, took it to pieces and even ridiculed it as though it had no living, feeling person behind it. It was why, once the party was over tonight, she was flying home to her parents, for it was hard enough trying to deal with this, without the press revelling in it the way they were.

'How long are you staying with your folks?' Forgon asked, as though reading her mind.

'Two, maybe three weeks,' she answered.

554

'It's always a good idea to take a break between jobs,' he commented. 'Gives you time to slough off the old skin and start toughening up the new one. Matty going with you?'

Ellen shook her head. 'Will you keep her at ATI?' she asked. 'Rosa said she'd take her on.'

Forgon shrugged. 'OK by me,' he said. 'What about the rest of your list? You've spoken to them all, I take it?'

'Yes. It's all sorted.'

Forgon nodded and glanced at his watch. 'So I guess that's it then,' he said, getting to his feet. 'Good luck with everything and don't lose too much sleep over McCann; his life's changing in ways he never even dreamt about, so he sure won't be losing any sleep over you.'

As his cruelty hit home, Ellen raised her eyes to his and, doing nothing to disguise her contempt she said, 'You really are a callous bastard, aren't you?'

His eyebrows flickered. 'And don't you forget it,' he advised and pulling open the door he stood to one side as she left.

She was still going over the end of their meeting as she showered and dressed for her party later. Something about it was bothering her and she couldn't quite put her finger on what. For sure, it was out of character for Forgon to show as much kindness as he had, though blowing it all apart the way he had at the end was vintage Ted. No, it wasn't his sudden morphing into a guardian angel that was particularly unnerving her, odd though it was, it was more the manner in which he had told her not to forget what a callous bastard he could be. It had sounded like a warning. And coming right after his assertion that Michael's life was changing in ways he'd never even dreamt about she couldn't help wondering if the warning was for him, rather than for her.

Except everything came back to Michael in the end and it would be just like her to create an issue where there was none, just so's she'd have an excuse to call him – or to give herself some vain and pathetic hope that Forgon might one day succeed in getting him to come to LA.

It was so torturous and cruel, the way her heart wouldn't let her give up, even though she knew they could never work out now, even if he were to come to LA. Michelle and their son would come with him – and that was something she really wouldn't be able to bear. But to see him, or just to hear him was a longing she couldn't get out of her mind. It was why, in truth, she had to get away, because despite all her efforts to convince herself and the world she was coping, she was in fact a very, very long way from it.

As far as Sandy was concerned there was only one aspect of Michael's and Michelle's reunion that was bearable and that was what it was undoubtedly doing to Ellen. And in truth she wasn't even sure about that, for knowing that Ellen's suffering was very probably greater than hers – and more justified – made her feel somehow diminished and cheated, and more resentful than ever at being upstaged by the American yet again.

At least Michelle had been on the scene before, which in its way gave her a prior right to Michael, especially now everyone knew they had a son, whereas Ellen had just stolen in and snatched him right from under Sandy's nose. So whatever heartache Ellen Shelby was enduring she damned well deserved. And as far as Michelle was concerned Sandy just couldn't see it working out, not when so much time had gone by and when Michael could never trust her not to go running off on her errands of mercy again. So there was just no way Sandy was giving up hope, for by the time it fell apart with Michelle, Ellen would very likely be involved with someone else and she, Sandy, would be running the London end of World Wide, the company into which Michael had sunk virtually all of McCann Walsh's profits and a good proportion of his personal wealth too.

He must know by now that she had bought into World Wide, though she wondered if he had any idea who had backed her. He wasn't going to be pleased about that, but at least it would show him how determined and worthy a partner she could be. Of course he was going to need some time to get over the shock, which was no doubt why she hadn't heard from him yet, and she had to confess she was nervous about what he was going to say when she did. His anger was going to hurt her, she knew that already, but she had to make herself see past it and remember that ultimately, what she had done was going to give them both all the rewards they had ever dreamed of.

Maurice had explained to her just a couple of weeks ago that McCann Walsh could no longer function the way it was, too many of its assets were invested in World Wide and the controlling share of World Wide now belonged to Ted Forgon. As payment for the information she had given him, Forgon had promised her the senior position in London, which meant that Michael, when he resurfaced from domesticity, was going to find himself, on the World Wide front at least, working for her. Naturally, she would allow him to make most of the decisions, as his experience was far greater than hers, and she was going to be at pains to let him know that would be the case. She didn't want there to be any antagonism, she simply wanted him to know that she loved him enough to hand back all that she had taken.

'In exchange for what?' Nesta had asked on one of the many occasions the two of them had sat discussing it long into the night. 'His hand in marriage?' She scoffed. 'You can't buy people like that, Sandy.'

'I'm not buying him, I'm just showing him how much I'm prepared to give him,' Sandy protested. 'On condition.'

Nesta rolled her eyes. 'Well, I suppose condition's a better word than blackmail,' she said. 'So what is this condition?'

Sandy coloured. 'That we become partners, of course.'

'So I was right. His hand in marriage.'

'In case you've forgotten, I'm in love with him, Nesta . . .'

'Bullshit,' Nesta cut in. 'You're no more in love with him than I am, and if you ask me you never were. He was just the first man you met when you came to London who was rich and powerful and good-looking enough to turn every other woman's head. You wanted him because you thought it would turn you into a somebody, because you had no confidence in yourself, no self-esteem or self-respect. You assumed, because he's the kind of man he is, that he could change all that. You never seemed to understand that it had to come from you, not from someone else. Yet you did it anyway. You've got your own business, you're successful in your own right, you've pulled off a major deal with Ted Forgon and Mark Bergin and you've stitched up Michael good and proper. You did all that yourself. OK, with some help from me and a lot from Maurice, but you're the one who runs the show, you're the real brains behind it, the one with a gift for recognizing talent and utilizing assets, and you're the one who's getting written up all over the place as the hottest thing since toast. We've got nearly two thirds of our acting list out there working and half the writers. Harry's producers and directors have hardly stopped and the drive, the energy, the guts it took to get the team together in the first place all came from you. You're incredible, do you know that? You go out there and give a performance that's got the whole world convinced you're going to be bigger than Salinger, yet here, behind the scenes, you act like a kid. So why not do yourself a favour and start facing up to the fact that not only are you never going to get Michael McCann, you damn well don't want him anyway. What's more you don't even *need* him. You've done it. You're out there, you're one of the tall poppies now.'

'Tall poppies get their heads lopped off,' Sandy reminded her.

'Well, you know what I mean,' Nesta responded. 'You're so far away from that pathetic creature I found weeping in a Barking bedsit, you've grown so much since then and so bloody fast it's frightening. But emotionally, Sandy, you're so immature I swear you're going backwards. Now for God's sake, put an end to this crush, or whatever you want to call it, and find someone who's right for you, who's really going to love you and appreciate you for the woman you are. And you're in there somewhere, I know it. You just keep hiding behind that star-struck kid who, by the miracles of fate and a rich man's infatuation, managed to take away the best part of Michael McCann's livelihood and is now trying to force him to live with her in order to get it back. Well, take it from me, Sandy, it's not going to work – on that basis it doesn't even stand a chance.'

Ever since that night Sandy had tried to put Nesta's words out of her mind, but they just kept coming back. It wasn't that she thought Nesta was right, but she had to concede that maybe she had a point. In fact, Michael probably hated her for what she had done and she could hardly blame him for that, when the last thing he needed, now he had a family to get used to, was to be trying to sort out the mess she had created.

559

Chapter 29

Zelda was standing on the balcony of Michael's apartment, idly watching the river flow by and listening to the late evening bird-song. The air was freshened by the invigorating scent of early summer and the music drifting from the hi-fi was suitably dreamy and filled with nostalgia. Closing her eyes, she let the rhythm steal over her, until the telephone sliced into the moment and hearing Michael go to answer it she turned to gaze downriver to Chelsea Harbour and the McCann Walsh offices.

'Sorry about that,' Michael said, joining her a few minutes later with two large gin and tonics. 'It was Michelle calling to say good-night to Robbie.'

Zelda smiled and took her drink. 'Did you wake him?' she asked.

Michael shook his head. 'He's had a busy day over at Colleen's with his cousins. He's shattered.'

'And Michelle? Where's she?'

Michael waggled his eyebrows in a teasing fashion, then, taking a sip of his drink he said, 'Michelle is at her sister's, in Wales.'

Zelda screwed up her nose. 'Wales?' she repeated, turning to follow him inside. 'I thought her sister lived in Spain.'

'That's the other sister,' Michael reminded her. 'There are three of them.'

Zelda nodded and sank into one of the sumptuous leather sofas. Evidence of Robbie was everywhere now, from the scattered toys over in his play area to the newly framed photographs on shelves and tables and all the childish drawings decorating the fridge. He'd shown her his bedroom himself, just after he and Daddy had finished doing it up together. He was so proud of it, with its Thomas the Tank Engine bunk beds, Winnie the Pooh and Power Rangers posters; his garage, his train set, his pedal car and big, shiny blue bike with stabilizers that he had assured Zelda he wasn't going to need for very long. He had so many toys and books and puzzles and games that like a child at Christmas he hadn't known which to play with first.

Though grateful for the incredible generosity of family, friends and even strangers, Michael and Michelle had tried hard to keep most of the gifts back, not wanting to overwhelm him, or to encourage him to become blasé, but as he was continually being asked what he thought of this action man or that drum set, they had given in and decided to let him be spoiled for a while.

Actually, Zelda reflected, he had settled in so well it was already becoming hard to remember a time when he wasn't there and she only had to look at Michael to see what a difference the child had made to his father's life. Gone was the guilt that had tormented him since the day Michelle left, gone too was the tension that had stolen a light from his eyes and an ease from his manner, which had been so much a part of him before. The real Michael was back, the man she had known and loved, laughed with, played with, taken risks with and triumphed with. His old energy was restored and it was so plain to see how much he was enjoying life now, and the pleasure he took in his son was so moving, that Zelda couldn't have been happier were it happening to her.

'What are you smiling at?' Michael asked, lifting his feet on to the coffee table between them.

'You,' she answered, 'and how relaxed you look these days, which, considering the unholy mess the agency is in, is no mean feat.'

Michael's eyes narrowed humorously, but instead of answering, he merely took another sip of his drink.

Zelda waited, certain he would pick up the baton any minute, but he didn't, so leaving him to get to it in his own time, she returned to the subject of his personal life, which he seemed more willing to discuss. 'How come Michelle didn't take Robbie to her sister's?' she asked. 'I'd have thought his aunt was longing to meet him.'

'She met him a couple of weeks ago, here in London,' Michael answered. He paused for a moment, then added, 'And Michelle thought it would be a good idea for Robbie and me to have some time without her.'

Zelda's eyebrows rose. 'Oh?' she said. 'Do I take it from that things aren't going too well, or is it just a bit of male bonding you're up to?'

Michael chuckled. 'Actually, both,' he replied.

Zelda pursed her lips and looked at him with her shrewd grey eyes.

'Cavan's gone to Wales with her,' Michael said.

'Oh, I see,' Zelda responded. 'Or do I?'

Michael grinned. 'I think you do,' he told her. 'That is, inasmuch as any of us see anything right now. I guess the easiest way to sum it up, though, is that Michelle is going through a bit of a rough time trying to decide between me and Cavan.'

Zelda's surprise was genuine. 'But I thought . . .' she began.

'That we had it all sorted out,' Michael supplied. 'So did I. So did she, until we started living together and it hasn't taken very long for us to discover that maybe we haven't made the right decision. At least not for us.'

'Och, dear,' Zelda muttered. 'And we all thought . . .' Her eyes returned to Michael's. 'Has she left you?' she said.

Michael laughed. 'I don't know that I'd put it quite like that,' he answered.

'But she's gone to Wales with Cavan. Does she still love him?' ·

Michael shrugged. 'I'm not sure even Michelle knows the answer to that,' he replied, 'which is why they're spending this time together. They'll stay a couple of days with Marianne, Michelle's sister, then they're taking a cottage somewhere, I believe. Actually, I should tell you at this point that having experienced first hand the kind of torture and abuse going on in the world, Cavan's now hell bent on getting back out there to bring down as many Pedro Pastillanos as he can. Needless to say, this holds great appeal for Michelle.'

Zelda was regarding him closely, searching for any signs of how he might feel about that, but the humour in his eyes was impossible to get past. 'I've got to say you seem very relaxed about it all,' she said suspiciously.

Michael nodded and sucked in his bottom lip, as though considering her remark. 'To a certain degree I am,' he said eventually, 'but that's only because the problem is less mine than Michelle's.'

Zelda waited for him to continue, knowing that at last she was about to learn the real reason he had invited her over tonight.

'So she tells me,' Michael said, cupping his drink in his lap and gazing absently out at the twilight, 'she had a sudden blinding revelation when we were in Rio that she had to come back to me, that it was all she wanted and that though she loved Cavan, it wasn't in the same way she loved me. She wanted us to be together as a family, me, her and Robbie, and she wanted, if I were willing, for us to try to love each other again. And, of

563

course, for Robbie's sake I was willing to give it a go. But we're not even a couple of months along the road yet and already it's pretty evident it's not going to work. We've changed. We're different people now and though I'll always care for her, love her even, I just don't feel the way I once did. And she senses it. She was the one who brought it up in fact, and I didn't want to lie to her. So, whether she's as torn between me and Cavan as she's now claiming to be only she knows. It could be a kind of face-saver, which wouldn't be very fair on Cavan, but would be human, and Cavan's big enough to take care of himself. Or it could be that by confessing I didn't feel the same way about her, I've now given her the freedom to do what she really wants. Except she genuinely is confused about that, because she doesn't want to leave Robbie, nor does she want to take him away from me.'

Zelda's eyes remained on his as she took a generous sip of her drink. 'Mmm,' she said, 'a dilemma indeed, and one made harder if she really is intending to return to the field.'

'I think she would like to, but she knows she can't take Robbie again. It's no life for a child and it's time he was at a proper school with other kids his age. She's not arguing that, obviously, but it's going to be hard for her to let him go and I don't want to force him to live with me if he'd rather be with his mother. At the moment, he's happy to stay with me, but Michelle's not very far away, they speak every day on the phone and I'm still a novelty for him. What it's going to be like if she takes off for Africa, or India, or wherever's next on her agenda, and the reality of Michelle not being there starts to set in . . . Well, it's impossible to say how he'll be.'

'Have you discussed it with him?' Zelda asked.

'Not really. He's too young to take it all in and besides, you've seen what he's like, he's flexible, totally

564

independent, far too good-natured and will do whatever we tell him to do. Of course, he can be as naughty as sin when he wants to be and he's got a wicked temper, but on the whole he's a well-adjusted kid – which considering the way he's grown up so far is pretty miraculous. But he seems so together at times that it would be easy to forget he's just as vulnerable as any other boy his age.'

'Vulnerable, yes,' Zelda said, 'but most kids are tougher than we give credit for, and as long as they're loved and given all the proper care and attention it's not going to matter much where they live. Africa and India wouldn't be a good choice, however, at least not in the conditions Michelle would be in.'

'Which is why we gave him the option of going to Wales with her,' Michael said, 'or staying here with me. It was a small test and not really that conclusive, but he didn't even hesitate. Whether it's going to be what he wants long term, though, we've yet to find out. For now, we've decided that he stays with me for a year, seeing Michelle and speaking to her as often as he can, after that we'll review the situation. If he wants to go back with her, she'll return to England and live with him here. If he wants to stay with me, obviously we'll just carry on with the arrangements we'll already have in place by then.'

Zelda inhaled deeply. 'My, you have been working things through,' she said, draining her glass. 'And what would these arrangements be, presuming you're intending to return to work one of these days?'

Smiling, Michael got to his feet and went to refill their glasses.

'And what about Ellen?' Zelda called after him. 'Have you spoken to her? Or is that all over now?'

'I will be returning to work,' Michael said, coming back with fresh drinks, 'but not just yet.'

Zelda shook her head in confusion. 'I don't under-stand,' she told him, mentally noting that once again he'd managed to side-step the issue of Ellen. 'You know what a mess everything's in and it's not going to get any better until you're back on board.'

'Have you seen anything of your new boss?' he asked.

'Not yet, but she's sure to put in an appearance sooner or later. So what I want to hear now is that you're going to fight for the agency and make damned sure that World Wide is wrested back from Sandy Paull's and Ted Forgon's control.'

Michael grimaced. 'I have to confess,' he said, 'Sandy gives me less of a problem than Forgon, but both can be dealt with and once I've told you how and provided you agree, I'll set up a meeting with Sandy ...' he grinned, 'And give her the surprise of her life.'

Running to the door in a stylish turquoise blue suit, black lace body and four-inch black suede shoes, Sandy suddenly remembered all the pictures she'd seen of Michelle and how casual and understated she always looked. Feeling suddenly gaudy and obvious she almost went back to change, but she didn't have the time. He had called at three this afternoon to invite her to dinner at a venue of her choosing and she hadn't been able to get away from the office until gone seven. It was now twenty past eight and she had ten minutes to get to the restaurant, which she could make if she found a taxi straight away.

She was in luck and settling back for the five-minute journey she tried to get her nerves in some semblance of order. But she couldn't. He had sounded so friendly on the phone, to the point of actually saying that he was looking forward to seeing her, that she just couldn't keep herself calm through the onslaught of expectations and emotions that had plagued her ever since.

It was going to be the first time she'd seen him since the day he'd fired her, and when she considered what she'd done to his agency since and the way she had stitched him up with Ted Forgon and World Wide, she'd have to be some kind of fool if she was expecting him to sweep her up in his arms. But she couldn't stop thinking about the phone call and the warmth in his voice. It had sounded so genuine and his pleasure on finding out she could make it at such short notice had seemed so sincere, that despite her efforts at caution her hopes were just soaring out of control. Actually, she might have better been able to temper them, were it not for the fact that just that morning she had read in the papers about his break-up with Michelle. Of course, it was only rumour at the moment, but when she'd called Jodi to find out if there was any truth in it, Jodi had said that all she knew was Michelle and Cavan were in Wales, and Michael and Robbie were in London.

Sandy gave a shiver of excitement as she considered what it might be like to be a stepmother. She'd never really thought much about kids before, but she was sure she'd get along well with Robbie; in fact, as he was Michael's son she'd make sure she did.

A bolt of pure nerves hit her heart hard as the taxi came to a halt at the busy junction outside the restaurant. She'd chosen it in the hope that the press would pounce on the fact they were together and make as much out of it as she wanted them to. Indeed, it could well prove the first time their names were romantically linked, provided it all went the way she hoped, of course.

By the time she was greeted, shown to a discreet corner table and brought a much-needed glass of wine, she had managed to calm down a little. But then she looked across the restaurant and saw him coming in and the sensation that suddenly pressed down on her heart was so profound that she was unable to breathe. She had no idea what emotions might be shining in her eyes as she watched him follow the *maître d'* towards her: all she knew was that the seeds of doubt Nesta had planted as to how she really felt about him were completely annihilated. She wanted him in a way that defied explanation; she felt linked to him, somehow destined to be with him, to share his life and his dreams, to be there for all his triumphs and tragedies, and be a part of them too. And it would happen, she knew that with the same certainty she knew that the sun would rise in the morning.

'Hi,' he said, smiling down at her as he reached their table, 'I hope you haven't been waiting long.'

Sandy shook her head and forced her voice through the congested emotion in her throat. 'Just a few minutes,' she said, watching him turn to the wine waiter to order a drink.

'Are you OK?' he said, looking across the table to see if she had an aperitif.

'Fine, thanks,' she said, glancing at the waiter, then returning her eyes to Michael, she felt her lips tremble as she smiled.

'So how are you?' he said. 'You're looking good.'

The laughter simmering in his eyes was disconcerting, but trying not to let it affect her she said, 'Thank you. In fact, you look pretty good too.'

He grimaced, then said, 'Zelda showed me an article about you – and your family – in last month's *Cosmopolitan*.' He laughed. 'So now we know who you really are at last. Or at least, from whence you hail.'

Sandy screwed up her nose. 'It's nothing to be proud of,' she told him.

'Nothing to be ashamed of either,' he responded.

She looked doubtful about that. 'You should try living with them,' she said. 'Or getting the calls that keep coming now, asking for loans they have no intention, nor any means, of repaying.'

They looked up as a producer they both knew suddenly spotted them. 'Hey, Michael! How are you?' he said, grabbing Michael's hand as Michael rose. 'It's good to see you. You look great, man. Fatherhood obviously agrees with you.'

'It's the best,' Michael grinned. 'And how's life with you?'

'Great. Just great,' he responded warmly. 'And Sandy! What a surprise seeing you two together. Terrific deal you pulled off for Emma Hodge, by the way, Sandy. She was telling me about it earlier. No question she's right for the part, but boy, did you do well to screw that kind of money out of Carlton. Best thing she ever did was get you as an agent.' He glanced awkwardly at Michael, clearly not sure whether he'd just put his foot in it or not. Michael's expression was totally benign, which did nothing to ease the man's discomfort. 'Right, well, I won't interrupt any longer,' he said. 'Great to see you guys. Enjoy your meal,' and he went off to rejoin his table.

Still laughing, as he sat back down and his drink was delivered, Michael said, 'Well, you certainly are the toast of the town these days, Sandy,' and raising his glass he saluted her too. 'Congratulations,' he said, 'you're fast becoming a powerful woman and once you get World Wide underway you're really going to be up there – not just nationally, but globally.'

Sandy was flushing and her glass was still firmly on the table. 'Yes, well,' she stumbled, not at all sure what she wanted to say.

Michael lowered his head and peered at her. 'There's no need to be shy about this,' he told her, 'we both know what's going on here, so let's have it all out in the open, why not?'

Sandy lifted her eyes to his and was more nonplussed than ever when she saw not even a trace of rancour in his smile. Then it suddenly hit her that maybe he was talking personally rather than professionally and a rush of nerves collided with her heart. 'So how's Robbie?' she said, sensing this might be easier territory for the moment. 'Is he settling in well?'

Michael rolled his eyes. 'He's a handful and to say he's settled in would be an understatement. He's taken over would be more accurate.'

Sandy smiled. 'I'd like to meet him,' she said and blushed as she realized how forward that must sound. 'I mean, one of these days,' she added shakily.

'Oh, there's no doubt you will,' he assured her, picking up the menu. 'Shall we order?'

As Sandy scanned all the deliciously exotic hors d'oeuvres and entrées, she was trying desperately to work out what was really going on. He sounded so sure she was going to meet Robbie, and he was showing such bewildering unconcern about her success and how she had clinched it, that she was actually daring to hope that all her faith in her dreams was about to pay off.

'Well, I guess there's no point beating around the bush any longer,' he said, after placing their orders, 'I've got a couple of proposals for you and the quicker we get to them the quicker we're going to find out how workable they are.'

Sandy looked at him, her large blue-green eyes showing how apprehensive she was inside.

Michael smiled, as though to put her at her ease. 'The first,' he began, 'is probably going to surprise you the least, though you won't think that until I've told you the second, but anyway, here goes: I'm not going to start getting involved in everything that's happened over the past eight months, it would be a wasted exercise and though you've certainly downsized us at

McCann's and created a lot of problems that are going to take some time to sort out, the wounds definitely aren't fatal. It's essentially mine and Zelda's lists that give the agency it's real value, which is how come you haven't managed to destroy us altogether. So I'm going to put it to you now that instead of continuing this vendetta we join forces and turn our agencies into one.'

Sandy's eyes started to dilate.

'No, hear me out,' he said as she seemed about to speak. 'Obviously, if you're agreeable, there are numerous ramifications to be considered, but to start the ball rolling on the simpler issues I'm happy to call the agency whatever you like, McCann Walsh and Sandy Paull, Sandy Paull and McCann Walsh – I don't have an ego about these things, so it's basically up to you. Obviously I've discussed it with Dan and Zelda, who are the other two major shareholders in McCann's, and they both agree that combining what is left of our resources with those that are now available to you, would be an extremely wise route for us to take.' He laughed, slightly self-consciously. 'Of course, you'll be wondering what's in it for you and the answer to that is you will be a senior partner, along with me, in both McCann Walsh and World Wide Productions. In fact, Dan is willing to drop his name from the agency so we can call the company Sandy Paull and Michael McCann, or whichever way around, if that's what you want; and considering that I will be concentrating much more on World Wide and the new productions coming in there, you will effectively be running one of the most prestigious agencies in London.'

Sandy's mounting disbelief and euphoria were lighting up her eyes in a way that made her look even younger than her twenty-five years. Indeed, she felt like a child, one whom Santa had suddenly come to visit with all the desires that had built up throughout years of neglect. Her cheeks were turning crimson as she struggled to find the right answer – she didn't want to gush, though God knew she felt like it, nor did she want to sound too cool or offhand.

'I've spoken to Harry and Craig,' he told her, 'and they're all for it too. So it just needs your agreement, then we can hand over to the lawyers.'

Sandy was confused. 'You spoke to Harry and Craig?' she repeated. 'They never mentioned anything.'

'Because I asked them not to,' Michael smiled. Then, with a shrug he added, 'OK, I confess I was sounding them out, checking to see if they thought you'd be interested. They thought you would be and quite frankly, with the way you've utilized the assets of other people's indiscretions, turned me upside down and built yourself an agency of impressive reputation in such a short space of time, I can't think of anyone I less want as an enemy, or would feel safer having as my partner. Why you'd want me is another matter, but you could do worse.'

As he grinned, Sandy felt her heart melting. 'I've always wanted to be your partner,' she told him softly, 'but I never dreamt it would happen so soon – or this way.' Then, laughing, she waved a dismissive hand at their drinks. 'Where's the champagne?' she demanded. 'We should be celebrating.'

Michael immediately raised his hand.

'Oh God,' Sandy said, pressing her hands to her cheeks, 'I can hardly believe this. I mean, I was terrified you were going to come here this evening and . . . Well, I don't know what I thought you would do. But after the way I took Harry and Craig and all their clients, and the best part of Diana's and Janey's lists too and then with tipping Ted Forgon off about World Wide so he could buy it out from under you . . .' She stopped suddenly. 'What about Ted Forgon?' she said. 'How is he going to take it, me joining up with you? I mean, he's the head of World Wide now, he's going to make the decisions on who runs it . . .'

Michael was smiling. 'Believe me,' he said, 'all Ted Forgon wants is to be my boss, which he now is, so I don't think he'll give a damn who's running the show on a daily basis over here in London. But if he wants to appoint you senior operative, then that's OK by me.'

'But I thought you wanted us to be partners?'

'I do, so I suggest we cross that bridge when we come to it. In the meantime, we should set about putting all three companies, yours, mine and the London end of World Wide, under one roof. I would suggest the Chelsea Harbour offices, but maybe you're finding it more convenient to be up in the West End.'

'Convenient, yes,' she agreed, 'but there's more space at Chelsea Harbour and now we're going to be a much bigger concern, we'll need to expand. Are those outrageously expensive offices beneath yours still to let? I'll bet they are, with the rent they're asking. Leave it to me, I'll beat the price down and snap them up before anyone else gets in on the act.'

Michael was laughing. 'Bring us a bottle of Dom Perignon,' he told the waiter who had just materialized, 'we've got some serious celebrating to get underway.'

Sandy watched the waiter go and felt her head starting to spin with excitement. It was beginning to feel as though she was coming apart from reality, drifting in some surreal, almost nirvanic state that was allowing her to see the people around her, and to hear them, but was somehow cushioning her from the noise and the harshness of colour. Her throat was tight and her heart was tripping in an odd, floaty kind of way. She felt humble, yet immodestly special as she realized how incredibly lucky she was, how charmed and blessed with good fortune. These past eighteen months, since she'd come to London, hadn't always been easy, but there was no question now that dreams really did come true, if you held on to them long enough, for she'd always known that once she was in a position to meet him on his level he would want her.

Her eyes returned to his and as he continued to speak she could feel her smile starting to drain and a curious sensation nudging her heart. He was making his second proposal, but his words were suddenly sounding strange and her aura of happiness was melting away, as though she were slowly losing conciousness. She blinked and tried to reconnect with the euphoria of what he had told her, but it was as though the world had suddenly turned on its axis and was rotating another way. Perhaps this was what too much happiness did – or perhaps she was just too afraid to believe it was all coming true.

The champagne came, so did the food, but as the evening passed her shock and disbelief remained rooted in the moment when she had finally registered the full meaning of his second proposal.

Chapter 30

'Did you find a home for all the pups yet, Mom?' Ellen said, coming in the kitchen door and going to the cluttered sink to wash her hands.

'Yeah, just about all of them,' her mother answered, letting her glasses slide down her nose as she looked up from the accounts books she had spread out over the table. 'Except the black one. Don't know how he got in there, but he sure gave us a surprise, I can tell you.'

Ellen laughed. 'He's so cute,' she said, gazing out to where her father and a couple of workers were checking on the ripening rows of soybeans.

'Why, you thinking of taking him back to LA?' her mother asked, returning to her paperwork.

'I wish,' Ellen replied wistfully. 'But I'm going to be so busy over the next few months that I won't be able to give him any time.'

Nina Shelby nodded absently and began prodding her calculator, while Ellen filled the sink with hot water to start washing up.

'Bessie Jane's coming over later,' Nina said, referring to the housekeeper who had looked after them since Ellen was a child, until she'd retired a few years ago. 'That was her on the phone just now.'

'Is she still driving, at her age?' Ellen asked, soaping up the water.

'No. I'll go pick her up. She'll be staying the night, so

I guess I'd better get the room ready, soon as I finish up here.'

'I don't mind doing it,' Ellen said. 'And why you pay an accountant when you do all that work yourself sure beats me.'

'Got to keep an eye on the old rascal,' Nina winked.

Ellen chuckled, for old Sammy Katz who'd taken care of the farm's taxes for close on thirty years was so honest he'd once turned himself in for late payment of a parking violation. It was a bit mean of Sargeant Brazier to lock him up the way he did, but everyone including Sam, once he was released, had enjoyed the joke.

'My, it sure is getting warm out there,' Frank Shelby commented, coming in through the door and stomping his dusty boots on the rush mat. 'Fergus wants to know what you're going to be cooking up for the fair next month, Nina. His wife's getting on to him for an answer.'

'Oh, sure, I'll go talk to him,' she answered, sitting back and sliding her fingers under her glasses to rub her eyes. 'Bessie Jane's coming over later,' she told him.

Frank grunted, then, shifting his eyes half-way towards Ellen he walked on through the kitchen and started to climb the stairs.

Ellen's heart twisted, for there was nothing she'd wanted more these past couple of weeks than to feel the comfort of her father's arms and to know that at last they were putting this silly feud behind them. The maddening part of it was that she was certain he wanted it too, but his pride was just too stubborn to back down and right now she was simply too vulnerable to try any harder.

'It's done him good, you being here,' her mother told her, as though sensing her despair and wanting to ease it. 'That bout of flu really took it out of him, thought he was never going to get over it. He couldn't walk for days, just lay there in his bed too weak most of the time even to speak, never mind eat. Well, you've seen for yourself how much weight he lost, still hasn't put a lot of it back on. To tell the truth, he was frightened half to death that he wasn't going to make it, not that he'd ever admit it, of course, but it was plain to me.

'Now, where did I put the list I made for Fergus's wife? Shame you're not going to be here for the fair, honey, it's been a long time since you took part in our annual madness. Do you remember the year you won first prize for your chocolate spongecake?' She chuckled nostalgically. 'Never tasted anything so bad in my life,' she commented, 'but it sure looked good and Mitzi Frankham was mad as hell, 'cos her custard pie didn't even get a look in, as I recall.' She chuckled again and began tidying up her books. 'Ivy Perry's talking about raising the price of her donkey rides to a dollar,' she went on. 'Don't know that the kids can afford it, but I guess she'll drop if they can't. Oh, Dad tells me Bob Gilbert's bringing out his old coconut shy. It'll be the first time we've seen that old thing since Fremont Fulbright was mayor and that's going back some. Boy, did Fremont love that old shy, turned into a great big kid every time he got near it. They say his son's organizing for a real carnival ride to come over from Utah this year, though why Utah no one seems to know, 'cos I'm sure we've got some mighty fine rides right here in Nebraska if anyone cared to look.'

Stacking everything in a disorderly pile, she turned to look at Ellen and found her staring down at the bowl full of water with her hands resting gently on the edge of the sink. She watched her for a while and wished with all her heart that there were something she could do to take the pain away, but there was nothing except be there for her and try to help her through it.

Hearing Frank come back into the kitchen, she glanced over at him and saw that he was watching

Ellen too and her heart weighted with sadness as she saw the helplessness in his eyes. Ellen was only going to be here a couple more days and Nina was praying with all her might that her husband would overcome that obstinate pride of his before she went, because it certainly was high time he did. In fact, if he didn't she was going to step right in there and make him, because this had gone on far too long now and it was time someone brought the old fool to his senses.

In truth, he appeared on the brink of giving way now, but to her dismay he merely ended up treating her to a punishing scowl before walking on out the door.

Turning back to Ellen she said, 'Are you OK, honey?'

Ellen nodded and lifting her head she forced a smile. 'I'm sorry,' she said, 'it just steals up on me sometimes and it's like I can't get it under control.' She took a breath, as though the small rush of air could ease the burn of the pain. Then, picking up a plate she began to wash it. She wanted to tell her mother how it seemed to hurt all over, not just in her heart, but in her eyes, her face, her hands – it was as though her entire body were being taken over by the longing and despair. The most difficult part of it was that it seemed to be getting worse instead of better, for she had only to picture his face, or remember some little thing he had said and the need would sear through her with an intensity she could hardly bear. She said nothing, though, for it troubled her mother deeply to know how much she was suffering and there had to come a time when she stopped discussing it, for going over and over it, the way she and her mother had these past couple of weeks, was never going to change it.

'I'll go get the room ready for Bessie Jane,' she offered, leaving the dishes and starting to dry her hands.

Nina smiled, for it was typical of her lately to leave a

task half finished without even realizing it. 'You know, it's going to be all right, honey,' she said softly. 'In my heart, I know it.'

Ellen nodded and stroked her mother's cheek as she passed. 'Of course it will,' she said. 'And being here with you has helped more than you know.'

An hour or so later Ellen was swinging gently back and forth on the porch swing, with the coffee and cookies her mother had brought out lying untouched on the table. She knew her mother wouldn't mind about the cookies, but she'd want her to make a special effort for Bessie Jane at dinner tonight, which she would, for the last thing she needed was Bessie Jane fussing and fretting over how much weight she had lost. At least her mother understood it was normal to lose your appetite at a time like this, even though she did all she could to encourage her to eat anyway. But it wasn't like she was starving herself, it was simply hard to get the food down, for every time she thought of Michael her mouth turned dry and her throat just closed up. And she'd been doing a lot of strenuous work about the farm since she got there, keeping herself busy, trying hard not to give herself too much time to think, so she was sure to have lost weight that way too.

In fact, it was only now, today, that she had run out of things to do and people to visit. Or maybe it was just that she needed a little time to take stock, work out exactly where she was going to begin when she returned to LA. She felt so unfocused right now that it would probably do her good to get back, even though, in her heart, she was dreading it. But of course, once she was there she'd be so busy, so bogged down with commitments and plans and meetings and strategies to get her new career underway she wasn't going to have time to be afraid.

Suddenly the phone started to ring inside the house

and her heart felt as though it was trying to leap from her chest, even though she already knew it wouldn't be him. Then, with a horrible, sinking sensation she found herself wondering if she would *ever* see or hear from him again. The idea that they were now on totally separate paths was so heart-wrenching that she couldn't bring herself to face it, but she would, soon, she just needed more time. And at least here, in the sanctuary of her home, she didn't have to deal with the press and the fear that she was going to pick up a paper, or turn on the TV, and discover that he and Michelle were getting married, or having another baby, or something else equally as devastating.

'That was Bessie Jane,' her mother said, slipping a cardigan on as she came out on to the porch. 'She's ready for me to go pick her up now. I'll be gone about an hour, unless you feel like taking a ride with me.'

Still struggling with the disappointment that it hadn't been him, Ellen smiled and shook her head. 'I need to call Matty,' she said. 'She's been filming in Phoenix, so I haven't spoken to her for a couple of days and I want to find out if she's heard from Matt Granger; you know, the director who's thinking of giving her the lead in his new movie.'

Nina nodded, kissed the top of her head and went off to get the car. Ellen watched her go and knew that she'd seen straight through the excuse, for what she really wanted to ask Matty was if she had heard any news about Michael. Except she knew that once she got Matty on the line she wouldn't ask, though whether it was pride and anger at the way he had just abandoned her that would stop her, or simply the fact that she wasn't up to any more blows, she couldn't really be sure.

Sighing wearily to herself, she watched her father standing over the car talking to her mother, then, as her mother drove off she let her head drop back and pushed the swing a little harder. She could feel the tears rising, the grief, the despair, the hopelessness and pain. In reality she'd hardly cried at all, but inside it was as though she never stopped. What frightened her the most was the way she held on to her pain, as though it was all that connected her to him now. In its way it was like a support, though in truth it was tearing her apart. She was angry at him for making her afraid to return to LA, even though she knew the courage had to be hers – and it was there, right deep down inside her, all she had to do was find it. But even if she did, would it bring back her drive, her sparkle and zest, all of which had been dulled by the hurt, as though the loss of her dreams had turned out a light inside her, leaving her spirits in a cold and darkened world? Maybe if she could stop torturing herself with wondering if he truly loved Michelle, or had gone back to her because of Robbie, she would find it easier to get on with her life. For what did his reasons matter when his choice had been made and whether he had ever really loved her was a question she would probably never know the answer to now.

Her eyes closed as the slow, cruel burn of loss embraced her heart again and the strength she normally found to break it failed her. It was as though there was nothing in her now but the need to see him, to hear him and feel him. She wondered if she really could find the courage to call him, even though she knew she wouldn't for she was too angry and too proud to want him to know how much he'd hurt her. She doubted she would ever be able to forgive him for leaving her the way he had, for not even caring enough to make a phone call, or bothering to say goodbye. She hated him for making her feel so unimportant when he meant so much to her and had allowed her to believe she had meant the same to him.

Her breath was starting to quicken and as she

struggled to keep control she heard someone walk up the steps to the porch and come to stand beside her. Opening her eyes, she looked up to see her father, and as he sat down beside her and took her hand in his there was nothing she could do to stop the tears falling. She started to sob, and putting his arms around her he rocked her back and forth, the way he always had when she was a child, right here on this swing.

'Can you forgive an old fool?' he said gruffly.

'Oh, Dad,' she choked, lifting her head from his shoulder and looking into his awkward but gentle grey eyes. 'Of course I can forgive you. Can you forgive me?'

His lean, weathered cheeks were wet with his own tears, as he said, 'Nothing to forgive. It's your life, I just had other ideas what you should do with it.'

Ellen's smile was shaky. 'Looking at me now, I wonder if you weren't right,' she told him.

He shook his head. 'Not right,' he said, 'just scared. I wanted to stop anything bad ever happening to you and I got mad because you wouldn't let me. You wanted to go out there and make your own mistakes, and I wanted to make them for you. I've learned now that you can't do that for a person, no matter how much you love them.'

Resting her head back on his shoulder Ellen gazed down at their joined hands and allowed the safe, familiar scent of him to wash over her. Just like her mother, she'd prayed during the past two weeks that this would happen, for in an irrational, almost childish kind of way she still believed that her father could make everything all right. But as special as this moment was and as happy as it was making her to know that at last they were friends, there was still an emptiness inside her that was refusing to be filled. As though to reassure him that he was giving her all she needed she squeezed his hand tighter and wondered how much her mother had told him about Michael, and Clay and

582

Ted Forgon, for she had confessed all the night after she arrived. She guessed her father probably knew more than he would want to talk about, but she didn't blame him for that, some things between father and daughter were best left unsaid. And all that mattered now was that they were sitting here together, gazing out at the endless rows of soybeans to a far and promising horizon that was as enticing and ephemeral as it was unpredictable.

They were still there, holding hands and idly chatting and laughing about the farm, their neighbours, the past when, over an hour later, her mother's station wagon came chugging into the distance. Ellen smiled as she thought of how happy her mother was going to be to find them together like this and for a fleeting moment she even dared to hope that maybe, one of these days, they might persuade her father to visit LA. But it wouldn't be wise to rush him and besides, she was wondering if now the silence was over she shouldn't stay on at the farm for a few more days. She needed to be sure first that she wasn't doing it just to put off returning to LA, but even if that were her reason it would still give her and her father some more time.

'Should get her a new car,' her father remarked, as her mother drove into the yard, 'that old jalopy's falling apart.'

'Mmm,' Ellen responded, gazing curiously at the windshield. Her head went to one side, as though to see past the reflecting sunlight and shadow, but though she could see her mother all right, she still couldn't get a clear look at the person beside her. Whoever it was though, it sure wasn't Bessie Jane.

Even before he got out of the car Ellen's heart was starting to thud – but she had to be dreaming, this couldn't be happening, grief and longing had obviously turned her mind to the point where she was beginning to see things. Yet he was standing there, looking across the yard to where she was, and even through all the confusion inside her she somehow knew this was real.

She started to laugh and sob. 'I don't believe it,' she said, getting to her feet. Then, clasping her hands to her cheeks she whispered, 'Tell me I'm not dreaming.'

'If you are, then so am I,' her father responded.

'Did you know?' she asked, still looking at Michael.

'Yes,' Frank answered. 'But your mother said I wasn't to tell you.'

Ellen stood where she was, watching as Michael opened a rear door of the car, then moved aside for a little boy to get out. 'Oh my God,' Ellen murmured, tears stinging her eyes. 'This can't be happening. How can this be happening without anyone telling me?' Not waiting for an answer, she began walking along the porch to the steps, her fingers pressed to her mouth, as hand in hand Michael and Robbie came towards her. She ran down the steps quickly, then took the last few paces more slowly, until she was standing in front of them and seeing so much love and irony in Michael's eyes that she longed just to throw herself into his arms.

'Ellen,' he said, holding her gaze, 'I'd like you to meet Robbie. Robbie,' he said, looking down at his son, 'this is Ellen.'

'Hello,' Robbie said, looking up at her with his father's devastatingly blue eyes and holding out a hand for her to shake. He glanced at his father, as though seeking reassurance and as she took his hand Ellen was dimly aware of her parents joining them too.

'Hello Robbie,' she said, smiling down at him. 'I'm glad to meet you.'

Robbie's eyes suddenly became big with importance. 'Daddy said I have to be a good boy,' he told her.

'Is that so?' she said, matching his earnestness. 'Well I'm sure you're always a good boy, aren't you?'

'Yes, I am. Well usually I am. But I have to be especially good today, because Daddy wants you to

584

come and live with us and if I'm a good boy and he's a good boy too, you might want to. And when we go to live in America-land he wants you to be married to him, but he thinks it might . . .' he took a breath, 'be too soon to ask. And he said when we get to America-land that Batman and Superman live there and you might take me to see them.'

Ellen and her parents were laughing, as rolling his eyes Michael said, 'Robbie, you just stole all my lines and gave away all my secrets.'

Robbie's eyes were still on Ellen. 'I forgot,' he told her. 'Well, that's OK,' she said. 'We all forget things sometimes, and I always think it's good sharing secrets, don't you?'

Robbie nodded. 'Me and Daddy share all our secrets, don't we Daddy?'

'Not any more, we don't,' Michael corrected.

'Shall I tell you something?' Robbie said to Ellen, as though his father were no longer there.

'Oh, yes please,' she said, her eyes dancing with laughter.

'Robbie,' Michael cautioned.

But Robbie was already underway. 'My Daddy saved me,' he said proudly. 'I was with all these really bad men who had guns and masks and there was this one man who Daddy hit and then he got the man like this . . . Shall I show you how he got the man?'

'No, thank you,' Michael interrupted. 'Why don't you show us all how good you are at introducing yourself instead, because Ellen's father is there and you haven't said hello to him yet.'

Robbie looked up at Frank. 'Shall I show *you* how Daddy got the man?' he said.

Frank chuckled with delight.

'Introduce yourself,' Michael said firmly. 'This is Mr Shelby and you are . . .'

'I am Robbie,' he said, pronouncing each word very deliberately as he held out his hand.

'Hello, Robbie,' Frank said, taking the hand. 'Didn't your daddy tell you you've already arrived in America-land?'

Robbie's eyes started to shine with wonder. 'Do you mean Batman is here?' he said, almost in a whisper.

Frank grimaced. 'Not Batman,' he said, 'but I do have something to show you, over there in the barn, and I think you're going to like them. Do you want to come see?'

'Yes, please,' Robbie said and without a backward glance he started to follow Frank across the yard.

Michael, Ellen and her mother watched them go and heard Robbie say, 'Mr Shelby, what's your name?'

'Well,' they heard Frank answer, 'my name's Frank, but I guess, if your daddy is going to marry my daughter then you can call me grandpa.'

'I haven't got a grandpa,' Robbie told him.

'Well, looks like you got one now,' Frank replied and they disappeared around the corner.

Ellen turned back to Michael and caught her lip between her teeth as a sob of pure joy tried to erupt from her throat. 'Why didn't you tell me you were coming?' she said. 'Mom, you must have known, how come you never said anything?'

Nina shrugged. 'He asked me not to,' she said.

'I thought you might refuse to see me,' Michael confessed, 'so I decided not to give you a choice. And I brought Robbie along, because I figured if I didn't win you over, he might.'

'Are you kidding?' Ellen laughed. 'He's adorable.'

'He's a lousy keeper of secrets, is what he is,' Michael reminded her, reaching out to take her hand.

'Well, I got a dinner to be putting on the stove,' Nina said tactfully. 'Frank'll see to your luggage in a while, Michael. Welcome to the farm, by the way. We got a room all fixed up for you. Ellen did it, but she didn't realize she was doing it for you. Will Robbie be OK sleeping with you?'

'That'll work just fine,' Michael assured her and as she turned away he slipped an arm around Ellen's shoulders. 'Is there somewhere around here I can kiss you?' he whispered, 'because I'm feeling the urge pretty bad.'

Laughing, Ellen took hold of his hand and started to run, leading him around the house to a quiet, shady backyard where she flung her arms around his neck and kissed him for all she was worth. 'You're crazy out of your mind coming here like this and I love you for it,' she told him breathlessly as he let her go for a moment.

'And I've got to share a bed with Robbie when I don't think I've ever wanted you as much as I want you right now,' Michael complained.

'They're God-fearing Catholics,' Ellen reminded him.

'And I'm a desparate man.'

'No more desperate than me,' she grinned. 'But wait until after dinner, then I'll borrow Mom's car and take you on a little tour of the area. There's a spot I know, not too far from here, where the pioneers hauled their wagons along the Oregon trail and no one goes there now except the ghosts of them old wayfaring cowboys. But first things first: you've got some explaining to do, Michael McCann, and I hardly know where to start asking the questions. I guess I should start with Michelle. Where is she? What happened?'

Pulling her closer to him he said, 'What happened is I love you and she sensed it. I don't know how long we might have carried on if she hadn't found the courage to bring it up, because I felt I owed Robbie and well . . .' he shrugged, 'for a while there he was all that mattered.'

Ellen smiled. 'I can understand that,' she said. 'I just wish you'd told me about him before, that's all.'

'I know, but I had it all screwed up in my head and I just couldn't talk about it to anyone. It was like I was trying to deny he existed, which was crazy, I know, but I did it to hurt Michelle and ended up hurting us all.'

'So where is she now?' Ellen asked.

'In London, at my apartment. She's going to stay on there for a while, until we're sure Robbie is settled and she gets a new posting.'

'So she's going back to her charity work?'

He nodded. 'Probably. Cavan'll go with her. It's a passion with them both and they're kind of in love. I say kind of because Michelle's all mixed up right now and Cavan's still pretty young.' His eyes suddenly softened as he gazed down into her face. 'God, you're so beautiful, do you know that?' he murmured, stroking her hair.

As his mouth touched hers her lips parted and they didn't speak again for several minutes.

'So what's all this about America-land?' she said, as finally he lifted his head to look at her.

Immediately his eyes started to simmer with laughter. 'America-land is where Batman and Superman live,' he answered. 'Robbie and I are going there to try to make our fortunes, and we'd like you to come and live with us when we get there.'

'Oh God, I don't believe this,' Ellen laughed, resting her forehead on his chest. 'You're going to LA?' she said, looking up at him again.

He nodded. 'I was about to tell you that when we were in Barbados, but then the phone rang and my whole life suddenly went crazy. Anyway, things have changed a lot since then, because I've got even more reason to ship out to LA now than I had before – as if you weren't enough of a reason.'

Pursing her lips with laughter she said, 'I could flatter myself and believe that was true.'

'Then flatter yourself,' he told her.

'So what happened to change your mind? I thought you hated the place.'

'I do, but I figured I could get to like it if you were around and now, with the way things have turned out, I've more or less got to be there.'

Ellen frowned her confusion, then laughed as her mother's voice shouted discreetly round the corner, 'Iced lemonade coming up.'

'It's OK, Mom, we're decent,' Ellen called back.

As Nina Shelby came round the corner she was trying very hard not to laugh, for that kind of risqué comment appealed to a humour she generally kept hidden. 'I'll set it down here,' she said, putting the tray in the shade of a dense old oak.

'Is Robbie OK?' Michael asked.

'He's still in the barn with Frank, looking at the pups,' Nina told him.

'Oh,' Michael laughed, 'we probably won't see him for days then.'

'Doesn't he miss Michelle?' Ellen asked, as her mother disappeared back inside.

'Maybe it's too soon for him to miss her yet,' he answered, drawing her down on to the grass and settling her between his legs as he leaned back against the trunk of the tree. 'Though there were plenty of tears when he said goodbye and I suspect there are a lot more to come. But for the moment he's enjoying the newness of everything and though it's obviously breaking Michelle's heart, I guess you could say this is her way of dealing with her own guilt for going off when she was pregnant, the way she did. Not that I want it to be that way, but it's time Robbie was in a proper school and living the kind of life other boys like him live. And Michelle agrees, because subjecting him to hardship and danger is going to do nothing to improve the lives of the children she wants to help; all it does is subject him to hardship and danger. He doesn't need that at his age and Michelle's not arguing the point. But she loves him, obviously, she's his mother and I'm never going to do anything to keep them apart. I want you to know that now, because if at some time in the future you decide to accept Robbie's proposal, you're going to be every bit as much involved in this as the rest of us.'

Ellen smiled at 'Robbie's proposal' and felt a quiet sweep of happiness steal through her. Then, turning to sit cross-legged facing him she said, 'Tell me more about LA. Why do you say you've got to be there?'

Michael's eyebrows went up as he started to laugh. 'You mean you haven't heard?' he said.

'Heard what?'

'About World Wide and Ted Forgon. Did you leave ATI, by the way?'

'Yes, I did. And now you come to mention it, Forgon gave me a kind of feeling the day I left that something was going down where you were concerned. In fact, he gave me the rest of the photographs and negatives he had of me, telling me some bullshit story that it was a lesson I needed to learn that someone would always be out there ready to pull another trick like that if I didn't take more care. Which reminds me, you told me once that you had something on him, if I ever needed it. I don't, but I wouldn't mind knowing what it is.'

Michael grinned. 'A man like Forgon has always got something to hide,' he told her, 'it's why he takes such pleasure in getting the goods on other people. He sees it as getting in first, I suppose. And frankly, all you have to do with him is tell him you've got something on him and he'll be eating out of your hand.'

Ellen was looking at him incredulously. 'You mean you were bluffing?' she said.

He laughed. 'I easily could have been and take my

word for it, it would have worked, because they don't come much more paranoid than Forgon. But no, what I've got on the man could send him to prison for a good long while.'

'You're kidding,' Ellen gasped.

Michael shook his head, then, pulling his brows together he said, 'Do you remember the secretary he had once, Carleena? It was a few years ago, maybe before your time.'

Ellen nodded. 'I remember the name. I never knew her, though. Wasn't there something about her bringing some kind of law-suit for wrongful dismissal or something?'

'I think there was,' Michael said. 'I'd forgotten about that. All I remember is that he fired her and tried to get her out of LA with some cock-and-bull story about her missing her folks and wanting to go back home to Nashville. Whereas the truth is she was seventeen years old and he'd been screwing her regularly for close on a year. And in California that makes him guilty of rape. Statutory rape, to be more precise, but rape nevertheless. And the six-year statute of limitations has yet to expire.'

'My God,' Ellen murmured, 'the man suddenly becomes putty.'

'Thank God,' Michael said, 'because he's just bought a controlling share of World Wide and made Sandy Paull the chief operating officer in London.'

Ellen stared at him, dumbfounded. 'Sandy Paull?' she said. 'The girl *you* fired . . .'

'. . . who, thanks to indiscretions she managed to find out about other people I was employing, has been systematically dismantling the agency ever since,' he finished for her. 'The same,' he confirmed. 'Nasty business this, isn't it? Maybe we should get out while the going's good.'

She laughed, then was serious again. 'So how did

Sandy Paull and Ted Forgon get in on World Wide? Jesus Christ, Michael, practically everything you've got is invested in that company and *they're* running it?'

He nodded. 'Certainly Sandy is in London,' he said, 'but only because I didn't want to leave any unpleasantness behind when I went and because she's turning into a damned good businesswoman actually. Not always ethical, it's true, but she's got her good points and frankly, I'd rather have her with me than against me – which is why I've invited her to become my partner and more or less run McCann's in London, as well as head up World Wide over there.'

Ellen stared at him, totally dumbfounded.

Michael picked up a glass of lemonade and passed it to her.

She took it, but didn't drink. 'You have left *her* to take care of your business in London,' she said. 'Are you totally out of your mind?'

'I don't think so,' he responded. 'In fact, from everything I hear about her she's a pretty good boss. Always ready to listen, willing to learn, never assumes her way is the right way, but isn't afraid to act on her instincts – all good qualities. And if Harry and Craig are speaking highly of her, then to be honest, I don't have too much of a problem with her either. And Zelda's still one of the major shareholders, so's Dan, and with Paul Patton on board now, plus the other agents she's going to have working with her, she can't really go wrong. Besides, I'm going to be keeping a pretty close eye on it all and don't forget, she's getting what she wanted, which is a partnership in McCann Walsh.'

'Michael, are you blind?' Ellen demanded. 'What she wanted was you. She doesn't care about the agency, nor about World Wide, all she cares about is getting you.'

'Wrong,' Michael responded. 'She's doing too well

592

now to want to see either company do anything but succeed and believe me, she's not going to let her personal feelings get in the way. That's not to say they aren't still there, because I'm pretty sure they are, but in her own peculiar and unscrupulous way she's as ambitious as the rest of us, so she's not going to do anything to jeopardize her future now.'

'But she's got no experience where a company like World Wide is concerned,' Ellen pointed out.

'True, but we're bringing someone in who does to advise her and don't forget, I've seen what a fast learner she is. So you watch, she'll hone up her talents quicker than you can say shoeshine and the next thing we know we'll all be making a fortune from the London end of World Wide, as well as from the McCann Paull Agency.'

'McCann Paull?' Ellen repeated.

Michael shrugged. 'It was what she wanted and Dan didn't object,' he said.

'So what's going to happen in LA?' she asked.

'What's going to happen,' he said, 'is we're going to find a house that'll give us enough room for a decent-sized study which we can use to get World Wide off the ground and to oversee the initial development of your projects. It could be that World Wide LA will be one of your first investors.'

'My God, this is amazing,' Ellen murmured. 'Is Chris Ruskin still involved?'

'Yes. He's going to be keeping his eyes open for new books or plays in New York and searching out investors from Wall Street or 47th Street, or wherever. Mark Bergin's about to poach someone from an Australian film distributor to start things rolling that end; Sandy's pretty well underway in London, so that only leaves Hollywood. Of course, we've got Ted Forgon at the moment, but I'll just whisper the name Carleena in his ear and I think he'll be happy to hand the reins over.

593

Ellen laughed. 'But what about all the directors you represent? Are you still going to be their agent?'

He grinned, then, looking kind of sheepish he said, 'I used them as a second carrot for Sandy. She gets to handle them personally, which considering what calibre of director most of them are is a huge step up for her in terms of prestige, and I get to go to Hollywood.'

Ellen watched him, waiting for the sting.

'I have to confess,' he said, 'when I put it to her I thought she was going to back out of the entire shebang, because it was at that point that I think she was expecting me to start getting more personal. I'm even willing to admit that I might have led her down that path a bit, knowing it would soften her up, but with Forgon taking over World Wide in LA there was no way I could stay in London while he called the tune; nor could I leave Sandy rolling about the decks like a loose cannon. So I've anchored her down with as fair and generous an offer as she'll probably ever get in her life, and into the bargain I've managed to get back two damned good agents in Craig and Harry.'

Ellen was laughing. 'My, you *have* been busy,' she remarked. 'And there was me thinking that all you had time for was getting it back together with Michelle and creating a new life for Robbie.'

'I did a lot of it from home,' he admitted, 'and I'm not going to lie to you, at first we were trying to make it work.'

'Meaning you slept with her?'

He nodded.

Ellen smiled past her jealousy and dropped her eyes for a moment. 'I knew you would,' she said quietly, 'I just wish you hadn't told me.'

Putting his fingers under her chin, he lifted her head up so he could look into her eyes. 'It was because we made love that she knew things weren't right between us,' he told her frankly. Then, running his fingers down over her neck he pushed a hand inside her blouse and caressed her shoulder. 'I love you,' he whispered, gazing into her beautiful, sunlit face.

'I love you too,' she said and covering his hand with hers she drew it down to her breast.

Through the fabric of her blouse and bra he could feel her nipple hardening, and pulling her back into his arms he laid her against his shoulder and kissed her deeply. Their passion was aroused so quickly that his hand was already between her legs and pressing hard into her groin before he suddenly remembered where they were.

Smiling as he lifted his head to look at her he said, 'I know I've taken a lot for granted where you're concerned, but do you think you'd be interested in moving in with us when we get to LA? I know it's probably come as a bit of a shock, having to take on a four-year-old as well, and if you'd rather have some time to think about it, believe me, I'll understand, because instant parenthood definitely takes some getting used to.'

As he finished, Ellen was laughing at the expression on his face as they could hear Robbie calling out for him.

'Daddy! Daddy! Look what I've got,' he cried, half running and half walking around the corner of the house. 'It's a puppy.'

'No kidding,' Michael said, as he carried the tiny little black bundle over to the tree.

'Grandpa said I could keep him, but I have to ask you first.'

Michael looked at the dog, then at Ellen.

'Please,' Robbie implored. 'He doesn't have a home to go to because he's black and he should have been white, but I like him because he's black.'

'So do I,' Ellen agreed, sitting up and stroking the puppy. 'In fact, he's my favourite.'

'Mine too,' Robbie told her eagerly. 'Please, Dad,' he added.

'Looks like I'm outnumbered here,' Michael replied, secretly considering it a great idea. 'So what are you going to call him?'

Robbie looked down at the dog, whose huge brown eyes were gazing up at him in sublime adoration. Its fur was long and silky, and entirely black. 'I know,' Robbie suddenly declared. 'I'll call him Spot.'

Michael's head went round to Ellen.

'Great name,' Ellen said, trying very hard not to laugh as she pictured Michael in an LA dog park calling out Spot to a dog that had not a single patch of colour on its entire body.

'I'll go and tell Grandpa,' Robbie said, and putting the pup on the grass he started to run on ahead. 'Come on Spot,' he called and to his delight the six-week-old puppy started chasing after him.

'Looks like we're about to become a regular family,' Ellen remarked, 'what with the dog as well.'

Michael smiled. 'All a bit different from the way I thought we might get started in LA, but like I said, I don't want to rush you. You can have ten minutes.' He shrugged. 'Hell, I'm feeling generous, take fifteen.'

Laughing, she leaned forward to kiss him. 'I made up my mind about you a long time ago, Michael McCann,' she told him, 'and right now I'm so excited about the future I can hardly wait to get started.'

'Really?' Michael said, feigning surprise. 'Personally, I can't wait to get dinner.'

Ellen frowned. 'Why? Are you hungry?'

'Not a bit,' he said, rolling her on to her back in the grass and lying over her. 'It's what's coming after that's interesting me.'

As he kissed her Ellen circled her arms tightly around his neck and refused to think any more about Sandy Paull – or how blind men could be when it came to women who loved them. There was going to be plenty of time for that in the months to come, in fact, if Ellen's instincts were right there was a very good chance it was going to become as big an issue in their personal lives as it undoubtedly would in their professional lives. But they would deal with that when they had to, for all that mattered now was that they were together again and as deeply in love as it was possible to be. She just hoped to God it stayed that way, because during that very brief meeting they'd had in LA she had sensed something about Sandy Paull that had made her extremely uneasy.

Standing behind what had once been Michael McCann's desk, Sandy took the glass of wine Nesta was passing her and gazed thoughtfully out at the activity in the well. Craig and Bertie were explaining something to Jodi, while Harry and Diana shouted into their phones and called up information on their computers. Zelda was over at the National, so Janey had slipped into her office to make a personal call. Frances and Janine, the bookers, whom she hadn't fired because she thought it might be worse for them having to work for her, were busy making their end-of-day checks, while the other assistants badgered them for dates and deadlines. Paul Patton, the new guy, had moved into Dan's office, as Dan never came in more than once a week and both were happy to share for that time.

'It's amazing,' she remarked as she sipped her wine and tried not to wish herself back to a time when Michael had been in this office, 'in fact I can hardly believe it, can you?'

'What?' Nesta asked, 'that you're here and this is your little empire now, or that Michael's just taken over as controlling officer of World Wide?'

Sandy laughed drily. 'Both, I suppose,' she answered. 'But I was thinking about World Wide,' and looking down to where the newspaper was lying open at a shot of Ted Forgon and Michael McCann shaking hands at the ATI offices in LA she said, 'That's got to be sticking right in Ted Forgon's throat, so what I want to know is how did Michael do it? I mean, all Forgon ever wanted was to destroy Michael and no sooner does he get the means to do it than he gives it all away.' Her eyes came up to Nesta's. 'Why?' she demanded.

'Does it matter why?' Nesta responded. 'Michael's going to be every bit as good running World Wide as Forgon, probably better, in fact.'

'I'm not disputing that,' Sandy replied, 'but it makes him my boss again. And if she's his partner, then that makes her my boss too.'

'Oh come on, Sandy,' Nesta protested. 'Look at all you've got going for you here. So what does it matter if technically he's your boss? He's over in LA and as far as London's concerned, you're the one in charge.'

'But I'll have to answer to him and maybe to *her* too,' Sandy said tightly. Her eyes went down as though to conceal their expression. 'This is the second time she's stolen him from me . . .'

'Sandy!'

'You don't understand,' Sandy told her. 'It's a point of principle now.' She raised her eyes again and looking at Nesta she suddenly started to smile. 'Remember the lunch?' she said.

Nesta frowned. 'Do you mean the one you had with Ellen Shelby in LA?' she asked.

Sandy nodded. 'That's the one,' she confirmed. 'I thought at the time it might turn out to be a clever move and guess what, I was right, because as soon as I'm ready Ellen Shelby is going to find out exactly what that lunch was all about.' And brightening considerably, she closed the newspaper and raised her glass. 'Drink up, Nesta,' she said, 'because this isn't over yet.

In fact it's so far from being over, it could be just the beginning.'

The Mill House

Susan Lewis

Julia Thayne is a valued and loving wife, a successful mother and a beautiful woman. She is everything most other women strive to be. But beneath the surface is a terrible secret that threatens to tear her perfect world apart.

Joshua is Julia's husband – a dynamic, devastatingly handsome man with great style, charisma and humour. He is utterly devoted to his wife and children, but as the ghosts of Julia's past begin to move into their marriage, he finds himself losing the struggle to keep them together. Then two telephone calls change everything.

Julia moves from London to a remote mill house in Cornwall, determined to break free from the past and save her fractured relationship with Josh. But it is here that she makes her own fatal mistake, and once more her marriage is rocked to its very foundation . . .

'Mystery and romance *par excellence'* Sun

'Erotic and exciting' *Sunday Times*

arrow books

ALSO AVAILABLE IN ARROW

The Hornbeam Tree

Susan Lewis

Just as celebrated columnist Katie Kiernan thinks life is over, it suddenly arrives on her doorstep in the shape of her sister Michelle, and all the intrigue she brings with her. Friction, resentment and old jealousies make life in their house doubly challenging, as Katie struggles to cope with a rebellious teenager and Michelle longs for the man she left behind.

After a devastating betrayal Laurie Forbes is trying to rebuild her relationship with Elliot Russell, when she is plunged into a whirlwind of passion that threatens to tear them apart completely.

Top journalist, Tom Chambers, the man Michelle left behind, faces the greatest challenge of his career when highly classified documents fall into his hands. Realizing how explosive the material is, Tom calls upon Elliot Russell to help with the investigation, and very quickly they are caught up in the deadly efforts to stop them going to print . . .

'A multi-faceted tear jerker'
heat

arrow books

Just One More Day: A Memoir

Susan Lewis

In 1960s Bristol a family is overshadowed by tragedy . . .

While Susan, a feisty seven-year-old, is busy being brave, her mother, Eddress, is struggling for courage. Though bound by an indestructible love, their journey through a world that is darkening with tragedy is fraught with misunderstandings.

As a mother's greatest fear becomes reality, Eddress tries to deny the truth. And, faced with a wall of adult secrets, Susan creates a world that will never allow her mother to leave.

Set in a world where a fridge is a luxury, cars have starting handles, and where bingo and coupons bring in the little extras, *Just One More Day* is a deeply moving true-life account of how the spectre of death moved into Susan's family, and how hard they all tried to pretend it wasn't there.

'Susan Lewis fans know she can write compelling fiction, but not, until now, that she can write even more engrossing fact. We use the phrase honest truth too lightly: it should be reserved for books – deeply moving books – like this' Alan Coren

arrow books